D0065057

BRIDEY'S
MOUNTAIN

BRIDEY'S MOUNTAIN

~

YVONNE ADAMSON

DELACORTE PRESS

Published by
Delacorte Press
Bantam Doubleday Dell Publishing Group, Inc.
1540 Broadway
New York, New York 10036

Library of Congress Cataloging in Publication Data

Adamson, Yvonne.
Bridey's mountain / Yvonne Adamson.
p.   cm.
ISBN 0-385-30850-7 (hc) : $19.95
1. Telluride (Colo.)—History—Fiction.   I. Title.
PS3511.D3956B75   1993
813'.54—dc20   92-41211
                                                                         CIP

Book design by Robin Arzt

Manufactured in the United States of America

Published simultaneously in Canada

August 1993

10 9 8 7 6 5 4 3 2 1

RRH

To those who live in the house of tomorrow
David, Leah, and Tim
Misty and Shane

This book was truly a collaboration. So much gratitude is due to *all* those who helped and especially to David Adamson, Richard Adamson, and Bob Ewegen. Elspeth MacHattie's careful reading and acute observations sharpened the narrative. Every writer should be fortunate enough to have an agent like Deborah Schneider, who read so many versions of this novel and came up with a hundred thoughtful suggestions. Every writer needs an editor like Damaris Rowland, who saw what the book should be. The Nature Conservancy and the people of Telluride deserve much praise for preserving the town's heritage and that beautiful valley.

NOTE:

Actual historical characters are used fictitiously in this novel to give it a sense of authenticity. All the other people are products of the imagination and any similarity to real people is entirely coincidental.

Telluride is, of course, a real town in Colorado. The events in its rich history that appear in the novel are reported as accurately as possible. The miners' strike and all the natural disasters took place on the dates given.

Its geography is also described faithfully, with one exception. A side canyon called Ute Rise has been added outside of Telluride, and is entirely fictional.

Ireland's geography has also been altered slightly. Daire, a small island, has been situated off the northern coast.

Listen. Hear the lilac sigh
As the trunk is opened
Unfaded white is the wedding dress
And the memories are petal fresh

ARI

CHAPTER 1

The glossy black and white magpies gathered in the elms high outside the window were usually piercingly effective alarm clocks. As the warming sun signaled a new June day, they uttered harsh calls of welcome to each other in the stately trees that lined the main street of the small town in Colorado.

Ariana MacAllister was blissfully asleep in her basement apartment. She knew all about those magpies and preferred their raucous caws to electronic buzzes. Still, the previous evening as she reached up to unlatch the small window near the ceiling above her bed, she'd hesitated. Planning a luxurious Sunday, she didn't want to be awakened early—by anything. On the other hand, the cinder block walls of her bedroom always exuded a musty smell. At last, Ari had voted for the sweet air and let the window down on its rusty chain, telling herself she would pull a pillow over her head if she heard the birds and just drift right off again. And that's what she'd done, nestling her slim, full-breasted body in a hollow in the lumpy mattress, reaching down with long legs to tuck the old quilt around her feet to keep out the fresh coolness of the morning.

Nothing was going to spoil the day, Ari had determined. It was to be her first true day of rest. For almost six years as she'd struggled to both work and attend college, weekends had been spent writing papers, studying for exams, frantically catching up on reading. Weekdays were a mad rush to catch the early morning bus to the campus in the next town and back again to work at the bank down the street. Summers were no vacation, since she'd worked full-time and taken classes she'd missed during regular term. But she'd graduated last week, and Ari wanted to spend a lazy Sunday—getting dressed late, reading the fat newspapers, picnicking on the high ridge overlooking the mountains.

Although she'd shopped at the supermarket on Saturday with her usual care, she did buy several things to treat herself. She felt she needed cheering up. Ari had found the longed-for gift of leisure was spoiled by loneliness. Her best friend, Janie, was an out-of-state student and had left after graduation for her eagerly sought-after job in a Chicago public relations firm. Then, too, Ari had been handed bad news on Friday.

So she'd bought a whole chicken and simmered it with rosemary, celery, and carrots for a soup to last the week. She took out the white breast to make a salad for her picnic. On Monday she planned to add a can of tomatoes, dried onion soup, and raw cabbage to the broth, and the rest of the meat. Growing up on a farm, she'd been taught how to cook and stretch a food dollar. Nothing was ever wasted.

At the store's produce section Ari had stopped before the Granny Smith apples, whose color had always reminded her of the crayon labeled "spring-green." And, thinking of the wonderful pies she and Mrs. Mac had made in the farm kitchen from the scrubby apple tree at the bottom of the garden, she'd chosen five fat ones, although they were expensive. With a smile, she realized she'd never made a pie for herself. Later Saturday afternoon, rolling out the dough, then smelling the cinnamony fragrance of the baked pastry, all the happy memories of her childhood and youth with the MacAllisters, her adoptive parents, welled up.

In her mind's eye she and Mrs. Mac were usually in the kitchen together, canning fresh vegetables, squeezing rich purple grape juice through a cheesecloth bag for jelly, making Brown Betty with leftover bread. After every step of every process hands had to be washed with surgical care with thick chunks of brown soap. And it was in the kitchen that Mrs. Mac ironed. She ironed everything—dishtowels, pillowcases, sheets, Mr. Mac's cotton pajamas. When Ari teasingly pointed out that everything would be wrinkled five minutes later, she'd only shake her head and smile, saying, "But it feels nice." Her gray hair was braided neatly in the morning and wound around her head, but as the day progressed, wisps came undone, and she would stop and tuck them in as she added a finished piece to the stack of linen.

In the summer they'd spent a lot of time in the garden and the old orchard behind it. As Mrs. Mac hoed the weeds out, she'd send Ari to tie up sweet peas, pull ripe tomatoes and squashes from their vines, throw bird-pecked fruit onto the mulch pile. And the two of them would take long rambles in the nearby fields toward the cottonwood stands with a metal Thermos of lemonade and sandwiches in much-creased waxed paper. On their way back Ari would pick the bright pinwheels of black-eyed Susans for the kitchen table. If it were autumn, Mrs. Mac pried open the bristly, plum-sized pod of a milkweed, pulled out the glistening fluff, and as she blew the small parachutes upward, she'd say, "Make a wish, Ari. Hurry, before they land, or it won't come true."

Since his accident in the mines Mr. Mac had been in a wheelchair. But a workbench the right height had been built off the kitchen and broad planks laid down in the yard so he could roll out to tend the beehives. He always dressed in light colors because he said that dark ones disturbed the bees. They had bad memories about hive-destroying bears, he said, and they would sting people dressed in black, mistaking them for bears. Swathed in white netting, he would continually converse in his soft Scots burr with the circling bees. After his funeral, when Ari, as was the tradition, went to the hives to tell the bees that the beekeeper was dead, she could barely blurt the words out. But she thought their answering hums held sorrow too.

With these recollections came the aching sense of loss she still felt for Lucy and Gerald MacAllister. Sitting in her own tiny kitchen, wishing desperately they were here now so that she could pour out her misery, she'd summoned up their understanding ghosts. Living alone, many times Ari had found herself sharing her internal life with them, murmuring about her daily concerns. It was a way of threshing out whatever troubled her. As she dabbed at her hot tears with the damp dishcloth she'd used to scrub the floury wooden pastry board, she explained to them, half-aloud, "It just wasn't fair that I was fired. 'Laid off,' Betty called it, almost smirking at me as she said it. I finally figured out *why*, but that doesn't help. I was counting on that job for now—working at the bank for another summer. Then I could have saved enough to move . . . fall's a much better time to find a decent job. They always kept me as a part-time employee, I won't get unemployment . . . two weeks' severance pay . . . what good will that do?"

Wholly involved with her painful reflections, she'd walked around the kitchen, gesturing as she talked, almost feeling the sympathy of her unseen listeners. She made some coffee, cut herself a large piece of pie, murmured as she ate it. "The worst is the cost of moving. First month's rent on a new place, probably a deposit. And there are no jobs here." Contemplating her current dreary prospects, she lifted another section of pie onto her plate. "Here I thought," she said, between satisfying chews, "that once you get the degree, some of the money troubles are over. They're worse. And all because of Betty D'Amato. Whom I hate."

Dipping her fork now into the pie pan, she broke off a flaky bit of crust, then followed that with a comforting piece of warm apple, and then another. "That woman"—Ari waved her fork in the air—"actually thought I wanted to stay on at the bank, as if I weren't sick of the place. *She* thought I was after the head teller's job that she's been dying to get for *years*. And she was jealous because Mr. Johnson's been talking about having me write the bank's history. I know that's why she got rid of me."

Ari looked down and, aghast, realized she'd eaten half the pie. A grin started, although tears still pooled at the corners of her eyes. She had a sudden sharp image of the tender laughter in Mrs. Mac's eyes whenever Ari had felt the entire weight of the world had landed unfairly on her shoulders. "Okay, okay. Enough self-pity already. I'll think of something to do."

Carrying her dishes to the small sink, she mused that it really had been an emotional week, graduating, having to say good-bye to a big part of her life—and Janie. Several times she'd discovered herself behaving against habit. At the supermarket, noticing the length of the check-out line, she'd gone back for some cheddar and, seeing the lottery ticket counter, she'd bought one. As she ran hot water into the stained metal sink and added detergent, she argued aloud, "Well, what difference was a couple more dollars going to make? It's never gotten up to twenty-five million before. Twenty-five million dollars!"

Ari stopped, held up the plastic plate to see if it were clean. But she was staring at it blindly, her head whirling with a vision of herself on a tall sailing ship rounding the isles of Greece, of a house of her own with a flowering garden, of closets full of shimmering gowns, of entire chests of drawers filled with soft hand-knit sweaters and satiny slips and lacy bras. With her soapy fingers she touched her right cheek in a daydream of hope. Then she sighed, rinsed the dish, and her grin returned, this time with a wry twist.

"Sure. Anyway," she went on aloud, "they're calling this contest a sweepstakes because the winner gets most of the money upfront instead of so much a year. The drawing's tonight, so somebody will wake up Sunday an instant multimillionaire. But I couldn't resist . . . the old

Sweepstakes mine on Bridey's Mountain. Wait. Come to think of it, that mine was a bust, wasn't it? No silver or gold. Still," Ari finished, "I don't feel bad at all about spending the money." She *did* feel a little guilty. The MacAllisters had always needed to be careful about small sums and had taught her to be too.

Talking it out had made her feel better. She decided to ride extra miles on her bicycle tomorrow to work off the pie. Caught up in this high-minded mood, she glanced around her small apartment and realized it'd been some time since she'd cleaned it. Since well before the last month's deluge of papers and finals, now that she thought of it. Pushed well to the back of her dusty, coffee-ringed desk was a stack of unopened mail, most of it, she'd gathered at a glance, from insurance firms who seemed convinced that new college graduates were very much interested in taking out a policy. Popcorn kernels were mixed with dustballs in the corners of the kitchen, and the worn linoleum floor felt sticky beneath her sneakers. Several invisible spiders had made their homes by the heavy, half-painted pipes on the ceiling. The Contac-paper-covered card table where she ate was ragged at the corners, and she remembered there was probably enough of the roll left under the sink to redo it. Sliding the broom and mop from their corner next to the antique Frigidaire, she set to work.

As Ari dusted off the frame of a picture in her bedroom, she stopped to smile at it. It was a charcoal sketch of a Colorado canyon, done by her grandmother. The scene showed a stream with trumpetlike flowers beside it, solid mountains with one peak warmly brooding over the others. That was Bridey's Mountain. She felt it was imprinted on her heart.

When she'd finished her housework, she contemplated her sparse living quarters with some satisfaction. It was clean—she'd scrubbed everything, including the greasy top of the refrigerator, even polished the dented toaster. She'd stacked everything neatly on her immaculate desk, including the unopened letters, putting that off until Monday. Although longing for a long soak in a tub, she'd sung cheerfully as she hopped about in the jerry-built shower installed in the corner of her bedroom. Happily choosing a novel she could read for the sheer pleasure of it instead of making notes in the margin for an assignment, she went to bed early. She made up her mind not to spoil Sunday by dwelling on the future.

Now, this morning, with the pillow tucked firmly over her head, she was dreaming. Her dream, like those that come after dawn, had pieces of reality jumbled in the fantasy. In this one, although she'd apparently set out to go mountain climbing, she was wearing a long white dress, old-fashioned and decorated with exquisite cobwebby lace. Her thick brown hair, usually wildly curling, was neatly upswept, and on her finger she had an ornate ruby-and-diamond ring. Ari actually had such a dress, long packed in tissue and lavender, in a trunk on the floor of her makeshift closet. She'd never had occasion to wear it. It had belonged to her great-grandmother, as had the ring.

In her mindscape she was walking beside a clear-running stream in a place she'd never been, an old mining town where she'd always wanted to go. The town was quite real. It was in Colorado, but miles away, in altitude and distance, from where she lived. Set strikingly in a mountain-ringed valley, the town had boomed and busted, and then boomed again for a hundred and some years.

The Ute Indians had considered these particular mountains sacrosanct. They'd been promised they could stay there as long as the streams ran and the grass was green. But when silver and gold were discovered in the San Juan Range, the Indians were forced to leave and were sent to a dry, sandy plain in the southwest. As Chief Shavano led the Utes out on their long, painful march, he turned in his saddle, looked back at the green valley and said bitterly, "No man will be happy here for a hundred and five years, and no family will survive here for four generations."

When the history of the town was considered, it did seem that Shavano's curse was working. Of course, some of the early prospectors were lucky. One man named Ingram noticed that two of the potentially best mining claims were five hundred feet longer than the legal limit. He staked his own exactly between them, gleefully calling *his* mine the Smuggler. It was the richest strike of all. Yet one of the first claimants went away with almost nothing.

The location of the valley was itself a problem. The passes that led into it were tortuous at the best of seasons, impassable at the worst. The town, once called Columbia, was finally named Telluride, although no one was quite sure why. That particular valuable ore, derived from the element tellurium, was not found there. Most people believed that the name was a shortened form of "To hell you ride" since it was almost impossible to get there.

But the town was situated on the Colorado Mineral Belt. That zone slices the state diagonally, starting around the middle in Boulder and creasing the heart of the Rockies to the glacier-carved basins of the San Juan Mountains in the southwest. It contained abounding deposits of gold, silver, zinc, and lead. So people came to Telluride. And it was a beautiful place, with hanging waterfalls that cascaded down to the shining San Miguel River, which meandered along the edge of the town. But hardly anyone managed to stay, because the wheel of fortune seemed to turn so rapidly there.

Although Ari had visited there only in her dreams, she had heard the town's history many times from Mrs. Mac. Lucy Wesley MacAllister had never been to Telluride either. It was hard for Gerald to travel far. And right to the day of her death there'd never been quite enough money for a long trip, and no one to look after the farm in any case. But Mrs. Mac had herself been told the stories of days in that high frontier town by her maternal aunt Isobel Ewen, who shared a history there with Ari's great-grandmother, Morna Gregory.

When Ari was small and tired, she would climb into Mrs. Mac's hard but comforting lap, be embraced by thin, strong arms. The older woman would repeat tales from the Grimm brothers of princes who were turned into frogs or swans, of princesses who slept in enchanted forests or lived on top of glass mountains. But Mrs. Mac usually ended with the story that she said was true.

"Long ago, Ariana Bridget Gregory MacAllister," she'd begin, and the child would wriggle in pleasure. She liked being addressed by her full name because it was so long and it made her feel important. "And from faraway too," the soothing voice would continue, "Morna Gregory came to live in the valley overlooked by Bridget's Mountain. She named it that because, if you look carefully, you can see the shape of a woman's face on top—her forehead, her nose, her mouth. And you can follow with your finger how her long hair flows backward. She has her face lifted to the sky. The name was shortened to Bridey's Mountain because that's a nickname for Bridget. Other people call the mountain something else entirely because they don't know its real name. Only you and I and Mr. Mac know that."

With her brown-splotched, veined hand, Mrs. Mac would stroke the child's springy curls. "Now, when Morna got the mountain, people had been digging into it because they thought it had something shiny inside, like silver or gold. One man called his mine 'Champion' but he couldn't find anything there that he wanted. Another named his 'Sweepstakes,' which is a lucky name, but he didn't have any luck. Morna didn't think the mountain liked holes poked in its sides and, to her, it was beautiful as it was. She wanted to make sure no one would do that again. She gave the mountain to her daughter, Bridey, to watch over. Bridey was your grandmother. She told *her* daughter, Trish, to take care of the mountain. Trish was your mother and she left the mountain to you. And it's really yours, to this very day!"

No matter how many times the story was told, the ending always brought a delighted, transfiguring smile to the child's face, and at that

sight Lucy MacAllister's heart would expand with love. She had regarded Ari's mother, Trish Gregory, as her own grandchild and adored
her, looking forward each week to her visit. But, because she herself
had raised Ari, Lucy thought of her as the daughter whom she herself
could not have.

As she rocked the little girl peacefully and went over the past, the
elderly woman would look at her and think what a gift she was. The
years when the MacAllisters had prayed for children, they'd had none.
But those were the years when Gerald spent all the daylight hours in the
dark mines, the years when Lucy had helped her widowed mother run
the farm. All the acreage had been planted then, and they'd also kept
dairy cows. There was never a spare minute. Only when they were old
enough to become grandparents had they at last had time to play, to tell
stories, to enjoy a child's growing discoveries.

As Mrs. Mac gazed down at the small face raised to hers, she
would see reminders of her cherished Trish. There was that delicate
nose, the rosebud mouth with a full lower lip, even signs of the determined jaw that Trish had inherited from her mother, Bridey, who had
been her own lifelong best friend. But Ari's unruly mop of curls was all
her own, she thought, and those amazing eyes, too, of the palest brown
imaginable. The color made Mrs. Mac think of the golden honey from
Gerald's bees, just scraped from the wax frames. The thick, surprisingly
dark lashes were a hallmark of all the Gregory women.

There was one difference, and although Mrs. Mac regarded it as
slight, she knew even before Ari started kindergarten that it would
make a larger difference to her. A port-wine birthmark started at the
child's forehead, circled the eye, and stained the right cheek. When the
two of them went into town to get supplies, people who didn't know
them looked at the little girl once, then looked twice. Soon Mrs. Mac
noticed Ari invariably turned her left profile to strangers.

The angriest moment of her life, Mrs. Mac recalled, was the August morning she'd taken Ari to be fitted for new shoes for school. Two
seats down Mavis Allert was waiting with a friend for a clerk. She was a
woman Lucy MacAllister instinctively avoided even at church socials,
the sort who saw God's displeasure in every crop-threatening storm, in
every dry spell. Mavis had nudged her friend, whispered loudly,
"Child's illegitimate. You see that blotch on her face and it makes you
think, doesn't it? The Bible says the sins of the parents shall be visited
on their children." When Lucy glared ferociously at her, Mavis had
turned aside, but she thought the woman had even mouthed, "The
mark of Cain."

The first day of school had been very difficult for Ari. All the children had stared, and one outspoken little girl on the playground had asked curiously, "What's the matter with your face?"

A pudgy-faced older boy, whose parents were new in town and who was therefore anxious to prove himself, noticed that the purplish-red mark on her cheek resembled three spread fingers. He declared, "Looks like somebody smacked her. She's probably a bad girl."

Ari had at first shrunk back from the unwanted attention, but that remark amazed her, then shook her with rage. "I am not!"

Seeing that several of his classmates had come up, the boy felt he couldn't resist the challenge. "You must be," he stated, taking one step forward.

Her whole body convulsed with a child's first experience of injustice, Ari's fist landed in his stomach. She still had a ferocious grip on his hair when a teacher rescued the surprised bully.

That afternoon, as Gerald MacAllister was sanding a hive frame at his workbench, Ari had marched up to him, eyes still bright with blinked-back tears. "Take it off," she said, pointing to her cheek, convinced of his ability to fix anything.

One look at her and he guessed the trouble, spun his wheelchair around, lifted her onto his lap. He looked sadly at his neatly spread-out tools and replied, "I canna' do that, my honey. It's a doctor's job to work on faces, and one day maybe one of 'em can."

Gently he had pulled the story from her, his own anger growing, but when she'd reached the end, his shoulders rippled with the effort to hold back laughter. "You did what?" he asked.

"I punched him." Shame in her voice, she looked down.

"Weel, now." Try as he would, a chuckle escaped. "It may be that wasn't the best thing, but it may be that was a lesson on him. We'll just go have some chocolate cake and talk it over."

After Ari had gone to bed, the MacAllisters had consulted together on the darkened porch, but they couldn't see what to do. From the beginning the doctor had spread his hands, calling the birthmark *nevus flammeus*. "It's only on the surface of the skin, but plastic surgeons don't know how to remove them yet. Maybe when she's older, who knows? But no one considers trying with a child."

Over the years the MacAllisters had not seen signs that the port-wine stain had made Ari less outgoing or slower to make friends, once she'd adjusted to school. And, ever the optimist, Gerald had even suggested to his wife that there was a positive side. "Ye know," he said, "it may be that's why she's so good wi' her studies. She wants to shine there. And, Lucy, she's inherited your good looks and that of the Gregory women."

"But, my dear," his wife interrupted, laughing, "she could hardly *inherit* anything from me. We're no blood kin."

"Oh, aye, she could," he'd replied with a twinkle, waving that away as a minor objection. "Same as she's come by your green thumb. And she's that like you in another way, and Bridey and Trish as well, ye canna' coop any of you indoors too long or not one of you'd be happy. There's one thing, though, ye can tell Ari's a Gregory when she gets that don't-be-telling-me-no look in her eyes. Stubborn, she is, for all her sweet ways. You've always been too good for your own good, Lucy. Spoiled me, ye have. But I'll not be having you fret over our Ari," he concluded with fatherly pride. "There's no cause."

But as Ari became a teenager, the birthmark made more of a difference than the tenderhearted MacAllisters hoped or knew, distanced by their age from the exquisite pains of adolescence. Although she was full of fun with girlfriends, she became shy and withdrawn in the company of boys. Even the idea of dating was a misery for Ari, convinced as she was that pity was at the heart of any invitation from a male. At first she'd experimented with cosmetics, but she found that over-the-counter makeup didn't work, and she looked in mirrors with sadness.

Even now as she slept, the pillow tossed aside after the magpies had winged away, the brown curls were tumbled over her cheek, as if to hide that stain. And in her dream, dressed in delicate white, walking beside the transparent water, she bore no such mark.

It was one of those delicious, sun-splashed dreams. She knelt down beside a clear pool formed in the rock-filled stream, and she saw reflected there the lace of the dress that covered her throat and above it a woman's face. But it was not her own, although somehow familiar. The woman was beautiful, smiling reassuringly. On the other bank were graceful blue-purple columbines that leaned forward to be picked. Ari turned and it seemed the high mountain before her was within reach. Simply by stretching out her hand she was sure she could trace its profile, run a finger down the forehead, the nose.

She glanced back again at the glassy water and saw it was rippling over what seemed a lump of gold in the bottom sand. A second look showed it was a man's pocket watch, shiny and round, with a fob chain glittering from its top. Thinking to retrieve such a valuable antique, she plunged her hand in.

But just as she did so, a fear that belonged to nightmares gripped her. The water ran blood-red. The ruby ring slipped from her finger, and she could not see to find it. The watch chain coiled around her wrist, manacling her.

Then the ground shook violently beneath her as if to bring down the mountain itself. Looking wildly up, she saw its face obscured with fog. Suddenly a woman's white hand thrust up from the water, the ring in her open palm. But the golden chain on Ari's wrist held her so that she couldn't reach it. A man's urgent voice called her name, once, twice, but was drowned out by the howl of a wolf reverberating through the canyon.

She covered her ears to block out its frightening echo, but it only changed in tone, became more bell-like. It was impossible to ignore.

Ari sat up in bed with a gasp. She was panting as if she had been running, and she pushed her hair away from her sweating forehead. The bell sound persisted. It took her a moment to realize it was the telephone.

CHAPTER 2

Rivers Alexander had questioned his decision to phone so early on a Sunday morning. Seated in his office in a renovated Victorian mansion in Denver, he'd sipped his coffee, putting it off. He realized that at this hour it was more than a little rude, but he considered that the woman might be a churchgoer, might leave for the day. And Rivers had been trying to reach her for several weeks, calling repeatedly, with no answer. He'd written two letters and gotten no reply. He'd even made the forty-minute drive to the little town of Louisville, just off the highway between Denver and Boulder, to see if he could catch her at home.

And he thought that the business proposal he had outlined in his letters had to be welcome news. When he'd seen the shabby frame house where she lived and had been told by Mrs. Barth, the older woman upstairs who owned the house, that Ari MacAllister was a working college student who rented the basement, he was sure of it. The price that his employer, Murdoch and Associates, was offering for the mining claims and accompanying surface rights on the mountain in Telluride was more than fair, even considering the boom that town was experiencing. To someone in these circumstances it would be a small fortune.

Rivers had attended to other less pressing matters before placing the call, paced a bit, stared out the window, abstractedly rumpling brown hair, still sun streaked from spring skiing. He was not yet thirty, his face leanly sculpted, with well-defined bones, a straight nose, clean jaw. His dark-lashed, blue-green eyes were what caught the attention, reflecting his feelings more than he was perhaps aware. His generous mouth, often twisted in a deceptively lazy grin, was vulnerable in repose. Women noticed that. Women's eyes always lingered on Rivers.

His air of self-confidence was warranted, but misleading. It implied that he had found life easy, and he had not. He saw complexities wherever he looked. So there was more than a little wariness in his stance, in the way he moved, his body only relaxing into grace in athletics.

In fact, Rivers was in the office at that uncivilized hour because he wanted to spend the rest of this glorious June morning mountain-climbing, and he wanted to do it with an untroubled mind. But he knew that Jonas Murdoch placed a high priority on getting the Telluride project started and that acquiring this last piece was essential. His employer was sure to inquire about progress the first thing on Monday.

After this was settled, Rivers himself would no longer be involved in that particular project. He was glad of it. In his view Ute Rise Canyon should be left undeveloped, its quiet beauty undisturbed. It was so near the center of the small town that residents and visitors could stroll there and remember wilderness. Joggers could run along the untrafficked road, and the upper reaches of the enclosing mountains could be given over to the more venturesome hikers and climbers. Telluride had magnificent ski slopes already and, he thought, in the recently built Mountain Village high above the valley, it had more than enough condos.

The town itself had preserved its own past wonderfully. If one took the cars away from the broad main street, it was like a Western movie set with square wooden storefronts stair-stepping down the short downtown blocks. The only change was that the stores now sold curios, bicycles, and ski parkas instead of hay, grain, and miners' gear. The handsome steepled brick courthouse was still used as the county seat. The Sheridan Hotel's bar continued its roaring business. The old Opera House next door was called that yet and was now a theater. The saloons along Colorado Avenue no longer had roulette wheels and poker tables, but they still sold liquor. The whorehouses had become restaurants, but the buildings remained the same. Along Popcorn Alley the tiny cribs where individual ladies of the evening had beckoned to men passing by looked no different, although they had a much different kind of renter. The elegant Victorian houses on the north side, refurbished to within an inch of their lives, had once housed the town's elite and now did so again.

Rivers especially liked going to Telluride in the fall, when the crowds of the Film Festival had left, and the skiers not yet arrived. Then golden aspen blazed amid dark conifers on the mountainsides, and the unmoving ski lifts looked very like the old tramways once used to carry ore down from the mines. Most of the stores closed for the season, and the town settled sleepily down. In the evening he'd wander down deserted streets. It almost seemed to him then that the ghosts of the ruffle-shirted gamblers, the laughing ladies, and the burly miners drifted back to their former haunts, drawn by the weathered wooden boards and aged brick.

But as he looked down at the office's parking lot, which had once been this mansion's garden, he reflected that Jonas Murdoch had not secured his place near the top of the list of *Fortune*'s 500 by passing up good opportunities to add to his wealth. Building in Ute Rise Canyon would surely do that. Rivers couldn't say he liked the cold-eyed, aristocratic-looking man in his early fifties, but he admired Murdoch's intelligence, his decisiveness, his grasp of business fundamentals. And he had to admit that he generally enjoyed his job, found the work diverse enough to be interesting. Moreover, Rivers knew that he was exceptionally well paid. He was sure that if he continued saving, he could start his own company a few years down the road.

Running his hand down the satiny wood of the window frame thoughtfully, he wondered if Murdoch found it ironic that he was employing an Alexander. The two families were among Denver's founders, but their fortunes were no longer equal. In fact, the three-story mansion on Grant Street that now elegantly housed these modern offices had been the Alexander family house. Jonas Murdoch had acquired it in one of Denver's real estate downturns for almost nothing. The upstairs tower room where Rivers was standing had been his mother's sitting room. Jonas's handsome office downstairs with its bay window had been the very spot where, as a lonely boy, Rivers would await his father's return from some political meeting, often into the late hours.

Whereas Murdoch's grandfather William had carefully tended to his bank, his near contemporary, Patrick Alexander, had lightheartedly let money drift through his spread fingers. William had set his own son, Enos, to work at twelve at his business, but Patrick hadn't even gotten around to marrying the mother of his sons until the oldest was nearly that age. It wasn't a matter of outright negligence. Patrick's first wife had an aversion to children and divorces were difficult to procure at the turn of the century. Apparently everyone had liked Patrick, both the ladies and the gentlemen. It was said he could always tell you which horse to bet on, which business to invest in, but he'd done very little of the latter himself. His easy laugh was often heard in the bordellos on Market Street, at the track, at the less stuffy men's clubs.

As if to compensate for this charming scapegrace, Rivers's father, Thomas, had been hardworking, idealistic, rather earnest. He believed in public service, rising rapidly through the ranks to a high position in the War Department during the dark years of the Second World War when people looked to their leaders to be true statesmen. Thomas Alexander had tried hard to be that, not even stopping to marry until he was in his early fifties. But the beautiful young Helen Rivers whom he'd fallen so in love with had died early. The grieving man had buried himself even further in the public's needs, and he'd used the slim capital left him by Patrick to augment his salary.

Thomas was continually pressed for time; he'd not been able to look after his growing son, often left to a succession of housekeepers, or to his own finances as he might have liked. So the once-proud mansion almost echoed with that embarrassing shortage of money faced by those with influence and social standing, but little cash. Everyone assumed there was money and saw the unmade repairs as a sign of carelessness, the refusal to spend as tight-fistedness. There was enough to pay for Rivers's expensive private education, but only just enough. He was always popular, always invited along, but usually could not afford to go. So the look of exasperated love that Rivers frequently turned on his aging father before his death was understandable. If the young man looked at good causes with a certain distance, it was the result of too many solitary hours curled in the window seat, longing for his father's return. All of this went a long way to explain Rivers's ambition, his desire to make his own fortune.

He was thinking at that moment that it was important to do it here in Denver. The original families that had prospered stayed. And they had long memories, the elders relishing the old stories at the two most exclusive country clubs. Whereas populous New York had had its famous "Four Hundred," Denver's elite had been called the "Sacred Thirty-six," two generations back. This was usually abbreviated to the "Sacred." Their approval was necessary. But Rivers was not yet sure of the kind of golden opinions he wanted. He only knew that he needed to accomplish something, and money was essential for that.

Plunging his hands into the deep pockets of his mountaineering shorts, he sat down in his swivel chair, stretched out long, muscular legs. He eyed his left knee, embroidered with surgical scars from a climbing accident, hoping that it would hold up well today. He'd have to take it easy, which made him impatient. The hope of getting out of the office made him reach for the telephone.

This had to be the right woman, he assured himself. Although the taxes had always been paid at the courthouse in Telluride under the name of Ariana Gregory, the address was the same as the MacAllister woman's. And there was that unusual first name. He punched out the number. He might wake her up, but she would be happy to hear what he had to say.

"Hello." The voice that answered was low, musical, throaty with sleep.

He lifted an eyebrow at the pleasing sound, smiled at the telephone, and said, "I'm Rivers Alexander from Murdoch and Associates. I'm sorry to disturb you so early, but I need to talk to Ariana Gregory. It's important. Have I got the right number?"

"Yes." Ari tried to clear her throat, shivering nakedly in the dankness of the basement as she stood by the table near the couch. The cord wouldn't reach to the bed. "That's me."

"And"—he paused, wondering how to address her—"MacAllister is your married name?"

"No. I was adopted." She finally managed to stretch the short cord far enough to snag a quilt off the bed and, cradling the receiver, wrapped herself in it. Holding the faded coverlet around her slender frame with one arm, she rubbed the sleep from her eyes and pushed back the thick curls from her face with the other hand. She was still half in her dream.

"Ms. MacAllister, I'm sure you've kept up on the changes in Telluride. Now that it's such a popular resort, land has become quite valuable. Murdoch and Associates wants to buy yours. I wrote you—twice, in fact—giving the details. Did you get my letters?"

"Um, no. Well, maybe." Ari looked guiltily at the teetering pile of unopened mail. "I've been truly busy. Final exams. But I'm not interested in selling."

Rivers raised both his dark eyebrows, thinking that this young woman had better take a look at the price being offered in the letters before saying that. But then he thought that maybe she had, and this was a negotiating ploy. "Let me explain," he said, attempting to sound friendly *and* firm. "Mr. Murdoch has owned several of the surrounding slopes for some time, and he's bought the rest. He'll be the only bidder for your land and, honestly, that's a fair price. You can look at market valuations, check with any realtor there. But with Murdoch's lock on the area, no one else will come in. The cost of the development will run near a hundred million, with the ski lifts, condos, roads, necessary improvements—"

Suddenly awake, Ari clenched her teeth at the idea of chalets on stilts jutting from the sides of Bridey's Mountain. "I'm not interested in selling," she repeated distinctly. "I don't think my mountain needs any 'improvements,' as you call them."

Now Rivers stared at the receiver, astonished. God help him, he thought, had he gotten hold of a dewy-eyed world-saver? No, there was a more likely explanation. She hadn't read the letter, perhaps thought she was turning down a few thousand, not hundreds of thousands. It was obvious from her voice that she was young. Maybe she was unaware of the cost of land near a popular ski resort. He backtracked hurriedly. "Look, I apologize again for shoving a business discussion on you before you've even had coffee. Could I drive out to Louisville now, take you to breakfast? In the meantime you could look at the letters, and we could talk—"

"That's not necessary, Mr. . . ." she jogged her memory for his name, pulling the quilt more tightly around her.

"Rivers," he supplied.

"Mr. Rivers, as I said—"

"Rivers is my first name," he broke in, "Alexander is the last. Please, I'd be happy to drive—"

"There's no point, Mr. Alexander. I want my mountain left alone. There must be plenty of other places in Telluride where they can put their houses and roads and ski slopes—"

"But there aren't," he interrupted, surprised at her remark, betraying as it did a lack of knowledge about the area. "The town's in a box canyon, as you know. The ski slopes have to be on the south so that the sun doesn't hit the snow. Ute Rise is very near the town's current ski runs and the only place that you could have a new one, without going some distance away."

"Maybe you're right. I don't know. I've never been to Telluride, but I've seen articles on the town and it looks like they've got more than enough ski areas nearby. And while I don't mind people skiing on the mountain—that doesn't hurt it—it's the other part I don't like. Turning a wilderness into little sectioned-off lots, tearing it all up. You have to dig into it to put pipes in for all those fake Swiss condos."

Score round one for the lady, he thought. "Well," he answered, "I can't guarantee someone won't opt for fake Swiss, but the houses will be custom built, very expensive, spaced among the trees. They'll be attractive. People are willing to pay a high price to ski to the lifts from their front doors. And," he added gently, "you'd be paid a very high price for selling the land to them. Not just a few thousand, Ms. MacAllister."

"No," Ari said quietly. "No. It isn't a question of money. I simply don't want it developed."

Rivers raked a hand through his hair. He had to give her round two as well. She wasn't rich but she stood by her principles. But she couldn't win this match. "There's one other thing you should know," he went on uneasily. "There are several mountains in Ute Rise. If Murdoch goes ahead and develops the area, puts in roads, sewers, and water, other property owners have to bear part of the cost. The only other one is you." He had a vision of that little house in Louisville, and he knew that if she had *any* money, she wouldn't be living there and commuting to the campus in Boulder. "That'll cost you a bundle."

Ari collapsed on the couch, the quilt slipping down from her shoulders. "You mean they can do all these things that I don't want done, and *I* have to pay for them?"

"I'm sorry," he said. "You'd have to get legal advice, but that's the way it's usually done. It's very possible."

The chill of the Naugahyde couch on her back made her tug at the quilt to get it back up onto her bare shoulders. "Look, there must be something that can be done to save the mountain. The whole canyon could be left as it is," she spoke rapidly, thinking aloud. "Mr. Murdoch could donate his land, and I'll donate mine. We could give it to the town if they promised to preserve it, or to The Nature Conservancy. They do things like that, I read about it."

"Wait." Rivers rubbed his forehead, took a breath. She had to be made to face realities. "That's a very generous idea. But you're talking about giving away hundreds of thousands of dollars. I'd be a lot happier if you'd take a look at my letter. We can talk later. If you're still in school, you can use that money and—"

"Just graduated," Ari stopped him. Then she sighed. "And of course I could use the money. I don't have a job, and I do have debts." The MacAllister farm had been sold long before Louisville had become an increasingly prosperous bedroom community for Boulder. There'd been no money left after Mrs. Mac died. Ari still owed for the funeral and had student loans as well.

"But," she went on, wanting to persuade him, "that mountain has always been in my family. I've heard the stories about it all my life. My great-grandmother didn't want the veins of the mountain opened by miners. She wanted its beauty. Everyone in the family needed money at one time or another. But no one sold it. Of course, it wasn't always worth this much, but you have to understand that I'd always feel bad if I was the one who lost it. I'd always have to feel I'd sold my birthright for a mess of pottage. Or, in this case, a mess of sewage pipe."

Rivers swiveled in his chair, glancing at the plastic louvers on the window, unwillingly knowing how she felt. He remembered sitting in this room next to his mother. There had been pale blue drapes against the blue walls, and his mother wore a blue dress, smoothing his hair, talking to him.

"Yes," he finally said slowly, "there are places that give meaning to our lives, and they shouldn't be destroyed. But," he added, turning impatiently to face his littered desk, "I have to tell you that Jonas Murdoch is not going to give away *that* expensive piece of real estate."

"Couldn't you at least suggest it? If you're buying land for him, he must have confidence in your judgment."

Yeah, he thought, *but he wouldn't if I told him to give his land away.* "This is a little removed from my usual job. He asked me to take it over because I know Telluride. I'm definitely not one of the 'associates' of the company's title. On the other hand, I don't know of anyone who could persuade him to even consider such an idea."

Ari jerked at the top of the old quilt. She was determined not to give up. "But if he's rich, he must give to charity. And we could name the park after him. I don't care. People would always think well of him," she finished hopefully.

Rivers thought of the few thousands Murdoch gave to the Symphony, to the Denver Zoo, to the Natural History Museum, aware that his employer gave only what he could claim as a tax write-off. "Yes, he gives some to charity." Then he added dryly, "I imagine he believes, however, that people really think well of you if you're very, very, very, *very* rich."

"He doesn't sound very likable," Ari said.

He countered, "I don't think that's a requirement for employers. Have you liked all your bosses?"

"No." Surprised at the question, Ari grinned. She thought of Betty D'Amato, her hair sprayed into a helmet. "Hated my last one. The one that just fired me." She sighed. "That's what money really gives you, doesn't it? Choice. Freedom."

"And couldn't you look at the sale that way?" he urged. "You're not giving up your inheritance, it's giving you something. The choice you mentioned."

"No." Ari abruptly remembered why this man had called her. She thought that no matter how pleasant he sounded, he was only interested in getting her signature. Anger welled up. "I'm not selling! Not ever. And you can tell Mr. Murdoch that."

"I can't see what option you have," he replied. "I don't think you can just give the mountain to the town or The Conservancy, surrounded as it will be by development. There's no access to it."

"I'll think of something," she gritted out, and banged the receiver down. She stood up, clutching the quilt around her, and stalked back to the bedroom.

CHAPTER 3

Gasping happily, out of breath, Ari tilted the bicycle, planted one foot on the ground, and looked with satisfaction at the muscles dancing in her bare leg beneath the khaki shorts. Then she swung her other leg over the seat and inhaled deeply. She'd ridden along the straight road from Louisville as if she were trying to escape the pull of gravity, and although the climb up the high hill had slowed her, she'd felt with each hard downthrust on the pedals that her anger and frustration were being pushed away.

Now, leaning her bicycle against the wind-smoothed trunk of an old pine, she gazed in delight over Boulder Valley. Her arrival had interrupted a meadowlark's liquid song, and now he flushed upward, his saffron breast gleaming. He veered west toward the rough mountains that rose solidly from the floor of the valley. The first tier were the Flatirons, aptly named thick slabs of limestone. Behind them more peaks reached up, holding perpetual snow in their crevices. The Colorado summer sky dwarfed even these summits. Its amazing lupine blue, without a scrap of filmy cloud, seemed to stretch to infinity.

Mr. Mac had quoted the psalm to her so often: "I will lift up mine eyes unto the hills, from whence cometh my help." Just for that moment she lived simply with her eyes. The morning sun, not yet at its highest point, poured over the front range of the Rockies, but there were still deep shadows among the clusters of sawtoothed peaks. Twin Sisters had a purplish hue and seemed to peer over the Flatirons. Just to the north Sugar Loaf Mountain's gunmetal gray shaded to violet. Long's Peak towered over the foothills, and the sheen of its snow, although it would not last much longer, was as white as on the day it had fallen.

The wind that ruffled the feathery grasses on the hillside was soft on her perspiring skin, and she pulled off the bandana that had tied back her long hair. The flyaway curls were gently brushed back as she lifted her face to the sky. The breeze touched her throat, flipped the banded collar of her cropped yellow shirt, and, as she raised her arms upward, slid along the bare flesh near her waist. The almost physical weight of worry fell away from her shoulders, and the peace of quiet nature wrapped itself around her.

Turning back to the tree, she loosened the tightly rolled bundles from the metal rack above the bicycle's rear wheel. First, she shook out the square of frayed canvas that all through her childhood had been taken along for picnics and spread it over the crinkling layer of shed pine needles. The embroidered quilt from her bed was laid over that, and within easy reach she tossed the two thick Sunday newspapers. From the front basket she picked up the silver coffee-filled Thermos, her lunch sack, and the white bakery bag, smelling wonderfully of the buttery croissants inside.

As she sat down, she put out her hand to slip the rubber band off the *Denver Post,* but that reminded her of the pages and pages of classified want-ads that she'd have to search through later. Instead, she unscrewed the cap of the dented Thermos and sniffed the coffee's welcome fragrance. As she poured it out, it occurred to her that this ringed metal container must be nearly an antique. Mrs. Mac saved everything, cared for everything she owned. This cup with its round handle looked to Ari very like the one her grandmother Bridey was holding in an old snapshot taken with Mrs. Mac's Brownie.

In that photograph Bridey's dark hair was arranged in a late nineteen-forties hairdo, the front swept over in a small roll, the sides pinned back, a style that flattered only those with cheekbones and even features. That she'd had, a true beauty of line. One could see the resolute shape of her lifted chin as she smiled at the camera, seated on a blanket before the MacAllisters' windowed west wall. One hand held the cup, the other circled her small daughter, Trish, her hair caught up in a curly topknot, her grin an echo of her mother's. Ari had studied the family photographs as she grew up, touching the faces, looking for resemblances to her own.

Now she sipped from the cup, smiling. Knowing Mrs. Mac, it might well be the very one in the picture. She imagined the two friends bringing little Trish to this very hillside, spreading out the old canvas and a blanket, gossiping as the child ran gleefully down to pick the scattered wildflowers. Now in June the slope held the tall stems of lacy wild carrot, the yellow and orange blossoms of butter-and-eggs, bright splashes of crimson Indian paintbrush. Ari felt she could almost see a little girl's curly topknot bobbing amid them.

She stroked the blue-and-white quilt beneath her which Mrs. Mac had made for Trish's bed, decorated with rows of sunbonneted little maids tending a garden. Probably, Ari thought, Mrs. Mac had sat sorting out gingham checked pieces for the skirts and bonnets, taking tiny stitches as she and Bridey chatted together in the evenings on the farm. Bridey had grown up in Telluride under the watchful eye of Lucy Mac-Allister's aunt Isobel. She must have talked to Mrs. Mac about the town in the days when its booming mines poured out silver and gold, gone over the stories Issy had told her about what had happened before her own birth. These were the tales Ari had heard, curled in Mrs. Mac's lap as they rocked together.

As she recalled these, she shifted her right hand so the rich red rubies of the ring blazed in the sun. The ring had belonged to Morna Gregory, her great-grandmother. It was the only valuable thing she owned. Just as she was leaving home that morning, Ari had gone back, pulled it from its hiding place securely pinned in the pocket of an old terry-cloth robe, and slipped it on her finger. Usually, she was afraid to wear it, worried that one of the glowing stones might be knocked from the ornate rose shape of the setting. But today she'd felt she needed it, and now, seeing its deep colors refracted by the sun onto the quilt, she was sure that she was no longer alone. She sensed that she was surrounded by this community of women who'd sent their love forward in time to her.

It was Morna who'd first seen the mountain in Telluride just before the turn of the century, her arrival there the start of the family legend handed on. So, Ari thought, sitting with her knees drawn up to her chin, it was natural that the place became— She stopped. How had the man she talked to on the phone this morning put it? Yes, a place that gave meaning to our lives. Well, she began fuming inwardly again, if this Rivers Alexander knew the importance of such things, how could he not see her point?

Fiercely, she tucked her breeze-tangled hair behind her ears and stared at the vista before her, glorying in the primeval power of those mountains, once thrust up from the earth's hot heart, a memory of the planet's past. Men had always marveled at the sight, drawing strength from that reminder. Now she narrowed her eyes, imagining each mountain bristling with houses, their sun decks cantilevered this way and that, saw the endless roads snaking between the lots, saw the beauty gone.

Perhaps, she thought, she should go personally and argue, not with Rivers Alexander, but his boss, Jonas Murdoch. She pictured herself taking a bus to Denver, finding his suite—no doubt in a glass skyscraper —getting by a secretary, marching into his office. But a vision of this unknown man, raising an incredulous eyebrow at her words, suddenly defeated her before she could even summon up the words she'd use. No doubt Murdoch was a man who would not listen to such a idea, would not back off unless faced with a wall of dollars as high as his own.

There was another problem. The port-wine stain on her face had made her shy, would rob her of courage. Ari shook herself mentally, her anger gone, trying to let herself off that hook. The birthmark wasn't the only reason she wouldn't face Murdoch down. But it was a big part of it. People did stare. At the University she'd pored over all the recent articles in Norlin Library, and she knew it could be removed now with lasers. But the operation was expensive and it wouldn't be covered by medical insurance at any job she'd get. It was considered cosmetic surgery.

Trying to regain her calm, she told herself that at least her problems canceled each other out. If she were forced to sell, she wouldn't have any immediate money problems. But the thought of selling brought an overwhelming feeling of betrayal and defeat. Somewhere, years from now, *she* could never tell her daughter the family stories. They'd always have to end with the bitter truth, "But I, my dear, sold the mountain, and it's forever changed."

With tears once again prickling, Ari straightened her back. A distraction was in order. She reached for the newspaper with one hand and the croissant bag with the other. Biting into the flaky layers of the roll, she savored its lightness on her tongue, licked a light brown morsel from the corner of her mouth. The taste made her glance at the stalk of butter-and-eggs near the blanket, with its golden curled cups. The hillside was bright with their snapdragon blooms, and Ari found herself grateful for these comforts.

She unfolded the front page, and immediately her eye was caught by the side box that proclaimed "Sweepstakes Drawing, page 6." It'd be fun to check, she thought, to see how close she'd come. If no one won this week, the prize would be increased. Then she'd find it even harder to resist buying another, particularly if she'd had any of the numbers this time.

Spreading the newspaper over her knees, thumbing for the page she needed, she went over the numbers she'd chosen. She'd picked 6 and 7 because she was born in 1967; then 10 since Mrs. Mac was born in 1910; 23 was her age; 25 was her birthday; last was 42. Her own mother, Trish, was born in 1944, but the highest number on the card was 42 so she'd settled for that.

The headline leapt from the page, but Ari quickly covered the article with her hand before she could read it properly. If, she told herself, she'd managed to get three of the numbers, next week she'd buy three tickets out of the small winnings. This *was* fun, she thought, it was easy to see why so many people bought the tickets. But she'd already seen the first number was 6, so she felt she was cheating a little with that promise to buy more next time. Still, it was hard to get *three* of them right. Slowly she pulled her finger along the line and saw the 7 and then the 10. In amazement, her eyes widening, she lifted her hand and saw 23, 25, and 42.

Her first reaction was disbelief. It must be a mistake, she was sure. She just hadn't remembered the numbers she'd picked properly. That must be it. It was a mistake. With a trembling hand she reached into her back pocket and yanked out her billfold. She knew she'd seen the ticket there when she bought the croissants and papers. But for a dreadful moment she couldn't find it, was sure she'd dropped it on the bakery floor. At last she pulled it from behind a dollar bill. She was quite literally holding her breath. When she could get her eyes to focus, she read the numbers out loud: 6, 7, 10, 23, 25, 42.

She couldn't imagine it was true. Perhaps it was a printer's error. Unable to take in any air, she snapped the rubber band off the *Rocky Mountain News,* found the front box, fumbled through to the indicated page, and couldn't find the article. No, she was on the wrong page, and she flipped the sheets nervelessly backwards. The numbers marched along exactly: 6, 7, 10, 23, 25, 42. She clutched the white Sweepstakes ticket so tightly that it was a wonder the ink did not indelibly print on her hand.

Like an automaton Ari replaced the small slip in her wallet, stuck it in her back pocket, and shoved it down hard. She looked up, and the scene before her seemed to spin like a kaleidoscope, the colors of sky, mountains, wildflowers, revolving, changing, re-forming before her dazzled eyes. She felt as she had when, as a little girl, she and her friends would whirl themselves around, arms spread out, until they fell giggling and dizzy on the soft grass. Finally, Ari took a deep breath, and the world reeled a little less.

But she felt disembodied, ran her fingers down her face, pinched her cheeks, whispering to herself, "Twenty-five million dollars." It would change everything. All her life her decisions had been made on the cost of things. If one bought this, one could not have that. This sweater, but no matching skirt. That pair of shoes, but no purse. This book instead of that book, but usually no books at all unless they were needed for her classes.

It was not as if she'd spent her life discontentedly longing for luxuries. When she was standing on a snow-whipped bus corner and a lipstick-red Porsche zipped by, the driver surrounded by warmth and music, she'd not yearned for that. But she had many times wished for a car, any car. And, on her way to the nearest thrift shop, passing by an expensive boutique on College Hill, she'd not felt her stomach ache for everything in the window, but she'd have really liked one whole new outfit. She was decidedly tired of stitching together graying elastic on brassiere backs.

Her thoughts now were simply incoherent. Visions, glittering visions, crowded through her mind, one replacing another with boggling speed. She'd always known that somewhere there was a party in silken rooms, with people wonderfully dressed, tables laden with delicacies, sparkling wines in crystal glasses. The people there said, "I'll have this, and that, and that as well." Outside, there was only a hint of the music, distant and seductive. Now she'd been given an engraved invitation.

Ari had no idea how long she'd sat there, numbed with joy. But the touch of her fingers still on her face reminded her of the one thing she'd always wanted. She jumped up distractedly, recalled that her bicycle had a rearview mirror. With clumsy fingers she tilted it up. Leaning into it, she saw that her eyes were huge, the lashes soaked with tears she had no memory of having shed.

As always, she covered the birthmark with one cupped hand, trying to imagine what she'd look like if it were gone. Now when she took away her hand, the stain already looked less red, as if the very idea of a laser beam, waved over it like a wizard's wand, had made it begin to fade. And that was the moment when she began to truly believe that she'd won twenty-five million dollars, the shining moment when she realized her wishes all could come true.

Pirouetting with arms outflung, much as she'd done as a child, she ecstatically whirled to the brow of the ridge. She felt as if she could embrace all she saw, touch the very top of Long's Peak. Her voice shaking, she whispered, "Oh, now I can go to Telluride, I can see Bridey's Mountain. It will always be *ours*. I promise. I promise."

MORNA

CHAPTER 1

It was a seltzer-clear Monday, morning January 1, 1900, in the prosperous mining town of Telluride, Colorado. The first day of the century, Isobel Ewen thought, turning from her vigil by her mistress's bedside to the window and gazing up at the sun-dazzled snow on the mountain peaks. Absentmindedly, she rubbed glycerin on her sore, reddened hands, easing the chafing from the cold water she'd repeatedly immersed them in the night before. She was exhausted but exhilarated, and that mixture showed on her homely, round features. Her almost lashless eyes, though puffy with weariness, were filled with a joyful light.

Things were going to be all right, she considered with a rare burst of optimism. A born worrier, Isobel usually dreaded any kind of change. But this particular change, she smiled to herself, was good. She was happy that the century was not all that was brand new in Telluride.

Never before had she enjoyed life as she had the last eighteen months here. Because of her quite strict religious upbringing, Isobel could not excuse all the goings-on, but somehow, secretly, she loved the town's exuberant, wicked heart. And she loved this high, isolated mountain valley. She thought it the most beautiful place on earth. The air itself was like tonic, and the sky an amazing bellflower blue.

Tucking behind her ear a frizzled lock of hair that was the color and texture of summer straw, she glanced quickly at the sleeping woman on the shiny, curlicued brass bed and then down at the almost deserted main street a short block to the north. She was thankful for the quiet. Any other weekday morning, men and mules would have been noisily lining the narrow strip cleared in the snow of wide Colorado Avenue, getting ready for the trek to the mines outside of town. The only holidays usually celebrated were Christmas and the Fourth of July.

But last night the town had exploded into a razzle-dazzle, once-in-a-hundred-years New Year's Eve party. Every alcoholic drifter musician appeared, ready to play. Bright lights and loud music spilled from every saloon and dance hall on the south side of town. The gambling casinos offered hot, fragrant bowls of Tom-and-Jerrys to all comers. The miners from Cornwall, always called Cousin Jacks, had gone from bar to bar singing lusty ballads and ending with a sweet "Auld Lang Syne." For once, the rigid ethnic barriers between the men were overlooked. The Swedes bought drinks for the Cornishmen, and even for the Finns, who reciprocated by treating the Swedes born in Finland, whom they normally ignored. Since there was the customary shortage of women, they even tipsily waltzed with each other on the cleared plank sidewalks of Pacific Avenue.

Just before midnight the fireworks began. Even the genteel citizens from the residential west end came in their carriages to see the display. Berkeley Glendower, who was a most popular gentleman already, had arranged a display of Roman candles that splashed fiery light on the steep mountain slopes. The Telluride Cornet Band—which was all brass because blowing horns was thought to clear dust from miners' lungs—jubilantly blasted in the intervals between rockets.

The town's leading madam, politely addressed as Miss Freda (but known as Swede Freda or even, affectionately, as Fat Freddie), sent steaming cups of laced cider and honey cakes to the carriages. The ladies, shivering despite their fur capes and bearskin lap robes, accepted gratefully. A few even smiled sideways at the girls who brought out refreshments. They knew them, since some of the "ladies" had once themselves been employed by Miss Freda. After their marriages to successful miners, they'd stopped painting their faces, put on high-necked dresses, and held sedate "at homes" in their Victorian residences a few blocks away in the proper part of town.

Of course, the notion of propriety had a distinctly practical side in a mining town. Because of the highly profitable whorehouses Telluride's citizens paid no taxes. Each madam was charged $150 a week, which barely dented the takings. And, as the west-end matrons whispered over tea, with delicate shudders, prostitution made the town safe for respectable women, what with all those bachelor miners. Everyone knew that accommodations had to be made here where life was raw and where survival during the eight-month winter was a daily challenge.

On a fair day even the most surefooted horse might not make it over the narrow passes out of the valley, and then there were the blizzards and the snowslides. The bodies of those who didn't make it were never found until spring. The fragile narrow-gauge rail link to faraway Denver could be taken out in an instant by an avalanche and require months to repair.

When that happened, meals at the miners' boardinghouses eventually became a monotony of deer, elk, and, occasionally, Rocky Mountain bighorn sheep. The men stared glumly at the plates of dried fruit, of cups of coffee made of ground beetroot or, if they were lucky, of parched chicory and barley. The canned condensed milk, mixed with two parts of water, still had the lingering taste of tin.

But, although the standards of Boston or the niceties of Denver society could not be maintained, the citizens of Telluride were proud of the progress they were making toward civilization. Two churches had been built, and services no longer had to be held in one of the gambling casinos with sheets thrown over the roulette wheels. Some of the traveling preachers were a little regretful, since afterward they had bet the money in the collection plate to see if they could double it. There was a brick courthouse and a school. The bank had not been robbed for eleven years, when Butch Cassidy and his Wild Bunch had galloped off with $20,000. And a newspaper editorial bragged that there were only two or three murders a year. Telluride called itself "The Town Without a Bellyache."

But in any town there would always be certain people with no sense of shame, Isobel thought, pursing her lips disapprovingly as she recalled some of the things she'd observed from this window last night. From where she stood on the second story, she could see along Pacific Avenue to the line of cribs. These were small wooden cabins where the lower-class prostitutes worked on an individual basis. If not engaged, they would sit inside with their shades up, advertising their wares. If the shades were down, the potential customer wandered past and on down the line. But the heady mix of alcohol and the turn of the century had caused shades to be up when they should certainly have been down. Giggling and half-dressed, some of the women rushed out on the sidewalk and danced wild tarantellas without their corsets. A few had even dragged willing passersby inside.

Even though she'd only been in Telluride for a matter of months, Isobel could see that this was what happened when there wasn't the proper sort of madam to supervise. Miss Freda might look like just a good-natured Swedish matron, but she was a strict manager and a sharp-eyed businesswoman. The girls she hired for her adjoining dance hall need only be fresh-faced and clean. All *they* did was dance with the men and were paid with brass tickets by the bartenders when they talked their partners into drinks. If more than a dance was demanded of the lady, a burly bouncer hustled the fellow right to the street.

But the courtesans in her parlor had to meet exacting standards in appearance and demeanor. Their wasp-waisted evening gowns of rich velvets, Japanese silks, and shimmery satins must always have the latest in necklines and sleeves. The trimming was usually exquisite Brussels lace. Miss Freda ordered some of them directly from Paris, but modistes from Denver arrived on the train with trunkloads as well for the madam to choose from. She really preferred this because she could stroke the fabrics with fat, sensual fingers, carefully check all the stitching. Then, too, she received a larger commission from these women than from the French couturières. Although Miss Freda chose the dresses, and took her cut, her girls paid for them. Quite frequently, they were considerably in debt to her.

Their undergarments, too, had to be of the best quality. The corsets were to be of whalebone (not steel) and silk batiste, the petticoats of soft sateen, their long drawers lace-trimmed with umbrella flounces. Their slippers were of kidskin or kangaroo calf with lace tops. It was an expensive place to work.

But it was a treat to watch them sweep down the wide mahogany staircase in the evenings, sweetly perfumed, their laughing mouths carefully painted, their hair piled up in gleaming masses. Although Isobel herself had to get up quite early to see to the baking and then attend Morna in the afternoons, she never went to bed until she'd seen them descend. Miss Freda, too, stood at the foot of the stairs, her eyes, almost hidden in the fleshy folds of her cheeks, never missing a slight droop in a hem or a frayed ribbon.

When they'd first arrived, Isobel had been shocked to her thrifty Highland core at the price of the gowns and the requirement to be constantly buying new ones. She'd protested to Morna, "Gentlemen don't ken fashion." Although she'd been taken from her native Scotland at four, thirty years of living in America had not quite erased all traces, especially when she was indignant. Holding up a chemise that was little more than a scrap of embroidered lawn, she continued grumbling. "It's pneumonia you'll be catching up here with this. Ye need a good piece of flannel on the chest."

"Oh, Issy." Morna Gregory's low, delighted laugh had welled up. "And should I put a mustard plaster beneath it? Persuade the gentlemen that the pungent smell was the latest French cologne?" Then her gray eyes had darkened. "What have I done to you? Bringing you and your sensible ways and your Calvinist conscience to live in a bawdy house!"

Isobel had turned hurriedly back to rinsing the chemise. "It's saving me, ye did," she replied in a low voice. She remembered the bleak day eighteen months ago when she'd sat waiting for Jock Campbell in the bare passenger area of Denver's Union Depot. That morning she'd arisen before dawn and stolen out of the house in the coal-mining town of Louisville without waking her father. Hailing a passing horse-drawn dairy wagon, she'd made the slow thirty-mile trip into the city. From the outskirts where she'd left the wagon to the station, it'd been a long dusty walk, and the old Gladstone valise that contained everything she owned was wearyingly heavy.

So at first, Isobel had dozed a bit, even on the hard pewlike seats. She was very thirsty, but she hadn't the money for a cup of tea. Soon she became too worried to think about eating the sandwiches she'd brought for their trip to Cheyenne. A uniformed railroad employee paced by her ever more frequently, his mouth set severely.

By late afternoon she'd realized Jock wasn't coming. And she knew that in the small town of Louisville, the gossip about her would be starting. They'd already be wondering how poor, plain Isobel Ewen had ever imagined that handsome Jock Campbell would run off with her, her a spinster of thirty and more. Even though she was miles away, she thought she could hear the town's buzzing, and her cheeks burned with the humiliation.

That feeling gave way to empty despair. She knew no one in Denver; she'd never been in the city before. Her father would never take her back, not now. The younger sister she'd raised had a minister husband who was, if possible, an even stricter man. Not only would he never allow her into his home again, he would forbid her seeing her small niece and nephew.

Unheeded tears squeezed from the corners of her eyes. Her trembling fingers plucked at the drab brown flannelette of her dress. In her misery she could not imagine where she could go, how she could live. All she could think of was the South Platte River near the station, swift moving now with spring snow melt.

"What troubles you? Can I help?" The woman who'd sat down

quietly next to her put a small suede-gloved hand over Isobel's agitated fingers. The voice was as soft as the gloves, and kind. That was how Isobel had met Morna Gregory.

She was dressed in the unadorned black usually worn by widows, the bombazine of her dress only relieved by the gray lace of a collar that completely covered her throat. Her hat had a modest satin bow in front, with fine illusion veiling that stretched tightly across her face but did not obscure her delicate features and pale porcelain skin. She had the light eyes that, as the Gaels said, "were put in with a sooty finger."

It was the expression in her eyes that caught Isobel, made her swallow a shy, quick denial of need, and overcame her ingrained hesitancy to impose. Because of that look that seemed to enter into her own feelings, she found herself pouring out the story. As she spoke, she felt that young and beautiful woman could see the cramped house with the bare, well-scrubbed wooden floors that Isobel had fled, could imagine the loneliness of the days that ended only with her dour father's silent return from the mines.

Isobel told her of the difference Jock had made simply by walking in the door. He'd come, smiling, to pick up the laundry she took in to make ends meet, always coming after her father had gone to have an evening pint with his workmates. She'd offered him tea, a slice of pie.

"He'd be saying his shirts were never so clean and praising my pastries to the skies. I do have a very light hand with them," Isobel had added earnestly. "My sister, Florrie, she says so too. And I told myself, over and over, that what he needed was a good wife to get over his wandering ways, and even if I wasn't . . . Ah, what will I do now? What will I ever do?"

Abashed at her outcry, she pressed her freckled, large-knuckled hand against her mouth. Gulping back the tears in her throat, she'd concluded in a desperate jumbled rush, trying to explain. "But wi' Florrie so far, ye see. She lives over in Lafayette and only on the rare Sunday do I see her and . . ."

The gloved hand squeezed hers tightly. "Being so alone is like ice and gray winter every day, isn't it? By the way, my name is Morna Gregory. What's yours?"

As she replied, Isobel looked in wonder. At her first glance, seeing the widow's weeds, hearing an assurance in the cultivated voice, she'd somehow assumed the woman was near her own age. But clearly Morna was just barely in her twenties. Noting the elegant arrangement of the dark hair, the rich silk of her dress, struck again by her beauty, Isobel could not imagine how such a woman could ever be lonely. She'd always supposed that wealth and social standing removed such a trial. But before she could arrange her thoughts, Morna had gone on.

"We do have a similar problem. Neither your light hand with pastry nor my little skills at the piano will keep us decently housed, let alone clothed and fed. At least, not in the usual way of things. Unlike you, I've had a great deal of time to consider the situation. We can't go back, so we must go forward. I have a plan."

She stared down at the eight tiny buttons on the wrist of her glove and slowly undid those on the bottom, as if to give herself time to choose her words. "What I intend . . ." she began, and then paused. "I came to the station," she started over, "to inquire about the train to Telluride. I'm told that town is thriving because they mine gold as well as silver and therefore they were not affected by the financial panic of a few years ago. Telluride is in the southwestern part of the state, you know, in the San Juan Mountains and at least three hundred miles from here"—she'd smiled slightly—"mostly straight up. My informant says Telluride is miles from everything—except the sky."

Here all of the liveliness went out of her face. "Its distance, and inaccessibility, is very much to my purpose. If you like, you can accompany me. I have enough for your fare. As for what you will do when we get there . . . well, I hope you will hear me out. But I feel that something satisfactory can be arranged. After all, we have very little choice. As for me, I am determined. Perhaps we could talk over some tea."

Once en route in the early morning Isobel had been unable to reconsider her decision. Or even to think. She was sure that the two of them were going to die. Jokingly, the conductor had remarked that Telluride had not been named for the mineral found with gold, but rather as a shortened form of "To Hell You Ride." Even though they were going in the opposite direction, it seemed terribly true to Isobel.

The small train jolted, ever upward, over the rugged terrain, hugging mountainsides where there seemed barely room even for the narrow track. The cars swayed on thin wooden trestles built up from plunging chasms. Morna exclaimed over the beauty of the cloud-scraping mountain peaks. Isobel closed her eyes and tried to pray, hoping God was still willing to listen to her. She vowed she would stay forever in Telluride, should they arrive, because leaving it would mean getting back on that train.

But when they were standing at the door of Miss Freda's stately red brick establishment, Isobel decided she would gladly reboard. She'd never been inside such a place. Moreover, what Morna was going to suggest to the owner would be unacceptable, she was sure. Faint-hearted, not knowing where to look, so pale her freckles were dark brown blotches, she waited in the mirrored foyer while Morna swept confidently into the madam's room and closed the door.

CHAPTER 2

Gathering her courage, Isobel had finally ventured a quick glance over her shoulder into the parlor. But the opulence of the room had her turning and gaping. She'd been raised in the austere fundamentalist belief that every object should be simple and utilitarian. Any appeal to the senses must be suppressed. Over and over she'd been taught that the flesh must not be pandered to in any way. Her father would never allow a rosebush to take space that could be used for cabbages in their back garden. In their church there was no stained glass or golden candelabras to distract the eye, certainly no sweet incense.

This parlor was a banquet of deep colors and light. The setting sun came through the fretwork of heavy lace curtains and was caught by the prisms of the enormous crystal and gold chandelier in the center. Rainbow tints splashed everywhere on the gleaming walnut floor and the solid wood of the side tables, as well as on the burgundy leather chairs and tufted velvet chaises. Glints of light touched polished andirons by the immense marble fireplace and were reflected back from the cut glass decanters and goblets arranged on a long library table.

Isobel stepped to the doorway and timidly leaned her head farther in. At the far end was a black burnished piano so large, it could not have fit into any of the rooms of the home she'd left. A richly patterned paisley shawl was draped across its top and on that was placed a bowl that held armfuls of erect white lilies. The tall metal candlesticks next to the flowers were themselves sculpted in the shape of lily stalks. Beveled glass-fronted cases containing more books than she'd ever seen in one place were set against the walls covered in paper with intricate red and gold whorls and spirals.

A delicate scent of dried herbs and flower petals mingled with the beeswax of floor and furniture polish. She could smell, too, from a distant kitchen in the back of the house, the crackling odor of pork roast, the brown sugary smell of baking apples. Retying her bonnet more carefully, Isobel stood stiffly in the foyer, not daring to sit on the graceful plush chair for fear that ashes from the train's small potbellied stove might be clinging to her cloak. She was now positive that Morna's plan was unworkable, and that they were lost entirely.

But the two women had emerged arm in arm, and Miss Freda was smiling delightedly. The madam was already dressed for the evening in a gown of black sequins that cascaded over her imposing bosom. Three strands of thick jet beads encircled her stubby neck. Her skin was Scandinavian fair, but large pored, and all trace of a chin was gone. But the roundness of her face added to her look of geniality and good humor. The ostrich feathers arranged in her faded blond hair bobbed as she bent her head.

She enveloped Isobel's hand in her beringed pudgy ones. "And to think I get a pastry chef as well," she exclaimed. There was a faint guttural sound underlying her rather affected manner of speech. "Welcome, my dear. The only cooks to be found up here are the Chinese who've tired of railroad building. They're quite good on vegetables and plank steaks, of course, and they do a nice roast, even of mutton, but you simply cannot teach a Chinaman to make a proper crust."

Then she gestured toward the velvet carpeted staircase. "But I'm sure you're both tired. I'll send to the station for your things and have dinner brought to your rooms. We can get acquainted tomorrow. In any case, I'll need an evening to prepare my gentlemen for your debut." Her feathery plumes dipped in anticipation. "I'm quite sure we'll be crowded tomorrow night. I'll have to order up more cases of champagne."

This had been their introduction to their new life at Freda's. Now as Isobel reached for the glycerin bottle on the bedside table, she reflected on how tender her hands had become since they'd been here. She was no longer used to the rough work she'd once known. She poured several more drops of the clear liquid onto her palm. No matter how carefully one rubbed it in, the back of the hands always felt sticky. Cocking her head, she listened carefully, but the entire house was still quiet. She darted a quick look at the cloud of loose, dark hair on the pillow, but Morna hadn't stirred. Last night had been difficult, and had more than frightened Isobel. But, satisfied at the sound of quiet breathing, Isobel slipped into the maple rocker by the bed and closed her own eyes.

She would never forget their first day—and evening—at Miss Freda's. Directly after the late breakfast customary at the house, all the dresses in Morna's trunk had been spread on the wide feather mattress. Freda had come bustling in, still wearing a matronly flannel nightgown under her embroidered velveteen robe. Although it was late in May, snow still limned the mountain ridges that seemed so near Isobel thought she could reach out of the window and touch them. The madam scrutinized each gown and one hand hovered over a raspberry satin. "Perfect for your coloring, of course, and the leg-of-mutton sleeves are good, but I like the little extra puff at the top of the sleeve that they're showing this year in France." She wheeled to Isobel. "How good is your fine stitching?"

"All I've done is ordinary dressmaking, and plain mending," she began hesitantly.

"Never mind," Freda went on decisively. "You'll have more than enough to do today. All these undergarments will have to be seen to as well. And then the petticoats are badly creased." She looked inquisitively at Morna. "You must have been traveling for some distance, or for some time." Morna merely nodded.

Freda touched the deep pink fabric lightly. "Lovely stuff. Imported, isn't it? Well, Colette's good at French seaming and—"

"This is the dress I'll wear," Morna interrupted gently, holding up a dress of creamy white peau de soie, simple in design. The bodice was unadorned except for the profusion of seafoam lace that edged the square neck and spilled from the fitted, straight sleeves that ended at the elbow. The gossamer lace had a pale ivory tinge.

"But, my dear," Freda protested, "that's not only out of style, it's decidedly old fashioned. It could have been your mother's!"

"It was," Morna replied. "It was her wedding dress, although it has been tailored for me."

"And it'll never show off that tiny waist of yours," Freda grumbled on. "You'd barely need to wear a corset with that one, and hardly a glimpse of bosom with that lace." She paused and peered at the neckline. "Although that is the finest lace I've ever seen. Better even than the handmade Belgian. Where's it come from? Alsace?"

"Ireland," Morna replied.

"Is that your home?" Freda asked, her small eyes alight with curiosity.

"It's where the lace was made," Morna returned. Slipping her nightgown off her shoulders, she pressed the dress against her body. The delicate tint of the lace set off the translucent alabaster of her skin, and the white silk of the dress emphasized the onyx sheen of her hair, which hung loosely about her shoulders. She looked ethereal, with an air of untouched innocence, her beauty so perfect, it needed no color.

Isobel, who had turned away, regretfully hanging up the satin dress that reminded her of fruit ice in July, stared at her in amazed pleasure. Freda's jaw dropped. Morna, unconscious of the effect she'd created, pulled gently at the loose waist of the bodice. "It is so much easier to sing without a tight corset. And here, at this altitude, I'm having some trouble breathing at all. In fact, I won't wear a corset at all if I'm going to sing the latest English dance hall songs. They take a lot of breath, if you do them right. But everyone likes them. The lyrics are a little naughty."

"No corset?" Freda's voice went up an octave and her eyebrows disappeared into her blond fringe. *Downstairs?*

"Now, then," Morna said briskly, pulling a brown velour robe styled like a monk's habit over her head, "would it be convenient for me to begin to practice? I haven't played for some time and I'm longing to try your piano."

"Wait." Freda had sunk deeply onto the feather mattress, but she raised an imploring hand. "What jewelry will you wear with that dress? I know the others would be glad to lend a choker or possibly a pendant with brilliants that would add a little style. As for shoes—"

Morna dived into the bottom of her trunk. "I have the perfect shoes." She straightened, holding a pair of white satin slippers with modish square French heels. "As for jewelry, I haven't a lot left. . . . I mean, I only have a few pieces. But"—she pulled a black leather drawstring bag from a compartment in the trunk and rummaged in it—"these seed pearls and earrings are quite right." She held up a single strand with matching drop earrings.

Freda sighed, closed her eyes, and wrinkled her plump face in thought. "The hair," she said at last. "If we did a quite elaborate—" Opening her eyes, she turned to Isobel, who was shaking out a tulle petticoat, and asked, "Have you done hair? We could pile it quite high and use some fake pieces for effect."

"I've often done my sister's, but it was a plain style indeed, and I'm not sure—"

They both turned to look at Morna, but she'd gone, and they heard from downstairs a silvery arpeggio.

"Well," Freda said, heaving herself up from the soft bed, "I'll send some of the girls along with their paint pots and bits and pieces of jewelry when you're helping her dress. But I have the feeling she'll persuade them, rather than the other way about. And perhaps, after all . . ." Freda was still talking to herself as she went down the hall.

For Isobel the day disappeared in a novel blur of bright colors, light laughter, unfamiliar perfumes. It was a Saturday and everyone was preparing for a busy evening. She hurried upstairs and downstairs, pleased to have her opinion sought on the placement of a rosette, a glittering pin, delighted with the compliments on the scones she'd made for tea, on her help, her efficiency. She was stopped at the door of almost every room—here to trim a ribbon, there to tie up a corset. Above the chatter she could hear snatches of song in Morna's sweet contralto.

Finally, Freda, herself resplendent in black satin with a high Spanish comb in her hair, a Madeira mantilla, and a fan dangling from her wrist, sent Morna up to have her hair dressed. Isobel had never seen curling tongs, but May, a Midwestern farm girl whose lumpish features were redeemed by flawless skin and a charming smile, showed her how to heat them. Colette, a French girl with a heart-shaped face and cat-quick eyes, came in bearing some sprigs of apple blossoms picked from the branches that a western-slope fruit grower had presented to Freda that morning.

Here was the odd thing that Isobel never forgot. She was standing in front of Morna, who had her back to the mirror, since they'd been discussing how the back hair should be done. Colette lightly dropped the blossoms onto Morna's lap and then quickly leaned forward to inspect her own face in the mirror.

But Morna looked down with an expression of horror, as if the French girl had laid squirming snakes on the white peau de soie material. All Isobel could see were delicately pink-tinged blooms, and she picked them up and held them out in wonder at her mistress's reaction. Morna gazed at them, shook her head, tried to smile, turned back to the mirror, and looked searchingly at Colette's reflection next to her own. The French girl smiled at her and went on with her application of lip rouge.

Then, although she was still pale, Morna gestured to the bewildered Isobel to suggest that only the sides of her hair be lifted to the top, and it was there that Isobel attached the fragrant blossoms. The back hair was curled into thick ringlets that fell to the shoulders. The result was much admired, but before Morna could add her jewelry or finish dressing, a distant chime sounded.

May and Colette had already finished their toilettes and they only paused for a last twirl before the mirror. They, and the others, had to be downstairs before Morna and they hurried off in a swish of silk.

CHAPTER 3

The two men in evening dress reclining comfortably in adjacent leather armchairs were watching Freda as she moved around the crowded parlor, always smiling, stopping to greet each of the gentlemen and make sure he was well provided with the drink of his choice. As she bent her head to listen to a low-voiced remark, the brilliants set in her comb glittered in the candle glow as well as in the illumination of the few widely scattered globes of electric light. Given the subdued elegance of her dress and her welcoming manner, she could have been mistaken for a society hostess.

"Freda has a distinct air of satisfaction about her tonight; one could even say of swallowed canary," the fair-haired one remarked idly. Although he was only in his early thirties, his forehead already reached the middle of his scalp. He made the best of it by combing a few strands of his side hair over the top and by cultivating a manner of quiet, bored worldliness beyond his years. As the only child of a flint-hard, determined father, the young man had early learned to keep still and out of the way.

And the role of observer suited him. His pale eyes had a lizardlike fixity as he watched others. He had long ears with sheared-off lobes that lay flat to his skull, and this, along with his near baldness, increased the similarity to a reptile's sleek head. His name was Stanton Caley. Although the elder Caley had made a fortune by driving steers from Texas and fattening them in Denver before slaughtering them, his son had been expensively educated in the East and his vowels were Bostonian.

"Not," he went on, rather enjoying his unaccustomed position of tour guide to the newly arrived Englishman, "that I believe for a minute her extravagant story about her new artiste, as she put it, who is appearing tonight. No, Theo, I brought you here because this is the best introduction to the town. If you plan to stay any length of time up here, you'll find that you'll naturally gravitate to Freda's of an evening. Give her credit—this is by way of being somewhat like your gentlemen's clubs in London. Quite a bit of serious business is conducted here. The mine managers bring along potential investors. Always one of the engineers here if you have the stray question. And the mine supervisors, who tend to be rather a superior lot—they're paid the princely sum of three hundred dollars a month—are often about. Most of the men don't have their families up here, of course."

With his whiskey-filled Waterford tumbler Caley gestured almost proprietorily around the room. "So Freda can get away with her demands that we wear tails on Saturday. If your family wants you to learn about American mining, this is where the insiders gather in Telluride."

His companion, Theo Manningham, some years younger and looking more so because of a thatch of sun-streaked hair and a round and amiable face, nodded in what he hoped was a knowledgeable manner. His family owned a prosperous wool-processing firm in Yorkshire and even had a distant claim on the peerage, but he was a third son. Therefore, he'd come, not to study the mining business, but to find an American heiress. He'd quite liked the girls from Boston's wealthy families, but he was a romantic with a hankering to see the Wild West, of which he'd heard so much. He'd been sent to Caley, who was a Harvard graduate and a friend of a friend, with appropriate letters.

Theo surveyed the scene, which was at once familiar and deliciously strange. It was an elegant drawing room, very little different from the ones he'd been entertained in in Boston. The men were attired in dark formal dress. The women in their rich jewel-toned dresses of emerald, amethyst, sapphire—with the sheen of white shoulders, more than a promise of bosom—looked and talked like other ladies. Yet the way they returned his glance, smiling gently and invitingly, was far more enticing than any flaunting could be. While this was not at all what he'd expected of a bordello, neither did it seem like a stuffy men's club. He was thoroughly enjoying himself. "Jolly nice," he murmured.

"Mind you, Miss Freda's prices are stiffish," Stanton shrugged as if that could hardly be of consequence, although in reality he was a man who was very pinch fisted with his many dollars, "but her liquor is the best and not watered. The food is superb—you should only consider eating here or at the Sheridan Hotel—and the ladies . . ." He paused and took an indulgent puff on his slim, dark cigar. "Well, as you can see, they're attractive and a few can even converse amusingly. It's said that Freda takes pains to teach them manners. Should you be inclined," he suggested, waving his cigar toward the staircase, "you'll be well entertained upstairs."

A number of questions overwhelmed Theo, but he wasn't sure how to phrase them. Ever since his first years at boarding school he'd been turning over what he'd heard whispered after the lights went out. There were remarks, tantalizingly vague, made by older men in smoking rooms about the congenial ladies in sporting houses. He was desperately eager, if inexperienced. At last, to have something to say, he asked, "When do you think she'll appear? The new, um, pianist, I mean?"

"Oh, not until the right moment. Freda makes her real profits on the liquor, so she'll want to wait a bit," Caley replied. "And things get more lively later on. But, as I warned you when I repeated the madam's claims, this new addition will hardly be a great beauty, let alone a 'lady to her fingertips.' No. Probably she'll be pretty enough and will sing and play passably well. Perhaps her mother was a housekeeper for one of the better families in the East. Now, Freda herself can ape the grande dame wonderfully. And I can't imagine where she learned to speak as she does—one suspects she grew up on a farm in Minnesota. Still, how could she know real breeding? As for the old dear's protestation that this lady's not for bedding"—his blond eyebrows ascended—"well, that, I promise you, is just a way to raise the price for her favors. Freda already charges ten dollars for the night—twice what's asked in Denver at the better places—and one's expected to tip the girls for bringing you your expensive drink."

Just then the madam approached them, both hands outstretched, and Caley put down his glass and cigar and rose to clasp them. "My dear Mr. Caley," she said warmly, "the evening doesn't begin until you've arrived!" He introduced Theo Manningham, and Freda beamed. Tapping the young Englishman playfully with her fan, she said, "We have an unusual treat in store for your first night with us. Being so out of the way, we rarely have artistes of this caliber." She turned to Caley with a hopeful note in her voice. "And can we expect Mr. Glendower this evening?"

"I doubt it," Caley answered. "He wasn't on this morning's train from Denver. But you of all people ought to be glad his business takes him there so often. Each time he returns, he comes with magnificent bouquets for you."

"He's very thoughtful. But I always miss him. I'm so happy *you* are here—and your friend. Now, if you'll excuse me—Miss Gregory prefers champagne and I want to make sure we have enough iced." She sailed off majestically with a backward smile.

"I also regret Glendower's absence," Caley remarked as the two men reseated themselves. He tucked his lips together dryly and then explained. "He'd have the mot juste to describe Freda's new find. Not that he'd hurt the old girl's feelings—he's very fond of her. But he'd manage to say just what he thought and make us all smile in the bargain. I met him at school—he was two years ahead of me at Harvard."

"Glendower," Theo repeated. "A Welshman?"

"Well, if so, one that came on the second ship after the *Mayflower*. Old Boston money, but I understand they've lost most of it. Not that Berkeley needs to worry. He's married to Olivia Hyde-White." Caley picked up and relit his cigar. "A fortune from a grandfather in fur trading." He puffed thoughtfully and added, "And her father doubled it in railroads. Now Berkeley is investing a sizable portion very successfully in these mines."

Theo opened his mouth and then decided to take a sip of his sherry instead. He was still unused to the American habit of discussing the source of other people's—and even their own—money. He never mentioned wool manufacturing.

"Story goes"—Caley leaned back with a reminiscent smile—"that Olivia's pater ran into Berkeley at a New York men's club. Stakes were ten dollars a point and Berkeley played as cool as you please, on credit. Won twenty-five hundred dollars in a matter of minutes. Old Hyde-White was impressed and thought anyone who could gamble like that should be out here in mining ventures." Chuckling, he tapped the ash from his cigar. "Berkeley told me later he thought he was playing for a dollar a point, although, mind you, he's a damned good poker player."

"But what if"—a slight crease dented Theo's smooth forehead as he imagined telling his father he'd thrown away that kind of money in a few minutes—"he'd *lost*?"

"He'd have carried it off, I swear! Handsome as the devil and as smooth." Despite his overlay of sophistication Stanton did not seem to have lost an undergraduate's admiration for an envied upperclassman.

"And he has a damn-your-eyes way about him. Sometimes the flowers he brings for Freda are the exotic tropical varieties, grown in the conservatory of none other than Mrs. Laughton Powell. *She* is Denver's reigning society queen. Amelia is no longer in her first youth, true, but she is formidable. You'll meet her soon."

Stanton took a long pull at his cigar and went on with more than a little pride. "I know Amelia, and I've secured an invitation for you, as well, for the summer season's parties. She's the leader of the Sacred Thirty-six. These women gather of an afternoon, supposedly to play whist, but really to pass judgment on the behavior of people who matter. But for Berkeley, orchids are the least favor Amelia would—" Here he stopped and was staring at the parlor's entry.

Theo followed his gaze. Against the candle-lit background of the foyer Morna in her white dress seemed almost an illusion. As she made her way down the length of the room to the piano, the dark wainscoting and deep reds of the parlor heightened the impression. She opened the piano, seated herself, and conversation slowly stopped.

The hauntingly plaintive notes of "Greensleeves" whispered in the room's quiet. "Alas, my love," Morna sang softly, "you do me wrong, to cast me off discourteously." The song, the simplicity of her dress, the blossoms woven in her hair, all suggested she belonged to another time, a longed-for place. But even before the sweetness of that melody faded, she'd begun the sprightly London street vendors' song: " 'Cherry-ripe, ripe, ripe,' I cry,/'Full and fair ones; come and buy.' "

That lusty Cockney invitation was followed by a medley of roguish tunes from the music halls that had the listeners laughing. Then they clapped and stomped their feet to her Spanish flamencos. At the close of a vigorous Gypsy rhythm she ran her fingers down the keys and stood up, eyes sparkling.

Although Theo clapped until his hands tingled, he still managed to be the first at the piano, handing her the glass of champagne that Freda had given him. Caley hurried after him, wondering how he'd gotten the impression the young Englishman was bashful. Despite his own quickness he was only at the fringes of the crowd. He heard Morna's warm response to Theo's first words: "Ah, but you're from Yorkshire. I can tell. From the Dales?"

It was quite a half hour later before Stanton Caley himself was able to speak to her. He'd repeatedly taken out his gold pocket watch, flipping open the initialed cover impatiently. He was able to meet her only because the other girls beguiled some of the bystanders into the dining room. When someone else successfully whisked her away for supper, he could not recall a single word they'd spoken. All that remained in his memory was the light in her astonishing gray eyes framed in dark lashes. During the meal he was surprised at the depth of his newfound dislike for the banker Edward Gibbons, who was monopolizing her conversation.

At the end of the evening he and Theo stood together at the bottom of the staircase, watching Morna ascend alone, the hem of her silken dress just touching the wine-red velvet of the carpet, watching until she disappeared down the corridor. "What's more," the Englishman said, implying an ongoing dialogue, although neither of them had spoken since she'd left, "I think she sings superbly."

"Yes," Caley replied abstractedly, "and one can stare at her the entire time."

"What do you think your friend Glendower will say?"

"Frankly . . ." Caley began and paused. He lightly brushed his fingertips across the wisps of blond hair on his scalp. Then he threw a fringed white scarf around his stiff upstanding collar and slid into his velvet-lapeled Chesterfield coat. "I hope he stays in Denver a good while."

CHAPTER 4

It was a full two weeks before Berkeley Glendower returned, and it was the first really warm day of the year.

As always, spring in the high mountains was very late. If everyone hadn't been waiting so impatiently, it would have been missed altogether. One day the inhabitants were glumly eyeing yet another snow shower, and the next, the buds had turned to tender green leaf and the steep slopes were decorated with the bright yellow of the snow buttercup, the earliest of the wildflowers.

Therefore, although it was the last of May, the few lilac bushes in Telluride had not yet bloomed. But, as he strolled with Stanton Caley through the soft twilight air toward Miss Freda's that Saturday evening, Glendower was carrying what seemed enough flowering branches to perfume the town itself. He was wearing one of the blossoms as a boutonniere on his formal tailed jacket. He was tall, with a natural grace, and more than one of the passersby thought the way he carried his leafy bouquet made lilacs seem a far better choice than the inevitable roses.

His unusual handsomeness would have bordered on beauty except for a strong nose and the angular lines at the corners of his jaw. His thick dark brown hair was brushed back at the sides. Even darker eyebrows and lashes emphasized changeable light brown eyes. His straight upper lip was clean shaven and the lower lip rather full. The lines on the sides of his mouth indicated a quick and frequent smile.

"Well, Caley, you've aroused my curiosity," he said, smiling now. "To quote Will Shakespeare, who always has the right phrase, 'Who is Silvia, what is she, that all our swains commend her?' I would substitute 'Morna' but that's short a syllable. That is her name?"

The younger man cast a sideways look at his friend, as if wondering if he was being lightly ribbed. He nodded and fingered his lapel, adjusting the carnation that now seemed to him too conventional.

"Theo Manningham certainly displays none of the expected English reserve in his praises of this lady," Berkeley continued. "Of course, having just met him, I've no idea what impresses him." Correctly interpreting his friend's disquieted glance, he added with a fine it-goes-without-saying air, "The fact that *you* agree, Stanton, truly interests me."

Reassured, Stanton answered with some feeling. "It's odd, you see, the effect she has. I can't explain it . . . how often she intrudes on your thoughts when you've something else entirely on your mind. You find yourself considering what she'd think of this, whether she'd like that. And d'you know, Edward Gibbons, Gibbons of all people, has been sending her flowers and gifts almost daily!"

"Hmm. I would have thought access to his heart would be as well guarded as entry to his blue steel bank vault."

As they went down the plank sidewalks, their strides matching, Caley reflected that since he'd met him ten years ago in college, Berkeley's life had been a triumphal march. Influential men sought him out; women adored him. What other men prayed for, he was offered. Although Stanton had often to choke back his own envy of his friend's fortune, Glendower himself seemed to regard such things lightly. It was difficult for Caley to gauge what Berkeley would do if he set his heart on a prize. It was even difficult to decide when he was serious. Now he told Caley, in a tone of mild interest, "But as to her mysterious origin, if she's really a person of some background, well, ladies just don't go missing in this day and age. Even if she's British, word would somehow flash across the Atlantic. We must find out. You haven't detected an accent of any kind?"

They had arrived at Freda's carved wooden door and Glendower was reaching for the brass knocker. "I try to listen," Caley replied, "but I only hear her voice. Even her speaking voice is music."

The door opened almost immediately and Freda's wide smile spread in surprised pleasure at the sight of the flowers. "Why, Mr. Glendower, lilacs!"

"You said once, dear Freda, that you didn't believe in spring until you smelled these blossoms." He filled her arms with the branches.

"Imagine you remembering." There was a slight tremble in her reply as she looked down at them. "But I am forgetting my manners. Please, both of you, come in, come in."

The two men were barely through the parlor entrance when Colette came fluttering up, small hands reaching out for Berkeley's. "Mr. Glendower, *mon cher*. You have been gone an age!" Kissing her cheek, he stood back, still clasping her hands, to admire her sherry-colored gown trimmed in ecru lace. The gold tint in the brown satin enhanced a cinnamon glint in her eyes, emphasized the chestnut of her hair, which Caley noted was let down in the back in Morna's fashion. She had a tiny nose, with odd, curlicued nostrils above an avid mouth that was now smiling widely.

"Colette," Berkeley said with cheerful approval, "I still can't believe France has not declared war on us, requiring your return."

Her piquant face alive with pleasure, Colette settled the two men on a velvety mohair couch and perched on a matching ottoman before them. Caley always tried to place himself near the French girl and usually succeeded in garnering her complete attentions, except when Glendower was near. She was vivacious and amusingly sharp tongued.

These were qualities he appreciated, and more and more so because of the time he spent in decorous drawing rooms both in the East and in Denver. The young unmarried women of his class were advised to be subdued in men's company, to remain demurely reticent. Then, too, other than a few art and music lessons, their education was largely neglected. Their training, he'd decided long ago, must consist solely of learning how to dress fashionably and smile modestly at wealthy bachelors like himself.

The company here was much livelier, and conversation was not limited to those topics considered suitable for the delicate ears of the gentler sex. The men talked about what really interested them, usually their daily occupation, and over time some of the women became quite familiar with mining operations. This added to Caley's pleasure in their society. He did not fear boring them, and he himself was not bored.

Before he met Morna, he'd once studied the ladies in the room, creating a composite perfect woman. He'd chosen Britta's thick blond hair, May's swansdown skin, Harriet's oval face, Jenny's responsive eyes, Alma's elegant nose, Daisy's sensual mouth, Jane Ellen's winsome magnolia manners, and combined all this with Colette's effervescence.

But now Caley realized that Morna Gregory came much closer to his image of the ideal. Her beauty was animated with genuine intelligence and real perception. To maintain her position here required those qualities, as well as the balance of a high-wire artist. Morna demanded, and was accorded, respect from these men, he noticed. She extended exquisite courtesy to each, allowed familiarity from none.

Stanton could not conceive how she managed it, and he'd given it a great deal of thought. Even if she'd been performing at a theater, such as Denver's Apollo Hall, well, everyone knew that *ladies* never went onstage. He'd decided that she had caused him to lose not only his detachment, but also his powers of analysis. He only knew that he reveled in her company, craved her approval.

Caley waited now in a ferment of impatience. He wanted to look at her, to listen to her sing, to hear her speak, even if she were talking to others. Several times he'd found that preferable because of the annoying flush that spread up his face and over his high-domed forehead when she looked directly at him.

He glanced at Glendower, who was leaning forward, listening as Colette turned an uptilted, radiant face to him. Caley tried, but failed, to imagine *him* tongue tied, disconcerted, by a woman's presence. He wanted Berkeley to meet and admire Morna as he himself did, to hear what he had to say. Yet he knew that if he could, he would have prevented their meeting. Supposing, he agonized, his friend did fall victim to her enormous appeal, and worse, much worse, she to Glendower's. Caley lit a cigar, forgetting that he already had one glowing in the ashtray, fidgeted on the soft mohair, and watched the parlor entrance.

When Morna did arrive, there was an almost audible rustle of pleasure. Her moire silk dress was of the palest lavender—almost all of the color seemed to be in the ripples of the fabric. Gathered in scalloped folds, the material just skimmed her shoulders in a puff of sleeve that left her arms bare. Tiny violets were scattered in her shining upswept hair, only a few dark tendrils curling to her bare white shoulders. An amethyst pendant had been attached to the single seed-pearl strand.

She seated herself quickly at the lilac-laden piano and began with Ben Jonson's familiar air, "Drink to me only with thine eyes, and I will pledge with mine." Then she sang some of the verses of the Cavalier poets that had been set to drinking songs, including Suckling's witty "The Constant Lover," who complained that he'd already admired his lady for "three whole days together."

During these and the Mozart interlude that followed, Caley repeatedly tried to catch Berkeley's eye. But his friend was sitting slightly
forward on the chaise, and his gaze was usually directed at the per-
former. One moment, Caley thought he was merely listening with polite
interest; at the next, he uneasily suspected an intensity underlying
Glendower's urbane manner.

At last, acknowledging with a smile a request for the dance hall
tunes from the first Saturday, Morna played those, ending with "Mrs.
Brown from Camden Town." She stood up with a happy flourish.

Accustomed now to the haste required to be the first, Caley managed to be at Morna's side almost immediately. But he found
Glendower next to him. Seesawed by his own emotions, Caley cleared
his throat and introduced the two. As Berkeley was presented to her,
Morna held out her hand and, noticing his boutonniere, remarked on
how much she enjoyed the scent of the lilacs placed on the piano.

Her face was lifted to his and her smile was warm. But Caley had
learned that he could not interpret that smile. She gave it as generously
to Theo, to himself, and for that matter, to portly, bespectacled Edward
Gibbons. Now it seemed to Caley that Glendower was silent for an
unusually long time, as he stood there looking down at Morna, still
holding her hand.

But just as Caley had begun to wonder if, struck by the force of her
beauty, the man had indeed lost his skill with polished phrases,
Glendower replied. To his friend's despair and envy he said, smiling, "I
was lucky in my choice of flowers, given your dress, but do you know,
watching you sing Ben Jonson's lyrics, I was reminded of his lines that
begin, 'Have you seen but a bright lily grow' and end, 'O, so white! O,
so soft! O, so sweet is she!' "

"A pretty compliment. Thank you," she responded, and as far as
Caley could tell, she was pleased. Glendower's eyes were on her face,
his hand as yet firmly clasping hers. "But as I recall," she continued,
"the character in that play was trying to seduce the lady. A *married*
lady, I believe."

Caley was overwhelmed both by her reply and its quickness. He
fumbled in distress through his memory, on which he'd always rather
prided himself, but drew a blank. What play was she referring to?
Surely an obscure one. He hadn't recognized the line, let alone which of
Jonson's many works it was from. Moreover, he suspected that Morna
was giving Berkeley a definite message, but he wasn't sure.

Gently, she withdrew her hand and looked down at the shimmering pattern of her dress. Her voice was, as always after singing, charm-

ingly throaty. "And despite the fact that we are told he was very handsome, I don't think the gentleman was in the end successful."

When she'd finished speaking, Glendower dropped his own hand
and remained quite still, one dark eyebrow lifted faintly. Caley tried not
to drown in his own sea of questions. What *did* she mean? Was Morna
mildly teasing Berkeley because of the very smoothness of his tribute?
Or was she warning him off? Perhaps there was a faint rebuke in her
tone because his stare had been too bold, his grasp more lingering than
propriety allowed. Had Glendower done so for effect, to show his admiration, or was he in fact so entranced that he'd genuinely forgotten
himself?

Abruptly, a large hand shot out and landed on Berkeley's shoulder.
"Ah, Glendower," Edward Gibbons said, his eyes behind gold-rimmed
spectacles fixed on Morna. "You'll forgive me for interrupting, sir, but
this is the least this lady deserves after such a performance." He held a
delicate flute of champagne in his outstretched hand and, with a slight
bow, gave it to her. "I hope you'll enjoy this, my dear. I brought the
bottle from my own cellar, and it's considered the finest France has to
offer."

Almost before she'd finished her graceful thank-you, Theo Manningham had slid in front of the tall, stout banker. Gibbons shrugged
regretfully and grasped Berkeley's arm. "Well, we'd best temporarily
give place here. I'm glad you're back, since I've something to discuss. I
understand you have leased some sections of the Smuggler mine for
cleanup. Clever of you. Should be highly profitable. I have an interested
investor who would like to go in with you. Let's find a quiet corner
before dinner."

Although Caley kept half an eye on the two as the banker animatedly conferred with Berkeley, Glendower managed to break away in
time to end up on Morna's right at dinner. Outmaneuvered, Caley sat
across from them with Colette on his left, and he strained to hear what
was said on the other side of the table.

Morna kept the conversation light and scrupulously divided her
attention between Glendower and the man on her left, George Fisk, the
manager of the Tomboy mine, a rabbity-faced man who sported thick
side whiskers to disguise the narrowness of his face. He was surprisingly talkative, Glendower unusually quiet. As course followed course,
Caley remained in anxious doubt. Was it possible that Glendower was
as lightning struck as he himself had been on meeting Morna? Or was
he, along with first the trout and then the sirloin of beef, swallowing the
easy words that had always sprung so readily to his lips in talking to

pretty women? Could he conceivably be just mulling over Gibbons's business proposal?

Meanwhile Fisk had happily launched into a description of the way the molten gold, freed of quicksilver, was at last poured into bar molds on the monthly Bullion Day. "It is exciting, Miss Gregory. I'd like you to see it. The crucible is lifted from the furnace with a chain block and swung over the molds. Then, with a pair of long tongs, it is tipped just enough to let the white-hot liquid flow into the molds. Sometimes there is a shower of golden drops." He added pragmatically, "Of course, when they cool and solidify, we sweep them up carefully."

Morna expressed real interest, remarking that she had not yet been out of Telluride itself, and Glendower broke in. "The road to the Tomboy is too narrow for a carriage and difficult even when the ground is drier. But I have several good horses, and I would be happy to accompany you. Do you ride?"

"Oh, yes. I'm sure I spent most of my childhood on horseback." Delight skimmed across her face, and for one brief moment she held his gaze. Then she lowered her eyes. "But you must excuse me. I cannot make appointments to do so. Freda has been kind enough to order up sheet music for some of the latest songs and I must learn them. As well, the summer gowns and their makers are arriving almost daily. There are endless selections, and then the fittings." She turned to Fisk and also thanked him for the invitation without accepting it.

It was during the dessert course that Caley felt, with a definite rise of spirits, that Glendower had taken an unwitting false step. Morna praised the pastries of Isobel Ewen, whom she'd said accompanied her to Telluride and, handing him a slice of pie, said, "You must try this apple tart."

"It's interesting," he commented, looking first at his plate and then at her. "Those raised in the British Isles call meat dishes with crust 'pies,' but if the filling is fruit, they invariably refer to them as 'tarts' instead."

Instead of the noncommittal smile or wry nod both Caley and he expected as a response, those two men, although no one else, saw a quick glint of alarm in her eyes. Putting down his fork, Berkeley said gently, "My dear lady, you are in a room with powerful men that you can claim as friends. And I would be honored to do anything to set your mind at ease. Would it not be better if you told us if you have anything that troubles you and—"

"Please, Mr. Glendower," she interrupted in a low voice that Caley just caught, "it would be better if you trusted my judgment on this matter. And it would be best if we now changed the topic of our conversation. How long have you been coming to Telluride?"

Afterward, brandy was served in the parlor. Cigars were lit and the talk and laughter grew louder. Another pianist had been hired to play dance music, and Morna was in such demand as a partner that there was no chance to get near her. Caley, feeling that he'd rather neglected Colette during dinner, spun her into a waltz. Soon, someone else claimed her for a dance, and Caley surveyed the long room. There was no sign of Glendower.

CHAPTER 5

Ⅰf Stanton Caley had risen early the next morning, he would have seen something that would have interested him greatly. But it was Sunday and he'd stayed late at Freda's, thinking that Berkeley had only stepped outside for a quiet cigar in the freshness of the night air and that he'd return. Caley had also nervously rehearsed a few things that he might say to Morna, if he were lucky enough to have at least a brief talk with her. But, disappointed in both instances, at last he'd given up and gone back to his lodgings at the Sheridan.

So he missed the dawn's aftermath in the valley, a pastel light because the sun's rays didn't reach down into Telluride until midmorning, and the tentative twittering of newly arrived birds. The spring breeze, which still remembered snow, briskly ruffled the manes of the two horses that Glendower was leading down Pacific Avenue toward Miss Freda's.

The gray mare, whose well-brushed coat resembled the silvery undersides of sage leaves, walked tranquilly, but the roan gelding took one step sideways for every two forward. It kept nudging its nose against the rough tweed of the man's shoulder as if to remind him they should be off and running, and when tied alongside the mare to the post outside of Freda's, the roan snorted in dissatisfaction.

It was Isobel who answered the door. She'd been up for some time preparing cinnamon rolls, which had to rise twice, for the lavish late breakfast always served on Sunday. Wiping her floury hands on her apron, she'd hurried from the kitchen, wondering who'd be knocking at such an hour.

The man had doffed the cap that matched his woolen jacket, and the wind brushed dark hair onto his forehead. "You must be Miss Isobel Ewen," he said gravely. "Last night at dinner the manager of the Tomboy, after tasting your pie, begged to hire you to cook at his boardinghouse. Ask Freda for a rise in your wages immediately. She knows you're worth the ore in that mine."

He paused and sniffed. "Johnnycake." He grinned with pleasure. "Coffee. Yes. I've brought these horses as a gift for Miss Morna Gregory, and since I have a few words of warning regarding *that* mischief maker"—he leveled a finger at the impatient roan—"I'll have to come to the kitchen with you. While you work and I eat johnnycake, I'll pass on what you must tell her."

Pure sauce, Isobel had thought that morning, seeing him standing on the doorstep with wind-tousled hair and smiling hazel eyes. But he'd always had such a way with him. Now, as she recalled the day she had met Berkeley Glendower, she smiled sleepily, tilting her head back in the rocking chair. It was wicked that a man so good looking should have such charm. Before he asked a question, every woman was answering, "Yes."

Well, she corrected herself, not *every* woman. Isobel opened her eyes and looked at the bed, listening to Morna's even breathing. Such a quiet sleep had to be a good sign. Reassured, she worked the tallowy glycerin into her knuckles and slipped back in memory. As she'd learned, Mr. Glendower had other qualities, and because of those, she herself had never been able to say no to him from that day eighteen months earlier to this.

That Sunday, before she knew where *she* was at, he was comfortably settled by the huge black stove, a slab of buttery corn bread in his hand, a thick cup before him, watching her knead the rolls. And she was soon telling him about Louisville, its coal mines and wheat fields.

"A beautiful valley," he agreed. "A whole view of the Front Range, mountain piled on mountain."

"Ah, I like it here too. The air's like it's just been laundered and the sky's that close." She pushed down on the soft dough. "But the spring's so late. I was just writing to my sister, Florrie, in Lafayette last night, saying that by now I'd have my whole garden in at home."

"Get the letter," he said, picking up the last crumb of bread with a moistened forefinger. "I'm taking this morning's train and I'll post it in Denver. That way she'll have it tomorrow."

Isobel had picked up the heavy brown bowl, and it almost slipped through her flour-coated fingers. "I—I don't send the letters to Lafayette. I . . . just write to her." She set the bowl on the stove top to rise again and avoided his eyes.

"Why is that, Isobel?" He leaned forward to see her face, but she wheeled back to the scrubbed wooden table she'd been working on. She ran an awkward hand over the pale reddish hair that frizzed onto the back of her neck. Her shoulders were stiff beneath the black homespun of her dress.

"Her husband, John Wesley, well, he's a preacher. A fierce godly man, ye see, and—" She waved her hand to take in the house, the bedrooms upstairs. "But Florrie, she'd just want to know I'm happy wherever I am. Still, he'd be getting the mail from the post office, more than likely, and be asking Florrie, and she's not one to lie. Just my . . . leaving was bad enough. He'll have had the whole church praying for me *and* telling them why. I can't be causing any more trouble for Florrie, ye see."

"I do see." Glendower rose, walked to the table, and stood very near Isobel. "Does Florrie even know where you are?"

"No. And I know she's right heartsick because of that." In her misery Isobel unthinkingly cradled her elbows in her hands, leaving flour marks on the long sleeves of her dark cotton dress. She blinked back the tears that trembled on her eyelashes.

"Let's think," he said quietly. "Now, Florrie, being a minister's wife, must occasionally visit the sick or do other good works about town. Isn't there a family she might drop in on, someone you know?"

Isobel considered, and her face, already damp from the stove's heat, now grew more shiny with hope. "The Tollivers. Harold lost his legs in the mines and his wife, Etta Whitby, that was, before she married, went to school with me. She's a good woman and not one to talk."

"Exactly. Mrs. Tolliver." He gently brushed flour from her sleeve. "You get your letters, the whole packet, and I'll see they're delivered to her personally with instructions about discretion. In small towns sometimes it's best to avoid post offices altogether, isn't it? That way if a friendly, if gossipy, clerk inquires about frequent letters from Telluride, Mrs. Tolliver need not invent a cousin here. And if no one asks your sister if she's corresponding with you, why, then she needn't lie."

Isobel flew from the kitchen, and when she returned with several fat envelopes, Glendower was waiting in the foyer. He removed his cap from a capacious side pocket and slipped the letters in. He patted his hip. "There. That'll be our secret."

Opening the door, he said, "Now, these horses. At any time their reins can be looped over the saddle and they'll trot happily back to Jackson's stable. They're well trained. Unfortunately, neither of them is well named. Greybird, the mare, does not have wings on her heels. But if Miss Gregory prefers sidesaddle, that little horse is reliable. And she can step lively when pulling a light carriage. She even likes the sound of bells on her harness."

He stepped to the roan and ran an affectionate hand down its shining flank. "Chevalier, here, is very fast, but not always a gentleman. He has to be ridden astride. He doesn't like carriages, and will not stay in traces. Still, he can be handled by the right lady. Be sure to tell Miss Gregory *that*."

He put on his cap and smiled up at Isobel in the doorway. "And mention to her that these horses come with reins, but no strings. No strings at all. Good-bye. I'm sure you'll hear from Florrie soon." Isobel stood in the doorway, beaming, until he turned the corner onto Colorado Avenue. Returning to her baking, she inadvertently poured an entire pint of cream into the icing for the rolls and ended with enough to frost three cakes.

When Morna came into the kitchen a short time later for her usual early breakfast, she was wearing her brown monk's-cloth robe. Her hair, in one long braid, was loosely wrapped around her head, and the effect was one of a rather solemn ascetic beauty. When Isobel put a mug of coffee in her hand and simultaneously burst out that Glendower had been there with two horses, her face became quite stern. "I told the gentleman," she said in a cold voice, "that I would make no appointments for riding with him."

"But no, he's gone! To Denver. The horses—both of them—are for you. A gift, he said. Without reins, I mean, strings. He said to tell you that especially."

"*Two* horses? A gift? I don't know that I can—"

"But, Miss Morna, I have to tell you what else he did," Isobel interrupted. In her excitement she forgot Glendower's parting words about the delivery of the letters being a secret, but she'd not thought, in any case, that such words applied to her mistress.

During this recital Morna said nothing, but kept her eyes on the other woman's delighted face. Isobel concluded with "Now you must come and see the horses. They are that beautiful. But I've been thinking

about the brown one, quite fast he said, and I'll not be wanting you—"
Isobel was beckoning her to the foyer as she talked.

Morna hesitated, then put down her coffee cup, and followed her. Isobel almost threw open the front door. "There!" she exclaimed.

Morna stared, and as Isobel faithfully repeated Glendower's words, she continued looking. The gray mare stood quietly, but the roan tossed his head and nickered hopefully, lifting first one front hoof and then the other. To Isobel's astonishment Morna did not utter a word, but turned and went rapidly up the staircase.

When she came down a few minutes later, she was dressed in a black velvet jacket over a high-necked tan blouse and a black split skirt. On her still braided hair she wore an English jockey's velvet hard-crowned riding hat.

Isobel, still mystified, had returned to the kitchen. She did not see Morna go out, loop the reins over the mare's saddle, and, with a quick pat, send her back to the stable. Then Morna ran one leather-gloved hand down the roan's nose, next along his neck. He turned to look at her and she whispered for some time in his ear. She slipped one foot in the stirrup and sprang to his back.

By the time that Isobel had worriedly returned to the hallway to check, she could just see the two of them turning the corner at a gallop.

CHAPTER 6

The soft Denver night was lit by the cold rays of the full moon illuminating the outlines of the house roofs along Capitol Hill, overlooking the city below. The new mansions of Millionaire's Row along Grant Street were lined up, one next to the other, almost jostling for place. Almost all were Victorian style, arrayed in the latest furbelows of curled wooden gingerbread trim and iron railings edging their roofs. Towers and turrets pointed grandly to the vast Colorado sky, and windows stared haughtily west at what the Indians called the spine of the world: the Rocky Mountains. Thrusting upward over lesser peaks, Mount Evans, adorned only with still white snow, gleamed back in perfect isolated splendor.

Capturing far more than its share of the moon's chilly illumination was the huge, thrusting profile of the Laughton Powell home. Four stories in height, its top lavished with every ornament an architect could envision, the Powell house was a marvel in red brick. The corners were trimmed with silver-bearing rock, which glittered like smiling teeth in the twin light sources of the moon and the lanterns placed atop the brick gateposts at the edge of the grounds. Nearly all of the windows were aglow, the mullioned glass panes in the conservatory sparkling like square-cut diamonds.

Inside the house Amelia Powell, née Wetherhill, of the South Carolina Wetherhills, was herself a jewel in the stately setting of the formal dining room. The subtle yellow silk wallpaper, ordered from Paris, framed elegantly by lustrous rosewood molding, had been chosen to highlight her chestnut hair, piled high tonight in a cluster of curls. That the delicate color of the walls, in concert with the candelabras suspended above, would also lend warmth to her pale, dramatic face had been noted by her at the time of its purchase.

Amelia, surveying the long table, which was bedecked with a daring arrangement of camellias and asparagus fern spread the length of the damask cloth, allowed herself a moment of rich satisfaction as her glance at last paused at the reason for the night's festivities. Berkeley Glendower, darkly handsome in tails and white shirt, cast her a smile, then answered a question from the Englishman, Theo Manningham, across the table. Olivia Glendower, née Hyde-White, was not present, having returned to her family's Newport residence for the summer. So, Amelia decided, the Powell mansion would be the site of many such parties in the next three months. Her cat-in-the-cream expression was silently remarked by every other woman present.

Around the table were, for the most part, what Amelia fondly thought of as her closest friends. In actuality, the forty people who had agreed as a matter of course to sup with the Powells, even for this small party on short notice, did have common interests and were used to each other. Most of them were fellow players in the central game of Denver society, in which only the "Sacred Thirty-six" held truly significant power.

Despite her spinsterhood Eloise Murdoch was a member of this group. But she was one of the banking Murdochs, second-generation Denver money. She always dressed as a widow, hair primly tucked under a black band, and she'd never been seen without her fingerless lace gloves. Frequently, she attended functions with her brother, William, whose own wife, Maud, was a retiring lady known for her delicate health. Like her brother in being a tireless whist player, Eloise even resembled William, although the sharp features and hard stare, so much an asset to him in his business dealings, were somewhat of a disadvantage for a gently bred lady.

But her plainness perhaps endeared her to the trio of very pretty young ladies who were also part of the group. Belle Alexander would have been beautiful had she any animation. Her carefully arranged thick blond hair was never disturbed by a toss of the head, her peach-blossom complexion unwrinkled by a sudden smile or lifted eyebrow. A local wit had remarked that her attractive and energetic husband, Patrick, had probably married her on a bet, determined to arouse a response. By all accounts he'd lost. But, if Belle were comfortably arranged, with everything she liked close at hand, she was sometimes capable of a malicious turn of phrase.

She was always seen with Jessamine Wyndham and Caroline Farnsworth. Jessamine was barely nineteen, the second wife of Quentin, who was himself not yet forty, and the two made a striking couple. But she'd cast herself as an adored darling, petted by an older man, and her soft pinkness, wispy curls, and petite figure fit her role. The bodice of her silk dress in a pale peony shade was ruffled to suggest a bosom and cut in to emphasize a stem thin waist. She always described eating as a troublesome necessity and vowed that if her dear Quentin didn't coax her constantly, she'd simply live like a flower on air and water.

Caroline Farnsworth considered herself the most intellectual of the three—she read all the novels labeled suitable for ladies—and as such felt she must advise the naive Jessamine, prompt the languid Belle. Her cameo face was only marred by thin lips and a faint separation between her front teeth that she tried constantly to conceal. She considered her hair a little too dark for fashion, but this evening had added to her upswept hair thin ribbons in a melon hue, which exactly matched her gown, for a lightening effect.

But the color of the dress had caused her much anxiety. Amelia, whom Caroline always addressed as Mrs. Powell, was very strict in requiring that no one else wear the same shade in which she would appear. And although this soirée had been hastily organized, the word had been put about that the hostess would be dressed in amber. Poor Caroline was faced with a quandary: Dare she attend in her lovely new pale orange dress? She called several modistes, one of whom ventured that amber was a deep gold. But she was still quite uncertain. No one would risk offending the doyenne of Denver society, and no one would ever forget the apple episode.

A year ago in the spring Amelia had planned her first garden party of the season rather early because her young trees would be in blossom. Her own dress was announced as a delicate shade of apple green with petals of white lace. First, the weather had proved unreliable. Although morning drizzles were unusual—Denver leaned toward abrupt thunderstorms or nothing—Amelia had taken no chances. Whole trees were uprooted, and the flower-laden branches had been hacked off others, and the garden was recreated indoors in the palatial music gallery on the third floor.

But worse was to follow. The young wife of an architect much favored by society appeared in a light chartreuse gown. Moreover, she'd thoughtlessly strayed near the bower that was serving as Mrs. Powell's backdrop. Amelia's frozen smile did not thaw. The architect received no more commissions for mansions, although he did make something of a name for himself in San Francisco, where he'd relocated some months later.

After fretting for three whole days—Caroline did so want to wear her new dress—she put the question to her husband. Rollo lifted his thick, triangular eyebrows and smiled broadly, "What you must do, my dear, immediately upon arriving, if you find the colors too similar, is faint. I'll mention to the coachman that you might be returning home shortly after we enter." Grateful for the idea, Caroline particularly mentioned to both Belle and Jessamine that she'd been taking Brown's Vegetable Cure for an inexplicable dizziness she'd been experiencing of late.

Amelia, who had unblinkingly eyed Caroline's gown, was again looking at Berkeley, whom she'd of course seated on her right, but he was speaking now to Rose Trimble on his other side. She'd been so placed by her hostess because all one could say of Rose was that she was present. Her husband, Orville, required her to be there and so she was, dressed in a prairie-brown taffeta. Amelia abstractedly pressed more of the creamy blue-veined Stilton on George Bender—whom she'd positioned on her left because he could be ignored—and wondered what was preoccupying Berkeley. He'd not commented on her new gown, which shone so richly against the jonquil wallpaper, and which exactly matched her diamond-encrusted antique gold pendant. She'd been looking forward to one of his usual wonderfully phrased compliments.

No doubt, she judged, it was the mining business that took him so annoyingly often to Telluride. It could be nothing else. The glittering reflection her mirror had given her this evening convinced her of that. And certainly he was as pleasantly attentive to her as ever. What caused Amelia to scheme night and day was that that was *all* he ever was.

Watching her with some interest, noting that her glances were lingering as always on his friend Berkeley, Patrick Alexander leaned back in his chair. Patrick had shrewd eyes, an irreverent grin, and a jutting chin set in a square jaw. His light streaked hair was combed straight back over a well-shaped head. Except for a gently curving mouth, his good looks were rugged. He continued to make the occasional judicious nod during Eloise Murdoch's monologue, but he wondered, not for the first time, what Berkeley made of the fact that Mrs. Powell doted on him.

It was obvious to everyone. And, if Amelia were not so truly rich, people might have been tempted to disapprove. If she were less beautiful, they would have even considered pitying her. As it was, the subject made for quite a bit of titillated gossip in their set. Amelia's husband, Laughton, seemed undisturbed by the situation. But then, very little seemed to bother that complacent man, and perhaps he was relieved that his forceful wife had something to occupy her thoughts. Laughton himself sought Glendower out, spent a great deal of time talking to him.

As for what Berkeley thought about it, Patrick reflected, that was a little hard to tell. Perhaps a man that extraordinarily good looking simply took women's attention for granted, had become used to it. Patrick chewed his lip in wry envy at the prospect of being so fortunate. Yet, mulling it over, he had to admit Berkeley wasn't vain. Possibly his friend just didn't spend much time sorting over people's emotions, thinking about why they acted as they did. Maybe he'd never had to. Everyone always seemed to like him.

It was, Patrick realized, the most conceivable explanation. It wasn't that Berkeley wasn't astute about people's reactions; playing high-stakes poker with him was definitely not a good idea. He just seemed to prefer concentrating on more matter-of-fact problems, finding useful solutions for them. Over brandy and cigars Berkeley tended to talk, and entertainingly at that, about such things as how the experienced Cornish miners could dovetail the timber in tunnels so that the mountain did not come crashing down on their heads. This practical mindset no doubt accounted for Berkeley's frequent presence in Telluride, where such problems abounded, Patrick had observed on his own infrequent visits. And there Glendower need not attend elaborate functions of this sort, which, he'd once remarked, bored him.

Patrick, on the other hand, usually enjoyed them. These parties afforded him, along with the excellent dinners and wines that he appreciated, quite a bit of food for thought. Here, amid the fragile china and polished silver, one saw the quick slash of unsheathed claw, the fierce grasp of talon. The female of the species, too, was proficient at the game. Though he was himself a kindhearted man, all this kept Patrick's interest.

Now, while again nodding agreeably at Eloise Murdoch, he turned his speculations on Amelia. It was certain that she wanted men's admiration, that she was not at all adverse to their ardent appeals. Still, he doubted that she ever accepted. It was the power to move men she wanted, a way of winning. But now all the passion of her passionate personality was narrowly channeled, directed at Berkeley Glendower. Patrick thought he would not like to have that force trained on himself. While it was not at all the thing one man said to another, he'd have liked to warn Berkeley that he ought to take seriously that woman's obsession.

Patrick eyed Amelia's high, rounded bosom beneath the sparkling pendant. It would be a challenge to bed her. But—he shrugged—someday a man would conquer Everest, too, and it would be just as cold and uncomfortable at the top as it'd been on the way up.

Just then, Eloise Murdoch's trumpet blast of a voice swelled over the quieter conversations. "Indeed, Mr. Alexander, wives today neglect the most important aspect of marriage. It was quite otherwise in my youth," she announced trenchantly.

"Whatever can you mean, Miss Murdoch?" Patrick Alexander's smile was engagingly open, but one rueful, sardonic eyebrow was lifted. "My Belle would surely be an exception to any such complaint." Amelia was certain his wife must have overheard. Everyone knew that Patrick longed for children and that Belle was trying hard not to oblige. Her expression remained blankly smooth. With her white shoulders rising from the mounded white satin of her sleeve tops, Belle looked like one of the elegant dessert meringues that had accompanied the macédoine of fruit.

"It is a wife's first duty," Eloise continued, ignoring the response, "to consider her husband's health. And although it pains me to say so, I have often had to point this out to Maud. She cannot let her own minor complaints blind her to my brother's symptoms. William's pulse flutters, he has palpitations, and I myself have detected a shortness of breath in him. But what is overwhelming evidence of his incipient heart trouble"—she paused impressively—"is that William told me just last week that he had dreamed of falling!"

"Good heavens," Rose Trimble interjected, a worried frown creasing her brow. "What do you recommend?"

"Dr. Echols's Heart Cure. The bottle clearly states the complete list of scientific indicators that I have just outlined, particularly specifying the dream. One must keep abreast of modern medical advances."

Amelia stopped listening and returned to her summer dreams. On her last trip to the East she'd tried to discover if Theodore Roosevelt would be available. It'd seemed likely—she'd brushed away the interference of the troublesome war with Spain. Although he was only at present in 1898 an assistant secretary of the Navy, it was rumored he would run for governor of New York in the fall. He loved the West, and he seemed pleased at the idea of a hunting trip with Laughton. Despite her husband's tendency to deliver ear-numbing monologues, he *was* an excellent marksman. At dinner, she thought, sighing inwardly with relief, Berkeley could talk to Mr. Roosevelt.

Then, too, with Glendower by her side, she would invite the smart set from Colorado Springs. Fancying themselves as the inhabitants of an exclusive spa, that group had to be shown how Denver could shine. It was not just his extraordinary good looks that made him such a desirable addition, although here she again let her eyes linger on his profile. The straight nose, the clean upper lip, the firm jaw—so admirably masculine, she thought. She disapproved of the way that so many society women chose male friends, like gossipy Cyril Harrington, who were rather effeminate.

Berkeley really was quite different, despite his graceful manner. That was obvious from the reaction of every woman who met him. The intensity of his eyes, his mouth—it was the fullness of his lower lip—here Amelia tried to change the direction of her thoughts. Only alone at night did she allow herself to dwell on the way his mouth might feel on hers, the touch of his hands. Everyone in Denver knew she wanted him; she had not been able to hide it. They all must see that she'd gotten him.

Her own rich brown hair, she considered, was set off by the black sheen of his. Returning to this safer ground, she went over the perfect setting she'd envisioned for the two of them this summer. The conservatory gardeners had been instructed to move the orchids outside for garden parties. Although they had pulled long, shocked faces because of the effect of the lack of humidity on the flowers, she had been firm. She'd had a watercolorist copy the fuchsia hue of the orchids and sent the drawing off to her favorite Paris couturière.

And for the end of the season gala she had a delicious idea. When Baron von Richtofen finished his castle to the east of the city, he'd released a thousand canaries to populate the neighboring plains and serenade his new bride. No one of consequence had attended the gathering, of course, because of his ill-advised choice of a wife. However, having heard of Roosevelt's interest in animals and such things, Amelia planned to import rare tropical parrots and let them fly and, she hoped, eventually breed in the stately conifers on Grant Street. Everyone would comment on the jeweled plumage against the dark green needles. What the parrots might think of northern pines did not concern Amelia.

Her attention was rather rudely wrenched back from her reverie by a faint but audible belch on the part of her left-hand dinner partner. It occurred to her that George Bender had emptied each refill of his wineglass with unaccustomed speed. He was now glancing ponderously down the table, his slightly bulbous eyes glassy, hectic color in his hearty face. Laughton had said something about his being heavily invested in real estate in Montclair, east of the city. If his finances were shaky, Amelia considered, she would have to rethink the couple's presence on her guest lists for the summer season.

Although not in the inner circle, the Benders had impeccable social credentials and had been counted on to regard an invitation to any of the Thirty-six's functions as a command performance. This evening even their daughter, Elizabeth, whose nondescript prettiness Amelia regarded as safely neutral, had been invited, since there were two young bachelors. Stanton Caley was a regular guest, and he'd brought his English friend. But both the Benders did seem to be under a certain amount of strain, Amelia thought. Charlotte, usually immaculately groomed, had a hurried, almost neglected air. The cascade of ribbons on one shoulder was loosely tied, and tiny tendrils had already begun to escape her heavy black chignon.

Caroline Farnsworth, head tilted, sparrow-sharp eyes trained on Charlotte's appearance, was exchanging significant glances with Belle Alexander across the table. Nothing was more agreeable than a departure from the ordinary. The possibilities for speculation were clearly intriguing them both.

The comfortable hum of voices, no longer punctuated by the sounds of silver against china, wavered. Recognizing a natural ebb in the after-dinner conversation, Amelia Powell felt it time to nudge the evening along. Without pausing for even a pretense of the obligatory glance toward her husband, she rose, in one fluid motion, to her feet. The light from the one hundred candles artfully ablaze overhead cast a multitude of shadows among the folds and tucks of her amber satin dress. She knew she looked her best, her creamy skin rising above the ivory rose-point lace that frothed along the décolletage of her gown. Her large, heavy-lidded brown eyes glowed and the dramatic slash of her cheekbones created interesting hollows that emphasized what she considered her best feature, her voluptuous, pouting mouth.

Amelia was aware of the eyes of her guests, the men in particular, and she held her head just a little higher, knowing that more than one had used the term *swanlike* to describe the graceful lines of her neck. The slight movement sent her earrings, faceted pear-shape diamond pendants, to tapping gently against her cheeks. From the corner of her eyes she now sought Glendower's approving gaze. But Berkeley, a frown drawing his long brows together, was listening to George Bender, not even noticing her.

The lines of petulance a little deeper around her mouth, Amelia nodded regally. "Ladies, shall we?"

As if on a sign the people at the table pushed back their carved mahogany chairs. The women clustered together on their way to the withdrawing room, their long skirts trailing over the burgundy swirls of carpet as if caught in an errant current.

The men, their voices already deepening and roughening as they approached the comforts of tobacco and brandy in the library, left without a backward glance.

The withdrawing room was papered in deep green silk, populated with the delicate, intricate furniture considered de rigueur for a feminine retreat. It had been transformed into a bower, nearly every surface bearing plants or cut blossoms from Amelia's conservatory that she'd had built some two years earlier. Since then she had become known for the astonishing variety of flowers that had distinguished each of her soirées, and many of Denver's other hostesses had been forced to petition their husbands for their own hothouses. Thus far, however, none had been able to obtain the kind of creativity for which Amelia paid so dearly in her staff of three indoor gardeners.

Tonight the heavy scent of magnolia vied with the dusky purple perfume of the irises banked near one window. A riotous arrangement of Lily of the Nile, Canterbury Bells, and Phantom Orchids held pride of place under the Gainsborough that Amelia had purchased during a recent trip abroad.

Eloise Murdoch, funereal in her black bombazine, followed Jessamine Wyndham to the gray damask love seat near the marble fireplace. The light cast by the gas lamps, crystal pendants suspended beneath them, lent grand shadows to the corner, adding the illusions of privacy and intrigue. "That quail pie was undercooked," she muttered to Jessamine's slender rose taffeta back. "Amelia needs to look to her kitchen."

Amelia, swishing across the Oriental rug toward the square pedestal table, which held an interesting array of decanters, heard the comment and smiled to herself. She was more than pleased with the efforts of her kitchen staff. Her latest success in acquisition involved the French-trained cook of William Murdoch, Eloise's brother. No Murdoch had ever been able to accept being the victim of superior strategy, Amelia reflected, flicking a glance at Eloise's tightened lips. The warmth of triumph flowed through her.

The fact that Eloise had sponsored her entrée into Denver society upon her arrival from Charleston made it all that more important to Amelia to savor her small victory. She had assumed that marriage to the Powell fortune would assure her place, but there was no such automatic acceptance on the part of the women. It had taken a nod from the

Murdochs to smooth her way into the rigidly controlled numbers of the socially elite in the Queen City of the Plains. That rankled, since the Wetherhills were themselves Old Money.

Denver's Sacred Thirty-six fought the fight of the nouveaux riches, Amelia thought with inbred, Charlestonian disdain. Here, on the edge of the frontier, Denver seemed always looking over its shoulder, afraid of being viewed as only an aspirant to civilization. In the South it was more gracefully done: everyone knew everyone, and one's launching into the world was never haunted by the specter of the wrong newcomers. Entrée was granted—at least to those with the right name and the money—with the ease that came with that security.

Eloise had pointed out that, since Denver men had positively made it a habit to marry for the wrong reasons, things must be done this way. "My dear Amelia," she'd reminded her, "when Horace Tabor had eight million dollars he married that—that Baby Doe. And *she* put marble statues—nude ones—on her grounds, which practically adjoined William's. My nephews could actually see them!" Amelia was not mollified, but later she herself made sure that the alluring second wife of the baron von Richtofen was invited nowhere. The men, of course, followed suit by denying the baron access to their tight-knit business world, although some of his ideas had seemed to them both original and promising.

"Ladies, we will, of course, have tea with the gentlemen when they return." Amelia's honeyed voice, her most treasured legacy from her South Carolina girlhood, paused. "And then Elizabeth Bender has kindly consented to sing for us. In the meantime, may I offer you a choice of cordials, or perhaps some ratafia?"

Eloise Murdoch shifted in her spot on the comfortable velveteen chair. "I prefer sherry," she announced firmly, having already noticed that there was none of that wine on the pedestal table. "I cannot abide that other treacle." As Amelia tugged the bell pull for a servant to fetch that decanter, Eloise turned to the woman in the small chair beside the love seat. "How are the children?" she asked. Having no offspring of her own, Eloise naturally had many theories on how the young should be raised, and she was always eager to share them.

Rose Trimble shook her head, and her wide, apple-cheeked face, framed by smooth wings of graying hair over her ears, lost its normally cheery cast. "Abigail has had such a malaise this spring." The lines around her blue eyes deepened into a fretwork. "I've tried everything to aid her."

Eloise had straightened at the mention of health problems, her coffee-brown eyes snapping with vitality. "Have you been taking her to

Dr. McBroom?" At her companion's nod she inquired suspiciously, "What did he prescribe?"

"Some sort of tonic," Rose answered. "But it has not had the desired results."

"I shouldn't think it would!" Eloise's thin features quivered with righteous indignation. "That man has never been able to deal satisfactorily with Maud's problems, even though she continues to see him, against my strict advice. As for his diagnosis of my condition, it doesn't bear repeating!" She nodded sharply, then leaned closer. "Does Abigail have palpitations?"

"Yes," said Rose sadly, "and she seems to be tired constantly. And"—her voice lowered to a near whisper—"her monthly courses are irregular."

Eloise nodded again. "I know the very thing," she declared. "Celery Malt Compound. Why, last year, when I was so fatigued . . ."

Caroline Farnsworth, having heard Eloise's opening questions, was quickly moving away to the corner where Belle Alexander was stretched out on a chaise longue with Jessamine in a stiff chair next to her. But her hostess forestalled her. At being so stopped, Caroline very nearly did faint, sure that the subject of their conversation would be the unfortunate choice of the color of her gown. Her tongue stuck to the roof of her mouth in fear.

But Amelia had merely decided that Caroline might have a modicum of information about the Benders, so she exerted her considerable diplomacy. "My dear Caroline, you are the only woman here who has such good sense that her husband confides in her regarding business affairs. And I was wondering, only because Laughton asked my opinion —can you imagine—what Rollo says about George Bender's investments in Montclair."

In relief Caroline put one small index finger to her lips as she thought, which she felt would make her look intelligent and had the additional advantage of hiding the gap between her teeth. She was trying to guess where Montclair could be, and wondering if Rollo had ever let fall the name. Her thoughts were whirling so fast she could not speak in any case. She was disappointed as well. She had so hoped that Charlotte Bender's distraction was due to something interesting, such as Elizabeth's decision to run off with someone totally unsuitable, instead of boring old business. But Amelia was no doubt right in her theory— she usually was—and besides, Elizabeth Bender was too much of a stick to do any such thing.

Amelia waited gracefully for a response, thinking that, although Rollo was toadlike in appearance, he was a sharp businessman and would be her most reliable source. Laughton was quite capable of forgetting what he'd heard. She was ruthless in her attention to detail, and she had no intention of letting the smallest thing, such as a miscue in her guest list, spoil her triumphant summer with Berkeley. It was already June, and she would have to move quickly.

At last she smiled purposefully at her still silent guest. "I am at home on Wednesday afternoons, you know. If you would tell me then?" Amelia swirled off even before Caroline could gasp out, "Oh, yes, Mrs. Powell."

Meanwhile, Jessamine, who'd asked only for a glass of seltzer, was excitedly leaning next to Belle Alexander's ear. "Do you know what I heard at dinner? I was next to Stanton Caley, and Stanton, you know, for a man, can be quite interesting. In fact, if he had a bit more hair, he would even be of interest himself." Taking the smallest sip from the crystal goblet, she giggled breathily. "Sitting next to him tonight was quite like eating with Quentin. 'My dear Mrs. Wyndham,' he said, 'you must try at least a bite of the veal. You didn't touch the fish, or the quail pie. Why, a breath of wind would—' "

"Jessamine," Belle interrupted, languorously raising a blackberry cordial to her lips, "exactly what did Stanton tell you?"

"But I was coming to that, Belle. He says that Amelia—why, I can hardly credit it, not that I imagine Stanton could be *wrong* about such a matter, but even for someone as high handed as Amelia—and when I think what dear Quentin would say were *I* to even think of doing such a thing—"

This time Jessamine interrupted herself, because she could see that Belle's eyelids were drooping. She finished in a rush. "He says that Amelia has obtained a portrait of Berkeley from his mother in Boston and commissioned a painter to copy it. And do you know where she is going to hang it?"

Belle's eyelids lifted fractionally. "Where?"

"At the top of the staircase!" Jessamine burst out fervidly. "And Stanton says that she says that is so she may look at it the last thing each night before she retires! When I think of what Quentin would think . . . and what do *you* imagine that Laughton thinks?"

"My dear," Belle replied, barely disguising a yawn behind a delicate hand, "no one knows what Laughton thinks, including Laughton. But," she added, setting her cordial glass on a dainty piecrust table next to her, "we must tell Caroline this. Do be good enough to bring her over the minute she leaves Amelia. And I rather want to know what she thinks about the extraordinary change in Charlotte Bender too. Really, if the woman cannot maintain appearances, she should not inflict herself on others."

Charlotte Bender was unaware of the whispers behind her. She was staring at the bouquet on the low table before her, her gaze losing itself in the curves and hollows of the trumpetlike columbines, thinking that she'd never been so provoked—and flustered—in her life. Before they'd come to the Powells, just as she was going in to dress, George had actually discussed his business affairs with her. He had said they might lose all their money. And to bother her with it now—just when she had her mind absolutely full with her planning on what might well be Elizabeth's last chance at a husband!

The arrival of Theo Manningham several weeks ago had, for Charlotte, begun a course of strategy more complex than the chess played by Colorado's monied barons. At twenty her daughter had already lingered on the shelf longer than most of her contemporaries. She had been introduced, without success, to every eligible bachelor in Denver.

The problem was, her mother reasoned, that although Elizabeth was quite pretty enough, she simply would not adopt the proper manner. One had to pretend to some complaisance, at least until the wedding day, and perhaps even to flirt, however shyly. To her mother's exasperation Elizabeth had sat like a stone next to Stanton Caley and later tossed her head at the idea that she should have tried to converse. She said that he would soon be quite bald. As if—Charlotte had thrown up her hands—his lack of hair could matter, given the Caley fortune.

With the coming of Theo, his tidy handsomeness, his distinguished background, and his flicker of interest in Elizabeth, Charlotte had taken heart. All still might be within reach. Although a younger son, there would surely be some Manningham money, and he *was* English. An advantageous marriage for Elizabeth might be just what was needed to push the Benders into the charmed circle.

Charlotte removed her eyes from the flowers. They only reminded her of George's miserly refusal a few months back to allow her to put in even a small conservatory. And now to upset her with this foolish talk of their losing their money. Surely, she considered, it would be in the bank where money was kept. Of course, she'd heard of such things— Horace Tabor had become quite penniless. But that was only justice. Hadn't he married that Baby Doe, who had no background at all? And George had selfishly interrupted her, before she had a chance to dress, and just when she was giving Elizabeth a much-needed talking to. She felt that never had a woman been so put upon.

Elizabeth Bender sat sulkily on a velveteen settee at the edge of the room, plucking at the rosettes on her pink organza dress. She was remembering, with much resentment, the scene with her mother. Elizabeth had almost completed her toilette, finally persuading her side curls to hang perfectly, despite having to listen to yet another lecture on the importance of smiling demurely and constantly.

In the midst of reminding her daughter to be more than usually attentive to Eloise Murdoch, a woman so boring she made Elizabeth's teeth ache, Charlotte had disappeared into her own dressing room. But before she'd really even managed to study the effect of the side curls, her mother had hurriedly returned. "Here." Charlotte had held out a rounded box of rice powder. "For your shoulders," she'd said with nervous firmness. "And what about scent?"

"Scent?" Elizabeth had stared at her uncomprehendingly. How many times had she been told that decent women wore no scent?

"Attar of roses. At least a trace. You need to capture his attention."

As Elizabeth raised the crystal glass of ratafia to her lips, she arched her neck defiantly. As if she needed such things. She would be singing tonight, and she would be the focus of all eyes. In preparation she'd soaked her hands for several days in dissolved almond-oil tablets for the whitening effect, and run through her pieces a time or two. And, even if it was the second time she'd had to wear the pink organza, she knew she was quite lovely. Elizabeth could hardly wait to display herself and her talents.

CHAPTER 7

The men had been well looked after in Laughton Powell's trophy-laden smoking room. In fact, as soon as Stanton Caley had settled himself in a cushiony cordovan leather arm-chair, he looked up to find the butler standing discreetly before him. "Port, sir, or brandy?"

Without hesitation Caley opted for the former. Laughton Powell's wine cellar was justly famous, but his vintage port was the rich ruby crown jewel of the cavernous kingdom belowstairs. On their frequent trips to Europe, while Amelia Powell was gladdening the hearts of the couturieres of London and Paris, Laughton bustled from one vintner's tasting room to the next. He'd even ventured off track enough to trace the smaller Spanish and Portuguese shippers of sherry, Madeira, and port at their source, leaving his wife alone with her modistes and seamstresses. A story made the rounds that at a London ball, the Prince of Wales—that rotund, jolly libertine—while raising Amelia from her graceful curtsy, had whispered a question in her ear. Eyebrows had twitched excitedly, but to everyone's disappointment (including

Amelia's) it was later learned that he'd fervently begged the name of her husband's new wine merchant in Oporto.

Standing before the baronial fireplace, the enormous opening now filled with a gleaming gold-plated fretwork fan, Powell nodded complacently. "Wise choice, that port, if I say so myself." He removed the lid of the satiny wood humidor on the table next to Caley, inviting him to choose a cigar. The Denver millionaire was a tall man who carried his middle-aged weight well and whose fair hair, Stanton always noted enviously, was still thick on his forehead. Although not even his skilled English tailor could hide Powell's thickening waistline, that comfortable bulge and the florid flush on his jowly cheeks was reassuring evidence to his guests that the man knew good food and drink. "Let me just clip that cigar end for you, Caley," he said, drawing out a silver cutter.

As he snipped the cigar, the small electric bulbs concealed behind candelabra sconces twinkled on the marquise diamond of his square onyx and gold ring. The light glinted, too, off the glass eyes of the heads of exotic animals mounted on all the paneled walls.

Because of the subdued lighting, which created only small pools of illumination in the enormous room filled with heavy woods and overstuffed furniture, it was sometimes difficult to distinguish the men standing quietly talking from the lifelike trophies scattered about. In one corner a grizzly that was a marvel of taxidermy reared up to its full twelve feet, menacing claws upraised. Across the room a gazelle, head turned, seemed to be eyeing the spotted leopard, its tawny coat glistening, crouched a few feet away.

"Thank you," Caley returned deferentially as he took the trimmed cigar. "And for the magnificent meal, sir. I've never had better salmon. The gherkin sauce was perfection."

"Enjoyed that, did you?" Powell beamed. "Damnably expensive to bring fresh fish on ice all the way from Oregon, of course. But worth it, worth it. You won't find salmon like that elsewhere in Colorado." He rocked back on his heels, then leaned down slightly, chuckling. "New cook. Very sound woman on sauces, Amelia says. She hired her away from the William Murdochs—with quite a substantial rise in wages. Not"—he interrupted his rocking—"that that's the reason *they're* not here tonight. No, no. Of course, everyone else is, despite the short notice."

He gestured with an expansive outstretched hand, as if suggesting that Caley could positively warm himself with the reflected light from the eminent gathering of some twenty men. "Real power here. Why, do you know, at the dinner table I heard of a multimillion-dollar endeavor that will change the entire direction of this state. Sugar beets. Growing and processing sugar beets. Came together this very evening." He paused and teetered in satisfaction. "But what was I saying before that?" Laughton looked at the cigar he was unwrapping as if for inspiration. "Ah, yes. Bill Murdoch. He's on his way to Washington, to talk to the President about this foolishness of the miners striking for higher wages. Why, I understand some are already paid three dollars a day. I must ask Glendower what the devil those men can be thinking. Berkeley's always sound on such stuff." His forehead furrowed. "Murdoch's bank is solidly invested in ore refining, as well as excavating. Having the miners off would shut the smelteries right down, you know."

His slight frown at the idea appeared and disappeared, barely creasing the imperturbable affability that made him such an excellent host. In addition, Laughton Powell was an accurate source of information on the things that really mattered to most of his guests. Not only could he reel off the great years for velvety Bordeaux wines, he could quote the odds on horses running in either the Kentucky or British Derby. Most importantly, he was an expert on Denver's restricted social elite, and he also knew who belonged to the beau monde in the major eastern cities and the basis and status of their fortunes. This made him an ideal consort for the fiercely ambitious Amelia, who having thoroughly conquered Denver society, now chafed at the smallness of her domain.

"This young Manningham you've brought this evening, Caley, family's in wool?" Powell was thoughtfully rolling the cigar next to his ear to check the freshness of the leaf wrapping the tobacco. "If I'm not mistaken, there's a chance of an inherited peerage there too. I should have a few words with him, see if the industry's on a sound footing." He moved off, and as Caley watched his host bear down on Theo, looking even younger with a bright western sunburn splashed across his nose and cheeks, Caley reflected that the Englishman would soon be as closely shorn of information as one of his family's yearling sheep. Laughton liked to know what others were doing.

Unlike his son, Amos Powell had himself been a doer, a man of much enterprise. Inhaling the mellow Havana smoke, Caley recalled the stories his own father had, with undisguised resentment, told of the senior Powell's success. While the elder Caley had grasped on to the idea of fattening cattle free on government land and very profitably shipping the beef to surrounding markets, Amos had seen that the key to the West lay in access to water. He'd turned the dry, dusty settlement of Denver into a little Venice by diverting the Platte River and digging canals and irrigation ditches through the city. The gorgeous mansions of Capitol Hill lay on real estate made possible by this insight.

But Amos also had wisely foreseen Denver's by now fabled boom-and-bust cycles. Before dying comfortably in California, he'd sold the green city lots and put his money into flour milling, smelter development, and railroads. After a disastrous flyer or two of his own Laughton now left business decisions to the army of lawyers and bookkeepers originally retained by his father. Berkeley had once remarked, and Caley had almost thought him serious, that Amelia would be far better able to handle investments than her husband.

Glendower, Stanton noticed, was standing at the end of the room, near French doors that opened onto the grounds, listening as patiently to Orville Trimble as he had to Trimble's wife over dinner. Although Theo, and Caley himself, had been reluctant to leave the daily delight of seeing Morna in Telluride, they'd been committed to parties in Denver. He'd seen Berkeley, although they'd had no chance to talk, at a number of these, including those given in his wife's honor, since she was leaving for Newport. Perhaps, Stanton thought wryly, the reason the Glendowers were childless was that they were rarely in the same state, sometimes not even in the same country. But Olivia apparently found little to interest her in the West, particularly any part ruled by Mrs. Laughton Powell.

Drawing on his cigar, Stanton was quite cheered with the rumors passed on by Jessamine Wyndham of Amelia's plans to stay in town for the season. That meant a frantic social pace and Berkeley, who was a good friend of both the Powells, would be much in demand here. Stanton conjured up a picture of cool summer evenings in the high mountain valley, wine chilling in an icy stream, and Morna Gregory gazing only at him. It was true that Glendower had not expressed any interest in her, but he preferred his friend three hundred miles away. Theo, of course, would have to be gotten rid of, but that could be arranged.

Caley now turned his pale unblinking gaze on two men talking intensely near a squashed-snout warthog with upcurling tusks and a bristly forehead. Quentin Wyndham had the chiseled profile of an English actor; his much shorter companion, except for his amiable expression, more nearly resembled the warthog. Rollo Farnsworth's dark bushy eyebrows were shaped exactly like isosceles triangles, which he raised and lowered animatedly in the course of his outpourings to Wyndham. Their thick points almost reached hair so black, it looked dyed. But what really captured Caley's attention was that another man, nominally listening to Powell's inquisition of Theo nearby, was instead desperately trying to overhear Farnsworth. And that man—George Bender—looked almost ill at the snatches of conversation he was catching.

"Drink up that excellent port, Stanton!" At that laughing command Caley turned to Patrick Alexander, one of his preparatory-school friends, who'd slid onto the arm of his chair. "It maketh up for a multitude of sins, including Mine Host's inquiries on your finances." Here he imitated Powell's deep rumble. " 'What are you investing in now? But is that sound, sir?' "

He blew a perfect smoke ring and went on blithely. "The inside of Laughton's head must look like an overturned hive—all the bees frantically trying to sort out the pollen and quite unable to make honey from it."

Sitting so near him, Caley thought that even in stiff collar and tails, one could catch a whiff of horse about Patrick. He further decided that it was a toss-up whether his friend was more taken by well-turned ankles when there were four of them, or just two beneath a lady's lacy petticoat. Maybe, after ten years of marriage to the lethargic Belle, Patrick simply liked anything with a show of life.

"I do believe," Alexander was continuing, after a swallow of port, "that Powell is the only man I know whose wife is far more attractive than his mistress. Maisie, for all her sweet plumpness, has a distinct wall-eye. When she's out and about in her new carriage, she fancies hats that dip over that eye. Except"—and he hit Caley's knee lightly in glee —"after the description of Amelia's dazzling ostrich-feather Paris creation in the papers, Maisie had a similar one made up. And damned if the two didn't drive by each other soon after. I understand that little episode cost Laughton that diamond pendant for Amelia. Don't know what Maisie got."

But Alexander's smile faded as he noticed Caley's glance still on George Bender. "Hard cheese on poor old George. Wish I could help."

"What's that about?" Caley gestured with his glass toward the two separate groups assembled near the warthog.

"Didn't you hear at dinner?" Alexander asked in surprise. "But no, you were administering to the underfed Jessamine. Luckily, Bender couldn't hear it, either, or it would have put him right off his feed."

He inclined his head toward the taller handsome man. "Wyndham has talked Farnsworth and old Trimble into sinking money into his sugar-beet venture. That means Bender is out of luck getting financing from them on the wide-open spaces he's so heavily invested in east of town. Since Richthofen died of a stroke last month, Bender's been frantically looking for another backer. He's up to his eyes in loans to Murdoch's bank."

"But the Benders are an old family here. His father was once in business with Murdoch Senior. Surely," Caley protested, "Mr. Murdoch will grant George an extension."

"Stanton, Stanton. Since when did old granite-heart Bill make business decisions on sentiment? Besides, if George's bubble bursts, the bank will get the land, as well as getting to keep that juicy down payment. Murdoch has a keen eye for other people's visions." Alexander shrugged broad shoulders ruefully. "I should know. We're by way of being cousins through marriage, and yet when I tried for a loan to build stables on Market Street—prime location—he turned me down flat."

Caley pursed his lips. "Perhaps that's because he's quite a religious man, Patrick. After all, every other house on Market is a bordello. Not to mention that one can openly buy opium and laudanum. Come to think of it, everything's for sale on Market Street."

"He is a bluenose, yes." Alexander flashed his rakish grin. "But that hardly entered in. He could see the wisdom of stables so close to the city center and that, moreover, the land would appreciate. He even muttered that it was a very busy street. No, what happened was that he frowned over my other investments with his glasses on his nose, throwing out words like *risky,* and *chancy,* and ended up saying a loan to me wouldn't be 'fiduciarily secure.' Then later on, I try old Trimble and he tells me he's just been asked to finance a stable on Market Street with— you guessed it—Bill Murdoch."

Sliding lightly from the chair arm, he stood and pulled both his trouser pockets inside out. They were quite empty. "Of course, it *is* true that my last venture took the wind out of my sails. But I have several prospects on the horizon that look ready for pillaging."

The imagery struck Caley. He could easily imagine Patrick, a sword between his teeth, ready to board a gold-carrying galleon. Not, he reflected disapprovingly, that that was any way to view investments. Ever since they were schoolmates, he'd distrusted Alexander's headlong dash at life, even though it made his company so enjoyable. His talents were almost up to Berkeley's, but unlike Glendower, Patrick never took anything seriously, especially his business affairs.

Alexander roughly shoved his pockets back in and looked with a grimace at Bender, now standing alone before the grizzly, his eyes closed as if in pain. "Bad spot for George. Who could help? I suppose the real question is, who would?" He surveyed the room thoughtfully. "Farnsworth and Trimble are out if they're going in with Wyndham. Sugar beets aren't a bad idea, of course, but they'll take a lot of water for irrigation. That will take money. Mind you," he added, picking up Caley's wineglass and sipping at it absentmindedly, "Trimble could do both, even given that he has his wife turn out a child a year. But he'd say real estate that far out was too long-term an investment, and meanwhile the money's not earning interest. Man's *too* conservative."

He polished off the last of Caley's port and nodded toward a reed-slim, almost foppish man with purse-string lips. "What about Cyril Harrington? Not married yet, and bound to have some cash. His father used to do a brisk trade in buying goods from failed prospectors who were heading downheartedly back East and then reselling to newcomers at fancy prices."

Caley shook his head. "Harrington's a careful man with both his nickels and his dollars, except for the clothes on his back. Takes after his father, who, I heard, ate the spoiled potatoes he couldn't sell."

Alexander reached over Caley and raided the humidor, sticking several cigars in his coat pocket, and then biting off the end of the last one before resuming. "Laughton's advisers always shy away from undeveloped Denver land. Of course, Amelia could help George with no trouble just out of her dress allowance." He grinned wickedly. "And maybe she would if Glendower asked her."

Caley responded, although he did not speak to Alexander's point. "Berkeley can't help Bender himself." His tone was faintly superior. "The money's not his. And his investors are eastern—they never like raw land out here. They prefer metals."

"What about you, Stanton?" Patrick Alexander suddenly wheeled to face him. "After all, that land in Montclair is bound to pay off eventually. Right in the path of Denver development eastward. You'll make your children rich."

Caley hurriedly sat up straighter. "No, no. Too speculative. I certainly wouldn't want to commit." He fidgeted, smoothing his side hair over the lobeless ears. "Besides," he went on with a self-justifying air, "George should have known what he was going into as partner to Richtofen. He was probably only letting George in on such a favorable basis as a way of getting in with us. And, aristocrat or not, the man was, well, foreign. George should certainly have foreseen this."

"Ah, yes," Patrick returned dryly. "Bender should certainly have foreseen the man would drop dead in his prime. Foolish of him."

"Gentlemen, gentlemen." Laughton Powell raised his genial voice. "Time to return to the ladies and to the evening's entertainment." He lowered his voice and addressed Farnsworth, chuckling. "Not, Rollo, that the ladies, bless 'em, ever tire of their little gossip, do they? We, on the other hand, have accomplished something here in our talks. Really, our after-dinner gatherings are just part of our business day, aren't they?"

*   *   *

Rather than use the outsized gallery with the spread-out seats reserved for the Powells' chamber-music evenings, Amelia had gathered her guests in the parlor, which also contained a grand piano. She was seated next to Glendower on a narrow Empire brocaded settee near the front. The room was about the same size as Miss Freda's, Stanton judged, but here the people were scattered about on French antique furniture that forced one to sit rather uncomfortably upright. It would at least serve to keep him awake, he thought, taking a long swallow of tea.

Elizabeth Bender began with several extremely well-known pieces that she'd often played for her ladies' academy recitals. She'd learned them carefully and she sang, at least as far as Stanton could tell, reasonably on key. But now he missed the vivid expression Morna brought to song, in her face, in her voice. The girl at the piano, who was very little younger than Morna, he realized in surprise, kept her eyes woodenly on the keys and gave each word the same value as the next.

It was during a Chopin nocturne, which he recognized from having heard Morna play, that it occurred to him that he must tell Theo about the Benders' downturn. The young Englishman was, after all, under strict instructions from his family to bring back an American heiress, and Stanton had introduced Elizabeth as such in good faith. Theo had responded with his usual polite attentions. Then Caley had a second thought. Perhaps, after all, he wouldn't mention the change in fortune. Young Manningham could then be encouraged to stay in Denver and continue his courting. He himself could return to Telluride quite alone.

Enamored of that idea, Stanton returned to his absorbing schemes for the summer with Morna. The first involved discovering if she ever left Miss Freda's. Accidental meetings, he mused, would be best at first. Then . . . he was still wrapped in this delectable daze when the polite applause signaled the end of the evening, and the guests were clustered in the palatial hall for their farewells. He hung back, waiting for Theo to finish congratulating Elizabeth Bender on her singing.

Laughton stood near the door, his hearty tone almost echoing throughout the entry. Amelia stood much farther back, facing a baroque mirror, with one light, imperious hand on Glendower's arm, as if detaining him as long as she could. Framed in the heavy golden swirls, she in her amber, he so dark, they looked perfectly posed. Amelia turned a laughing profile up to him and said something quite low. Caley could not hear his response, but he saw Amelia Powell's face shatter in the mirror.

Stanton hurriedly moved closer, but he could not catch her strangled words. Glendower's reply was, however, plain. "No, I really cannot. I am sorry. But my business affairs will keep me in Telluride for
most of the summer."

CHAPTER 8

As each June morning dawned in Telluride, the sun rose a moment or two earlier. The cool crystal air in the valley grew more brilliant, and every daybreak it was a degree less sharp. The increasing warmth and light threw the natural world into intense activity. Every bird, butterfly, and bee hurried, well aware of the shortness of summer's stay in the high mountains. The gray tundra of the alpine heights burst into tiny, exquisite wildflowers. Stalks of penstemon and monkshood transformed the valley bottoms into purple blue meadows.

Samuel Goler, the ostler at Jackson's stables, used the sun as his clock, but he did not begrudge the lost minutes of sleep these days. He threw off the rough horsehair blanket he still needed for the chilly nights and brushed from his heavy woolen flannel shirt the straw of the stall in which he slept. He tossed a few small chunks of wood onto the glowing ashes in his fat-bellied stove. Pouring cold water from a bucket into his battered coffeepot, he plonked it on top of the black stove so that it would be boiling on his return. Then he carefully splashed some of the bucket's contents on his face and finger-combed his raggedy pepper-and-salt beard. Mr. Glendower had instructed him to have the roan gelding saddled and ready outside the lady's place first thing every day.

But he was thinking, as he picked up a handful of fresh straw and cleaned as much manure as he could off his boots, that it wouldn't do to be too early, either, because then he would just have to tie the horse up and leave without seeing her. It was a treat, the sight of her with her hair almost all tucked up under the jockey hat, the pretty lace at her throat, and the divided skirt. The first time, he'd almost gawped, never having seen such a thing before, and the skirt only came to the top of her ankles at that, although all he could see were her boots no matter how he craned his neck when she swung onto Chevalier's back.

And Mr. Glendower was right, too, because it wouldn't do having her trail over to the stables, especially with the mule skinners on the main street, shouting and cursing, as they loaded up their pack trains to go to the Tomboy mine as soon as the sun was up. Who could tell what they'd be remarking to her, knowing that she lived on Popcorn Alley, not knowing *she* was a lady.

But Sam Goler knew. That first day, out she walked with that smile, and when he put the packet of bread and a tin flask in the saddlebag for her, he'd sniffed appreciatively because the bread was fresh baked. Every blessed morning since then she'd handed him a thick slice to take back and have with his coffee. It was delicious. Now he felt honor bound not to try and get a peek at her legs.

Besides, he considered as he led the prancing roan to Freda's, he was really twice-paid for his services, not even counting the free breakfast, a fact that troubled him. Then it struck him that he hadn't come up with any ideas on nearby places for her to see, pretty rides to take. He knew that she was getting impatient to go farther up the slopes, but that made him uneasy. It was mud season still, and the earth was loose. Rock slides could suddenly cover any of the trails that were at best just ledges hacked out of the mountainside.

She was not only a good rider but a sensible one, that he was sure of. The roan never came back with a raw, tender mouth from having had the bit pulled too hard. She must be giving him his head at the right times, letting him feel his way. But this horse was young, and even experienced mounts took missteps, plunged over mountain cliffs, taking their riders with them. Men familiar with the terrain knew when to lead the animal, when to trust it.

So, as he held the stirrup for her, he tried to explain that she'd be better off staying in the valley, maybe following the San Miguel River west, or going east along the main road to the mills at Pandora. She heard him out, but she shook her head and grinned. "Sam, I've got my heart set on seeing Bridal Veil Falls from the top today. And so I will. Excelsior!" Happily, she pointed one finger skyward. Mischief flicked in her eyes. "Higher. Ever higher. Now, who said that? Some Roman, probably. Perhaps the same Roman general who once told his men— without taking a vote on it, mind you—'It's necessary to sail; it's not necessary to live.' "

"Now, don't you be saying any such stuff, Miss Morna," Goler replied, although he wasn't at all clear on what she had said. He was pleased that she was in her customary good spirits, even though the idea of her going up slippery, winding Black Bear Pass Road alone fussed him considerably. "If you'd just wait until somebody could go with you and—"

"You mean some *man*, right, Sam?" Still smiling, she turned the roan's head lightly and they were gone.

Goler started back to the stables, thinking that it was sometimes impossible to understand the woman. Of course he'd meant a man. After all, the only women he'd seen riding astride were squaws in leggings when a few Indians came for the Fourth of July celebrations. And they didn't count. It'd be a day's outing for ladies going sidesaddle to get up that trail. Horses had to plod with riders balanced like that.

He tore off an irresistible piece of the bread crust and munched it. By the time he'd reached the wide door of the stone stables, Sam had decided that, after all, it was right to take the gentleman's money to tell him where she went of a morning. At least that way somebody knew where she was likely to be in case of some accident. He wasn't going to feel guilty at all about telling. No, sir. Sam now felt that he'd squared his running account with his conscience.

As it happened, anyone on the high ridges overlooking Telluride on that June day could make out the single horse and rider far below going east. The mists of dawn that hung over marshes and wove through the dark pines had gone. From that sunny vantage point the whole valley could be seen and it looked as if it'd been formed by a giant hand reaching down and scooping out the center of earth, leaving a deep bowl surrounded by sky-touching peaks. It was, in fact, a box canyon, and it dead-ended abruptly at broad-shouldered mountains.

Sparkling streams had carved crevices down these, along which water glittered as it fell. Like a silvery needle Ingram Falls slid down one craggy peak. The cloudy spray of breathtaking Bridal Veil Falls was at a right angle, slightly to the southwest. These were the pristine head-waters of the San Miguel River, which was also fed by other mountain streams as it meandered westward. First it was joined by Bear Creek and, when the San Miguel skirted Telluride, by Cornet Creek, which tumbled through the town itself.

Below Ingram and Bridal Veil Falls mills were situated on the valley floor in an area called Pandora. There silver and gold were extracted from the huge chunks of rock that came down, by aerial tramway, from the mines high above, whose outbuildings clung precariously to vertical slopes. "Ten times out of nine," the Colorado saying was, "silver comes at timberline." It was fortunate that this valley was so wide that the mills could be located on the level and yet away from the town itself. The river carried away as much of the mine tailings as it could, although the clear water was turned gray with the sludge from then on.

The man high above Pandora on the switchback road that snaked ever upward to Bridal Veil Falls was seated on an enormous black stallion. He was wearing a brown scaled-down version of a cowboy's Stetson, with a flat crown and a narrower brim. His dark buckskin jacket was tailored and unfringed. As he drew on a thin black cigar, he gazed broodingly at the smelting mill and the surrounding clutter of offices, barns, and boardinghouses below. Then he shifted his eyes to the rider fast approaching Pandora.

But as he watched, he decided that the horse was not going at a full gallop and therefore was being paced. Its strength was being saved for a high climb. Therefore, its rider undoubtedly intended heading up the Black Bear Pass Road on which he himself stood. He entwined his fingers, more tightly than he intended, in his own mount's heavy ebony mane. As the stallion threw its head up in quick complaint, he slid his hand soothingly down its neck. "Sorry, Druid, I had my mind on other matters," he murmured. Tossing the cigar onto the rocky scree below, he tugged at the reins and began the short ascent remaining to Bridal Veil.

After tying the horse to a stunted tree he moved to the ledge of the precipice, with its collar of spring-green alpine grass above the cliff's rough-hewn gray surface. He stared, impassively but impatiently, at the filmy glory of the falls. In the past he would have had his mind contentedly on the prospect of harnessing the water's power for the mines below, a project he'd often discussed with the manager of the Smugglers-Union Company. But all he was doing now, he knew, was concentrating on the roan's approach.

Too often, in the last weeks, he'd tried unsuccessfully to order himself to stop thinking of Morna Gregory. In curiosity and amazement he'd discovered he could not. As he rounded each mental corner he met her distracting image. And because she inhabited his mind, he found himself seeing the familiar differently. Once again, as he had not for some time, he saw the water's splendor.

There was only one solution. He would win her. If he could not understand *why* he felt so driven, at least he could turn his mind to *how* he could accomplish that objective. Analysis of a problem had never failed him, he reflected. He paused. Would an intellectual approach work in such a situation? He had no idea. The experience was quite new to him.

Still, he would consider what he knew. The reason for her well-guarded fences was clearly fear, although he did not know of what, or whom. But her look of alarm at the thought of being traced was unmistakable. Legally, she could escape parental control, although she could be disowned. But he had the distinct impression that Morna would not *fear* that. Quite the contrary. Since it was almost impossible for a woman to earn any kind of a reasonable wage, she might even see it as a challenge.

The explanation that was left had already haunted him, and considering it now, his angular jaw tightened. He began to prowl restlessly along the ledge in long, angry strides, the heels of his boots crunching viciously into the graveled surface. The images that unwillingly sprang to his mind's eye filled him with fury. He swore to himself that from this moment he'd protect her, even feeling a wholly irrational urge to reach back in the past and there surround her with his strong, encircling arms.

Leaning down, he picked up a fist-sized rock and threw it forcibly over the cliff. How could he persuade her that he could help? He did not doubt that he could.

He remembered the quick joy she'd shown at dinner when contemplating a spirited horseback ride, and he'd seen, for that instant, the delighted and delightful young woman who lived behind that extraordinary reserve. How to reach her? Elaborate compliments were not the way. That had been proven. He must make her like him first. Trust could be won later. But never in his life had he thought about being likable, about deliberately setting out to do that. He had no idea of how to go about it.

Then, although the noisy headlong surge of the falls covered the sound of the horse's hoofs, he was suddenly aware of her presence. He turned, but before he reached her to help her dismount, she'd already done so and was coming toward him, gloved hand extended. His heart lurched against his ribs, but try as he might, he could not snatch even a glimpse of what feelings lay behind her unruffled mask of courtesy. Was she pleased at seeing him? Or annoyed at his intrusion? Did his presence matter to her at all?

"Mr. Glendower. I didn't know you'd returned," she said composedly.

"Miss Gregory," he replied with a smile of real pleasure, taking her hand only lightly and briefly, "I am just back and came immediately to one of my favorite sights." He suspected that her back beneath the fitted velvet jacket stiffened slightly, and he gestured vaguely toward the falls. While he congratulated himself that his words, at least, were absolutely truthful, he reminded himself to be studiously impersonal.

"It is lovely." She seemed to relax and looked over the precipice at the water pouring down hundreds of feet. "Incredibly so." At the far bottom the descending cascade then sprayed upward as it foamed over the gigantic boulders below. "As sheer and as white as the veil it was named for. Up here the water is so clear."

They stood for a while in silence, and although he took care not to stare at her profile, he was struck by her resemblance to a pre-Raphaelite painting. She need only undo her hair and put on a floating gown to pose for Rossetti. She possessed that same unearthly beauty that he himself supposed the artist had only seen looking inward and then superimposed on a model that was vaguely like. Yet here was the living woman.

But he reflected that Caley was quite right—her beauty explained nothing. By itself it did not account for the prickle of his skin, the sheer aliveness of his body next to hers, the vividness everything took on when she was near. He could see, with extraordinary clarity, the fine hairs on her cheek, could detect a faint flush on her skin, perhaps caused by the ride here. But he could not understand the almost uncontrollable desire he had to touch, and yet not touch, her.

He recollected that *that* part of the problem was not open to analysis. He was supposed to think about how to win her and not why he so much wanted her. He stood, cursing his slow wits, and could not summon up a single acceptable thing to say.

"I want to thank you for Chevalier," she said at last. "I've so enjoyed my morning rides, the freedom. Sometimes when I'm away from the town, or these mills, I feel I'm the first person to set foot on a given patch of earth."

"You're most welcome." He replied too stiffly, he knew, but he had the odd sensation that someone else was speaking. "And you may well be the first, with the outside chance of a stray Ute Indian or a wandering prospector. I'm not entirely sure all these mountains have even been named."

"Good. Then I'll do it. There's one in a canyon just before Pandora that looks to me like a woman's face raised to the sky." She lifted radiant gray eyes to his and then looked too quickly away. "Her hair is tumbling backwards, and she has a high brow and a well-shaped nose. *I* call it Bridget's Mountain."

"Odd, I've seen that mountain many times, but never noticed the profile. Now, I don't see how I could have missed it. But why Bridget?" he asked with interest. "Who is Bridget?" Too late he feared the question was unwise and would have called it back. That name, after all, was surely Celtic.

But her response was quiet. "She was, and wasn't, my mother. Mothers enhance life as well as give it. My own died at my birth, and it was Bridget who raised me. When I was very small, she read to me endlessly—fairy tales, myths, poetry. And I sat next to her on the spinet bench, listened to her play and sing and soon learned to accompany her. She had a glorious voice and always asked what I'd like to hear."

Pausing, she stripped off one glove and held out her fingers. "Do you know that later I heard that young girls were usually taught to play the piano by being made to drill endlessly on scales? Their fingers were snapped with birch switches if they made mistakes. And they practiced their pieces with coins balanced on the backs of their hands so that those who watched them perform could admire the pretty position of their hands. Little wonder that most of them hate to play. How I wish I could thank Bridget now for my love of music. And for the way she admired my every childish drawing."

In the same fervent tone, still with her gaze over the valley, she continued, "She let me ramble with my brother over the moors, on foot, on horseback. We saw the beauty of every season, talked to anyone we met. I had the happiest of childhoods. Then, one day, my father emerged from his study and noticed that I wasn't a boy." She lifted a rueful shoulder. "From then on I looked out windows. But at least I was permitted my choice of all our books. I know now how unusual *that* was, since only the most insipid novels are regarded as appropriate for ladies."

She stopped suddenly, as if she'd said more than she'd intended. Assuming that, he searched desperately for a suitable change of subject, but discovered none. He twisted in his hands the hat he'd removed when she arrived, then brushed back the hair that had fallen on his forehead. He twisted the hat again.

In the lengthening silence he found he had to avoid her eyes. Now that he had her here, he would keep her, but no topic of conversation seemed neutral. She was too near and too much in his mind.

Hoping for inspiration, he glanced away at the nearest mountain slope where the pale, asparagus-thin aspen groves stood out from the surrounding deep green of the conifers. Above the tree line the gray solid peaks thrust upward like the valley's sentinels. Discussing the landscape might be trite, he thought, but it usually kept the foot out of the mouth. On the other hand, if he observed that it was the feeling of rockbound safety that attracted some to the mountains, she might regard that as a reference to her own situation.

Just as he was about to clear his throat and say whatever words came to his tongue, she interjected abruptly, "The mountains are in fact not safe places to live, are they? Sudden storms, avalanches. It's even hard to breathe here."

Stupefied, he stared down at her. Had he said aloud what he was thinking? He hadn't. Over his shiver of joy at what he'd discovered, he tried to reply in a normal tone. "What's safe? Tidal waves strike the beach, there are tornadoes on the prairies. And the air feels heavy at sea level after a stay in the mountains."

"You're right. One feels secure where one feels at home." She paused and added, "Wherever that is."

"Home's not always the place you've grown up and gotten used to, is it? Some people are born in their homes, but others have to find them." He hadn't known he believed that and didn't notice their silence while he considered it.

Now it was she who seemed to want to end the quiet, at last asking, "Is there any gold in Bridget's Mountain? I hope not. I want that left untouched, unmined."

"I think you'll get your wish." His throat was dry, but he was determined to keep talking. "That mountain must be in Ute Rise Canyon and no one's had any luck there yet. L. L. Nunn had high hopes of a mine named Champion, but it wasn't one. The Sweepstakes mine brought the owner no fortune. As far as I know, all the claims have been abandoned. Still, there is high grade ore all around." He gestured at the Smugglers-Union mill below in Pandora. "They've hit one vein after another. And, of course, there's the Tomboy in Marshall Basin just over those northern peaks."

Pleasantly caught up in his subject, almost forgetting that it was she he was addressing, he described the Bullion Tunnel, how expertly timbering needed to be put in to avoid cave-ins, given the length of the tunnel. But halfway through a recounting of the precision required to blast out a further opening, he stopped, embarrassed, sure that this dry recital must be boring her. Trying for some conclusion, he added, "But the discovery of all this gold argues that Telluride seems to be the one place that has escaped the Ute curse."

She turned to him with more gravity than he'd expected. "You mean the Indians put a curse on these mountains?"

"Well, the San Juans were the last piece of their vast lands the Utes surrendered, after Chief Ouray made countless efforts to keep what they'd been promised by a number of presidents. These mountains were sacred to them and they'd been assured they could keep these 'as long as the grass grew and the streams ran,' in return for agreeing to give up the eastern plains. But silver was found throughout the range and some gold. So, twenty years ago, the entire tribe was escorted out of Colorado by U.S. military along the Trail of Sorrows to a reservation in northeastern Utah."

"And what were they given in exchange?" Morna did not take her eyes off his, and he could see her troubled absorption.

"The reservation is large, but the land there is dry and rather flat. In any case, as they left, Ouray's successor, Chief Shavano, looked back and said that for one hundred and five years, no man would be happy here and no family survive more than four generations."

"Do you believe this?" She tugged a little at her lace jabot, loosening it around her throat, but did not drop her gaze.

He started to shrug, to put on a graceful dismissive smile, as he normally would have. But the intensity of her expression changed his mind. Surprised even as he made the admission, he answered, "If you look at what's happened, one can easily believe it. These are called 'the silvery San Juans,' and there is plenty of silver. Men came here and, at great effort, dug it out. The mountains do not give up precious metals easily. Quite a few men died trying. And they squabbled endlessly over it. But after the Panic of Ninety-three silver became almost worthless overnight. Such a reversal, creating instant paupers as it did, makes you think that's someone's revenge."

She swept a long wisp of hair away from her mouth and looked at the green reaches of the western valley, nodding.

"Then too," he went on, "most men don't bring their wives and children to these isolated camps. They simply try to make money and move on. There's little chance any family would stay for four generations. Most women"—his own expression was bleak—"despite this beauty, don't want to come up here."

"Is this home to you?"

Her straightforward return to that subject took him unaware, and he answered immediately. "Yes. I'm going to stay." In his enthusiasm he began to talk faster, his eyes glinting with the excitement of his plans. "As I said, so far Telluride has escaped the curse. They've found a great deal of gold to replace the silver, and we've had almost none of the labor strife they've had elsewhere. Here there are things to be done, problems to be solved. Until someone had the idea of building those tramways that hop and skip over cliffs and chasms, all those huge chunks of unrefined ore were laboriously brought down on the backs of mules. There's always a better way of doing something, and you can figure it out."

"Is that what really interests you?"

"Ah, yes. Somehow I need to keep my mind stretched. And repetition bores me. I consider it a flaw in my character that I so dislike doing the same thing twice. At first, investing money engaged my attention, but that usually is a matter of explaining the same things over and over, as you sit in stuffy offices and drawing rooms with well, frankly, *stuffy* men." All he could think of now was how overwhelmingly important it was that she understand. He sought out her eyes. "And, in the end, what you've accomplished is moving this pile of money from here to there. Almost all of the already rich prefer the safest commitment of funds. They're not willing to back anything new or inventive. They positively dislike risk. But here on the frontier there are some who enjoy it. I am one."

"So here," she asked reflectively, "you at least are not subject to the curse? You are a happy man?"

"At this moment the happiest I've ever been."

She took a step away, and he could have bitten his tongue. He realized that throughout this conversation he had again forgotten to be careful, he'd spoken truthfully but without deliberation. Perhaps now his very sincerity might have threatened her.

But her response was simply "Yes, moments are probably all we have." Then she added, pulling on the glove she'd taken off and starting toward the roan, "I must go back."

"Wait." When she stopped, he had no idea of what he was going to say, but he could not let her leave. "This is your first visit to the falls and there's a long-standing tradition to be honored on such occasions."

"What's that?"

He strode hurriedly to his stallion and began unbuckling a saddle-bag. He pulled out several sacks and began opening them as he walked back. "You have to eat fruit."

"Eat fruit?" There was the beginning of a smile on her lips. "Why is that?"

"Because," he replied, grinning himself, "that's what I've brought for breakfast. And there's plenty for two. In Denver there were shipments from the southern markets. See"—he showed her the contents of one bag—"dates from silken Samarkand. Although Mexico is more likely. And grapes from California. Plus, still to come, cheese from Holland."

She hesitated, and he broke off a small clump of Tokay grapes and offered them to her. As she brought one to her lips, she said, "I rather think it was eating fruit, six pomegranate seeds or something, that got Persephone in trouble after she'd been carried off by the Lord of the Underworld. If she just hadn't done that, she could have gone back to her mother, Ceres, and, I believe, we would never have had winter."

"These Greek myths are not to be relied on as patterns of behavior," he replied, returning briskly to the stallion. "Even the gods carried on scandalously. I'll just get Druid's saddle blanket so we can sit down. Do try that grape."

She hesitated again, but popped it into her mouth and then gave him a brilliant smile. "I have some of Isobel's bread. We'll share."

CHAPTER 9

It was two o'clock in the morning, which was Miss Freda's favorite time. The unfailing coolness of the Colorado night poured through an open window covered only by the loose netting that kept out the occasional fluttering miller moth. She settled herself in the wide seat of her golden oak office chair and rolled up the top of her desk. Taking out a buttonhook, she leaned over and undid the high lace tops of her patent leather shoes and eased her swollen feet out of them. She wiggled her toes, still encased in silk stockings, and pulled her account book toward her.

After she'd figured up the sums taken in from the liquor served both in her parlor and in her dance hall, she need only make out the orders to be sent to Denver on the morning train. In summer she could get most of the food—although not the alcohol—from local merchants, whom she patronized whenever possible. That policy, and her generous contributions to town causes, was a wise use of money, she considered. One got lovely fruit from the nearby western-slope growers. By mid-July—she glanced at the calendar—just three weeks away, fresh peach cobbler would be on the table.

After making out the Denver order, she would go directly to the kitchen, pour out the warm milk Isobel always left on the back of the stove, pick up the covered dessert dish from the sideboard, and climb the stairs.

Her nightly ritual included scooping bran from a linen bag that had been soaking all day in boiling water and washing her face carefully. The subsequent rainwater rinse was guaranteed to keep the complexion soft and fine. Freda had learned this long ago from her first madam, and although the procedure seemed to have little effect on her own rather coarse skin, she did it faithfully.

Nor did she ever neglect taking Dr. Wilden's Stomach Remedy for her dyspepsia. These chocolate-covered tablets contained, according to the box, sodium bicarbonate, powdered rhubarb, powdered gentian, and powdered willow charcoal. Freda kept several boxes on hand. She was a practical, imperturbable woman who believed that although most of life's problems could not be solved, they could be faced if one's digestion was in good working order. When her young women poured out their troubles, she listened sympathetically, then gave them a comforting maternal hug and a tablet.

Once she'd swallowed her medicine, then, and only then, could she relax corsetless in her bedroom, drink her milk, and savor her evening sweet. One of the desserts that evening had been carrot pudding, which Freda had often had as a child on the family farm in Minnesota. But Isobel's version was much richer. To the grated carrots she added nutmeg, cinnamon, almost a full pound of sugar, and a dozen eggs, as well as melted butter and thick cream. The whole was poured into a deep dish lined with puff paste. Freda had what she called a sliver when it was served, and she was greatly looking forward to the rest.

Now, as she added up the numbers, which she wrote large enough to fill two of the allotted spaces, she enjoyed the quiet of the house. Since it was Wednesday, none of the gentlemen had elected to spend the night. If they were not going to do so, customarily they all left by this time. But—she dipped her quill pen into the ink with a smile—last summer Berkeley Glendower had given her quite a surprise.

Just as she'd had her foot on the bottom stair, she'd looked up and in the faint glow of the gas lamp at the top, she saw him buttoning up his trousers. His coat and shirt were draped over the heavy wood banister. Even in the dimness of the light she could see the heavy bones of his bare shoulders, the bulge of his forearms. In his clothing, she remembered thinking, he looked leaner than he was.

Catching sight of her, he'd gently pulled the door to Jane Ellen's room completely closed, scooped up shirt and coat, and slid lightly down the banister. Before she could say a word, he'd taken the japanned tray from her hands, put it on the floor, and wrapped her in powerful arms. Her face was pressed against his naked chest and he smelled of wind-dried sheets and clean sweat. He pulled back. His hair was rumpled and his dark-fringed eyes were warm and sated. Planting a firm kiss on her forehead, he said, "I love you, Freda, but your feather beds are much too soft—for sleeping, anyway."

He'd gone out, and she'd stood, staring through the stained-glass side panel by the door, watching him shrug into his shirt with his face lifted to the night sky. A dangerous man, she'd sighed, and would be even if he were only half that good looking. Some men, and there weren't many, she considered, always got around you because they thought the way women did, maybe without knowing it. Or perhaps they just had good imaginations. They made you laugh, besides.

The ink had dried again on her pen, and she poised it over the gold-rimmed crystal pot, but her mind wasn't on her work. Berkeley was used to getting what he wanted, and what he wanted, she knew it in her bones, even if he never betrayed it, was Morna Gregory. She would have bet a month's take on her bar, which was well over $3,000, that he knew what would win Morna's heart.

Really, she couldn't help but think it'd be a good thing. Freda nodded her head as she turned over the question. Morna wasn't at all one of those skittery, high-strung girls whom no sensible madam would have in the house, but still . . . For all the pleasant friendliness she showed, Freda had noticed that, except when she was dancing and lost in the music, Morna had a way of gently avoiding other people's touch. As if she imagined she had some kind of sickness they'd catch. Or maybe she thought they'd keep holding on, not let go.

Freda herself did not pretend to understand that young woman, or what she was running from so determinedly, but she was worried that with Morna's eyes fixed on what was behind her, she couldn't see what was in front of her. When she'd first arrived, Freda had seen Morna's quick intelligence and believed then that she had more natural cunning than even Colette. No doubt, Freda thought, the first marriage had been an unhappy one, and for a lady—and the madam was convinced Morna was one—there was little recourse, unless she belonged to a very rich and helpful family. Lacking that, women simply bore their lot. But Morna was not only spirited but unconventional, which she'd demonstrated a little too often for Freda's comfort, and she had simply left. Then, Freda had assumed, she must have decided that rather than selling her youth and beauty piecemeal, she'd hold out for one high bidder. Freda had quite approved.

Telluride was the place a smart woman would choose. There was a great surplus of men, some of whom luck and wealth had just that moment touched. Moreover, these men were close to desperate for women. As one prospector had said, stumbling into town after an isolated winter in his cabin, "I'd give a ten-dollar gold piece for a glimpse of a servant girl's petticoat a mile away."

But that assessment of Morna Gregory had been wrong. If it was marriage she was after, why, she had Edward Gibbons, that stony-hearted old bachelor, gasping like a trout in shallow water. All she'd need do was reel him in. The tiresome first husband could be paid off, and no one up here the wiser. It was true that the ladies of Telluride had closed their ranks against some of the girls, although not all, who crossed over to the north side of town. Then the poor new wife had been doomed to a cruel, boxed-in loneliness. Forced to give up her old friends, she had no new ones. Ignored at the Opera House and all church events, she was never invited to anyone else's at homes. No one attended hers. But with Morna's social graces, and the banker's money, that would never happen, Freda knew. Even the most sniffy folks in an isolated mining camp couldn't afford to be *too* exclusive.

But—and here Freda threw her eyes up to the heavens—even for blue-steel security, how could any woman deny Berkeley Glendower? Nor would he let her worry about the future; that was definitely a problem that could be solved. Freda delicately scratched beneath her elaborate pompadour, enhanced by a hairpiece, with the wooden end of her pen. The situation mystified her.

As she turned back to her additions, she heard the floor creak in the room above her, but the sound could as well have come from any of the rooms along the front. This was the original part of the house, and the dry old beams supporting the first story were each of one piece that ran the length of the floor. Years ago, hearing queer noises in the small hours when she was alone bothered Freda. It put her in mind of a story Sam Goler had told her, even if she was never sure he hadn't been pulling her leg. And the sounds made her recall that two of the girls, when newly hired, had told her on separate occasions about seeing a strange woman in a nightgown wandering down the hallway, a woman who didn't know where she was going, who was feeling her way along the wall.

But she'd told herself then that the girls had probably been half asleep. After all, women looked quite different with their hair down and no makeup. After she undressed at night, Freda didn't even like looking in the mirror, preferring her daytime self.

Now, she merely glanced up worriedly, remembering that May still had a weak chest after a bad winter's bout with pneumonia. Then she shrugged off the slight noise. No doubt someone had gotten up to use the chamberpot.

The recorded numbers, even though she had made them large, blurred before her eyes. She could no longer persuade herself that it was merely fatigue, although she seemed to be getting tired earlier and earlier in the evening. She needed spectacles. Perhaps it was even time to think of selling up and retiring. Back in Minnesota her immigrant parents, who spoke only Swedish, were still farming, and the money she sent back regularly had enabled them to acquire acreage and young laborers to help. They never asked how she came by these handsome sums. They, too, were practical people.

Rubbing her eyes, she stood up, her toes sinking into the velvet carpet, walked to a closed window, and threw up the sash. This one lacked netting, but except for the annoying bluebottle flies swarming over the mule manure in the main street during the day, there were few insects to keep out.

Leaning out, she inspected a sky so black that it seemed to have substance and weight, holding stars so large and low that it seemed possible to pull one down. The new quarter moon had already slid behind the mountains, but left an outline of light on the ridges. She would hate to leave Telluride, she realized. It was never hot; Freda hated heat and the thick humid air of summers elsewhere that made clothes a torture. The chemise under her corset would get soaked and stay soaked. Although the Telluride winters were long, she did not have to suffer from the lowering gray skies found in the northern country. Here the sun spangled the snowy mountains. Then there were those moth-sized mosquitoes in Minnesota. There was a further problem: who would pay her large asking price for the business?

Colette had more than once hinted she would be happy to take over and pay in monthly installments. Freda had considered it and told her that she would have to find a backer to provide at least half the money in the beginning. The French girl was quite capable of keeping accounts, of ordering food and liquor, she thought. But the handling of the girls was another question. It was the kind of business for which you had to have a cast iron head but be sometimes soft, as well. Then, too, Morna's popularity had already put Colette's delicate nose with those curlicued nostrils out of joint. What would happen as her own youth faded, and she was surrounded by blooming beauties?

Pulling her head back in, Freda returned to her desk. One might as well be jealous of the butterflies as all those pretty young girls, but for all her shrewdness Colette was unlikely to learn that, she thought. Marriage to one of the nice steady mine managers was the answer for that girl, although Freda suspected that Colette had more grandiose schemes in mind. The madam lowered herself back into her comfortable chair, determined to get on with the night's work.

It wasn't long before she realized that the light, almost uncertain step somewhere above her was continuing. She glanced up, slightly annoyed. If someone were troubled, or not feeling well, why not come down? She herself couldn't decide who was up and she didn't want to disturb anyone else by opening doors. Freda struggled out of her chair and went to the foot of the stairs.

She saw nothing, but what she heard was the insistent brushing of fingertips against the flocked wallpaper of the upper hallway. And that odd but gentle sound caused Freda's breathing, already shallow because of the corset, to almost stop altogether. She grasped the banister to support her trembling knees.

She was not a superstitious woman, but she immediately recalled— she'd never been completely able to forget it—that story she'd heard when she'd first bought the house. Sam Goler, one of Telluride's few natives, had been hired to shoulder up some of the heavy furniture. Stopping to wipe a sweating brow, he'd stroked the back wall of the front bedroom and called her attention to the fact that only that section had new plaster. "Folks say the owner strangled his young wife, walled her up, said she'd gone home to her family."

He'd leaned near and Freda could smell the pervasive odor of the stables, then added, "But, see, she weren't quite dead, and the man could hear her all the time in there, fumbling, trying to get out. Maybe she does. That's how come it was for sale. But nobody'd buy it. When you go to add on to this place, I'd jest leave that wall alone."

The groping sound of the fingers came again, and she was not able either to keep her eyes wide open or totally close them. One minute there was nothing there, and then the empty shadows seemed to move. Freda moaned, rather than shrieked, when she saw the indistinct figure in the white nightgown outlined against the gas lamp. It was the hurried caution in the way the woman walked, flattening the balls of her feet to try to prevent creaks, the way she felt lightly for the banister as though there were no light, that transfixed the terrified madam.

It was not until the apparition was halfway down the staircase that Freda realized it was Morna Gregory who was floating toward her, dressed in a filmy shift. Before she could clear her dry throat, to chide the girl for so startling her, Freda noticed how queerly she was behaving. She made no effort to hold up the nightgown's lace-trimmed edge that might trip her, gave no sign that she could see Freda in the light spilling from her open office door.

Morna reached the bottom and sailed purposefully on toward the foyer, walking even faster now. Freda realized from her blank stare that she was walking in her sleep. She would have to stop the dreamer from going out, but one wasn't supposed to awaken a sleepwalker suddenly. She hesitated and then sped around Morna and stood before the door. "No, my dear," she whispered.

"I must go," Morna replied in a low passionate voice, terror now in her dark-fringed eyes. "He'll get him too. He's quite mad, you know."

"Who?" Freda breathed, before she could stop herself. Without answering, Morna reached blindly for the doorknob. The older woman took her elbow gently but tightly and turned her back to the staircase, guiding her with quiet reassurances. As they went up, Morna offered no resistance, although she murmured ceaselessly in agitation.

The next morning Freda told only Isobel what had happened, so that she could keep an eye out for any further occurrences. Later, she told herself that the scene had disturbed her so much, impressed her so vividly, simply because of the reminder of the old ghost story. Yet she could not forget the dread in Morna's eyes, and she was no longer so sure that this could end well.

CHAPTER 10

Stanton Caley was very suspicious, although he had nothing on which to base his misgivings. He was broodingly watching Berkeley and Morna waltzing across the polished walnut floor of Miss Freda's dance hall, which the madam had closed for this Friday evening because she was giving a private pre–Fourth of July party for her best customers.

The national holiday was a three-day celebration in Telluride. All the mines were closed—the only time other than Christmas that they did not operate around the clock. The streets were crowded until three in the morning, and parades, band concerts, baseball games, rock-drilling contests, and horse races filled the time, ending in a grand fireworks display. This year, with the Fourth on a Monday, the weekend promised to be a gala of fun and merrymaking, and the residents had been preparing for weeks.

Morna's flag-blue gown was conspicuous as she swirled; most of the other women had chosen resplendent reds or summery whites with bright sashes of the other two colors. And it wasn't, Stanton considered, that she and Glendower were not maintaining the proper distance as they circled in time. Nor did it seem that they were trading anything more than the casual remarks that this stately version of the dance allowed. It was simply the way they moved together that set his teeth on edge.

The previous tune had been a lively polka, which had left Morna and George Fisk, who had partnered her, giddily breathless. Certainly if one were to be jealous of her closeness to another man, it would have been at the conclusion of that round, when she and Fisk had clung together in helpless laughter. Or one could cast a cold eye on the banker Edward Gibbons, whose gift of starry sapphires encircled her neck.

But in the three weeks since he'd returned to Telluride, Caley had noticed evidence of some sort of—he didn't know how to phrase it, even to himself—communion between Morna and Berkeley. Together in the same crowded room, as they usually were, there were no significant glances, no whispered conversations. Indeed, she spent no more time talking to him than to anyone else, did not encourage him at all. But even when she was smiling warmly at someone else, and Berkeley was engaged in some business affairs in a far corner, Caley felt that Glendower was really by her side, quietly and insistently saying the right words to her. And Morna could hear those unspoken words, had to listen whether she would or not.

Or so Caley fancied as he sleeplessly paced his hotel room in the middle of the night. But in the morning, although it was always nearer noon before he awoke from a troubled doze, he reminded himself that this was not possible, and it was all a figment of his own exhausted imagining. Even if Berkeley could so court her, as focused as a compass on her true North, they must meet alone at some time. And that was equally impossible, he was sure.

Caley saw Morna go unattended up the stairs every evening. He knew all daytime visitors for Miss Gregory were turned firmly away. On the pretense of looking for Berkeley himself, he'd asked most particularly several times if Glendower ever called and was told he did not. With some difficulty, since Isobel Ewen was also one of the cooks, Caley had managed a few words alone with her maid. But she would not answer the most innocuous of his questions. When he tried to ingratiate himself by offering her some silver coins, Isobel indignantly refused. He felt himself lucky that he'd escaped without a box on the ears.

Stanton had had no better luck with Sam Goler at the stables, although he'd impassively accepted a coin. The ostler pointed out Morna's horse, a pretty mare named Greybird. He said it was the only horse that could be ridden sidesaddle, and even volunteered the information that he sometimes hitched the mare to a carriage and took it over to Freda's. But another coin only elicited the response that it was the other girls who rode in it. "Miss Morna don't, sir. Not usual, least-ways," he'd added laconically.

Given Caley's own observations, the mare was really underex-ercised. Although he'd wandered by the stables at several different times of the day, once even quite early, she was always contentedly munching in her stall. He began to feel he saw more of Greybird than he did of Morna.

In the long mirror above the dark, glossily polished bar, the reflec-tions of the gaily whirling couples spun in a kaleidoscope of red, white, and blue. Buntings of those colors draped the antlered deer heads above the bar. Stanton shifted his gaze to avoid seeing that bright blue gown and Morna in Berkeley's embrace. The sight seemed to make his stom-ach spin, too, in time to the music. Even the hands of his pocket watch circled too quickly. Or perhaps it was the champagne, of which he'd drunk rather a lot as he brooded.

He studied the patterned tin ceiling, whose almost lacy moldings blended into the red textured wallpaper. Huge oil paintings, mostly of plump, smiling nudes, had streamers around their frames. Even the enameled stove in the corner, like an ornate handleless teapot, had been decorated for the evening.

The marshal in his sober navy suit and six-sided star, leaning amia-bly against the bar, seemed part of the decor. He'd clearly already taken in more than his share of the free liquor that Freda was offering for her party. His usual services, a demanding job of keeping rowdy miners in line here at the dance hall, were not required this evening, since the mines would not shut down until Saturday morning. He was the only still figure in the room, and Stanton kept his eyes fixed on the marshal, to avoid the nausea caused by his stomach's gyrations, to distract him-self from the mirror.

Miss Freda, on the other hand, was trying to catch a glimpse of her own reflection and, when she did, was quite satisfied. As she'd un-packed the box from Paris, she'd been a little worried that the cardinal red of the gown, so shiny with sequins, might be too garish, but it did set off the blond in her graying hair. Although it had taken two of the strongest girls to lace up her corset, the bodice was quite slenderizing, she decided. The top half of her bosom was pushed up, setting off her ruby necklace, while the bottom half, although mashed very uncomfort-ably against her rib cage, seemed to have disappeared. And the color would do nicely for Christmas as well, she thought, provided she didn't gain too much weight before then. The sleeves, of course, would have to be changed when she saw the fall fashions.

Thoroughly enjoying her own party, she tapped her red lace slipper to the music and inspected the long buffet table. The shaved ice beneath the fish dishes seemed to be holding up. Inroads had been made into the gleaming coral of the enormous whole salmon, and she congratulated herself on having ordered several from Oregon. She thought she'd best try it and put a large slice on a plate and covered it with the fresh shredded cucumber in soured cream. What was that called? Ah, yes, she remembered, gherkin sauce. Sweet white-fleshed crab chunks still remained in abundance, but she passed these up in favor of the fat shrimp. The oyster shortcake had already been served, hot and buttery from the oven as the guests arrived. Really, she thought, recalling it with a mental smack of the lips, Isobel was a genius with pastry.

Freda moved down the table, musing that, after all, she was right to put the minced truffle and greens dish with the fish, rather than the salads, since it did contain mussels. The champagne added with the chives and parsley at the end kept it lovely and moist. She reached the meats. The crispy cones of the chicken croquettes were the proper rich brown, she noted, and were a good idea since they were quite as nice cold as hot. Plucking off an outside bit of the succulent ham, she nodded happily at the tart sweetness of the orange-honey glaze.

The waltz ended, and she turned to watch the dancers separating. She was glad that she'd announced the party as informal, given that it was held in the dance hall. The men looked more comfortable in their light summer suits and smaller collars. A few had substituted wing collars with red striped ascots held with pearl stick pins. Except for Berkeley Glendower. The scarf tucked into the vest of his white linen suit was royal blue. Now he seemed to be merely nodding a polite thanks to Morna Gregory, but Freda was not fooled.

His right hand still lightly rested on his partner's waist, and Morna need only take a graceful sidestep to be away from his warm touch. But she did not move, although she looked poised to do so. Again the anxiety Freda had felt that night a few weeks ago swept over her.

She turned back to the table. Perhaps a dessert might soothe her stomach, she thought. The molded strawberry custard, decorated with crystallized rose petals, looked wonderfully creamy. She'd best have a helping, she decided.

"Ah, M'sieu Caley, at a party you should not be sitting and staring by yourself." Stanton looked up to see Colette, playfully wagging a scolding finger. Her skirt was made of layers of ruffled white tulle, and over the tight-fitting bodice she had arranged wide ribbons in the tri-color of France. They were fastened at the side of the low-pointed waist with a medallion showing the helmeted woman who was the symbol of

France. Colette's own shining brown hair was arranged to mimic the woman's headpiece, and her even features were not unlike those of the engraved portrayal. She had spent half the evening standing in profile, hoping that Berkeley would comment flatteringly, and she was put out that he hadn't noticed. She'd had yet another glass of champagne and gone looking for a more appreciative audience.

Leaning over Caley so that her décolletage was displayed effectively, she pointed to her ribbons. Her speech was a little slurred. "How nice that our colors are the same as yours, eh? And, since Bastille Day is July fourteenth, we can celebrate together! Let me get you some champagne," she coaxed prettily, "and cheer you up. It is not often that Freda gives anything away. Not," she added, running soft fingers along his chin, "that *I* intend to follow her example. But, especially for a *cher ami,* I could think of something . . . French, and quite different."

Caley tried to paste an uneven smile on his face, but Colette's feline glance quickly caught his underlying wretchedness. "Ah," she exclaimed angrily, flouncing down next to him, quite forgetting to straighten her ruffles before doing so. "But you are wasting your time trailing after La Gregory! I have seen you loitering in the foyer half the night to make sure she sleeps with no one. She does not, she will not, I tell you. She could insure her future, even retire while she is still young. But no! She sings instead for her supper."

She let out a disdainful, very Gallic puff of air, but envy sparkled in her hazel eyes. "And the so rich banker gives her jewels for a smile, but for me, not even a little ring! All my pearls are merely *faux,*" she added self-pityingly. She threw up her hands. "And I believe the woman is so demented that she would refuse even the beautiful Glendower."

Relief, as well as intense interest, spread across Caley's features. "Did she . . . I mean, do you know that he has been refused?"

"Ah," Colette said again, swallowing her own vexation. She could see, as she put it to herself, how that wind was blowing. Not only was this man sick with frustrated desire, but very jealous too. Her innate calculation set in. Perhaps this situation could be turned to her advantage.

She'd been eyeing Caley speculatively for some time, wondering if he might be willing to back her and buy out Freda. He was not at all a generous man, she knew too well, but he might invest in her venture, seeing it as a good use of his money. She'd been bethinking herself as to how low an interest rate he might accept. If now she became his confidante, things might move nicely in that direction.

Or, perhaps in even a more promising one. Colette ran a pink-tipped index finger down her delicate nose. Marriage. To her. Colette had reviewed several of her customers with that possibility on her mind, although that was the last thing on theirs. Most of them had been salaried men, and it would have meant a lifetime of tiny economies to live in both style and comfort. She had no desire to do that.

But Colette had not, up to this point, seen Stanton Caley as even an outside hope. Despite his own wealth he was likely to expect his bride to have a comfortable income of her own. Besides, he was at heart a very conventional man, who only thought of marriage in terms of his own social class, no doubt to some dull but acceptable girl. So it would surely be wise, she reflected now, to have him at least start thinking along the right lines, even if it was just now of the wrong woman.

"Mon cher," she murmured, nestling closer, outlining his flat ear with her soft fingertips, being careful not to disturb the combed-over hair, "you are such a student of human behavior, an observant man who so carefully considers all the sides to a question. So wise of you, and the reason *I* have always been so attracted to you. But you are too modest. That is your problem. Therefore you do not see that an intelligent woman, like my sweet *amie* Morna, would choose you over Monsieur Glendower."

Stanton looked at her in amazement. He thought himself clever enough, but certainly less so than Berkeley, and he hadn't any illusions about his appearance. He'd never before heard Colette say downright foolish things, even at the end of the evening when she'd not yet garnered a partner for her bed.

But before he could respond, she went on. "You have something priceless to offer her. Yourself," she whispered, "your hand. He is married, is he not?"

This time Caley gawped at her. The idea of proposing to Morna had never occurred to him. It was true, that was the one thing Berkeley could not do. A divorce from Olivia and her money would surely ruin him. Well—he stopped himself—perhaps not, if Glendower waited a suitable length of time and then remarried an equally rich and proper wife. Denver society would overlook a divorce—for a man—under the right circumstances. Olivia Hyde-White had no supporters in the Sacred Thirty-six. She'd made no attempt to ingratiate herself. Quite the reverse. But for him to then marry Morna, who had no money . . . Stanton suddenly realized that, while he'd been digesting this novel idea, Colette was looking at him expectantly.

"Yes, he is married," he replied, with a dawning satisfaction. "His wife is an heiress. He, of course, has few resources of his own. And it would be utter folly for him to even consider divorce."

"Exactement," Colette murmured. "But for a man like you, a man

of such means of his own, a mind of his own, no such problems exist." She stopped, flattering herself that now she knew how to bring him along step by step, although she devoutly wished she'd not drunk that last glass of champagne. Still, drinking wine tended to make her accent a little more pronounced, and she'd found that many men felt that any utterance that sounded French was somehow more insightful. "You do not know, you cannot know, M'sieu Caley, how I 'ave worried myself over you. Suppose, I say to myself, that this man of such intellect, such sense, should marry a . . . lesser woman. A woman not of his quality."

"What d'you mean?" Stanton blinked his colorless lashes in an effort to clear his head and struggled to sit more nearly upright. "I would never marry without carefully investigating the girl's back—"

"No, no, no." Colette smiled sadly, took his hand, and gave it a caressing pat. "You do not have my meaning. I was not thinking of social class." She clicked her fingers as if to dismiss such an insignificant idea. "You must be besieged in Denver by women of the proper circumstance. But can they appreciate a man who sits quietly, who thinks? A man of your intellectual power? I cannot imagine it. No, no. Their only thought is how many new dresses they could buy with your fortune, of the mansion they will build with your money. And for you to be harnessed—for life—to one of these."

Caley shifted uneasily on the velvet chaise at these words, especially at the idea of anyone spending his money, but Colette went on relentlessly. "Think of it. It makes me weep. You will sit with her, night after night in the drawing room, trying to converse, trying to tell her of your insights, and she will stare at you with the glassy eye, her head filled with . . ." Colette could see she had Caley's complete attention, but she could not think at all of the word she wanted. "Frivols!" she finally burst out.

"Trifles," Stanton said automatically, but he was not at all aware of correcting her. Instead, he was staring with horror at the future Colette had conjured up for him. It was, in fact, very near his own experience as a bachelor at interminable dinners and social functions.

"So, my dear, dear, M'sieu Caley, I can understand your interest in our friend Morna. Only she—and I, of course—can appreciate a man of superior mental power, who could raise us up, fill our days with the delights of his wisdom." She threw her head back and lifted two graceful white arms heavenward.

These speeches had made Colette decidedly thirsty, and besides, she felt Stanton needed a little time to rearrange his preconceived notions. It would take some days, perhaps months, of course, but she felt that she'd made a nice start. "Do let me get you some more champagne, *mon cher*. For you, I know that Freda will insist a new bottle be opened. In one moment I will return."

She sailed off with her tricolor sash fluttering. Although she had momentarily worried that she might go too far and induce Caley to dash over and offer his hand to Morna on the spot, she had placed her faith in the fact that he was not a man of action, but a sitter on the sidelines of life. Furthermore, as difficult as it was to conceive of a woman behaving so against her own best interests, she believed Morna Gregory would refuse him.

Now with his head whirling, as well as his stomach, Caley searched for a glimpse of Morna. She was not far from him, near the lavish buffet table, talking to Edward Gibbons and the New York investor he'd brought with him. The easterner was clearly so entranced that he stood stockstill, gazing at her, with a plump shrimp hovering somewhere near his half-opened mouth. In his mind's eye Caley could see her just like that, as Mrs. Caley, beguiling the influential men of Denver.

He could picture them coming home, her curling up on a cushion by his feet in their sitting room, looking up at him with her dark-lashed eyes bright, while he recounted the men's smoking-room conversation, pointing out the flaws in their investment approaches. He could almost feel the softness of her hair beneath his stroking hand.

But out of the corner of his eye he saw Freda in her sparkling red gown approaching the group, and his dream shriveled. What was he thinking of? Everyone would soon know—the Sacred Thirty-six would surely spread the word—that she'd come from a whorehouse in Telluride. It wouldn't matter that Morna had wit, charm, and beauty. It'd almost be better if she hadn't.

Stanton closed his eyes in pain at the thought of the whispers, the snubs. He'd be ostracized, cut from every invitation list. There'd be no more inside information on the financial world dropped carelessly over the cigars and brandy. True, his inherited wealth was substantial, but as the elder Caley, now dead, had been fond of saying, "There's no such thing as too much money." And suppose by some dreadful mischance he should lose his fortune? He had no confidence that he could imitate his father and make a new one.

There was ample evidence of the power of the ladies of society. Baron von Richtofen, with his dishwater-plain German wife, had been originally welcome. But when he'd discreetly persuaded her family to take her back and acquired a dazzling bride with no antecedents, he'd become a nonperson. All his business schemes, some quite brilliant, were allowed to wither without help from the bankers and tycoons.

And when Horace Tabor became overextended, no man stretched out a hand, all because of Baby Doe. Horace went back to being a common laborer, shoveling slag in a mine he'd once owned.

Massaging his now throbbing forehead, Caley opened his eyes. For some reason he was struck with grief when he saw Morna. It was as if he'd won and lost her in an instant, had been permitted a glimpse of Paradise before iron gates had slammed shut. She was flanked by Gibbons and his investor, with her back to the dance floor. But she was turning slightly in that direction, although the musicians had not yet started the next set.

And then Stanton could see Berkeley making his way slowly toward her, stopping here and there to have a smiling word with one friend or another. There was no way she could know he was approaching, but she was aware he'd soon be at her side, of that Caley was sure.

Anger licked his stomach lining, sent blood surging to his face. He couldn't explain his overwhelming feeling that Berkeley had now succeeded where he himself had failed. It made no sense. He had not tried because he couldn't think of how to do so. So why should he feel defeated? But still he sat, trembling with rage, hating Berkeley Glendower.

CHAPTER 11

Isobel would never forget her first fourth of July celebration in Telluride in 1898. As she sat rocking dreamily, still keeping an eye on her pale, sleeping mistress, she smiled as she recalled the events.

No one in the town had slept Saturday night, which was only the second of July, or Sunday, the third. Those few who had tried were doomed to failure because of the sporadic booms of dynamite crackers and the continuous gaiety of those who thronged the streets until nearly dawn. Pitchmen called incessantly to attract people to their games of chance, and medicine men loudly hawked their elixirs. The food vendors, working around the clock to satisfy the appetites of the swarms lining up before them, shouted to helpers for more shortening, flour, firewood, or ice.

Cold pork pies, strawberry ices, fry bread, as well as cobs of corn on pointed sticks—boiled briefly in kettles, then buttered and salted—sold fast on the streets. Booths offering sweet sarsaparilla, freshly pulled sticky taffy, and spun sugar did a land-office business, although Telluride, like most mountain mining camps, had few children. Regular meals, even at Freda's, were out of the question. But, as usual, her larder was full. In the days just before, Isobel herself had stored a supply of green apple tarts and berry pies on the clean straw of the ice house.

When she was a child, Isobel's favorite holiday had been Independence Day because it came during the summer. Christmas meant shivering in an unheated church much of the day with the misery of chilblained fingers and frozen toes, although there was the rare treat of cocoa afterward and a package containing new shoes or undergarments to be opened. But on the Fourth, Louisville always had a parade, baseball games, and a small fireworks display. Families gathered around groaning picnic tables laden with fried chicken, deviled eggs, corn pudding, and homemade ice cream in thick metal containers packed around with rock salt.

Yet it was nothing like this dizzying whirl of noise, smells, and high-pitched laughter. A circus, knowing that their trip would be well worthwhile because of the free-spending bachelor miners, arrived amid banners and fanfare. Besides the band concerts and baseball games, every day had its assortment of races: bicyclists pedaled furiously around their course, Indian squaws astride their ponies tore down the street, the firemen's spindly-wheeled carts with tightly wrapped hoses careened behind the volunteers dressed in tights.

The size of the prizes they competed for would have shocked the conservative citizens of Louisville, Isobel knew. The winners of the miners' double-hammer drilling match would take away $350. The five-mile cowboy race paid $300 for first place. While the last event of the long holiday—the prestigious mile horse race—only had a purse of $100, the side bets were often more than a coal miner earned in a year. Perhaps, she considered, Telluride celebrated so feverishly because here at the stroke of midsummer, the townspeople remembered that there would be few golden autumn days at this high elevation to lead into the long winter. Each person was therefore determined to enjoy each brief, bright hour to the fullest. And they did. Everyone was giddy with lack of sleep. Isobel had never before felt this carefree tingling.

By early afternoon on Monday, the actual Fourth, she was still upright in one of the parlor armchairs but quite droopy eyed, and her head had a tendency to fall abruptly forward. Normally at this time she would be sitting in this very chair, doing her mending and listening to Morna practice on the piano. Today she was just listening. Morna was dreamily playing a melody whose title Isobel always forgot, but it made her think of a bell-like stream that wandered through green meadows and under rustic bridges. Some days the song came out sounding as if there might be trolls hunkering down under those bridges. Misshapen, ugly trolls who'd snatch at the feet of those who crossed over. But not today.

Now that Isobel thought of it, she hadn't imagined those trolls for several weeks, ever since Mr. Glendower had returned. Several times Miss Morna had come back from her morning rides looking almost rosy cheeked. That morning before the parade, when they saw him across the street and he'd doffed his hat and bowed, she'd smiled wonderfully.

Morna had on her short military blue jacket with the white silk facings on the reveres and cuffs and Hussar braids stitched across the chest. The matching skirt had darker taffeta bands in a square pattern around the circular hem. Wearing a smart hat with a severe blue bow, she looked far more elegant, Isobel thought, than any of the north-side ladies clustered together, their skirts clutched closely to their bodies as if a touch of the common folk would contaminate them. Isobel herself wore, for the first time in her life, a wash silk dress. She'd found that even with saving from her wages what once would have seemed unimaginable sums to send Florrie, she still had more than plenty left.

The excursion train bringing 250 citizens of Ouray, the town east of the Dallas Divide, had been late, but as soon as it pulled in, the bands struck up. Cornets and tubas blared, drums banged. They marched and countermarched in intricate formations down flag-lined Main Street, followed by a contingent of Navahos in native costume. Because it was nearly twelve, it was judged better to skip the reading of the Declaration of Independence. A window-rattling explosion of giant powder before the Courthouse made the Fourth official promptly at noon.

By then Isobel and Morna had returned home to relax and refresh themselves. They'd decided to avoid the jostling of the crowds trying for a good view of the drilling contest. Each mine backed their own crew, placing huge bets to see who could drill in fifteen minutes the deepest hole in the large block of granite set up in the middle of Colorado Avenue. One man knelt, holding the sharpened bit of steel upright, turning it a fraction as his partner brought down each mighty sledgehammer blow. With lightning speed and no break in rhythm they occasionally changed places. Even now, several blocks away, the cheers of the onlookers were ringing as loud as the pounding.

Besides, the evening's festivities promised to be long. After the late-afternoon horse race the town picnic would begin, followed by patriotic music played by the Brass and Cornet Band and then the fireworks.

"Ah, Isobel, there you are. Thank heavens." Freda bustled in, her entire face so flushed that the usual two spots of rouge on her cheekbones were lost in the general red. Although she never strayed far from dark colors, her navy dress of a material called nun's veiling was embroidered in front with white French dots and elaborate swirls. Around the top of her shoulders was a puffy boa of Brussels net that bobbed about like lace pompons when she moved. She pulled a large pearl-tipped pin from her tilted saucer hat, also filled with flowers made of the same net, and laying it down on the parlor table, carefully patted her hair.

With an exhausted whoosh she sank down next to Isobel, saying, "Morna, my dear, I'm sorry to interrupt, but I'm still organizing the picnic." Every year the Methodist ladies, a group that as yet did not have a church, and the Congregationalists, who did, combined forces to feed the citizens and raise money for their causes. Freda contributed regularly to the two assemblages, and donated both ginger beer and the far more popular kegs from her dance hall's supply. The temperance movement had never caught on in Telluride.

"The shortcakes will last, but surely not the strawberries," Freda lamented. "We'd best send over the pies we've got. If you would, Isobel, when Sam Goler comes for the beer, have him load them onto the wagon too. You can ride over with him to where the tables are set up by the river. Pity it's so murky there with the mine tailings. But it's a pretty spot and big enough for the crowd. And at least there's no mosquitoes. If you wait there, you won't be in a bad position to see the end of the race." She fanned herself with a dainty handkerchief pulled from her sleeve and finished complacently, "Of course, no one will have Morna's view of the finish."

Morna ran an index finger gently along the keys and said nothing. When Edward Gibbons, appointed the head judge by the race association, had asked her to share his specially built narrow platform on the finish line, she'd been hesitant to accept. "Be foolish not to," Freda had insisted. "You'll look lovely standing up there. Maybe you can help. Even with his new double spectacles your young eyes are better than Gibbons's. You'll have a grand view, and the race is always exciting."

"Do you know," she said now, trying discreetly to massage the middle of her back through her corset, "Berkeley Glendower won't be in the race. They've made him the second judge. He'll be exactly across from the marked pole and mounted himself for a good sight line. Well, he's a fair man and well liked. Maybe if he's one of the officials, there won't be the arguments we've had some years when it came down to a nose. Probably why they picked him."

"Perhaps"—Morna swiveled on the piano stool to face them—"they were also afraid he'd easily win the race. His stallion, Druid, is surely a blood horse. At least fifteen hands high, I'd guess, and very fast."

"Ah," Freda said, her eyebrows climbing to her blond fringe, "I've never seen his horse." Morna leaned down to pick up a fallen piece of sheet music, and when she sat back up, her face was pink tinged.

"One thing," Freda went on after a pause, "Mr. Glendower is surely right about. He thinks the fireworks display is too near the town, and if a rocket went astray and hit the ones not yet set off, there'd be a fine how-do-you-do. But people'd fuss if they moved the location. They want to be just underneath for the full effect. And with the band playing beside the river after the picnic, everyone can just stay right where they are after they eat. Speaking of the picnic"—she levered herself up—"I'll just go along and see how things are going and get a good spot for the race."

Morna returned to her playing, and Freda leaned close to Isobel's ear. "That blue suit is perfect, but"—she gestured to Morna's simple high-collared blouse with a faint polka-dot pattern—"the shirt is so very plain. Do you think you could talk her into some jewelry? The sapphires?" she ended hopefully.

Isobel shook her head. "I don't think so. She might do the pearls."

Edward Gibbons had brought a small spray of white and red roses to be pinned on Morna's lapel. When Freda saw her standing next to the banker on the rough wooden platform just above the heads of the crowd, she entirely approved of the flowers on the blue jacket. She would have liked the sparkle of showier jewelry, a more eye-catching hat, but she had to admit that Morna had never looked more beautiful. When the horses paraded by the finish line on their way down Main Street to the start on the western outskirts, she was as dignified as a queen inspecting the troops.

Gibbons seemed to agree because, except when he was peering about through his opera glasses, his eyes were fixed on her. Berkeley Glendower was just below them seated on his black horse. He was turned in his saddle, with his flat-crowned Stetson off, his face raised, talking to Gibbons and Morna. Dressed in a soft tanned buckskin jacket, he held on to the thin railing of the platform as his stallion shifted his hooves and swished his tail to keep away the bluebottles. His hand, Freda noticed with a smile, was between the banker and Morna, as if to fend off any touching by Gibbons.

It would be a good quarter of an hour before the race started, the madam judged, since the riders were letting their horses canter slowly to the start a mile away down the main street. But there was plenty to see, and she'd yet to place her final bet with one of the oddsmakers. Touts with bits of paper marking the agreed-upon odds stuck in their derbies worked the packed throngs on both sides of the wide avenue. The odds shifted continually as the spectators eyed the prancing horses, each man sure that his superior eye had detected a flaw in his neighbor's choice.

Freda did love to take a flyer on the horses and had won fifty dollars last year on George Fisk's beautiful chestnut gelding. Sam Goler had said it was the best horse, but she'd bet on it because it was the prettiest. This year Axel Nordstrom, who owned the thriving men's haberdashery in town, had a shining gray that had caught her eye. The local ranchers grumbled that the wealthy citizens of Telluride had all brought in blood horses, but several of them entered their fast, sturdy ponies anyway. She considered a spirited pinto owned by Homer Dunlap from Norwood, an agricultural area some thirty-five miles away, but at last settled on the gray and beckoned to a nearby bet-taker.

Adjusting one side of her wide-brimmed saucer hat a little higher and plucking up her puffed boa, to the dismay of the short young miner behind her, Freda surveyed the crowd. Some distance past the finish line the carriages of Telluride society were lined up. As the horses thundered down the stretch, the ladies and gentlemen could stand and have a good view. They were on the same side of the street as Freda, so it was necessary for her to crane forward to inspect the women's hats. Across from them, on the north side, there was no room for spectators because of a wide drainage ditch. Just beyond the ditch, in a wide meadow, stood the wagon containing boxes of Roman candles and rockets.

Freda had already admired the befeathered and flowered creation on the head of plump Grace Nordstrom as her sleek two-seater had gone by, pulled by a high-stepping sorrel. Grace had, as always, slyly tipped her ruffled parasol at the madam. When Grace had first arrived in Telluride, she was Greta Hjalmar and worked for Freda, who was always sure that the success of Axel Nordstrom's clothing emporium was due to his competent wife. Farther down, Ivy Wildon's narrow-brimmed pie-plate hat with—Freda sniffed to herself—a bow as stingy as the lady's lips could be glimpsed. Ivy would have cut Grace dead, she knew, but Axel had bought the downtown block adjoining Wilbur Wildon's. Then, too, Ivy might have been afraid that Grace wouldn't have noticed the snub, since everyone else flocked to the Nordstroms' splendid dinners.

Except for the ache in her tired feet Freda was truly enjoying the day. The sun was brilliant in a gemstone sky and the mountains rising at the eastern end of the valley looked as sharply drawn as if they'd been chiseled. The slight wind was coolly soft on the skin, and it was laden with a not unpleasant mixture of smells—hot oils from the cauldrons of fried foods, the quick-growing tall grasses along the river, and fresh manure. Still, she, like the throngs lining the street, was impatient for the race to begin.

Then a tremble ran through the crowd from west to east, moving even faster than the horses, indicating that the leaders must have entered the far side of town. Muffled shouts could be heard, then the cheers started, louder and louder. A few too brave souls near the finish line sped to the middle of the course for a quick look down and then scurried back to report to those near them. "Three," the word went around, "three leaders. The rest are out of it."

Those at the finish could now even feel, or thought they could, the thud of approaching hooves on the hard-packed dirt of the street. Edward Gibbons was leaning forward, his belly flattened against the flimsy railing and his opera glasses pressed to his spectacles. "Fisk's horse is neck and neck with the gray," he bellowed. "Pinto's a couple of lengths behind."

Berkeley rose in his stirrups, Morna excitedly stood on her tiptoes. "The pinto's catching up!" Gibbons burst out.

A sharp whine and then an enormous bang rocked the air. No one ever discovered who set off the dynamite-filled cracker. Mischievous adolescents, the miners who were lining up against Fisk's refusal of the eight-hour day, or even a losing bettor—all were possibilities. But what happened then followed with blurring speed. The pinto reared, its front hooves stabbing at empty air. The chestnut veered in panic, crashing into the gray and sending them both heading across the broad street into the packed sidelines near the judge's stand.

With unblinking thought Glendower threw his huge stallion into their path before they could plunge into the horror-stricken spectators. The two terrified horses, seeing the black insurmountable hurdle, could not stop, so the gray swerved back into the chestnut and they, with both riders, fell with bone-jarring force onto the dirt.

At the same time the fireworks exploded. The ominous wham of that cracker meant that it had gone off too soon and too low. On its downward spin it slammed into the wagon full of rockets. They blew up with ear-numbing booms and wild cracklings. Some thumped harmlessly into the bank of the drainage ditch in front of them, but others soared over, sizzling like burning arrows toward the crowd.

Amid the screams people pushed, shoved, elbowed, in all directions. Scrambling frantically, they knocked on both sides against the unstable supports of the viewing stand. It rocked violently to and fro, like a storm-tossed boat. Turning Druid to avoid the onrushing hordes from the western end, now running unthinkingly toward the excitement, Berkeley saw Gibbons thrown through the railing at the back of the high platform, his arms flailing, his opera glasses flying. Morna was barely erect, clutching the thin bar in front. He spurred the stallion forward into the now cleared space before the stand and, with an outflung right arm, encircled her waist and yanked her down from the teetering stand. For a moment she dangled breathless in his grasp, then kicked one leg free of petticoats and swung it over Druid's haunches.

With eyes rolling, the stallion tried to rear, but to keep him down Berkeley hurled his own weight forward, with Morna now desperately clinging to his back. Druid's front hooves struck the ground, and goaded by both his master's sharp heels and the fear of the fire and noise to his left, the horse charged forward.

Jerking her head to the side, Morna saw Telluride's most spectacular fireworks display. Many of the rockets had soared skyward, not all of their brightness lost in the smoke billowing from the wagon. They blossomed in glowing reds and brilliant whites against the light-filled heavens, and they blasted with the roar of repeated cannon shot.

Stampeding ahead of Druid were three of the carriage horses that had bolted. Two of the traps were empty, the passengers having been unceremoniously dumped, and these thin-wheeled carriages careened aimlessly behind the speeding horses. But one well-rounded, hatless woman gallantly held to her reins, standing upright, arms outstretched, as her sorrel galloped madly.

Berkeley tore after her. As they drew abreast, he shouted, "Grace, Grace, have you got him?"

Without turning her head she nodded vigorously, and the sorrel was indeed slowing. But Druid was not. On he raced down the flat road toward Pandora. Abruptly, Berkeley tugged on his rein and the stallion swerved and thundered over the wooden bridge across the river and up Ute Rise Canyon.

"Berkeley," Morna almost pressed her lips against his ear. "You must stop him! We have to go back. To help."

Glendower turned so that her lips almost brushed his cheek. "Help with what? Adding to the confusion?"

"People might be hurt," she said urgently. She'd lost her hat long ago, and her hair was tangling down.

"Best leave them to those who know what they're doing," he said, the wind almost whipping away his words. "Druid doesn't want to go back just yet and neither do I."

His shoulders started to shake. Gripping his waist even tighter, she leaned forward anxiously to see his face. He was strangling with laughter. "Unless you want to go back to bind up poor Gibbon's wounds," he gasped out. "He went right over on his backside."

"That's not at all funny! He could be badly hurt."

"And so is whoever he fell on." Roaring with mirth, he lifted his face to Bridget's Mountain just ahead. The stallion carrying them both sped toward it.

CHAPTER 12

"Here," Berkeley said matter-of-factly, without turning around. He led Druid off the dirt trail that wound up Ute Rise Canyon and onto the grassy edge. "This is a good place."

He'd dismounted some distance back and was walking alongside the now almost calm stallion.

Morna was still astride, her skirt and beflounced petticoats bunched before and behind her. Despite all her shiftings and tuggings the hems were too narrow to drape over the wide saddle, and it'd proved impossible to balance on it sideways. So, although her cheeks burned, she'd decided to ignore the fact that her black silk-stockinged legs swung uncovered above the dangling stirrups. Dust was liberally sprinkled over her delicate kid shoes and the two bows that kept them on. Her hairpins had given up the losing fight to the wind and the speed at which they'd galloped, and her dark hair sprawled over her shoulders. A few grimy streaks of fireworks soot smudged her face, despite her efforts with the small scrap of lace handkerchief always tucked in her sleeve.

But, in spite of her embarrassment Morna had found herself as little disposed as horse or rider to return immediately to the uproar they'd left. After all, she'd reasoned, Isobel would have been quite safe by the picnic tables near the river, and would certainly look after Freda if the redoubtable madam needed help. It would be more sensible to go back after dark, when she could slip unseen to her room, and no one would know how long she'd been there. The wrong construction would surely be put on her present disheveled appearance, given that she'd left clinging to Berkeley Glendower and had not returned for some time. That would be all some narrow souls would remember, disregarding his quick-thinking courage in saving her from, at the very least, a bad fall.

Tomorrow morning all she need say is that Mr. Glendower had put her down safely on the edge of town. It was not necessary to say *when* that had occurred. Then she could listen with sympathy to the stories everyone would be eager to recount. Explanations, however true, that would not be believed were best avoided, Morna knew.

And as soon as she collected herself, she'd thought, she would find the right words to tell him how grateful she was for his action.

When Druid had finally slowed his breakneck pace, she'd looked up to see the tranquil, sky-lifted face of Bridget's Mountain in front of them. Thin streaks of snow were still left in the rock that resembled hair tumbling down. Serenity was carved in that upthrust profile. A red-tailed hawk dipped and wove in the slice of blue above them. The cool green quiet of the isolated canyon began to relax her too-quick heart-beat.

But, although she was trying not to think of it, her forearms quivered yet from the tightness with which she'd had to clasp Glendower and from the feel of his hard flesh beneath the supple leather of his jacket.

The horse nickered, wedged his nose beneath Berkeley's elbow, and lifted insistently. Although the tumbling waters of Ute Rise Creek could not be seen behind the leafy copse of aspen, its enticing rush could be heard. "Right, boy," his master reassured him, "drinks all around. But ladies first."

Glendower assumed that was enough notice to Morna that he was about to turn around. As he'd paced the horse to cool it, he'd carefully refrained from even a glance over his shoulder to see how she was managing. The unavoidable display of sheer stocking clearly upset her, although she was aristocratically disregarding it. It didn't matter to her, he reflected, grinning to himself, that, in any case, proper society would already have believed her hopelessly compromised by her place of residence. The lady had her own standards, and it was certainly true that every man in Telluride accepted them in their treatment of her.

By the time he wheeled around, Morna had succeeded in gathering up the froth of material in front of her and swinging both legs to the side. He swallowed both a smile and an unexpected lump in his throat. With her smudged face and wild hair she'd never looked more vulnerable, or more beautiful. She slid stiffly into his uplifted arms.

Eyeing the thin soles of her shoes as he set her down, Berkeley gestured to a rounded boulder near the overgrown road. "You could sit there and I'll bring you a hatful of water. The creek's just back of this grove, and it's the clearest and cleanest in the county. Not so sure about the hat." He swept off his leather Stetson and ran the back of his hand across his sweating forehead. "I'll let Druid have a short drink before I rub him down."

"I'll come too," Morna said, slipping off her jacket, and rolling up her sleeves as she followed him to the stream. "I think I need a face wash."

Now, with the water droplets still clinging to the black tendrils around her face, her cheeks pink from the icy water, Morna was seated on his jacket beneath the overarching aspen. She'd unlooped the gold braid from her jacket and tied back her hair. Her handkerchief had served to sponge off a few spots from her skirt and the dust from her shoes. She was feeling much more in command of herself.

The rough horse blanket, sweat dampened, was drying on the upthrust rock behind her. Berkeley had laid aside his brocade vest and, with a wry apology, stripped off his shirt to rub down the stallion's shivering flanks and legs. Catching her comic grimace at the idea of using the sheer lawn fabric as a rag, he clicked his fingers at his own memory lapse.

"Right you are," he said, crouching down and unbuckling the saddlebag next to her. "And Druid will like the feel of this flannel better anyway." He pulled out a folded plaid shirt and then fished out a knife, a packet of butcher paper, and a squat silver flask. "Emergency supplies," he said, unscrewing the top of the bottle. "This is recommended for shocks to the system, as well as being guaranteed to save you from snake- and frostbite."

He held it out to her and looked up at the lengthening afternoon shadows. "It is definitely getting chilly. Take two sips. One can't be too careful, even in July."

The first drink was fire in her throat and Morna almost gasped. But the second burned a little less and sent its relaxing warmth down to her fingers. "Thank you." She handed it back and sprang up. "But now I need some more water."

"Wait." He unrolled the oiled paper. "I didn't show you dinner. Beef jerky."

She eyed the brown dried strips of leathery meat. "Oh, Isobel and I stuffed ourselves at the food booths at lunch," she said, hurrying to the stream, convinced that he was grinning as he moved toward the horse.

Morna did not immediately reseat herself. It would be easier to say this now while he was busying himself, and at some distance away, she considered. Her sincerity might make him uncomfortable. "I cannot thank you enough for what you did," she began. "I was thoroughly frightened on the platform, sure that when it toppled, I'd fall beneath the feet of that trampling crowd. Had it not been for your judgment and speed, I would have."

"I was thankful I was there," he replied seriously. They both fell quiet.

She watched him dry the horse, murmuring to it. The thin-strapped lisle undervest he wore clung with perspiration to his chest and narrow waist. As he wiped down the thoroughbred's strong legs, the powerful muscles in his shoulders moved in mesmerizing strokes. His soothing hands stilled the nerves that quivered and danced on Druid's gleaming flanks. His dark hair fell over his forehead, and as he raised his head, concentrating on his task, she could see in half profile the heavy lashes against his cheeks, the determined upper lip, the sensual lower one, the hardness of his jaw.

By force of will she turned back to the fast-rushing stream and forced herself to stare instead at the glassy clarity of the water and the masses of graceful columbines that lined the other bank. The starry white cups of the flowers lifted upward, their purple outer leaves and trailing tendrils fluttered in a breeze turning chilly, but she was only barely aware of them. The sun and its warmth had gone behind the canyon walls, and she'd have liked her jacket on, but it lay near him.

"There's something I want to say to you," he said, breaking the silence. Over her shoulder she could see him in the middle of the aspen bower, putting the flannel shirt in the saddlebag, straightening up. She could see the gleam of his bare flesh. Standing near him was, she knew, unthinkable at that moment.

Quickly untying the bows of her shoes, Morna slipped out of them. Gathering a handful of skirt and petticoats in her hand, she put one foot tentatively on a fat rock a step away. "I don't think I've ever seen so many columbines," she said, striving for her usual tone. "I'll gather some. Their scent is lovely." Carefully but hurriedly, she stepped with her other foot onto the next rock, and then the next.

"Wait," he called in alarm. "You'll slip in those stockings. That water's frigid. I'll pick them for you."

The rounded stone over a deep pool, she calculated, was the best choice, even if a bit of a stretch. From there she could leap to the opposite bank. With her right hand holding the skirt and her left arm extended, she reached out with her foot. It was then, balanced on two rocks behind her, he caught her arm to steady her. They both catapulted forward into the water.

The water was only waist high, but it was an icy surprise. Soaked and gasping, Morna sat up and then jumped upright. Berkeley, although he'd avoided any rocks, had hit a shallower part and had had the breath knocked out of him.

"Are you all right?" She stumbled toward him, impeded by her sodden skirt, her feet sliced by the sharp pebbles on the bottom. He struggled up, and now in knee-deep water, his boots on the gravel, he again grasped her waist. Hitching her onto his hip, he waded toward the bank, saying between rasps for air, "We can't make a habit of this."

On shore, Morna trembled with cold, vainly wrung her skirts, rubbed her forearms beneath the drenched blouse. Shivering himself, Berkeley handed her the horse blanket and the flask. "Here, take a quick drink, then remove those wet things and wrap yourself up." He stripped off his dripping undershirt. "If today is a portent of things to come, I must remember to bring more brandy on outings with you."

Her teeth chattered so that she could hardly drink, but she swallowed and then dived for the thickest part of the grove. As she finally managed to free herself of the last of the clinging petticoats, she heard him say, "But this is a heaven-sent opportunity. You'll hardly rush out to stop me talking. I want you to know that I did not bring you up here for a brief seduction."

Angrily she whirled around, unthinkingly parted the leaves before her face, and snapped, "The length of time is irrelevant. That will not happen. And no gentleman would take advantage of this situation!"

He was standing a few feet away. Although his thigh-length jacket was discreetly buttoned from his chest hair to its hem, his muscular legs and his feet were completely bare. It only incensed her further that he still managed to look like one of the lords of the earth.

He took off the top of the flask, smiling meditatively. "Yes, *brief* was not at all the word I wanted. It wouldn't apply to any undertaking that involves getting your cooperation. I recall it took three weeks of long morning talks before you stopped calling me Mr. Glendower.

Imagine then the length of time required for cooperation. After some months we would be missed, search parties sent out. Nor is there enough beef jerky for an extended stay."

Despite the fact that she'd disappeared, he continued and his voice had lost its laughing tone. "*Seduction* was the word I intended to deny. I am proposing marriage. I mean this, Morna."

No response came. The aspen leaves between them whispered and swished, but that might have been the rapidly cooling wind. In a way he was thankful that she had not interrupted, knowing this had to be said first. "It will take some time before I am legally able to ask for your hand. But before she left, I told Olivia, my wife, that I did not think we could continue. When her anger cools, she will agree. She has never desired to leave her family, nor does she want a husband—at least not one like me, who does not share her wholehearted interest in the gossip and parties of society. She does not want children." His pause seemed full of remembered pain, but then he went on, his voice quickening. "I have already talked to men here in Telluride about working for them. They have agreed. Without my eastern backers the nature of my work will change, but I'm looking forward to that."

When at last, still hidden, she answered, her voice was shaking. "Berkeley, you do not know the problem, the impediment—"

" 'Let me not, to the marriage of true minds, admit impediments,' " he quoted with conviction. "Morna, listen to me. We share a mind. Even if I wanted, I could not stop loving you. And I had not thought it possible to love anyone as much as I love you, to want anyone as much as I want you. Without you, I will not know one happy day. You—"

"Please, please, don't say this to me," she returned, low and pleading. He bit his lip in angry frustration, and then it occurred to him that her voice still shivered with cold.

"Very well, I'll keep still now. But tomorrow afternoon I'll call at Freda's and you *must* listen. Wrap that blanket around you and come out."

"I can't. My undergarments will soak the blanket, but the corset strings in back are tangled and swollen and won't come loose."

He reached quickly for his knife, unsheathed it, and pushed aside the sheltering branches. She stood, shivering, with her back to him, her arms clasped in front of her.

The pale moon, just off full, had looked so transparent on rising that the twilit sky seemed visible behind it. But it had gathered its light in the darkening and now it gleamed on Morna's bare shoulders, making them as shining as the pearls that encircled her neck. When he put out one hand to steady her, lest he cut her, her skin was cold as snow. "Hold still," he muttered gruffly. He sliced through the wet cords, and then, pulling the lace of the underneath shift to him, slit through that as well.

Leaning down, Morna scooped up the coarse throw as the corset and chemise fell away, and held it gratefully to her body. As she did so, he saw the cruel red ridges of the stiff whalebone imprinted on her back. Unable to stop himself, he reached out and ran his fingers over them as if to erase them.

She felt the warmth of his hands on her goosefleshed back and then the uninsistent lightness of his healing touch on her numbed shoulders. One second she willed him to stop, the next inwardly begged him to continue.

Had he grasped, held, she felt that she could have called up the strength to push away. But she was powerless to move from his stroking hands. She had stayed so long in an arctic world, kept herself there by a fierce tenacity to live on her own terms. She could not believe his fingertips could so immediately thaw her icy resistance to any closeness.

But his touch held so much more than aching desire, and his hands were more eloquent than eyes or mouth could be. He reached around, ran his palms down the sides of her face, along her throat, slid over her collarbone, briefly cupped the edges of her shoulders. Without a word, although she could feel the warmth of his breath on her neck, he deftly massaged the skin nipped daily by the corset. She was so used to the discomfort of that garment, but so absolutely unused to this luxury after its release.

He stopped each time just at the roundness at the top of her slender hips. Her sides, and then her thighs, began to crave the same silken touch. An incandescence flowed upward. Her skin glowed as if from the June sun, and the very memory of January's freeze was forgotten.

Still, he said nothing, asked nothing. The fingertips circled, the palms were unemphatic. He brought no pressure from the strong bones of his hands or heavy forearms. And she could not tell if the heat she felt emanated from him or simmered from her own flesh.

Her blood was now brandy in her veins, her marrow was liquid coursing silver. She felt if she pressed her mouth on his she would burn his flesh. And at that very moment his right hand explored her cheek, then the ring finger outlined her lips. Again and again. It lingered at the corners with a tenderness that was now not enough.

When she finally leaned back against him, she could not tell if that shudder, that groan, was his or hers. Just as the blanket slipped from her grasp, he caught it and threw it on the grass. He spun her to him, iron fingers on her arm, but even that force was not enough.

As if he knew that, he pulled her down to the blanket in that unrelenting grasp without a kiss or word. He flung off his jacket and now pressed the full length of himself against her. He had the hardness and heat of new steel, and she was like one who, almost frozen, now stands much too near the fire and revels in it, though it burns.

He kissed her like a starving man, not letting either of them breathe, his fingers knotted in her hair so she could not pull back even if she wanted. When he caught her lower lip between his teeth, she would not have had him stop, even if he'd bitten through it.

She had not known her own passion before, had never guessed her body could move and flow without her consent, had never imagined this consuming ache. Nor had she dreamed that the edges of the self could blur so that she felt his flesh, the smooth skin of his back, was her own.

He lifted his face. His lips scalded her throat, sent wildfire now through her breasts, seared across her stomach.

But this now was not what she wanted. Her own hands dug pleadingly into the corded muscles of his shoulders, trying to pull him back up so he would lie on her, enter her. Her nails raked across his back when he would not comply.

His tongue blazed on the skin of her inner thighs, on the softness inside her. But this was not enough, her fever too intense. "Berkeley, you must," not sure if she screamed or whispered the words.

He raised himself up, thrust into her, and she melted into him.

CHAPTER 13

The morning sun, as bright and fresh-minted as the new century, streamed through the fretwork of the heavy lace curtains, but Isobel dozed peacefully in the rocking chair. Her reddened hands, still clutching the glycerin bottle, lay folded in the lap of her brown linsey-woolsey dress. Somewhere in the distance a firecracker saved from last night's New Year celebration popped noisily, but it disturbed neither of the exhausted women sleeping in the bedroom. Morna Gregory, her dark hair tangled on the creamy satin of the pillow slip, did not even stir.

But the faraway bang gently invaded Isobel's half-dreaming memory, and she was back again at that Fourth of July a year and a half ago. She'd been standing on the thick boards of a makeshift picnic table, well back from the street, hoping to catch a glimpse of the end of the race. Suddenly, the cheers had stopped and half the town seemed to be screaming. The crack of the fireworks had so startled her that she wasn't sure where she was. Then she'd thought she'd gone daft, seeing Morna behind Mr. Glendower on the back of a black horse that ran as if chased by demons.

But Sam Goler had pulled her down promptly and, upending the table, tugged her with him to the shelter of those heavy boards. It took her another minute to realize that the tears he was wiping from his streaming eyes were only partly caused by the acrid smoke. He was choking with laughter. "Told 'em, he did. Durned fireworks too close to town." He popped his head up for a quick look at the explosions, then crouched down, slapping his thigh with glee.

When she finally decided it was safe to stand, the grass around the river was already littered with people clutching an injured arm, leg, or ankle. Some had been knocked down in the panicked crush, a few had burns from the rockets. Miss Freda, her hat cockeyed, her pomponed boa waving down her back like a decorated mare's tail, was issuing orders like a field general. Isobel had sent Sam, happily scooping up the inside of a crushed berry pie with his fingers, back to the house for ointments and bandages. Then she'd hurried to Freda's side.

That night the dance hall had been converted into an improvised sickroom, since those with broken bones were in no condition for the long, steep horseback ride to the Tomboy. More than one young miner, Isobel suspected, claimed to be in far greater pain than he was in order to spend the night on a velvet chaise being fussed over by the girls. But the winner of the rock-drilling contest, on whom Edward Gibbons had landed so forcefully, did have a badly cracked collarbone.

Run off her feet as she was, it was quite late before Isobel noticed to her surprise that she'd not seen Morna all evening. When she worriedly slipped into her bedroom to turn down the coverlet, Isobel saw her mistress sound asleep, one hand resting on the leather jacket she was sure she'd seen Mr. Glendower wearing. It was not until two days later that it occurred to her that there was no sign of Morna's blue suit. Or her petticoats.

But by then Isobel was extremely busy arranging their move. The very next morning Berkeley Glendower had arrived with a field of columbines in his arms and even more waving from his saddlebags. That flower's scent was so light that she'd never realized how fragrant it was until she'd put them in every available vase and carried them to Morna's room. And, despite the wild disorganization of the kitchen with so many breakfasts to prepare, he'd managed to follow her soon with a steaming silver teapot and two cups on a tray. With one finger on his smiling lips he'd waved her away, opened the door, and closed it firmly behind him.

Later, as she'd hurried down the hall to the linen closet for fresh towels, she'd heard Morna's voice raised in protest. But when her mistress finally appeared in the kitchen, she was smiling so delightedly that Isobel had decided that some agreement had been reached.

The house, which Isobel realized must have been rented that very morning, had once been known as Valborg's Folly. The stolid Swede who'd ordered it built was a quiet bachelor who'd sold his claim very profitably to the Smuggler-Union mine when that company incorporated, and then he had stayed on as an engineer. When the sheer size of the place became evident during its construction, the townspeople tittered. Moreover, he was quite mad, they said, to put an expensive and elegant house on Pacific Avenue near the saloons and cribs. All the best houses were on the north slope to catch the south sun, and it was the only place a respectable woman would conceivably want to live.

Then there was the question of what woman of any sort would want to live with Valborg. He was a hulking man with a badly pockmarked face that had been pitted in an explosion. His hair sprang up in wild blond curls, his bleached blue eyes looked lashless, and his nose had, at some point in his life, been mashed decidedly to the left. He was a quiet, morose man who, although liked by the other men, never stopped in for a beer with them. Valborg never patronized the bordellos or the cribs, never gambled. Each evening he went to the sauna and then played checkers for hours with his friend Klas.

As the three-storied house neared completion, there was a tinge of awe in people's laughter. There were seven bedrooms and three baths, all with enormous clawfoot tubs and the latest in indoor plumbing. Moreover, in the expansive kitchen a gleaming steel hipbath stood next to a coal-fired range that could have heated enough water for a boardinghouse. On the ground floor there was a parlor, back parlor, dining room, sun parlor, and library. Outside, on either side of a wide balcony, was a six-sided tower with rounded glass windows. The whole was painted a sunny yellow and the elaborate wooden trim was decorated with white alpine flowers and Wedgwood blue leaves.

It sat on the largest—and prettiest—lot in town. At the south end the river gurgled below steep banks. Between that and the latticed back porch lay fully a half acre that could be planted in flowers or vegetables, given the fertile soil the river had once deposited. At the bottom of the lot, before a small stand of aspen trees, Valborg had erected a lacy wooden gazebo and planted daisies around it. Such grounds were not possible in the better part of town because the narrow lots there were carved out of a rising mountainside.

More than one of the ladies of the evening from the nearby houses found occasion to stroll past during the day when Valborg was inspecting the workmen's progress. They, too, would have much preferred a home on the north slope, but this house was a marvel. A man's face, even an extraordinarily ugly one, could be overlooked. But Valborg never struck up a conversation. He was a very shy man.

Then the rumor went around, no doubt put forth by Klas, who was bursting with the news, that Valborg had sent for a mail-order bride. It was a not uncommon arrangement, and although there were some shady companies, there were a few reliable ones, patronized by settled workingmen who could afford a wife. Usually a description of the lady was provided, but prior correspondence was not allowed since there were always men who took advantage of this by writing improper letters. The prospective bride's return fare was guaranteed if she did not like her first look at the groom.

On the Saturday morning the train carrying the lady pulled in, a surprising number of onlookers gathered. Klas was not good at keeping secrets of this magnitude. Valborg had purchased a new brown serge suit, and the color didn't flatter his complexion. But, given his size, it was lucky that Axel Nordstrom had anything at all that fit. As it was, both the sleeves and trouser legs were slightly too short. He'd just been to the barber and the fresh shave had turned his scarred cheeks quite red.

Since ladies traveling alone were rare, everyone knew it was she when the conductor helped her onto the small metal stool and then onto the wooden platform. Dressed in gray and black, the last stages of extended mourning, the woman was small, nearer thirty than twenty, but quite passably pretty. Her blond hair was neatly wound in back and a black straw hat with a black dove was perched on her pompadour.

As she neared the giant Valborg standing alone at the end of the platform, her steps slowed. He was tugging at the edge of his jacket with his left hand, and the derby clutched in his right bounced against his leg. When she was three feet away, she stopped. Story had it that she took two steps back.

Valborg cleared his throat. "I'm a hardvorking man." He'd never lost his Scandinavian accent. "And I've got some put by. I don't drink or gamble." He fell silent. She said nothing, but she half turned to go. Everyone waited for him to tell her about the wonderful house. But his next words were simply "I don't talk much. I vill always provide for you, and," he finished in an agonized rush, "I vill always be good to you."

Whether it was the man's shambling dignity or the small plea in his last words, no one ever knew. But she took his arm and pointed out her valise. They drove off in the carriage he'd hired.

In the next decade the couple had seven children and the townsfolk stopped calling the house a "Folly." Valborg was always seen with a grin and one small blond or another clinging to his massive hand. But hired help was almost impossible to find in Telluride and his wife clearly needed an army. Valborg decided she looked peaked and something would have to be done. They'd regretfully moved to Denver.

But few people needed a house that large, it was expensive to heat, and the location was all wrong. It had been standing empty for some time.

At first sight Isobel adored the kitchen with its immense black range and capacious pantries. Morna loved the whole house. A smiling but non–English-speaking Finnish woman with very red cheeks had opened every window and was removing the dustcovers from the furniture, polishing tables as she went. The smell of beeswax filled the air, and dust motes danced in the sunlight streaming in. Perennials from the neglected garden added their scents to the back rooms.

Clutching the side of her white, cornflower-sprinkled skirt so she could run from room to room, up and down staircases, Morna exclaimed over everything. She insisted that Berkeley and Isobel follow her to admire the tile in this bathroom, the molded ceiling in that bedroom, the size of the airing cupboards in the upper hallways, the carved newel post at the bottom of the stairs, only a little scuffed by climbing children's shoes. She was enchanted by the view from the tower windows in front, the sound of the murmuring river from the nursery rooms in the back. The gazebo would be perfect, she pronounced, for summer picnics.

Whirling with delight in one of the bedrooms at the top of the house, she stopped long enough to say, "Berkeley, each time I've passed this house, I've had to stop and stare at it, it's so beautiful. Like a ship about to take off under full sail. And I thought what a pity that it was empty. But how did you arrange on the fifth of July, after such a weekend, to find someone to open it, let alone someone to air it?"

"Why, it was nothing," he replied, grinning hugely and obviously pleased with himself. "If I put my mind to it, I can do anything." With mock theatricality he struck the histrionic pose so common with emotional actors, one arm upflung. "Shakespeare even had Owen Glendower—no doubt my ancestor—declare, 'I can summon spirits from the vasty deep!'"

Morna was at the doorway and about to leave the room for further exploration. But she paused long enough to answer over her shoulder. "Ah, yes, and I remember Hotspur's retort: 'Why, so can I, or so can any man; but will they come when you do call for them?'" Her light laugh followed her down the stairs.

"I knew," he said thoughtfully to the empty room, "that there was *some* reason we didn't educate women."

While she was admiring the filagreed chandelier in the dining room, Berkeley called to her from the overstuffed mohair couch in the parlor that he'd finally stretched out on in exhaustion. "Morna, my dear," he pleaded, "please come here. We do have to discuss something."

As she came into the room, he noticed that the hand holding up her skirt was, as she approached him, almost clenching the fabric into a knot. He sat up and, when she stood before him, gently unloosened her fingers. It was clear she was not looking forward to certain topics, their marriage for example, and was prepared to resist.

He took her hand, pressed his lips against her palm, pulled her down next to him. He ran her fingertips lightly over his own mouth.

"Yes?" she said expectantly. She was sitting upright, her back quite straight, even a little stiff. The small hand between his trembled slightly. "What did you want to discuss?"

"Wallpaper," he said gravely, slipping his fingers between hers, lacing their hands together. "That flowery pattern in the main bedroom will not do. Valborg must have been an excessively sentimental man to have chosen it. And then all those tangly vines and leaves. It makes one dizzy to look at it. Now, here"—he let his eyes wander speculatively around the room—"this silk has a nice golden sheen, although the design is quite rococo."

"I had not thought," she began, striving for equal gravity but with laughter bubbling up, "that while lying in bed you planned on staring at the walls. But I do assure you that if—"

It was then she discovered he'd slipped a ring on her left hand. The diamond was not large, but it sparkled in an ornate bed of deepest rubies, veined by the glittering metal that held them.

As she stared wordlessly at its glow, he said, "A rather old-fashioned ring, you see. This belonged to my mother, who wore it till her death. It wouldn't do for a modern marriage, but then our union is old. It began long before we met and will never end. The rubies are appropriate, Morna, for you are my heart's blood."

When Isobel hurried in from the kitchen she saw them entwined in each other's arms. She turned back promptly and continued her one-sided conversation with Helga, the smiling Finn. She was sure that if she raised her voice and enunciated carefully the woman *would* understand eventually.

And so had begun those happy months. The garden had become Isobel's Eden. Although the tomatoes remained miserably small without the warm nights they required, all the faster-growing plants sprang up in the rich soil. Peas and beans, onions and squash, grapes and berries. The branches of the fruit trees Valborg had planted were weighed down in the fall. Isobel hoed and weeded, then steamed and blanched, pickled and canned. What she could not grow, Berkeley brought in bushels from Denver, but he also talked to gardeners, brought her seeds and cuttings.

Not only the wide pantry shelves, but half the basement next to the newly built wine cellar, had jeweled jars of plums, pears, marmalades, applesauce, and jams of all kinds. All winter they had summer's bounty: raspberry-rhubarb pie, peach cobbler, cherry crisp. The sun parlor was now heated in the winter so Isobel had her own conservatory. She had pots of cheerful geraniums, double violets, tiny peppers, and fresh herbs.

She found they needed all her efforts could produce. Berkeley Glendower was a hospitable man, and most of the businessmen coming to Telluride came alone. So he brought them, friends and clients, to dinner. And Morna asked them about their families, their work, played on the gleaming new grand piano in the parlor for them, sang their favorite songs. Everyone who came to the mining town looked forward to their next trip.

The ladies on the north side, of course, did not come, but when Grace Nordstrom visited, as she frequently did, her next at-home was so crowded that there was no room to sit. The women of quality were forced to stand, teacups in hand, straining to hear what Grace had to say about the couple who lived in what had once been a long time ago, Valborg's Folly.

Morna had made the lovely house bloom again. Under her eye some of the rooms were repainted and repapered, some of the furniture removed. On his trips Berkeley unendingly searched for the lamp or table whose exact specifications she'd given him. The handsome, solid pieces of oak and mahogany were now surrounded with airy space and bowls of fresh flowers. Paintings of dramatic vistas of mountains and lakes in enormous gilt frames enlarged the parlor and dining room.

Only a few modern touches had been needed. A telephone was put in, and the steam heat extended to the sun parlor so that Isobel could use it as a small conservatory in the winter. Electric lights, which already brightened the downstairs, were added to the upper floors.

When Freda came to tea, Isobel always sent her back with a package of scones, but she still grumbled endlessly about the quality of her new cook's pastry. She even declared she was losing weight. Isobel was smiling at that thought when she jerked awake as the glycerin bottle fell from her fingers and rolled across the carpet. And she heard the first tiny whimpers from the crib next to Morna's bed. Even before she reached it, she was whispering soothing Scots phrases.

CHAPTER 14

"Oh, Issy, do let me hold her now." Wincing, Morna pulled herself up and, settling herself gingerly, leaned against the pillows piled in front of the ornate brass headboard. Her pallor seemed even more extraordinary against the black sheen of her now unruly curls, the deepened gray of her eyes, and the darkness of her lashes. Yet she seemed to glow inwardly, and there was a liveliness in her voice as she pushed up the lace-trimmed edges of the leg-of-mutton sleeves of her nightdress. "Surely the doctor can't object to my sitting up a very few minutes. The second she's ready to be fed, I'll lie right back down to nurse her."

"Weell," Isobel drew out the word grudgingly before putting the baby, dressed in a tiny crocheted cap and a long white gown with the same crocheting at the collar, in her mother's stretched out arms.

"Isn't she beautiful," Morna breathed, trying not to clutch the infant too tightly in her joy. "My beautiful, beautiful Bridget. Not only is your name, Bridget Isobel, the prettiest name, but you've grown more lovely every hour since you were born. First child born in this new century! Oh, my dear Bridey, just wait till your father sees you. Surely that's his nose, Issy, and the jaw too! I can't wait until he gets here, although I suppose tomorrow is the soonest, if he gets the letter on today's train."

Isobel nodded happily, but she thought privately that it was a very good thing that Berkeley Glendower had been in Denver during the actual birth. He'd have been out of his mind with worry, and there'd have been no way of keeping that man out of the room. Some things it was best not to see, if there was nothing to do about them. Morna had had a hard time of it, the baby's head in the wrong position, and Dr. Wade unreachable up at an accident at the Tomboy. He'd only arrived after the event and given Morna a few drops of laudanum to send her to an exhausted sleep.

But it'd all come right, Isobel thought. Still, if it'd not been that Morna had insisted on a brief walk to see the New Year's fireworks, against all of her own objections, they would not have been near Freda's when she'd crumpled up in pain. And without Freda, Isobel was not sure all would have turned out so well. And May, too, who with her experience on an Iowa farm, had known how to help. She herself had only been at one birthing, an easy one of Florrie's, and was not aware of the dangers of a baby getting caught in the umbilical cord.

So it'd certainly been best that Mr. Berkeley had been sent off so firmly after Christmas. Miss Morna had said that, after all, the baby wasn't due for three weeks and there she was in no size or shape to be attending any turn-of-the-century fêtes, and he had business to look after. Now, as Isobel sank back down in the chair at the foot of the bed, she couldn't think of a blessed thing to worry about.

But she immediately leapt back up in alarm at Morna's muffled cry. Having gone from examining each tiny fingernail, the proud mother had taken off the baby's cap and was looking at the back of the small, perfect head. "Oh, Issy, Issy, what have I done? It was my walking through the cold, I'm sure, and now she's marked. It was all my fault! I should have listened to you. Look!"

Isobel peered at the dark red blotch on the back of the infant's head, clearly visible through the fine dark hair. "It's a strawberry mark," she said matter-of-factly.

"Strawberries!" Morna gasped. "I ate bowlfuls last summer. I knew better. I'd heard that one shouldn't, but then I didn't believe it. Of course, I wasn't just sure then that . . . But anyway I should have—"

"Now, now, you'll be upsetting the bairn," Isobel interrupted sharply, as the tiny girl whimpered. "I can no' believe it's what you ate. You have the same mark yourself. Haven't I seen it often enough brushing your hair? Give her to me." She took back the baby proprietorially.

"I do?" Morna said in surprise. "I've never seen it."

"And no more will little Bridey but when she looks for it. With the hair you've got, not to mention Mr. Berkeley's, she'll not be able to find it." She covered the little head with one freckled hand and rubbed her cheek against the newborn's satiny one. "We'd best put the cap back on, a bit of a chill in here. I'll stir up the fire and put on another log. Let her suckle—it'll bring in your milk."

At last, with the baby back in her crib, and Isobel gently swinging it with her foot, the peaceful crackle of the fireplace pine became the only sound in the room.

That was interrupted by frantic knuckles rapping on the door. Berkeley Glendower burst in, and before Morna could more than raise herself on her elbows, she was enveloped in an embrace of the fresh coldness of his broadcloth coat and the warmth of his panting breaths. "Oh, my dear, are you all right? Of course you're not." After raining kisses on her face, he caught sight of her unusual paleness. His own face turned ashen. "I'll never forgive myself for going. How could I have?" He almost crushed her in anxiety, and she could not get a word in to reassure him. "And yet, it was the strangest thing," he said, his face in her hair. "There I was, toasting the new century, and I suddenly put down the champagne. I heard you, Morna, I swear! But the early train was late and—"

"Mr. Berkeley!" Isobel tugged at his shoulder indignantly and almost pushed him into the wooden chair she'd brought up by the bedside. "Flat on her back she should be, the doctor said."

Distracted, consumed with apprehension because despite Freda's reassurances when he'd come, he'd seen her tired eyes and grim mouth, he sat looking from one to the other dumbly. Morna reached out and stroked his cheek, and Isobel fussed him out of his coat. But the panic he'd endured during the long hours of pacing at the train station, cursing the distance that lay between him and Telluride, did not vanish, only lessened a little. Morna's fragility was too evident, and the shock of pain lingered in her eyes. He felt he had to hold her, to infuse his own vigor and strength into her by that touch, as well as to reassure himself that she was here and alive.

Then Isobel scooped up the infant and laid her in his awkward arms. He stared at his daughter in besotted wonder. Pink satin ribbon had been threaded through the soft yarn of the tiny crocheted cap on her head, and the face framed by it seemed to him wholly flowerlike in its delicate perfection. But the skin beneath his fingers was softer than new petals, the mouth far more exquisite than any rosebud, he thought. "For months," he said as if to himself, "I've been peering at babies whenever I got the chance, but I could never have imagined this . . . amazing child. And she's *ours*."

Watching him like a man enchanted, unwilling to move or breathe lest a dream might fade, Isobel swallowed hard. "I'll get some tea," she said, and hurried out with an attempt at briskness.

By the time she returned with a tray laden with milk toast for Morna and much thicker slices with melted cheddar for him, Berkeley was lying full length on the outside of the bed, still dressed in his black formal attire of the evening before. His once stiffly starched waistcoat was now wrinkled, but his trousers with the silk braid were still neatly creased. He'd only removed his shoes, and lying there with his feet in black silk socks hanging over the end of the damask coverlet, he looked elegant as usual, but not at all his usual self. Bridey lay snuggled uncomplainingly between her parents, each of whom had a hand curled over one of hers.

"I must think," he was saying, studying the ceiling, "what to get her for such a birthday. First child of the century. And, come to think of it, a Monday's child. Fair of face. Of course, with such a mother, she'd have that no matter what day of the week she'd been born." Raising himself up, he continued, "Don't scold, Isobel. It was the only way to keep Morna down. She would be leaning over every five seconds to point out the baby's fingernails, toes—"

"But I have to sit up to eat," Morna interjected, "and I'm starved."

"Good sign," he said approvingly, edging off the bed so as not to disturb the baby. "And if you are very good and eat every bit of this lovely . . ."—he eyed the soggy toast doubtfully, but continued, "well, it smells deliciously cinnamony—then comes the surprise."

Isobel whisked Bridey off with her to the rocking chair, feeling it was definitely her turn to hold her namesake. Morna struggled to a sitting position, smiling at him. "I could have *that* first. It would improve my appetite."

"No, no, my girl." He placed the white wicker tray legs carefully over her lap and put two enormous sham-covered pillows behind her. "Tea and toast now. Surprises are always dessert."

Then, to keep him from hovering over her until she'd swallowed every morsel, Morna waved him to his chair, saying she had to hear about the success of his current venture. Although the Hyde-Whites and their set had pulled their funds from western-slope mining ventures at the news of Berkeley's divorce, he had a number of Denver backers interested in his expertise. But what excited him far more were the engineering problems at the mines. He often worked for the huge Smuggler-Union Company as well as for the Tomboy, which had been bought by the Rothschilds of Europe under the name of the London Exploration Company. He found a ready listener in Morna, who loved his eagerness in exploring efficient solutions. And right now, feeling the agitation he tried to hide, she knew how much he needed distraction.

Between approving crunches of his own toast he described the interest shown by the bankers in his sketches for hydroelectric power. In his enthusiasm some of his color returned, his dark hair tumbled unnoticed over his forehead, and his brown eyes were flecked with light. "And," he finished triumphantly, "Lord Rothschild himself will be coming in late spring to have a look. The haut monde of Denver is already atwitter. Laughton Powell is communing daily with his wine cellar. Elaborate dinners are being planned. But, I know this, he won't get better food than Isobel's when he arrives here."

Although Isobel swallowed dryly at the thought of a lord coming to dinner, she'd become an accomplished all-around cook. She kept up a constant recipe exchange with Florrie in Louisville, who picked up good ones in her rounds as a minister's wife. Then there was the occasional prized cookbook—although few were published—that Berkeley found in his forays through the book stores as he added to their library. Red-cheeked, cheerful Helga, although her English was still uncertain, knew her way around in the kitchen, and even though Isobel brushed the happy compliments of the guests away lightly, she was delighted by them.

"Do you know, Isobel"—Glendower was now leaning over her for yet another amazed look at Bridey—"that Patrick Alexander says he still dreams of your whitefish fillets in gooseberry and sorrel sauce? Between your cooking and the way the moon rises in his eyes when he sees Morna, he'd give me every spare dollar he had to invest so that he could come weekly to Telluride. Being Patrick, of course, he never has a *spare* dollar. He grumbles that it's due to the size of his wife Belle's dress allowance. I myself think the problem may be that Patrick likes a chancy interesting investment more than one that simply pays interest. But, my love," he said, smiling at Morna, hopeful at his every glance that she would look less wan, "he sends his best regards to you, as does Theo Manningham."

Unsure whether a second cup of tea was on the allowed list, Morna was pouring herself one quietly so that Isobel wouldn't notice. "How is Theo?" she asked, wanting the conversation to go on, wanting that newly etched furrow to disappear from Berkeley's forehead. "It must be fully a year since I've seen him. He's married now, isn't he? Happily, I hope?"

"Yes and no." Berkeley thoughtfully loosened the white linen bow tie around his high wing collar as he paced before the fireplace. "His father-in-law, George Bender, had serious business setbacks, which were not evident until after the marriage. Theo must have blanched when he learned how bad things were. His own income is not sizable, I think. At any rate, his young wife, Elizabeth, openly complains at what she sees as a narrow style of living."

"But"—he paused in his restless walking to poke at the fire— "Theo has, of necessity, thrown himself into promoting the Montclair lots that had not been selling well. Not only does he like it, he's quite good at it. I detect a first-class business mind behind that fresh and guileless face. I doubt that he ever had much interest in the Yorkshire wool industry, and now he's been forced into congenial work. Their fortunes should improve eventually."

Taking three conifer cones from the basket-weave oak mantel, he put them into the flames and waited for their piny scent to snap through the room. He tried to think of what else to say to engage Morna. He could not stop the feeling that she'd somehow been hurled a dark distance from him, and that he needed to pull her back to their warm hearth. "Ah, yes," he added, "Theo's had a recent letter from Stanton Caley. He's still in Europe." When Morna and Berkeley had taken the house together, Caley had left town abruptly and never returned.

"Is Colette still traveling with him? Did he say?"

"Yes, indeed. Stanton groaned for several paragraphs at the cost of her wardrobe. And she's found an expensive new process to lighten her hair. Apparently, she has also taken to calling herself Céline and has become the very model of a respectable French lady. Somehow I'm not surprised."

He turned to inspect Morna's tray. "Yes," he said, lifting it off the bed, "I believe this empty dish merits the dessert course." Putting the tray on the nightstand, he walked quickly toward the door, but paused before opening it. "Now, you mustn't be put off by the box. I'd intended to find one of hand-tooled leather in Denver, but some people *will* rush things and have babies before they are due."

When he returned, he was carrying a shiny rectangular metal strongbox, and he handed it to Morna without a word. The small heart-shaped padlock was loose on the hasp, and she slipped it off and lifted the lid. Inside lay a collection of thick parchment, each piece with a bright gold seal. Studying them, one by one, she looked at Berkeley in amazement. "Why, these are mining claims! Here's the one for the Champion mine. And for Sweepstakes!"

"Yes," he said, unable to hide his pleasure. "Every one that has ever been recorded on Bridget's Mountain. It took some time to find each owner and see if they were willing to sell. But now no one can lift a pick there without your permission."

Running her finger over the embossed seals, she breathed, "Berkeley, it must have taken you months. And it's wonderful to own these. I can't believe this. How long do they run for?"

"Forever. Or as long as you pay a small fee at the courthouse each year to record them." He settled down beside her on the edge of the bed and stretched his arm around her, looking at the box's contents with her. "To be honest, they're not worth much. None of those who tried found either silver or gold anywhere in Ute Rise Canyon. That's why they were all willing to give them up and were, in fact, surprised anyone would pay for them. But now you own all the mineral rights, as well as all the rocks on top of whatever is there."

"Not worth much!" Words poured from her in her excitement. "Berkeley, this is a priceless gift. One I would have wanted above all, and never could have imagined receiving. And it's for me and for Bridey. She can give it to her daughter, and she to hers. Its beauty can be enjoyed every day, it will never change or diminish. The joy of seeing it will never be less." She was gazing at the inside of the box as if it held the magnificence of the mountain. "And if any of the Utes return to their sacred mountains, they will find that one, at least, just as it was when they left their homeland."

He brushed aside her hair so he could kiss her cheek. "I'm happy that you're happy. As for the Utes, I can say this. Without any producing mines the water in that stream will run as clear as the day—that fortunate day—when we both fell in it."

She turned her face to his. Before kissing him she murmured in delight, "Thank you, my love, for Bridget's Mountain. Though now we'll call it *Bridey's* Mountain. What woman ever had such a present?"

He put both hands on her cheeks and returned the kiss. "Thank *you* for Bridey. She's the best gift by far."

CHAPTER 15

"Bridget Isobel, be reasonable," Berkeley implored the toddler astride his knees facing him, "this horse is tired. He needs his oats, although from the delicious odor of chicken and sage wafting from the kitchen, I don't think dried grass is what Isobel is going to give him for dinner, thank heavens." He took a deep breath, inhaling the scent.

Bridey pressed one dimpled finger hopefully on her father's her-ringbone trousers and looked up at him under thick lashes. She had the delicate elfin charm so often misleading in tiny girls because it can disguise a resolve usually thought of as masculine. At two she had eyes so shiny brown, they held the light, hair not quite as dark as either of her parents'. She'd inherited her mother's fine features and, under a childish roundness, her father's determined jaw. As evidence that this was not simply a physical characteristic, she tapped his thigh again and asked sweetly, "Giddyap?"

"One last time," he sighed and began by enveloping each small hand with one of his. "This is the way the farmers ride, hobbledehoy, hobbledehoy." To imitate the plodding gait he lifted first one knee and then the other, slowly bouncing Bridey. She pressed her lips together in gleeful anticipation of the next step of the game, her current favorite.

They were in the back parlor, and the burning logs shone on the polished crimson tiles surrounding the fireplace, picked up bright threads in the glossy wallpaper, turned the incised flowers in the beveled edges of the mirrors into prisms of light. High on the wall electric bulbs in lily-shaped sconces cast a diffused glow on glass-framed panels depicting golden birds and scarlet butterflies. The room held the comfortable leather sofa and chairs already well worn by the Valborg children. Because of its snugness, its warmth of color, the family gathered here in the evening.

"And this is the way the ladies ride, la da da, la da da," Berkeley sang, knees pressed together in a prim jog. The child held her back erect, a grin starting. The rich reds of the room tinted her white flowing nightdress with its elaborately tucked bodice a rosy pink and touched her cheeks with the same color.

"This is the way the gentlemen ride," her father pronounced in a deepened voice, "clip, clip, clip." Bridey's small body rose in the brisk canter, and a giggle escaped with each uplift. "And this is the way the cowboys ride, whoo-ha, whoo-ha, whoo-ha." Now screaming with laughter, the toddler almost flew in the air with each high bounce. When Berkeley stopped in exhaustion, she slid forward, now clutching his lapels, still hiccuping joyfully. He stroked her tumbling curls happily.

Isobel stood frowning in the doorway. "It's nae been so long since she finished her porridge, and it's lucky that's not down the front of your wool suit."

"Not my fault," he said, raising a hand. "She insisted, and it's not in me to say no to beautiful women. Speaking of which, her mother promised to try on her new gown quickly before dinner, and where is she?"

"Oh, this is perfect for tomorrow night's performance, Berkeley!" Morna's voice floated down the staircase ahead of her, and then her heels clicked across the terrazzo floor of the foyer and down the hall. She hurried in, paused for effect, and then swirled in a circle, saying happily, "I can't imagine how you always know just what I want!"

The white satin princess gown was nipped in at the waist, then spread out to a wide embroidered hem. The enormous billowy sleeves were black lace over white satin, and wide black velvet ribbons started over each shoulder, were bowed at the sides of the lace that just covered her bosom, and fell in long streamers to the edge of the dress. Her exquisite pale face was framed by the stiff ruffle of ebony lace that encircled her neck, and there were snowy bird-of-paradise plumes in her dark upswept curls. Her white suede gloves were elbow length, and she carried a feathery white ostrich fan.

Bridey scrambled from her father's lap and caught up the end of a velvet ribbon in one chubby hand, dancing sideways as if it were a Maypole band. Morna peeked playfully down at her over the edge of the spread-out fan. Berkeley announced with satisfaction, "You are a poem in black and white, my dear, and far too elegant for the loft of Stubbs and Jakway's warehouse. Still, it's because of your far too well-attended musical evenings that they're finally building a true Opera House in the spring. I can't wait for the comfortable box seats they're promising."

Isobel was examining the covered buttons on the back of the dress, but apparently the workmanship met with her grudging approval. "Needs a bit of pressing on the seams, more than likely," she reflected. "And now, Miss Bridget"—she reached down for the child—"it's time for a bit of warm milk and bed."

Eluding her grasp, Bridey rushed over and clung to her father's calf. "Giddyap?" she asked him again, sure that where her doting father was concerned, it was worth a try.

"No more tonight, my love," he replied. "But tomorrow, perhaps the two of us could ride on Druid." He looked at the two women who were eyeing him severely. "For the end of February it's quite a thaw, and you could bundle her up well. She'll sit in front of me, and I'll wrap her in the sides of my beaver coat. We'll just stop by at Freda's and a few stores," he said persuasively.

When neither responded, he continued, "In the morning I only have to go to the Liberty Bell, and as it's so close, I'll be back to take her just as she's up from her nap. Poor child, she's been cooped up all through this last storm. She'll be as skittish as Chevalier when he finally got out for exercise."

Morna had to grin at the comparison. Because of the constant snow she and Berkeley had not been able to take the horses for their usual brisk runs. She'd declared yesterday, that if she'd not held him so tightly, Chevalier would have pranced with her to California.

But he could see that Isobel was framing her familiar worries about the cold air, being of the school that regarded it as unhealthy for children as it was for flowers. Before she could get in even one of her many words on the subject, he ended with an emotional appeal. "Besides, with the black wreaths everywhere, the town's so gloomy. All the merchants will be cheered by the sight of her."

Three months previously a fire at the Smuggler mine had killed twenty-eight men, some of them would-be rescuers. A load of hay had burst into flame at the mouth of the Bullion adit and set fire to adjoining buildings. Drafts sucked flame and smoke down the heavily timbered tunnel. Two mule drivers immediately cut their animals loose from the ore carts and whipping them furiously while hanging on to their tails, were pulled roughshod to safety. The rest of those inside were suffocated, as were the men who went in to save them. All the streetlamps in the town were draped in evergreen boughs with black bows, and the winter had been a long unsmiling season for everyone.

"Well," said Morna, with a glance at Isobel, both remembering how few children lived in the camp, how warmly Bridey was welcomed everywhere.

Berkeley leaned down and rubbed his nose against his daughter's pert one. "That's settled. We'll go to the clothing emporium and see Uncle Axel."

Bridey beamed and managed to get out a version of "lollypop." "Yes!" Berkeley responded with as much pride as if she'd rattled off a paragraph. "He will definitely give you a lollypop. But you must go off now with Isobel. Tomorrow cannot come until you sleep."

"Horse," she reminded him firmly over Isobel's shoulder as she was borne off.

Morna slipped the feathers from her hair and began stripping off her gloves as she sank into the plump couch next to Berkeley. He put a hand into the inside pocket of his suit jacket, saying, "The dress is not all I brought from Denver. See here, you've been reviewed quite favorably in the *Denver Times*. I'm sure you were unaware you were performing last weekend for an out-of-town critic. He exalts you over Miss Jenny Lind, the Swedish Nightingale."

He handed her a clipping that was headlined boldly AN AMERICAN NIGHTINGALE! The reporter mentioned that he had been in Telluride to bring back mining reports and had happened to wander into the upstairs of a lumber warehouse, which, to his expressed amazement, had the effrontery to call itself an Opera House. But, after looking down his nose at the rough wooden boards that comprised most of the seating and the knocked-together stage, he waxed effusive over the singing of Miss Morna Gregory.

Here, dear readers, he enthused, *on this crude platform, was a singer with hardly an equal. Hers is a voice of transcendent sweetness, variety, and the supreme power of impressing itself on the inmost fiber of our beings.* He praised each of her selections—from ballad to dance-hall tune—throwing in frequent references to the liquid notes of the bird extolled by Keats, Wordsworth, and Coleridge, and ended with a reference to Shelley's skylark.

"Goodness," Morna said, clearly pleased, but unable to suppress a giggle, "I little knew I could 'bring the listener into a mysterious sympathy with things beyond our understanding.' Perhaps the man didn't catch all the lyrics."

"Well, the poor fellow was overcome with your beauty," Glendower pointed out with some pride, "as he notes. You have avid fans everywhere. Stubbs was telling me that the photograph of you in the glass case by the door was pilfered. It wasn't a good one, anyway. That elaborate hat obscured your face. We'll have a new one taken in this gown."

But Morna shivered at what was obviously a troubling idea. "Why would anyone steal that picture, Berkeley? You don't think it was that reporter and that he plans to run it later in the paper? Who knows, a copy might find its way abroad."

"Morna," he pounded his knee with an angry fist, "I promised you I would bury this subject because it ends in either your tears or your silence. But it maddens me that you live in this state of fear. It has been four years that you've been here. Why will you not tell me where—"

"No." She sprang up in agitation. "No, I will not. And to sue for divorce would require me to disclose my whereabouts."

She whirled and knelt before him, taking his hands in hers, forcing him to look into her eyes. She knew she had to tell him now enough of the truth and not too much. "Whether he finds me or you find him, it will end in tragedy. Four years is nothing. He has the patience of a saint, as well as the cunning of the devil, and all the fiendish concentration of the mad. It is for that reason—that he *lacks* reason—that I'm doomed to protect him if I can."

The white satin of her dress pooled in the firelight, taking on its color, so she looked surrounded by a ring of flame. Suddenly, the serenity of that civilized parlor was swept away, and in her transparent gray eyes Glendower saw the image of a man, one who loved her as he himself did, one who felt, too, that he could not live without her. With a chill of empathy he seemed to hear that man's bitter howl echoing over land and sea. Yet that understanding did not prevent a fierce, feral upsurge to fight and destroy him, by gun or knife, or most satisfyingly, bare hands on the throat. He sat still, shaken by that desire, that awareness.

"I know he will not give up, would die first," Morna was saying, her low voice urgent, desperate to press her case. "But he would come here, and he is plausible. That is what is so frightening. He would even find supporters. He would goad you every day. Eventually, Berkeley, you would win. You always have. But how could I live happily, knowing I was responsible for his death?"

Morna shut her eyes in pain, but also so he could not read there all that she dreaded to dwell on. Bridey kidnapped, taken to the island where the laird she'd married was the law. He could maintain that the child was conceived while they were married and was therefore his. She could as well imagine Berkeley in a dock, in a court that would not look kindly on a lover who had killed an outraged husband. And there was the too vivid nightmare, which she was not sure was merely dream or true vision, of Berkeley dead by the laird's wiles and deceit. In that case she felt she could not live at all. But these were things she would not say. She had never even told Berkeley her husband's name.

She added only, anguished tears sliding from her closed eyes, "For now, please, my love, do as I ask!"

With the lace ruff, the too pale face, she looked like a stricken Renaissance queen. He pressed her head to his chest. "For now," he muttered unwillingly.

In the morning there was a promise of sun in the predawn sky on the edge of the mountains and an unusual warmth for the last day of February. Fetching in the wood for the back-parlor fireplace, Isobel was surprised at the almost spring feel of the air on her cheek. She was taken aback, too, because she'd barely put the johnnycake on the coals when she saw Berkeley cranking the kitchen phone and talking to the operator. It was only a little more than half after six, and he usually waited to have a proper breakfast with Morna when he had only the Liberty Bell to go to. It was much the closest of the three big mines, only a mile from town up a steep trail. But then she remembered he'd wanted an early start to take Bridey riding.

He waved away the eggs and sausage she'd taken out to cook, wanting only the cake and coffee. And that wasn't usual, especially because last night she'd noticed that he, and Miss Morna for that matter, had picked at their dinner and she had left most of the chicken. Of course (Isobel's thoughts raced ahead), that would do cut up fine for Bridey's lunch with plenty left over for some nice light chicken fritters. And a soup, maybe velvet soup, because with Morna singing that evening, *she'd* be in no mood to eat.

At this hour of the morning Isobel always planned the day's food; it was hard for her to get her mind on much else. So much had to be begun early. And usually when Mr. Berkeley was there in the kitchen with his coffee, he'd insist on hearing the menu, saying it set him up for the day, knowing what he had to look forward to. He seemed to enjoy watching her checking the larder and the root cellar, inspecting the level in the flour bin, peering in her pride and joy—a wall chest of spices— with one drawer for each, that had been filled at the end of summer.

But this morning he'd only gulped his coffee and shrugged his beaver coat over his heavy suit before hurrying out the walk on his way to the stables three blocks down. She had to run after him with his wool muffler and a wrapped piece of johnnycake for Sam Goler. Halfway back to the kitchen she recalled she was clear out of pearl sago for the velvet soup. That concern had pushed all other considerations aside, until it occurred to her that rice, cooked well and pulverized, would do as well for a smooth base. And she was again launched well into the new day.

Berkeley was already on the slippery path to the mine, staring moodily as he rode at the frozen gray contortions of Cornet Creek alongside him, when he heard the thundering roar of the avalanche. After the sudden shock that made him pull the horse up, stop while the air itself seemed to vibrate, he told himself that it was not the disaster it seemed. An avalanche was almost to be expected, given this winter's heavy snows, and now this slight warming. South-facing slopes were dangerous under these conditions. He knew that the Liberty Bell had routinely survived other slides.

The one flat place on that mountainside where all its wooden buildings had to be crowded was only two acres at best. A large boardinghouse, another bunkhouse, the ore crusher, the tram terminal building, and the shops and offices were huddled under the sawtoothed outline of St. Sophia's ridge. But there was a gulch, some twenty feet deep, that sliced down from that ominous ridge and then veered off to the right. Usually the slides just filled the gulch and then boomed off down the course away from the mine. In the back of the buildings was a stand of trees that showed no sign of avalanche scars. It was only the noise that was appalling.

But there was something about the quality of silence after the deafening boom and then the sound of panicked shouts that caused Berkeley to 'dig his heels into Druid's unwilling sides. They made the best speed possible up that vertical track, and what he heard as he neared the flat froze his marrow.

At the top he could barely take in what he saw. Most of what had been a busy cleared worksite was now a forbidding mountain of high-piled snow. The tall boardinghouse braced on stilts, which must have been filled with men changing shifts, some going to bed, others getting ready for the day's work, had been swept down the slope and covered. It was as if it had never existed. The ore crusher and tram terminal were gone. The bunkhouse, pushed aside as if by a huge, swatting hand, lay in crumpled ruins. This time the gulch had filled too rapidly and the overflow had come crashing down on the Liberty Bell.

Some men were yelling, pawing frantically at the snow to dig as quickly as they could to save those still alive. Others were wading hip deep through drifts, struggling to the shop to find shovels and poles to locate their buried workmates. But Berkeley could see, even as he tied the horse and ran forward, that there were not enough to help. Rescue had to come quickly, if it came. Even if a man survived the violence of the impact and was lucky enough to be surrounded by an air pocket, thirty minutes was the most he could last buried alive.

As he dashed through an open space toward the shop, he caught sight of the still-intact telephone lines. Already the firebell would have clanged, rounded up the men in town. Dr. Wade might already be on his way up. A chance, a chance. All he could think of was the desperate need to hurry. He felt his own throat constrict at the fate of the entombed men, crushed beneath a paralyzing weight, gasping for air, unable to push away the deadly, suffocating snow.

Grabbing a pile of sturdy saplings stripped for just such an emergency, he began pulling the scrambling diggers nearest him into a ragged line. He thrust a pole into their hands so that each section of the ground could be probed.

But before he could plunge into the drifts to join them, a short, bearded miner staggered into the clearing, eyes blind with shock, lungs gasping for breath in the thin air. Slung onto his back, clutched by one arm and leg, was an unconscious man. The snow behind the rescuer was stained with red blood, almost obscene in its brightness, pouring from the injured man. "Wait, wait," Berkeley shouted. "Put him down here. Let's have a look."

In a stupor the rescuer obediently laid his burden, not ungently, on the hardpack of the clearing by the shop. They both gaped at a jagged stump where there'd once been an arm. "I din't know, I din't," the miner gabbled. "Just tugged him out, humped 'im on me back. Mebbe I can find—" He dazedly turned as if to lurch back.

"No, never mind." Berkeley caught at him, trying to keep his own voice calm. "It won't do any good. Get a piece of kindling from that woodpile, bring it here." Kneeling down, stripping off his gloves, yanking off his tie, he began to fashion a rough tourniquet below the shoulder. He took the thin twig he was handed, tightened it, prayed the spurting blood to stop. His own hands were covered with it, his shirt cuffs soaked with it, and yet there seemed more than one man could hold already crimsoning the icy ground.

The rescuer was stooping beside him, and with his thick mitten he clumsily but carefully brushed snow from the injured man's eyes and nose. As he peered down, unnoticed tears soaked his gingery mustache and the prickles of his beard. With the snow wiped away Berkeley recognized with pain the young face of an engineer in training from the Colorado School of Mines. "He alive?" the miner asked with more fear than hope.

"You saved him," Berkeley replied with more assurance than he felt. "The doctor'll soon be here. We've just got to get him to someplace warm." Between the two of them they trundled the injured man into the office, already a hospital, then rushed back to help the others.

Miners and clerks, managers and assayers, and every available townsman worked frantically. At first they were heartened by success. Whenever a pole struck an inert object, they began a frantic shoveling. Eight survivors were pulled out. But as hours that seemed minutes passed, and all their discoveries were corpses, they did not let up their breathless pace. It was the hope that some man lay beneath a lucky brace of broken boards that let in air, held up the weight, that kept them going. The dead, they knew, would wait, and some of them would not be found until the spring melt.

For the women waiting in Telluride the morning was interminable, each hour a day. The first news, after the foreboding clangor of the firebell, was brought to Isobel by a white-faced Grace Nordstrom, come to collect whatever they could supply for the townswomen setting up the Sheridan Hotel as a makeshift hospital. Then Isobel, clutching Morna, repeated and repeated that Berkeley must be safe. By seven-thirty he could only have been on the trail to the mine, she knew.

But Pacific Avenue, where they lived, was lined with four-room bungalows, five of them the homes of married miners who worked at the Liberty Bell, none with phones. Morna sent Isobel and Helga, whose brawny Finnish husband worked at the distant Tomboy mine, to their doors. They gathered the shaken women from their houses, drew them in for coffee, fresh-baked scones that went largely uneaten, and a difficult wait by the telephone.

Isobel, who normally would not let even Helga make a crust in her kitchen realm, pleaded she needed help with the cold meat pies to be sent to the Sheridan when the injured were brought down. In the homely tasks of flouring hands, kneading and rolling, the time passed.

On occasion a harassed Dr. Wade at the mine would have to ring through to the central operator to get her to arrange supplies to be taken to the Sheridan, ready for when the pack train arrived with the injured. He also gave her the names of those he was treating. The operator would call immediately with the news.

The two women who learned their husbands were at least alive tried almost guiltily to hide their joyous relief in the somber house. Morna played a ringing hymn of thanksgiving. As their voices rose in "A Mighty Fortress Is Our God," all found comfort in hope.

Bridey, as children do, knew from the adults' stony gravity that she should be quiet too. She even seemed to accept what Isobel said about her looked-for ride being put off until another day. There was no shortage of willing laps to hold her, eager fingers to turn the pages of her favorite picture books for her. Everyone ached for a distraction. Small animals were cut out for her from the leftover scraps of pastry and then baked. After lunch, replete with the sugared treats, she went without a complaint to her nap.

It was just as Isobel was closing the door to the toddler's room after putting her down that Morna came flying, ashen faced, up the stairs. She stopped at the top, and her eyes grew unfocused, her arms clutched her opposite elbows as if she would otherwise split in two. "Oh, Issy," she was gasping, incoherent, "something's very wrong on the mountain. . . . It's Berkeley—"

"But I didn't hear the phone, nor the door. How d'ye know?" Isobel's arms goosefleshed even under her brown woolen jersey at the sight of Morna's staring eyes.

"I don't know . . . but I'm *sure*. I was just going into the kitchen, and it was as if I was struck blind and deaf. But it's him, it's him, not me."

"Nae, nae," Isobel soothed, gathering the shaking woman into an embrace. "It's not himself that's hurt or going to be. It's just that he's there, with all those poor souls, and he feels it too strong. And now you feel it too." Being Gaelic herself, she'd never doubted that some were gifted, or cursed, with flashes of second sight.

"I'll brew up some tea," she went on. "You feel chilled through. But it'd be best if ye'd lie down a bit in the bedroom under the quilts."

Morna looked at her oddly and replied slowly. "Yes, I'd better go to the bedroom. I need to change."

"Weel, yes." Isobel eyed the thin cashmere of the dark blue dress. "Best put on the purple kersey with the double sleeves. It'll be good and warm. I'll be up in a bit with the tea. Likely everyone could use some."

But when she opened the oaken armoire, Morna took out her winter riding habit. She let her dress fall to the floor and quickly slipped on a high-necked, tea-rose suede blouse. She knotted a matching scarf around her neck. Slipping on her black wool divided skirt, she sat on the bed's edge and tugged on calf-high black boots. Then she donned a shirred beaver vestee and, over that, a black bolero jacket. But she left her riding hat on the wardrobe shelf and, standing by a north-facing window, gazed fixedly at St. Sophia's Ridge.

By early afternoon Berkeley's arms felt like leaden weights and the sweat was a torrent beneath his clothes. He'd long ago taken off his bulky outer coat, but he was layered in a tweed jacket, vest, and heavy underwear. The young assayer laboring next to him, his stiff collar wildly askew, was dripping, too, and they stopped together to wipe a handful of snow across their faces. Berkeley savored the coolness on his eyelids that eased the ache of the snow's insistent gleam. Opening his eyes, he found the glare, along with his extreme fatigue, was making his vision shimmer.

Hearing a disturbed whinnying, he glanced over to where the horses were tied some distance away at the head of the trail, suspecting it might be Chevalier. The gelding, along with all the horses stabled at Jackson's, had been commandeered to bring volunteers to the mine. Extra horses would be needed as well to bring down the disabled. The roan, he knew, would be unhappy at the long, cold wait.

He saw the gelding's head upraised, tugging fiercely at the reins looped around a tree. To his amazement he could see Morna standing next to Chevalier. He blinked, sure that his exhausted eyes were betraying him. No, it was she in her customary riding apparel, rose scarf tied around her throat. But she was hatless. It could only mean, he thought, his heart dropping, that something had happened to Bridey, and she'd raced up to get him, forgetting all else.

But even as he dropped his pole, ran wildly toward her, his thoughts jumbling, he wondered how she had come. He reached the path's icy surface, slipped sideways, looked down to get his footing, looked up to call out to her, and found she was gone.

It was then the mountain shrugged again. Berkeley could see the men, staring up, open mouthed in horror, at the snow roaring down toward them. The young assayer he'd been standing next to had not even time to throw up his hands in a vain attempt to ward it off when the white death slammed down.

Late that night, when Berkeley with numb lips told Morna what had happened, he finished by saying that the assayer had been swept far down, killed instantly. "If I'd not thought I'd seen you and run to the horses, I would have died as well," he said, his voice unsteady. She only clung desperately to him, saying nothing.

Some years later, repeating the story to Isobel, he approached some understanding of what finally happened. Isobel understood even more clearly.

CHAPTER 16

As he walked with a measured pace up the newly raked gravel of the circular drive, Stanton Caley was surprised at the sense he had of something radically changed in the Powell residence in the six years he'd been abroad. He slowed his steps even more because he was early, and that wouldn't do for an afternoon visit, so he looked over the grounds, trying to put his finger on what was different.

He had allowed himself plenty of time to dress because he knew he'd be unsure of his attire. In the past he'd always dithered over this because Amelia never disguised the disapproval in her eyes if one made the wrong choice. Moreover, he was unused to making these decisions by himself now.

At last he'd settled on his new bespoke English tan walking suit with the fitted waistline and thigh-length jacket. The color was all right, he was convinced. Black surely would no longer be required. But the suit, although a lightweight worsted that was perfect for a London summer, already seemed uncomfortably warm in the Colorado sun. He glanced quickly down to check his tan spats and the gleam on his black calf shoes. Caley had already decided that he'd made one mistake. He should not have brought the slender Malacca cane that had almost become an extension of his hand in Europe. In his stroll here from the Brown Palace Hotel, he'd not seen any other gentlemen with walking sticks. But he realized that what was making him most uneasy was that soon he'd have to remove his dark brown homburg, settled so expertly over his still thick blond side-hairs, and reveal his now entirely bald crown.

Stanton again let his eyes roam over the house. There was, of course, the dark wreath with a funeral ribbon on the wide doors with the stained-glass fanlights. But that was to be expected and didn't account for the change.

It was an alteration he simply couldn't identify. The mansion sat as solidly as ever, like a plump and stately dowager with flowing skirts, the porticoes and verandas spreading into the lush grounds. The embedded silver of the square rocks outlining the projections of gables and towers and turrets, as well as all the many windows, dazzled like jewelry in the late June sunlight.

As usual, it was beautifully maintained. The elaborate balustrades of the balconies, the fretwork, the carved overhangs, looked as if the painters had just taken away their scaffoldings and left. In the pruned gardens there were no traces of leftover spring flowers, no drooping blades of daffodils or tulips. The colors of summer were richly displayed in the brilliant pink of peonies, the impossible reds and creamy whites of roses, the full-throated orange of daylilies, the imperial purple-blue of delphiniums.

Perhaps, he reflected with a corner of his attention as he checked his watch once more, it was having seen the resplendent castles of Europe that made this house seem less grand than he remembered it. He'd taken in the storied manors of England, the cloud-hung citadels of Scotland, the Gothic châteaus of France, the classic palaces of Rome. Not that he'd gone to look at them, of course. His purpose had been solely to avoid seeing or thinking about what he'd left.

Six years ago he'd known what was bound to happen, even though he could not bear holding the idea in his mind. He'd known at their meeting that Glendower would claim Morna Gregory. But the fact of it, the searing pain of the fact when it happened, was not to be borne. When he'd learned of it, nausea almost doubled him over. He'd staggered, clutching a sturdy walnut table for support. At last he'd sunk into a chair with his head in his hands and only one clear thought. He must not give any sign of the emotions that convulsed him. Not the gnawing jealousy, the impotent anger, the numbing loss. Even if the straitjacket of convention—which he'd never questioned—allowed it, vanity would not permit it. His first concern was that none of his friends, no acquaintance or member of his circle, suspect how he felt. He had no close relatives who might notice.

But under the circumstances, he could not imagine, either, taking part in the rounds of summer parties and amusements that always filled his days and evenings. If he could not go out into society, he did not know how he could occupy his time. What reason was there to get out of bed at all?

The news had come in the form of an airy note, full of misspellings and gossip, from Colette. Caley had been observing the Fourth of July celebration in Denver since Amelia Powell had gone ahead with her season, although now planning on cutting it quite short. When the envelope had been delivered to his suite at the Brown Palace Hotel, he'd stared at it, the very idea that *Colette* would write him filling him with a dismayed foreboding. She'd apologized endlessly for the liberty, pleading that everyone in Telluride missed him. In the second paragraph she mentioned, as if it were a matter of passing interest, that Monsieur Glendower had taken a house and that her *chère amie* Morna had moved there as well.

At that point he'd dropped the letter on the table and sat down. Later he'd canceled all his upcoming engagements on the grounds of ill health. It wasn't until the second day, as the porter removed another untouched tray and sent the note fluttering to the floor, that he listlessly picked it up and finished reading it. Colette had gone on to protest how much she missed her beloved France, how glorious it would be in Provence in September, how she longed to return, even though she knew she could never afford to do so. She ended with many, many expressions of affection.

Going abroad had not occurred to Stanton. His father's intense distrust of foreigners, including the English, whom he believed talked queerly on purpose, had meant that the family had never gone to Europe. And his mother's long decline before her death kept Stanton in Colorado after college, when he might have ventured there. In any case, his life consisted of the people he knew in the Denver elite, watching them, listening to them.

But in his current state, buffeted by passions he could not control or display, a continent full of strangers might offer some comfort, he realized. Left to his own devices Stanton would not have made the decision to go. Feeling as apathetic and withdrawn as an invalid, he knew he could not cope with tickets and trunks and several foreign languages. Colette could, however, and he felt somehow sure that she would see how he felt and never refer to the cause. He sent her just enough for the fare to Denver and a little over, and met her with his own luggage at Union station. They departed within the hour on their travels.

Being abroad had distracted Caley but he found, on the rare occasions when he was detached enough to explore his sensations, that he was not at all cured. A numbing fog of grief and loneliness surrounded him, and everything he observed he saw through that grayness. He tried to reason with himself, saying that after all he'd only known Morna Gregory a few months, repeating inwardly that this woman who haunted his dreams was beautiful, but not the only beauty. But if he caught sight of shining dark hair above an elegant dress, he'd almost run to see if the face, by some miraculous chance, was her face. The smallest thing recalled her, the graceful twitch of a hand sweeping up a skirt, a musical laugh, another woman's light eyes with dark lashes. All the sweet singers of Europe merely brought back memories of her voice.

A fear that he refused to dwell on gradually overtook Stanton. The appalling thought was this: Perhaps he had always lived in that grayness, gazing through it at people, and was accustomed to it. Only in the brief time he'd known Morna had he caught sight of the true and shining world. Now the fog was back.

Colette had done all she could to divert him. He could not fault her. While busily educating herself at the same time, she'd dangled all the treasures of Europe before his unhappy eyes: art, opera, horse racing, as well as the cooking of France, the winter sun of Spain. Because of her competence he'd hardly had to make a decision. He'd even grown to depend on that. True, he railed at her for the astonishing expense of her clothes, but he had to admit that she was careful about money in every other way.

If Stanton had thought about it, he might have wondered how she managed to overlook his almost constant ill-humor. When she said she preferred the name Céline, he sourly took to calling her C-C, for Colette/Céline. Examining her face in the mirror, she'd said calmly, "You are quite right as usual, *mon cher*. C-C it shall be, spelled C-e-c-i. The nose, you see"—and she looked with some satisfaction at its pertness and the dainty parentheses of her nostrils—"gives me the look of the gamine. So it fits me, this name Ceci. Especially with the new hair coloring." Turning this way and that, she'd admired the effect of the blond tint on her once brown curls. Slipping on a newly purchased hat with huge drooping willow plumes of rose and blue, she thought she'd never looked more attractive.

With the tip of his cane Stanton made a vague half-circle in the gravel of the driveway. Although traveling without her was a distinct inconvenience, he was glad she'd stayed in Europe, saying she could no longer put off the long-delayed trip to her home. He was sure she had not wanted him to meet her family, and he had no intention of bringing her with him to Denver. In any case, he'd been growing increasingly restive abroad and wanted to come back to his old pursuits. He knew he would need to reestablish himself with the Sacred Thirty-six. So this particular visit, also delayed, was the first one he had to make, and he'd come promptly to do so.

"Stanton, my dear, dear Stanton, I've been longing to see you." Amelia Powell stood in the doorway and then came forward onto the portico to greet him. He hurried forward in amazement, hastily removing his hat and gloves as he did so. Not only could he not remember her ever using his first name before, she was actually admitting him to the house herself!

"Permit me to offer my condolences, Mrs. Powell." Caley recovered himself and, taking her smooth ringless hand, launched into the words he'd planned. "The dreadful news of Laughton's death shocked me more than I can say, but I did not receive the letter for several months, as I was moving about. Otherwise, I would have returned immediately."

This was almost true. He had been en route by train to Italy and Theo Manningham's cable arrived at the same time as his longer letter, giving the details of Laughton Powell's sudden death from a heart attack. That had been almost a year ago now. But plans had already been made for the London winter season, and Ceci had her heart set on that. To avoid the fuss he'd decided to wait, since the funeral was long over.

Now he added some further words about pressing business affairs in England, and Amelia nodded as if she quite understood.

She was, of course, still dressed in black, but the Irish lace that completely covered her throat and her shoulders were delicately sheer. The dress was quite in the height of fashion. The scallops of lace with a cape effect ended above her elbows. The long Bertha Bishop sleeves that billowed from beneath the fragile scoops were tightly cuffed at the wrist. The skirt was also scalloped in a fitted hip yoke and fell in inverted box pleats in the latest French style. The mourning brooch pinned at her neck and the pointed velvet band at her waist were deep black and in some contrast to the almost gray hue of the dress itself.

Nor did Amelia's manner seem quite like that of a widow, Stanton considered, as he handed his hat, gloves, and cane to the waiting butler. There was an air of suppressed excitement about her that seemed downright cheerful. The six years had wrought immediately noticeable changes in her face, longer lines at the side of her mouth, a fretwork of faint wrinkles around the eyes. Although she was nearing forty, her rich brown hair showed little sign of gray, and the dramatic, sculptured bones of her cheeks still lent her beauty. From the way she held her head and neck it seemed likely that she was as aware as ever of that, he thought. And her increased vivacity almost erased the years.

But he was at a loss to explain this warmth that she was clearly extending to him. Before, although Laughton had always condescended to chat at length with him, Amelia had been aloof, talking to him only as long as being a good hostess required. Stanton had always thought he'd been invited so frequently to their dinners because he was a useful extra man. He had been happy just to be included in the inner sanctum. He even began to wonder if Amelia was so welcoming because, given her widowhood, she herself had slipped down the social scale. That was hard to imagine, because she was such a formidable woman. And, too, being a single woman had never affected Eloise Murdoch's position. Still, he would have to investigate this possibility before he committed himself to any parties when she began to entertain again.

As he followed her into the familiar parlor, where the tea service was already laid out, Caley noted with some surprise, given Amelia's former passion for redecoration, that nothing seemed changed. Surely the stiff-backed antique Empire furniture was the same. He'd often studied this room, admiring the opulence of gilt and silk, the glitter of prism and mirror, the objets d'art scattered everywhere. Now he recognized that the decor was influenced by the magnificent palace of Versailles and felt somehow that the effect was lost on this smaller scale. But he told himself that the room might seem less splendid than he recalled because of the crepe streamers draped everywhere over pictures as a sign of mourning. Most of the bibelots were also covered in black.

As if she divined some of his thoughts, Amelia waved a hand around the room almost dismissively. "Laughton and I"—and here she wiped away a tear that he hadn't seen with a bit of lace—"had left the house closed up and spent our time almost exclusively in New York before his untimely death. There was no sign, no sign at all, of any illness. He was always so well fleshed, you know, and had that wonderful high color in his cheeks. He was, of course, a great deal older than I, but to pass away in his prime like that, a man not yet fifty!"

Stanton murmured suitable commiserations and took the seat across the low carved table from her that she indicated. With a sudden ache he recognized the metallic-threaded brocade sofa as the one he'd sat on while he listened to Elizabeth Bender's recital so long ago and planned a blissful summer alone with Morna.

As she poured from the heavy teapot through a silver strainer so fine, it seemed lace and not metal, Amelia exclaimed, "Now, dear Stanton, and you *must* call me Amelia—we're such old acquaintances and have such *close* friends in common—tell me all about your travels. I'm so anxious to hear."

Before coming Stanton had reviewed several stories he might recount to her. The thought of being alone with Amelia had been rather daunting. He reminded himself to be careful to say "I" and not "we." It had been bad enough that he'd been forced to register Ceci in all the respectable hotels as Madame Caley, and he certainly did not want it known here that he'd had such a companion. To frequent bordellos was one thing, but he knew that he'd stepped over the line by their protracted travels. Of course, mentioning such an arrangement to a gentlewoman would be the really unforgivable transgression.

Caley had hardly begun when he noticed that Amelia was not really listening. Her newly acquired pleasantness kept her from displaying her lack of interest; still, there it was. He was here to ingratiate himself. Obligingly, he interrupted the story. "But, Amelia"—and he was pleased that he did not falter over her name—"after my long absence what I'm eager to hear is the news at home, and of the sort that only *you* would be able to tell me. I was able to receive so few letters."

This was true. Stanton had given his fixed *poste restante* only to Theo Manningham, who'd faithfully reported business doings, and Patrick Alexander, who'd occasionally scrawled an amusing note. Caley had confined himself to postcards and notes without a return address, explaining that he was moving around the continent. No one had sent him news of Berkeley, since they assumed the two old friends would be corresponding. To his relief he'd heard not a word about Morna.

Refilling their cups and putting the tray of cucumber sandwiches and petits fours within his reach, Amelia began by reminding him that she, devastated by her husband's loss, had gone nowhere, and that only a few select friends called regularly to share her sorrow. Stanton was not incapable of sympathetic understanding, and he could imagine how hard this last year of mourning, rigidly enforced by convention, had been for her. Forbidden by custom to attend any social function, to entertain, or seek any kind of diversion, confined to the house and the same daily visitors, Amelia must have found the tedium of her days well nigh unendurable. Even had she been wild with grief at first, and that was hard to picture given the composed Amelia across from him, there would have been no escape from that grief. The fact that this year was ending might account for her present uplifted spirits, he thought.

This time her dabbing at the eyes was quite perfunctory. "But I felt, for Laughton's sake, that I had to bear up, and that even in my depressed state I should keep in touch with events. My friends still came to me for advice and counsel, of course. Social leaders have responsibilities, you know." Amelia met his eyes and Stanton nodded on cue in quick agreement, although the question as to who took over those duties when she was living in New York did occur to him. He was a little taken aback that he'd had such a thought, which implied a slight criticism of her conduct. She continued, "And dear Eloise Murdoch naturally has kept me informed. I'm sorry to say, dear boy, that you will find things are not as they were. The whole tone of society here has sunk far below those standards set for us by New York and Boston."

Amelia leaned forward and set her teacup down to emphasize the importance of what she had to say. "Why, do you know, the women of our circle are being criticized for not involving themselves in these misguided attempts to help the indigent! They wish *us* to become active in such groups as the Ladies' Relief Society and the Ladies' Union Aid Society. A woman named Rachel Peterson came and spoke at, of all places, the Trinity Methodist Episcopal Church, urging us to give our time and money. She waved her chapped red hands about and told terrible stories about the unemployed, the destitute, unable to feed their children. A well-meaning woman, perhaps, but very weak headed to think that *we* are unaware of the cause of this. The poor are simply indolent! These people live in disgusting conditions near the smelters along the Platte. They are depraved, too lazy to find work, and most of them are foreigners."

Caley had heard a form of this speech many times from Laughton over port and cigars and had always nodded judiciously in assent. But now he found a quibble surfacing. The Denver leaders had established a Bureau of Immigration for the express purpose of attracting those very foreigners. Many were hired to do the backbreaking work in the city's factories and the coal mines of outlying areas. The recent economic depression Theo had written of must have thrown many of them out of work. Hastily he repressed this line of thinking, realizing that if he wasn't careful he might find himself actually disagreeing with Amelia!

Taking his raised eyebrows and sad shake of the head as a sign that they were of one mind, she launched into a more specific dissection of the failings of members of society. Soon Stanton found his attention going astray. ". . . Eloise being most upset," Amelia was saying, "since she had always praised Cyril Harrington as just the sort of man who would marry wisely. Now, some might have called him 'foppish' and one has to admit that he did gossip freely, but his fortune was solid. For him to choose this *gauche* woman—and that is by no means too strong a word—from Idaho! Her father's lumber holdings are extensive, but she thought, the poor girl actually thought, that Albert Bierstadt, our most famous *artist,* was a German brewer. Cyril was saved by the fact that her health was delicate, and Eloise was too kindhearted not to share her remedies with her old friend's wife. They've become quite close. I shudder to think what this means. *I* will be forced to invite her as well."

Stanton stole a glance at the ormolu clock on the mantel and found that only twenty minutes had passed. It would be unthinkable to leave before an hour was up. Wrenching his attention back, he noticed that whatever the topic of conversation was now, it involved a rather forced tender smile on Amelia's face. "Quite the dearest babies, I'm told, but Caroline naturally has not the time for reading she once had. I don't believe she keeps up with events at all. No matter the larger issue being discussed, she interrupts with stories of her darlings' latest prattlings. And these . . . confinements"—she hesitated over the word—"have meant that we hardly see her for whist as before. So inconvenient not having the proper number to play. But surely you'd heard that the Farnsworth family had grown by three in your absence?"

Realizing that actual words were called for, he searched his memory frantically. "Ah, yes," he finally managed, "Patrick Alexander did mention that news." Patrick had in fact remarked that God was good and the children did not take after Rollo. Then he'd added with great pleasure that his own mistress was again pregnant.

"No doubt sweet Patrick must have sounded very wistful on such a subject. He and Belle have not been blessed with offspring. Belle remains the beauty of our circle, of course." Amelia paused and looked down modestly, obviously hoping for a polished compliment denying that assertion. But Stanton was meditating about Patrick's wife. If, as was commonly believed, gentility was measured by how little a woman did, then surely Belle Alexander was the best bred. Her flair was for lowering herself slowly onto a couch and staying there.

He only realized too late that he'd stumbled from grace. Amelia was continuing with some asperity, "But then Patrick must also have told you that Jessamine and Quentin Wyndham have a daughter, Lillian Amelia, my godchild."

The narrow face and wispy figure of Jessamine came immediately to Stanton's mind because he could never forget the many dinners he'd spent sitting next to her in which the sole topic of conversation had to be what Jessamine ate, or rather didn't eat, unless prettily coaxed. "Both mother and child are flourishing, I hope," he said, trying in some panic to focus his attention.

Amelia sighed, although she did not seem at all unhappy at whatever prospect gleamed in her inner vision. "I had hoped that my namesake might be raised here in this very house. Quentin had spoken to Laughton about the possibility of buying it because even then I had begun to see that a more classical style of architecture was more suitable to my, our rather, *our* manner—" This time, as if overcome by sorrow at the memory of her husband, Amelia pressed her handkerchief to her lips and turned her head aside. But this time there was no mistaking the theatricality of her gesture. It was required of her and she duly paid homage to custom.

This was all the more evident in the speed with which she returned to her topic of conversation. "Forgive me, dear boy. I'm still overcome when I remember the happy past. As I was saying, the Wyndhams would have been ideal for this house. But poor Jessamine's been so fragile that she thinks it best to spend most of her time in Baltimore near her mother. I myself think her doctor here was a little harsh in demanding that she follow a strict regime in eating, but she bloomed, she positively bloomed. After my charming little Lillian Amelia was born, however, Jessamine declared that the *idea* of food quite horrified her. So difficult for Quentin. With the success of his sugar-beet company he naturally was looking forward to a son to carry on. He remains here for business reasons, of course, and his brother has gone into the company with him."

Amelia's glance moved around the room and at last landed on Stanton. "Now, if you were just established, how wonderful to have you living here! I'm very much surprised that your heart was not captured in your travels by some suitable young lady, perhaps even one of noble birth." She lifted one eyebrow archly. "Tell me the truth. There must be some explanation for your long absence. Did you not meet someone who struck an inner chord?"

This was not a subject he wished pursued. "I find this talk of your selling the house disturbing, Amelia. It cannot mean that you would *think* of leaving us?"

"Ah, as to that, I cannot be sure." Her lips curved in what only could be described as a girlish simper. "Such decisions are not always up to one alone. You know"—and she met his gaze directly—"that Laughton would have wanted me to take up my life, to once again be happy."

At these words Caley immediately understood the source of Amelia's new vivacity. She was planning on remarriage and she was delighted with her choice. Without question she would be an extremely wealthy woman and there would have been a field of suitors, although it was obvious that she had already settled on one. No doubt it was someone she had met in her long visits to New York, someone with whom she'd conducted a sedate flirtation. The favored man must now be very pleased that she was in the market for a husband, Stanton reflected. Since she was still in mourning, no mention could be made of a name, but Amelia was obviously preparing all her friends for the announcement after the proper amount of time had elapsed.

This insight did not explain her cordiality to him personally, but he considered that her felicity, like a welcome rain after a drought, was falling on everyone. Indeed, now that he saw it, he was bemused that it had taken him so long to understand. Once he would have been sensitive to her moods, as aware of any variation in the lives of the Thirty-six as a spider is of the twitch of a dewdrop on the farthest reach of its web. This was a momentous happening.

Were he invited to a dinner in town this evening and he simply murmured his suspicions, he would become the immediate center of a group, Caley knew. The size of Laughton Powell's fortune would make his widow's plans the sole topic of discussion over port and cigars among the men. Speculation over the identity of Amelia's preference would be the subject of conversation at every women's tea, every at-home, every garden party.

But Stanton found himself absolutely indifferent. He did not care whom she married. This realization came so like a thunderclap from a sunny sky that he would have dropped the Limoges teacup if he had not set it down a moment earlier. Moreover, it was plain why all of the preceding chatter about these people had bored him. They and their opinions had once been at the center of his world, but he didn't care about them either.

Six years ago he would have thought that missing the latest financial moves of these captains of industry would have been a vital loss. Yet while he was gone, his fortune in the meat-packing factories his father had founded had been competently handled by an accountant and his clerks. But he'd known even then that it was not investment advice he'd wanted, but approval. And that simply did not matter to him anymore.

But if it didn't, he did not know what did matter. All during the years abroad he'd been simply marking time, hoping his numb pain would disappear. Then he could come back to the solidity of his former day-to-day life, take up his real concerns. He sat in stunned silence, trying to absorb his change in attitude, looking at Amelia's animated face without seeing a single feature.

Rapt in her own satisfying plans, Amelia did not observe that Stanton's mind was elsewhere. With her pink fingertips on her chin, she was now discussing the various styles of architecture for her proposed new dwelling. ". . . haven't grasped that Queen Victoria's death three years ago was the end of an era. Now in 1904 we must move into the modern age, and I feel that the Greco-Roman mode, that enduring classical look, will be what people who are ahead of their times will choose." She stretched out a graceful hand, and the full, almost transparent, sleeve of her dress fluttered.

She did not notice, nor did he, that his hands were trembling. Following that first upheaval in his thinking Caley was suffering a further revelation. Once again he was back in Freda's dance hall seeing Morna lean forward as she spoke to Edward Gibbons's mesmerized friend, her white shoulders glowing against the blue of her gown.

The remembered pain flooded him again as it had when he'd perceived that the Thirty-six would not have accepted her, that not one female foot would ever have crossed the threshold if she was his wife. Because of that he'd not gotten up from the velvet couch, crossed the room, and proposed. Yet if she'd accepted, he could have gone to Europe with *Morna*. With her beside him he would have seen the splendor fall on castle walls, the sun splash on the wine-dark seas that surround the Grecian Isles.

She might not have accepted, of course, he told himself to push away the thought of what he'd missed. But an inner voice played devil's advocate, pointing out that he'd been able to see that she was frightened, and he could have offered her the security of his wealth, surrounded her with that fortress. So she might have said yes, grateful for his kindness. He had loved her at first sight, and she might have come to love him too. But he would never know because he had not asked.

He had not asked because thirty-six people would never have sanctioned it. The rest of the world, however, would have envied him. Everywhere else they went, in London, in Paris, in New York, men would have looked with discreet longing at Madame Caley, women would have unbent at her warmth. Morna's charm, her wit, would have made him shine.

Today, *he* did not care about those thirty-six people. The thought of it made him want to run howling into the street. He might have done that, but for the fact that he would have had to collect his hat, cane, and gloves from the butler, and he did not know what possible excuse he could make to Amelia.

So he sat, and self-disgust, like sweat, sprang from his every pore. He could not bear such a feeling. He squirmed and shifted on the couch until once again his hatred, like a spear, was aimed at Berkeley

Glendower. Caley, writhing at the thought, recalled that he himself had seen Morna first, loved her first. And what had he done? He had waited for Glendower's opinion! That he had gotten, and immediately, although he'd refused to admit it then. Glendower had without a moment's hesitation gone to the front of the room, taken Morna's hand, and not let go. Although Caley's lips were firmly closed, he ground his teeth, knowing that if that room had been filled with the titled peerage of England, the moneyed barons of America, staring aghast at his action, Glendower would not have cared.

Caley suddenly realized that Amelia had just spoken that name. She was finishing a sentence. ". . . hardly seen our good friend since his divorce was final. One quite understands that, of course, under the circumstances." Her smile was sweetly regretful, with more than a touch of coyness.

"What?" Stanton blurted in amazement. He had not even been aware that proceedings had been initiated. But then none of his other friends would have written that, assuming that Berkeley himself would have done so.

Amelia misunderstood his surprise, thinking that it was merely a comment on the quickness of time's passage. "Oh yes," she replied, "it has in fact been a full two years since Olivia was granted a decree on the grounds of desertion. An unpleasant matter, so dear Berkeley might not have mentioned it to you in his letters. It was a mere formality in this case, since it was *she* who refused to return to Colorado. As you can imagine, Berkeley had the full sympathy of everyone here, and no door has ever been closed to him. With his usual exquisite tact he has chosen to spend most of his time in Telluride during this period. But with so many here in Denver wanting his advice, he has come down for business engagements, I understand, but has not accepted social invitations." She adjusted the mourning brooch at her throat as if that explained all.

Then, with her eyes cast down, her smile no less demure, Amelia said, "But that will change soon, won't it? With you, his old friend, here —and I have waited for your arrival for just this purpose—and *I* at your side, together we'll welcome him back to his rightful place in Denver."

Amelia was going to marry Berkeley! At the thought joy ran through every vein in Stanton's body. That had to mean he was no longer with Morna. Perhaps it was not too late. Perhaps she would now listen to his own suit. He would forgive the past. It would be hard, but she would have even more cause to be grateful to him. All he needed to do was find her. He leapt to his feet and, in his excitement, burst out unthinkingly, "When did he leave Morna? Where is she now?"

Amelia gaped at him. It was as if he'd poured the pot of cold tea over her. First incomprehension, then a dawning suspicion, swept across her face. At last her features turned to stone. "Who," she asked frigidly, "is Morna?"

That abrupt question congealed Caley's warm joy, stopped his very blood from flowing. Of course Amelia would not know of Morna's existence. No man who knew would have mentioned that illicit union to his wife, and even if a rumor had reached a gentlewoman's delicate ears, it would not have been a possible subject of discussion among ladies. The prudish William Murdoch would never have breathed it to his spinster sister, Eloise. No doubt the affair would have been brought up over port, but Laughton would not have thought it fit to tell even Amelia. Men presented a united front on such issues. Berkeley was being divorced, and therefore some such arrangement was inevitable in their eyes. Hardly any of them would have known Morna personally. In any case, the Powells had spent their time in New York, and as spicier scandals occupied Laughton's thinking, that story might have slipped his mind.

But, as Caley stood there, looking blankly down at Amelia, another possibility formed. It became a conviction. And all his hope vanished. Berkeley was still with Morna. He would not leave her. It was hard to believe anything else. Surely Theo or Patrick would have written the news of any breakup, thinking that it would be too painful for Glendower himself to mention it.

That meant Berkeley was quite unaware of the rosy future Amelia was planning for herself—and him. She knew only that he was divorced, and now she was also free to marry. Bored and lonely, she had sat in the black-draped rooms and built an airy castle with a classical façade on that flimsy foundation.

"Sit down, Stanton," Amelia commanded, her lips thin. "I asked you a question, and I will have an answer. Who is Morna?"

CHAPTER 17

Caley's head and stomach were still whirling the day after the interview with Amelia. The orders—and there was no other word for it—that she had given him were explicit. He was to separate Berkeley from "this woman" and do it immediately. Consequently, Stanton was at that very moment on the train to Telluride.

He had told her very little, only that Glendower had been living with a woman for some six years now, a woman who had been employed as a singer at a house of ill-repute. Caley had been taxed to the limit to get that much out. It was one thing to realize that having Amelia Powell's good opinion was not the be-all and end-all of existence. It was quite another to face this commanding woman with bad news. He felt very much like the messenger of olden days with a similar task, who as he still stood before the enraged queen, heard them sharpening the ax to cut off his head.

Then he'd had to hem and haw for some time before coming up with a term to describe Freda's establishment, one that he desperately hoped would not further offend. As he spoke, Amelia's face was per-

fectly blank. Her prominent cheekbones seemed to stand out a little
more sharply. Her topaz eyes were as hard as that stone, but not an
eyelash flickered.

As a matter of fact, his word choice was hardly at issue. Amelia
was so taken aback that she could barely absorb what she was hearing.
She sat frozen, far more agitated by this news than she would ever
betray. She was far more disturbed than she herself knew.

The thought that "her" Berkeley could do such a thing caused the
doors and windows to slam in the dream castle in which she'd lived for
so long. This display of what she saw as weakness on his part, of giving
in to base appetites, opened cracks in all the walls of her world. Men
were capable of the most inconceivable actions, as Amelia and Eloise
Murdoch so frequently agreed, but she herself had certainly expected
better of *him*. Briefly, she even wondered if he were deserving of her.
Her hands were so tightly clenched in her lap that it was well she'd
removed her elaborate rings as a sign of mourning.

Nonetheless, she had always taken pride in the belief that she was a
sophisticated woman, one who knew the ways of the world. After all,
men were men, to every decent woman's regret. The affairs of the
Prince of Wales with the actress Lillie Langtry and others too numerous
to mention were common knowledge across the length and breadth of
England, and now that he was King Edward VI, he had not changed his
behavior! If the queen could overlook such indiscretions, so could she.
In Berkeley's case they would end after marriage, of course. She summoned up the cherished mental picture of him standing next to her
beneath the marble Grecian columns of a majestic new mansion.
Amelia rallied and gathered up the pieces.

She began by explaining to Caley why this had happened, and soon
convinced herself of its truth. "Our good friend, our poor Berkeley, was
after all involved in the drawn-out process of divorce. We must remember this, Stanton, because it will help us understand. During this time—
and it did take several years—he was alone in Telluride, an outpost
of civilization. There he naturally needed . . ." Here she paused. Finding the proper and delicate expression for exactly *what* Berkeley
Glendower had needed was the only difficulty she now perceived in the
whole situation.

She began again. "He needed *solace*. Therefore he ill-advisedly, it
has to be said, entered into this liaison with this woman. In his favor
one should point out that she had no reputation to lose, being already
compromised by her choice of . . . workplace."

Stanton had, Amelia thought, referred to the woman as a "singer"
merely out of respect for herself. Women in such places did not only

sing. And, from a different kind of modesty, she could not add her inward certainty that once Berkeley knew of Amelia's continuing tender regard for him, he would be most eager to end the relationship. Moreover, after such a length of time, he must be weary of such a person, she was sure.

Out loud, she laid out the solution, which she now regarded as simplicity itself. All one had to do was offer "Moira," as Amelia now continually referred to Morna, a substantial sum of money to leave. The woman would no doubt be delighted because, as Amelia pointed out, she could then go elsewhere and with such a dowry find herself a husband and set herself up respectably.

When Caley had not instantly agreed with her, but instead sat there, struggling for words, opening and closing his mouth—quite like a fish, Amelia had thought privately—she did her best to clarify it for him. "Dear boy, women of this sort cannot be expected to have the grasp of things that we do, but she cannot be entirely stupid. Obviously, she cannot hope that Berkeley himself would *marry* her. Her best hope is to find someone who is not aware of her past. Perhaps she could move to California. I understand they have no standards at all in that state, excepting in San Francisco, of course. There, she could pass herself off as a widow and find a miner or a farmer. Someone not too particular."

As if dismissing such an unimportant subject forever, she brushed the air with her fingertips. But this was not quite what she believed would happen. Once such a woman had her hands on a sum of money she would surely spend it immediately and sink right back to her former occupation. But then Amelia was glad that she had not said that. In the course of his stammerings and pauses she finally deduced that Caley himself had strong feelings about "Moira." In fact, she began to think that when Berkeley ended the affair Caley would take up with her himself!

At first she could not credit such an idea. Indeed, she found it necessary to ring for the maid and have the tea things removed and the sherry decanter brought in, hoping that during this activity she would have time to arrange her mind. Although she'd never in the past spent an instant's reflection on Stanton Caley, she'd always assumed he was a reasonable man. His income was secure, and he was a friend of Berkeley's.

By the time she was pouring the sherry, an explanation had occurred to her. This impressionable young man had had too large an exposure to the decadence of Europe, where one man might, she supposed, take up with the mistress of another. She shuddered inwardly.

Stanton would have been so much better off to confine himself to just a brief foray to the continent and then only to Switzerland. Now he would have to be forcefully reminded of how things were really done.

But just as Amelia opened her mouth to point out to him that, under such circumstances, she and Berkeley would not be able to receive him, that his having such a mistress would soon be *known,* she stopped herself. For she realized that she would need a go-between in handling this sordid affair. It would not do for her to reveal her own feelings to Berkeley himself, and she had absolutely no intention of speaking to such a woman. While Caley would probably handle it all simply as a favor to Glendower—and herself—it might be even better if he felt he himself would benefit.

After her marriage, Amelia considered, she would have to come up with some excuse for not inviting Caley to parties. She could not imagine ever enjoying his company again, even after he recovered from this folly and married properly. No doubt Berkeley would object at first. He had been at college with Stanton. But she would be firm. Berkeley would perhaps never be aware of what she'd gone through for him, yet he should have to pay in some way for this ordeal.

Stanton at this point had been in an extraordinary quandary. He patted his high-domed forehead, now glistening with sweat, with his pocket handkerchief. There was no way that Amelia could be made to understand that her assumptions were wrong, and that she was badly mistaken in her proposed solution. But then she told him something he had not known.

She followed this piece of information with a low-voiced statement, uttered distinctly. And, although the statement was delicately phrased and delivered in Amelia's usual polished tones, it was a threat. A threat that she could and, he knew, would carry out.

This was what sent Caley back to his hotel to pack hurriedly and then make a brief stop at his club to make sure her facts were correct. In the morning he'd boarded the train to Telluride with renewed hope for his own marriage to Morna in his heart.

CHAPTER 18

The summer sky above Telluride was a deep gentian blue, and it lent that hue to the stone grays of the enclosing mountains. All the season's bright colors seemed twice as intense in the thin, soft air. The spring-green of the new aspen leaves lightened the wintergreen of the surrounding pines, and Indian paintbrush splashed scarlet on the foothills. But as he stepped off the train onto the long wooden platform, Stanton was too edgy to notice. What he'd heard about Telluride's troubles made him nervous. Stray gunshots were a possibility, he supposed, given the explosive clash here between the Western Federation of Miners and the huge Smugglers-Union Mine Company.

The rumbles of this conflict had reached him even abroad through Theo Manningham's letters. Two years ago he'd written in alarm, saying that Arthur Collins, the manager of the Smuggler and a man Stanton knew well, had become a victim of the struggle. A shotgun blast through his living room window had killed the manager instantly. What Collins had done had infuriated all the miners. After long negotiations the owners had finally agreed to an eight-hour day and a three-dollar daily wage. However, Collins had then switched to the Cornish fathom system, whereby the miner only received this if he removed all the ore from his vein. But the Smuggler's veins were unusually wide, and this could not possibly be done by a man in eight hours. The union had called a strike. Theo had added, "The guilty miner was clearly of unbalanced mind, but the town is hardly the peaceful and prosperous place we once knew."

In the very last letter Caley had received before returning to Denver, Theo had sadly concluded, "The citizens of Telluride had so welcomed in the new century. But the last four years have been terrible in the valley. Between the fire at one mine, the avalanche at another, and now this labor war—because that's what it is—I imagine that every person there wishes that one calendar page had not been turned and it was still 1899."

But Stanton soon shook off his twinges of apprehension in the freshness of the June day and his joy in the fact that he must be only within a few streets of Morna. And Berkeley Glendower was not even in the town. As Amelia had explained yesterday, "Eloise tells me that dear Berkeley no longer recommends the mining companies in Telluride as investments for our Denver financiers because of the labor unrest. He now spends his time consulting on the subject of mine safety in other areas of the state. He's often in Durango, I hear. But he goes as well into the territory of New Mexico searching for other secure investments for the Murdoch Bank and its trustees. I believe, now that he's divorced, that's the chief source of his income."

Caley, having heard this, was almost breathless when he'd arrived last night at his club because of his haste to hear more. He had no reason to doubt her words. Although no one who knew would have mentioned Glendower's personal life to her, his business comings and goings would be just the sort of thing Amelia would have learned. What Stanton really wanted was news of Morna. But neither in the dining room nor in the comfortable paneled bar was there a sign of the men who could have told him. Nowhere did he see Rollo Farnsworth's genial warthog visage or Patrick Alexander's easy grin.

Checking the club room, he caught sight of William Murdoch, who at least could expand on Amelia's information. But Stanton paused. Talking to him would mean forgoing a relaxing drink as well as exercising a great deal of patience. Murdoch was known for his sermons and soda water. Stanton approached reluctantly.

Upright in a heavy leather chair, the banker was frowning over the *Denver Post,* a seltzer bottle and glass within hand's reach. He was a sparse man with thinning hair and not enough neck to fill his stiff collar. Murdoch adjusted his half-glasses farther down his nose and looked up at Stanton with much the same dollar-hard stare as if he'd merely seen him the day before instead of after a six-year interval. "What the world is coming to, Caley, I cannot imagine," he said abruptly, without any greeting. "Judgment Day is nigh. It must be so. Only last evening when I was doing my Bible reading, I opened to the Book of Revelation wherein the Apostle John speaks of what will happen to those men who fornicate, those men who live deliciously. They will be cast into the fiery lake, Caley."

As Murdoch expanded with some gratification on the fire and brimstone that awaited these sinners, Stanton seated himself in the next chair, all the while nodding soberly. He remembered with an inward groan that the banker's favorite deadly sins were lust and sloth and that once started on these, he was difficult to distract. Now Murdoch brought his open palm down hard on the leather armrest. "And this dread Day will be coming soon." He shook his newspaper as if he'd seen written proof of his words there. "State militia has had to be sent back to Telluride again! Mark my words, Judgment Day approaches."

Caley cleared his throat. "That's along the lines of what I wanted to discuss with you. Telluride, I mean," he added hurriedly.

"What's happening there is exactly the sort of thing the Apostle warns of." Murdoch smacked the chair again. "Those miners wanting their shifts cut to eight hours a day *and* asking for a full three dollars per day! And with this money and this life of ease, what will they do? Why, every God-fearing person knows they will wallow in the beds of the brothels that line those streets and lead lives of idleness. The governor did the right thing when they went on strike—sent six railcars of state troops up there, closed those saloons and bawdy houses, and put the strikers in a bullpen in the middle of the main street. Then they ran them out of town on a rail. Problem is some of them keep sneaking back. Say they want to see their families." He snorted. "Hang every man jack of 'em, I would. I was telling my sister, Eloise—" Luckily for his agonized listener, Murdoch stopped for a swallow of his soda water.

"I'm sure you're right, sir," Stanton inserted quickly. "It's just that I was thinking of putting some of my money in mines, and I gather you think this would be unwise."

"Well now, Caley"—the banker almost sputtered out his seltzer in his haste to correct that impression—"I wouldn't go that far. No, indeed. I didn't realize you were actually thinking of moving your money around. I can be of some help to you there." Even Murdoch's eyeglasses glinted acquisitively. "Those mining companies are still solid, you know, quite solid. Even after the avalanche and the rebuilding—and

having to pay three hundred dollars to the families of each man killed—
the Liberty Bell still cleared a dollar sixty-two a ton. This strike business
will blow over soon. Miners been out almost a year now—they can't
hold out much longer. What's more, the mineowners have hired a
whole passel of gunmen."

His smile now a real attempt at joviality, the banker smoothed his
blue sharkskin-suited trousers. "Nothing for you to worry about. You
just turn over your money to me and I'll see that it's put to work safely.
Moving some of it out of meatpacking? How much were you thinking
of?"

"I heard, sir," Caley replied, avoiding the question, "that Berkeley
Glendower wasn't recommending investing there now, that he was
looking elsewhere for your group."

"Well, now," Murdoch said earnestly, "there's an example of how
carefully we look after your money. Glendower is a sound man, and he
felt we should hold off for the time being. If he'd said we should put
more money in now that the stock's depressed and the owners hungry
for cash, I would have listened and done it. He would have earned some
substantial commissions, so I have to believe him. His own income is
suffering mightily because we're following his advice. There can't be
any question that he's supporting the *miners*. No, no, he's a sound man.
Right now he's in the Southwest, but he's been there awhile. Bound to
be back soon. You ask him about this. He'll tell you it's temporary."

"I'm sure you're right, sir," Caley said once more, standing up
with relief. "I will have a word with him, and you and I can discuss this
later. By the way, do you have Berkeley's address in Telluride?"

Murdoch had. Stanton was now blithely strolling through the almost too-quiet streets of Telluride toward the house on Pacific Avenue.
He intended to just walk past and then settle into the Sheridan Hotel
and send a note from there to Morna asking if he might call. As he went
along, he was going over Amelia's last words to him. She had made it
perfectly plain that if matters did not turn out as she envisioned, steps
would be taken. At a murmur from her, Berkeley would no longer be
working for the Murdoch group. The size of the fortune the bank ad-
ministered for her made Amelia's wish their command.

Moreover, although Glendower's qualifications made him eligible
for any mine manager's position, the financiers at the top were a close-
knit group. All Murdoch need do was shake his head doubtfully, mention that this man *might* be sympathetic to the labor movement, and
doors would be tightly closed from Colorado to California. Berkeley
would either marry Amelia or face ruin.

Caley stopped, wishing that he'd brought his Malacca walking stick. He was used to tapping it, swinging it about, and these switchings helped him think. It was a pity that gentlemen here had not taken up the fashion, he reflected, which made him reluctant to carry his own. Although he wasn't aware of it, his hand made the same movements with an imaginary cane as he considered the best approach to Morna. Should he tell her what the future certainly held? Would this make her more disposed to consider his own proposal?

Or should he delicately explain the situation to Berkeley himself? Contemplating that idea gave Caley a great deal of pleasure. He flicked his wrist, and the stick he did not have swished satisfyingly through the air. Not only would his onetime friend have to hear that he would have to give up Morna, he would even have to be grateful to the person who told him. Stanton imagined himself looking into the handsome face of the man he so envied and saying quietly, "Of course you must understand, Berkeley, that since Amelia is aware of the situation, it would be best if *I* saw to Morna's future and well-being. I will devote myself to her happiness. I promise you that with me never again will she have to face a moment's concern about money."

Of course, in a way, he would be doing Glendower a great favor. The man who married Amelia Powell would, to all intents and purposes, control the fortune, and make him a man to be reckoned with anywhere in America. And she was a beautiful woman. Here, if he'd had his slender Malacca, Stanton would have tapped the ground dubiously. He simply couldn't picture any man stroking Amelia's hair, her face, the way he longed to do with Morna, nor would this man be likely to be basking in any sweet glances. No, he couldn't conceive that Berkeley would regard this change as a favor, exactly. But then, Caley thought as he began walking again quite briskly, Glendower hadn't any choice.

Before he could make up his mind how to handle the matter, Stanton realized that he needed to know why Berkeley himself had not married Morna once he was free. There was her past to consider, and the explanation must be that there had been a shortage of money. Yes, that was it, Caley nodded to himself. A husband somewhere, no doubt in the far reaches of the British Isles, who'd demanded a small fortune in return for her freedom. The whole affair had begun too precipitously and not been managed with forethought. If Berkeley had just taken care of that before letting go of Olivia Hyde-White's wealth, they would have married. But since he had not done so, he did not have the requisite sum.

That line of thinking brought Stanton to a complete stop. Since *he* wished to marry Morna, how much was it going to cost him? His hand holding the phantom cane wiggled unhappily. It occurred to him that some time had passed, and now this husband might be more open to reason. Perhaps he was a member of the impoverished aristocracy or squirearchy and could be bargained with. After all, Morna had been living with Glendower for some time, and even a high-handed Gaelic laird must realize that he would not get another offer.

Now, although he had a keen eye for errors in Amelia's thinking, Caley did not realize that he shared an unquestioned assumption with her. It was simply this: that enough money would buy anything. His own fear that his inheritance, once lost, could never be regained naturally influenced his view. And he believed that life would be insupportable without all that he had. Stanton Caley was convinced of this, even though he had very recently discovered that his own life was quite bleak, despite all he had. Without examining this, he proceeded cheerfully toward Pacific Avenue.

He was very close when two small children came racing along the path toward him. The boy in front had an angelic face, blond hair, and panic in his blue eyes. Close on his heels was a delicate brunette, alive with anger, her long brown curls flying behind her, determination in her set lips. Just as they reached Stanton, the boy veered off the path onto a patch of grassy lawn, scampered onto the bare boards before a small house, and disappeared inside.

He would not have made it to safety had not the girl, reaching out to yank at his hair, caught a shoetip in the long white pinafore that covered a flowered dress and gone sprawling into the grass. She landed with a thump on her stomach.

Stanton had had very little to do with children, and in fact didn't want to, but the little girl did not get up immediately. There was no adult in view, and no sound from the house, so he supposed he should do something. He leaned over her and asked cautiously, "Have you hurt yourself?"

She pushed herself up with her forearms and, with an agile twist, ended in a sitting position. Unspilled tears sparkled in brown eyes that seemed gold flecked, and there was a tremble in the cherub mouth. She was, he thought, a remarkably pretty child. She appeared to be thinking his question over. At last she shook her head, and he stretched out a hand to help her up. The hand she held out was grubby, but she rose almost with a lady's airs and graces. "Thank you," she murmured.

She glanced down at her grass-stained pinafore and saw the wide rip where her shoe had caught the ruffled hem. "Oh, dear," she exclaimed in dismay. She lifted up the edge, poked one small finger sadly through the gaping rent, and repeated with even more emphasis, "Oh, dear! I will get a scolding. I'm not supposed to be fighting, especially with Ivor." She looked up at him without a trace of shyness and added, as if politeness required an explanation, "He's Helga's nephew and he comes to play so his English will get better."

No doubt she was some superior servant's child, Stanton thought, given her manners and language. He noticed that the small pinafore, although starched and neatly ironed, was already much mended in other places. While he had no idea how to talk to children, he somehow wanted to coax a smile from this enchanting little girl. He said soothingly, "It is rather badly torn. Perhaps you can get a new one now."

"Oh, no," she said firmly, tossing her head so that some of the tangled dark curls fell forward. "Mother says we can't get new things now. All the miners' families need help. But I don't feel like helping *Ivor* after what he said. He lied."

"Well, then," Stanton replied, "your mother might then overlook the, um, fighting and the torn dress."

She caught a bit of lip between small white teeth and considered this idea. "No." She sighed reluctantly. "She'll still say I shouldn't have lost my temper." Now her upward gaze took him in as if he were a trusted friend, and it was important that he understand. The look quite won Stanton's heart.

"He said I didn't have a father," she continued, "and I wouldn't have gotten mad, but he kept saying it. He *knows* I have a father, although he isn't here just now. But"—and a shadow of guilt swept over her fine features—"maybe that isn't what he meant. His English isn't very good yet. And now I've made him miss his tea. We have scones and we were going to have them, just the two of us, outside. Both Mother and Issy will be cross because I ran him off. *That* was rude." Again there was the glint of unshed tears in her long-lashed eyes.

Stanton suspected that the vanished Ivor had overheard grown-ups talking and, catching their tone, had intended to insult his playmate, but that his English wasn't up to it. Partly because of that and partly because of her charm, he found himself saying, to his own surprise, "Would it help if I went with you and explained to your mother that there'd been a misunderstanding and then"—he gestured toward the torn ruffle drooping on the ground—"an accident? She'd be able to see you were really sorry before the whole story came out."

A wonderful smile spread across the little girl's face. She could see the advantage, simply in terms of distracting attention away from herself, of having a gentleman in hat and gloves accompany her. "Oh, yes," she replied instantly. "And you could stay for tea." With one hand she gathered the pinafore up so it wouldn't drag, exactly the way a lady gracefully lifted her skirt. She offered him her other hand. "I'll show you where we live. I'm Bridget."

"I'm delighted to meet you, Miss Bridget," he responded with the same gravity. "I'm Stanton Caley. But I won't be able to stay." He pictured the shock of an unprepared mother, well-trained servant or not, faced with a complete stranger coming to tea, and wondered again at the amazing assurance of the child.

"You'll like the scones," she answered persuasively. "They're filled with raspberry jam. I'll get Mother to tell you one of the stories she tells me. You'll like that too. My favorite is about Castle Connemara and a princess named Bridget who lives there." She gave a wholly contented smile. "It's really me, and—"

They'd only passed four houses and were approaching the gabled lemon-yellow one on the corner, when the gate of the picket fence on the side flew open and a woman called, "Bridget Isobel! I've been *that* worried. Where did you go? You weren't to leave the garden."

The woman hurried across the lawn toward them, trying to tuck the ends of the grizzled straw-colored hair back into the bun they'd escaped from. She was older than Stanton had ever expected this small child's mother to be, but there was every sign of maternal alarm in the freckled features. As she reached Caley, an expression of recognition came to her eyes, as if she'd met him once but couldn't recall where.

Looking at her, Stanton had the same sensation. The little girl tried to tuck the torn pinafore out of sight and began, "Now, Issy, don't be cross. I—"

But then the polished front door opened wide, and another woman came sweeping down the stairs. "Stanton Caley! Why, I'm delighted to see you."

Bridget let go of his hand and threw her arms around the skirt of white violet-strewn cotton, as if sure of a more lenient judge. "Mother," she said very quickly, "I had a small accident, and"—she finished the sentence winningly—"I've invited this gentleman to tea."

"How nice of you, Bridey. He's an old friend of mine," Morna answered, and with that smile, and the sound of the low musical voice that had echoed in his memory, Stanton could only stand and stare like a man struck dumb.

CHAPTER 19

In a state of happy light-headedness Stanton sat in the front parlor on a sofa of gold. If he'd looked carefully, he would have noticed that its sheen was faded, as was the wallpaper's. But he didn't, and it only seemed to him that the room was filled with preserved sunlight. The scent of the still blooming lilacs that bushed so extravagantly under the open windows, combined with that of the flowers themselves in cut-glass vases everywhere in the room, contributed to that airy feeling. But it was really the presence of Morna, he knew.

She looked like summer itself. Her dress of sheer white lawn, with its sprinkling of small violets, had a filmy lace insert at the top, gossamer sleeves, and a wide ruffle at the bottom. Her hair, which had been brushed up into a loose mass of curls, was held by combs of etched columbines. Around the lace at her throat were strands of amethyst beads, and they added a tinge of that color to her gray eyes. The details were lost on Stanton, but the memory of the way she looked was forever preserved in the shimmer of lavender. He remembered that afternoon the rest of his life.

Bridey had gone off quite readily with Isobel, sure that this good behavior would help when the account of her misdemeanor had to be told. Over her shoulder the child called smilingly back to Caley, "Don't forget. Ask for the story. You'll like it."

But it was he who told the stories of his travels. Morna was so full of questions, so genuinely interested in what he'd thought of all he'd seen, that he found that he hadn't stopped talking once, despite the fact that he'd downed three scones and as many cups of tea. He could see that these tales were often really quite funny because he didn't mind showing to her that on one occasion or another, he'd been more than a little naive or foolish. He didn't mind because her expressive eyes and happy laugh assured him that she knew these things happened to the cleverest person; that when abroad for the first time, everyone was an innocent. Since this was true, the wise man would simply smile, shrug, and later turn the experience into a joke.

With such an appreciative listener he felt as if he were at last a witty man and, feeling so, he somehow became one. He quickly forgot to say "I" instead of "we" and when Morna inquired after Colette, it seemed quite natural to include her in his accounts. He mentioned the French girl's steely stare when confronted with a high-handed, over-priced couturiere, ending with the remark that Ceci had out-hauteured the Parisienne. " 'Ceci,' " Morna said with a light snap of her fingers. "What a perfect new name! It fits her. When Freda told me she'd gone with you, I was so happy, remembering how she used to dream of shopping in Paris, and I thought how wonderful that at last she could."

With Morna beaming at him like that Stanton now also felt like a generous man. It occurred to him that she'd changed in only one way. The reserve she'd always shown was gone, and her face mirrored each delighted feeling. It made his heart catch in his throat. Aware that he might be displaying his own emotions too openly, he took a deep breath. "How is Miss Freda?" he asked with interest.

Her laugh was gleeful. "What I'm about to tell you sounds like a sad story, but it isn't at all. You know Freda, Stanton." He couldn't recall when the two of them had slipped onto a first-name basis.

"You are aware," she went on, "that, when the miners struck, the governor ordered all the Telluride saloons, casinos, bordellos, and dance halls closed? There was no recompense offered by the state, and quite a few of the owners eventually left the valley. But when they sent an officer to Freda's to enforce the order, she fixed the poor young colonel with a gimlet eye and said, 'Surely you don't mean to shut down my restaurant as well?' He was taken aback, never having heard that her establishment contained any such thing. And, until that moment, of course, it hadn't. He hemmed a bit, and she stepped nearer. He trod backward, frowned, and then said, as fiercely as he could, "Very well, but no liquor may be sold.' In her best grande dame manner Freda drew herself up, took a step even closer, and replied haughtily, 'Drinks with dinner are entirely complimentary.' He turned on his heel and marched out."

Caley chortled at the idea of the militia officer retreating from that imposing bosom, and Morna giggled as she continued, "So now she charges the earth for her wonderful food and serves the very best wine with dinner. I assure you, it's constantly crowded. The ladies from the north side were quite reluctant at first, but they'd always wanted to see the inside of Miss Freda's. Some of our old friends did leave, but Jane Ellen and May stayed and make superb waitresses. May does complain she'd planned on a bit of rest and now is run off her feet."

"I am happy to hear all's well with them," Stanton answered, and meant it. "But I should think it's more than a little dangerous here for you and for Bridey."

"It is dangerous, Stanton, but not for me and Bridey. It is for the poor miners who've gone on strike. The owners of the Smuggler have brought in strikebreakers—scabs, I believe they're called—and it's dangerous for them too. A good many of them were immigrants who can't speak English and they came, happy to find work, not knowing the circumstances under which they were hired. To punish the strikers the mineowners pay these new men what the original miners asked for and were not given. Now the strikers fight with the scabs and the owners' hired gunmen shoot at the strikers."

Caley stirred uneasily on the pillowy sofa. He was not a brave man. "But with all this gunfire about I think you should leave."

Morna shook her head decisively, her gray eyes intense. "Oh, I couldn't. Berkeley is not in one place very long, so that Bridey and I cannot accompany him. And I have work here. The Opera House is packed each evening it's open." She stopped and grinned wryly. "I would tell you that's because everyone loves to hear me sing, but really, there's nothing else for people to do with almost everything closed. In any case, I am paid reasonably well, and with all the miners' families in such dire straits, I can help them. Issy—and Helga—are the real mainstays of those families, though. They've turned our kitchen into a cannery. They and Freda together feed the women and children whose husbands are out of work and, in most cases, not even allowed into Telluride."

Caley gaped at her. "But why should *you* stay here and help these . . . people?"

Her smile was lit by a joy of memory. "Berkeley said once that some of us are born in our homes, others have to find theirs. He swears this valley is his. And it's mine. I found it, I chose it." Her laugh rippled. "I even own one of these mountains. A whole one. And," she ended earnestly, "that makes these people my neighbors."

This turn of the conversation jolted Stanton upright and brought him back to his purpose for being here. Faced with the happiness that added such glow to her already shining beauty, he could not tell her how soon her stay must end. But Berkeley would not find employment here, or anywhere else for that matter. He must marry Amelia. Morna's own wages would hardly support herself and the child in any comfort. No, neither of them had a choice that he could see. But he vowed to himself that he would make it up to her. Only a moment's consideration convinced him how much better off, in fact, she would soon be. *He* could offer the best finishing schools for Bridey, the richest clothing for them both, lay all of Europe at their feet. He thought it best to insinuate that idea now.

Caley began, "Bridget is really the most remarkable child. I'm thinking that she needs advantages."

"Ah, thank you," Morna exclaimed, now on a doting mother's favorite topic. "Do you know that she's not yet five and can already read? And, although I say it myself, her horsemanship for one so small is amazing. She has already told us quite firmly that, when grown, she intends to have a ranch nearby. With lots of horses, she insists. She *is* lucky to be growing up here with all the advantages I myself had, books and music, natural beauty, fresh air, freedom, and," she added, smiling at her own bias, "horses."

Stanton was nonplused. She had not caught his meaning at all. He tried again, choosing his words carefully. "But I worry that, if something should happen . . . if Berkeley—" He stopped himself at the shadow of anguish on her face. "I meant," he stammered, "if circumstances should change, financial ones, or . . . anything." He paused, and at last blurted out, "Morna, promise me something. If anything happened, you would . . . allow me to care for you."

Her equanimity restored, Morna's eyes softened at his words. She rose from her chair and, seating herself next to him, took his hand. "What a generous offer, Stanton. You are a true friend. Berkeley's—and my own. But you must see that I cannot promise that. It wouldn't be fair to you. You're a young man and will marry yourself, have children of your own. Your wife would not appreciate such an obligation and might misunderstand. It could even cause a rift. But I do thank you."

Her nearness, her touch, her lilac perfume, made his head spin. The thought that soon, even if she could not know it, she would be *his*, made him even dizzier. Yet he remembered that there were still formalities to be dealt with. He must find her husband and free her. "But I wish to be assured, for my own sake, that you would never be in want. I need to return to Europe; I have business matters there." He had the arrangements he'd need to make to disentangle Ceci in mind, but he did not say that. "To set my mind at ease, would you allow me to speak to your family and—"

The soft hand in his quivered. To hide that she removed it from his and smoothed her skirt. "No. That is not possible. But again, thank you."

He was now truly at a loss. In desperation he glanced up and was shocked to see the mantel clock. He'd been here well over two hours. Apologizing profusely, he stood up. He caught sight of a small elfin face peering around the archway. Her mother did, too, and rising, beckoned to her.

"You may come in, Bridget," Morna said, now smiling.

Bridey rushed in, clasping her hands over a now clean pinafore. "Did you like the scones? Did she tell you the story? The one about Castle Connemara?"

Morna's movement was slight. Her back stiffened, her petticoats rustled only a little. But Caley knew. He knew that, in an unthinking moment, telling her daughter a bedtime tale, she had given her home its true name. Everything would soon be possible. Soon Morna would be Mrs. Caley. That idea even consoled him for having to leave her.

"No, we hadn't the time. But"—he smiled broadly at the child, already feeling a sense of proprietorship—"I'll hear it later, I hope. Next visit, perhaps. I have to take the morning train to Denver."

"Oh, Stanton," Morna said with genuine regret. "I had no idea your stay here would be so short. Berkeley will be sorry to have missed you. I expect him back in a week or so."

"Unfortunately," Caley replied, trying to look genuinely regretful himself, "I may have to go back to Europe before then. Ceci is there, of course. But give Glendower my regards. I'm sure to have news of him, given all our close friends. I will write. And you must too. I'll send you an address quite soon, one that will always reach me."

He bowed over Bridey's hand, which made her giggle happily. "Miss Bridget," he said, "when I return, I will bring you a lace pinafore to replace the one you've lost."

As Morna saw him out, he pressed her hand in both of his, saying, "You must write when . . . *if* I can be of any help. I am wholly at your service."

"How kind you are," Morna replied. "I will."

Setting his homburg on at a jaunty angle, Caley hurried down the stairs past the lilacs. But before he'd reached the street, he turned and rushed back. "Morna," he blurted out, sweeping off the hat and flushing beet-red, "I wish to be quite plain. I have always wanted to marry you. And I very much still do. When, I mean, *if* your circumstances change, you need only say the word and you will be Mrs. Caley."

Before she could even recover from her astonishment, he dashed down the path and out to the street. Giving her a flurried wave, he strode off.

By the time he'd reached the hotel, he was already planning his immediate passage to the British Isles. Let Amelia herself deal with Berkeley, he thought happily. She would handle it quite efficiently. He intended to drop her a note to that effect just before he left Denver.

CHAPTER 20

Amelia was so enraged by Stanton's note that she'd torn it into small pieces before the butler, who'd brought it in on a silver tray, had even left the morning room. This was by no means easy to do, since Caley's stationery was of heavy gray parchment. Although the butler's rigid back and steady pace did not alter in the slightest at the sound of the ripping, immediately after shutting the door he hurried to the kitchen to warn the cook that lunch today should be superb. Mrs. Powell's moods, always difficult to bear, had been especially trying for the servants since she'd been confined to the house by her widowhood.

Pressing her back so hard against her Louis Seize chair that its rococo carvings almost imprinted themselves on her skin, Amelia cast her eyes in fury to the ceiling. Stanton had written that when he called on Miss Gregory in Telluride, he had not found it possible to broach the subject of her leaving. He'd concluded, *Believe me, dear Amelia, no amount of money will persuade her to do this. Berkeley himself must be made to see that this is in Miss Gregory's best interest. This can be done. Unfortunately, I myself am departing for Europe posthaste and I cannot oblige you in this matter. I leave it in your capable hands.*

So like that parsimonious man, Amelia fumed. "No amount of money," indeed! What had most probably happened was that the wretched woman had asked for quite a large sum, and Caley, being Caley, had boggled at it. The actual figure that should be offered had not been discussed while he was in Denver—that was far too lowering —and Amelia had not even considered doing so. Still, she would have thought he knew that she herself would pay, and that he would not be required to contribute.

Or, she reflected, tapping her fingertips on the piecrust table next to her, perhaps Caley had not even gotten so far as to discuss sums. If he were so besotted with the wretched creature, he might wish her good opinion after the affair was concluded. He might not want to be held responsible, even though he himself planned to benefit by taking Berkeley's place. That was possible. Men were so weak. In any case, she thought, a Denver lawyer would now have to be dispatched to Telluride with carte blanche as to the amount, and the woman gotten rid of that way.

But even as she reached for the bell to call the maid, she paused. The question of who should be sent stayed her hand. Although there were two attorneys in the Thirty-six, either of whom she would trust not to talk, the chosen man might himself think that she'd "bought" a husband, in a sense. *That* would injure her pride. And how could one trust a stranger's discretion?

With an irate swish of silk Amelia rose from her chair. How could Caley have so disappointed her? She'd been quite comfortable with the idea of his handling all this. She'd assumed his silence would be mandatory because he would be too worried about her cutting him out of the circle. When she eventually did—as she'd had every intention of doing —everyone else would follow suit. If he talked then, it would only be to people who didn't count. He wouldn't be believed by those who did, since it would seem that he was merely being vengeful.

His defection caused another problem, she realized, pacing to a window that overlooked the massed glories of her gardens. She'd been depending on Caley to delicately convey to his old friend that she was disposed to be courted by Berkeley. Amelia never questioned that this hint would be all it would take to bring that fortunate man, hat in hand, to her door. But that was a simpler business—even Eloise could take care of that. Finding the right person to deal with this Moira, or Morna, or whatever her name was, was pricklier.

Suddenly noticing a gardener trundling a wheelbarrow past a rosebush whose deadheads definitely needed cutting, she rapped sharply on the window. Only her sternly leveled finger and a snipping motion with the other hand finally made it clear to the man what needed doing. It was then that Amelia knew who should go to Telluride, the one person who would be sure to manage the matter effectively. She should go herself.

Although she certainly didn't dwell on this inwardly, the fact was that Amelia was quite jealous and more than a little curious. Berkeley had been living with this woman for some time—six years, Stanton had said. And Caley—who was quite particular—now wished to take up with her himself. What *did* she look like? When Amelia had finally gotten a glimpse of Laughton's mistress—and she'd known who the strumpet was when she saw that her own Paris-designed hat had been copied—she was frankly astonished. Plump and good-natured looking, that was to be expected, but the woman was walleyed!

Staring unseeingly at a bed of opulent dahlias, Amelia clearly imagined a pillowy blonde, one who was certainly a little coarse if she'd been willing to live in a mining camp, the sort of woman who was not too particular about bed linen. Although it was beyond her own understanding, men seemed attracted to a looseness, an indifference to what really mattered. Now that the idea was conceived, Amelia was really quite eager to squelch such a person.

She hurried up the staircase, but she paused as always on the landing, staring at the full-length portrait of Berkeley Glendower at the top of the stairs. The heavy gold frame with its serpentine leaves and intricate cutwork had been shipped from Europe—it had taken her months to find one that satisfied her. The painter had managed to suggest that the man himself was about to step from that enclosure and come walking down the steps to meet whoever was coming up.

Amelia would have preferred that Berkeley had been portrayed in evening clothes, for she thought him a man born to wear white tie and tails. But this had been a copy of a portrait his mother had owned, and in it he was dressed in a rich, satiny brown frock coat with matching cravat and trousers. The folded-back wing-collar of the dazzling white shirt was opened a little at the throat and around his neck was a flowing, dark tie. On his hands were pale tan kid gloves.

His shining dark hair was brushed smoothly back, except for a tuft that had sprung loose and feathered across his brow. The painter had caught the warmth in the odd shade of brown of his eyes, and he'd exactly reproduced Berkeley's smile. The curve of the lips was confident, but not self-esteeming. Instead, he looked as if he were about to speak, to continue a conversation he could share only with the person before him.

Her eyes fixed on that sensuous mouth, Amelia almost shivered with pleasure, knowing she would soon own the man portrayed. All through the dull months of her widowhood, each night she'd stood here and imagined him walking down the stairs to her, slowly pulling off the gloves, then his long fingers caressing her face, then cupping it to his.

Now, in determined haste, she swirled up the rest of the stairs and along the corridor to her sitting room. She opened her Marie Antoinette secretary and seated herself before its gleaming ebony fold-out top. A list was called for because arrangements of the kind that she was wholly unused to making would have to be thought out. For Amelia Powell had never, in all her life, set foot unaccompanied outside the grounds of any of her estates, neither as child nor adult. A woman of her station would never go beyond her garden alone. It was unthinkable.

If anyone discovered she was going to do it now, and to such a distance as Telluride, they would be convinced that her mourning had unsettled her mind. It would take some planning to hide this trip from the servants, who would gossip ferociously to their counterparts in other households. Therefore, she decided on sending her personal maid on the train to Colorado Springs, some sixty miles south, with the requisite bulky trunks for a longish stay. She would imply that she herself would be traveling down with a friend, by carriage. And she would be, with only two days' delay.

Pulling a piece of ecru linen notepaper from one of the gold-encrusted small drawers in the secretary, Amelia began her first task. She took malicious delight in choosing her hostess in Colorado Springs, a woman who would be thrown into a state of feverish anxiety at the news that, on short notice, Denver's social leader would be coming for a visit. Apologizing daintily, Amelia explained that she could think of no one she would rather stay with, now that her mourning period was at an end. Really, she thought with a great deal of pleasure, this was turning into one of the most satisfying adventures of her life.

Halfway to Telluride, Amelia was finding it one of the worst experiences she had ever undergone. Since no one could know she was going to the train station, she'd had to hire a carriage. That turned out to be only a pony trap. The driver had ignored her order to go more slowly and she'd been hurtled about in the backseat. Her carefully done hair was loosened and her hat tilted askew. At the station the porters had studiously overlooked this woman traveling alone, which was highly suspicious in any case, and hustled after the gentlemen from whom a tip would be forthcoming. In a state of shock, she'd had to carry her own valise.

These humiliations were followed by a nightmare journey. Amelia had spent a great deal of time on trains en route to the East Coast and back, but it had always been in the same car—the Powells' own parlor car. This resembled a suite of rooms on wheels and had been magnificently furnished by Amelia herself. The commodious red velvet chaises in the sitting area were amply overstuffed. Two servants always accompanied them. Before today, however, she'd always chafed at the discomforts even of this mode of travel. The rooms were so cramped, there were frequent stops, and the motion jerky in the places where roadbeds were in need of repair.

The ride to Telluride had begun badly and got worse and worse and worse. In outrage, she pointed out to the conductor that all the small hard seats were covered with a thin layer of coal dust. A sixtyish man in need of a closer shave, he looked her up and down and grinned, exposing uneven, mossy teeth. "Glad t'oblige a lady," he responded. His intonation on the word *lady* suggested that was a little joke between the two of them. Then, swiping at one of the seats with an already filthy, wadded-up handkerchief, he performed a mock bow.

No sooner had they left Denver than he found occasion to lean over the empty seat next to Amelia to point out one of the views. His breath was stale sausage and onion. When she lifted her umbrella with a threatening motion, he wandered off, chortling that he *did* like a spunky one. On his trips down the aisle, whenever he caught her eye, he winked.

As the train ascended higher and higher, she was thrown from side to side in her seat because of the winding required. Moreover, the ash that covered the seats now was sprinkled liberally over the once immaculate beige of her broadcloth suit. She spent an hour composing a long, vitriolic letter of complaint to the president of the railroad, whom she knew, and then realized she couldn't send it without revealing she'd been on the train alone.

But as the grade grew steeper, the tribulations of the journey were almost forgotten in the sheer terror she felt on looking down. The drops were dramatic. Just enough room for a narrow track had been hewn out of the mountainsides, and the trestles spanning the chasms were not an inch wider than they need be. Each lurch of the train caused a horror of tipping right over and plunging down.

Travel stained, nettled, and exquisitely uncomfortable, Amelia was only sustained by the anticipation of squashing the contemptible slattern who had subjected her to this ordeal. Calling up a mental image of the woman she'd imagined, her lips curved in a smile of creamy expectation. Probably the woman was pretty enough, and no doubt thought she was a great deal more attractive than she was—Amelia pictured her in a frumpy teagown, blond hair untidy. How her painted mouth would gape at the sight of Mrs. Laughton Powell, especially because that was not at all the person she believed was coming to call.

Amelia had sent a note on plain paper to Miss Gregory at Berkeley's address, having learned from William Murdoch that Glendower was still in the territory of New Mexico, and asked if she might call at four o'clock to discuss a matter of mutual interest. Mentioning a long friendship with Berkeley, she had not signed the letter. Moira or Morna, or whatever, would be expecting a man. Given her calling, she would be looking forward to the banter, the usual coarse compliments that men paid women of her sort. And she would be dressed accordingly in some sort of cheap, frayed satin.

But all along Amelia had intended to arrive shortly after three. Unready, in the midst of her toilette, the woman would therefore be at a disadvantage from the start, and Amelia had planned her remarks—and her outfit—so that the great difference between the two of them would be further emphasized. Unfortunately, she had not taken into account the effect of coal dust on her light tailored suit or the white shirtwaist beneath it. Still, the cloth itself was obviously expensive, and she felt that any other woman would recognize how beautifully it was cut. Black velvet lapels and matching ribbons that marched down the jacket and skirt, as well as a single ebony aigrette plume on her hat, were her only ornamentation. She'd been pleased with the idea that the severity of her clothing would underline the businesslike nature of her call.

Reminding herself continually *not* to look out the window, Amelia spent the last hour of the trip pleasantly enough in rehearsing the upcoming visit. First, she would ferret out the sort of sum the woman would regard as munificent. Then she would coolly offer to double it if the move from Telluride were accomplished immediately and without a word to Berkeley. Amelia debated whether such a person could be counted on to live up honorably to the latter part. But, if he discovered the truth, Berkeley could be told—and Amelia could imagine herself pointing this out with just an edge of sorrowful reproach—that such a relationship was sure to injure his business standing. Consequently, she would say, she'd acted as a friend in freeing him from it.

Soon this began to sound like the truth to her. Really she was doing him a favor, she was sure. And now that the moment of actual confrontation was approaching, she found herself warmed by spiteful eagerness. She could hardly wait.

When the train finally settled with a hiss of brakes next to the platform, Amelia swept off, ignoring the conductor's outstretched hand. She walked briskly into the depot, intending to freshen up to the extent she could and get someone to find a carriage.

At that moment Morna was staring at her image in the cheval glass, patted the sleek shoulders of her emerald-green silk dress and said, "Issy, you have outdone yourself on these sleeves. I could never have told they originally were great puffs of material. And this lace from my old shawl is glorious at the elbow. But you don't think the bodice is too low cut now?"

Behind her, adjusting the back of the dress and doing up the last button, Isobel replied, "Nae, nae. Perfect for the Opera House. Jane Ellen has the latest Godey's pattern book and they showed one more deep in front than that. For the evening, you ken, with the big pearl choker to set it off. But I've got a bit more of a surprise."

From beneath the piles of material on the chair behind her, she pulled out a high-necked yoke of lace and fastened it around Morna's neck. Tiny rows of shirring covered her throat and shoulders, and the lace that matched the ends of the sleeves cascaded over her upper arms and across her bosom. "Rest of the shawl," she said, looking at the effect in great satisfaction. "Wi' that, you've got an afternoon dress. Nice and plain, except for that lovely bit of lace."

Morna turned and embraced her warmly. "You are an angel, Issy. That must have taken you hours. And you shouldn't have, with all the other work you do. But I love the way it looks. Grace Nordstrom is coming to tea tomorrow and she will love it too. And that reminds me, some friend of Berkeley's is coming this afternoon."

Isobel nodded and started putting away the sewing materials. "Hmm, the Cornish fruit loaf is left and that's nice toasted and buttered. And I could whip up a seedy cake."

"He said he'd be here at four. But it was an odd note and he didn't sign it. It sounded as if it were a business matter, but I can't imagine why he'd want to talk to me. And it was certainly a woman's handwriting." She shrugged and adjusted a tortoise comb in her neat upsweep. "Anyway, I shall just practice till then."

Fifteen minutes later Morna was playing "Maple Leaf Rag"—a current favorite at the Opera House—with so much gusto that neither she nor Issy heard the horse's hooves or the sound of the creaking carriage wheels outside. The grizzled, bearded driver scratched at the bit of gray Union underwear showing beneath the open collar of his flannel shirt, smiled, and turned to his fare, saying, "That's Miss Morna. Don't she play a treat?"

Without responding Amelia Powell stepped down and marched up the pathway. Sam Goler, for it was he, called at her back, "Could ya' tell her I'm here?" He'd quickly caught the delectable aroma of the caraway in the baking seedy cake. Amelia whirled indignantly and spat out, "I am not accustomed to delivering such messages!"

Sam nodded agreeably, figuring that meant he could invite himself around to the kitchen door and wait inside. Isobel was an equally soft touch. He walked up the path side by side with his fare, only veering off to skirt the lilac bushes and go in through the garden gate.

Before he'd finished crossing the lawn, Bridey had caught sight of her favorite ostler through a narrow staircase window and ran to her mother. "Mr. Goler's here," she announced with pleasure.

"Let him in, please," Morna responded, paying attention to the intricate rhythms of the ragtime.

So it was that Bridey opened the door to Amelia Powell. That matron stiffened, finding it inconceivable that a servant's child, no matter how pretty, should be allowed to greet her. What had Berkeley sunk to, she wondered in indignation. "Where's your mother?" she asked with a cold stare. Although the exterior of the house had been quite a surprise, the way it was run was just what she'd imagined.

Bridget had not seen the lady because the lower half of the door was solid wood, but she quickly recovered her manners. "Please come in," she said. "Mother's practicing, and I'll get her."

The music stopped shortly after the little girl disappeared into the parlor. Amelia reeled with shock. If the pianist was her mother, no doubt the child was Berkeley's! She had simply never considered the possibility. So overcome was she that she had to grasp the carved newel post for support, did not even glance around the entry hall or into the parlor to notice the furnishings.

But the sight of the woman coming through the archway of that room now stunned her with a tidal-wave force. The fashionable dress, the aristocratic carriage, the sheer beauty of her face and form made Amelia's tongue cleave to the roof of her mouth. Only her iron self-discipline enabled her to unstick it. "I," she said frostily, "am Mrs. Laughton Powell."

Morna smiled in delight. "Oh, Berkeley has so often spoken of you. How do you do? I'm Morna Gregory." She gestured gracefully toward the parlor. "Won't you please come in?"

Amelia was seated in the airy, sweet-scented room before she was really aware of it. In her rehearsal on the train she'd planned to address the trollop rudely by her first name and usher *her* to the nearest convenient seat. But she found that she'd again forgotten the name, being too taken aback when it was given.

Briefly, faced with the woman before her rather than the one she'd conceived of, the idea of changing her approach did flash through Amelia's mind. But several things kept her from doing so. Although Amelia was an intelligent woman, her thinking did tend to run on rather rigid rails in terms of class. She was, after all, one of the Wetherhills of South Carolina, a rather long line—for America—of patricians. She never questioned that she was made of exalted material and that, while a given individual might parrot the manners of the upper class, mimic their style of dress, inevitably such a person was made of coarser stuff. She steadily maintained this belief despite living on the edge of the frontier, where new fortunes—and new aristocrats— were constantly being formed from mining, smelting, and meat packing.

Having been told that Berkeley's paramour had been not only a singer, but one in a house of ill-repute, she really could not see any point in proffering courtesies, despite the woman's appearance. No doubt, to please Berkeley, this Moira or Morna had acquired a few social graces. But such a person, in her view, could not really understand anything but money.

Then, too, it was one of the rare occasions in Amelia's life when she felt less than perfectly attired. Looking at Morna's elegance, she was acutely conscious of the fact that her own hair was coming undone, of the smudge on the cuff of her shirtwaist, of the black specks on her skirt, and the dust on her shoes. Being at such a disadvantage distracted her. She'd begun to feel as if the situation was not under her control. That was also very unusual. This complex of unpleasant sensations not only clouded her judgment, but raised her temper.

"I'll have Issy bring in the tea," Morna said, smiling. "Could I—"

Amelia interrupted her. "Sit down. This is not a social call."

Morna withdrew her hand from the bell, raised her eyebrows, but said nothing. She did not, however, sit down.

Thus forced to crane upward at her, Amelia nonetheless launched into her prepared speech. "Berkeley Glendower is a man of much promise. In addition, before my husband passed away, he was a good friend of Laughton's, as he is of mine. I was therefore quite distressed to learn that his personal life is in such disarray. It can only harm his social standing and consequently his business life. This must end. You must leave. I am prepared—"

"I beg your pardon, Mrs. Powell," Morna interrupted, her gray eyes now as hard as stone. "If these remarks were to be made at all, they should more properly be addressed to Berkeley."

"Let me finish." Amelia's eyes took in the expensive lace, the cut of the silk gown, and she determined she would have to double the highest amount she'd envisioned. That did not trouble her, but this woman's assured manner stung her. Amelia felt as if she were being treated as an equal. Even the plume in her hat trembled in indignation. Her voice became even colder. "I am at present prepared—out of friendship to Mr. Glendower—to offer you any sum you name. Given the child, I will be most generous. You, and she, will be able to live in comfort. But this depends on your instant and complete cooperation."

"And if I refuse?" Although Morna's tone was itself still frigid January, she'd become curious indeed. Mrs. Laughton Powell was implying she was acting from a disinterested motive, but she was high-handedly ignoring the feelings of a man she claimed to want to protect. And she had come personally on such a journey, one that she'd obviously not enjoyed.

"I would be forced to inform all those for whom he invests that he is . . . unreliable," Amelia shot back. "Moreover, I cannot believe then that any man of prominence would be willing to employ him in any capacity whatsoever."

Although quite taken aback, Morna looked closely at the woman, the tightening of the prominent cheekbones, the ruthless line of the mouth. When her eyes met Amelia's glare, however, she caught the slight sideways shift. She also noticed how tightly clenched the gloved hands were on the umbrella handle, the way its point dug into the Oriental rug. *Mrs. Laughton Powell is more than angry, she is jealous,* she thought. *She wants Berkeley, wants him very much indeed.*

"Let me understand you," Morna said, clasping her hands together. "In order to enable Berkeley's business affairs to prosper, you feel that I should leave him. Out of friendship for him, and a desire to see him succeed, you are offering me money so that I will do this."

"Quite correct," Amelia returned, her throat tight with enormous vexation. She knew that she'd given something away in the staring contest, which normally would never have occurred, even with women she saw as her peers. But she did not doubt that in the end, *she* would win. A large amount of money—or whatever this person considered a large amount—would carry the day. "How much do you require?"

Morna waved away the last question with a quick sweep and continued with a knife edge in her voice, "But if our relationship does not end, you will see to it that he is unable to earn his living. You would ruin him to save him? Mrs. Powell, that is not an act of friendship. It is a threat."

"Mere words," Amelia ground out between gritted teeth. "Do not ape the style of your betters. How much?"

Morna moved to the archway of the parlor, her dress rustling over the rug. Amelia was certain that she was pacing, considering a sum, and waited.

At the door Morna turned and said dryly, "I conceive my 'betters' to be men and women who are more magnanimous, more generous, more kind than I am, *not* more rich. But you are right about one thing, Mrs. Powell. This is not a social call. You have been far too uncivil. I will tell Mr. Goler you will be waiting for him in the carriage. You may see yourself out."

CHAPTER 21

Candlelight would be the thing, Berkeley decided, leaving on only the dimmest of the electric bulbs on the wall of the back parlor. And a small fire to take away the chill of the late summer night. He knelt down on the shaggy sheepskin rug before the hearth and started the thin white aspen logs that Isobel had laid out before retiring. Then he rose and, brushing bits of clinging fleece off the knees of his black worsted evening trousers, surveyed the room with enormous satisfaction.

Outside, from the bottom of the garden, came the soothing, constant murmur of the river. In here the gentle crackle of the fire added counterpoint. The flames winked on the transparent squares of the cut-glass decanters on the library table and added a tint of orange to the freshly opened yellow roses. The candles cast their honeyed glow on the gloss of polished tables, the dull gleam of leather sofas. Returning only hours ago from his travels, he'd just had time to bathe and change before accompanying Morna to the Opera House. Now he was beginning to wrap himself in that sense of harmony home brought him.

But tonight he did not relax into the worn comfort of his afghan-backed armchair, instead walking the length of the room and staring out into the darkness. Something was troubling Morna and he could not even guess what it might be. He'd seen it in the absence of the crinkles of amusement usually at the corners of her eyes, in the presence of a worried set to her mouth. He'd felt it in her prolonged embrace on his arrival. He'd heard it in every song she sang that evening, even caught it beneath the merry jingle of ragtime.

As he'd watched her onstage, he'd tried to decipher the nature of the problem. Not well? A noticeable pallor? But that was impossible to decide with her. The fashion of the time that decreed women should, in daytime, be absolutely covered from chin to toe, but décolleté at night, wholly suited Morna. Covered from the sun, her skin in evening gowns was white rose petals in moonlight, he thought with delight. Her neck, her shoulders, her breasts, gleamed against the rich emerald green of the silk dress. The froth of lace at her elbows was not as white as her arms. Entranced by this pale shining, by the sure sweetness of her voice, he'd forgotten for the moment to be concerned.

As he paced, he smilingly recalled when they'd first met and he could not read her expressions, he who'd prided himself on his acute observations at cards with other men. Now he knew each eyelash flicker, each twitch of the soft mouth. He was surprised at this riddle. He heard her footsteps in the hall, returning from looking in on Bridey. Busying himself with getting a decanter, warming a snifter in the palm of his hands, he waited until she had sat down.

"Berkeley," she said edgily, taking the brandy he held out, "I find that I am not the only contender for your heart."

Of all the possible openings that one had never entered his mind. "That's only fair, my love," he replied, trying to catch her eyes, but failing. "I thought I was going to have to empty Telluride of men to gain possession of yours. But in my case the contest was over the moment I saw you." Although he could not imagine what lay behind her statement, his first feeling was a flush of pleasure at the idea that Morna was jealous. He'd never seen any sign of that in their years together.

Adjusting the tails of his black evening coat, he seated himself on the couch across from hers so he would have a better chance to explore this when she lifted her glance. Now he filled his own snifter and waited for her to meet his eyes.

Over the rim of the fragile glass she finally did so. He saw anxiety there, but not doubt, he thought. The fierce elation that came from knowing she was very sure of his love was far better than that light-fingered touch of earlier pleasure.

"Who is this lady of such taste and intelligence?" he asked, hoping to brush away whatever was upsetting her.

"Amelia Powell," she replied, setting down her glass and unfastening the back of one pearl eardrop. She bent her head to unclasp her wide pearl choker and did not look up when she added, "Perhaps she does not find living alone to her liking. In any case, I believe that she has chosen you for her new husband."

He ran a little of the smooth liquor across his tongue before swallowing it. "Hmm," he answered. "I would be happy to oblige Amelia in most matters. In this instance I cannot. What makes you suspect this?"

Morna removed her other earring and put it on top of the translucent pile of pearls on the table. She told him of the first part of Amelia's visit, ending with "She expects me to leave instantly, but she is prepared to make it all worth my while financially."

He put the snifter down carefully, but his fingers clutched it so whitely before he did so that it was a wonder the thin glass did not snap. Then, in a panther leap of controlled rage, he was on his feet. He only barely contained his shaking voice. "She came here and spoke to *you* this way?"

"Wait, there is more I must tell you." Morna ran the palm of her hand over and over the deep green silk of her dress as she repeated Amelia's threat. As his lips pressed together in a narrow line of fury, she rose quickly and took his hands in hers. "Oh, Berkeley, she means this. She *will* do it. She will take away your livelihood."

Dropping his hands, she turned away from him and walked to the windows, looking out to the river so that he couldn't see her anguished face. "In the beginning I felt an odd sympathy for her, despite her . . . manner. Then anger overwhelmed me. But later I could see that you and I would have to discuss whether—" She had to stop, to swallow the tears that scalded her throat, almost choking her. Although she had repeated the words to herself earlier, she now found she could not say them.

With her back to him she could not see how wrath swiftly darkened his handsomeness, the force with which he gripped the sides of the mantel, as though to rip it from the wall. He kept his voice dangerously low.

"Whether what, Morna? Whether we should part so that I might acquire the Powell fortune? So that I could—how shall I say it?—maintain my position in society? Have all the investors begging for my advice on the grounds that I must be a brilliant man to have married so well?"

Morna heard the bitter ire licking his words, but she would not turn. During several sleepless nights she had decided she could not bear asking him to give up his work, all that so interested him for her sake. On the other hand she could not bear giving *him* up. Tossing and turning, she'd remembered his intense pleasure when he talked of solving mining problems, the exhilaration in his eyes when he planned creating hydroelectric power from Bridal Veil Falls. That he loved her, she knew well, but had in agony faced the question of what would happen to love purchased at such cost. Forced into a post that bored him, might he not come to hate his daily life, and *her*?

Rising each gray dawn, she'd shivered at the recollection of the Ute curse, that for one hundred and five years no man would be happy here, no family survive for more than four generations. Going over in her mind all that the valley had suffered in the last five years—the fire, the avalanches, the families torn by the labor wars—fear had rippled through her. The echo came remorselessly: No man will be happy. At last, that morning she'd determined the decision must be his. And he must understand that she knew what he was sacrificing for her if he chose to stay with her. Now she said, through trembling lips, "What would you do without your work?"

"I see." He bit the two words out. In some cooler part of his mind Berkeley was aware that this question could be interpreted in more than one way, that Morna could be asking him if he could be content doing something else. Since he was a man who had extraordinary confidence in his own abilities, he was untroubled by any fear that he could not earn money. But, partly because he suddenly suspected *she* might not share that trust, partly because his outrage at Amelia Powell's behavior was spilling out, he responded, "You're assuming we would be in some trouble without my current employment, worried that I could not care for you and Bridey. On the other hand, you are thinking that we could both live more grandly apart. Given my new 'position,' I could easily afford to support you sumptuously as well. Then you wouldn't have to fret about money."

"Ah, Berkeley," she cried out, running back to stand before him, no longer caring that he'd see her tear-stained cheeks. "How can you think—"

But the sight of her grief inflamed him further. Beyond all reason now, he blamed her for what he insisted on seeing as a lack of trust. He sought to wound her. "Or has another country been heard from? Bridey was prattling to me as I slipped into my vest that Mr. Caley had called and was going to return with a lace pinafore for her. Six years would not dampen his ardor. You plan to change partners, live elegantly on *his* large fortune?"

She had at first tried to interrupt him, one hand out in entreaty. But with each sentence she'd become paler and now her gray eyes seemed onyx in her white face. Her outstretched hand whipped furiously across his cheek.

"You cannot believe that!" she cried. "Not for a moment did I consider his offer."

He grasped her by the shoulders so hard that it seemed that his fingers not only dug through the bare skin but clutched the bone. "What kind of logic chopping is this, Morna? I can only assume that you were not even planning on telling me this part. Not even so much as a 'By the by, my sweet, Stanton Caley dropped in and, over the tea and crumpets, he proposed.'"

His blood pounded at his temples, for at this image Berkeley himself now felt a wild flash of jealousy. There was nothing of pleasure in it. Describing jealousy as 'green eyed' implies a certain coolness, but he was blinded by that emotion's red haze. His arms so shuddered with the force of his passions that her head was jerked back.

"But *I* was given"—his voice was almost a hiss—"no such latitude in my decision. Not at all. You expected me to coolly discuss whether I would leave you for Amelia. That signals a distinct lack of trust."

Morna's eyes at first widened in surprise at his interpretation. Then anger flooded her as well. *This* was his response to her concern for him? His hot breath scorched her cheek, his grip sent stabs of pain down her arms, and he was shaking her like a rag doll. "You *purposely* misunderstand," she spat back. "And you insult me. And you are hurting me. Let me go at once."

"No. I will not."

At the hardness of his tone, even through the blaze of her own fury, Morna felt a jolt of astonishment. So accustomed was she to his urbanity, she had never known his force except in lovemaking.

Before she found her voice, he said, his words sounding as if they were ripped from his throat, "You are mine. I will never let you go." His kisses were so cruel that his teeth almost cut her lips. They awoke the ache she'd felt during all the long days of his absence.

At last, twisting her face sideways, she ran her tongue over her bruised mouth and said fiercely, "You do not *own* me, Berkeley Glendower!"

He spun her backward onto the couch and, in a second, was above her, his hair down his forehead, his eyes hot. "Yes, I do. Because you are half me."

"Get up!" She tried pushing him with her forearm. "You are crushing me—and my dress!"

"Yes." His voice was distinct and low. "So I am. Take it off. Now."

CHAPTER 22

"Berkeley," Morna said sternly, "you mustn't think this means I have forgiven you." Since she was lying next to him on the deep pile of the sheepskin, curled spoon fashion, her bare back against his chest, this statement did not have the severity it might have in other circumstances. Furthermore, as she spoke she was making sure with her free hand that the afghan that covered her was also spread over him.

"Then," he replied, tucking his right arm around her waist, and turning her toward him, "I will have to repeat the performance"—he brushed his lips lightly down her cheek—"again"—his mouth nuzzled her neck—"again"—his tongue flicked at her breast—"and again until you finally—"

"You must be serious for a moment," she interrupted, although her fingertips were caressing the long bone at the base of his throat, tightening on his shoulder. She winced as she saw the teeth marks, which were hers, and tried to smooth them away. "You *know* what worried me was that you would be miserable without work that challenges you."

"Yes." He supported himself on an elbow, putting his face in his palm so he could look down at her in the fading light of the fire. "But Amelia Powell cannot take *that* away from me. She will sever my relationship with the Murdoch group, true, and the mines here, I think. She is not a woman at all used to being thwarted. Everyone has always scurried to do her bidding. She will be most unhappy with me when she receives the stiff note I'll send tomorrow—one that will end our friendship. Even close acquaintances of mine, here and in Denver, will only bow distantly to me from across the street."

"Berkeley, I'm so sorry. I—"

"Don't be," he stopped her, stroking her hair. "You are as aware as I am that such people are no loss. I have several interesting possibilities in the territory of New Mexico, although they're not yet lucrative. In the meantime I have an ace up my sleeve." He paused, then laughed as he laid his head back down on the thick sheepskin and looked at the ceiling. "Not, come to think of it, that that's the expression I should choose, given what I'm about to tell you. Do you know what I do to while away the evenings when I'm traveling?"

Grinning, she tangled her fingers tightly in the mat of his chest hair and tugged. "Do I want to know?"

"Ouch. Yes. I play high-stakes poker. Over the last months I've been putting my winnings into a fund for Bridey's ranch, and I was amazed to find that the child could very nearly buy one tomorrow. 'Manna from heaven,' I'll tell her when she's grown. In the meantime, if I play a little more, we can manage quite nicely."

She'd turned her head so quickly toward him that her last hairpins caught in the rug. As she sat up in surprise, her hair spilled down in a black tangle around her face. "Do you mean that? Would you like that?"

"Ah, Morna," he reached up and entwined his fingers in her curls, brushing them back over her shoulder. "I think the reason you've been suffering lately is that you imagine this change for me would be like asking you to give up your singing. An almost unendurable loss. But it's not at all the same. I enjoy the skill involved in that kind of gambling, the concentration, the excitement, and in any case it's only temporary. Things will move fast in New Mexico—it'll be a state in a very few years."

He pulled on her shoulder, and she slid back down into the circle of his arm. "But it does mean, my love, fairly continual traveling for a time." He looked laughingly at the ceiling again. "One has to move on, give the rich land barons a chance to forget how much they lost on the last go, and let their confidence build up so that they imagine they can beat me on my return. Which they are unlikely to do. Still, I can arrange long stays here between trips. Can you approve?"

"That is your decision," she said earnestly, and then, feeling him turn his head toward her, rose, putting her fingers on his mouth lest he interrupt. As she spoke, she ran a fingertip over his long, straight upper lip, circled the fullness of the lower one. "I want to say this. Earlier, I only wanted to explain to you that I could appreciate the sacrifice asked of you, that I could at least understand your choice, no matter what you decided. So many times during the last few days I've thought of what you said once in talking about Bridget's future. You hoped for her a man she could love and admire, but work, as well, that would give her a reason to live. So I concluded—"

"No." He groaned, squeezing her hand, his arm crushing her to his side. "Don't throw my own words back at me, even though that's fair, I suppose. God, yes, the importance of work." He brushed his hair back and rubbed his forehead with his fingers. "What I was thinking was that she might not be as lucky as we are, might not find that man. Or, having found him, not be able to have him. So she would need something else to sustain her. Then, too, I had in mind these idle gentlewomen, with their empty souls, who lead a cursed existence and call it luxury."

He sat up and raised her upright to face him so she could see how serious he was. The firelight behind him lit his dark hair, cast his brooding face in shadow. Only his thick-lashed eyes shone. "You know, Morna, you know well how it is with a loved child. You try to foresee every blow life might deal her, try to protect, prepare, and in the end you can't. All we can hope is that Bridey will make *her* right choice. Most of all, I'd want her to have the happiness I've had with you. You are what's most important to me. I would give up the round earth itself, and all that's piled on it, rather than let you go."

She stroked his face, touched the winged brows, the high cheekbones, the perfect mouth, remembering the first time she'd looked up into that face and been alarmed at his effect on her. She'd tried then to convince herself that it was his sheer handsomeness. All she'd wanted was to escape his presence, hoping to find later that was it, that he was only beautiful. Now she loved Berkeley for what he was and knew what she'd seen at first had little to do with it, and knew she could only be happy in his presence. Drawing him to her, she curved her hands around the nape of his neck. "But, my dear, I had to hear you say that. Not at all because I doubted you, but because it was a choice you had to make, not one I could make for you, as much as I love you."

"Then promise," he said, his lips burning her ear, "you would not leave me."

Over his shoulder she looked at the flickering fire and then at the images of the flames on his smooth muscular back. She closed her eyes against the thought of how vulnerable the strongest was, of the thousand doors in the flesh that let death in. "I would to save your life," she said passionately. Then she leaned back to smile into his eyes. "But not to save your livelihood. That I can promise. It's clear, knowing you, that was never a requirement. Still"—and her anger sparkled again at the thought—"it's not at all fair that they can do this to you, not at all just that they will now question your competence, say you would make unwise use of their money, whereas *I* am the investment they object to."

He swooped her over onto her back and bent close, his smile wicked. "Now, that's an idea I hadn't considered, Morna. *You* as an investment. Why, were I to parade you as an example of my successful venturing, they'd all have to concede I do very well indeed. No additional overhead—I had to live somewhere. And all this time I've had the use and enjoyment of you at very little cost. You buy your own dresses from your earnings. You save me a housekeeper's wages, overseeing this establishment, and you decorate *and* put fresh flowers in vases, besides. You—"

"Berkeley, this is not funny. They—"

He cupped his hand firmly over her mouth. "You brought it up. Let me finish. By producing a healthy and beautiful child you have increased my stock. Best of all, you have not depreciated in value at all. Were I to turn you over to Stanton Caley, he'd pay me a good round sum. Ow!"

She'd clamped her teeth into the underside of his ring finger, and he jerked his hand back to rub it. "I won't mention the biting part. That would lower your price. Except for the nips of passion. Probably a good selling point."

"If," she responded sweetly, rising up on her elbows, her hair tossed back, her eyes glittering, "we are to continue this conversation, I could say that *I* am the one that shines as an investor. You cost me nothing. You can earn your keep with only a deck of cards. And one of America's richest women will play high for hearts. Think what she will pay for you just as you stand." She let her eyes move down his naked body and lifted an eyebrow when she reached his groin. "Especially as you stand. I could turn you over as is. Even undergarments need not be included, I should imagine."

He rolled over on top of her, pinioning her firmly. He grimaced at her remarks. "Hmm. Let's not continue. Put the shoe on the other foot, and it pinches painfully. But first, I don't think I included in the appraisal one of the chief advantages I enjoy."

She wriggled beneath him in protest. "I thought we were not going to continue."

"Continue *talking* is what I meant, Morna. Talking." He began to kiss her deeply and slowly.

CHAPTER 23

Half the world away it was already midmorning in London and Ceci, who now always thought of herself as Madame Stanton Caley (and was, in fact, so registered at the hotel at which she was staying), was supremely disquieted. It seemed to her that her chances of achieving that actual legal status were slipping away. She was too shrewd to think that Caley had ever had any intention of marrying her, but she had thought that under the right circumstances it might be managed. At the moment, staring down at busy Sloane Street from the window of the Cadogan Hotel, she felt the circumstances were not at all right.

During their six years together Ceci had set aside a goodly sum (which she inwardly referred to as her "competence") in case of this eventuality. She had done this by bargaining couturieres down to the lowest possible price and having them bill Stanton at their original figure. Moreover, she had practiced innumerable small economies, slipping coins into a separate purse, which was not easy because he, too, was conscious of costs. When the amount had grown respectable enough, she'd taken part of it to a London firm and explained that her husband was an invalid who needed to have his money conservatively invested. Watching her nest egg grow had become one of Ceci's chief pleasures.

She had also envisioned that Caley, given the towering tantrum she planned to stage if the evil day arrived, would give her a sizable parting gift. Altogether, this dowry would enable her to come by a husband who was reasonably prosperous, if that's what she chose. Or she could live economically with her parents until their deaths increased the amount. However, the latter arrangement was, she'd found after only a two-week stay in the dismal apartment in the very unfashionable arrondissement in Paris where she'd been raised, quite impossible.

Her mother and father both had been outraged at her return, because of the talk it would create, and avidly curious at the extraordinary elegance of her clothing. They'd grudgingly allowed her to stay in the spare bedroom, at the same price for which she could have roomed at one of the better hotels, telling her *they* could hardly be expected to bear the cost of her upkeep. The room had once been hers, but was stripped of the few pictures taken of her, as well as any remembrance of her existence. Ceci—her parents continued to call her Colette, but she ignored that completely—realized that avarice had won when the childhood pictures reappeared, hung again in the exact places where the wallpaper had been slightly less faded.

But the narrow rooms, dark even in the midst of summer, the dreary evenings, when her mother sat disapprovingly turning shirt collars and her father rationed his reading of the newspaper as carefully as the single glass of wine allowed at dinner, had immediately reminded her of why she'd left ten years earlier. But at that time she'd been accustomed to the weekday soup, made from Sunday's bones, enlivened occasionally by a fresh vegetable from a vendor's cart, and served each evening. She'd been used to going to bed at darkness to save on kerosene and candles—the endless skimps and savings—which she knew would be a set way of life even with a husband of a better income than her father earned as a clerk.

Before coming back to her home she'd imagined that she could adapt again, telling herself that, after all, she lived rather frugally with Stanton. It was Ceci herself who had urged they keep rooms at the Cadogan, rather than at Claridge's. While the Cadogan was very near Mayfair and on the edge of elegant Belgravia, it had a slightly racy reputation, which kept the cost down. Lillie Langtry had had her town house there, and it was from the hotel's Turret Room that Oscar Wilde had been carted off to prison. Moreover, like a good French housewife, Ceci often brought in cheese, pâté, and fresh fruit for lunch in their rooms so that they need not be put to the expense of taking each meal out. Now she realized that, by comparison, she had enjoyed the wildest luxury with Caley.

Fleeing back to the suite of rooms he'd kept at the Cadogan against his return, she'd determined to do all that was in her power to continue in that lavish life. Ceci began plotting, assuming that Stanton would be gone for several months. To her surprise she'd barely settled in herself before he, too, rushed back.

He'd been equally taken aback at seeing her and had been almost brusque in his greeting. But he'd relented slightly as she hurriedly bustled about, arranging everything for his comfort, soothing nerves jangled by the long Atlantic crossing. After settling him into his smoking jacket and putting the whiskey and cigars near his armchair, Ceci had probed delicately regarding events in Denver. At first she was overjoyed to learn of his change in attitude toward that city's society leaders. That definitely was to her advantage should he be persuaded to go back with her on his arm. But the next exchange sent her spirits to the soles of her grosgrain-bowed pumps.

"And M'sieu Glendower, what of him?" Ceci moved a plate of salted biscuits within easy reach and smiled, encouraging him to talk.

"I didn't see him. I believe he travels a great deal." Stanton waved a dismissive hand, and Ceci did not like at all the contented pull he took of his drink.

"*Chère* Morna? Is he still with her?"

"Telluride is such a distance," Caley replied evasively. Ceci noted immediately that he did not say, however, that he had not made the trip. He added, "But, yes, she is still there."

It was the half-smile of elation that he could not suppress that told Ceci clearly that he did not think that situation would last, that he meant to change it. That evening he slept alone in the rather Spartan accommodations of his dressing room.

The very next morning, which was a Tuesday, Caley left in a hansom cab. He did not come back for some hours, nor did he volunteer where he'd been. He did, however, look enormously satisfied with the outcome of the day's business.

On Wednesday she followed him. It was not easy. The cobbled streets of London near them were crowded with the carriages—and the occasional motorcar—of the affluent residents of the area. But as the two of them, one behind the other, clopped briskly along the Strand, she guessed he was on his way to Holborn and the lawyers of Lincoln's Inn. By urging her driver to pass his cab and arriving slightly before him, she even managed to find an alert street urchin to penetrate those dark passageways and discover the name of the solicitors' offices into which Caley had subsequently vanished. The ten-year-old couldn't read, but had had the wit to ask what the nameplate said. Reaching up with a grimy hand for the coin Ceci offered, he repeated in careful Cockney, "Morton, Aldwych, and Briggs."

But this information had gotten her no farther. That had been ten days ago, and not one word had passed Caley's lips concerning the business, whatever it was. For the first week he'd placidly accompanied her on their usual rounds of opera, theater, and museums, on long walks around the city. But for the last three days he'd hardly been willing to venture as far as Hyde Park for a constitutional, saying he was expecting a message. He could not disguise his eager anticipation, and what truly added to her disquiet, he did not even trouble to do so.

Now they both waited in their quiet hotel sitting room, the only sounds being the intermittent snap of Stanton's watch cover as he checked the time, and Ceci's rustling petticoats as she paced, looking down at the street scene. She herself very much wanted to be amid the fashionably dressed throng below, strolling up toward and down from Knightsbridge. Her yellow chiffon dress was new and superbly designed to emphasize the S-shape, which was the last word in style. By thrusting the bust forward and throwing the hips back, the corset beneath admirably supported this curve. In addition, a pleated ruffle on her gown started at the shoulders and swirled forward, making the bosom even more commanding. A frilly white lace sash widened charmingly over the gathers in the back of the hips, further delineating the curve. She wanted to put on the yellow flowered hat that picked up the gold glints the hairdresser had introduced to her brown hair. Stanton's refusal to leave the suite added pique to her indignant spice-colored eyes. But, because she was so set on plumbing the mystery, she would not have left the Cadogan short of a general alarm fire.

To calm her anxiety and irritation Ceci wished she might have one of the thin, dark French cigarettes she enjoyed, but Stanton had been adamant on that point. "Although it was done at Miss Freda's, proper ladies do not smoke in the company of gentlemen," he'd stated flatly. Instead, she stared longingly downward, took three steps forward and three back.

When there was a hurried, but discreet, knock at the door, they both started. Stanton almost leapt from his armchair; she whirled from the window. Although Ceci could not hear all the hotel porter's words, she recognized his voice, particularly since his h's bobbed about when he was uneasy. That he must have been, for his message was difficult to decipher. All she caught was the name of "Briggs." Even Stanton seemed a little disturbed when he turned to her and announced, "There's a gentleman below who wishes to see me urgently. On business. But why the devil he should have come here, rather than sending for me . . ." Caley rubbed his domed forehead in puzzled distraction.

"Do not trouble yourself on my account, *mon cher*." Ceci smiled graciously and picked up some needlework she'd left on the settee. "I shall retire to my sitting room." She retreated to that small nook off her dressing room and closed the door behind her firmly. It was not until she heard the bustle of Briggs's arrival that she opened it a crack, slowly and with exquisite care.

The solicitor's first words were compelling, but delivered in a low voice. All Ceci could gather was that he was apologizing to Stanton for the personal call, and that he was returning most of the money he'd been offered to retain his services—less travel expenses—and that he refused to act further in the matter. In a slightly higher and more agitated tone he urged that no further visits should even be made to Lincoln's Inn, as Caley might be traced back to his hotel in that manner.

"But I don't understand at all," Stanton said clearly. "Why is that a concern?"

"Sir, I will explain, if only to impress on you that you should follow my advice and go to the Continent immedjitly with no forwarding address. Stay there for some time." Briggs spoke loudly, as if to persuade. He was silent for a bit before he asked, "Early as it is, might I have a whiskey?" Ceci heard Stanton's startled murmur and the faint clink of decanter and glass.

"Thank you," the solicitor said, and then went on. "Originally, I had thought this matter could even be handled from London as the . . . laird"—here Briggs seemed to have trouble bringing out the very word—"sent my first letter back unopened, with a note to the effect that he had a financial man, named James Farringdon, in the City, who looked after all his affairs. Naturally, I called on that gentleman, and here I should have known there was something singular. Farringdon, a queer little weasely chap, said he never communicated with his client except at the laird's instigation—that the man himself refused to be bothered with mail. Very rarely, he came down to London to confer. When I pointed out that I had something very much to his client's advantage to hear, Farringdon only let out an oozy chuckle and said, 'That's as may be. The laird can add and subtract, as I have cause to know. You'll have to go there, then.' And he refused to say anything further!"

Briggs paused, and given the shaky sound of his voice, Ceci could imagine him gulping his drink. When he began to speak again, he was muttering ". . . demmed island off the north coast of Ireland, impossible to reach . . . never go again."

"What was it like there?" Stanton's intense curiosity came through his question.

The solicitor set his glass down hard and groaned. "God Himself hasn't been back since He made it. If He did. A mist that goes to your bones and makes you unsure of what you see and what you don't, sir. You only know the sea surrounds it because everywhere it pounds on rocks or hisses away. And, mind you, this is midsummer. Getting to Castle Daire itself was not easy and then, of a sudden, it looms up at you like some rock-hewn pile formed from the sea's leavings. It's a grim medieval fortress, but as much a place to keep people in as to shut them out. I asked the driver to wait, and sullen as he was, he did. Thank the good Lord!" he added fervently.

"And inside?" Stanton pressed, now with a shiver in his own voice. He must then have held out the decanter because Ceci again heard the ring of glass.

"Thank you, yes." Briggs seemed to be thinking over his answer, because he waited before continuing and then spoke haltingly. "Well, at first, you know, it was hard enough talking my way in, but the elderly servingman who answered was red cheeked, hale enough, and finally he told me grudgingly to wait. So I looked round at that great hall beyond where I was standing. You recall we checked what must be the lady in question and her descent in *Burke's Peerage*. Her own family in Connemara—a lovely bit of Ireland—was ancient and well founded, but no longer prosperous. A family, I discovered, known for its anti-English sentiments. Perhaps this was due to the . . . evictions and the various difficulties that the Irish aristocracy have had . . . in holding on to their lands."

Ceci only heard the eagerness in Caley's voice in wanting to hear the rest, but not his question.

"Sir, I want to tell you what I thought first, because later—" He halted, as if to refresh himself. "You had such interest concerning the lady, and I wondered what her father, who is now dead, had thought leaving her there. Eager to have her marry one of their own, he might have hoped for the best. Now that hall, with a roaring peat fire and good company, might have been merry, I suppose. The castle itself seemed . . . reasonably kept and, located at land's end as it is, safe. No Englishman would want to live there."

Ceci did not catch the ambiguity in his tone, but she could hear the shudder in his words as he went on. "Even when I first saw the laird himself, I thought him a likable man. And handsome. Clear eyes, dark

well-trimmed beard, warm handshake. He insisted I take some Irish
malt whiskey—though it's not to my taste, it was the best I've ever
drunk—to take off the chill, he said. There was a seeping cold in those
stone-walled rooms. But this, this is what you must understand, Mr.
Caley. The man listened to me. Heard me through, sat with his legs
crossed easily, sipping at his whiskey. I told him that his wife wished
her freedom, and that an American gentleman would pay for any possible expenses, plus a generous amount for any . . . trouble he might
suffer in the process. No doubt I concluded with some conciliating
phrases to the effect that such things happen, and men of the world
agree to overlook, and profit, from these experiences. I stressed the
word *profit* so that there should be no mistake."

Ceci again heard a liquid being poured, but she had not heard any
offer of a drink by Stanton. The decanter rattled on the glass rim. She
could only assume that the solicitor had now helped himself.

"Sir, the laird walked over to my chair with his smile still in place.
He reached down—I swear I thought he planned to refill my glass—and
began strangling me with my own cravat! 'Where is she?' he asked in
the most pleasant of tones! I could not have answered. I was choking.
He lessened his grip just a little and I gasped out that I did not know.
Indeed, Mr. Caley, you know that I do not! He tightened his grip,
though my hands clawed at his, and said, still smiling, 'Then where is
he? And what is his name?' He meant you, sir!"

Briggs now was nearly sobbing. "'Pon my honor, Mr. Caley, I have
never betrayed a client's trust. But I would have told him how to assas-
sinate King Edward himself, if only he would let me breathe. It is the
most awful sensation. See here"—and Ceci imagined him pulling open
his collar—"the marks are still on my throat. I said, 'Stanton Caley. In
London.' Luckily, although you'd given my clerk the name of your
hotel, I had not glanced at it. He twisted my cravat again, his eyes now
as glassy and mad as any in Bedlam's, saying, 'But where is *she*? I want
her. I *want* her.' I am sorry, Mr. Caley, but I would have told him had I
known. He would never have stopped twisting. And then I could imagine him tossing my body off the tower into the sea, and sending the
coachman away with the same smile, saying that I intended to remain."
Now the solicitor did let out a sob.

"B-but, how did you get away?" Stanton's voice was equally
shaken.

"The old butler came in. When he saw what was happening, he
began to strike *me* with a gnarled fist, shouting, 'You shouldna' cross
him, you shouldna'!' I could only rasp out that I hadn't meant to, that I
didn't know what he wanted me to tell him, and then the old man

whispered in his ear. Abruptly, the laird let go. I have no idea what the servingman said. But what was almost worse was the coachman's snarl when I finally staggered back out. The old man said something low to him as I sprawled in the seat. The driver looked back at me with bared teeth and said he'd take me to the ferry but I was not to come back! I can only think they all protect him. Perhaps he lets them smuggle contraband. What else they could do, I don't know. A sheep couldn't live on that cloud-covered rock."

It was Stanton's voice next, and he sounded as if his own throat had been closed by force. "And you think I should go . . . abroad?"

"Yes, yes, Mr. Caley. Through you he may trace his wife. If you value the lady, you must stay as far away from her as you can. He will already assume she is in Colorado because I told him that was your home state but he will not know exactly where. I myself believe he will go there, but he may not locate her, if the state is as large as you say. And then, he does not know the name she uses. But certainly he will come to London looking for you."

Here Ceci quietly shut her sitting-room door. She did not attend to Briggs's departure, but instead sat on a small chaise, thinking. She recalled the last time she'd seen Morna Gregory, and for that matter, Berkeley Glendower. It was only several weeks after the two of them had moved into the house on Pacific Avenue, one that Ceci herself had always admired for its graceful exterior. Freda had asked Morna to return for a farewell concert, as the madam had put it, and Morna had, to Ceci's amazement, agreed. Berkeley had come, also, elegant as usual in his tucked shirt and tails.

Most of the evening had faded from her memory, but two things the Frenchwoman had never forgotten. Morna had worn the white dress, plain except for its lace, that she'd had on when she'd begun singing there. It had always irritated Ceci—that habit Morna had of choosing simple gowns, barely stylish except for the sleeves—yet when one stood next to her, one felt overdressed. Putting real flowers in the hair, too, hardly imaginable when plumes, combs, and jewelry were what was required by fashion. Ceci recollected that on the night the two women first met she herself had brought a spray of apple blossoms for Morna's hair, almost as a joke, and she'd actually worn them, to all the men's admiration!

The night she came back to sing, crimson roses had been entwined in her tendriled upsweep and the color of those flowers was an exact counterpart of the fiery rubies in the unusual ring on her left hand. An old-fashioned ring, but exquisite—Ceci had known instinctively it had been Glendower's gift. It shone brilliantly on her white hand as she played.

Later, as they prepared to leave, Ceci had also been in the foyer because that's where Edward Gibbons was, and she had not let *him* out of her sight all evening. She had every intention of consoling the banker for the loss of Morna and perhaps later on interesting him in her scheme of purchasing the business. The four of them were exchanging parting pleasantries, and Glendower was arranging Morna's light evening cape around her shoulders.

It was a dolman wrap of scarlet peau de soie with a high stiff collar in back. Ceci remembered it vividly, as well as what happened next. All Glendower was doing was draping the wrap, as he might have done for any woman, making sure as a normal courtesy that the collar did not disarrange her hair. But his manner made clear what he was doing was enfolding her in an insistent embrace. That Morna knew what he meant was evidenced by the sudden blush on her pale cheeks, which turned as scarlet as the cloak. She reached up as if to pull the wrap more firmly onto her shoulder, and her fingertips only lightly brushed his, almost accidentally, one might have thought. But she had answered his touch with an equally fervent yes.

Ceci was facing Glendower, and she saw his expression. First, amusement flared in his eyes at Morna's blush, and then a look of impassioned love blazed out. The Frenchwoman knew all about a man's desire and the tricks that called it up. But no man had ever looked at her like that.

Envy as sharp as nausea had welled up in the pit of her stomach and climbed to her throat. It was not only that Ceci would have wanted that ring, that house, and that very man, but now she longed most for that extraordinary and passionate adoration. And she knew she would not get it, would perhaps never have it from anyone.

Gibbons seemed also to have caught the exchange, for he turned on his heel and went to fetch his hat and left immediately, his shoulders drooping disconsolately. Ceci had gone to her room alone, her vanity injured now too. But she had sat on the edge of the bed for a long time and then conceived the desperate measure of writing Stanton Caley in Denver. And this, thus far, had worked. She had at least had luxury.

She was determined, with all her soul, to keep it. But what had happened to Glendower that now made Stanton think he could replace him? And what would happen, she wondered, if this demented Irish lord could not find Morna? Would not Stanton always be yearning for her, convincing himself that one day he would have her? Ceci got up, opened a small tapestried reticule, and took out a cigarette. Lighting it, she inhaled deeply, concentrating. She pinched her curlicued nostrils together. There must be something she could do.

When she thought of it, she hesitated only very briefly. Stanton would be enraged if he ever learned of her action, but then Ceci did not think he would. And by then, they two might even be safely married. But now, she reflected, Morna's husband must be notified of her whereabouts. It was the only practical thing to do. She stubbed out her cigarette, quickly crossed to her small secretary, and drew out notepaper and three envelopes from an inlaid drawer. The first, in her looping, unformed handwriting, she addressed to James Farringdon, Esquire, The City, London. A short note went in it, explaining that the enclosed letter should be given to the laird of Castle Daire. And *that* letter stated only that the woman he sought was Morna Gregory and she resided in Telluride, Colorado, in the United States.

On the third envelope she wrote out Morna's complete address. With a small smile Ceci made sure that her script itself was flurried, as if done in haste. She told Morna, her dear friend, that Stanton had, perhaps foolishly, given her present location to the laird of Castle Daire. She added her concern and, of course, her best love. For the last time in her life, she signed a letter "Colette."

Just as she finished, there was a knock on her sitting-room door. Sliding the envelopes under her blotter, she rose and opened to Caley, who stood before her with sick and frightened eyes.

"Ceci," he said, with an attempt at a smile, "I'm thinking of a trip to Greece."

"But *mon cher,* a magnificent idea! How do you always know exactly what I have in mind? Only this morning I was thinking that sun and sea air might improve my health. I didn't wish to trouble you, but I had noticed while at home a tendency to be . . . unwell in the mornings."

This was not true, but Ceci intended that it soon should be. The prospect of becoming a father usually got a man's attention. Now she continued with a Gallic shrug. "Only a liver upset, I assume. Nothing to concern you. You know my health is superb. So. I shall pack instantly. Just allow me to post some letters."

CHAPTER 24

"G'Night, Miss Morna," Sam Goler called again from the pony trap. "Call if you need anything."

Morna waved and smiled over her shoulder with an attempt at cheerfulness before reaching up to turn the square tab that shut off the porch light. But she paused before going into the quiet house. It was always hard to return alone just after Berkeley had left, but tonight it seemed almost impossible. She'd put it off as long as she could, using every ruse she could imagine to distract herself, to console herself.

Earlier, at the Opera House, she'd begun with two of his favorite ballads, "Greensleeves," and "Drink to Me Only with Thine Eyes." She'd kept her gaze on the back wall, pretending he was, in fact, one of her listeners. Then she'd sung a popular tune, well liked by the audience, "Love Among the Roses," which Berkeley had helped her rehearse the previous evening. He had a robust baritone and liked to stand behind her as she played, keeping time with his fingers on her shoulders, leaning over to turn the page for her.

Although the cloying sentimentality of much of the current music made him cast his eyes to the heavens, he'd joined in the refrain of this one last night with some gusto. "And how we met, I'll ne'er forget,/ T'was love among the roses." He'd bent down, dropped a kiss on her hair, and said dryly, "T'was actually lilacs, you know. On the piano. And *t'wasn't* love on your part. I distinctly recall the cool reception you gave me."

"Ah, yes"—she had grinned over her shoulder, pulling the piano top over the keys—"it must have discouraged you badly, because only a few hours later you came calling with Greybird and Chevalier. But on this subject it's the columbines *I'll* ne'er forget, when I was trying to put the creek between you and me. Without success."

"Now that you mention it"—he'd crowed with pleasure, slid her off the bench, whirled her, and hoisted her on his hip as he had in the stream—"I can truthfully say I went through fire and water to win you."

"Fire*works,*" she'd corrected him laughingly, embracing him as she had not on that first occasion.

"A trifling difference," he'd replied, making for the staircase, still clutching her waist in the crook of his arm, her feet dangling around his ankles. "Instead of niggling, you should swoon at the memory of my bravery."

"Berkeley, I shall swoon," she'd managed to gasp out as he'd climbed upward, "between the tightness of this corset and your grip."

"Never mind," he said, marching toward the bedroom. "You'll soon be out of it. The corset, I mean."

As she sang, the memory of their laughter rang in her ears, but tears starred her eyes. She wanted to call him back just long enough to say, "But you do understand—I *did* love you when first I saw you." It had taken his fire to melt the cold walls of fear so she could recognize it. At that thought Morna had had to motion to the audience to join in the refrain. They had done so, quite loudly, so no one was aware her own voice was breaking.

After the performance, because there was a full harvest moon, she'd asked Sam to drive her to Ute Rise Canyon road so she could see Bridey's Mountain lift its profile in the white glow. On the way the only sound in the moon-drenched valley had been the horse's hooves. The aspens' autumn gold was bleached by the light, but on the slopes those slim trees had still stood out like candles from the blackness of the pines. The night's soft peace enclosed her like the protective mountain walls, but she could not feel it, longing as she did for Berkeley's encircling arms. Underneath the ache of his absence she was aware of a tremble of unease. But she refused to dwell on that, telling herself it was caused simply by the length of the journey he'd set out on that morning, by the fact that he would be facing winter's dangers on his return.

When Sam stopped at the entrance of the canyon and she could see the mountain's strength against the sky's dark indigo, she did forget that troubling sensation. With her finger floating on the air, she traced the face she saw outlined, knowing it comforted her because it was a way to merge frail humanity with the enduring rock. Too, it reminded her of the first Bridget and all the blessings of the distant past. And it would be a gift to her own dear Bridey, a gift to the future. Most of all, the stone's indestructible thrust to the heavens meant the power of the love she'd found here, meant the man who gave it to her. She felt so forcefully Glendower's presence that he might almost have been in the carriage beside her.

But coming back, the brief serenity seemed to drop away as they drew nearer home. She closed her eyes, hoping the sway of the carriage would lull her, make possible the forgetfulness of sleep when she arrived. Somehow, though, an annoying wind had sprung up, and through the rush of air from the open two-wheeler, she heard its sibilant hiss, which chased away any hope of drowsiness.

Now, although Sam's farewell and the crunch of the carriage wheels had long faded, she still stood, her hand on the doorknob. She crossed the veranda and leaned her arms on the railing to take one last look at the calm, illumined sky. But that persistent wind murmured at her, unsettling her. She stared at the unmoving leaves of the lilac bushes. It was not a breeze, she knew now, but the sound of the too-familiar swish of the sea around the rough-hewn boulders where *he* lived. In common with the other islanders, she did not refer to the laird by his name. *"He,"* they all said when speaking of him. It did not take her long, after arriving at the place she thought accursed, to adopt the habit.

Convulsively, she clenched her arms across her chest, digging her fingertips into her velvet wrap, remembering. The air on that rocky outcropping always had Iceland on its breath. The ocean there was always foaming, tearing at the shore, then withdrawing only long enough to snarl back. Waking or sleeping, when she lived there, she heard its smashing fist and then the menacing whistle when it pulled away for a new attack. It was a destroying sea, and its sound was not at all like that at the strand near her beloved home in Connemara, where the sea sighed and could offer mother-comfort. But for so long now that pounding ocean, that sunless island, and its lord had only grasped her in nightmares. Half awakened at her tossing but unaware of the cause,

Berkeley would sleepily enfold her, and in the darkness she would feel only his warmth, and she would hear only his steadily beating heart.

Stopping her ears, Morna almost fled into the house that would still hold his presence, just as the pillows held his scent. She pressed her back against the door until her breath slowed. Mechanically, she took off her wrap, hung it on the hall tree, then decided not to look in on Bridey until she'd had a chance to collect herself. She put her small fringed evening bag on the letters Issy had left on the hall table, thinking she'd read them later too. Now she needed to sit by the fire laid in the back parlor, try to find its usual peace.

Humming loudly to herself to keep out any unwelcome sounds, she set the logs alight. She continued kneeling on the fleecy rug, watching the shadow of the slender flames make a pattern on the ivory silk of her gown. To cheer herself up she had put on her own mother's dress when readying herself for the Opera House. Its delicate lace-trimmed bodice was once again stylish, although yards of fabric had to be removed from a skirt made for the crinolines of her mother's day. She pretended that all she need do was lean back a little, and she could rest her head on Berkeley's shoulder, hear the reassuring crinkle of his stiffly starched evening shirt.

Perhaps a little too loudly she sang the rest of the lyrics of one of her opening songs: "But leave a kiss within the cup, and I'll not ask for wine." The color of sherry, she thought, that warm golden brown, was the true color of his eyes. Had she ever told him that? Once, he'd said of her gray ones, quoting Byron, "And all that's best of dark and bright/ Meet in her aspect and her eyes:/Thus mellowed to that tender light/ Which heaven to gaudy day denies." As her fingertips traced the soft whorls of the rug, she thought of Berkeley's smooth urbanity and the rough passion beneath it.

She held out her hands, which still trembled, to the fire. As if stroking reassuring beads she went over the August days they'd just spent together. In his company it was always high summer to her, but this month had been hours, days, weeks, of radiance. Like competing jockeys the two of them had raced up to the tableland overlooking Wilson's Peak and Sunshine Mountain. They picnicked as the day flamed into twilight by Ute Rise Creek. Taking Issy and Bridey, they'd hitched a fast team to a four-seated carriage and gone spinning out of Telluride to the high, warm mesas near Norwood. Bridey had sat on her father's lap, her hands over his on the reins, and the two of them would gravely discuss likely locations for a ranch. Here, he'd pointed out, the growing season was much longer than in their sheltered valley, not many miles away. Issy and Morna had lifted their faces to the sun, the child's delighted laughter as she helped Berkeley drive blowing back on the wind.

But though Morna tried desperately, all her memories of joy and love in this light-filled mountain fastness could not keep away the dreaded recollections of the mist-dimmed island that so insistently intruded tonight. And once again she could see the laird in one of his moods, watch his restless leopard prowlings through the castle, in and out of rooms, down corridors, and up the stairs, stopping only to gaze at her. The stone walls would echo with his footfalls, his wild shouting and ravings. If quiet fell, it was almost worse, because then she did not know what he was doing.

When she played the softest tune on the piano, he held his head in pain. When she picked up a book, opening the pages, letting the story swallow her, he would tear the volume from her hands, fling it across the room, bury his face in her lap, and sob for hours like a helpless child. She did not know if she most pitied him, feared him, or hated him. She had felt as storm tossed by her emotions as any wracked ship near the island's currents.

Then, shortly after her father's death, her young brother, Liam, had come for a protracted stay, Liam who was her childhood companion and dearest friend. Although the laird had been a model host, unusually charming, Liam's merry eyes had grown flintily sober after a few weeks at this castle. He quickly made plans to take her away when he left, although only the two of them knew, pretending all was well. But Liam had not come back from the last day's fishing. Drowned, the laird said, and there seemed a world of sorrow in his sea-colored eyes when he told her.

Through the following months, when she was half crazed with grief, Morna would look at her husband each day. One moment she was sure he'd killed Liam, or ordered it done. The next she was not sure, knew she had no cause for thinking so. Truth on that island was obscured in mist, like everything else. Neither vision nor dream gave her the answer. She feared that if she knew, she'd grow as mad as the laird. For had she not taken a vow, a sacred vow, to care for him, in sickness and in health? How could she then wish to destroy him? But what if *he* had killed Liam?

But she had known she would leave, had planned it carefully, waited only for the opportunity. When it came, she had fled, careless of which end of the universe she went to, provided only that *he* could never find her.

Suddenly Morna leapt to her feet, covering her ears. With that fear-haunted reverie the susurration of the sea came back to her, the muttering as it pulled back before it slammed into the rocks. As she pressed her palms to her head, she prayed this was only a fancy, a result of the too-vivid imagination her father had often told her she had.

She hurried to the windows to look out at the peaceful fall garden with its chrysanthemums, zinnias, and asters. The flowers raised their fringed petals in the moonlight, the only shadows those thrown by the gazebo's lattice. Slowly she lowered her arms and, raising the sash, found to her relief that she only heard the crickets' call, the San Miguel river's soothing murmur.

After a few quiet moments she decided she must do something, anything, to keep from brooding in this fashion. It had all been brought on, she persuaded herself, by Berkeley's absence and by her awareness of its length. The letters on the table, she thought. Carrying the envelopes back, she settled on the rug by the fire and glanced at the top one from London. She lifted the flap and slipped out the note.

Ten seconds later her fingers dropped it nervelessly into the fire. The edges of the paper curled, and Ceci's rapid scrawl writhed like snakes before being consumed. Had the flames themselves caught Morna's fingers, she might not have moved. She sat, unbreathing, as still as a figure carved on a monument. And now she heard the ocean's full roar. When at last she stood up, she did so as jerkily as a puppet, and only the desolation in her gray eyes showed she was painfully human.

With that same motion she turned toward the windows, and for one brief instant she took a quick, reviving breath. For it was Berkeley in that moon-washed garden walking toward her. She rushed toward him. But, no, the room he was crossing was illuminated like day from blazing chandeliers, and he was moving past green baize-covered tables. He did not see her. His expression was that easy smile he extended to strangers.

The hand he held out was suddenly clamped to his shirtfront. The smile dissolved in surprise, and then amazement, as both hands, clutched to his chest, could not hold in the bright blood spurting between his fingers, staining the shirt, spilling onto the floor. He slipped to his knees. Morna herself crumpled by the sill, reaching forward in agony, but her fingers touched only the empty air of night.

Her keening shriek, which she thought would burst her own eardrums, must have been silent, for no lights came on, no dog barked. Her forehead pressed on the hard marble sill, she folded her hands over her head, and her body shook in wracking sobs.

She did not know how long she knelt there, but when she stiffly rose, she moved purposefully, if slowly, into the library that adjoined

the little parlor. Sliding back the roll-top of the desk, she took out
envelopes and a sheaf of papers. The first envelope was addressed to
James Farringdon in London, and she included a letter to be given to
her husband. She said only that she was leaving Colorado and could be
reached in care of general delivery in San Francisco. The name she
signed was not Morna Gregory.

Dipping her quill pen in the black ink, she wrote the next letter as
carefully as she could, addressing a grown-up Bridey whom she could
only imagine. Then she slipped off the ruby ring. But she could not bear
to look at its crimson depths because she could once again hear Berkeley saying, "You are my heart's blood, Morna." All she knew was that
she would not let that blood be lost. Closing her eyes, she entrusted the
ring to Bridey.

But this envelope she sealed carefully and put it into another with a
note to Isobel. *I hope,* she said in this, *that Bridget need never read my
letter to her. Give it to her if it's necessary, and when you think best. I
trust you so. Dear Issy, when I saw you at the station all those years
ago, I felt your pain and knew our lives were entwined. What I did not
know was how fortunate that would be for me!*

But the next paragraph she began by begging Isobel never to repeat
its contents, to anyone. She described what she'd seen in the garden. *I
tell you this because I believe it a true vision, and you will then understand why I must leave. You know how hard this is for me, that it cuts
me in two. But staying would be harder because of what I saw in the
moonlight. Still, tonight when I look at my Bridey, it will take all the
determination I possess to go out her bedroom door. She is the sign of
love between me and Berkeley, and the dearest thing I own. I give her
to you, until she is returned to me, because you love her as your own.*

Morna wrote the last salutation rapidly, *Dearest Berkeley.* She began the letter, shakily but clearly, by saying she had been told that her
husband was on the way, and that she was going to meet him. She
insisted that she was entirely sure this was the best plan. The situation
would be resolved, and then she would return, although she could not
say when that would be.

But when she started the next part, tried to tell him in words, in
pen strokes that seemed too thin to hold all she would say about how
much she loved him, her hand faltered and slowed. How could she
thank him for the years of joy he'd given her, she asked herself, apologize for the pain she now was causing him? But, although she wept, she
kept writing, the blotting pad she pressed over each page absorbing the
tears and ink equally. His thoughts would complete hers as they always

did. "We share a mind," he'd once said. She would be gone, but she would be only here, and she was sure he would know that.

She did not write that she would shield him from her future thoughts, as she had hidden her past. But that would be necessary, she was certain. Her one belief—that no mist could ever obscure—was that love must at all costs preserve life, nourish it, protect it. Therefore, she would do all in her power to safeguard Berkeley. Near her, he would meet death, she was convinced. But she did not write that either.

At the end she wrote, *Although I am leaving, you and I can never be parted. And I promise I will return to this valley and you. Then we will always be together. You know I am careful of my promises, so you will believe this one. If, on a dark day, I seem far away, go to the mountain. I wait for you there.*

Her handwriting had become hopelessly illegible, but she added, *And I will love you long after the sun is dark and the mountain crumbled.* She could barely see to sign it.

It was not long after she'd sealed that envelope that she returned downstairs with a packed valise. She was wearing a black dress and a hat swathed in disguising veils. But no one saw her leave. She walked into a light that was not yet dawn.

CHAPTER 25

"Isobel," Freda pleaded earnestly, "you must listen to me. It has been almost three years since Morna left. After seeing Berkeley Glendower yesterday on the street, I decided to be quite straightforward on the subject of the future with you. At least we should discuss it." She would have stood up to emphasize her words, but she'd slipped off her patent leather pumps under the kitchen table, and it was very difficult to shoehorn her bulging feet back into them. She nudged May with a stocking foot to encourage her to chime in, but May, her amiable face puckered, was looking at Isobel in sympathetic distress.

"He looks . . ." Freda searched distractedly for the word she wanted. Although she'd prepared herself for this conversation, she didn't know how to begin it. At last she finished with what she was aware was not the best choice, ". . . drawn."

"What d'ye mean?" Isobel came back sharply, implying that she was taking the remark as a criticism of her own care of Mr. Berkeley. She knew it was not. But since she was already fretting herself to the bone on this very point without coming up with a solution, in her stubborn Scots way, she refused to admit to the problem out loud. For of all the dark moon phases the man had undergone, this one made her the most heartsore.

The day he'd returned and read Morna's letter, he'd only asked a few questions, his tongue thick with pain, and left immediately. Isobel had known he was sure he could find her and, worse, was herself terrified that he might succeed. When he'd come back alone, weeks later, he'd said only that he could trace her no farther than Durango, not many miles on a crow's flight from Telluride. A train conductor remembered a widow getting off about that time, but no one knew where she'd gone from there, or had any idea if that was Morna who'd stepped off the train.

Berkeley was then, Isobel recalled with anguish, bedeviled by grief and rage. During the daylight hours, for Bridey's sake, he kept the black demons bottled up inside. But at night he'd shut himself up in the small library. She would hear wild mutterings, pleas, and curses, drawers being slammed shut, books thrown down. In the morning she would find that the decanter she'd just filled was empty. Sometimes, herself drifting in and out of sleep, she would hear him fling himself out in the wee hours, although it was the dead of winter, and ride off she knew not where. The odd thing was that often he was then better in the morning than when she'd hear his dragging footsteps going off to bed early.

It was fortunate that the mining companies, once again prosperous because the labor wars had ended successfully for the owners, had decided to go in together and build the hydroelectric plant at Bridal Veil Falls. Although not a word could be said to the Denver financiers about his hiring, the manager of the Smuggler had begged Berkeley to help oversee the project. And, because he absolutely refused to leave Telluride, and Bridey, he'd taken the job. That was the period Isobel called the time of hoping.

Each evening he would come in the door, and Isobel could tell just by the way he hurried up the path that he was expecting Morna to be there, her arms lifted for an embrace. But when he saw that she was not, he'd simply turn and put his overcoat on the hall tree. Bridey would rush in from her play, he would swing her up and they'd go off to the back parlor for a chat before supper. Although the child would occasionally prattle of plans, things they would do "when Momma comes back," she seemed to know it was best to talk of other things with her father.

It was the hours when Bridey was not with him that were hard for the little girl. In the middle of the night she would come weeping to

Isobel's bed or, suddenly in the kitchen, climb into her lap, bury her face in the apron's bib, and wail for her mother. Isobel's own tears would fall on the child's shining hair as they rocked together in grief.

It was during this period that Isobel worried most. She would creep down the stairs and now and again hear Berkeley behind the closed library door talking to himself. She would stand there, nervously pleating and repleating her nighttime braid, unable to catch his words, but hearing the quiet cadence of conversation—the pauses, the interrupted sentences. She feared that his mind had snapped, or would. At last, shivering, she would go back to bed and eventually doze off. But then she was happy that he was outwardly calm, and grateful for the unfailing hope he had.

Then toward the end of one night, one terrible night, when it was almost morning, Isobel heard him give an anguished call. It was not loud, but so piercing that it seemed to sliver the wooden floor beneath her room. There was such agony in that word, *Morna,* that she was sure the demons had come back, were tearing at him again. Shrugging into her flannel robe, she all but tumbled down the stairs. But by then he was out the front door. Nor did he return until the evening, and she could not bear the look in his eyes. Ever since then he'd had that look, the one Isobel knew Freda was referring to.

"Mr. Berkeley eats right well," she answered now defiantly. Isobel waved her thin freckled hand around the kitchen as if to show that the existence of all the food in itself was proof.

A pork roast, judging by its enticing aroma, was slowly crackling in the oven. On the counter next to the enormous black range stood jars of home-canned green beans and applesauce waiting to be opened. Scrubbed new potatoes were in a bowl by the gleaming jars. And despite both Freda's and May's earlier nibblings, there were three different kinds of fresh-baked cookies still piled on the crockery platters.

"And if he dinna' eat," Isobel said with an air of closing the matter, "Bridey most likely would be telling him that *she* wouldn't clean her plate either. A tongue she's got, for all she adores him. And I never saw such a child for not finishing her vegetables. Get rickets, she will, if she keeps it up."

"You know," May said, patting Isobel's arm, "my brothers and sisters were just like that about anything green. They did like corn, though. And the corn at home in Iowa was so good. But every one of them grew up healthy as horses, so I wouldn't—" She stopped abruptly and, to cover her confusion, reached for a lace cookie. Freda had just given her a distinct prod with her big toe to remind her to stay on the agreed-upon topic.

"Besides, Isobel," Freda went on resolutely, "I didn't say he was *thin.*" Nor, she thought, calling up the way he'd looked when they met on the street, was that at all what she meant. Certainly, any stranger would call Glendower a fine figure of a man, and the only change those who knew him slightly would see was the brush of gray hair about the temples. His cheekbones seemed a little more prominent perhaps, and he didn't smile as readily, and it didn't touch his eyes anymore. But it was the look in his eyes, Freda had decided, that had made her spirits sink. Not pain or hopelessness, that wasn't it. It was as if the essential part of him was remote, somewhere else, waiting.

The more Freda had mulled it over, the more she'd thought something should be done. That man, of all men, should be happy, and she longed to see again that golden smile that he'd once had. Although she had a romantic corner to her soul, her practical side took over, and she'd announced to Jane Ellen and May that they should talk to Issy about it, at least see what *she* was thinking now that all this time had passed.

Jane Ellen had flatly refused, for despite that gentle southern charm, she had her own mind about things. "You'll only upset her. Miss Freda, not once have we ever gotten Isobel to say anything except 'Miss Morna's coming back to us. She promised.' And then she closes her mouth. Maybe someday she'll say something else, but you have to leave it to her. When she's ready, she will. She sees us often enough."

That was true. Almost every weekday afternoon one or another— or all three—would walk down Pacific Avenue and have tea in the warm kitchen where Isobel waited for Bridey to come home from school. Freda's restaurant, The Silver Pick, was closed until the dinner hour, and preparations for evening were by then in hand. It'd become an agreeable habit, and the women regarded the little girl as a favorite niece to be petted, slightly spoiled, and her progress with her studies thoroughly discussed. Freda, especially, now that she'd settled into the pillow of respectability as a restaurant owner rather than a madam— she'd even sold off the dance hall—regarded herself as an expert on child raising.

If Bridey found this array of aunts formidable, she gave no sign of it and was eager to discuss with one, or all, her day's activities. There was an intensity about life in the valley for children and adults alike, perhaps because three of the seasons were so short. The brief, sweet-smelling spring, the shining summer, the glorious fall, all had their charms and pleasures. The winter, if long, was bright, and Bridey would come in from sledding or skating with the Nordstrom children, red cheeked and glowing with excitement.

Jane Ellen, in her soft accent, had raised a question about the amount of time Bridey spent at the stables. But May and Freda were farm girls both, the daughters of immigrants who had followed the same occupation for generations in the old country, and saw nothing wrong with that. All agreed that Sam Goler kept a watchful eye on the girl around the more spirited horses. As to Bridey's clothing, Jane Ellen was allowed the last word and was forever ordering new patterns and stitching them up.

The house itself still had its soothing atmosphere. Nothing about it had been changed, and May—who was not given to notions or fancies—had more than once remarked on the way back that she wouldn't be surprised at all to see Morna walk into the room, smiling, pulling off her gloves, as if she'd only been gone for the afternoon.

This afternoon, Freda had finally induced May to go along with her plan, although the younger woman's pleasant round face had compressed uncertainly. May had become much plumper, perhaps through the necessary tastings in the restaurant kitchen when she'd become the cook. But this fullness suited her, and it smoothed features which once seemed overly large. Her amazing skin still seemed milkmaid fresh, and she wore her light hair braided in a coronet. So did Freda now, although her blond hair was now more white than gold, despite regular rinses in lemon juice. The two looked rather like mother and daughter, and they often acted that way. Freda had never lost her grande-dame air, however. In any case, May's good nature was no match for the former madam's force.

Still, on the way to tea, May had ventured, "You know, Isobel never really talks about Mr. Berkeley. Oh, she says a good deal about all his work building the power station at Bridal Veil Falls, and what he says to Bridey and what the two of them do of an evening. But as to what he *thinks,* she doesn't. And honestly, I don't know what Issy can do—"

Freda's interruption was rather acerbic, because she didn't know either. "The point, May, is to discover what Isobel *thinks.* For all she seems down to earth, she has a queer view on . . ." She let her voice trail off and began again a little aggravatedly. "I don't know why it is—the English are sensible enough—but the rest of them from the British Isles! The Scots, the Irish, the Welsh, even all the miners we have from Cornwall, talk of 'long-sightedness' and 'the second sight.' And they believe it. I swear they are all quite *used* to seeing things that aren't there."

Freda paused to catch her breath. Even a short walk winded her. "Anyway, one worries that Isobel is letting such stuff influence her decisions. What are they all going to do? Sit and wait forever? I've said often enough, I who even hate to think it"—and the quaver in her voice attested to that—"that Morna Gregory is dead. Or else she'd be here, or at least have written to spare the worry."

This was something Freda *had* despairingly brought out before. The first time May had quite practically responded that any letter would be postmarked and Mr. Berkeley would be gone there in an instant. Freda had then replied that Morna could have written to *her,* that discretion was the one thing she'd learned in her many years in the business. Being kind, May had never once pointed out that Berkeley Glendower would have gotten it out of Freda in a heart's beat.

Now Freda put down her teacup and returned to the issue. She started firmly, "Isobel, what I meant was that it seems to us that, being a man, Berkeley needs"—but here she couldn't quite manage to maintain her resolve—"friends," she finished.

"Oh, that he has, and plenty." Isobel's furrowed forehead ironed out with relief at this turn of the conversation. "Mr. Wells, from the Smuggler, he drops in often, and the other men Mr. Berkeley works with on the power station at the Falls. They play cards of a weekend with him, them not having family here. And then Mr. Alexander comes from Denver now and again. He's the one—Mr. Patrick—who can even make him laugh again." Issy blinked her colorless lashes rapidly as if a tear hovered now that she had unwittingly veered onto the very ground she had been avoiding. But she rallied and chatted on volubly, as if to avoid the next question. "Mr. Patrick's quite the gentleman in Denver, and would have the largest fortune of all, Mr. Berkeley says, if it weren't for his spending ways. Anyway, he's got two bonny boys, and he brought them, telling them to watch how Miss Bridey rides and maybe they'd learn to do it proper."

But Freda, despite having momentarily weakened, had had too much trouble gathering her mettle for this conversation to back down now. "You know, Issy, that that's not what I'm talking about. Berkeley Glendower is a young man still, the fair side of forty. Surely he should be . . . making other plans . . . thinking of other women."

Isobel rested her elbows on the oak table and locked her hands over frizzled hair that had only streaks of red left. "He canna' choose to do that," she whispered, as if talking to the scrubbed wooden surface.

Freda swallowed, feeling more than a tinge of regret that she'd embarked on this course. There was genuine pity in her voice. "But surely he *can*—a man like him has a great deal of choice. Do you mean he doesn't want to, or that you don't want him to because of Morna, or . . . Bridey?"

When Isobel raised her head, she looked directly at Freda. Only the strength of her burr showed her intensity. "He *canna'*, I tell you, and if he could, he wouldna'. Ye know well Mr. Berkeley. Though he says no so smooth that you think he said yes, for a' that, you no can budge him. But on this, it has nothing to do wi' me, nor Bridey, though he thinks a silver floor's not good enough for her to walk on."

Then she added, and the matter-of-fact tone that the Scotswoman had sent a shiver up Freda's stolid Scandinavian spine, "He doesna' want another woman because he has Miss Morna and she's the only one he ever wanted."

"Issy," Freda expostulated, with an irritated glance at May, who was nodding gently in agreement with those words, "that's contrary to reason. He doesn't *have* her because she isn't here. Wherever Morna is, she certainly isn't *here*. That's not what you mean, is it?" she finished uneasily.

"Aye, it is," Isobel returned firmly. "The way he loves her means she canna' go elsewhere. And because she loves him, she willna'. And here is where she is."

CHAPTER 26

"Issy," Bridey hurried into the kitchen, the blue satin sash on her white organdy dress fluttering behind her, the usual adolescent impatience in her voice, "where *is* Papa? I've been ready for *hours!*"

Sifting flour into a mixing bowl almost as large as the table, Isobel replied with her mind on the cookies, "Not *hours,* I think, missy. It's not been more than fifteen minutes since I heard the tub being emptied. And, mind you, it'd best be spotless the next time I look at it. Your father's got his hands full today. Being head of the Fourth of July committee means he's right now got to be making sure the street's clear after the parade so the horses can race down it. And he's always been good as to time."

"Why are you making cookies now?" Bridey asked with good-humored exasperation. "You won't be ready when it's time to go to the race and the picnic."

"Sure and I will. All I need do is whip off the apron. But the last *two* years they've run out of dessert. It was always planned proper before Freda went and retired back to Minnesota, but those church ladies and their committees spend more time fussing at each other than counting pies. But ye can hurry me along if you help here. Put on an apron so your dress doesn't get mucky and crack these eggs. One at a time in the cup, mind, so ye can check for any spoiled ones."

As Bridey dutifully donned an apron and bent her head over the eggs, Isobel inspected her hairdo with approval. The front had been neatly brushed back from her forehead and fastened behind with a blue bow. The long shining chestnut curls at the back spilled over her shoulders and down around the lace that marked the end of the squared bib of the dress. Lovely hair, she thought, and she was saying inwardly to Morna, *See, and wasn't I right, that hair's too thick to show the strawberry mark beneath. And you so worried the day she was born.* Aloud she asked, as she stirred the beaten eggs and vanilla into the dough, "Did ye have enough of the ribbon, Bridey, to trim your hat to your liking?"

"The hat! I forgot to do it." She sent the long apron flying in the general direction of the hook she'd taken it from, then rushed out of the kitchen and up the stairs.

When she returned, Isobel was putting four cookie sheets into the massive oven. She shut the range door, folded her veined hands over her apron, and ordered, "Turn around."

Smiling, Bridey twirled slowly. The wide, drooping brim of the beige sun hat was laden with silk daisies, dried cornflowers, and delicate baby's breath. The flag-blue ribbon hanging down the back matched the sash of the dress. At fourteen she was losing the gangling look of a young girl, rounding into womanhood, and Issy thought her wholly beautiful. Exactly as old as this new century, she mused, both of them born the same day. Pleased as she was at the sight of this maturing, this blooming, she also felt a nostalgic pang at the loss of the child. Her inner voice murmured to Morna, *Still and all, doesn't she look like the pair of you? The brown of his eyes, but your curling lashes. Your nose, his mouth, and that jut of the jaw that's Mr. Berkeley all over. Thank heavens she has those pretty ears, tucked nicely to her head, just as yours—*"

"Well?" Bridey asked, taking off the hat and putting it on the sideboard.

"Good job," Isobel pronounced a little gruffly, to hide her filling heart. "Make sure you pin it on tight or what with the crowds these days for the holiday, it'll get knocked off and stepped on. And don't be eating all that batter," she finished as she saw a spoon dipped into the bowl.

"As good as the cookies." Bridey grinned and popped a sugary lump into her mouth. She paused, and then asked, her question coming from nowhere, "Do you think that Papa is the handsomest man you ever saw? Aunt Freda always said *she* thought he was."

Isobel pursed her mouth, considering what she should say. She was now used to this unsettling habit of Bridey's of bringing up whatever was on the front of her mind but, having herself been raised in the preachy school of moral lessons, had a tendency to answer in that fashion. "When I was in grammar school, we had to copy many a time in our commonplace books, *Handsome is as handsome does.* The morning we met, I thought him too good looking for his own good. But that day he left me thinking, *Aye, he is the handsomest man.* Your mother took that bit more persuading. But then she could never find a fault with him. Not," she added hurriedly, "that he's without his faults. All men have them. But the best father he's been, and you should give him no more sass about attending the Ladies' Academy."

This was a very sore point indeed, and Issy instantly regretted she'd brought it up on the holiday. But to her, September was as close as tomorrow, and she was trying to ease her own aching pain at the thought of losing Bridey for long months at a time by facing the issue. That was what was on the front of *her* mind.

A few weeks back Berkeley had pointed out that Bridey needed further schooling and mentioned he'd visited a boarding school in Colorado Springs. Although that small and pleasant city was near Denver, it was many hours by train from Telluride, and Isobel regarded it as a world away. The fact that Bridey had had the same horror-stricken look as she herself had when the subject was mentioned only added to the older woman's sorrow. But Isobel had to agree that it was the right thing, and she always did her duty, though this time it felt as if a stony hand were squeezing her heart.

In the silence between them at the thought of a leave-taking, the house itself seemed to hold its breath. Only the gently swinging pendulum of the wooden-framed clock by the range tocked back and forth. The quiet spread from the comfortable kitchen to the adjoining back parlor, the two rooms that were the center and held the echoes of the family's joy and grief. It touched the arrayed books in the library and infiltrated the glassed-in porch, trailing over Isobel's tender green plants like the motes in the sunlight. The stillness settled in the darkened drawing room with its shrouded piano, containing the memory of music.

Outside, even the wind that had snapped the bright flag fluttering on the veranda seemed to have died down. In the garden the heavy heads of roses, the scalloped tops of snapdragons, the small bells of lily-of-the-valley, were unstirring. The celebrating crowd's hubbub a few blocks away on the main street receded.

Then Bridey slid onto a chair, spread out her skirts, and managed a smile. "Don't let's talk about this now, Issy. It's the Fourth. Anyway, September's months away. Today, I'm only sorry that Viscount isn't entered in the race. He's the best of Chevalier's line. Why, the other day I beat Piers Nordstrom by a furlong on a race to Pandora! But Sam says we should wait until next year because of Viscount's strained hock. Sam thinks a bay gelding belonging to one of the Norwood ranchers will take it today. I'll have to ask Papa what he thinks about that bay. He'll have had a good look at it by now. Oh, I *do* wish he'd hurry."

Isobel peeked inside the oven and nodded in a satisfied fashion, saying, "These are done. I'll just whip in the next batch. And," she scolded automatically, "stop eating the batter."

Issy had no sooner done that and turned back to the table, than Bridey asked broodingly, putting down the spoon, "What do you think it feels like to die?"

Disconcerted, the older woman sank onto a chair. "I canna' guess, child. My own mother went so peaceful, probably glad of the rest she'd be having. You could ask your father."

"I did," Bridey responded, reaching now for one of the hot, buttery cookies. "He said he talked to a prospector once who almost froze to death. The man told him that he'd been fighting through the drifts for so long and he was so cold and so tired. Then, with the last of his strength, he made a cave of pine branches and crawled inside. After a while he got sleepy and toasty warm. He knew he shouldn't let go, but gradually he did, and he slid into a black tunnel, soft as fur. Then he saw a bright light, and he was wanting to get to that in the worst way. But a couple of mule drivers had seen his pack and burro, and pulled him out and were shaking him. Said it made him so mad, he never thanked them."

Isobel watched her munch on the cookie meditatively and waited, thinking a question about her mother might come next. But instead of asking anything, Bridey said, making a circle with her finger on the table in spilled sugar, "I've been dreaming of Momma a lot lately. Same old dream, and it always makes me happy. She's standing in the door-way of my room, looking in, just as she used to do when she came back from singing. And, of all her beautiful gowns, she's always wearing the same dress, that white one you packed away for me with lavender and tissue."

"Aye, her mother's, that was." Isobel blinked, and got up too quickly to check the cookies. "Already we'll be having to add a lace ruffle to the bottom, you're getting so tall."

The sound of the front screen door opening came through to the kitchen. Bridey sprang up and, going to the sideboard, began adjusting her hat, using its glass front as a mirror. "We're in here, Papa," she called.

"I hope," Berkeley said cheerfully, coming down the hall, "that the ladies are ready. I've bribed one of the local boys a fearsome sum to save us a front-row place for the race."

When he walked into the kitchen, Isobel looked up to give him a brief greeting, but then she almost let the cookie sheet slide from the pot holder in her hand. She hadn't seen him that morning, since he'd had to leave early, and now she thought that not for years had she seen Berkeley Glendower look like that. Was it the white ice-cream suit, she wondered, the dark blue ascot neatly tucked into the cravat, that made him look so young? Although in his early forties, he looked ten years less. But no, she could swear it was his old smile back, the corners of the eyes crinkled, the brown again lighted with gold.

And he had the same laughing note in his voice as he spun Bridey around to look at her. "I shall be," he said with fatherly pride, "the envy of the multitudes with such a glorious girl on my arm. The hat is perfection."

"Well, Papa," Bridey said, with a happy blush of pleasure on her cheeks, as she straightened the scarf around his neck slightly, "you look wonderful yourself. Been drinking at the Fountain of Youth?"

"Not at all," he replied with a grin, "although I was tempted. But, in the interest of avoiding the blind staggers, I turned down some of Telluride's best home-distilled whiskey, no doubt fresh made yesterday, which Sam Goler says they're going to export to New York as soon as the nation goes dry. It's too bad Colorado jumped the gun on Prohibition—I could certainly have used a little brandy in my coffee to get through *this* morning. Still, bootlegging has created a nice cottage industry for the town, now that the mines are slowing down. One shouldn't grumble. Is there any coffee around, Issy?"

"We haven't time," Bridey almost wailed. "Do let's go."

He picked up one of the star-shaped cookies and nodded resignedly while he chewed.

Issy reached into the icebox and poured him a half glass of iced tea, saying, "I'll just finish up the last batch here, take them to the picnic grounds, and give them to May. I'll meet you later."

He patted her cheek and gulped his tea. "Don't hurry. There's time, despite this filly's impatience. We're by the viewing stand." He took his daughter's elbow and said, sketching a bow, "Miss Bridget. We'll be off. Your admirers await."

As Isobel watched the two of them go down the path arm-in-arm, Bridey's giggle floating back, she said aloud wonderingly, "Weel, I would surely think, from the look of him, that he was going off with you. Now, why is that?"

It was several days later that Berkeley came into the kitchen rather early, even for him. He motioned to Isobel to stay seated, poured himself coffee, and topped up her cup. Sitting across from her, he said, "I'm going to have to be off the end of the month, and it'll be a long trip. Even the cleanup leases at the mines are getting thinner. If the veins play out, it'll be hard times here." He sipped his coffee and sighed. "I've seen it happen before, even to towns as bustling as Telluride with five thousand and more people. Suddenly there's no work. A short time later there are only empty houses with an unlatched door banging in the wind."

He lifted his eyes to hers and added, "And I don't like this recent news from Europe. If there's a war, we'll somehow get involved, I'm sure."

But, even as he sat frowning over the future, Isobel thought he still had that transformed look to him. *Is it just,* she asked herself, *that he's newly shaved, his wet hair hiding any gray? Could it be that which gives him this morning freshness? No, it* is *his eyes,* she decided at last. *He doesn't look faraway anymore, but instead here and happy.*

"Anyway"—he shrugged slightly and set down his cup—"these are the plans. Tell me honestly what you think. Like it or not, Bridey has to go off to the Ladies' Academy in Colorado Springs in the fall. You'll go with her, I hope. She couldn't stand it otherwise." He put his hand over hers and squeezed it briefly. "And that way she needn't board. Patrick Alexander writes that he's found a widow who lives nearby, where the two of you can stay. Talks a lot, he says, but a pleasant woman. Will you mind?"

Isobel couldn't breathe for delight while she listened, and then burst into words. "Why, I never thought I'd be going with her! All I was thinking was that she must do it. With your reading to her over the years, she knows more than the teachers here, I kept saying to myself. Oh, aye, I'll go. I'll not mind the people at that school taking over some of the lecturing, and keeping after her. She'll be right glad to come home to me at night. But—"

"Dear Issy," he interrupted, grinning at her, "the *two* of us have always been glad to do that. You're our mainstay. But I'll be all right, if that's what you're going to ask. Helga and her husband, with their two children, are cramped for room down the street. They can move in, have the third floor here, take care of the house. And you know, in the Springs, you'll only be sixty miles away from Florrie in Lafayette. If I'm not here, you and Bridey could even spend the summers there."

"Why, now, that's a thought." Isobel stood up with a wide smile of pleasure. "Now that John Wesley's passed on, I could be some real help to her. Her youngest, Lucy, is still a wee tyke and Florrie's got her hands full, though the oldest boys help out at the farm." Her head buzzing with plans, Isobel opened the oven and took out a johnnycake with a long-handled spatula. As she set it on a plate before him, her forehead furrowed, and she added, "But Bridey won't like leaving the valley, especially with knowing your journey is long."

"No, she won't," he responded, spreading butter on the steaming cake. "But I intend to bribe her royally. First, I've arranged with Sam Goler to have Viscount shipped down to her when she arrives in Colorado Springs. There's a stable not far from the school. Best of all, though, Issy, and this is a secret that I'm not telling her until she agrees to go uncomplainingly off to school, I've bought her ranch."

"Mr. Berkeley!" Isobel sank joyfully down on the chair. "She'll be that happy!"

"I hope so," he said, clearly delighted himself. "I'll take the two of you to see it next week, pretending it belongs to somebody else. The view is magnificent in all directions, with her familiar mountains on the horizon. The house itself is rather charming, and the widow who sold it to me wants to stay in it for a while. Homer Dunlap's got a big spread not far away, and he'll be running his stock on Bridey's ranch for the next few years. That'll make the payments. But Bridey's ranch account at the bank's grown over the years, and it's got plenty for start-up funds when she's ready."

He finished his coffee and stood up. "Is it settled, then? Can you be happy with these arrangements?"

"Aye," Isobel answered, relaxing into the relief that she need not be parted from her dear girl, thinking of long visits with Florrie. "Even Bridey will bear with it, after a bit."

"Good." He started out the door and then came back and planted a kiss on Isobel's lined cheek. "I don't think I told you that first morning we met, but you make the best johnnycake in the world."

CHAPTER 27

That morning the July sky was almost black, lowering, obscuring the top of the ridges on the north slope. The jagged edges of the Sawtooth Range were blotted out, and the buildings of the Liberty Bell mine, which still hunkered precariously on a ledge before the mountains, could not be seen even from a short distance away along the man-made sides of Cornet Creek. Slightly to the east the greasy clouds hid the entrance of the high road that wound painfully upward for five miles to Savage Basin and the Tomboy mine. They swirled even farther down the steep incline that held the residences of the wealthy on Galena Avenue, one of the highest streets on the north side of town: Victorian towers and gables and balconies, which usually commanded the sun, were blurred and veiled by the thick mist.

Such weather was almost unknown in the bright summer and would have been unusual even in the spring and fall, when there was the occasional overcast. Moreover, these heavy clouds and the pelting bursts of rain that tore from them had persisted over the weekend. When this Monday came and it was no better, Telluride citizens eyed the irascible skies glumly and stared down at streets that had become a soup of mud.

Summer cloudbursts were not at all uncommon, crackling through the valley with electrical force. But they were always brief storms, and there was something vibrant about their energy, causing the fine hairs to rise on people's arms as they craned through windows at the exciting turbulence. Then, almost before the rain stopped at one end of the valley, the sun had come back on the other. Rainbows would arc above as a reward.

Thunder had come rumbling in with these clouds, too, and lightning flashed. But the bolts came sizzling unexpectedly through the murky sky almost without light, and the thunder seemed to gather itself almost wearily, after three days, before building up to a battering roar, its echoes pounding back and forth between the high ridges.

The whole valley was waterlogged. The gulch beneath the Sawtooths, which in the winter was piled with the snow the mountains shrugged off, was now a lake. The storage reservoirs were overflowing, as well as the water dam owned by the city on the north by Cornet Creek Canyon. That particular stream had been diverted long ago and a new course built for it so that it met the San Miguel River more efficiently at the bottom on the western outskirts of town.

In the time of the Utes, however, Cornet Creek had run clear and wide on a diagonal eastern course down the mountainside. But the sun-attracting north slope had been taken over by the homes of the well-to-do, and the old channel filled in. A small dirt dam at the top reminded the creek of its new route. Today, heavy with mine tailings from the Liberty Bell, the sludgy water pitched slowly downward, slopping over its banks onto the nearby trail, a few blocks from the wooden houses perched on its former terrain.

From the glassed-in back porch Isobel was looking up at the sky with edgy impatience. She liked to do the laundry on Monday, and she had plenty of wash, since Mr. Berkeley would be leaving in two days. Finally, she decided to do up his shirts and hang them on the covered porch. But, as so often is the case, when one small problem is disposed of, the next one occupies the mind. Now, she stared at her drowned garden in dismay. The vegetable patch had become a pond. The neat furrows between the rows had filled, and when the soaked earth could absorb no more, they'd run over. All the ripening squash on the ground was submerged; the strawberries on the edges would never recover. Even the flowers looked defeated. The hollyhocks had drawn their fragile red petals together, the sodden heads of the butter-colored snapdragons were leaning drunkenly against each other, and the pansies had turned their velvet faces to the wet ground.

The unaccustomed moisture caused Isobel's hair to kink annoyingly, and spirals of graying red sprang from her neat bun at the back. Sighing, she tried unsuccessfully to tuck them back. The real cause of her uneasiness, however, she had pushed away as mere fuss-budgetry on her part. She did not like Bridey being out and about in what she called "wicked weather." Come snow or cold, wind or rain, Isobel liked to have Bridey in the house. When, after a hasty breakfast, the girl started on her usual dash to the stables, Isobel had handed her some cinnamon rolls for Sam Goler and gotten so far as to open her mouth. A knowing twinkle sprang to Bridey's eyes—she knew what the next words would be. So Isobel had simply closed her mouth. But that didn't mean she couldn't worry. And she did.

"Isobel," Berkeley said, coming in behind her through the small parlor, "I have at last sorted through the desk papers and managed to confine all the documents that you might need to one metal box. Sorry, make that two. Could you come and have a look?"

They both stopped at the door to the usually tidy library. Piles of paper were stacked on every surface and most of the floor. Berkeley surveyed the scene with satisfaction, since he saw order. Isobel saw a muddle. That Berkeley had worked hard she could tell from his rumpled hair, which fell, like a boy's, onto his forehead. He had a habit of lifting the sides with his fingers when he concentrated. His string tie was undone, shirtsleeves rolled up, the paisley vest unbuttoned. His face looked less gaunt, as if he'd gone backward in time, and she saw he had the contentment in his quick smile that she'd noted for the last several weeks since the Fourth. He even seemed to face his coming journey, the first one since Morna had gone, with resignation.

The only thing that troubled him was that his daughter did not face their separation in at all the same spirit. But Bridey tried hard to confine her tears to Isobel and the kitchen.

"In this one"—he tapped the fatter of the two metal boxes—"are documents you'll need for Bridey's enrollment at the Ladies' Academy in the fall. Birth certificate, eighth-grade diploma, and, most importantly, her formal adoption papers. I always tell her," he said, grinning at Isobel, "that not only am I her father, *I've* got the papers to prove it. Few fathers can say that. But she may wish to enroll as 'Bridget Gregory' because I think that tie to Morna is very important to her. Let her do so. She is mine, no matter what her name."

He opened the box and his smile grew wider as he ruffled the parchment stack. "Here as well is the deed to the ranch." He paused, and added happily, "Wasn't she pleased when she knew the place was hers?"

"Aye," Isobel agreed, smiling with him as together they recalled the girl's joy, "over the moon she's been for ten days now. She talks of nothing but the horses she'll buy. Had to run to the stables in the wet first thing this morning for yet another talk with Sam Goler."

"Well," Berkeley replied, and his fingers tousled his hair further, "we'll all have to become much more interested in *cows* if the place is to pay."

She nodded abstractedly. For her, cows were a useful source of cream, but even more importantly, fertilizer. Ever since seeing the fertile acres out the back door of the ranch house, Isobel had been mentally laying out the grandest garden. Rows of fresh corn and tomatoes sprang up in her mind, which were not possible here because of the valley's short growing season. Some fruit trees had already been in place, but were badly neglected, and she was mentally pruning them back when Berkeley pointed to the blue cardboard squares on the top of the box.

"Last, but not least, the bankbooks. Your name is on both accounts. If you have any questions, the young president who's replaced Gibbons is quite a reliable man. I've already sent a tuition check to Colorado Springs. As for the rest of this clutter"—he flipped casually through the documents—"will, deed on this house, insurance papers . . . Wait, the woman's address in Colorado Springs, yes, Mrs. Ellis. You'll want to write her next week. And Patrick Alexander's Denver address is in this little leather book. That's it."

He closed it, pushed it aside, and his face reflected aching nostalgia as he gestured to the other steel box with its heart padlock. His fingertips touched the lock gently. "The mining claims on Bridey's Mountain. They have to be renewed every year, but Bridey knows the tradition well. She's gone often enough with me to the courthouse. She'll never forget to do it, proud as she is of her own high peak. Where is she, by the way? Still at the stables?"

"No," Isobel answered as she walked to the window and looked worriedly at the sharp-edged rain. "She called from the Nordstroms to say that she'd dashed up there when it let up a bit. But, getting there, she saw the muddy climb up Fir Street seems to have bothered Viscount's bad . . . ankle"—she waved away all knowledge of the horse's anatomy while peering upward at the sky—"and she sent him packing back to Sam Goler. Now she'll have to come back on foot in all this muck, and catch pneumonia, besides, more than likely. She was telling me the rain would stop, but it won't."

Berkeley glanced at her, squared a teetering pile of papers, and said, "I'm going to Pandora soon to deliver these to Wells at Smuggler-Union. They're original drawings of the power station that he'll probably be glad to have. I'll need a closed trap for that, so I could as easily pick her up first and drop her here."

"Ah, would you?" Isobel's face cleared for the first time that morning. "But ye'll need lunch first. I'll cut a nice slice from the Sunday roast and—"

"No, no, Issy. Not after that breakfast you gave me." Berkeley held up his hand. But, seeing Isobel pluck a little at her dark cotton sleeve, he added hastily, "I'll be back for tea. Be nice on a wet day."

"Aye." She drew the word out in satisfaction. "I'll make scones. Bridey was telling me I haven't done them all summer. With the new raspberry jam."

The corner of his mouth quirked, and he embraced her with one strong arm, warmth bringing gold to his brown eyes. "Isobel Ewen, I am the luckiest man ever born. To have Morna and Bridey and *you*. I'll just fetch my coat, and then my daughter."

There was very little warning when it happened. The reasons that it occurred were simple. The Liberty Bell was in a bad place, as anyone could see, and as the avalanche had shown. But that had happened only the one time. That site was where the silver was, so that's where the mine had to be. It was the only thing to be done, the owners agreed. The gravel, the scree, all the refuse that came from the mine had to go somewhere, so the tailings were put into Cornet Creek, which was very handy, to be carried away. This meant the water was sludgy and couldn't flow swiftly and freely on its way to the San Miguel.

Moreover, it had made good sense to change the stream's channel. What difference did it make *where* the creek met the river? People wanted to live in the sun and could pay to do so. Cornet Creek was therefore moved westward so it wouldn't cut through the expensive lots. Perhaps if it'd still been a pretty stream, they might have left it, charged a little more to have it flow past the small back gardens. But because of the tailings it was murky, cinder colored.

Then there was the weather. Just when it seemed it could not possibly rain any harder, a looming cloud above the pinnacle of Sawtooth Range split open and poured out its contents. This waterspout, eight to ten feet high, roared down Cornet Creek Canyon. The nearby city reservoirs could not hold one more drop. The dam gave way, the storage tanks were torn from their moorings. This weight of water added to the raging flood now spilling down beside, but missing, the Liberty Bell.

Boulders weighing half a ton were easily carried along on the crest of the mass of mud, mine tailings, and debris forced on by the irresistible rush of the water, each second gaining speed as it swept down the mountainside and through the narrow canyon. Huge timbers and trees were tossed as if they'd been mere chips of wood. And the new route was too slow, too clogged. The small dirt dam set up to keep Cornet Creek in its man-made bounds was washed aside as if it were a straw.

It was then that the engorged creek remembered its old, preferred path to the east. And that's the way it went. Sheds, lean-tos, fences, and whole houses were muscled aside or swallowed up like kindling in the flow, as thick as lava, but far faster.

There just wasn't time. The telephone operator at the mine had put in a frantic call and the firebell in Telluride clamored in panic. But it sounded almost tinny beneath the water's paralyzing thunder. The residents on the favored north slope tore outside even before they heard the bell. A husband and wife made it to their garden gate. Although he was thrown aside by the onrush, she was instantly crushed against a back building.

Berkeley was halfway up steep Fir Street on his way to the Nordstroms on Galena Avenue when he heard the roar. Ten seconds later he saw the wall of water. Just ahead of it, running wildly from the house, was Bridey. His yell was wrenched from his throat as he leapt from the carriage and had only just caught her in his arms when they were engulfed.

Briefly, the strength of his legs held them up, but the sheer bulk and weight of the water pulled them under the next minute. Twice she was sucked away from him by the swirling current, and twice he clutched her again, hauling her head up, gasping for air, as they were rolled and driven by the furious flood. There was not time for anything but the frenzied thought that he must, he *must* grip tightly, pull her to the side and safety. He hung desperately on to her, trying to shield her with his own body from the slamming rocks and bruising logs. It was all he could do. The stoutest tree was jetsam, as helpless as they were, spun adrift as they were, and grabbing it was useless.

But a huge house had been tossed like a toy upended on its side, and he just managed with an upflung right arm to grasp a porch railing as they swept past. With his other, he held Bridey, and though he felt as if his arm was being wrenched from its socket as the current insistently snatched at her, he would not release his grasp. The tendons in his wrist that clenched the wood stood out like cords. The flood seemed malevolent in its determination to batter them, to divide them. Inch by inch he dragged her nearer to the haven of that tilted porch. Finally, he yanked her from the quicksand water and, with the last of his strength, thrust her up onto the splintered boards.

But to do so he'd had to let go of the railing himself, and though she immediately flung out her own mud-caked, beseeching young arm, he could not catch it before being hurled along again. Her anguished cry carried even above the water's roar. He heard that. Had there been time for reflection, he might have thought that was what the fortunate few hear as their last sound. It was a wail of love and despair at being separated.

But all that flickered through his mind was the enormous relief that she was safe. She was the child of his heart. He would never have hesitated to do what he'd done. Not a second's deliberation was needed. He knew, as Morna did, that to love is to preserve life. He was running out of time, but not love.

Perhaps, though, in that instant when he relaxed in his relief at Bridey's deliverance, Berkeley might have let go a little, his body too tired to struggle as it should. Now he was conscious of the water's bone-numbing cold, of the pain screaming in his useless right arm, of the mangled flesh of his hand. Still, the boulder was smashing down toward him, and it seemed unavoidable. One glance at it and he saw death. His last thoughts were what the prospector had told him about it.

Yes, here was that soft black tunnel, just as the man who was freezing had said. And it was warm and comforting. In it pain did disappear. He even found he couldn't imagine pain anymore. And then the peace, yes.

But there was no brilliant light. Instead, the darkness paled little by little into a dawn gray. And in that shining gray something happened that the prospector hadn't told him. For he was filled with joy, fierce and uplifting joy. No one could have told him what that soaring was like. No one could have described it.

The brightening gray was Morna's eyes. She stretched out her hand. And he reached up to her.

BRIDEY
and
TRISH

~

CHAPTER 1

The slowly climbing sun deepened
the Dresden blue of the sky, and a flock of fluffy clouds clustered like
quiet sheep across a china-smooth field. Patches of early mist still
wisped the floor of the mountain-edged valley. Stopping her mare on a
ridge overlooking it, Bridey Gregory pushed back her weathered Stetson to feel the soft touch of the sun on her cheek. She loosened the stray
tendrils of chestnut hair clinging damply to the collar of her chambray
work-shirt, letting the breeze cool her neck. Then she was still, absorbed in wind and sun and in her own thoughts.

The moment of peace shattered into motion and sound from the
land below. Cattle surged over a rise in an untidy mass, their reddish
brown hides a bright, moving contrast to the green, rolling foothills.
The whoops and shouts of the riders herding them cut through their
bellowing complaints like raucous birdsong.

A yearling broke away and tumbled into a hollow hidden by thick
grass. It tried to struggle out, now bawling in panic as its forelegs scrab-
bled on the loose dirt of the incline. The calf would need to be urged
out, pushed from behind by the thrust of a shoulder. Bridey could feel

the animal's warm side against her, hear its heaving breath, see— She pulled herself back from her memory to the present moment. A year ago she would have been in the thick of a spring roundup on her own ranch outside of Telluride. She would have been rescuing that imagined yearling. As it was, that cattle drive was only in her mindscape.

The scene Bridey was actually looking down on was Boulder Valley, some thirty miles from Denver. The fields spreading in all directions were sectioned off into rectangles of newly planted wheat. The sleepy lowing was that of dairy cows in their small pastures. She was whole mountain ranges from faraway Telluride in the San Juans. And from the land she'd turned into the flourishing Double B–G ranch, named for Berkeley, Bridey, and Gregory—for her mother.

But with her Bridey had brought the self-reliance that had sustained her through droughts and blizzards, through blighted crops and sickly calves. Work and experience had sculpted the early softness of her features into a stubborn beauty.

Her palomino was restive beneath her, but Bridey tightened the reins. She recalled the first time her father had shown her the spread he'd bought for her. She'd jumped up from the carriage seat, thrown her arms wide in youthful enthusiasm, exclaiming, "It's mine! I'm going to live on my own ranch."

Berkeley's happiness in her joy had brought that hint of gold to his hazel eyes. "But," he said, holding her hand so she wouldn't fall over the side of the buggy in her excitement, "it won't be easy. You'll be up at dawn every day, and your pretty hands will grow calluses. You'll smell of cow instead of rose water."

"I don't care if it's hard," she'd declared, bouncing back down beside him. "It's what I want."

"That's my girl," he'd replied, his smile flashing. "There's a proverb: 'Take what you want,' God says, 'and pay for it.' But everybody ends up paying something, so listen to the first part and take what *you* want. Most folks don't figure that out, and they end up with what somebody else told them to want. They paid the same price, and they never got their heart's desire. But I did and so will you."

Now as she settled her worn boot more firmly in the stirrup, Bridey considered that. By her early thirties she had gotten what she wanted, even if it'd cost more than a few calluses. Every morning she'd walked out onto her own land, seen the sturdy livestock she'd raised, the strong fences she'd built, and the stable barns filled with hay she'd baled. She and Issy had turned the neglected ranch house into a warm and comfortable home, and Issy's overflowing garden fed them well through the long winters.

On the Double B–G, Bridey had her pride of ownership and the security of solid ground beneath her feet. For the last fifteen years she'd devoted herself to winning that stability. She'd never forgotten the day she watched in a daze of horror as the swiftly churning water carried her father off, the current pulling him away with the crumbling rock of the mountainside. In her desperate grief she'd vowed with every ounce of her will never to be in so vulnerable a position again. Love could be lost, quickly and finally. Thereafter, Bridey told herself that her heart's desire would revolve around her work.

As she leaned forward to stroke the mare's creamy neck, Bridey's long lashes were thick against the strong curve of her cheek. She bore the inheritance of her parents in her face. Its oval shape was Morna's, as was the straight nose and full-lipped mouth. The brown eyes with the glance of gold recalled Berkeley's. The firm angle of the chin was his. She'd needed that set to her jaw, moving as she had in a world of men— of cowhands, feedstore owners, cattle buyers, bankers. All had been caught by her beauty. But they'd discovered they couldn't cross the boundaries she drew. To protect herself she'd built very high fences. No man had been permitted within.

Bridey had already learned from looking at the lives of her parents that love exacted the highest price of all. What she could not afford to see was that her true heart's desire was the love that Berkeley and Morna had shared.

Glancing up, she had her favorite view of Long's Peak, the reigning giant overlooking Boulder and Louisville. Soaring above the mountaintops below it, the diamond shape of the peak's east face caught the morning light. The dramatic upward thrust of the horizon eased her yearning for Bridey's Mountain and faraway Telluride.

And for her lost ranch. As the slow tide of the Great Depression flooded despair across the nation, the Double B–G had gone under. Despite her hard work and Issy's constant strength Bridey found she *was* defenseless against financial ruin. She and Isobel were forced off the land and had moved to Louisville in the Boulder Valley near Denver to live with Issy's sister, Florrie. Like so many in these new, hard times, they had been compelled to begin again.

Tucking her blue shirt more tightly into her faded denims, Bridey remained still, her thoughts turned back to those events of a year ago. The palomino lifted impatient feet, turning to question this long inactivity. "Hush, Anna," her owner murmured, brushing the ivory mane.

When Bridey had been told that the Double B–G would be auctioned unless she could raise enough money to pay off her debts, she'd raced home from the local bank in Norwood. She could see Issy, sun-bonnet knotted beneath her chin, in the far reaches of the garden. More than anything she wanted to turn to her for comfort, as she always had, but Bridey stopped herself. She couldn't yet find the words for news that would break Issy's heart too. She'd climbed slowly to her bedroom closet, pushing the hanging clothes to one side. Falling to her knees, she'd opened the lid of the leather-covered trunk that Morna had brought to Telluride at the turn of the century. The scent of lilac sachet filled the small space.

The metal strongbox was nestled beside the cloud of tissue paper holding Morna's lacy white dress. The box was as shiny as when Berkeley had presented it at Bridey's birth. The heart-shaped padlock swung gently from the hasp as she placed it on the bed. With the back of her hand she wiped the tears from her cheeks, recalling her mother's luminous gray eyes as she sang bedtime lullabies. For a moment the old grief at her loss overwhelmed Bridey, almost submerging her new sharp pain. The never-answered questions arose again. Why hadn't she ever come back? What had happened to her? But then her glance fell on the letter Morna had left for her with Issy. It had ended, "You have the mountain, Bridey . . . our gift of love. One that will give you strength. Whenever you feel downhearted, remember that."

Inside the box were the deeds to the mines on Bridey's Mountain, worthless now in the heart of the Depression. Not that Bridey would ever have considered selling them. After the mines' production slowed to a trickle of ore, Telluride had become a ghost town with tumbleweeds blowing down the empty streets. Bridey had some time ago deeded the family home to Helga, whose large family had outgrown her tiny house a few doors away. Otherwise, it would have been boarded up, falling into disrepair. But the mountain would always be hers.

She lifted out the small velvet box containing Morna's diamond and ruby ring. The brilliance of the stones had blurred as she faced the end of her dream.

On the day of the auction Bridey slipped the ring on her finger to give her strength. The summer sun had beaten down on every item put up for bid. She and Issy grew numb as pieces of their lives were pounded into sale by the hammer of the auctioneer. Local banker Walt Merrick had stood beside them, gray faced at the loss of his friends' home. He'd been powerless to help. Ranch after ranch on this fertile plateau outside of Telluride had gone on the auction block, bringing their hardworking owners next to nothing. As he'd told Bridey, Merrick didn't know whose money was behind the faceless Denver company that had refused to extend the loans until better times. He couldn't imagine who was so rich now when everyone else in the state was so poor.

No one noticed when a boxy black automobile slid up the lane, stopping on the edges of the crowd. In the backseat, his identity hidden by shadows, sat Enos Murdoch, of the powerful Colorado banking family.

Ramrod stiff in the Ford's backseat, Enos had examined the scene before him with close-set, emotionless eyes behind a pince-nez. In the area to survey his new holdings, he'd decided to attend the foreclosure of this sizable addition. He'd noticed that the original buyer was Berkeley Glendower, whom his father had often mentioned. William Murdoch had said that, despite the man's wrongheadedness in terms of marriage, Glendower had ended up well off. Enos figured there might be something here worth his while. Jewelry, a good horse, a piece of art. Everything would be going at a basement price. Such information was frequently as valuable a resource as money in the Murdoch way of doing business.

Bridey had borne up under her growing losses as the auction proceeded. But her composure slipped as Anna was led forward to be sold. The mare minced with nerves at the unaccustomed sight and sound of so many people, tugging at the stranger's hand on her halter.

Anna had been her favorite from her first shaky moment on new legs, her future elegance and personality only suggested. Bridey's hands clenched tightly, and she felt the constriction of Morna's ring around her finger. She remembered that Morna had ridden her Chevalier as if the two of them were one.

The afternoon heat seemed to gather itself into a knot of tension at the base of Bridey's neck. Looking over her shoulder, she saw a somber figure stepping out of a black Ford. "Who's that man?" she asked Walt.

Walt's blue gaze narrowed as he followed her line of sight. "Enos Murdoch." He couldn't bring himself to add what he suddenly realized. This was the new owner of the Double B–G.

"Murdoch?" Bridey remembered the bitter twist of Berkeley's lips whenever he'd said that name. The family had owned the smelters and a good piece of the mines. The Murdochs had been able to dictate the wages paid and who would get to work. The miners' families had often gone hungry while the Murdochs grew richer. She watched as the Denver banker ran a proprietorial eye over the nearest barn, even peering nearsightedly at door hinges. Gripped by fierce anger, she, too, knew who had foreclosed on her ranch. Murdoch adjusted his stiff collar and walked closer to inspect the spirited horse held by the auctioneer.

Bridey turned to Walt in sudden decision. "Would you be willing to buy a piece of jewelry?" The sunlight was captured by the rubies and center diamond of Morna's ring, then refracted into starry rays on the band of gold. Although her heart was thundering with distress, Bridey knew as clearly as if Morna had spoken that she would understand.

"I don't have that kind of money, Bridey. My salary—"

"Give me whatever you can, Walt." Her voice was resolute. She couldn't save her ranch, but this she would have. "I want to buy Anna."

On the day Isobel and Bridey left, Walt Merrick had promised to arrange Anna's delivery as soon as they were settled.

"That's my farewell present," he told Bridey as he said good-bye. "That and the promise that I'll hold your mother's ring for you. One of these days you're going to want it back." He smiled, but his eyes were sad. "You take care of yourself, you hear?"

They'd stopped off in Telluride before catching the train in Montrose. Bridey had wanted to say good-bye to her mountain. Heart full at the view of the face lifted to the sky, she said farewell to her legacy. Everything except Anna was gone, but she still had her mountain.

When they first caught sight of the old farmhouse outside Louisville, Bridey and Issy had felt a sense of homecoming. It was a snug place, dormer windows atop the second story, flowers and vines diverting attention from dingy white paint. The porch surrounding the first floor seemed to smile in welcome.

Their relief had been short lived. The man who opened the door to their repeated knocking identified himself as Dr. Bertram Ramsay. His shoulders sagged as he said that Florrie had gotten a bad case of scarlet fever and that he hadn't been able to save her.

Isobel froze at the news. Her first thought was that now all she had of her sister were the carefully preserved letters sent over the years, the yellowed pages filled with loving words. She burst out, "I dinna' even get to say hello. Or"—her voice faltered—"good-bye."

"Aunt Isobel?"

Lucy MacAllister was in the doorway, her husband, Gerald, behind her. She was parchment white, her brown hair escaping from the long braid over one shoulder of her faded rose dressing gown. The shock of grief had aged her beyond her twenty-seven years.

Isobel made her way over to her niece. "My poor bairn," she murmured, her thin arms going around her. As they embraced, Issy knew she still had a part of her beloved Florrie here in Lucy.

Bridey was roused from memory when Anna snorted, her long legs dancing with nervousness. She patted the arched neck. "Anna, what is the matter with you this morning?" she scolded gently. "I've never seen you so jumpy."

As she guided the mare through a grove of pines, Bridey reflected that she still had much to be thankful for. The greatest gift of the past year had been her growing friendship with Lucy and Gerald MacAllister. They'd slipped into a routine of farm work that was comfortable for them all.

The huge vegetable garden was thriving. The cows were producing so much cream that Issy was at her wit's end inventing new delights to use up what they didn't sell. And the price of butter had risen a half cent a pound.

A meadowlark sang as it soared above. Bridey lifted her face to the sky, and she felt she was addressing Berkeley as she said with a smile, "I'll just have to find something else I want. I'll be glad to pay what it costs." Nudging Anna away from the lowest of the branches, she reminded herself that right now there were chores to be done and she'd have to hurry back.

Suddenly, a loud noise sounded to her right, and Anna started wildly. Before Bridey could react, the mare plunged off through the trees "Whoa." Bridey pulled back on the reins. "Easy, girl."

Anna clenched the bit, galloping across an opening and into a stand of cottonwoods. When Bridey heard the loud, popping sound again, she realized it was gunfire.

She pulled with all her strength on the reins, but Anna was out of control. Her hooves thundered on the dry dirt as Bridey dodged one branch, then another, leaves flapping in her face, thin branches whipping at her arms and head.

Suddenly, a man stepped out from the shelter of a thick cottonwood. Anna reared up, whinnying. The reins were jerked out of Bridey's hands, and she slammed back in the saddle, then tumbled to the ground.

She lay sprawled, her head spinning, barely aware of the receding sound of Anna's hooves. Her eyes cleared, and her gaze traveled up dark trousers and a white shirt with sleeves folded to the elbows, up to a tanned, angry face. The dark eyes glittering down at her were shaded by the brim of a brown felt fedora. Bridey blinked. The man was holding a shotgun.

He looked down at her with narrowed eyes, and when he spoke, his voice was edged with exasperation. "Who the devil are you?"

CHAPTER 2

Bridey pushed herself up into a sitting position and her hair tumbled around her face, pins flying like confetti. "I might ask you the same thing," she returned roundly, rubbing at the pounding rhythm in the back of her head. Ignoring the man's outstretched hand, she levered herself to her feet. "And I'd add another question." Her voice gained firmness as she glared up at him. "What kind of idiot are you to step in front of a runaway horse?"

He'd taken off his fedora and a swatch of dark brown hair fell over his forehead. Black brows hitched in a frown over coffee-brown eyes lashed paintbrush thick. He looked down a long, straight nose at her and the mouth underneath it was wide, the muscles bunched in a square jaw. A gleam of humor sneaked into his eyes, and his lips twitched at the corners as he surveyed her with frank interest. "I *was* trying to stop the damned thing!" he said. "Sorry."

Bridey opened her mouth to respond, but at the rustling sound nearby he threw one lightning glance over his shoulder, then launched himself at her, knocking her to the ground. "Are you out of your—"

she started, and found a lean, hard hand jammed firmly against her mouth.

"Be quiet," he hissed into her ear. He shifted his weight, his hand pressing against her lips. She could taste the salt of his skin. His legs moved against her as he pushed up, and his shirt, still crisp and fresh with starch, dragged across her face.

Bridey was riled, both at his high-handed force and at her own sudden awareness of his feel, his smell. She tried to roll out from under him, swinging her legs for leverage. He sat on her thighs, one hand snaring and holding her wrists with easy strength. He lowered his face to hers, frustration in every line of his expression. "Will you be still a minute?" he demanded in a low, harried voice. "We've got trouble here."

She strained against his hold, her eyes flashing retribution, but his were scouting the stand of cottonwood trees some ten yards away. "Come on," he said abruptly, jerking her to her feet. "For God's sake, if you don't want to get shot, keep your mouth shut. You can yell all you want when we're out of this."

His manacle hold on her wrist did not weaken as they ran to the trees. Bridey stumbled over a rock but he simply pulled her all the harder, and she somehow kept from falling.

When they reached the protection offered by the crowded gray trunks of the cottonwoods, he bent in a crouch, tugging her down beside him. Bridey was breathing heavily, whether from anger or the running she didn't know, but he showed no shortness of breath.

"I hope you're not hurt"—he pitched his voice low—"but if you are, try to hang on. I already have a situation here and I don't need to be worrying about you."

"What's going on?" she insisted, trying to keep her own voice down. "I've got to get my horse before she—"

"Hush! You can't worry about that now. Not far from here," he said, his mouth near her ear, "is a man named Earl Beacham, who's drunk a bottle of his own white lightning. He resents my trying to keep him from making more of the stuff." He paused and listened intently. "Since he has a gun," he went on after a moment, the brush of his breath against her skin creating shivers down her neck, "and he's been doing his drunken best to shoot me full of holes, that makes this game dangerous." He slanted a look at her. "If I leave you here, will you stay put?"

Seeing her eyes blaze at him, he grinned and gestured with one finger to his lips. "Quietly."

"Who are you?" she demanded. Her head was spinning, but she

was aware of a laundry list of insults she'd like to loose upon him. Not that she'd do it till he put down the gun.

He flipped a silver badge from his shirt pocket and held it out silently.

Bridey stared at him, nonplused. He was a U.S. marshal? The position was a political appointment and in smaller towns usually given to men of retirement age. This man was not that much older than she. But she had time for only a flash of memory of the graying, slow-moving marshal she'd known in Norwood, and then she was being pulled along almost in a crouch. "Come on, move." He led her to the remnant of a stone wall nearly overgrown with wild plum and pussy willow. A grasshopper leapt from the crumbling edge of the sandstone rock where he sat her down next to him. He held her there for a moment, one strong hand on her shoulder, her hair brushing his collar, and she was again aware of the sharp tang of his sweat.

He held the gun with a tight hand, tensed as he strained to hear his quarry. Then he went down on one knee in front of her. "I'm going to try to get around him on the other side of those trees. Sit here and I'll come back for you as soon as I've found the old fool." He stood up and replaced his hat.

She shot him a resentful glance at his certainty that she would fall under his command. He was too sure of himself, and she didn't like the way he loomed over her. Worse, she was too aware of his urgent physicality. This stranger made her feel as if he'd just leapt over her barbed wire fences. "I've got to find my horse and get out of here," she muttered.

His lips curved with amusement, and Bridey was ruffled at the laugh that lit his eyes. She was convinced that he'd read her thoughts correctly. "First we settle this, then the horse," he ordered. "We'll even pick up your hat."

He loped off silently toward a stand of poplars, his long legs covering the ground with speed. Soon she could barely see his outline among the trees.

He moves like a hunter, Bridey thought, her eyes trained on him. As soon as she could no longer make out his figure, she pushed herself off the rock. She couldn't just sit there. Anna might come back and get hit by a bullet gone astray.

Walking as quietly as she could toward a flowered thicket, Bridey kept alert for any sign of the mare. Her head still ached, but she'd fallen off too many horses to let that affect her. She was irritated that she'd let the marshal get under her skin.

At a heavy rustling from the dense bushes she spun around. From the fountainlike branches of forsythia she saw the barrel of a gun pointed straight at her. "Who're you?" came from the bush in muffled tones, and the gun barrel moved jerkily, as if to threaten her.

Her eyes narrowing Bridey stared into the bush. "Who are *you*?"

"I asked first. Don't you try goin' nowhere, girlie." A short, stocky old man extricated himself from the foliage, his gun on her all the while. Shaggy gray hair hung over his forehead, nearly obscuring the rheumy blue eyes viewing her with suspicion. He wobbled slightly, then ran the torn sleeve of his grimy work shirt under his bulbous nose. "What're you doin' here?" he demanded, his words slurred. Then he broke into a cackle. "Don't tell me Devin Lowell's taken to bringin' along females as his deppities." He wheezed appreciatively at his own wit.

"Devin Lowell?" Bridey repeated.

"The fella you was jawin' with!" the old man snorted. "Don't try playin' me any tricks, girl. You tellin' me you don't know him?"

"I don't know him," Bridey declared. "I'd never seen him before he made me fall off my horse." She was suddenly very aware of the morning silence. Even the birds had stopped singing. Her instincts told her to keep talking. "I don't think we've met," she said to fill the quiet. "My name is Bridey Gregory, and I—"

"Well, how-de-do." The old man's eyes were bloodshot slits. "And ain't it a lovely day?" The gun barrel dipped like the handle of a pump and came back up.

This unrepentant drunk must be Earl Beacham. Bridey, too, was struck with the absurdity of attempting polite conversation while staring into the deadly eye of a shotgun. Her lips quivered with an almost irrepressible desire to laugh.

"Well, cat got your tongue?" He wavered again, and belched loudly. "'Scuse it," he mumbled automatically.

"No, it's a lovely day, and I'm delighted to meet you, and now I need to find my horse. If you'll excuse me—"

Somewhere behind him the sound of a loud thud was followed by a rustle, and Beacham lurched around to see what it was, nearly falling down in the process. He took a few staggering steps toward a plum bush that, some ten yards away, was still quaking as if it suffered from St. Vitus' dance. "What the hell is that?" he growled.

A pebble hit Bridey on the shoulder, and she jerked around. From the trees where he'd disappeared a few minutes ago, the marshal summoned her with an impatient arm. She ran lightly across the clearing to him, glancing back behind her to see the old man prodding the bush with his gun. Devin Lowell grabbed her hand and pulled her into cover.

Beacham, having discovered the blamelessness of the shrub, set up a howl at having lost his hostage and stamped around looking for her.

"How did he find you?" the marshal demanded in a fierce whisper. "I told you to stay put."

Bridey pointed back at the thicket. "He was hiding right behind the forsythia."

Devin Lowell grimaced. "I should've been able to smell the old bastard." He suddenly remembered his manners. "Sorry."

The apology provoked her. Considering how he'd already treated her, his being a stickler about language now seemed like condescension.

"I don't mind the term *bastard*," she replied crisply. "He's the second one I've met today."

Devin Lowell raised an eyebrow. He was a man who'd accepted the responsibility that people instinctively gave him. He thus took for granted, without arrogance, that they would always follow in his lead.

"Keep your voice down." He was reflecting that he'd been shot at enough times for him to think seriously about his lack of a last will and testament. While Earl would not deliberately shoot either one of them, his gun might go off in their direction. As they ran quickly from bushes to clumps of trees, he felt his hands itching to grab this sharp-tongued woman, either to shake her or hold her. He wasn't sure which.

"Watch out," Devin whispered as they crouched beside a grove of dogwood. He thought that where she was concerned, he should take that advice himself.

Gunfire sounded, loud and close, and Bridey barely restrained a yelp of surprise. They scrambled down the bank of the stream, taking cover in a tangle of Virginia creeper.

"Damn the old coot," the marshal muttered. "I don't want to have to shoot him." But he was afraid that as drunk as Earl was, he might have to wing him just to get his attention. He should have been able to bundle him into the car and down to the county jail without any trouble, or so Earl had given him cause to believe. He'd come staggering out of the woods with a boozy smile, carrying only a jug. But when Devin turned to open the backseat door, Beacham had scampered off, grabbing a shotgun he'd hidden behind a rotting tree stump. Now the stakes were higher, Devin thought uneasily, because he had an unwilling partner to look after.

For her part, Bridey was not used to being protected. She could see that Earl was unlikely to hit anything he aimed at, even if it was a whole mountainside. She was only worried about her wayward Anna being in the line of fire.

When she heard the sound of breaking twigs above her on the

other side of the creek bed, she glanced up and saw the mare, reins dangling. Unthinkingly, she rushed to scramble up the muddy bank. The next thing she knew, two hundred pounds of U.S. Marshal landed on her back, slamming her upright into the loose soil. "You're even dumber than that horse," he bit out. If he hadn't been whispering, he'd have been shouting.

He flipped her over, but because of the incline of the bankside, his mouth was only an inch from hers. He knew then how much he wanted her. Twigs were caught in her tumbling hair, her face and shirt were grimy, and her fiery brown eyes were flashing the sure and certain promise of murder. She was beautiful. In that second he couldn't ever remember wanting anything so much.

Devin stepped back quickly, then pulled her across the stream into the vines. Bridey was still swallowing the bile in her throat and trying to scrape the squishy mud from her boots when he disappeared up the near bank and into the trees. When she craned her neck to see where he'd gone, she saw Earl Beacham staring blearily down at her.

"What're you doin' down there, girlie?" he asked, peering the length of the streambed. His hands tightened on his shotgun, a look of foggy cunning on his face. "You lookin' for my still?"

"No," Bridey answered testily. She stood up, brushing the dirt from the legs of her denims, trying to find a firm place to stand on the rocks of the shallow creek. Looking up at him, she enunciated precisely, biting out each word, "Far from it. I'm trying to catch my horse and get out of here. As fast as I can."

Behind Earl, stalking silently, the marshal moved from the cover of the trees. His eyes signaled to Bridey, and she jerked back into speech. "She was on the far bank a minute ago." She waved an arm behind her. "Any sign of her?"

As Beacham scanned the woods across the stream, Devin's hand snaked out and yanked the shotgun away before the old man could react. "Now then, Earl," he said dryly, "you come along with me." Breaking open the barrel to remove the shells, he went on, "No more tricks. Not with a lady present."

Beacham stumbled a step backward, his rheumy eyes on Bridey as she climbed lightly up the bank. He nodded, his face creased in a crafty half-smile. He edged a little farther away as if to give her room on the verge. "We met." He made an ineffectual pass at his nose with his ragged sleeve. "But I don't rightly recall the name."

Bridey repeated it, her sense of humor returning at the old man's attempt at crestfallen politeness. She added, "I live a couple of miles from here, on Florrie Wesley's place. At least," she corrected herself, "that's what it used to be. She died last year."

Earl looked down. "Sorry. She was a nice lady, but that preacher husband of hers was a Bible thumper. Never touched a drop of liquor." His voice was full of mournful incredulity.

"Let's go, Earl," Devin ordered. "You know where the car is."

An expression of affability stole over Beacham's face. "I left a present for you beside that flivver you drive."

"A jug of that rotgut you call whiskey?" The marshal cocked a dark eyebrow.

Earl cackled until he started coughing. One minute he was bent slightly over as if trying to catch his breath and the next he was heading off with amazing speed into the trees.

"So help me, I'll shoot you in the back," Devin bellowed after him.

"Betcha won't," came the reply, and then he was gone.

The marshal cradled Beacham's shotgun with a resigned shrug and pocketed the shells. "Well," he said, the corners of his mouth lifting at the old man's neat turning of the tables, "I got this. At least it'll be a while before he saves up for another one."

"Don't you think that even *you*"—Bridey's tone was sweetly venomous—"might be able to catch one old man?"

His lips registered her gibe, but he replied evenly, "He knows every inch of this land and it'd take some time. Might as well let him sleep it off in the woods instead of in the jail at the county's expense. Without a gun he's harmless." Pulling out a pocket watch fastened to his belt loop with a leather strap, he finished, "Besides, it's nearly eight-thirty. I'm supposed to be at the electric plant by nine."

"Then, of course, there's the little matter of finding my horse." Bridey brushed again at the dirt on her pants, the edge returning to her voice. "Not to mention my hat. Just where is this 'flivver' of yours?"

As they approached the dirt road, she heard the marshal groan unexpectedly. But her attention was completely taken by the sight of Anna, grazing contentedly by a gleaming gray Chevrolet. Hurrying forward, she noticed the mare was favoring a back leg as she stood. Bridey murmured soothing words and stooped, running sensitive hands down that leg. At last she straightened up, remarking worriedly, "I think she's strained a hock. I'll have to walk her home."

It was only then that she noticed how low the car sat. The two visible tires were flattened in the dust. The marshal had been watching her. Following her glance, he said, "All four of them." He held up the hand pump, its hose shattered by a shotgun blast. "Earl's 'present,' " he added wryly. "We'll both be walking. If you have a telephone, I'll come with you."

They set off down the road side by side in silence. The horse paced behind them, the reins held loosely in Bridey's hand. She was finding that she was more than ever bothered by this man's presence. He was walking at quite an acceptable distance from her, but perhaps because of his size, he seemed much too close. As if to push him away with her voice, she said acerbically, "Anna probably hurt her leg rearing so sharply when you stepped in front of her."

"I am sorry, Miss—it is Miss?—Gregory. But, under the circumstances, maybe you could forgive me. I sure hope Anna will be all right."

The reasonableness of his reply only stung her further. "It was the gunfire that startled her. She's hardly used to that. What good is a marshal if you can't keep the peace? I was only out for a little early-morning exercise. *I* wasn't breaking any law."

"You might have been trespassing on someone's land. I'd have to check." There was no mistaking the wry humor in his tone.

Bridey's color rose. *Now he's making fun of me,* she fumed inwardly. She'd been chased around all morning by a drunk with a gun, thrown all too roughly in the dirt, and now this arrogant excuse for a lawman—But he hadn't been arrogant. He'd let Earl scamper off with an amused shrug and hadn't let his own pride get in the way. He'd even dismissed his deflated tires without rancor.

She grimaced; she couldn't allow herself to start defending him. His ease with his own place in things seemed to draw her in, to enclose her. Moreover, there was the way he'd just taken charge this morning. And she could still feel his powerful length against her body. She stared straight ahead and increased her pace.

Devin was relieved that she was not looking at him. Quite unconsciously, he'd raised his hand to pick the dried grass from her hair and brush the clinging dust from her shoulder. He dropped his arm abruptly. The unthinking familiarity of his gesture took him aback. He kept remembering the warmth of her skin under his hands. He'd been noticing that the sun brought out the red in her glorious hair, that her mouth was invitingly full lipped, that her breasts were high and rounded beneath the tightly tucked-in shirt. But it was obvious from the set of her mouth that her barbed wire was in place. Maybe, he thought ruefully, fences weren't a bad idea.

He couldn't resist adding, "When I get back to the office, I'll look up that piece of property. The owner might be willing to let you off with a warning."

Although she knew it was a giving in, Bridey's lips twitched. "I could always say that I'd been deputized." She let a fleeting smile touch her lips. "After all, I did save you from Earl Beacham."

Devin tugged at the brim of his fedora. "Hmm. Yes. *You* saved *me*." He made a sweeping gesture down the deserted road. "Then why is it that I don't feel safe with you now?"

CHAPTER 3

Bridey and Devin had settled into
an edgy silence by the time they arrived at the MacAllister place. She
found that even conventional phrases seemed to have larger meanings.
He was cursing himself because his feelings tongue-tied him when he
had a lot he wanted to say. As they approached the shabby old farmhouse, the screen door slammed and Isobel hurried down the walk.

"Where have you been?" she asked. One thin hand patted the
white apron bib over her gingham housedress. Under the fringe of grizzled hair her eyes were worried. They widened at Bridey's appearance.
She was on foot, Anna limping behind her, her clothes covered with
dust and her hair cascading down her back.

"Slight accident," Bridey replied briefly. "I'm okay." She patted
Issy's shoulder gently. Seeking an explanation, Isobel looked up at the
massive, ruggedly handsome man. As he smiled reassuringly at her, she
was convinced she'd never met him before, but there was something
about him that made her think she had.

"This is Devin Lowell," Bridey told her. "*Marshal* Lowell. We met
. . . on the road. Marshal Lowell, this is my friend Isobel Ewen."

Devin tipped his hat, and it was the warmth of his eyes beneath the recklessly flaring brows that made Issy realize why he seemed familiar. That smile reminded her of Berkeley Glendower's. It won her heart instantly. Here at last was a possible match for Bridey. Before she could say anything, Bridey went on, "I'm really fine, Issy. But I've got to get a poultice on Anna's leg. The marshal needs to use the phone."

Bridey extended her hand to Devin, but Issy noticed she avoided his eyes. "It's been an interesting morning. Good-bye." Without waiting for his reply Bridey led the horse away quickly. She was determined to get away from this man and sort out her thoughts.

Taken aback by Bridey's unusual abruptness, Issy made up for it in a burst of hospitable chat. By the time she'd showed him into the living room, Devin had already heard the story of the Double B–G. Imagining what a loss that must have been to Bridey, he recalled how she had scrambled up after falling from the horse. This woman, he thought, still feeling her strong fingers clasping his, got right up when she'd been knocked down.

As he glanced about the room, he could envision her here, curling up in the worn, deep-cushioned sofa. The furniture was solid, unpretentious, and chosen for comfort. He found the sense of home as seductive as Bridey herself, and he felt his own loss because he had nothing in his own life like this. Nothing at all like her.

Promising him lemonade, Isobel disappeared into the kitchen. Devin followed her there. The scent of fresh bread was strong in the high-ceilinged room, and its source was the black iron cookstove dominating one wall. On the table in the center of the floor was a cooling rack that held six loaves of bread, a sheen of butter on the crusts that had been applied with a brush just before baking.

As he sipped the cold, tart liquid, Devin's eyes kept straying to the open door of the barn across the yard. There was no sign of Bridey. Isobel followed his glance, gazing at him with bright curiosity. Several questions trembled on her lips. But she began politely, "There's the phone. If your deputy canna' come to get you, my nephew Gerald will be back soon and he can drive you."

"I haven't any deputies, ma'am," Devin replied with a grin. "Pretty peaceful county. Being marshal is just a part-time civic duty. I work at the power company."

"What do you do there?" Issy inquired as he reached for the telephone.

"I'm the president," he answered absentmindedly before asking the operator to connect him to the Northern Colorado Power Company.

After he'd arranged his ride and hung up, Issy suggested that he wait outside in the grape arbor. "A wee bit cooler there than this kitchen, what with the stove on." Holding open the screen door, she added pointedly, "Bridey's already in the garden too. Anna mustna' be ailing too much."

As Devin walked quickly through the arbor, then along a path walled in hollyhocks, he saw Bridey kneeling to hand-weed the new rows of vegetables. Her chestnut hair was tied off her neck with a blue bandana, her hands encased in canvas work-gloves. He stopped briefly to look at her, to inhale the perfume of growing plants, and then he released a long breath of contentment. How many years had it been, he wondered, since he'd felt this sense of belonging?

Bridey looked at him across the seedlings. She was aware of a rising resentment because he seemed at home here. This part of the garden was hers, a refuge. She'd planned it and planted it, and always arranged her thoughts as she worked. It was why she was here now. She wanted to rail at him to go because just the sight of him made her feel restless and dissatisfied. Her eyes, when they met his, reflected her emotions. "Hasn't your ride come yet?" she asked unnecessarily.

Devin didn't reply. He felt an odd sort of tenderness for her because she was fighting as if he were a danger to her, whereas he was touched with peace. As he took a few steps toward her, she rose abruptly and hurried toward him.

"Stop! You'll step on the okra plants." Her tone was sharp.

She tugged off her glove, reaching out for his sleeve as if to physically pull him along the flagstone path and back toward the house. Then she dropped her hand and marched through the arbor ahead of him.

"I'm usually a careful man," he said mildly, following her.

"You couldn't prove that by this morning," she returned as she spun to face him. She knew it was unfair, but there seemed no way to bolt the gates against him. He was so tall that the unfurling vine leaves brushed his hair, and he filled the latticed space.

"No, Bridey," he said quietly. "No more of that."

She was sure she was resisting the arm that drew her to him, the hand that lifted her face. But all she was aware of was opening to his kiss like a plant unlocking itself to sun and rain.

Isobel saw them from the kitchen. She quickly beckoned to her niece, who'd just come downstairs. "Lucy," she said in amazement. "Come look at this."

The sound of footsteps drew Lucy's attention to the hall outside. She smiled at Gerald as he approached her, casting off his beekeeping gear as he came. He landed a kiss on her cheek, his lean, kind face quizzical. "What are the both of ye staring at?"

"He's kissing her," Issy murmured. "What *do* ye think happened this morning?"

Gerald peered over her shoulder. "Who's kissing?"

"Devin Lowell," Issy answered, a gleam of satisfaction now in her eyes, "is kissing Bridey."

"Marshal Lowell?" Gerald's voice rose. "Marshal Devin Lowell is kissing our Bridey?"

"So it would appear," Lucy answered in a pleased voice.

Gerald's face was creased with trouble. "Lucy, Devin Lowell is a married man."

CHAPTER 4

Louisville was a sagging dowager
of a town, its clapboard buildings dingy in the summer light. The dirt
streets were nearly deserted except for an old yellow dog that moved
with the shade as the sun climbed. The dust kicked up by the occasional
car moving down Second Street was as fine as talcum powder.

Bridey made a token motion at brushing it off her skirt, then left it
alone. She'd pinned her hair up to keep it off her neck, but she was hot
in her taupe gabardine suit. Her creamy skin was flushed from the heat.
The sooner she could complete her errands, she thought wistfully, the
sooner she could go home and change out of her town clothes. The
worn wooden expanse of sidewalk shook under her shoes as she made
an effort to hurry.

A shiny gray Chevrolet hummed down the street, then made an
abrupt U-turn. Bridey had a sudden, certain knowledge that its driver
was Devin Lowell. It came as no surprise when the car pulled up just
ahead of her. The engine died, leaving abrupt silence. The door opened
and Devin got out.

He wore a lightweight suit, and his Panama hat was tilted at an angle. Bridey could almost see a twinkle in the eyes shaded by the smooth straw. She remembered him so, his eyes as dark as coffee, but with a light of laughter flashing like sun on water.

The memory of being in his arms had haunted her summer, and she'd avoided him entirely. He'd come to the farm, but each time she'd told Issy to say she was out. Glimpsing him across the floor filled with swirling square dancers at the Grange a month ago, she'd melted into the groups of onlookers. When he'd come purposefully toward her at the feed store, she followed the clerk to the back to examine a plow blade she didn't want and couldn't afford.

One evening she and Issy had gone with Lucy and Gerald to a Chautauqua lecture, only to learn that the Egyptology expert had canceled, and Devin was the substitute speaker. His explanation of the Rural Electrification Act was both helpful and witty. Forced to stare at him while he spoke, Bridey heard little of it. She was still hurt that his actions had lied.

Gerald, gray eyes distressed, had told her about Devin. "Just after he took office last year, I met him," he said that evening. "And he's a good man, responsible. We're lucky he moved here. But people in town say he has a wife in Denver. They don't live together, but married he is."

Bridey was aware of an irrational rage against fate. Devin had awakened something she'd never allowed herself to feel before. More, he'd demanded a response. Then she'd learned he had no right to make any demands.

The two came within speaking distance, the powerful man in the tan suit and the slender woman in beige.

Bridey thought of the kiss they'd shared, and now that he was here, it seemed moments ago. She knew suddenly that she didn't want to talk to him. As Devin approached her, she nodded, but didn't slow her pace.

"Bridey," came the low, amused voice that had echoed in her head since early summer. "If you want me to follow you down the street in order to talk to you, I'll do it."

She paused, feeling the color rise in her cheeks. "There's no reason to do that," she said coolly, not looking at him. "We have nothing to talk about."

"That's where you're wrong." His weight caused the wooden walk to tremble as he came toward her. He stopped in front of her, but Bridey stubbornly kept her eyes trained on the shiny black buttons of his vest. His silence forced her head up.

Under the frowning slashes of his brows his eyes met hers measuringly. "We have to get some things straight."

"That's ironic, coming from you."

"Maybe." A quiet insistence was in his voice. "But I have to be sure you understand."

"I understand perfectly," she countered. "You kissed me. And I kissed you back. The fact that you're married was pointed out to me later. That's the end of the story."

She started by him, but he caught hold of her arm. "No, Bridey, it's not. What I've been trying to do ever since that day is explain. It's important to me."

Bridey could hear the appeal underlying the controlled words. She hesitated. In a town this size, she knew they'd be bound to meet occasionally. If he felt it necessary to make an apology, perhaps it'd make future meetings more comfortable. "All right, let's talk."

He nodded, his hand slipping down her arm to cup her elbow as he helped her into the car.

The Chevy roared up the hill separating Louisville from the Boulder Valley. Before Bridey's blind gaze, pastureland singed with the heat of late summer spread on either side of them. Straight ahead the red slabs of the Flatirons pressed against the foothills overlooking Boulder, as if to keep the mountainsides from falling onto the town below.

Devin parked beside the Baseline Reservoir. Looking straight ahead, one large hand tight on the steering wheel, he said nothing for a moment. Bridey wished he'd make the polite gesture that he seemed to feel was necessary and get it over with. She was already regretting having agreed to this. In the line of his jaw, in the force of his shoulders, was a primal energy at odds with civilizing tie and shirt. He seemed to draw her toward him, and the effort to resist that was far more difficult then she could have imagined. To distance herself she wanted to move closer to the door, but she was sure he'd interpret that movement correctly. So she sat perfectly still. The collar of her suit scratched her neck and a trickle of sweat slid between her breasts.

When he turned toward her, Bridey instinctively edged away. "Don't," he said quietly. "If you think that what I did was just about a guy getting his hands on a beautiful woman, you're wrong. I've been thinking how to say this all summer." He paused, but only for a second, and then went on firmly, "You're mine, I'm yours. According to the rules I didn't have any right then and I don't now. But I'm staking a claim."

Bridey's breath was taken away. Instead of the meaningless apology she'd expected, she heard genuine conviction. She simply stared at him.

He took off his hat, spun it into the backseat, and wiped his brow with the back of his hand. "I talked to my wife—again—about giving me a divorce. She won't because she wants to keep what she calls her 'social standing.' The lawyer says if she won't consent, the court won't grant the decree."

For the first time he looked down, the lines around his mouth etched deeper. "It'd be bad enough with me being divorced. Still, the people here would come around when we got married. But if we were together without the legal papers, most of them would pass you right by on the sidewalk without so much as a nod. You know that. We're both settled in Louisville, but even in a bigger place, folks still think there are some rules you just don't break."

He faced her. There was determination in the dark depths of his eyes. "None of that matters to me. Bridey, you're all I want."

In that moment Bridey could see that what he offered was what she really wanted. Her heart's desire was this kind of love that crossed all boundaries. Despite the risks she could not deny her need.

She shifted in the seat, and he put out his hand abruptly as if he thought she intended to leave and he was going to hold her until he had his answer. But she was only turning toward him. Her gaze was direct. There was a quiver at the edge of her mouth, yet her voice was steady as she replied, "My father was a gambling man. He bought our ranch with the proceeds from poker. And he gave me some really good advice about what I should do when I wanted something." *Take it and pay the price.* Her lips curved into a smile as she remembered Berkeley's words. Bridey knew the man beside her was worth whatever she would have to pay.

Before he could respond, her fingers touched his sleeve. "You're right. *We* make the rules." She paused, knowing what she risked. "I have only one rule. If the day comes that you want something more, you'll tell me."

"Does that apply to you too?" His face was solemn.

"Yes." She knew what she wanted. To be in his arms.

He reached for her. "But you have to say it face to face," he insisted. "That way I can argue you out of it."

He was holding her so tightly that she felt his next words rather than heard them. "Bridey, the day will never come when I want something more than you. Never."

CHAPTER 5

The next morning Bridey woke to joy. The early breeze, fresh from the cool mountains, lifted the dotted Swiss curtains of her bedroom window, and she leaned out as if to a new world. Even the magpies' coarse calls from tree to tree sounded sweeter. Thinking of Devin, she began to plan all they would do together. As she hurried into a work shirt and denims to start the chores, her head was full of how different things would be.

But before anything could change, everything changed.

During the last few days Isobel had seemed to feel the late summer heat intensely, complaining of headaches. Still, she'd gone on with her canning, piling the kitchen table with heaps of bright green snap beans.

When Bridey and Lucy came in to lunch, the Mason jars were bubbling in hot water on the stove, but Issy had slumped forward onto the table, her hands still full of the viney ends of the beans. Bridey helped her to bed and Lucy put in a frantic call to the doctor.

Issy's temperature spiked to one hundred four and cold compresses couldn't lower it. She was delirious by the time Doc Ramsay arrived.

He moved quickly around the bed, rapidly assessing her condition.

"Swollen glands under the jaw," he muttered, his deft fingers moving carefully over her neck. He viewed her throat with a small flashlight. "Red, swollen." He glanced at Lucy and Bridey and jerked his chin toward the door.

Out in the hall he was blunt. "It's diphtheria. The membrane is already forming in her throat. I've given her the antitoxin but, well, she's not a young woman."

Over the next few days Issy struggled against the disease with characteristic grit, but she was failing. Her already thin frame had been pared to the slightness of bird's bones. She wandered in and out of consciousness.

Sleeplessness left dark smudges under Bridey's eyes, worry had drawn lines on her forehead, and the corners of her mouth were tensed. As she carried a glass of ice upstairs to Issy, each riser seemed to her a step toward inescapable pain. *What will I do without her?* she repeated dully to herself. She could see Issy mending clothes, needle flashing like a small rapier wielded against unraveling; her worn fingers culling cucumbers that would evolve into pickles; Issy nurturing canna lilies in a weedy field.

She slipped around the bed to the chair beneath her sketch of Bridey's Mountain. Issy had always said she liked to see it first thing in the morning because it brought back all their happy days. As the slow minutes passed, Bridey watched the nearly imperceptible rise and fall of the frail chest. How large a part, she thought with the clarity of fatigue, this small woman had played in her life.

Bridey's eyes felt weighted. If Isobel died, she reflected, sleepiness protecting her from the pain of the idea, her last link with the past would be gone. She wanted to reach out and hold her physically in place.

"Bridey." The sound was whisper soft. "Bridey, lass."

Bridey jerked awake and bent forward over the bed. She tried to smile as she held out a sliver of ice. "Take this. You must be thirsty."

Isobel obediently opened her mouth, and her throat quivered with the effort of swallowing even the trace of liquid. Her eyes were cloudy, but they were fixed on Bridey's face. "I've been thinking about Devin Lowell. You shouldna' mind my bit of advice. Like my own bairn you've always been, so . . ." She gasped for breath, her nostrils fluttering.

"Issy, I know. And you know how much I love you." Bridey's own throat hurt, salt tears choking her. Her hand slid across the muslin sheet to clasp Issy's thin fingers.

Issy's eyes glowed bright for an instant. "Aye. Weel, he's a good man. I was just saying that to your mother, and Morna—" This time she stopped herself. "Nae. I couldna' been speakin' to her, could I?" She made an effort to smile at the idea, but her glance searched the room as if she were not so sure she hadn't been.

"Now, Bridey." Her voice was thin as a thread. "You belong with Devin Lowell. Don't be worrying." Her lids drooped. Shallow breaths skimmed in and out, yet her chest was nearly still under the light sheet.

"Issy?" Bridey bent toward her, her hand tightening its hold.

"I'm just . . . resting." Isobel's eyes opened, their blue-green color crystal clear. "You mind what I said." A listening intentness had come into her face. Her features sharpened and she cocked her head, as if hearing something far away. Then she murmured, "I'll be right there. . . . Tell Mr. Berkeley I'll be making scones for tea."

A long breath eased from her, and then she lay still.

The silence in the room was profound, as if time itself had been suspended.

"Issy?" Bridey's ears roared and her fingers clutched the still hand. "Issy!"

She slid from the chair to kneel beside the bed, trembling at the force of her grief. Her eyes burned for the release of tears. She tried to cry, but no tears came.

The moment was split by the sound of footsteps on the stairs. They were firm, determined, intruding into the guarded atmosphere of the sickroom.

Devin paused in the doorway, his hand tight around the brass knob. Bridey's golden-brown eyes were empty, her face as pale as sand. He moved swiftly toward her.

At the heat in Devin's hand on her arm Bridey pulled back. She felt an instant of resentment. He was too large, too alive for the moment, his health and energy sharp reminders of living. The loss of Issy's unwavering support was too fresh. Then he lifted her to her feet, and his hard, safe arms enclosed her, pressing her to the shelter of his body.

"I'm sorry, love," Devin said simply. He held her close, then cupped her chin, intent on her face. His brows drew together over eyes dark with worry. "I couldn't stay when I brought the quarantine signs. Doc Ramsay had me hunting down all the people Issy might have been in contact with." He rested his chin on the top of her head in a rush of tenderness that threatened to destroy what little composure she had.

"Bridey?" Lucy's voice floated up the stairs, and Bridey lifted her head. *Lucy doesn't know,* she thought. Issy had slipped away before saying good-bye to her and Gerald. "I've got to tell her," she whispered painfully.

Devin nodded. "I'll help you." The words were simple, but in them was the weight of commitment.

The presence of Devin Lowell at Bridey's side at the funeral of Isobel Ewen caused raised eyebrows. Murmurs rippled through the small congregation paying their last respects at the Louisville Cemetery.

". . . name of the Father, the Son, and the Holy Ghost. Amen." The minister nodded at the family mourners.

Lucy groped for the comfort of Gerald's hand, and his fingers closed around hers. He steadied her as she bent to pick up a handful of earth, then helped her toward the open grave. The clods of dirt thudded against the wooden coffin. "Rest in peace, Aunt Issy."

Bridey, Devin at her side, was next to perform the ritual. She moved stiffly, unaware of the expressions on the faces behind them. Her eyelids scraped across dry eyes.

As she scattered the dirt over Isobel's coffin, Bridey heard the lighthearted trill of a redwing blackbird, one of Issy's favorites. "Keep the scones hot for me, Issy," she whispered huskily.

The house was quiet following the wake; Gerald and Lucy had gone upstairs to rest. Bridey walked through the kitchen. Outside was a different world, one untouched by death. The garden, past the barrier of the screen door, was burgeoning. With each step Bridey took, she imagined Issy, a basket on her arm, become a part of the place she'd loved.

Devin was waiting for her by the lilac bush. As his arms closed around her, the barren grip of grief released its hold.

The sound of the Chevrolet's door closing broke the September afternoon silence. A crow, shiny as a top hat, flapped his way over the two-story stone house perched on the rise extending north from Louisville.

Devin's gaze lingered with satisfaction on one portion of roof that poked like a witch's hat over the back corner of the house. The architectural whimsy had resulted from Bridey's teasing remark when she'd first seen the house. "It looks like a little castle. But where's the turret?"

Elated at the laughter in her eyes, he promised, "I'll build one."

He realized how still the place was. "Bridey." His deep voice echoed off the house wall. "Bridey!"

". . . out here." Her voice drifted from the weather-beaten structure they'd grandly dubbed the stable. Morning glories covered the faded wood, their tendrils clinging to uneven surfaces. Bridey knelt in the fresh straw of one stall. She smiled at him over her shoulder. "You're early."

Devin felt his mouth go dry. Sometimes he couldn't believe his good fortune. The willowy lines of her body were concealed by the tailored tweed of her slacks, and the yellow of her long-sleeved cotton shirt added a burnish to her chestnut hair. She'd braided it, but wild little wisps curled with abandon about her glowing face.

She was feeding a colt. He sucked the bottle's rubber nipple, sugar-laced milk moving down his throat. "Hey, little one, take it slow and easy."

"He's a greedy beggar," Devin said. At Bridey's speaking glance he added, "Don't tell me, he's your favorite."

"Of course. The ones that give the most trouble are always my favorites." She savored his fuzzy coat. "What are you doing coming home now?"

"I felt like it." Devin was aware of a tightening in his body at the sensual satisfaction on her face.

"Oh," she teased. "A command decision, eh?"

He raised a brow, slowly pulling one end of his tie. "He's done with the milk," he pointed out silkily.

Bridey patted the gawky colt's rump as it moved, wobbly legged, out of the stall. She reached up and caught hold of the loose ends of Devin's tie, her eyes shimmering with mischief. "Since you're here, let me see if I can think of something for you to do."

"Man's work is never done." His smile widened.

She pulled him down to her. "Workers of the world, unite."

His long fingers deftly opened the small buttons of her shirt. The gap between the edges of the shirt revealed her lacy camisole. Her breasts were smooth and creamy above the delicate filigree.

One by one she undid the buttons of his tattersall vest. "Let's get you undressed for manual labor." Soon his bare skin pressed against hers.

The single-mindedness of desire thickening his voice, he muttered, "Reporting for duty, ma'am." His strong hands clutched at her hips.

"Devin."

Her trembling breathlessness weakened his control. Then power surged through him. Always he was consumed in the fire. It meant losing his control, losing himself, finding the source of the sun.

Bridey jerked his mouth to hers and, burning, went with him.

"You're awfully quiet." His voice rumbled under her ear.

"Hmm." She pressed closer to his side, nestling down in the fragrant straw. Devin's arms tightened around her and he watched the dust motes float lazily in the air.

For the last year they'd been wrapped in sunlit happiness. Bridey still worked with Gerald and Lucy, even as she'd started her own herd of horses, and he'd continued at the power plant. Lillian Lowell had again refused to consent to a divorce. She'd threatened to countersue Devin for adultery if he charged her with desertion. No divorce would be granted. That meant, as Devin had feared, the small community in which they lived firmly excluded Bridey. Still, basking in the joy of being together, the two of them had ignored such shadows.

But the ominous rumble of approaching war across the Atlantic could not be shut out. Like most Americans, Devin and Bridey heard the news with growing anxiety as Hitler's troops stormed across one European border after another. The radio and the newsreels carried the whine of diving planes, the thunder of tanks. The papers were filled with grainy black-and-white photos of bristling battleships and shark-shaped submarines.

Now Devin stirred, breaking their moment of peace. As he sat up, Bridey saw something in his face. "What's wrong?"

"I got a phone call today from an old friend," he said. "Thomas Alexander is laying the groundwork for a seat in the House of Representatives. He's exactly the man we need in Washington at the moment. And he says he needs me. He's asked me to manage his campaign."

Bridey's throat tightened. Devin had always been active in local politics, and the knowledge of their relationship had not affected that. But this new position would thrust him into a larger arena. She sat up and pulled on her camisole, avoiding his eyes. "Do you want to do that?"

Devin had slipped into his pants and was buttoning his shirt. He stopped, leaned over, and gently picked the straw from her hair. "First thing, I told him about us, and said that if he invited me, he invited you."

She didn't reply for a moment and made a slow business of standing up and putting on her own clothes. In Bridey's view it was not just Thomas Alexander who needed a man like Devin, but a nation that soon might be involved in a war. She could only think what a hindrance she would be to him. At last, she looked up. "What did he say?"

Devin tucked in his shirt and grinned. "He said he'd be pleased— he could speechify at you and get your vote. I want to help him. Thomas thinks as we do, that we can't let the Nazis overrun Europe, that we'd just be next." He caught her hand in his. "What I told

Thomas, I meant. I want you to come with me to the fund-raiser this weekend."

Bridey shook her head. "You have so much to offer, but unless you keep me in the background, you won't get the chance."

"Listen to me." Devin cupped her cheek. "I'm proud of you and me. I won't let what we have be threatened. You have to come."

She searched his face. Like her, Devin wanted to set the terms. She knew there'd be no use in arguing with him—he'd clearly made up his mind on this point. Whatever happened, they'd face it together. "Of course I will," she replied, then added, "But you may want to rethink this. I haven't a thing to wear. I'll need a whole new outfit, and unless I sell this yearling, I can't afford it."

Devin smiled broadly. "Sky's the limit. And"—he began patting his pockets—"I brought you a present, something I think you'll like." The package was small in his hand.

Bridey took it, her fingers tearing away the brown paper, revealing a small velvet box. "What have you done?" she began in mock disapproval, but her voice died as she pulled open the spring top.

The stable swirled around her as she stared down at the ring. The diffused light was captured in the diamond encircled by rubies. Dancing fires of white and red shattered into mist as her eyes filled.

Early on, Bridey had told him about her mountain, Morna's disappearance, her ivory dress, and the rose ring she had left behind. She'd described the Double B–G auction, how she'd sold the ring to save her beloved Anna. Devin had seen the pain in her eyes, kissing her till the memories lost their sting.

Now delighted tears spilled on her cheeks. "You—oh, Devin, you . . ." She bent her head, striving for control. It was as if part of her mother had been returned to her.

"Walt Merrick sends his love," Devin murmured. He took the ring from the box and reached for her hand. When she looked at him, he began, "With this ring I thee wed."

Bridey focused on the love in his eyes as he continued, the words laden with feeling, "To have and to hold from this day forth, till death us do part."

Slipping the ring on her finger, he dipped his head to take her lips, tasting the salt of her tears. Lifting his mouth from hers, he looked into her eyes, into her soul. "My Bridey," he whispered. "My wife."

CHAPTER 6

Enos Murdoch polished his pince-nez before resettling it precisely on the narrow bridge of his nose. Even with the help of his glasses, only those faces nearest him in the crowded drawing room of the Alexander mansion were distinct. But he was not here to socialize. He was here to sabotage the candidacy of Thomas Alexander, whom this reception was honoring.

Enos was a very rich man. The Depression that had ruined so many had increased the power of the Murdoch banking empire. His foreclosures on the western-slope ranches alone had made him many times a millionaire in the ten years since the 1929 stock market crash.

To him public servants were just that. He intended to fire Alexander. *His* policies, in Enos's outraged view, were too close to those of that absolute scoundrel, the Democratic President Franklin Delano Roosevelt.

However, Alexander was the rising Republican star and ousting him would take some maneuvering. He was well liked. It wouldn't do to alert the man until Enos's own plans were set.

The problem had been choosing Alexander's replacement. What

was needed was a businessman, one who would clearly see the danger to profits posed by Roosevelt's programs. There was someone coming today who had the right qualifications. He was the head of a company, which meant he was ambitious. And the banker couldn't imagine any right-thinking man turning down the chance at a national office, even if it meant making a few changes in his personal life.

The man Enos had in mind was Devin Lowell.

That Lowell and Alexander were friends didn't affect Murdoch's strategy. To him, such things as love or loyalty were beside the point. He remembered Lowell, whom he had met on social occasions a few years ago, as quite tall, with a commanding presence. Enos was himself slight, and his extreme short-sightedness caused him to stretch his neck forward, giving him the air of a bespectacled turtle. It gave him pleasure to have powerful men under his control.

Of course, to bring it about, Lowell's estrangement from his wife would have to be ended. But when Lillian Lowell suggested Devin's name, she'd eagerly promised Enos that their marital conflict could be resolved. Enos intended to speak to Lowell on the question today. Arrangements for his move back with his wife should be made this week. While Murdoch didn't think women had any place in politics, the Wyndham sugar-beet fortune could finance the campaign. That way Enos himself would not have to donate too much.

As he stood alone, contemplating this tidy wrap-up of the problem, conversation hummed around him. It was muted, with a somber tone unusual for a political rally. No fanfare, no laughter. The reporters around the drinks table smoked constantly as they quietly exchanged the latest news from troubled Europe. Everyone feared that France would be the next to fall before the German juggernaut. Everyone knew that England alone could not withstand it.

Enos was uninterested, having made up his mind on that question. It was a foreign war, definitely not America's concern. Besides, he knew the outcome was a foregone conclusion. Germany would win. He'd acted on that belief by filling safe deposit boxes with German bonds. America's business was business. Hitler was an entire ocean away.

Yet Thomas Alexander insisted that the United States must aid England. He even agreed with the President's plan to send them a convoy of destroyers! To calm himself Enos circled the large bay-windowed room, peering up at the portraits, noting that several of the antique frames were quite expensive. Although the room was beautifully proportioned and filled with well-polished Victorian furniture, his eye had been caught by the fading green silk wallpaper and the worn areas of the Oriental carpet.

Enos shook his head. He should have known that backing an Alexander would be a risky investment. The family was old Denver, but there was that unpredictable strain. Above the fireplace was a picture of Patrick Alexander, looking down at the gathering with his amused smile. Enos twisted his own thin lips. Had Patrick been serious, he could have made a fortune. Not only had he failed to do that, he'd fathered three sons out of wedlock, only legitimizing the relationship on his first wife's death.

Here was Thomas, the younger son, who had every chance to feather his own nest *and* do well in Washington. Instead he sounded like Roosevelt—that class traitor—a rich man who spouted nonsense about the need to take care of the poor. When Enos had made an acid comment to that effect at a recent dinner, Ceci Caley had looked at him with that French cat's smile of hers and said, "Ah, but one understands." Her tone was cynical, but indulgent. "Thomas wishes to . . . improve the world. So different from the *très charmant* Patrick, who cared only for pleasure. But he is handsome like his father, *non? Les femmes*—they will vote for him."

Enos had had difficulty swallowing the bilious retort that almost escaped him. That dreadful woman now had the notion she was a political expert. He disapproved of everything about her, including that cloying perfume. Yet she had ruled Denver society for the last twenty-five years. Sourly, he eyed her elegant, petite figure standing regally before the fireplace, as if she were waiting for Thomas Alexander to finish with the crowd that surrounded him and come to consult her.

Ceci Caley caught Enos's testy glance, but ignored it. She turned to use the glass of the picture above her to adjust the tiny veil on her hat's shirred brim. She didn't look her sixty-five years, and although she imagined herself as a perennial forty-five, no one would have guessed she was a day over sixty. Her silvery hair was sleekly styled. The black Chanel suit emphasized her youthful shape, her trim legs were set off by silk hose and fashionable platform shoes. During her years at Miss Freda's everyone had admired Colette's chic. Now all Denver did.

She was thinking that Enos Murdoch dressed like one of the clerks in his own bank. To continue wearing the stiff collar, so long out of style! And it drew attention to a neck as wrinkled as that of the *tortue*. Not only that, he parted his hair in the exact middle. The man was *maladroit* in every way. The humor was that he regarded himself as knowledgeable in politics, a field that above all required finesse. Ceci smiled inwardly, knowing how much he disliked her.

Luckily, she had not needed Enos's good opinion thirty years ago when she and Stanton had returned from Europe, well and truly married. She had recognized immediately that it was Murdoch's aunt, that formidable spinster, whom she would have to court to establish herself. It had taken discipline. Eloise Murdoch was engrossed by health remedies and, as she grew older, became unnervingly forthright in her questions regarding bodily functions. Ceci had endeared herself by consulting Eloise daily during her pregnancy.

The time of her arrival had also worked in her favor, Ceci realized. There was a vacancy at the top of the social order once known as the Sacred Thirty-six. Amelia Powell had met an Italian prince in New York and eloped with him. The fact that the man had proved not to be a prince in any sense of the word was Amelia's misfortune. But this humiliation meant she would never return. And Eloise was quite elderly. It was a perfect opportunity for a coup d'état.

Dazzled by Ceci's continental airs and graces, and the rumor (which quickly became fact) that she was a member of European aristocracy, Denver's elite attended her. To entertain them she spent a good piece of the Caley meat-packing fortune. Eventually it paid off in information gleaned from the city's magnates. Issuing orders under her husband's name, Ceci shrewdly handled the family's investments. Stanton himself had just sat with port-glazed eyes at their lavish affairs, occasionally running his hand over his bald head as if to smooth the vanished hair. After he'd handed around the cigars and drifted off to bed, no one missed him.

Satisfied now by the sight of her hat in the portrait's glass, Ceci noticed the subject was Patrick Alexander. *Un vrai gentleman,* she thought. He could easily have told the world where he'd first met a certain young Frenchwoman. But he'd treated her with exquisite courtesy and never so much as let an eyelid droop in her direction. Occasionally, when she was present, he would recount news of his friend Berkeley Glendower. So she'd learned of Morna's departure. But Ceci had known the moment she came to Colorado that her own letter to Morna must have been destroyed. Otherwise Berkeley would have shown up on their doorstep the next day with ice in his eyes. As it was, neither she nor Stanton had seen him after their return to Denver.

At first Ceci hardly dared to breathe when the town of Telluride was mentioned. But the years passed without even a whisper going around. By this time she'd told the story of her privileged childhood in a French château so often that she herself could see the pony on which she'd galloped through the manicured grounds of the surrounding *parc.*

Her pressing concern now was that she might lose her social leadership in another way. There was always a younger woman ready to take over. Across the room she saw the showy feather in Lillian Lowell's turban. It reminded Ceci of the plume in the helmets of European generals. In the past she would have organized fêtes and elaborate galas to which she'd invite old friends and new allies. But with the Depression and the European war looming, entertaining had been scaled down. A few people even said such diversions were altogether inappropriate.

It occurred to Ceci that there were other ways of exerting power. Politics, for one. Unfortunately, the same idea must have struck Lillian Wyndham Lowell, or why would she have come today? Never in the past had she shown the slightest interest in such affairs. She was now attentively bending her head down to hear Enos Murdoch's words with a charmed smile on her bright lipsticked mouth.

Ceci considered her rival objectively and didn't at all like what she saw. Lillian's silky fair hair curved under in a pageboy beneath the turban that exactly matched a blue suit direct from the Paris spring collections. Not only did she have that cool blond beauty, she was rich in her own right from inherited money. Her background was all that it should be. Ceci had found on her arrival that all the people who made up Denver society had known one another from childhood. They'd attended the same schools, belonged to the same country club. Lillian was one of them. While they didn't particularly trust or necessarily like each other, they closed ranks against outsiders.

All Lillian lacked was a husband on the scene. Ceci knew that was a real disadvantage. One needed a host and an escort. And while so far there'd been no breath of scandal, other women nervously eyed their husbands when they talked to Lillian. Divorce for her wasn't an option. She'd be invited nowhere and she'd even lose her membership in the country club.

Smiling openly for the first time, Ceci recalled Devin Lowell. He was unlikely to return to his wife. A large man, handsome in the rugged western fashion, she'd noticed in the beginning that he was bored with society's games of ins and outs. And Lillian had the cold Nordic temperament to match her hair. The latest gossip was that he had a very pretty *petite amie* with whom he lived in Louisville.

Thomas Alexander had told Ceci that he'd asked Devin Lowell to be his campaign manager. So he would be coming today. What a pity, she thought as she pulled a man's large gold pocket watch from her small purse, that he could not bring the lady with him. It would be *très amusant* to see Lillian's face. But that was never done. She checked the time, running a finger over the incised *S* and *C* on the watch's case. It'd been Stanton's, and it pleased her to use it, since it was a reminder that it was she who had triumphed in the end. He had still been relatively young when he'd died of a stroke.

Of course he never would have married her if he hadn't believed in the pregnancy. Eventually she had become with child, and Ceci could never see why he'd taken so against her because of that little deception in beginning. Their daughter, Jacqueline, had been a disappointment because she was not a son. Ceci's brow creased, thinking that Jacqueline was still a disappointment. She spent her afternoons at bridge and her evenings soaked in gin. And this Sutherland she'd married had nothing to recommend him except his thick hair and blue eyes.

She frowned at the watch. Surely Devin Lowell should be here by now. Thomas would be waiting for him before he began speaking to the reporters. She moved nearer the door, glancing through the bay windows, but saw only a spring breeze whipping last year's leaves across the empty sidewalks. Around her the news of the movements of Nazi troops swirled like a baleful wind. But Ceci was far more concerned with her own private war with Lillian Lowell.

She could not imagine why she and Enos Murdoch still had their heads so closely together. Lillian had spoken to no one else since her arrival, not even Thomas Alexander. Ceci considered that he would be surprised indeed when he noticed Lillian's presence. No doubt so would her husband.

That Lillian should be having an *affaire* with Enos was out of the question, though it was known how much the straitlaced little banker enjoyed the company of pretty women. Ceci suspected the lust was all in his heart. It would pain him too deeply to pay to keep a mistress. Still, thinking of his wife, Alicia Farnsworth Murdoch, she considered that Enos would be sensible to do just that. Alicia never left the gloomy pile of a mansion that had belonged to William Murdoch. On the rare occasions when she had a small reception, she would sit quietly with brooding eyes. Stanton had said the Farnsworth women were all intellectual, but Ceci was sure that the abstracted gaze came from innumerable small glasses of sherry rather than deep thought.

In any case, Lillian had no need to be *that* nice to Enos. It was true that without a husband beside her, she was forced to be gracious to people she would not otherwise have wasted a smile on. One could not so treat a Murdoch, but a woman of Lillian's standing could get by with an insincere stretch of the lips. Ceci knew the exact degree of warmth required for any given member of society. What, she wondered, could those two be plotting in the corner of the room? And where was Devin Lowell?

The front door almost blew open with the force of the breeze behind it, and Devin and Bridey stopped just inside, laughingly trying to arrange their windblown hair. He was clutching his fedora in his hands, obviously having given up the effort to keep it on. She was hatless, the smooth roll of her hair now in tendrils that wisped onto the shoulders of her ivory silk shantung suit. Thomas Alexander hurried over to them.

His wide grin softened his lean, even features. "Well, Devin," he asked with mock seriousness, "is this the kind of support I can expect from you?"

"We're so sorry," Bridey said quickly. "We had a flat tire and then when I got out, my hat blew off right down the road. We chased it, but it landed in a ditch full of water." Her rueful grimace lit her hazel eyes as she looked apologetically at Thomas.

Devin put his hand on her arm, smiling. "He won't believe us, Bridey. He'll just think we had better things to do than huddle with reporters in a smoke-filled room. Even on behalf of a real statesman. Which Thomas is." He shook his friend's hand warmly and introduced Bridey.

Alexander took her arm, saying, "Statesmen are *dead* politicians, Devin. Let me get you a drink, Bridey, and then I'll have to take him off and throw him to the wolfish press."

"No. Please." She gently disengaged her arm from Thomas's and said, "They've already had time to sharpen their teeth. Don't keep them waiting any longer."

As the two men walked forward, a crowd quickly formed around them. Bridey stood on the edges, observing. Both Thomas and Devin were tall, both wearing dark blue suits. It was immediately obvious that they shared political views. Even their differences complemented each other. Thomas's answers to the journalists' questions were thoughtful and carefully phrased; Devin's were direct and quotable. Thomas's quiet, level voice commanded attention, Devin's deeper, rougher one reached out to demand it. She watched Devin with pride and with pain, thinking how effective he was, how much he was needed. The idea that she would be a burden to him was a dull weight on her heart. For the first time Bridey sensed that the cost of loving Devin might demand her leaving him.

Although she was not aware of it, three people in the room were attending only to Bridey, ignoring the press conference altogether.

Lillian Lowell had just moved away from Enos toward the drinks table when the front door opened. She continued steadily walking to the bar, but the brief glimpse of her husband and his companion had caused her face to turn blank white, her pallor heightening the slash of rouge across her cheekbones. Even her fingertips were numb with the coldness of her anger. Over and over she repeated inwardly, *How dare he bring that tramp here? How dare he?* That Devin could never have imagined Lillian would come did not affect her thinking. Self-absorbed, she lived in a palace of mirrors, and she was indifferent to the world behind that reflecting glass.

She had, however, considered during the last few weeks how to tempt Devin to return. Without him she was in a societal limbo. Ceci Caley ruled Denver society, but then, the widow of a prominent man was respected. Lillian remembered that her godmother, Amelia Powell, had once complained that Denver's society was very *small*. Let Ceci have it, Lillian declared to herself, oblivious to the whiff of sour grapes. In thinking about larger cities where she could become established, she recalled that Devin had always shown an interest in politics. Instantly she saw herself as an influential Washington hostess. She began planning her new wardrobe. Visions of ballgowns danced in her head. It would mean that she'd have to generously finance her husband's campaign for some office or other, but it would be worth it. Murdoch had been surprisingly easy to enlist in this cause. He could approach Devin and smooth the way. Lillian had no idea why Enos had agreed and didn't care. Nor did she bother to wonder what Devin might want.

When Lillian saw Bridey's magnificent ring, she froze for an instant. But she reminded herself that the woman would have to be bought off with expensive gifts, since Devin could not offer her legitimacy. Surely, when he saw what was at stake for him, Devin would resume the marriage. Lillian swallowed her rage, convinced that she would succeed in the end.

Ceci Caley at first had been wholly delighted that Bridey had attended. She'd not been near enough to the door to hear the woman's name, but she'd taken careful note of her appearance, intending to make an exquisite story to delight her—and Lillian's—circle at the earliest opportunity. She'd gathered from gestures that the woman's hat had blown off. Under such a circumstance Ceci herself would not have come into the house at all, but it made the story she would tell more *piquante*. She so hoped Lillian would behave badly. It would add such spice to her account.

In spreading this delicious gossip she need not even exaggerate the attractiveness of Devin's paramour. Ceci approved of the shantung suit and had to admit that the windblown look added to the freshness of the complexion and enhanced the sparkle of gold-tinged eyes.

But then she noticed the ring. The color drained from Ceci's face as well. The past rushed back on wings of fear. Those rubies and the diamond at the heart. It was surely the ring that Berkeley had given Morna. Did its wearer know who Ceci Caley had been?

As she sidled closer to look at it, she tried telling herself that the original craftsman might have made more than one, or that it could have been bought at an estate sale. But a cold inner voice reminded her that Patrick Alexander had mentioned Berkeley's daughter, that she would be this age, that those eyes were very reminiscent of Glendower's. She'd never heard what happened to the girl.

Ceci vividly remembered the day she'd learned of Berkeley's death in the Telluride flood. Stanton had had the story from Patrick and when he told her, he repeated Patrick's last words about his friend: "Alive, he was the luckiest man." Stanton's tone made it plain he shared that view. Until then, Ceci had never realized how much she hated her husband.

Bridey reached up in an abstracted effort to tuck her hair into place. Standing behind her, Ceci was sure it was the same ring. Her first thought was to leave so that her name would not come up in conversation. Then there would be no reason for this woman to dredge from her memory any story she might have heard from Berkeley about a woman who'd been a friend of Morna's and married a man named Caley. After all, she would have been a young girl when her father died and wouldn't be likely to remember such details.

But this attempt to reassure herself could not calm Ceci's fear. She'd have to relive those terrible years when she'd worried continually about her past being discovered. If it were revealed now—despite how far she'd come—no one who mattered would speak to her again. She had to know. She would have to introduce herself and watch carefully to see if her name brought a flicker to the woman's eyes. Then a quick defensive attack might be made.

Enos Murdoch was quite close to the door when Devin and Bridey arrived. His nerves quivered with moral outrage. This woman was mingling with respectable people and it was an affront to decency. That Lowell would countenance her doing so shook Enos. Could he support him as a candidate? Had his assumptions regarding Devin Lowell's pragmatic approach been wrong?

But then Murdoch began to reconsider. Lowell was definitely the best choice and perhaps the only one at this point who could rid him of Thomas Alexander. No doubt it was *she* who had insisted on coming. Although Enos could not see Bridey very clearly, he noted that she was very shapely. Men would do amazing things for an attractive woman.

With *her* background Enos was convinced she would have no understanding of finer feelings. For Murdoch knew who Bridey Gregory was. She was the illegitimate daughter of a woman from a brothel. When he decided on Lowell as a candidate, he'd made it his business to check on her as well. Information was valuable. His mind was filled with safe deposit boxes containing other people's secrets.

Her father, despite his talents, had made a foolish mistake. Berkeley Glendower could have married Amelia Powell and her money. Her capital would then have remained in Colorado. In the Murdoch bank. When Amelia left, his aunt Eloise had bought the entire estate cheaply, but that hardly made up for the bank's loss of control of the Powell fortune. Now that Enos thought of it, he had Amelia's portrait of Glendower stored away somewhere. The frame was genuine gold leaf. Eloise was always maundering about how obsessed her dear friend Amelia was with Glendower and declared the Italian prince she'd married bore a passing resemblance to him.

Murdoch glared at Bridey's back. With her here it was impossible to speak to Lowell about returning to Lillian. He noticed that Ceci Caley was standing quite near the Gregory woman and thought acidly how appropriate that was, since to him they were two of a kind.

For Enos was the only person in Denver who knew Ceci's true history.

One night long ago Stanton, while pouring his fourth glass of port with a trembling hand, had bemoaned his ruined life. William Murdoch had sipped his soda water and listened. Although he didn't catch the entire story, he learned exactly where Stanton had met Madame Caley. But William and his son were aware that this information would have to remain guarded in the Murdoch mental vaults. If Ceci were exposed, she would leave Denver, taking the Caley fortune from the bank. When she spoke of her *chère maman, la comtesse,* Enos ground his teeth but sealed his lips.

Then Enos realized that in this case, he could deal directly and firmly with Bridey Gregory. While Lowell would undoubtedly be subjected to her tearful fits when he told her the facts of his new political life, Enos would not have to put up with any such nonsense. He made his way purposefully through the crowd and grasped Bridey's arm.

Startled, she turned. The sight of that precisely parted hair and the chilly eyes behind a glittering pince-nez instantly brought back to Bridey the painful day she'd lost the Double B–G. She quickly stepped aside, a flush rising to her cheeks, but Enos held her sleeve, saying in a grating whisper, "I wish to say something that will benefit Devin Lowell. We can talk in the library." He turned on his heel without waiting for her response.

Bridey hesitated, glancing at Devin, still surrounded by the press. She was sure that the banker must be a generous supporter of Thomas's campaign. Deciding that she would have to listen for Devin's sake, even try to be pleasant, she walked out of the crowded parlor into the small book-lined room adjoining it.

Without preamble Enos introduced himself, adding, "I know who you are, Miss Gregory. Let us not mince words. We have opposing interests, but you need not lose in this matter. I will see that you do not. To begin with, you must keep what we discuss in the strictest confidence. Thomas Alexander must not learn of this. You must cooperate fully."

He emphasized the last word, standing quite close to her, his small, cold eyes on a level with hers. He continued, "Devin Lowell has a most promising future. He should run against Alexander in the primary for the Washington seat."

Bridey stared at him, her flush deepening. "Mr. Murdoch, Devin is Thomas's friend, he has pledged his support—"

With a flick of his dry fingers Enos dismissed loyalty and friendship, interrupting her. "If Lowell were to seek office himself, you would stand in his way."

Bridey's furious rejoinder died unspoken. Those were the exact words that had been burning in her own mind as she watched Devin.

Enos pulled up short as an idea presented itself. This close to her, he could see that she was uncommonly attractive. The color in her cheeks brought flecks of light to her eyes. The ivory silk of her blouse clung enticingly over a full bosom. The notion grew in appeal. Enos had never kept a mistress, despite his occasional longings. But Miss Gregory was, as he phrased it to himself, in need of a position. She was really quite lovely, he decided. Beautiful, he'd have to say. If she was provided for, she'd cause no fuss, he was sure. It would be a satisfactory arrangement for all of them. Lowell needn't be told the details, and in any case he'd soon be in Washington.

One worry did crease his brow. When she realized how very much richer than Lowell he was, her requests for clothing and jewelry might increase accordingly. He'd heard of that sort of thing happening to other men in his circle.

Forgetting entirely that all these plans were confined to his own head, Enos said flatly, "We would have to set a sum in the beginning for your, um, services."

Bridey had no idea what he meant. Was he, she wondered, offering her a clerical post in the campaign so that others wouldn't question her presence? It was hard enough to speak to this man, remembering that he was the cause of her loss. That she or Devin would disguise their relationship bordered on the insulting. Still, trying to keep her voice steady, she asked, "What services?"

Enos was taken aback. Did one, in these arrangements, have to *specify*? Or did she want to know what days he would visit? Perhaps she merely wished to be assured she'd be well rewarded. Some enticement might even be expected.

"Um, the usual," he blurted out. And he'd become so enamored of the delightful future he envisioned with her that he even threw financial caution to the wind. "Clothing . . . I would be most generous. Jewelry . . . some jewelry. You could choose a house. Move in this week. I would come to you on Tuesdays after the bank closed and—"

Bridey now knew what he meant. Drawing her arm well back, she slapped Enos Murdoch's face so hard that his clamped-on glasses flew off, landing some distance away.

He stood, blinking at her in outraged amazement.

CHAPTER 7

Murdoch and Bridey still stood glaring at each other, as Ceci Caley whisked into the library. "Enos," she said as if blithely oblivious to the tension in the room, "I 'ave been *looking* for you." Actually, she'd followed Bridey and eavesdropped outside the door. Their voices were too low for her to catch all that went on, but she'd overheard something important. Now she wanted to get rid of Enos.

Spotting his pince-nez on the carpet, she lifted a platform shoe and brought it down exactly on top of the fragile spectacles. At the scrunch of glass she stepped back in feigned horror. "What 'ave I done? *Mille pardons,* Enos. To be so clumsy!"

But by then she was talking to his back.

Ceci stepped in front of Bridey, who was also about to march out of the room. "Ah, permit me to introduce myself," she said, with an entreating smile. "*Cher* Thomas is one of my true friends, and I am so 'appy to see other women interested in helping his cause." Pronouncing her name quite clearly, Ceci watched for the slightest reaction.

Bridey, her breathing quick and uneven, managed to get out her own name in reply. She was not at all sorry for what she'd done. Murdoch's behavior richly deserved it, and there was more than a little satisfaction in having given that particular man a sharp slap in the face. Still, she knew she might have made a powerful enemy for Devin. She had already resolved not to tell him what had happened. His anger directed at the banker would only make the situation worse. At the moment all she could think was that she was a burden to the man she loved.

Talking vivaciously of the campaign, Ceci motioned to some nearby chairs where they could sit. She was reassured because her name had not seemed at all familiar to Bridey, although one had to take into account that the young woman was distracted. The Frenchwoman had heard the distinct sound of a slap, and she could imagine that Enos had made a serious faux pas. So typical of the man, she thought derisively, but the more foolish miscalculation was his belief that he could persuade Devin Lowell to run against his friend Thomas.

Ceci was too shrewd to think that would succeed, but it explained the plotting by Enos and Lillian. Ceci was delighted at the plan that lay behind it. Lillian was clearly giving up on Denver society and setting her sights on Washington. Since Ceci truly wanted her to go, it would make them allies. In her view, Thomas couldn't be defeated, but that wasn't necessary for the plan to work.

Ceci could see a more likely sequence of events. For all Enos's ranting, America would soon be in the war. When Thomas went to the Capitol, he would need Devin Lowell. Lillian could follow on some patriotic excuse. If the lovely young woman before her were separated for some time from her lover, Ceci thought the breach could be made permanent. Lillian would have her husband, and Ceci would have Denver.

But first she had to befriend Bridey Gregory. It would accomplish two things. If her childhood memory stirred, Ceci would deny any connection. With Devin gone Ceci would be there to insinuate, with a rueful Gallic shrug, that absence did not make the heart grow fonder. All the time she was thinking this over, she was warmly urging Bridey to help with the Alexander campaign.

As Bridey listened, she became convinced that this vivacious older woman was acting out of genuine kindness. She must have overheard Enos, despite her manner when she sailed into the library, and was now going out of her way to reassure and include Bridey.

With that idea in mind Bridey was drawn immediately to Ceci. The Frenchwoman was clearly making an effort to put her at ease. As she waved her jeweled fingers, she told several witty stories about her new involvement in election campaigns. "We women could tell these men a thing or two. Politicians, they are not always so *politique*." Her delicate curlicued nostrils lifted in an amused smile. She leaned forward and Bridey caught the springtime scent of her apple blossom perfume.

Applause from the outer room signaled the end of the press conference. Bridey saw Devin making his way through the crowd. He was stopped by an exquisitely dressed woman in a blue turban. As Bridey turned back to Ceci, suddenly a vision of a blooming apple tree sprang to her mind. Coiled in its branches was a glittering, diamond-backed serpent. Ceci was now standing, saying, "We 'ave plans to make for this election, you agree?"

Bridey almost had to blink before she replied a little distractedly, "Yes, yes, of course."

Ceci was leaving as Devin came into the library. He was smiling, but Bridey thought his eyes had a certain grimness. "There you are," he said with relief in his voice. "Let's get a drink. Talking to reporters is dry work."

But before he could turn, the turbaned blonde appeared at his side. With a familiar, proprietorial gesture, she put a red-nailed hand on his sleeve. "My dear," she said, "since we'll all be working together, you must allow me to introduce myself to your . . . friend. I'm Devin's wife, Lillian Wyndham Lowell."

Before Bridey could respond, Devin coldly interposed, "This is Bridey Gregory. Lillian, you'll have to understand—"

"Forgive me, M'sieu Lowell." Ceci hurried over, interrupting with a charming, apologetic smile. "I must rush off, but I need Miss Gregory for one moment." She twined her arm through Bridey's, drawing her off as she said, *"Chérie,* we must set a date for this party for Thomas that you and I will give. I told him that we would choose a time now. He will soon be so busy."

Enos Murdoch was waiting irritably on the edge of the crowd for the reporters to end their questions. Without his pince-nez all the faces near him were a blur. That contributed to his wrath, which had grown, not lessened, since his encounter with Bridey. That woman, he thought determinedly, was going to find herself out on the street. Starting tomorrow. He was going to speak to Lowell immediately. Hearing the name spoken near him, he put a commanding hand out to the tall man in the blue suit.

"I need to speak to you in strict confidence," he said, gesturing him aside. Anger sent Murdoch's words out in machine-gun clips. "No one else must know this yet. Hear me out without interruption. Any scruples you may have are not to the point here. Spare me any words on loyalty. What I offer is in your own best interest, as you will surely agree when you have had time to consider it. We can talk tomorrow to see if we think alike on the major issues. That is a requirement. Then, I will put my entire financial support behind you. I propose that *you* run for the House seat instead of Thomas Alexander. He will not vote as I see fit. He is quite the wrong man—"

The man Murdoch was addressing broke in with cold amusement. "I *am* the wrong man." It was Thomas Alexander's quiet voice. "At least," he continued, "not the one you want, Enos. But then, with your conditions, *I* don't want you—or your support."

As they drove home, Bridey could see an unusual exhilaration in Devin. His thick hair fell across his forehead when he turned to her to make a point, and his dark brown eyes were alight with the challenge of the campaign. She listened, and responded, but the afternoon's skirmishes had left her emotionally raw.

Worse, she imagined a crack opening, like a wound in the earth, between Devin and herself. That political world seemed exactly where he belonged and was needed. She recalled him standing before the press, and she'd felt his force energizing the room. When she compared that scene with their peaceful farm, the horses grazing in sunlit pastures, it seemed too fenced and narrow to contain him.

Bridey was convinced she didn't belong in his new world. It was his wife who did. She couldn't dislodge the cool, supercilious image of Lillian Lowell from her mind and couldn't tamp down the blood's heat when she thought of her. Until today Lillian had been featureless, and Devin never talked about her or their years together. Now it was clear that her beauty and wealth would open doors for Devin.

Bridey was, in fact, experiencing an emotion she hadn't felt before and didn't recognize. So she was defenseless before it. It was the fox fire of jealousy.

Abruptly, Devin sent the car down a sheltered side road, turned off the motor, and pulled on the emergency brake. "It'd be nice," he said, one brow raised, "if we went home together."

Startled, she only looked at him.

"Come on, Bridey. You're not even in the same car with me. What's bothering you? That Lillian was there?"

She pressed her lips together. She couldn't tell him all that had happened, and she certainly wouldn't tell him what she was feeling. She didn't even want to admit to herself the inward scorching.

"Look," he said, his tone quiet, reasonable, "I never dreamt she'd come. Neither did Thomas. She's never shown the slightest interest in politics. I can't tell you how—"

Bridey bit out, "There's a lot you didn't tell me. That she was beautiful." The heat now in her throat kept her from saying any more.

"For God's sake. You . . ." Devin lifted one mute hand, then banged it on the steering wheel. He thought of the years with Lillian, in the same house, the same room, the same bed, and how desperately lonely he'd been all that time. He'd never been able to tell Bridey the sense of oneness she'd brought to his life. The phrases that had come so readily to his lips all afternoon failed before the onrush of feeling.

"And that remark you made to Thomas when we walked in!" She whirled to face him. Her hair had come completely down, her color was high, and her eyes glittered. "You said we had better things to do— What was he to think? That we spend all our time in bed? That all I am —am is your mistress?"

"How can you say that?" He grabbed her shoulders roughly, shaking her. "You know I love you. You know—" His mouth came down hard on hers. His teeth sank into her lips to make her take back those words.

The fire that ignited Bridey was now of another kind. She had one blind idea. He was hers. She'd make sure he knew it. She ripped open his shirt, grabbed his mat of chest hair.

Devin shoved himself across the seat. Lifting her with fierce hands, he brought her down on his lap. She plunged her hands under his open shirt, digging her nails into his shoulders.

He shoved up her skirt and rasped his zipper open. As he ripped the crotch of her panties, she straddled him, her legs tightening against his.

When he thrust into her, her fingers clutched at his hair. Her mouth was ravenous on his. Together, they fought to fuse.

CHAPTER 8

Bridey stared through narrowed eyes at the innocent mailbox at the lane's end, as if threatening to knock it down if it disappointed her again today. With all her heart she was willing it to contain a letter from Devin.

As soon as the thunderclap of war burst over Pearl Harbor, he'd gone to Washington in answer to Thomas Alexander's urgent call after Thomas had won his House seat. But Bridey knew then she should stay behind to help on the MacAllister farm. Now, besides Gerald's already long hours in the coal mine, he did chores at night. Lucy was doing the work of three men in every precious daylight hour. Because the young farm workers had become soldiers, food shortages were alarming.

In the months before the war's quick and brutal start, Bridey had helped behind the scenes on the Alexander campaign. But she'd resisted Ceci Caley's efforts to persuade her to appear at Devin's side. When Bridey pointed out that the whispers about their living together outside of marriage took people's attention from the real issues, the Frenchwoman flicked the idea aside with her jeweled fingers, saying, "Let people talk. Love—*l'amour*—that is all important."

But to Bridey, loving Devin meant caring about what he wanted. Her feeling deepened that she was in the way of his getting it. Although she did not tell him, she sensed they were divided by that slowly eroding ravine. She closed her eyes to it, telling herself she could reach across it with the arms of love.

The day of Devin's departure he and Bridey had only a brief moment to say good-bye in Denver's high-ceilinged Union Station amid the chaos of people and luggage. Hundreds of soldiers were leaving. It seemed to her that the pain of separation filled the echoing depot, and that this tearing apart was the first wound of war.

His hands were tangling in her hair, reducing the smooth back-twist to loose chestnut waves, as if he could hold her that way to the last second. "Listen," he said urgently, "if you need me for anything— *anything*—promise you'll call." She'd nodded, but knew that with the country's overloaded long distance lines it would take a presidential order to get through. "I'll write, I'll write, whenever I can," he repeated.

Devin's mouth was in her hair, but she'd felt each syllable in the marrow of her bones. "I love you, Bridey. It'll take more than a war to keep us apart."

In answer she clung to him more tightly, her unspoken fears clear in the way she pressed against his chest, in the way her arms refused to let him go. She managed to get out "I love you too." Bridey's cheek ground against the wool of his coat, and she cherished the bar of warmth from his sleeve against her back.

"All abooooooard!" came the conductor's cry. The weight of all the words she had to say to him filled her throat, but not one came out. He kissed her until she was breathless, then pulled himself away to stride to the gate. Bridey watched numbly until he was gone.

Suddenly she couldn't bear to see him go without one last try to reach across the inner gulf that would now be widened by the miles between them. She ran past the conductor, down the platform, frantically searching the long rows of windows for him. Finally, she caught sight of him, head and shoulders over the other passengers in the aisle. When he saw her, he leaned over the soldier in the seat and pressed his palm against the glass. She put her open hand on the outside of the window. The train began to gather steam and then pulled forward, taking Devin with it. Bridey stood alone on the platform, hand out-stretched, scalding tears on her cheeks.

During the first year his letters had been brief, but frequent. He said little about how he felt, but she was used to his engineer's habit of giving only factual information when he wrote. He described the capital's frenetic pace, and the downward slope of his handwriting showed his fatigue. Thomas Alexander had given up his congressional seat and gone to the Department of War. Devin soon had his own post there, and it became clear to Bridey that he was being sent on missions outside the country. He wasn't allowed to say where he'd been or why he'd gone, but she read between the lines and knew he'd made more than one trip to England. In her nightmares silent torpedoes from a U-boat snaked toward the ship that carried him.

Ceci Caley wrote from Washington regularly, her long letters filled with gossipy tidbits about national figures and fizzy accounts of parties she'd attended. When she left, she had said she could no longer simply sit in Denver and worry about the Nazi occupation of France. Raising her aperitif glass, her silvery bobbed hair shining above the rich silk of her Lucien Le Long suit, she'd explained to Bridey, "The French Resistance has need in the Capitol of those who speak the language. Me, I will make contacts with the powerful, so I will speak both *le français* and *l'influence*." She'd promised to keep an eye on Devin to make sure he was caring for himself as well as for the country.

But Ceci's faithful correspondence did not always bring welcome news. Whenever she reported seeing Devin at an evening affair, it seemed to Bridey that Lillian Lowell was also there. She, too, had secured a posting at the War Department. At the beginning Ceci had reassured Bridey, "Do not upset yourself, *ma petite*. Your Devin and she don't work together. He is almost unknown in the office, being sent on vital missions. She is an assistant to the secretary, and she keeps unimportant people away from this important man. One imagines Lillian is efficient at that."

Ceci was well aware that such reports would distress Bridey, whom she always referred to as her dear friend. It was true that she didn't dislike her. She had spent some time in her company determining that this daughter of Berkeley's had never heard the name of Caley. If asked, Ceci would even have said she enjoyed their luncheons during the campaign, since Bridey had taste and intelligence. But it was to her own advantage that Lillian stay in Washington after the war. So she was arranging that.

Bridey rattled the old pickup to the mailbox and rolled down the truck window, wincing as she did so because wrestling hay bales all day had left her with a decided crick in her back. Most of the time she was grateful that the hard physical work left her too weary to notice the lonely house, too tired to do anything except fall into her empty bed. At the moment, she was relieved that the haying was over, thanks to the help of two teenaged boys too young to be drafted. If it hadn't been for the bright hope of word from Devin, she would have sped right by the mailbox and slid immediately into a hot bathtub.

Neither of the letters was from him. One envelope was addressed in Ceci's tiny script, one in the rounded hand of an old friend named Dolores Wolsin. Bridey eyed the first one warily and let it drop on the seat beside her. Then she tore open the second with pleasure. Dolores was the niece of May Tibbett, whom Bridey always thought of as her own dear aunt.

As a child Bridey had hurried home from school, knowing that her three "aunts" would be in the kitchen having tea and scones with Issy. Miss Freda would inquire about her grades, Jane Ellen would make sure her hemlines were the right length, but soft-cheeked May would just embrace her warmly. When visiting in Telluride, Dolores came too. Although the "aunts" had retired to Minnesota when there was no longer enough business for Freda's restaurant, Dolores had fallen in love with the high country and lived in Leadville, not far from Aspen.

Now, Bridey, she wrote, *don't say no until you've read this all the way through. I really need you desperately. The Army is building a whole new base here, called Camp Hale, to train the Tenth Mountain Division—soldiers on skis. I'm in charge of local food procurement. I could use a staff of ten, but I'd settle for one smart woman. Could the MacAllisters spare you for just a few months until I get organized? My landlady has an extra room.*

Bridey stopped and tapped the letter against the steering wheel as she thought. Lucy and Gerald would have the two boys to help and could get by for a couple of months. She grimaced, aware that the hardest part for her would be leaving the house inhabited still by Devin's presence. Many mornings, she slid to his side of the bed in drowsy happiness, thinking he was in the kitchen making coffee.

Her mind still full of Dolores and Leadville, she picked up the other letter. Abruptly the vision of a blooming apple tree with a diamond-backed snake looped in its branches arose, and it was so real, she almost thought she saw it through the windshield. Bridey shook her head to clear it. Why that image of treachery should come up in connection with Ceci she couldn't imagine. They were good friends. Easing the vellum paper out, she decided she was just tired.

Behind the words on the page she could almost hear the Frenchwoman's light laugh. *These soirées are so fatiguing, and at my age to have to attend so many! Still, so much diplomatic business is done over the cocktails. Last night, Eleanor Roosevelt attended, and I spent much time trying to mentally refashion her appearance to my liking. That untidy hair and the dress so shapeless. But then she has not the figure feminine. I threw up my hands.*

Frowning, Bridey rubbed the small of her back, wondering why Mrs. Roosevelt's clothes should be important. The First Lady had been a symbol of strength for the nation during this war, and that was what mattered. But then she shrugged this small criticism of Ceci away. Perhaps it was impossible for a Frenchwoman not to think of fashion.

But I myself am reduced to wearing the same ensemble several times. With the shoes being rationed and silk hose impossible to find! I envied Lillian the exquisite gown she was wearing. She said she'd found a clever seamstress. I immediately took down the woman's name.

Her eyes stinging from a day in the field's powdery dust, Bridey skimmed over the next few paragraphs. Then her eye was caught by this: *You could not guess who also appeared that evening. Enos Murdoch. Still with the part in his hair so precise in the middle!*

Bridey pressed her lips together. Nothing had brought home to her so sharply how little a part she could play in Devin's political life as Enos Murdoch's words at the Alexander mansion. Still, her mouth curved upward as she remembered his pince-nez flying off after that satisfying slap.

Ceci went on, *Because he invests in the defense plants in Colorado, Murdoch haunts the War Office, hoping for contracts. But Thomas has been cool to him ever since their contretemps during the campaign. Enos has no influence here.* Ceci had witnessed Enos being snubbed with delight. In writing about it, she'd recalled that it was his faux pas with Bridey that had led to his dreadful mistake with Thomas. She'd smiled, but had not added that.

Bridey saw Devin's name and read each word hungrily. *He came in at the last moment. He was not wearing a tuxedo, but a gray suit, wrinkled at that. He looked très, très fatigué and quickly took Thomas Alexander aside. Still, you should not worry, ma petite. A few minutes later Lillian gave him a drink and when she made some small remark on his attire, he did laugh. He has his sense of humor yet. The war drains all of us, but we go on bravely.*

Sitting there, Bridey was gripped by pain that had nothing to do with her wrenched back or sore muscles. She saw Devin tired to the bone and, in anguish, wanted to close his eyes with kisses, to make him forget for a few brief moments all the sorrow of war. Then she imagined him standing next to the exquisite blond Lillian in her exquisite gown and was tormented by the thought of how easy it would be for him to seek comfort from her. They were still legally married.

Trying to shut out that idea, Bridey shut her eyes. Inwardly, she saw Devin on the day by the reservoir, reaching for her, saying, "I'll never want anything more than you." It was she who'd insisted that he must tell her if he did. She wondered now why she'd made that rule. Didn't it mean she didn't trust love to last? Those she'd loved, she'd lost. Morna, Berkeley, Issy. Had she been protecting herself by admitting at the beginning that there could be an end to love?

Bridey didn't want to think about that. She had to *do* something.

She slammed the truck into forward gear, her weariness forgotten. She was not about to let Devin go that way, not without a battle. She muttered under her breath. *Fine. If he wants her, that's fine. But he'll damned well have to think about it and tell me right to my face. I'm not going to let him just fall into her arms.*

Packing a quick suitcase, she decided that she'd go to Union Station and take the first train they'd let her on that was going East. It would probably mean standing up for three days. But, from Ceci's letter it sounded as if Devin had just returned to Washington. The chances were good that he'd be there for a little while. There was no point in trying to call him. She'd never get through. She was going to see him, no matter what, that she was sure of.

But, three days later, climbing down just before dawn from the train she'd been shoehorned onto, a host of uncertainties attacked Bridey. If Devin were gone, no one would tell her when he'd be back. Sometimes a month went by without a letter from him and that meant he was not in Washington. What if he were there, but staying with Lillian? What if he answered his door, stood there, and then put on a forced smile of welcome?

A light but steady rain was falling on the capital. Without the kindness of two soldiers Bridey never would have gotten one of the few cabs still able to get the strictly rationed gas. With the blackout directive the other vehicles crawled in the shadows around them, their headlights narrow slits. This thick darkness seemed to make it even more difficult for her to breathe.

Carrying her bag up the stone steps of Devin's brownstone, Bridey felt her arm quiver with the tightness of her hold on it. She hesitated before pushing the elevator button in the drafty lobby. She told herself she *had* to know how he felt, but right then she wasn't sure she wanted to know. The brass cage creaked slowly upward, although it arrived all too quickly at his floor.

It took all her courage to press his doorbell. But after doing so she heard no sounds from inside. She tried again. Nothing. Once more she leaned against it, this time not taking her finger off the button.

The noise of the dead bolt being rasped across startled her. Devin's voice was growling even before he opened the door. "What the hell's the matter? I said—I haven't had any sleep for—" Unshaven, he was wearing only pajama bottoms, and his thick hair was close cropped in a crew cut.

She was about to set down the bag she was still clutching with clenched fingers, but by then he had her, suitcase and all, in his arms.

When Bridey awoke, the rain was falling harder. She lay listening to its drumming muffled by the closed windows, but was really only aware of the rhythm of Devin's breathing. His arm lay across her and his warmth was against her back. Her worry at the exhaustion in his face, her need to talk to him—all that could wait while she luxuriated in his nearness.

Nestling into the pillow, she felt that it was the first time she'd relaxed in days and weeks and months. His lovemaking had been so fierce that her body seemed imprinted by his in a pressure of oneness. Content, she started to drift back into their cocoon of sleep.

The bedside telephone shrilled next to her ear, and her arm jerked automatically to grab for the receiver. Devin shifted restlessly but didn't awake. "Hello," she said quickly and quietly.

The pause was slight but definite before a woman's voice asked, "Have I the right number? I'm calling Devin Lowell."

Even with those few words Bridey knew it was Lillian. "He's asleep," she whispered tersely. "Could you leave a message? I'll have him call back as soon as he—"

"Wake him up. He's got a telegram here at the office. It's marked top priority, and he has to answer right away." Lillian's animosity crackled through the phone.

Bridey shook Devin's shoulder and handed him the receiver when he half opened his eyes. The cord was stretched across her and, feeling his body stiffen even before she heard his curt responses, she knew he was going to leave.

"All right. I'll be ready." He tossed the receiver near her to hang up and swung out of bed. Devin looked down at her and at that moment he seemed a stranger. She'd noticed last night how much leaner he was. Now his skin was tight on the bones of his face, and this spareness and the shorn hair emphasized the jut of his nose, the strong jaw. His eyes, without their usual warmth, had a black intensity. Devin had always been direct, even blunt, in pressing his views, but he'd regarded others with a saving humor. There was no trace of that in the man before her. He seemed not so much a person as an embodied will.

His words were clipped. "It's bad news. What we feared. The Nazis have a new weapon. God help us, Bridey. We could lose this war."

She could feel his anger and pain but, without knowing more, could say nothing to help. It was only later that a knife twisted in her own heart as she wondered if Lillian shared what he'd heard and could understand better. All Bridey sensed then was his distance from her even as he stood beside her.

His voice was emotionless. "I have to go. And it'll be weeks before I get back."

"A few more hours?" she stammered out.

"No. They're sending a car. You can stay, rest up. Or if you want, I can drop you at the station."

There was no time for anything but rapid-fire talk as he rifled through dresser and closet for clothes, stuffing them into a leather valise. He rarely met her eyes, and she was not sure if he could not bear the grief he saw there or if he were hiding what he thought.

On the long way back to Colorado the train wheels seemed to be repeating her fears, her unanswered questions. Bridey imagined that even her skin was rubbed raw by her unhappiness. Only sleep provided cotton wool against it. She found she could even doze off standing up and the jolting stops didn't waken her. On the third day a smiling sailor reached out to catch her as the train swooped into a station. "Oops," he said, holding her upright. Then he ran his fingers again over her forearm. "Boy, you've got a temperature. You must have picked up the flu on this trip."

CHAPTER 9

Opening her eyes from the hot colors of a fever dream, Bridey saw that the polished grain of the bedroom's wood molding was shifting and rippling like stream water. She knew she was thirsty. And she was sick. That was all she was clear about. She had no idea how long she'd been back. Could it have been two days, or even three?

She faintly recalled getting a ride to the house from the county mail carrier, Will Jenkins. He'd burbled along in a friendly monotone, adding when she got out, "I'll bring by the bundle of mail I've been saving till you got home."

She'd said, "No hurry, Will." He'd drawn his wispy gray brows together then, apparently noticing her hectic color. "Just the flu. Don't worry," she'd reassured him. Opening her front door, she'd swayed a little as if still on board the train. The sound of the wheels spun in her head. Going to Washington, they'd repeated *Hurry, hurry, hurry*. On the way back they'd revolved to *Worry, worry, worry*.

Frowning, she considered those rhymes. Perhaps she hadn't come back with Will and had only imagined the words.

Still, she remembered how the dusty air in the abandoned house had a physical weight, making it too much of an effort for her to pick up the phone and call Lucy and Gerald. She knew they wouldn't be expecting her anyway. Yes, that was right. She'd wanted just to get to sleep. She'd wanted to sink into the darkness so she wouldn't have to think about Devin. That was really why she'd gone to bed.

Now it was hard to lift her head for a sip of water. The walls themselves seemed to be moving. As she lay dizzily back on the pillow, Bridey reminded herself to lie quite still. Otherwise, she'd fall into the steep crevasse between her side of the bed and Devin's.

As she slipped gratefully back into sleep, she was walking upward. She was going up her mountain. Bridey's Mountain. It was not an easy climb. The peak was cloud capped, and she couldn't see through the mist. She had to step carefully not to crush the white wildflowers. Then she realized they were snow covered, and that didn't make sense. Nor did the surrounding scent of lilacs. It wasn't spring. Still, that fragrance made her keep going. She knew she had to because Devin—

His name shook her out of sleep and made the waking painful. She sat up, aching, and decided that she should get out of bed and make some tea. Slipping on a soft cinnamon sweater warmed her, and she pulled on pants, heavy socks, shoes.

But as she put on the kettle and then went to the mailbox, Bridey found she was still walking carefully as if among the frosty flowers in her dream. The outside air was hazy, almost silver, in the anemic sun. Glancing upward, she saw a sparrow hawk circling in narrower spirals, intent on some prey below, and the cold deep inside her returned.

She laid the mail on the table and saw Dolores Wolsin's earlier letter there, waiting to be answered. Trying to think what to do about that, she automatically tore open an envelope. It was only when a clipping fell out that she noticed the new letter was from Ceci. Laying it aside without reading it, she picked up the newspaper picture. It showed a tuxedoed Devin with a smiling Lillian on his arm.

For a moment Bridey felt she could not force air into her lungs at all. She stood paralyzed. Then the doorbell chimed, and the photograph stayed in her throbbing head as she moved to the front door. As it swung inward, she was facing Lillian Lowell.

Lillian had planned everything about this interview exactly, starting with her outfit. She'd gone shopping, but because the war had wreaked havoc on the fashion industry, she hadn't been pleased. Instead, she'd put on one of her Paris suits that had been retailored. She'd made sure the skirt touched her kneecap at the newest level. The crown of her matching red hat was pierced with a cocky dark feather, and her blond hair was smoothly upswept. Her nail polish and lipstick were the same shade of cardinal red.

Trying to infuse her voice with feeling, Lillian asked, "Miss Gregory, I *need* to talk to you. May I come in?"

Bridey stared at her wordlessly, wondering if the woman before her was part of a fever dream. The feather in her hat reminded her of something she'd just seen. Yes, the swooping sparrow hawk. She needed to sit down and think about it. She definitely needed to sit down. With that need foremost in mind she nodded and ushered her in.

As Lillian walked into the living room, she was concentrating, remembering what she was to say. Immediately after the shock of hearing Bridey's voice on the phone in Washington, she'd called Ceci Caley. For a moment the older woman had been silent and then replied, *"Chérie, we must launch an attack. I will help you plan."*

At first Lillian had strongly resisted the idea of a long, uncomfortable trip to Colorado. But Ceci had said, "Now is the time. Tell them at your office that some family member in Denver is sick and you must go at once. Did you not just say that your 'usband will be gone for some time? Think. That means there will be no letters. She will hear only your words."

Lillian seated herself stiffly on the edge of an upholstered couch without waiting to be asked. She wanted to take in the room's furnishings but she didn't want to lose her train of thought. She was already a little put off by Bridey's appearance. She'd visualized catching her rival off guard, caught in the middle of cleaning, wearing some frumpy housedress. With sly pleasure she'd imagined her turning pale at the confrontation, trying hurriedly to rearrange her hair.

Instead, a flush lighted Bridey's dramatic features and the warm tone of her golden brown angora sweater brought out those colors in her eyes and her tumbling chestnut hair. Her eyes did seem unnaturally bright, Lillian thought, but she seemed, if anything, composed, even a little remote.

"If it weren't for the war, what's happening to America—" Lillian began, and then stopped abruptly. She was supposed to say that, but she wasn't supposed to start with it. How had Ceci told her to begin? She'd gone over it endlessly on the train. Then she remembered, even stretching out her hand in candid appeal as she'd rehearsed. "Miss Gregory, my husband and I are making an effort to put our marriage back together. We see now that we can . . ."

Again Lillian paused. She was supposed to emphasize *Devin,* what he could achieve, how only in this way would he be satisfied in the future. When talking to Ceci, Lillian had questioned the approach. But the Frenchwoman had insisted, "Miss Gregory will make the beau geste. Yes. She will give him up if she thinks finally this will make him happy. It may destroy her, but she will. I tell you that."

But Bridey's lack of expression, her almost tranquil silence, unnerved Lillian. Careless of the planned order of her arguments, she plunged on. She emphasized Devin's abilities, having seen that he could be a man of real influence in Washington. That had filled her head with images of her own bright future as a hostess in the nation's capital.

Leaning forward, she continued, "Devin's trusted there, and liked. He'll be very much needed in Washington in the future. Arranging the peace—when it finally comes—will be as much of a challenge as fighting this dreadful war. Devin will see that as part of his duty. He won't want to come back to Colorado."

Bridey nodded. She was listening, and the words appeared with shimmering clarity in her mind. This woman—if she was actually sitting here—was saying just what Bridey herself had been thinking. The new Devin that she'd just left in Washington—the one she didn't know anymore—would want to use his abilities.

"And you can see," Lillian went on, "that for you to accompany him would be . . . really impossible." She waved that idea away with red-taloned nails. "Oh, he could find you a small house on a back street and visit occasionally, but if it were known, the scandal would ruin his career."

Her argument was true, as far as it went, but Lillian wanted to get over this point quickly. Because Devin's domestic arrangements wouldn't be known. Reporters never even hinted in print at this aspect of politicians' lives. Men in public life were only expected to maintain the façade of a happy marriage. If Devin were to continue to spend most of his time with Bridey after their reconciliation, Lillian knew she herself would just have to close her eyes. Ceci had been blunt about this in their council of war.

Lillian was familiar with such situations. What she found shocking was that Ceci had discussed it openly. She excused it on the grounds that Ceci was a Frenchwoman. The important thing to Lillian was that it was *she* who would attend official functions with him. And she truly needed Devin for that. Marrying someone else was out of the question. No candidate seeking election would marry a divorced woman.

Lillian feared that Bridey might counter that it was quite possible for her to move to Washington with Devin. But what she found really insupportable was the very idea of talking about it. Bridey could well mention it. Enos Murdoch had said more than once that such women had none of the finer feelings.

But Bridey didn't respond and her calm silence shook Lillian badly. She was prepared for sharp comebacks. Ceci had said that Bridey might question whether Devin would choose politics on a national level. "Miss Gregory knows your 'usband well. I myself have watched him." She'd blown smoke from a thin brown imported cigarette as she went on. "He's the kind of man who, as one says, calls a spade a shovel. In wartime, he is a man who will do his duty. But will he want to stay on? He has not Thomas's patience in letting fools talk."

Lillian had assured herself that Devin's "rough edges just needed some polish." That was how she had planned to answer Bridey. As it was, all she could think to do was rush on, keeping Ceci's last words in her mind. "Leave her thinking this is a fait accompli. You and Devin will reunite. But say that he has found it hard to tell her because he feels *obliged* to her. She is a proud woman, an independent one. That will not sit well." Twitching at her red skirt so it skimmed her knees properly, Lillian managed to stammer out a version of that.

Bridey's lips parted but she said nothing. Lillian waited, growing ever more restless. Suspicion sprang into her mind. Perhaps Ceci Caley had betrayed her. She could have written Bridey, or pulled strings and gotten through on the phone, warning her what Lillian would say. And now the woman was secretly laughing at her, sitting there watching her go through the parroted speeches. It was the kind of thing Lillian could well believe Ceci would do, despite all her new assurances of friendship. The logic of it convinced her. That was it. The two of them were making a fool of her.

Unable to bear that idea, Lillian jumped up. "I'll see myself out." Her heels clicked angrily down the hall and the door slammed behind her.

For a moment Bridey still stared at the sofa. She decided that Lillian had really been here; she could smell her heavy perfume in the air. But somehow it didn't seem to matter. Wrapping the afghan on the chair arm around her, she leaned back and fell asleep.

When she awoke this time, her body felt curiously light, as if she could float. She realized the fever's hold was broken. But there were only a few seconds of release before memory returned. It pinned her in place with its leaden weight. She was aware that she'd come to a decision while she slept. She would let Devin go. He could no longer be happy with her here. She had lived with the fear of that, grown used to it, and it convinced her where Lillian's rehearsed speeches never could have.

As the house grew dark and cold around her, Bridey remained, trying to imagine a world where she was without Devin and the sun still rose. It was impossible to conceive, and she gave up the effort. At least it was the right decision, she told herself, and the worst was over. It was better than waiting, watching him struggle to find anguished words to tell her. That would be harder yet.

The odd thing was that the words she thought seemed to echo, to bounce off the bones in her head. She wondered if she were still sick after all. Then she understood she was empty inside.

The love that filled her hadn't lasted. Right at the start with Devin she'd feared it wouldn't. Now she was left alone. She would have to accept that and rely on herself, she thought. But she'd always been able to do that. She would again.

Bridey had the sense of lucidity that comes with convalescence. Pushing herself upright, she determined that she would write Dolores. Accepting the job in Leadville would mean moving. And she had to leave the house as soon as possible. She would write her immediately. And she would write Devin too.

Sitting in the kitchen, Bridey did the first letter quickly. The second took hours. Then, buried under the crumpled sheets of her discarded attempts, she saw the clipping about the Washington party that Ceci had sent. She unfolded it, almost hoping that anger would rush in and fill her hollowness. Instead, she felt only loss when she looked at Devin. He had found something he wanted more, though he'd once said he never would. She could see it had nothing to do with Lillian. At that moment Bridey could even have wished for jealousy or envy to pour in. But what Devin was reaching for was something beyond what he had now. Perhaps success or fulfillment. Perhaps he was being driven by duty, patriotism. In any case, she must let him go toward it.

Picking up her pen, Bridey gathered her resolve. She would go forward herself. She did not need Devin.

She would keep her pride in the process. With her hand hovering over the paper Bridey realized how difficult it would be to be strong if she had to face him, to listen to words she so wanted to hear but that he could not mean. She knew Devin, and she had to agree with Lillian that he would feel a sense of obligation. He would return, at least for a time. So she had to make clear in her letter that there would be no need for that.

Always before in writing Devin, Bridey's pen had flowed over pages. Now all she could manage was a few stilted words: *Thank you for the past we shared. I am grateful to you. But we cannot have a happy future together. I have a good one elsewhere. There is no need to discuss it. Please don't write. I've asked that mail from you not be forwarded. I wish you well.*

CHAPTER 10

The Continental Divide extended across the horizon like the crown of the world. Mount Massive lay asleep under a cover of snow in the afternoon sunshine. Suddenly, a line of men on skis appeared atop a ridge, dressed entirely in white, their eyes protected by the smoky lenses of their goggles. One by one, as silent as thought, they flashed down the long slope toward the base of the mountain. Their skis etched winding paths on the shining surface, their turns splashing showers of diamonds.

Bridey watched from an Army jeep parked on the road to Camp Hale. "They're magnificent," she murmured. Created to combat the expert German alpine units, which had been so effective in the ranges of Europe, the all-volunteer Tenth Mountain Division was an elite corps.

The supply sergeant in the driver's seat grinned at her. Very few saw these disciplined troops training in this stronghold in the high Rockies, but those who did were always impressed. Even he thought the Tenth was amazing. His smiling blue eyes narrowed against the sun's glare. "Those're the men you been feedin', ma'am. Now y'see why they eat so much."

For the first time in all the weeks since she'd arrived in the Aspen-Leadville area, Bridey felt an excitement, a sense of life's grace, even though she was an onlooker. Her heavy work schedule filled her waking hours and absorbed all the space around her. Dolores constantly expressed her gratitude—and relief—at her efficiency. Bridey knew that she must smile because others smiled back at her. But ever since writing to Devin, she'd only been aware of her inner darkness.

She'd called Lucy that night to talk to her about the Leadville job and then told her that she and Devin had decided on parting. Bridey knew that information should best be given over the phone. Had Lucy seen the ravages of the flu, she would not have let her leave quickly, and her friend would surely have wanted to discuss her decision regarding Devin. "It's the best thing for both of us," Bridey had insisted, trying to disguise the hoarseness brought on by her sore throat. "But, Lucy, if he does write, it'll be much easier for me if you don't forward his letters. Keep them until I get back. Just now I can't face them. And *promise* me that you won't tell him where I am."

Lucy had protested at length at that. Both she and Gerald were close to Devin. But Bridey had been adamant. "Promise me on Issy's grave, Lucy." At her friend's reluctant agreement Bridey had gotten off the phone hurriedly, saying, "I'll send you some money for the neighbor boys' help with the horses. Give Anna an apple for me and tell her I'll only be gone a few months."

Bridey had missed her horses, but when she arrived, kitten-weak from the flu, she was glad that her present job was sedentary. Ordering supplies for the military meant sitting and filling out endless forms, and she and Dolores drove to nearby ranches to inspect the sheep and cattle they were buying. But as the weeks went by, Bridey was surprised at how long the effects of her illness lingered, and how little she minded not having her usual vigorous exercise.

Not only did she sleep dreamlessly for long hours, she had to fight off doziness in the afternoon. She was uninterested in food and sometimes the thought of it made her queasy. Dolores who had inherited, along with her aunt May, a midwestern farm girl's sturdy frame, eyed Bridey's slender fragility with envy. Kneading her own solid hip in dismay, she said, "You'd think that after looking at cows all day, I wouldn't want to eat one at night. But I sure do. And I suppose tonight Mrs. Wentzel will fix macaroni and cheese. Again." Their landlady, along with housewives across the nation, was strict in her patriotic wartime observance of three "meatless" days a week.

What concerned Bridey most about her continuing listlessness and lack of appetite was the fear that it stemmed from her ongoing depres-

sion. She locked up her memory during the day, but alone in her room
her thoughts flew straight as springtime swallows to Devin. More than
once she'd told herself that they should have faced each other at a final
parting. Perhaps the pain of an endpoint would have allowed her a
chance to heal and to forget. He *had* promised to do that. But there'd
been no time at their last meeting.

Waiting for sleep, she remembered the passion of the night in
Washington. She had to admit that was probably sheer physical need.
She'd caught him off guard. There were the unendurable pressures of
war.

Again, she longed for anger because that emotion would at least
make her feel *something*. She found she couldn't even blame Lillian for
her visit, which she only dimly recalled. When she did, Bridey reasoned
she must have thought Devin had already broken the news of their
reconciliation. It was all understandable. He would need his wife in his
new career. Even the sharp prick of envy because it was Lillian that
could help him didn't pierce Bridey's numbed senses.

She was sure now that he'd accepted the manner of their parting,
probably with great relief. Lucy hadn't mentioned any letters from him.
While her friend had agreed not to forward them, Bridey knew Lucy.
She would have mentioned letters if there had been any, and would
have badgered Bridey to accept them. Lucy just sent on all her other
mail regularly with cheery notes.

On a piecrust table in her room at the boardinghouse, Bridey had
arranged her favorite photographs. Issy in her garden, Lucy and Gerald
at their front door, and Anna cantering up, her ivory mane flying. But
she'd firmly tucked away Devin and his smile in the drawer.

One evening, as Bridey was closing her door on her way to dinner,
Dolores came from her own room. Even the upstairs corridor was redo-
lent with the aroma of Mrs. Wentzel's mutton stew, spiced with marjo-
ram. Dolores sniffed appreciatively. Bridey suffered a wave of nausea so
acute, it stopped her in midstep. When she emerged from the bathroom,
Dolores glanced down at the other boarders chatting in the hall below
and waved Bridey back into her room.

Lowering herself onto the bed, Bridey began, "I don't know *why* I
can't shake this stomach trouble. Before that flu I was healthier than all
my horses and—"

Dolores planted one hand on a no-nonsense hip and interrupted,
"Now, when you arrived here, coming up to three months ago, you
were sick. But we both know that's got nothing to do with this. Since
you told me about your man staying in Washington, I can see why you
haven't wanted to discuss the situation. But I just want to say you've

got nothing to worry about. It's true that you won't be able to go out to Camp Hale once you start showing. The military wouldn't have that— war or no war. But there's the paperwork here—"

Finally realizing what Dolores meant, Bridey broke in, "No, no. Honestly, I'm not pregnant. I can't—"

Dolores overrode her. "Let me finish. We've known each other since we were ten. And I've kept my mouth shut for six weeks anyway. But you have to know that I'll help all I can. Not that I'm supposing you'll need me. Although I only met Lucy and Gerald the one time I visited, I can see that if you went back and lived with them on the farm, you'd have to fight for a chance to hold that baby."

Bridey only shook her head in denial. "Dolores, Devin and I hoped and hoped, but we finally had to accept the fact that it wasn't possible. After all, I'm over forty."

"So what?" Dolores grinned. "You can't fool a farm girl like me. When did you have your last period?"

Bridey thought. "Well, I don't . . ." One day had slid into another and each dreary week had looked like the one before. It hadn't occurred to her. Now it did. "I could be," she said slowly.

Then joy began to flash through Bridey's narrowest veins. She leapt up. "I am! Dolores, I'm pregnant."

After squeezing her in a tight hug Dolores said, "After I eat, I'll bring you some tea and toast and we'll talk."

"Thanks. *Thanks.*" Bridey was breathless in her exuberance but she went on, "I'm going to sit here and start telling her everything."

"Her?" Dolores turned on her way to the door.

Bridey paused then nodded in surprised assurance. "Yes. Her. I even know her name. I always planned on calling a girl Morna Patricia, for my mother. I'll christen her that, but I'll call her Trish, so she'll have a name that's hers alone too. And there's so much to tell her. About my parents. And Bridey's Mountain. Her mountain."

Dolores's grin grew wider. "You might want to wait until she's actually *born* before breaking the news."

Even as she closed the door, Bridey was hurrying to the piecrust table. Taking out Devin's picture, she said, "I'm so happy. Now I'll always have you. And although you won't know—" She stopped because tears began dropping on the glass of the photograph. Scrubbing them away with her sleeve, she went on, "It's *better* if you don't know. But I'll say only good things. Like how very much I loved you."

CHAPTER 11

Dressed only in a white slip, Bridey sat on the edge of the brass bed gently patting her well-rounded stomach. She was considering how to convince Dolores, who always came up with some new reason for her staying, that it was time to leave. Bridey was longing to go home. She hadn't yet told the MacAllisters about the baby because she was looking forward to seeing their faces light up when they learned. She whispered to the baby, "Trish, you'll love them and the farm. The horses. Someday you'll have one of your own."

That thought brought up other reasons why she had to return now. She'd have to sell one of the horses to pay for the hospital costs. And spring planting would take place soon. Lucy and Gerald would need all the help she could give. Bridey brushed out her hair in vigorous strokes as she mulled it over.

Dolores would have to agree to her leaving. She was at the moment going through her own closet to find a yet larger top for Bridey to wear to dinner. But disguise would soon be out of the question. Wrapping the bed's yellow quilted coverlet around her while she waited, Bridey prepared her case.

At the knock on her door she smiled, saying, "Come in. We have to talk."

The door opened. It was Devin, unsmiling, unshaven. He replied, "We sure do." After closing the door he leaned against it with crossed arms.

His wool overcoat, damp with April snow, hung open over a blue pinstripe suit and white shirt. Staring at him, Bridey could only wonder how she could have forgotten how tall he was, how broad his shoulders, how he filled the room. The angles of his face had the sharpness she'd noticed in Washington, but his dark hair had grown enough to fall over his forehead. His eyes still were that unyielding black.

She hurriedly bundled the quilt in front of her. Her first thought was that if he knew she was pregnant, he would insist on staying with her. No matter how much he'd have to give up or how little he wanted to be with her, he would stay. Her only words were "How did you know I was here?"

"That's not the first question, Bridey." His tone was harsh. He strode to the windows and stared down, his stiff back to her. "The one I had was: *How,* in God's name, could you do this? After six months I finally got back to the States and that was only because Eisenhower needed— Anyway, I expected a thick pile of letters from you. There was only the one."

Bridey thought that as long as he didn't turn around—as long as she didn't have to look at him—she could be strong. But hearing the dry ache in his voice was more than she could endure. Why had he come? And then clearly she saw him reading her letter, feeling her pain. That would have been hard for him. There would still be some love left for her despite his new focus.

Clenching the quilt's material into two tight hand-holds, she told herself that what she had to do now was let him talk and soon he'd see that she'd accepted it was for the best. Then she could tell him to go. Despite her hope that they needn't ever talk, she'd nevertheless imagined this conversation. The reality was much worse.

He jammed his fists into his coat pockets, the fabric taut across his shoulders. "I got on a military plane, told them it was a matter of life or death. That was true enough. The first thing I saw when I walked into the kitchen was that damned clipping. The picture of me and Lillian. Right away I got Lucy on the phone."

Watching him pace, never meeting her eyes, Bridey felt that he was giving her the chance to take back her decision. He would have to be sure that it hadn't been made in hasty anger, that she wouldn't have regrets later. For a few brief seconds she let herself imagine the exquisite pleasure of telling him the truth, of saying that she didn't want to live without him, that most days she didn't think she could. She would tell him about the baby. He would embrace her, and she could sleep in his arms.

Bridey closed her eyes against that overwhelming desire, then forced them open. That would only be spreading this pain in smaller pieces over the years. In any impatient gesture he made, she would see his dissatisfaction with the narrow world she'd forced him to choose. She could not live like that. She could take care of herself and Trish.

In profile his lips had a bitter twist, but there was a touch of his old humor in his voice. "Lucy would only say she promised not to tell, even when I talked myself hoarse. But finally she mentioned that when your mail came to her, she sorted it and put what you'd want in an envelope in her own box. And Will Jenkins took it. When I caught up with Will and told him I'd been a darned fool and didn't bring your new address with me, he said how sorry he was that all he had was your post office box number in Leadville. It's a very small town, Bridey."

He stopped abruptly, his attention caught by the photographs on the piecrust table, his own in the center. She winced, wishing she'd left it in the drawer. Now he would think she was hanging on to the past.

When he at last met her eyes, she immediately let her own slide to his coat. But that was the one he'd worn the day he left, and she could remember the wool against her cheek, the feel of him. So she looked at the quilt and strained out the words to send him away, "Devin, you needn't have come here. But this way I can assure you that I really agree that you've made the best choice for you. And, because that's true, for me. You're needed in Washington and will be even more so later, if this terrible war ever ends. During Lillian's visit, I—"

"*Lillian's* visit?" he burst out. With one long step he was gripping the brass foot of the bed. "She came to see you? When?"

Bridey detected guilt in his anger. She assumed it was caused by the way she'd learned of his reconciliation with Lillian. Bridey bit her lip. Now she would have to explain or else he'd think she'd left out of pique because of the way in which the news had been delivered.

With enormous effort she kept her voice flat. "Devin, she couldn't have known how short a time I was in Washington. Naturally, she assumed that you'd told me you two were patching up your marriage. It doesn't matter that it was she who told me. I see it's for the best. With your new career she can help—"

For a moment Bridey thought an earthquake had hit Leadville.

Then she realized it was Devin's white-knuckled grip on the bed's brass footrail. When he let go, the bed was still quivering.

He was suddenly in front of her, leaning over her as she sat clutching the quilt before her. She could have sworn he was roaring, but his lips were hardly moving. "Dear God. She said—But how could you—? How could you believe that, Bridey?"

He jerked upright and was back by the windows, while she was still staring at the spot where he'd been. But she heard the furious words as distinctly as if he hadn't moved. "I couldn't make sense of your letter. I couldn't. When I got home and saw that damned picture, courtesy of Ceci Caley, I got more than a hint. What I was afraid of was when you saw *that,* you'd gone off with . . . that your new future meant some other guy. All the way here, I was going over not whether I'd kill him, but *how.*"

At that she would have jumped up, but her feet were tangled in the quilt. She choked out, "That's crazy! How could you imagine while you were away I'd—"

He was again standing before her, shoving his hair from his forehead. "You think *that's* crazy? How about your believing I'd spend the rest of my life with an empty-headed clotheshorse like Lillian? Help my career? She'd be standing at some do or other thinking about what to wear to the next goddamned thing. I had to grit my teeth to smile at her, let them take our picture, but I hoped that way she'd listen to me long enough so I could talk her into a divorce."

His anger spread through the room, pulling out the air. Now her own was filling the vacuum. He was making her the target. Bridey couldn't bear the unfairness of it. Kicking at the bottom of the coverlet, she stood right before him.

"And how was I to know what you were thinking, Devin?" Her bare shoulders rising from the slipping bedspread heaved, as she tilted her head to glare up at him.

"You broke our rules!" His eyes were shining black as onyx. "We agreed. If I found something I wanted more, *I* was to tell you. You had no right to decide what *I* wanted."

He clutched the ruffled edge of the quilt around her in his fists and his trembling shook her. "If I'd thought I had to keep doing what I'm doing—You know how I make myself do it? Every day I get up and think the same thing. That soon I'll be coming home for good, that I'm going to be somewhere with my arms around you. And I don't care if all I'm doing then is watching a horse munch grass. As long as you're there. But I'll tell you, Bridey Gregory, that part of your leaving was that *you* didn't want anybody thinking you needed a damn thing. That, by God, you were going to take care of yourself, with or without me!"

Enraged that that was how he saw her actions, and that there was a kernel of truth in it, Bridey threw her arms up, completely forgetting her hold on the quilt. "That's right! I don't need you. I want you. But if I had to think you were with me because you felt obliged—"

The quilt was on the floor. Devin stared at her. He opened his mouth as his eyes moved from her waistline to her face. But he said nothing.

Her anger increased by what she'd revealed, Bridey's words still spilled out. "I can take care of the baby too. It's yours, but I am perfectly capable of raising her by myself."

"That night in Washington," he said. It was not a question.

She could only nod.

As his expression flashed from wonder to joy, Bridey finally took in what he'd said. *I'm going to be somewhere with my arms around you.* She started to reply that was all she wanted, but by then her mouth was muffled in his coat. And then he wouldn't stop kissing her.

Later, as she lay with her back against his chest, she decided that it was a perfect way to go to sleep. With his large warm hand on her stomach the baby was peacefully still, not kicking at all. She was quiet herself as she thought, *I do need Devin . . . I love him. That's the right kind of need. If I trust the love it will last.* Wrapped in his arms, she knew she'd found her heart's desire.

After a while she stirred and smiled, remembering something, "Devin, Mrs. Wentzel doesn't even allow men in the rooms, let alone having them spend the night."

His mouth was against her ear. "I'll just explain to her that I'm a VIP and, more importantly, a father-to-be. Men in my condition get tetchy, especially when they hear boardinghouse rules."

"Speaking of rules, how about a new one?" Bridey tucked one of her feet around his calf to draw him closer, even though it wasn't possible. "Once a year, maybe on New Year's Eve when the Louisville firemen let off the siren, you could say you still want—" She stopped, realizing that she no longer needed to have him say it.

"No changing rules in midstream," he answered sleepily. "Besides, I already told you I'd never want anything more than you. Let's stick with the ones we've got. 'From this day forward,' " he began, tightening his hold on her. "Wait a minute, the 'till death do us part' is wrong. I might die, but I'm not leaving you."

CHAPTER 12

In the mountains above Boulder, Gold Hill nestled like a reverie. Colorado's first mining town, it had become over the years the home of part-time university students and artists' communes. Reached by driving up the winding, pine-shaded canyon road from Boulder, the village was remote from the tensions of the sit-ins and Vietnam War protests on the campus itself.

At the edge of town was a cabin of log and stone surrounded by mountain wildflowers and old-fashioned blooms. A young woman in blue jeans and a scarlet shirt plied a gardening trowel, digging out weeds among lavender anemones, pink sweet williams, and a host of others. A breeze brushed by and she stopped to swiftly plait the long, dark hair it tossed around her vibrant face. Her eyes shone with a sensuous pleasure in being alive.

At twenty-two Morna Patricia Gregory—always called Trish—had Bridey's thickly lashed, golden brown eyes alight with Devin's humor. Her nose was delicate above the curve of her mouth.

The angular brown woman sketching her from the shade of a nearby pine drew Trish's full lower lip, then smudged the line with one thumb to suggest its generosity. Becca Blue nodded in silent satisfaction, the gold hoops at her ears swinging against sharp cheekbones exposed by pulled-back black hair. Her pencil captured the protective posture of Trish's body as she bent over the young plants.

Leaning across a clump of saxifrages, Trish hummed to herself as she tugged at a length of bindweed. At first she'd moved self-consciously, aware of Becca Blue's almond-shaped eyes watching her. But the feel of the earth beneath her, the scent of the flowers on the thin mountain air, had worked their familiar spell.

As the image of Trish took shape on her sketch pad, Becca became aware of a longing for her oil paints. She hurried the pencil over the paper, securing the tree shadows extending toward Trish like reaching fingers. But she had a nagging urge to return to the commune for her palette. The remembered colors swirled in her imagination, pulsing at bright yellow.

Her gaze lit upon a cluster of alpine buttercups not far from Trish. "No," Becca muttered, hand drawing unceasingly, "not yellow. Gold." Gold flashing off fragments of gemlike colors. "Jewels." Her mind's eye conjured the shimmer and glitter, and then the notion was gone. The pencil stopped moving, and she looked down at the sketch pad.

Her gaze skipped over the Trish she'd caught, flowers around her. In the lower right corner of the paper was something in a much different stroke, almost a scrawl. She studied it, not knowing what she'd drawn. Then she realized that it was hair, a person's hair, and with uneasy insight, that it was supposed to be gold.

"Hey," Trish called. "How about a break?"

Becca jerked at the sound, then shook her head at her own imaginings. "Okay." As she stood up, necklace of tiny bells chiming, long denim skirt shifting around her ankles, she felt a flutter of apprehension.

"Well, have you immortalized me?" Trish asked teasingly as she drew near.

"I'll show you when we get to the cabin."

At the edge to Becca's voice Trish took a closer look at her. Her face had an unaccustomed pallor to it, brown skin bleached to café-au-lait. The dark eyes avoided her gaze. "Fair enough. I'll make some tea."

"That'd be real nice." As they walked to the cabin, Becca tried to convince herself that the strange moment of drawing the unknown was an accident. She'd been off balance all day, maybe because of the visitor to the commune the night before. Her lover, Tympany, had brought home a man who'd sparked her nerve endings, inspecting the family as though assessing their value. At the thought of Caley Sutherland, Becca shivered, just as she had upon meeting him.

"How's Starshine?" Trish opened the screen door to the cabin and the scent of freshly baked bread.

The thought of her two-year-old daughter allowed Becca to complete her smile. For all the trouble Tympany had caused her, he'd given her Starshine. "She's bright as a new penny."

Becca relaxed inside the cabin. Trish had made it welcoming, with objects she valued on display. Above the saddleback leather sofa she'd hung a framed charcoal sketch of a mountain in Telluride. Bridey's Mountain, Becca remembered. When Trish told her about it, she'd felt a twinge of yearning for something handed down that way, through generations. There were no such legacies in her family. Born in Georgia of a black, unwed mother and a white father, she'd gone in search of a place of her own after her grandmother died. It had taken her years to find it at the Spring Gulch commune in Gold Hill.

Becca's glance went to the shadowbox fixed to the wall over the rolltop desk. The items kept in it evoked Gold Hill itself for her: a chunk of white quartz shot through with iron pyrites; a twisted railroad spike crusted with rust; a canning jar filled with old buttons.

One box held something she hadn't seen. "You got a thimble." Becca picked it up, thin fingers gently stroking the forget-me-nots painted on the chipped white china.

"Yeah, I found it a couple of days ago." Trish was drying her hands on a bright green towel. "In a clearing not far from the old cemetery. I think there must've been a cabin there a long time ago."

Becca set the thimble carefully into its niche, thinking that a woman she'd never known had used it. Now it pleasured the eye in the home of her friend, giving a sense of continuity, suggesting an endurance for times to come. Trish had put hope on display in those little boxes, Becca thought, visualizing the chain of years linking her to the long-ago needlewoman.

She lightly touched the doll seated in the tallest box. Dressed in calico, with features sewn onto cotton with embroidery thread, her red-stitched smile was faded from repeated kisses. Trish had told her that the doll, named Ariana, had been her favorite, a birthday gift from her mother. Trish had sewn one as like it as possible for Starshine.

Relieved to see that Becca was looking more like herself, Trish ducked back into the kitchen to set the kettle on. It was her favorite room, a galley of pine cabinets her father had made for her. The wide-silled window over the sink held herb pots started with cuttings from Lucy MacAllister. "I'm going to put in some hyssop," she called to

Becca, pulling a packet of the dried herb from a divided drawer. "That'll put the bloom back in your cheeks."

Becca appeared in the doorway, her necklace of bells sounding at the quick movement of her slender body. "Is that your favorite tonic? My grandma was a believer in chamomile."

"It doesn't matter what it is as long as it works." Trish stretched for the teapot on the top shelf, her red shirt tightening over full breasts.

They sat at the short, round coffee table in the living room on two of the six fat cushions tucked around it on the floor. Trish poured the steaming tea, then offered the plate of oatmeal cookies she'd made the day before. She bit into one, savoring its sweet crunchiness. Retrieving the old book she'd found in a used bookstore, Trish showed Becca the pictures of ancient household tools. They laughed at the tortured ingenuity of some.

Becca finished her tea. She did feel better, but not just because of the hyssop, she thought. To her, Trish's cabin was like a good painting, balanced and constant. Then she recalled the uneasiness her sketch had given her. "I want to show you what I drew," she said suddenly.

Sliding her sketch pad across the table toward her, Becca murmured, "I drew what I saw."

Trish looked at herself in the middle of massed flowers as if among friends, the lines of the sketch rooting her to the earth itself. The dreamy pleasure on her face caught her by surprise. In a few strokes Becca had rendered the marrow of her on paper.

Her smile held shyness. "I think it's wonderful."

Becca's dark eyes registered satisfaction.

"But what's the scratchy thing here in the corner?" Trish's finger touched the snarl of lines.

Becca shook her head. "I don't know. Here I was drawin' you a mile a minute, and I started thinkin' about gold, and then gold light bouncing off jewels." She trailed off uncertainly, then looked up from the sketch. "What I drew was this hair, supposed to be blond, and it had a scary feel to it." She shrugged uncomfortably. "I guess you'd better watch out for folks with blond hair. I don't know."

Forty miles away in Denver the strains of Mozart were nearly swallowed in the cavernous dining room of the Caley mansion, issuing from speakers hidden behind ornate doors. Almost every visible surface was wood—the polished mahogany of the long table, the oak tongue-in-groove flooring, the rosewood paneling of the walls. Red velvet draperies at the windows could not soften the overpowering sense that a whole forest had been sacrificed to create the room.

Ceci Caley sat like royalty at the head of the gargantuan table. Now ninety-one, she had shrunk into a gnome of a woman, her narrow shoulders rounded, silver hair sparse on the small head peering at the world over Stanton's gold chain and watch that she wore like an amulet.

Very little interested Ceci these days. After decades as a leader of Denver society, she'd known the respect of every new generation of the old families take its rightful place. But the endless games of ambition and power no longer fascinated her. Only the old animosities piqued her attention now, only the old rivalries stirred her to action. The adamant hatred of Lillian Lowell and the disapproval of Enos Murdoch, now a University of Colorado regent, were the spice in what had become a quiet life.

The object of Ceci's doting gaze was her grandson. *He is so very handsome,* she thought with the mix of complacency and wonder that was her first reaction to the boy whenever she saw him. His mother, Jacqueline, had never been more than passable in looks and his father had resembled a shop-window mannequin—a discount shop at that. But Caley, she exulted, ah, he was *magnifique.*

Ceci marveled silently that the partnership struck between her and Stanton Caley had produced such a creature. Caley even had a few features in common with his grandfather: the pale, almost transparent eyes and the ears that lay so flat to his skull, their lobes nearly nonexistent. But Caley also had a strength in his face that pleased her, a strong jaw, well-formed nose, and thick sandy eyebrows. Moreover, he had abundant blond hair, its gold strands gleaming in the light from the chandelier above those strangely penetrating eyes.

"Caley," Ceci snapped suddenly, her own eyes narrowing, looking beyond the light blue oxford shirt and the navy-and-red tie he wore. "Your hair is disgracefully long."

The smile on Caley Sutherland's chiseled lips was knowing. "Grandmère," he returned, a note of reproach in his low voice, "didn't any of those early Denver tycoons of yours wear their hair down on their neck a bit?"

Ceci blinked, heart still catching at the memory of Berkeley Glendower as she'd seen him in Telluride more than sixty years before. His dark hair had extended over his collar, had brushed against his dark brows above brown, heavily fringed eyes. Her mind lingered over the sudden, clear image of him, a wave of reminiscence hovering at its edge.

"Besides," Caley continued reasonably, "don't you want me to be in fashion? You wouldn't want anybody on campus to think I'm in the military, would you? Only the ROTC guys wear short hair."

Ceci's disconcerting recollection vanished in laughter along with her frown, and she summoned Caley to her with an imperious motion of one twisted hand. "You graceless boy," she gasped after regaining her breath. "You think you can do anything because I love you, *hein*? Well, you are probably right."

Caley approached her along the polished length of the table, his face impassive. Love, he thought coldly. What the old witch loved was to see herself as the indulgent grandmother. She loved to tease him and pet him with those gnarled, arthritic paws, but then it was, *Go away, Caley, go make something of your life. Your grandfather handed along a fortune, Caley, and much of it has kept you while you've grown up. See what you can do to make it bigger.*

He gently took Ceci's proffered hand in his own, bending over it, barely brushing her swollen knuckles with his lips. "Surely not graceless?" he murmured, timing his laughing glance upward into her eyes. As he had hoped, Ceci melted, her smile quivering around the edges.

As he lifted his head her mouth was working, and Caley knew it was time to speak. "Grandmère." He drew out the word with affection. "I have a small problem." He lifted one brow in the way he knew she loved, with the quizzical, flirting glance that made her curlicue nostrils flare a little. "I hate to ask again, but could you advance me something on next quarter's allowance?"

A lifetime of dealing with men had taught Ceci a great deal about them. Starting with her experience as Colette in Miss Freda's Telluride house, she'd learned that one got what one paid for. Her grandson could be charming and deferential, but for that he expected her to plump his pockets. Even though she knew this quite well, it never failed to irritate her.

She pulled her hand away from him, and her mouth firmed. "How much do you want?"

Caley paused, on guard at the astringent note in her voice. "How about a hundred?"

Ceci's eyes snapped. "A hundred, is it? A bit much for a kiss on the fingers, but then you do count your favors high, *n'est-ce pas?*" A small measure of satisfaction came with the color that rose in Caley's cheeks. "I'm afraid you'll have to do with fifty." She ignored his tightened lips and the angry flash in his eyes as she retrieved the small bag hanging over the back of her chair. Like the keys of a chatelaine Ceci's beaded evening bag was always with her, in it her cigarettes and a lighter, as well as a thick roll of bills. She peeled off two twenties and a ten, throwing them on the table, a twist to her lips. "See if you can avoid going through it all at once."

Caley bent at the waist in a slight bow that mocked them both, his fingers pulling the bills toward himself. "Thanks so much, Grandmère," he said colorlessly. "Your generosity is overwhelming."

"As is your devotion," she said in the same tone. For a moment the two looked at each other with identical expressions that combined distrust and a comfort born of met expectations. Then Caley was moving back toward the huge double doors to the room.

"I'll come visit you again soon, Grandmère," he threw over his shoulder.

"I have no doubt of that," she returned.

CHAPTER 13

Promise scented the morning air as Trish awoke. Snuggling in the feather bed that nearly filled her small bedroom, she stretched luxuriously under the lightweight quilt Lucy MacAllister had made. The dark silk of her hair trailed over her arms as she flexed them, fanning across the pink T-shirt she used as a nightgown. Her full lips curved in a smile of pure freedom.

It was here, the vacation she'd promised herself for the last two years of college. The work for her degree in history was behind her. She knew she would find a job teaching, and she would do her best at it. But now she had to satisfy her yearning for an interval, a "King's X," before beginning the next stage of the game. She needed to bridge the different parts of her life, to hide between milestones. This summer would be her magic time, when anything could happen.

A dog barked nearby, and Trish glanced out the window, noting the angle of the light. Casting aside the soft cotton cover, she scrambled into jeans and a yellow shirt. Gerald MacAllister had given her the bees to set up her own hive, and early morning was the best time to visit them. Afterward she would begin her first project of the summer. In the

old household-hint book she'd shown Becca Blue was a recipe for sachet, and she knew where to look for the lilac blossoms to make it.
Come winter, she mused, her dresser drawers would be scented with the
memory of this spring.

Trish ambled through the garden that was just awakening to the
mountain growing season, then crested the hill above her cabin. The
sun had loosed the nose-tickling aroma of butter-and-egg blossoms, and
already bees were at work in search of pollen. The barking sounded
again, but closer.

She was nearly at the bottom of the slope when a bright orange
disk floated groundward. A woofing, reddish-brown streak crashed
through the brush and raced toward the Frisbee, now drifting gently to
rest in front of the wooden box housing Trish's beehive.

Tranquillity vanished in an instant. The dog, an Irish setter with a
red kerchief around her neck, galloped across the clearing, intent on
retrieving the toy. Trish saw that it was Tulip, the dog at the Spring
Gulch commune. Her tail thumped against the hive as she scratched at
the Frisbee to flip it up so she could take hold of it with her teeth.

"Get away from there," Trish shouted to her in warning as she ran
toward the hive. "Go on!" She heard an ear-splitting whistle close behind her. The bees inside the hive were swarming out to see what was
threatening them. The dog howled as one defender found its mark.

"Tulip!" A man hurtled by her.

Madness reigned in a flurry of fur and bees, the two people collid-
ing as they struggled to grasp the kerchief collar of the setter, now
twisting in a frenzy.

Trish felt a stab of heat on the back of her neck, then on one hand.
The dog howled again. "Grab hold of her," she urged the man beside
her. "There's a pond over the rise." She pointed up the south slope.

Tanned fingers snared the dog's kerchief and pulled. Trish's wrist
was clamped in a tight hold and she, too, was tugged behind jeans and a
gray shirt up the rise, away from the hive. When she tripped, nearly
falling to her knees, a strong arm swept her up and carried her along.

"Hey!" Trish was jarred by his stride, but before she could try to
get loose, she felt his arm muscles tense. He took three more long,
running steps, then jumped. She, the man, and the dog all catapulted
into the pond.

Formed by the spring runoff from high-country snowfall that had
collected in the ravine, the pond was cold. Trish gasped as it splashed
around her. She struggled to her feet, but they slid out from under her
on the slick bottom. She sat down fast, water surging to her chin.

Delighted at this game, the dog barked joyously and bounded toward her, flinging drops everywhere.

"Hold it, hound." The man had plunged forward, grabbing Tulip's makeshift collar. "Quick," he advised Trish, humor edging his voice, "before she washes you under."

Trish steadied herself against the mudbank at her back and stood up. She pushed flowing hair back from her face to look at her companion. Water dripped from his shaggy blond hair over high cheekbones, firm jaw, straight nose, down to a stubborn chin. His soaked gray shirt was open at the throat and hung on well-knit shoulders.

Tulip wriggled excitedly, roiling the pond's muddy green surface, pulling out of his hold. Then she surged toward him, her long pink tongue lapping at his face. He jerked backward, grabbing her forelegs, and braced her against him. "Enough, you silly dog." He glanced back at Trish, laughter in his green crystal eyes. "I don't know about you, but she's having a great time."

Trish grinned. "It beats getting stung by bees." Even as she said it she saw red bumps swelling on his neck and forearms. She scooped clay from the bank behind her and started toward him to apply it to the stings as a poultice.

He was still tussling with the dog. "It's all your fault, isn't it, Tulip?" He let her drop back into the water. When Trish dabbed the cold silt onto his arm, he started, and then the light of adventure dawned in his eyes. "Ah, want a little mud fight action, do you?" Quicksilver fast he dredged up a fistful from the bottom.

Bee stings. That was what Trish had started to say when a blob of pine-scented mud landed on her cheek. Without even thinking she flung back what was in her hand, spinning to grab more when it slapped against his neck. War raged as Tulip barked ecstatically, plunging back and forth through the water between the two of them.

"Truce . . . truce!" Breathless, he lifted one dripping hand.

Her stomach sore from laughing, Trish let her ammunition slide between her fingers into the water. "You didn't say 'uncle.' "

"Okay, okay. Uncle." He waded toward her. "You're quite a warrior." His eyes danced with fun, seeming even greener in contrast with the mud on his face. Water trickled from his hair, creating small tributaries of bare skin down his smudged cheeks.

"Medic, not warrior," she returned. "This was supposed to be a healing experience. You know," she added pointedly, finger lightly tapping the one red bump on his arm not covered with dark clay, "for the bee stings."

"Oh," he said in elaborate surprise. "Why didn't you say so?" He shifted closer, water eddying around his waist. "I think you missed some." Shucking off the dripping shirt, he bared a muscular chest. Half a dozen bee stings dotted the tanned skin. "Maybe it was your technique?"

"Couldn't be." Trish was already patting mud on the bumps. "I studied at the best schools."

"I think I have some more." His hands went to the waistband of his jeans.

Her gaze flew to his face. A wide grin flashed white amid dirt. "Nope," she said. "You'll have to take care of those while I clean up."

"Here, let me. I'm an expert with mud." Cupping his hands, he carried water to each of her cheeks, rinsing them off. His long fingers lingered over her skin. "What's your name, Doc?" he asked softly.

"Trish Gregory." The scent of pine was on his hands. "You a doctor too?" she teased. "By the way, what's *your* name?"

"Chris Roth. I'm a sculptor. Knee deep in mud most of the time." His fingertips smoothed her forehead, then he tilted her chin up so he could look at her full-face. "What d'you say we continue this consultation on dry land? Now that I've had time to think about it, I'm freezing."

Trish reached up easily to wipe a smear from his chin. "But oh, so clean."

Back at the cabin they took turns in the shower. When Chris came into the small living room, he was wearing a worn white dress shirt that Trish had appropriated from her father for a work smock. His tattered jeans had progressed to mere dampness. Rubbing at his drying, caramel-colored hair with a towel, he surveyed his surroundings.

With pleasure he recognized the care that had gone into the comfortable room. His fingers savored the cool grain of the leather sofa, then brushed across the woolly crocheted afghan folded over the back. As he studied the sketch of Bridey's Mountain, he absentmindedly stroked the edge of its plain frame. His nose twitched appreciatively at the delicate scent of herbs on the air. Walking to the kitchen, he let his fingertips skim the gloss of the smooth pine wall.

Trish met him at the door. "You ready for some hot tea?" Faded jeans encased her slim legs and the rust-colored shirt she wore set off her golden-brown eyes. She'd pulled her dark hair back with a tan ribbon, exposing her flawless complexion.

He knew at once that smooth skin wouldn't really be defined for him until he'd memorized the texture of her face. "Tea would be fine."

They talked as Trish prepared it. Chris had been wandering across the country since the death of his widowed father, and was visiting his friend Jake Shimberg at the Spring Gulch commune. "I've got a carpentry job in Boulder," he said. "Until I earn enough to leave." He paused, staring out the window at the garden behind the cabin.

Trish glanced up from the teapot, seeing how he cradled the abandoned robin's nest she'd found the summer before. Later, as they shared fragrant cinnamon tea, he amused her with details about some of the places he'd seen. *He's so eager to touch what attracts him,* she thought. It almost seemed as if he wanted to settle in among such things.

As Chris followed a frisky Tulip back to Spring Gulch, he relived the moments in the pond when his hands had smoothed the mud from Trish's face. Her skin had been wet, its softness cool. He envisioned pink, veined marble. No, he thought, that was too hard, and couldn't begin to equal the warmth and resilience he'd felt. Perhaps the glossy elasticity of rising bread brushed with butter. All the way to the commune he tried to think of a texture even close to the feel of her skin.

Drawn together by a tantalizing sense of awareness, they saw one another daily, rambling with Tulip through the hills. Their conversations ranged as widely, lighthearted exchanges mixed with confided aims and fears. All the while they spoke on yet another level, hand touching hand, eyes revealing secrets, bodies attuning to each other.

The day they hiked to Sugar Loaf Mountain to pick lilac blossoms for Trish's sachet dawned sunny and calm. The quiet isolated them, only the birds and chipmunks sharing the hillsides. The mountain summer had outlined the trees and thickets with buds and the sun warmed the air. They stopped at Horsfal Hill for coffee and the cinnamon rolls Trish had baked the day before.

Christopher spread a thin blanket from his day pack in a clearing ringed with pines. They talked idly as they ate, then lay back to bask in the sunshine. "I can't think of any spot I'd rather be." He turned his head to look at her, eyes the shade of new pine growth.

"I can." Trish grinned at the surprise that flashed in his face. "Only in the right company, of course." Her hand found his. "It's called Bridey's Mountain."

His fingers tightened around hers. "Tell me."

Trish described the mountain whose face always gazed at the sky, and recounted the history of Morna, Berkeley, and Bridey in Telluride. A gentle breeze set the treetops to swaying, and the enchanted circle enclosed them with the beauty of the day as well as the events of the past. "They never did learn what happened to Morna," Trish concluded. "Mom has always held on to the mountain, no matter what, and someday she'll pass it along to me for my children."

She glanced at Chris, a smile in place against the old sadness the tale roused. His lips curved in response, but he saw the shadow. Brushing her eyelids shut, he placed a careful kiss on each. "It won't happen that way with us," he whispered.

Trish was caught in the multitude of crystals forming the green of his eyes. He bent to kiss her, simply, generously, flavoring her mouth with cinnamon. When he lifted his head, it was to reveal the promise in his face.

Then his lips were shifting, the tip of his tongue tracing her mouth, wandering down the line of her neck. "You're such a creative person," he murmured, cherishing the hollow at the base of her throat. "Have you ever sculpted?"

Trish moved her head side to side in a slow negative, breath catching at the journey his hand had begun. "Maybe you could give me lessons."

His fingers pulled delicately at the buttons of her shirt, releasing the blue cotton that covered the cream silk of her skin. "Yes," he agreed on a long breath, heating the valley between her breasts. "I'm a good teacher." He lingered over her softness.

She was the clay, he the artist. Patient hands stroked and shaped hot visions, forging beauty from beauty. Eager to learn, Trish mimicked his technique until her own inventive forces could take hold. When they did, she rediscovered that creativity amply rewards the creator.

His skin was slick beneath her skimming fingertips, his muscles a marvel of design. Careful in her craft, Trish returned to the challenge of his chest, the curve of his buttocks. Her clever hands, her caressing lips, learned the textures of his hair, the hidden pulse points of release, the rhythms of inspiration. She found her design in the sizzling energy of his crystal gaze.

CHAPTER 14

As the days simmered to midsummer, Becca Blue uneasily observed the intimacy growing between Chris and Trish. She'd liked Chris from the first, his quirky sense of humor, his enthusiasm and impulsive generosity. He'd promptly dubbed her "Big Mama" and ate as much of her corn bread as he could get his hands on. Trish she simply loved as a treasured part of home.

Still, whenever she saw them together she felt an edge of anxiety. And twice more her hand had drawn unplanned details into her sketches, as it had that day with Trish. No golden hair or images of jewels, as she'd done the first time. Now it was more like a chain of fragmentary links, leading to nothing and nowhere. The second time she thought she was sketching apple blossoms, but looking at the scribbles in the corner of her drawing of a weathered pine tree, she couldn't be sure. Before long her disquiet had spread to Spring Gulch itself. But for that she held Caley Sutherland accountable.

He'd been a frequent visitor over the last few weeks. In fact, Caley's black Corvette had snarled up the lane only an hour before. Tympany had appeared before Caley could even open the car door.

Working in the garden near the house, Becca noted Tympany's furtive relief as Caley handed him a package. More grass, she thought, since it had been brought every time so far. She knew the two were up to something, and she wasn't sure she wanted to know what it was. Like the thunderheads that massed each afternoon over the western mountains, the sense of threat was deepening. What frightened her was the helplessness she felt with it.

Becca tore leaf lettuce flounces from a straight row, a breeze blowing the skirt of her gauzy yellow dress against her legs. She was at a time in her life when she had something to lose. The tiny community at Spring Gulch was her family, its hodgepodge structure her home. The old cabin built of rounded river stones with its small wood geodesic dome was the birthplace of her child.

The door to the dome opened and Caley Sutherland stepped into the heat. His chinos were wrinkled, and he'd unbuttoned his white shirt. The air ruffled his hair, sunshine turning it to spun gold. Becca stiffened, fighting back a wave of hostility as strong as any emotion she'd ever known.

"Hey, Becca, looks like you're working hard." Caley put a cigarette to his mouth, cupping his hands to shield the flame of his lighter. His pale, expressionless eyes regarded her unwaveringly.

Becca repressed a shiver. Oh, but he made her nervous, this pretty white boy, she thought, unconsciously assuming the impassive face with which she'd survived her early years. "Guess so."

Caley cursed under his breath. Becca Blue had been a problem from the first time he'd come to Spring Gulch. And as things stood now, the commune was the linchpin to the success that would change everything for him.

Following the humiliation of Ceci's treatment a few weeks before, Caley had undergone a transformation. Barely able to control himself that day until the massive front door of the Caley mansion had swung shut behind him, he had flung himself into his car. His fist had tightened fiercely on the money his grandmother had given him so grudgingly, and then he'd pitched it onto the floor. "Damn her to hell!" he gritted, heat coursing through his veins. "I hate that old bitch . . . *hate* her!"

His temper was still bubbling when he arrived at the party at the Spring Gulch commune that night. One of his women was invited and she'd asked him along, promising good food and better drugs. By the time the party was over, Caley had seen how to pick up the gauntlet thrown down by Ceci as surely as he'd retrieved the crumpled money from the floor of his car.

It was during an overheard argument about the unreliability of a drug source that Caley's conversion to what he considered capitalism occurred. The Boulder area, especially the University of Colorado campus, had a large market for illegal substances and few dependable suppliers. Suddenly he grasped that the entrepreneurs of the day were the people who could guarantee regular delivery to their patrons. Ceci wanted him to fulfill his destiny as the heir to Stanton Caley's millions, to take risks to augment the family fortune. He would do both by becoming a dealer. It was a good way to make big money fast, he thought, and a damn sight *better* way than digging for gold and silver like the bygone bastards who'd made their piles in the good old days.

Caley discovered he had a talent for the work, easily selling his first consignment of marijuana and speed. He'd found his sources surprisingly close to Denver. But he had to find a place outside Boulder to store the shipments. Given the growing vigilance of the authorities, keeping anything in the town itself was asking for trouble. To transport his wares from Denver would be courting disaster.

Then Caley had remembered Tympany Weiss. Becca's lover was a small-time user because he couldn't afford to be anything more. For a minor amount he would allow drugs to be stored near Spring Gulch and Caley could move them out slowly without the others who lived there ever knowing.

The only snag in the scheme had been the savvy, suspicious woman watching him with almond-shaped eyes. Caley could feel her distrust. Tympany wasn't strong enough to go up against Becca and win, and Caley even wondered if he was smart enough to keep his mouth shut.

Caley threw a glance of dislike at Becca Blue, taking a final drag on his cigarette. He'd been contacted to arrange a large shipment for delivery at the end of the summer and it would take time and money to set things up. Either he left the situation as it was or he found a new hiding place.

Becca ignored him, continuing down the row of lettuce. Caley sourly recalled the animated expression she'd worn two days before, her laughter as she talked with the woman Chris Roth had brought to dinner.

Caley's pale eyes muddied sullenly. Trish Gregory had a lush promise to her that had captured him instantly. Her long dark hair, her passionate mouth, made him tighten with greed. When she took his outstretched hand at their introduction, her skin was soft, her scent enticing.

He'd shifted his body to block Christopher's gaze, tightening his hold on her fingers. "What're you doing later tonight?" he murmured, flashing what had always been his fail-safe smile.

Trish had pulled away, eyes darkening. At first he'd thought her careful, playing both ends against the middle with her boyfriend around. But as the evening progressed, and she avoided him, Caley simmered. Women had always paid attention to him, had constantly sought his notice. Here was a little hippie princess running hot and cold, figuring he'd go along with it.

Never able to stomach discomfort for long, Caley pitched his cigarette butt to the ground. He would deliver the big shipment coming in and he would be very well paid. Miss Gregory would make up her mind when he started spending some of that money. He relished a surge of pleasure at the idea of taking her on.

Caley's Corvette peeled out of Spring Gulch at a wicked pace. As he veered around the hairpin curves of Sunshine Canyon, he made his decision. The setup at the commune was too good, and it was late in the game to start looking for another one. Becca Blue could be dealt with and he was the man to do it.

For Caley, being thwarted provoked a craving along his nerve endings. He wanted to show them, he *would* show them all. Someday his grandmother would come to *him* for money and he would make her beg for it. Trish Gregory would beg, too, but not for money.

The roiling dust kicked up by the wheels of his car was snatched by the breeze as he raced down the mountain.

CHAPTER 15

Autumn was nearing the high country, drying the wild grasses, flecking the aspen leaves with yellow. Overlooking the Boulder Valley from Big Horn Mountain above Gold Hill, Trish could almost detect the ripe scents of crops in the air. But for her, spring had come again. She was pregnant with Chris's baby, and the world promised to begin anew.

When she thought back to just a few months before to the unfocused yearning she'd felt, Trish glowed at the rightness of all that had happened. She'd found the freedom she'd hungered for with Chris. He'd begun to sculpt her, saying he was incorporating her into his life through his fingertips. They'd begun to talk about marriage, and now that she was sure she was pregnant, that would include their child. The summer had been the magic time she needed, moments as vivid as shining beads threaded together in her memory. She would add one more to the string tonight when she gave Chris her news. And tomorrow she could tell her parents.

She would see them when she took Bridey's ring back to her. At her mother's request Trish had stopped off at the jewelry store in Boulder to pick it up. The prongs that held the diamond and rubies had to be tightened. Bridey had laughed a little over her reluctance to remove the ring. "I haven't taken it off since your father put it on my finger twenty-six years ago."

At the jeweler's Trish had held the circlet with its flashing stones, feeling as always the love passed along from Berkeley and Morna, from Bridey and Devin. Now there would be another to inherit that love in the future.

Trish noticed the fading light and slid off the rock to go back to the cabin before dark.

When she opened the door, the warmth of the cabin embraced her. Then the sound of a triumphant voice from across the room chilled the air.

"I've been waiting for you." Caley Sutherland slouched on the sofa, oddly formal in dark slacks, white shirt, and a tweed sports coat.

"How did you get in here?" Her eyes sought the door to the kitchen. "Where's Chris?"

"Up at Spring Gulch." Caley's lips smiled, but something else was in his eyes. "He'll be right back."

Reassured at the implication that Chris was gone only temporarily, Trish came farther into the room, pulling off her sweater. When she felt Caley's glance on her arms, on the peach jersey skimming her breasts, she cupped her elbows. "What do you want, Caley? I mean—"

"I want us to have a good time." Caley was jazzed, flowing with energy. That afternoon he'd received the shipment of acid and speed that would set him up for the big time. He exulted that he was indeed a businessman.

Driving up the canyon, Caley had pounded a victorious tattoo on the steering wheel of his Corvette. In his mind was the image of his grandmother, for once viewing him with admiration. In his jacket pocket were tabs of blotter acid. Tonight he would take a trip fueled with his success. But first he would seize the prize he'd promised himself since Trish Gregory's rejection.

It had been simple to set things up. Tympany had asked Chris Roth to the commune, where he'd slipped him a tab of acid. Chris was flying high, giving Caley the chance to visit Trish's cabin. Picking the lock had presented no challenge; he'd been waiting for over an hour, gaze steady on the uncompleted bust of her on the coffee table.

Now that Trish was in the room with him, Caley savored the itch she constantly aroused. Rather than the yes-I-will blondes he usually favored, she was dark haired. With those challenging eyes, he knew at first she'd say no-I-won't. But he would change her mind.

Uncomfortably aware of the way Caley's gaze ranged over her body, Trish wished that Chris would return. A cold breath of warning raced along her nerve endings. "Maybe you'd better come back later."

"I don't think so." He got to his feet, pulled down the cuffs of his shirt.

The confident smirk on his face annoyed Trish. "I'd rather you did." Her voice tensed. "I want you to leave."

When he came toward her, Trish instantly saw the coiled menace in him. Before she could move away, he grasped her arm. Then his fingers curled, squeezing her flesh.

"We've never had the chance to talk just by ourselves. I've got what Chris doesn't—money." When she shook off his hand, his eyes chilled, yet inside he felt a surge of excitement. "You might like me if you got to know me."

"Not a chance." She jerked out of his grasp, heart pounding. He frightened her, but she knew it would be fatal to show it. "I've seen the wrapping—I'm not interested in the package."

The judgment in her voice evoked his grandmother; color mottled Caley's cheeks. He seized her hand, jerked her to his body. "You're *gonna* see the package."

His breath was hot on her face. Trish pulled away and aimed her other fist at his Adam's apple, but he caught it, twisting her wrist. "Let go!"

Caley's blood hammered at the pain in her voice, at the command in her eyes. "Trish," he muttered thickly. Forcing her closer, he pushed his mouth against hers with bruising strength.

Trish bit his lip hard. When Caley dropped her arm with a howl of pain, she shoved past him, lunging for the door.

Before she could get the door open, Caley caught her hair, whipped her around. "I'll make you pay," he panted, bottom lip bloody. He swung his outflung arm, striking her cheek openhanded, sending her flying toward the desk.

Trish slammed against the rolltop. Caley hurled himself at her, seizing her by the waist. She strained to reach the shadowbox on the wall, fingers grazing the quartz rock, clinging to the railroad spike. At the cold feel of metal she went slack, letting Caley swing her around, the spike clenched in her hand. He bore her down to the couch, on top of her, his clutching hands forcing her to her back. One leg hit Chris's unfinished sculpture of her, sending it crashing to the floor.

He loomed over her, spitting venom. "Can't beat me, bitch." He leaned his whole weight on her, trapping her arms at her sides. Rubbing against her, shoving himself between her legs, he snarled, "You by-God won't forget me."

Trish fought to release her arms, shuddering at the thrust of his wet mouth. She couldn't breathe, he was too heavy. On a surge of panic she wrenched one arm free but lost hold of the spike. He pressed her down and she felt its rough edge under her hipbone. She went limp.

Scenting victory, Caley dragged his hands to her breasts, then to the neck of her jersey. He ripped it down the middle.

Trish's fingers curled around the spike. She brought it up fast, smashed it against his head. Caley's stunned eyes jerked to her face, then he slumped on top of her.

Stomach heaving, lungs straining for breath, she pushed at him frantically, finally twisting free. She staggered to her feet. A twitch of Caley's muscles sent her running for the door.

At Spring Gulch, Becca Blue pushed herself up from the floor and looked down at Christopher Roth lying on the mattress at her feet. He was at last breathing evenly, released from the nightmare visions that had plagued him for the last few hours. His hair was disheveled, his clothing rumpled, his face bore an expression of strain even in sleep.

Becca put a hand to her forehead, shivering with fatigue. Stains spread down the front of her yellow caftan and the cornrows of her hair were damp with sweat. She headed toward the kitchen for some water, pausing beside the pallet where Tympany tossed and muttered.

Staring down at him, Becca was sick with rage at what he'd done. Tympany had babbled Caley's plan to her while riding his own acid wave, caught on the rusty teeth of his conscience. He'd only just finished telling her when Chris's shout had come from the other room.

Unused to psychedelics, Chris had fought the waking dreams, frenzied at his loss of control. Becca had worked for hours to soothe him, sending everyone else away to keep things quiet, patiently guiding him back from the drug-induced landscapes in his mind.

Now, staring at Tympany's thin, troubled face, Becca weighed her discovery of a few days before. Tympany had unknowingly led her to what he'd shared with Caley, the boarded-up mine shaft in the gully west of the house.

She'd followed him through the piñon pines past the dry spring bed giving the area its name. He'd pulled several boards aside and crawled into the tunnel, returning a short time later. When Tympany went back toward the house, she'd retraced his path, finding the boxes of marijuana, plastic bags of pills, tabs of acid, covered with a tarp.

Tympany had blown it and she wouldn't jeopardize Starshine or the commune to protect him. Something had to be done to stop Caley, and Becca knew the time was now. Ignoring the tears trailing down her cheeks, she dialed the phone number she'd looked up earlier. The police had never done much for her, but they could stake out the Spring Gulch mine and catch Caley Sutherland in the middle of his stash.

When the call had been made, Becca turned to see the crystal bead curtain at the doorway swaying. A chalky face appeared behind the shifting strands.

Becca froze, then moved fast. "Trish! What happened?" She pushed through the curtain to her side. Her gaze skimmed over the swollen cheek and panicked eyes, fell to the torn shirt. She put her arm around Trish's quaking shoulders, shocked at the chill she felt through the cloth.

Safety had the power to do what terror could not, loosen Trish's control. Bolting from the cabin, she'd stumbled to the car, faltering when she remembered that the keys were still inside. As if in a nightmare she'd fled to the commune. Now in the sudden warmth the chill inside her intensified. The bruises on her legs throbbed, her cheek stung from Caley's blow. "Have you seen Chris?" she whispered.

"In here, honey." Becca Blue guided her into the bedroom, pushing past the paisley fabric serving as a door. Chris lay face down on a mattress on the floor.

Trish started forward, but Becca put out a restraining hand. "Wait a minute. He was slipped some acid, not knowin', and it's been bad for him."

"What?" Trish knelt shakily, hand going to Chris's back. "Is he all right?"

"Trish?" Christopher turned, wounded eyes slowly focusing. Trish lay down beside him and took him in her arms.

Becca swallowed painfully at the way they held each other, rubbing away tears with the back of her hand.

Chris shifted restlessly as he registered the bruises on Trish's face. "Help me up." Command was in his voice despite its weakness. "Who hurt you?" he asked Trish when they'd got him to his feet.

She started to speak, then shook her head. He was swaying, striving to maintain his balance, and the green of his eyes had nearly disappeared. She knew he had the courage to take on anything, but he was still under the effects of the drug.

Chris laid one trembling hand on her cheek, but his jaw squared with anger, his mouth grim. "I'm not so spaced out that I can't tell somebody's hit you. Tell me who it was."

"Caley," she whispered. "He came to the cabin."

Chris's gaze shifted to Becca at the sound of her quick breath. Her eyes hard, she told him the rest. "He got Tympany to put acid in your drink to get you out of the way. He's been real busy."

A dog started barking and before any of them could move, they heard steps in the next room. "Quiet, Tulip! Hey, Becca." Jake Shimberg pushed the paisley curtain aside. His long brown braids swung gently. "Oh, hi, you guys." He frowned at their appearance but said, "Caley Sutherland's coming up the lane, mad as fire, growling for Tympany. What's going on?"

Chris's crystal eyes went flat. "I'm going to kill the son of a bitch." He brushed past Trish and then he was out the door, staggering but moving fast. Jake threw a look of consternation toward Becca and followed him.

Trish whirled toward Becca, but before she could say anything the other woman's face creased in dismay. "My God, what did I do?"

"What?" Trish demanded anxiously. The bruise stood out on her ivory face like a brand. "What do you mean?"

"I turned him in," Becca said in a trembling voice. "I called the cops and told them where Caley hides his drugs." She drew one shaking hand across her forehead. "Chris is still high on acid, and him and Jake are gonna walk right into the middle of a bust."

CHAPTER 16

The news of Caley Sutherland's arrest spread rapidly, appearing the next day on the front pages of both Denver newspapers. He, along with Chris Roth and Jake Shimberg, had been picked up by the police staking out the old Spring Gulch mine. Ceci had done everything she could to suppress the story, but her influence with the press had faded since her wartime activities and neither daily paper's society page editor had helped her.

Nor could she even obtain bail for Caley. The Boulder authorities had found the drug cache the biggest they'd ever encountered, and the district attorney was proceeding very slowly.

It was two days before Caley was released from the county jail. As he left the building accompanied by his grandmother's lawyer, he reflected bitterly that Ceci had let him rot without a word, probably to teach him a lesson. Well, he'd learned it. His wrinkled wool jacket was open over a shirt that hadn't been clean for several days. Blond stubble blurred the handsome lines of his face. He knew for certain now that the old woman would throw him to the wolves.

Caley's long gait checked when he saw Trish Gregory approaching the jail. She didn't see him as she hurried toward the door. A gust of wind blew her raincoat open as she passed, and he glimpsed her slightly rounded belly. She was pregnant, he knew it. She'd been anxious enough to hop into bed with somebody else, he realized in dawning rage, but couldn't be bothered with him.

Caley had brooded over where things had gone wrong. He always came back to Trish. That night in her cabin she'd hurt him, made him look like a fool. And he knew she had to be the one who'd told the police about him. When he was goaded by how close he'd come to success, he yearned to get even with her.

Walking faster, he reached the family limousine and flung himself into it. There was nothing for him here now. Nothing but jail and snubs from everyone he knew. He took one long look back where Trish had been and cursed the day he'd ever heard of her.

Caley badly wanted a cigarette. Rifling through the manila envelope holding the possessions the jail clerk had returned to him, he felt something unfamiliar and pulled it out. It was a ring, a diamond surrounded by rubies. He'd taken it from Trish's cabin after he'd come to, trashing the room before discovering that she'd gone.

Holding the ring up to the light, Caley studied its rose design, wondering how much it would bring. He'd gotten something out of that night, he thought sourly, but it wasn't enough. He shoved the ring into his jacket pocket. Not enough at all.

Trish drove Chris back to Gold Hill, talking all the way to make up for his silence. "They won't make you and Jake go to trial," she said again. "Once Becca explains what happened, all the charges will be dropped."

Chris nodded absently, his gaze fixed on Boulder Creek as her Volkswagen chugged up the canyon.

"We'll all help pay your legal expenses." Trish glanced again at his profile, then back at the road. "Everybody will chip in." She couldn't understand why he was so quiet. "You know you have friends in Gold Hill."

"Dammit, Trish." Chris stopped, one clenched fist on his thigh. He hit his leg once, then again. "I can pay the legal expenses."

Trish saw a wide spot in the shoulder of the road and pulled over. "Okay," she said firmly. "I want you to tell me what's wrong."

She waited without speaking. When Christopher turned toward her, her breath caught at the misery darkening his crystal green eyes. "I let you down," he said in a low voice. "That night Caley hurt you and I wasn't able to help you."

"Are you crazy?" Fire flashed gold in Trish's eyes. "You were drugged and you ran out after him anyway. He could've killed you!"

Chris shook his head. Trish had told him about the missing ring and that had added to his sense of unfinished business. He wanted to make Caley pay for what he'd done.

Trish reached for his hand, bringing it to her mouth. "I'm just so glad you weren't hurt," she said softly. "Where could I get a father for my child if you weren't around?"

"What?" Chris turned in his seat, reached for her, his face vivid with joy. "You mean it? You're pregnant?"

Trish nodded and his arms tightened around her. In a moment of pure happiness they held on, complete in their gift to one another.

Lillian Wyndham Lowell had read the accounts of Caley Sutherland's arrest with acute pleasure. She could use it as a way to strike at Ceci, further weakening her power over Denver's Old Guard. Its members had no tolerance for the rebelliousness of the young the 1960s had produced. Within moments Lillian was talking to Enos Murdoch, the most conservative of their set.

As a regent of the university Enos was in a position to see that an example be made of Caley Sutherland. That he willingly entertained Lillian's notion of abandoning Caley to such punishment as expulsion and the loss of his student deferment was unusual. The normal response would have been to close ranks with Caley as a member of his own circle, little though he might like the boy. But Enos was genuinely appalled at the drug-possession charges against Caley, seeing them as symptomatic of the unraveling fabric of the nation's social order.

His eyes cold behind the thick lenses of his glasses, Enos carefully calculated the risks he might incur in making such a decision. At ninety-one Ceci would be unlikely to go to the fuss of removing her money from the Murdoch bank. He could safely support Lillian's position, thereby ensuring her continuing goodwill, and indulge his own outrage as well. Enos smiled coolly. He would see to it that no one lifted a finger to save Ceci's grandson from disgrace.

Lillian replaced the receiver fastidiously. She lifted her glass of brandy in a salute and drained it, slamming it onto the table with a thump. "That's one," she said aloud. "Now there's only Bridey Gregory left to deal with. Then," she added vengefully, "I'll be even with them all."

Caley pushed past the housekeeper with an obscenity that had her thin eyebrows climbing for her hairline. "If I know Grandmère," he said carelessly as he strode across the foyer, "she's in the dining room counting her gold pieces."

Half of the heavy double door crashed into the rosewood paneling as it flew open. At the far end of the long dining room table, Ceci glanced up at her grandson. "What a pleasant surprise." Her voice was desert dry.

"Isn't it?" Caley paced down the room.

Ceci watched her grandson's approach impassively. She was flawlessly dressed, as always, Stanton's gold watch and chain gleaming against her black Dior suit. But she was tired, her strength drained with trying to save Caley from the consequences of his own actions. Her attempts to pull the strings of old influence had resulted in checked moves on nearly every front.

It was that afternoon, with her fifth call of the day to Enos Murdoch, that she'd finally seen the pattern in the predicament. "I'm sorry," the harried secretary had said. "Mr. Murdoch is in conference with Mrs. Lowell."

Lillian Wyndham Lowell was behind the continued blocks to Ceci's efforts on Caley's behalf.

Ceci had spent the last hour reflecting upon the long battle between Lillian and herself. The abrupt appearance of her grandson was offensive, too much for her to deal with at the moment. She waved her twisted fingers in his direction. "Go away, Caley. I do not wish to talk with you."

Caley halted at the end of the table. "Tough shit, Grandmère." His very posture was insolent, and the contemptuous expression on his face was deliberate.

"*Sacré Dieu!*" Ceci grasped the edge of the table to push herself to her feet. "Are you drunk? Crazy? You come here and address your grandmother as if she were nothing but a low creature." Summoning all of the power at her command, Ceci leaned toward Caley, eyes fiery. "I have bent all of my energies to saving you, *une grosse bête*. Get out of my sight, Caley. I have no patience with you today."

Caley stood his ground. "Oh, no, Grandmère, not this time. I'm leaving tonight. Canada looks a hell of a lot better to me than Vietnam. If I lose my student deferment, that's where I'll end up. And don't forget the drug charges. You're going to give me the money to get out of the country."

"Canada. Money." Ceci shook her head fiercely. "Always it is money. Why should I finance your spinelessness?"

"Why?" Caley stepped closer, and she could smell his unwashed body. "Because I'm your grandson. I got into this mess trying to be what you wanted—the great businessman, like Grandfather. You owe me, and you'd better pay off."

Ceci stiffened in defiance, ignoring the sharp thrust of pain under her left breast. She'd not ascended to the position of respect and authority she now held by giving way to such demands. She raised one arthritic hand, struggling to snap her fingers. *That* for what I owe you."

Caley stared at her in frustration, and then what remained of his control broke. "Do you know what I've done because of you? And what I have to show for it?" He thrust both hands into the pockets of his slacks, pulling them out, empty white flags of defeat. He repeated the gesture with his jacket and Morna's ring fell onto the table. The rubies and diamond flashed in the light of the chandelier.

Ceci's attention was caught by the brilliance of the stones. Then she recognized it, one hand flying to her throat in horror. *"Where did you get that?"*

"I stole it," he spoke with biting precision. "From a bitch named Trish Gregory."

Gregory. Ceci heard the name and was thrust backward in time. Was this the reprisal for what she'd done to the Gregory women? For the letter she'd written to the laird of Castle Daire revealing Morna's whereabouts?

The memories were overcome by the pain swelling in her chest. Darkness hovered at the edge of her vision, and she leaned heavily on the table. From a distance she heard the voice of her grandson. "The hell with it."

Ceci was aware of movement behind her. Her legs lost their strength and she fell to the floor, her face slapping against smooth oak. She caught fragments of words as Caley rifled through her bag, hanging from the back of her chair.

"How much?" muttered Caley as he tossed the contents of the bag to the floor. A lighter went flying, then an almost empty pack of cigarettes.

Caley found the thick roll of bills at the bottom of the bag, and he counted it feverishly. "A little over a thousand," he said aloud. "Enough to get out of the country."

His grandmother lay gasping at his feet. Perhaps he ought to get one of the servants, he thought. A lifetime of demands weighed in the balance with the measured rewards he had received from her. He'd almost decided to help her when her twisted hand tightened convulsively. As it always had on the reins of his life.

The light reflected off his grandfather's pocket watch from the chain she wore. It was solid gold and valuable. He knelt to pull it from her neck. "The servants will find you soon enough," he told her. He went to the door, opened it, and left.

As the jarring of her grandson's footsteps faded from the planks of the floor, Ceci opened her eyes for the last time. Her gaze roamed the room seeking help or comfort. They found neither.

CHAPTER 17

Chris climbed from the bed, quietly picking up his clothes from the chair. He gazed down at Trish, asleep on the pillow next to his. In the moonlight shining through the window she looked as though she'd been carved, her silky dark hair framing the perfect outline of her face.

Bending toward her, he skimmed her cheek with his fingers, then tiptoed from the room. It was the work of a few minutes to dress and get his backpack from behind the leather sofa. The note he propped on the mantel was brief. *Trish,* he'd written, *I've got a lead about where Caley Sutherland's headed and I'm going after him. I'll do my best to get your mother's ring back. Take care of yourself and the baby. I love you both. Chris.*

As Jake Shimberg drove him to Denver's Stapleton Airport, Chris reflected grimly that what he'd written was true. But what had sent him looking for Caley was the sight of the sculpture he'd been working on, the bust of Trish. He'd picked up the fragments of clay, letting them fall back into the box where she'd put them, choking back rage. Not because of the wasted work, not because of the love he'd put into every curve. All he could think was that it could have been Trish herself, broken beyond repair due to Caley's actions. He couldn't let him get away with it.

It took Chris a month to track Caley down using the contacts he'd made in the antiwar underground during his travels across the country. Through the cobbled streets of Montreal he followed one tip after another, finally finding him in a dilapidated boardinghouse near the river. For five dollars the skinny, suspicious landlady let him look at the register. His heart beat faster when he saw Caley's sprawling signature on the grimy page. Another five dollars bought him the information that Caley was out, but due to return. Chris waited across the street in a deserted doorway.

A seasonless moon rose, throwing harsh light on the cobblestones, paving the way with shadows. Caley walked carefully across the uneven surface toward the rooming house, hands jammed in the pockets of his parka. Inside one was the ring he'd taken from Trish Gregory's cabin. He'd kept it, regarding it as a talisman, fondling it obsessively.

Life on the run hadn't suited him. He discovered that no one in Canada knew who he was, or cared. This Caley had found more frightening than anything that had happened.

When he reached the bottom step of the house, Chris stepped out of the shadows. "Calcy," he yelled. "Caley Sutherland."

Caley spun at the sound of his name, his jaw dropping in astonishment. "Roth? What the hell are you doing here?"

In the moonlight the two men looked eerily alike.

Chris drew closer, hands clenched at his sides. "Did you really think you'd be able to just walk away from what you did?"

"What *I* did?" Caley's short laugh was surprised. "I didn't do anything so bad. It was just business. If it hadn't been for your girlfriend, nothing would've happened."

Chris stepped closer. "I don't mean the drugs, Caley. I'm talking about assault, attempted rape." His eyes shot sparks of contempt. "Or don't you think that's worth consideration? I do. Trish did."

"Trish." Caley spat. "That little bitch—" His head jerked back as Chris hit him in the jaw and he went flying.

They fought hard, trading blows until they both were tired. Chris scraped his knuckles against Caley's teeth as he swung in with his left hand. Caley fell to the ground and Chris scrambled to hold him down, kneeling on his chest, one hand gathering up his collar. "I want the ring," he demanded breathlessly. "I know you've got it."

Caley shook his head back and forth and Chris slapped him open-handed. "Give it to me," he growled. "I'll hit you all night if I have to."

Hatred heating his pale eyes, Caley reached into his pocket, taking out the ring. Chris grabbed it, stuffed it hard into his jeans pocket. "Now, you bastard," he rasped, "I'm going—"

Caley scissored up one leg, catching Chris in the thigh. In a reflex attempt to avoid a hit to the groin, Chris shifted his weight to one side. Caley grabbed him by the lapels and pitched him over his shoulder.

Chris hit head first against a stone wall and lay still.

Fighting for breath, Caley rolled over and pushed himself to his feet. Suddenly the night was dead quiet, except for the wheeze of his own breath. He staggered toward Chris, grunting as he bent down to grab his shoulder. Turning him over, Caley suddenly realized he might benefit from the situation. He fumbled at Chris's back pocket for his wallet, pulling it out with difficulty.

"Eighty bucks," he muttered contemptuously as he went through it. "Last of the big spenders." It was when he caught sight of Chris's driver's license that the idea came to him. They were both blond . . . both about the same age. He could switch wallets, use Roth's name. Getting a visa at the embassy would be a cinch, and he could leave for Europe with no one the wiser.

Caley smirked. By God, his luck wasn't out yet. He bent again to grope in Chris's pockets for the ring. Trish wouldn't get it back if he had anything to say about it, he thought viciously, roughly shifting Chris to one side.

A policeman's whistle tore at the night. Caley threw a look over one shoulder, saw the figure at the end of the street. In a flash he pulled out his own wallet, sliding it into Roth's back pocket. He made one last attempt at finding the ring. When the whistle blew more loudly, he scrambled to his feet and ran. As he hugged the shadows, he tried to feel good about having stolen Roth's identity, but what stayed in his mind was the image of the ring.

Chris was unconscious when admitted to the hospital, but his vital signs were good. Left to watch him while the emergency-room staff dealt with the results of a multiple car crash, Eugénie Arnot was careful to monitor his breathing. As a weekly volunteer she rarely got to assist with actual patients, and the skin around her faded blue eyes puckered with worry over the responsibility. She was extremely relieved when his lashes fluttered.

As Chris opened his eyes, he had a confused impression of sounds and smells. At his light groan he heard a soft voice quaver, "How do you feel, young man?" A white-haired little woman was staring anxiously at him above a pink pinafore apron.

"My head hurts," he whispered, and then the memory of the fight with Caley came back to him. "My pocket," he muttered. He tried to lift his hand, but couldn't.

"What is it, dear?" Eugénie saw that he was distressed over something and her heart quailed. "Is there anything I can do for you?"

"Ring," Chris whispered. "In . . . pocket."

Eugénie found it after probing gingerly in several of his jeans pockets. "How pretty," she began.

"Send it," Chris said faintly. "You must . . . to my . . . girl." He looked at the old woman, wondering how he could make her understand.

The appeal in the boy's green crystal eyes melted Eugénie's heart. "Of course," she said. "Just tell me where to mail it. I'll send it out tonight."

Chris gave her the address. "Tell her I love her," he said finally. "Chris loves her. I'll always love her." He fell silent.

Eugénie waited beside him until a harried ER nurse took him for treatment. As she walked away she mused that Chris must be a nickname. The name on the gurney was Caley Sutherland. She mailed the small package to Trish that night, sliding it into the corner mailbox with a prayer for its sender.

Chris was now and then aware of a bright light or a sharp sound. He drifted, mind wandering through memories of textures, of sensations. He was dreamily aware of trying to name one thing that could compare to the feel of Trish's skin. He'd never been able to. Warm clay, risen bread, polished marble—no. And then he remembered the silver-green leaves of a plant warm from the sun, magically soft to the touch. Lamb's ears, he recalled with satisfaction. He slipped away on the softness. He never regained consciousness.

Seven months later Becca Blue hurried into the Boulder Community Hospital, lilac branches in her hands. When she reached the room, Trish brightened at the sight, her face glowing. "Where did you find them?" she asked in surprise. "It's still too early for lilacs."

"You just enjoy them," Becca told her. There was no need for her to know that she'd hunted those lilacs for two days. When Trish's mother, Bridey, had called to tell her about the baby, Becca had known that something special was in order.

"Thank you." Trish breathed in the fresh, promising scent of the flowers, remembering the first time she'd been with Chris.

"Well, do I get to see this child or not?" Becca demanded. "Somebody told me you had a baby."

Trish smiled. "Listen. Here they come."

Soon Becca was holding the small, warm bundle, looking at the beautiful little girl whose face was half covered with a port-wine stain. She thought of the sketch she'd drawn, a face obscured by shadow, and forced a smile. "You know what they say?" she asked Trish. "That a child born about four o'clock on a Saturday afternoon will be rich as can be."

"As long as she's happy," Trish murmured. "It's not money that matters." She looked once more at her baby, her Ariana Bridget, and felt a warm completion, a peace she hadn't known since Chris had gone. So much had happened so fast, getting the ring, the frantic trip to Montreal, learning of Chris's death. Then nothing except the months of slow, aching grief.

Now, at last, she could begin again. "I thought he was here with me when she was born," Trish said softly.

Nodding at the baby, Becca smiled. "He'll always be with you now, honey."

The laughter of a child pealed in the quiet. From the door of the old stable burst a tiny dynamo dressed in a blue snowsuit, the hood pulled back from her head, springy brown curls bouncing as she ran. "Granda, Granda," Ari chimed. "Catch me!"

Devin Lowell watched from the doorway as Ari ran to the house. His brown eyes held a gleam of amusement.

Ari stopped short of the back door and shot a flirting glance back at her grandfather. "Catch me, Granda!"

"You're too fast for me, punkin," he replied. "I'll have to find you when I get there, won't I?"

Ari glowed at the variation on her game and darted away.

Devin was feeling his age now, and an air of fatigue bound him in his seventy-ninth year. He was still tall, although his broad shoulders were rounded, and he appeared thin even in the heavy denim jacket.

As she watched him from the house, Bridey's hands went still in the dishwater. She, too, showed the passage of the years. At seventy her slenderness was heightened, and there was a new, fine-drawn quality to her. The chestnut in her hair had given way to gray.

As Bridey studied Devin's careful gait, her smile faltered. Then she heard the rapid pitter-pat of Ari's feet.

"Gan, where are you?"

Bridey stepped briskly into the kitchen. "Right here, lovie." She held out her arms for Ari's sturdy little body.

"I need a cookie."

Laughing, Bridey set the child down on the counter, then lifted the painted brown head of the teddy-bear cookie jar so that Ari could peer into its depths. Dimpled fingers dug for thick oatmeal cookies.

When Devin came in, he heard the murmur of Bridey's voice. For an instant he was cast back to the years long ago when Trish was a toddler, he and Bridey still caught up in the first flush of parenthood.

Ari saw him in the doorway. "You want a cookie, Granda?" In her outstretched hand was her own.

Devin recognized the sacrifice. "No, thanks, snippet." He rested his big, gnarled hand on her head for a moment. "I think it's time for my nap."

Ari's smile was reflected in the faces of her grandparents. "Me too?" One of her favorite things was to lie on the big bed in their tower bedroom and to cuddle with them, looking out the window at the mountains while they told her stories.

Devin raised one hitched, grizzled brow. "I think maybe there's room for you, punkin. Want to race up the stairs?"

"Okay!" Ari squirmed impatiently for Bridey to take off her snow-suit and set her down on the floor. "Mark-set-go!" Devin started after her.

"Hold it." Bridey snagged him by a belt loop on the back of his slacks. "No racing."

Devin turned, surveying her down his nose in the old sardonic way. "Hush," he ordered softly, and dropped a kiss on her mouth. Then he slowly followed after Ari.

Trish arrived home from school an hour later to a quiet house. She started to call, then set her books on the foyer table and walked up the stairs. Standing in the doorway of her parents' bedroom, she looked at the three on the bed, a lump forming in her throat. Devin was stretched out on his side and Bridey had curled within the curve of his body, held close by his arm across her waist. Snuggling next to Bridey was Ari, small face aimed toward the window where, in the distance, the slabs of the Flatirons thrust to the sky.

Trish went silently back down the stairs to the kitchen. She'd never anticipated the satisfaction of witnessing the circle formed by her child, her parents, and herself. The sense of continuity was sustaining.

She filled the kettle for tea, enjoying the heat of the sun's rays through the window over the sink. Since her days in the Gold Hill cabin she'd cut her hair, the dark strands swirling around her face at shoulder level.

Following Ari's birth Trish returned home to live with her parents. Bridey and Devin had welcomed her, reveling in being a part of Ari's earliest years. Having Lucy and Gerald nearby had meant both extra help and love while Trish worked as a teacher.

The kettle whistled and Trish poured steaming water into the teapot. *I have a good life,* she thought, not for the first time. She still missed Chris, not for just herself, but for Ari as well. Her glance fell to the clay figure Ari had made several days before, gravely assuring her it was a dinosaur. Trish touched the painted clay, warm from the sun, and smiled through her tears.

That night Lucy and Gerald MacAllister came for dinner and Ari got to stay up late, finally ending up on Devin's lap while all of them played Monopoly. Gerald teased Trish as he bought Boardwalk, as he always did. When Trish carried Ari up to bed, he blew her a kiss.

Trish went back downstairs, meeting her father on the landing. "Where do you think you're going?" she demanded playfully. "I still have another game coming."

Devin shook his head. He was pale and moved slowly, as if in pain. "I need to lie down awhile," he said huskily.

"Okay, Dad, but don't forget you owe me a game." Trish kissed his cheek as he passed her on his way to his room.

After a few more minutes of play Bridey pushed her chair away from the table, and the other three looked up at her. "I'm going to check on Ari," she said casually. "She ate a lot of popcorn tonight."

Surprise flickered in Trish's eyes. "I can go up, Mom. Did she say anything about a stomachache?"

Bridey waved her offer aside. "I'm just being a grandma." As she left the room, she admitted to herself that she was worried about Devin. He'd laid a reassuring hand on her shoulder when he left, but she hadn't been able to put the fatigue in his face out of her mind.

The shadows on the stairs seemed especially thick as Bridey walked up the steps, and she could hear their creaking. The sound teased her memory, and then the past overcame her. She was climbing the stairs in the MacAllister house, on her way to the room where Issy was dying.

Bridey moved her shoulders uncomfortably, trying to dispel the recollection. At the top of the stairs it was dark. She glanced up at the wall sconce, but the bulb was still alight. When she turned into the hallway, she saw a soft glow at the end, near the window. Then she realized that Devin was standing there, straight and tall.

"Oh, you're feeling better, love." Bridey's voice was laden with relief.

Devin gazed at her tenderly, love heartfelt in his eyes.

Bridey shivered again and smiled ruefully. "If you'll wait for me to get a sweater, I'll go back down with you." She saw him raise one hand, then she went into their bedroom.

Devin lay on the bed. He was very still, his face gray.

CHAPTER 18

For Bridey, late spring and early summer passed in a blur of pain. She'd always been strong, but now she wandered through her days with no sense of purpose. It was the small details of life that brought her back.

At the dinner table Ari was full of her day's adventures. "Mrs. Mac let me *kneel* the bread," she announced proudly. "Mr. Mac said it was the best bread in the world."

Bridey glanced at Trish. "Mr. and Mrs. Mac?"

Trish rolled her eyes. "Uncle Gerald took her with him to the hardware store last week. Mel Cooper's always referred to him as Mac, and he sent his greetings to Mrs. Mac." She ruffled Ari's riot of hair affectionately. "Guess who's been calling them that ever since?"

Bridey smiled at Ari's pleased laughter, but she wondered forlornly how many things she'd missed.

The next afternoon she came upon Ari seated on the bottom step of the stairs. The little girl was tugging at one of her curls, her round face serious.

"What's the matter, sweetheart?" Bridey bent to sit beside her. "You look unhappy."

Ari scanned her with troubled eyes. "Who will tell me stories?" she asked urgently. "Mama said Granda went to heaven, and you're too sad."

"I'm not too sad to tell stories anymore," Bridey said with difficulty. "Let's go upstairs, and I'll tell you one right now." Together they went to the bedroom, lying on the bed as they always had, Ari's face turned to the window.

At first Bridey fought tears, feeling the empty space behind her where Devin had once nestled. But as she spun a tale for Ari, a pleasing illusion spread through her, a sensation of familiar warmth against her back. She could almost believe that Devin was there with them. Bridey kept her gaze on the mountains, their outlines blurring as her eyes filled, feeling the comfort of that sensory echo.

Bridey turned slowly from grief. The love from Trish and Ari, from Gerald and Lucy, warmed her frozen heart and she began to relish life again. And then she received a letter from her lawyer.

Lillian Lowell had filed a challenge to Devin's will. Bridey stared at the cramped, up-and-down lines of the lawyer's signature, instead seeing an image decades old of Lillian's blond hair, blood-red lipstick, dark eyes filled with malice.

Bridey telephoned the lawyer. Since he'd drawn up Devin's will he'd received a copy of the letter regarding Lillian's action that afternoon. "I was about to call you, Miss Gregory," Cliff Morrow said amiably. "It's come up because the will has made it through the preliminary stages of probate. If there's going to be a challenge, this is the time."

He reiterated the main points of Devin's will. "You inherit the house, as well as being the main beneficiary of the two life-insurance policies. Let's see . . . the survivor benefits of his pension . . . He left cash amounts to your daughter and her child, as well as small bequests to Mr. and Mrs. MacAllister."

Morrow paused. "Now, Miss Gregory, there *might* be a bit of difficulty with the items regarding spousal benefits. Since Mr. and Mrs. Lowell were never legally divorced, she may be able to collect on them. I told him at the time he made the will that those were sticky points as far as the law was concerned." He didn't add that Devin hadn't believed that Lillian would challenge his wishes.

They arranged to meet in Morrow's office the next week. Bridey's hand shook as she replaced the receiver.

The afternoon sun poured through the west windows. She studied her ring, Morna's ring, its center diamond surrounded by ruby petals, all sparked into life by the light. Her father had given it to Morna so long ago. Devin had put it on her finger. She whispered, "I'm seventy years old."

Lillian had craved only the powers of wealth and privilege, and for that she'd needed Devin. She'd manipulated them both, and now she wanted to claim the benefits of the life Bridey and Devin had made in spite of her.

Bridey felt a surge of her old energy, her spine stiffening. Years ago she and Devin had sidestepped the battle with Lillian, choosing not to risk Trish to widespread censure. This time would be different. If Lillian wanted a fight, she would give her one.

Several weeks later the hearing was held in the chambers of Judge Morton Reese. He observed the people before him through glacial blue eyes, as if they were specimens.

Lillian's lawyer had repeated her claims several times. "Since the wedding in nineteen thirty-three, my client has been the legal wife of the late Devin Bannister Lowell. She petitions the court to award her the benefits allotted."

Bridey sighed inwardly, wearied by the flood of words since her arrival nearly two hours before. Beside her lawyer, Lillian nodded.

Lillian was in fine spirits, her dark eyes glowing with pleasure at having her enemy at her mercy at last. She'd prepared for the hearing by donning a severe black suit and elegant black felt hat, viewing them as weapons. She wanted to remind stuffy old Morton Reese that *she* was the widow.

Her tactic had not been lost upon Bridey. She and Trish had dressed simply, but not in mourning colors. Trish's rose knit suit made her bloom, and Bridey's teal blue dress had been one of Devin's favorites.

"Your Honor," Cliff Morrow said. "My client doesn't deny that Mrs. Lowell was still the wife of Devin Lowell in the eyes of the law at the time of his death. But," he pointed out, "we remind the court that Mr. Lowell attempted more than once to persuade Mrs. Lowell to a divorce. Most telling of all, he chose to live the last thirty-three years of his life with my client."

"Thirty-one," snapped Lillian. "He was in Washington during the war. With me."

Bridey stiffened, biting back anger.

His freckled face stern, Cliff Morrow ignored the interruption. "Devin Lowell considered Bridey Gregory his wife in every sense of the word. He made out his will exactly as he wanted it." He touched the paper in front of him. "Mrs. Lowell has no grounds for attempting to set it aside."

"Devin was under *her* influence," Lillian spat. She didn't glance toward Bridey. Her lawyer laid his hand over hers.

"That's an insult!" Trish said abruptly. She'd seethed throughout the proceedings, welcoming the anger as a way to combat grief. "My father loved my mother and wanted her to have what was his."

"How do you know he was your father?" Lillian inserted slyly. "As I said, he was in Washington during the war."

"Devin Lowell was my father." Trish met Lillian's eyes forthrightly, and the older woman's gaze fell.

The judge watched them impassively.

"Your Honor," Stephen Towbridge said, "I believe that all of the salient points in this case have been addressed. It's our request that the existing will of Devin Lowell be overturned in order that his lawful wife, Lillian Wyndham Lowell, be given what is guaranteed to her by the laws of the state of Colorado."

Cliff Morrow answered quietly, his eyes never leaving the face of Judge Reese. "Your Honor, as you know, the purpose of the law is to protect the rights of the citizens who live under it. In this case, however, the law itself falls short. Lillian Lowell may have been the legal wife of Devin Lowell, but that is the only regard in which that title can be applied to her."

Morrow's kind eyes narrowed. "Bridey Gregory shared the bed, the board, and the life of Devin Lowell. In every sense but the legal one she was the man's wife. Had Mr. Lowell been unmarried and lived with her under the same circumstances, she automatically would be considered his common-law wife. Additionally, we claim that it was through her efforts together with Mr. Lowell that the current estate was accumulated. Before her retirement Miss Gregory raised and sold horses from the property now in question."

Morrow added, "Morna Patricia Gregory is Devin Lowell's daughter. She was conceived during the time Mr. Lowell lived with her mother, and he acknowledged her at all times as his child."

As he stressed the points of their defense, Bridey's attention wandered. *Devin,* she thought, *I've never missed you as much as I do right now. If it weren't for Trish and Ari, Lillian could take everything. If only you were here, I wouldn't care.* In her mind's eye she saw him, brown eyes gleaming under mobile brows, mouth bracketed with lines carved by smiles. Then Bridey deliberately dispelled the image. She would not cry in front of Lillian.

"In conclusion, Your Honor," said Cliff Morrow, "we move that Devin Lowell's will be allowed to stand as written. He distributed his property according to his own wishes. The court should not tamper with those bequests."

Judge Reese let his gaze travel over each of their faces. Then he nodded curtly. "I'll take the case under advisement, counselors. This hearing is recessed."

Bridey and Trish followed Cliff Morrow out into the hall. As the door closed behind them, Morrow took Bridey's hand. "I did my best, Miss Gregory, but there's no way to tell how it went. Judge Reese is famous for his poker face." And for his harsh judgments, he reflected glumly.

Morrow knew that if it were up to him, he'd decide against the woman still in the judge's chambers. He'd been moved by the combination of challenge and serenity in Bridey's face. In spite of the strain she'd been under, he'd seen her remain both calm and dignified.

"Thank you for your efforts," Bridey told him. "You've done everything you can." She shivered, chilled by the institutional green walls of the hallway. She touched Trish's arm. "I'm tired, honey. Let's go home."

Trish had worried through the hearing, aware of Bridey's flagging energy. Now anger came as a relief. "I wanted to slug that woman," she growled. "No wonder Dad left her. She's a witch."

Bridey summoned a smile. "No, she's unhappy."

The door to the judge's chambers slammed. "Well," Lillian Lowell sputtered. "I thought you'd have had the decency to be gone by now."

Cliff Morrow's face hardened. "Mrs. Lowell, you have no right to speak to my client that way."

"No right?" Lillian's sharp chin rose. "Young man, this woman stole my husband from me, and made me look like a fool in front of the best people in this city."

Bridey shook her head, eyes rueful. She'd already achieved a victory, regardless of how the case was decided. She surveyed Lillian calmly. "Devin left you long before I ever met him. And if you've looked like a fool, it's only because you wouldn't divorce him. You and I both know that's true."

Fury boiled under Lillian's tailored silk blouse. Over the years she'd come to see herself as the abandoned wife battling for her proper due. That her mortal enemy would counter that interpretation was insufferable. "You're going to lose this case," she hissed, stepping closer to Bridey. "I'm going to see to it that you end up on the streets where you belong."

"Stop it!" Trish exploded. Bridey's hand on her arm kept her from saying more.

For the first time Bridey felt a stab of pity for the woman. "Lillian, you've never known the real value of anything. The fact that you're here trying to prevent Devin's final wishes from being carried out proves it. Even if you win this case, you lost a long time ago." Ignoring the other woman's strangled outrage, she added, "You had your chance with Devin, and you threw it away. I never took anything from you."

Lillian stared at her. A sliver of fear that what she said might be true made her spin and stalk down the hall. She wanted a drink. She very badly wanted a drink.

Bridey rubbed both arms, hugging herself in reaction. "I want to go home."

As they left Denver behind them, Bridey mused, "I don't know if I care whether we win or not."

Trish flicked the signal light off as she changed lanes, glancing away from the road for an instant toward Bridey. "This will all seem a lot more manageable when you've had a chance to rest."

"I suppose so." The scenery flashed by the car window, autumn colors softened by winter the night before. Red maples that had flamed had been extinguished. Fat pumpkins peeked through snow.

She'd been awakened that morning by Ari, beside herself with excitement at the storm. "Snowman, snowman, I'm going to make a snowman," the little girl sang.

"When it stops," Bridey had reminded her. She resented the hearing in Denver, wanting to bundle up and play with her granddaughter. The MacAllisters had come over to stay with Ari during the time Bridey and Trish would be gone.

Ari had escorted her mother and grandmother to the car, cheeks red in the snapping air. She'd hugged them both, her small mouth planting a sloppy kiss on Trish's cheek, then on Bridey's. Her golden eyes glowed as she waved. "I love you," she called, waiting for them to echo the words. Then she'd run toward Lucy.

Now Bridey thought she'd have been better off to stay home. The judge had seemed uninterested.

Trish turned on the windshield wipers as they approached Broomfield. Heavy, wet flakes of snow had begun to fall. "Mom, it might do you good to get away. You haven't gone anywhere since before Dad died." Worry was in her eyes. "You've been through so much."

Bridey smiled and patted her daughter's knee. "So have you, honey. Maybe we both ought to pack up and leave town for a while." The image of her mountain formed in her mind like a promise, and she felt a longing so intense that she closed her eyes. "Bridey's Mountain," she murmured. "Our mountain."

Trish envisioned its face uplifted to the sky. "Of course, Telluride." She'd been there only a few times, but its very air was charged with the stories she'd been told. The knowledge that it was their mountain had always created a special sense of home. "We could take Ari. She's never seen it." Her hands moved abruptly on the steering wheel. "There's some slick patches along here."

"It's not as warm up here as in Denver." Bridey relaxed as Trish took the Broomfield turnoff. The snow was thicker, but there would be little traffic on the way to Louisville, since the connecting highway had only two lanes.

They came to a stop at Broomfield's one traffic light, then headed up the hill outside the town. The heavy snow was becoming less feathery, but the smaller flakes were swirling with the gusting wind.

"Let's go to Telluride," Bridey said yearningly. "Getting back to Bridey's Mountain would help me see this thing through." She glanced almost shyly at Trish. "You do understand, don't you?"

Trish's face softened with memories. "Of course I do. The mountain's magic, Mom. We've always known that."

They came down the slippery hill slowly, Trish clutching the steering wheel tightly. The sides of the highway were barely visible through the blowing snow.

"When the weather clears," Bridey planned, scarcely noticing the conditions outside, "we'll go up for a week, stay at the Sheridan Hotel. Helga's daughter will let us see the house, and we can show Ari where her great-grandmother Morna once sang."

Trish was hunched over the wheel in an effort to see the road, but she smiled. "Let Lillian Lowell try to find us up there." Braking slowly as they approached the crossroads at the bottom of the hill, she wiped at the fog spreading across the windshield. "We own a mountain. There aren't very many people who can say that."

Bridey recognized her daughter's efforts to encourage her and her heart brimmed with love. "Better to say the mountain owns us."

Neither of them saw the semitrailer truck barreling toward the intersection from the west. Having built up momentum from the slope of Dillon Road, the driver was finding it difficult to slow the heavy rig. He had no way to stop when the truck began a skid across the sheet of ice yards from the stop sign.

"No matter where I've gone, the mountain has always been home," Bridey said. "And I need to go home." The full force of the loaded truck smashed into their car, crushing the metal shell as it hurled forward, ramming it against the telephone pole on the other side of the road. The impact slammed the horrified driver against the steering wheel, and he collapsed against it.

The desperate sounds of the collision faded, and the muffling silence of the storm resumed. The snow thickened, blanketing the site.

Bridey lay outside the car, flung onto the shoulder of the road. The cold snowflakes dusted her eyelids, after a while bringing her around. She opened her eyes and looked up into swirling white.

Memory returned slowly, of the drive, of the crash. She felt no pain. *If it were serious, I'd be hurting,* Bridey reasoned carefully. Just as the idea settled, instinct quickened. *Trish.*

Bridey wrenched herself to her side. Fear deadened the slash of agony along her ribs. Her eyes frantically searched the mass of crushed metal in front of her. Through the curtain of snow she glimpsed her daughter's dark hair beyond the listing telephone pole.

Breathing shallowly, Bridey forced her arm out in front of her. She tried to push herself up, not seeing the jagged bone that stabbed through her skin. Gritting her teeth against rising pain, she bent one leg, shoving her body forward with her foot. Her ribs protested agonizingly. She rolled onto her stomach and thrust her other arm forward, grabbing at a wet clump of dead grass to pull, pushing once more with her foot. Again and again she labored through each awkward motion, slowly crawling. She left a broad crimson trail along the snow.

When her outthrust fingers touched Trish's cheek, feeling the warmth there, Bridey sagged in relief. *Thank you, God,* she thought. Then she forced herself closer, bent over her daughter, struggling to control her heavy panting. "Trish," she whispered with difficulty. Her hand lifted to stroke dark hair back from the calm, unmarred face.

Trish lay as if sleeping, her massive injuries all internal, no outward sign of the punishment her body had received in the crash. She had died instantly.

Bridey cradled Trish against her, cautious to keep from jarring her, pulling her gently into the shelter of her coat. *I've got to keep her warm,* she thought painstakingly. *Someone will come soon.*

The snow sifted silently, covering the mangled car. Bridey held Trish to her, crooning words of comfort, her fingers lightly stroking her daughter's cheek. Beneath her coat, the blood from her side soaked steadily into the ground. *So tired,* Bridey thought hazily. Then, a slow realization came, an awareness that she was dying.

It will be all right. She felt a welcome comfort at the knowledge. *Trish will take care of Ari, and she'll have Lucy and Gerald to help.* Her mind's eye formed an image of the little girl in her mother's arms, the two of them in sunshine. A smile curved her chilly lips. Trish had always been such a good mother.

Against her fingertips Trish's skin was cooling. For a moment Bridey's cocoon of security was torn away by the icy, gusting wind. She tried to tighten her arms around Trish, to make her warmer.

After a while her arms slackened, thoughts drifting to Devin. She could almost see him now, standing with the loose-knit grace he'd always had, the amused smile in his eyes. Behind him was the outline of Bridey's Mountain and she wondered drowsily what he was doing in Telluride. Then she saw Trish beside him. *We can all be together,* she realized, and felt a surge of love. Warm now under the white blanket, Bridey welcomed the solace of winter's sleep.

ARI

CHAPTER 1

Now that it was almost dawn, the storm that had crackled through the night, slinging arcs of lightning over the front range of the Rockies, had thundered its way out to the eastern plains. It left an aftermath of soft rain. That gentle sound did not lull Ari to sleep in her basement apartment in Louisville, nor had the bluster before disturbed her. She was gloriously oblivious, turned inward, riding the swells of emotion from just learning that she'd won twenty-five million dollars in the Sweepstakes. This morning, unlike yesterday's, she wouldn't have noticed an entire convention of magpies croaking raucously outside her window.

Ari had gone to bed only a few hours earlier, and although she was exhausted by the day's excitement, wanting to rest, she could not stop the tide of thought. There was too much to absorb in her brand-new world. Sleep tried to catch her off-guard, to pull her down more deeply. But just as she'd start to doze, she'd find herself awake, tossed high in the bright daydreams of the future. And in that fluid state of mind her real memories merged with vivid imaginings.

One moment she was a child again, in the comforting fields of the farm, hurrying toward the shelter of the house and the MacAllisters. But when she opened the door, she saw herself as she'd been two days ago on Saturday, alone in her own cramped kitchen, unhappily rolling out the pie dough. Then the walls of the room dissolved, and she was outside again walking beside the mirror-clear stream in the Telluride canyon that in reality she'd never seen. The next instant she was shivering by the phone in her apartment as she had on Sunday, hearing a warm voice give her cold news about the development plans for Bridey's Mountain. Before she could recall the words of the conversation, she was spinning dizzily along the grassy ridge overlooking the Flatirons, exulting in the sun, realizing that she'd won.

Restlessly, she tried for a new position on the bed, ending up spread-eagled on her stomach on the mattress, both arms outstretched as if clutching its sides for balance. Her tousled brown curls were touched with gleams of light from the rips in the plastic shade of the bedside lamp she'd forgotten to turn off. Her hair obscured the purplish-red of the birthmark on her cheek and clung a little damply to her neck and bare shoulders. Her long dark lashes were wet, too, moistened by quiet unconscious tears of joy. The faded blue quilt that Mrs. Mac had lovingly stitched with its squares of sunbonneted maids in gingham skirts was wrapped around her. The early morning air was cool, wet with the rain plinking against the screen behind the window, ajar on its rusty chain.

The bed itself was an island in a sea of chaos. The sparse room's tidiness, which she'd surveyed only yesterday with such satisfaction, had disappeared beneath scattered brown grocery bags stuffed with clothing. Books lay in random piles on the once immaculate desktop beside the now jumbled pile of unopened mail. Open newspaper sections were spread in the next room on the stiff plastic of the couch and chair. Even the phone receiver dangled from its cradle. Because she'd finally tumbled into bed so late, Ari had taken it off the hook, intending to sleep until noon. And she wanted no more calls from Murdoch and Associates regarding their plans to tear up her mountain. Now she had plans of her own on that question.

All day Sunday, after seeing the article with her Sweepstakes numbers, she hadn't been able to settle in one place for two consecutive seconds or complete a coherent thought. On the hilltop, gathering up her canvas, her quilt, and the remains of a largely uneaten picnic, she'd stopped repeatedly to check both Denver newspapers lest those magic numbers be somehow a figment of her imagination. Then she raced home, her long hair flying wildly, pedaling so fast that she almost slipped her bicycle chain a dozen times. Banging through the side door that led down to her basement rooms, she immediately called Chicago, where her best friend, Janie Schmidt, had taken a job with a public relations firm after graduation. Since there'd been no answer, she'd dialed every fifteen minutes, or more often if her eye lighted on the phone.

Spreading out the travel sections of the papers, Ari had begun poring over cruise and airline specials. Then, grinning wryly at herself, she realized she needn't look for bargains. She could now afford to go anywhere, and first class at that. But before she even picked a destination, it occurred to her that she'd want to move before leaving on a trip, and she flipped excitedly to the house and condominium ads. Halfway down the first column she was suddenly aware that she wasn't sure whether she wanted to live in Boulder or Denver or neither. Then, her heart leaping higher than her pipe-laden ceiling, she knew that none of that mattered, anyway. She would go to Telluride. At last she would see Bridey's Mountain, especially now that it was threatened. That was a first priority. When she came back, she could make up her mind about everything else.

And at least once an hour she had studied her face in the cracked mirror above the bathroom sink, cupping her hand over the birthmark and trying to imagine it gone. Then she'd stood before the glass in profile, firmly tucking her thick tangle of curls behind her ear, and made an effort to be objective. Out of the corner of her left eye, she'd pored over the unblemished side of her face, wondering if she'd be really pretty when the right side matched it.

The third time Ari had done that, just when she was giving up on it because it gave her a crick in her neck, she recalled an article she'd saved on the Denver plastic surgeon who specialized in such cosmetic surgery. Dumping her box of files on the card table in the kitchen, she'd searched feverishly for it, scattering the papers every which way, and then leafed through the phone directory for the number. It was only when she reached Dr. Herron's answering service that she remembered it was Sunday and hung up in confusion.

Finally, as a way of calming down, she'd taken refuge in the familiar weekend chores. But getting out her wash to take to the Laundromat, she stopped. The cotton blouses were faded, the T-shirts stained, the summer skirts tired looking. Everything she owned came from the Thrift Shop and had been chosen, not because she liked the color or design, but because the item was wearable, not too badly damaged. Gleefully, she stuffed everything, including the threadbare towels, into a black plastic trash bag.

Turning to her closet, Ari began pulling clothing off the hangers, then folding it into sacks to be taken to Goodwill. Except for a comfortable pair of sneakers she stuffed all of her shoes into an old pillowcase and added that as well. But even as she was smiling with delight at the thought of her upcoming shopping sprees, she looked at her discarded possessions strewn on the floor and felt a pang. It was not that she cared for the things themselves, but she had the uneasy sensation that she'd shed her skin and was becoming a new Ari. She did not know who that person was.

She brushed that aside and laid out on the bed what she would save. A cable-stitch sweater that Mrs. Mac had knit as a gift for their last Christmas together; the warm terry-cloth robe that was the first thing put on in the morning; her favorite jeans; and two presents from Janie—a silk scarf she'd given her for her birthday and a T-shirt brought back as a souvenir from Mexico.

All that was left on the shelf above the tiny closet were the boxes that contained the family photo albums and Ari's school awards carefully saved by Mrs. Mac from first grade onward. Shoved as far back into a corner as it would fit was the frayed leather-covered shipping trunk that Morna Gregory had first brought to Telluride almost a hundred years ago, which had been too solid and useful to part with. In it was stored the metal box that held the mining claims on Bridey's Mountain and, somewhere near the bottom, packed in tissue and lavender, the white lace-trimmed dress that had belonged to Morna's mother.

As she emptied the closet, Ari had been tempted to open the humpbacked lid, look at the yellowed pieces of parchment that certified her ownership of the claims, even take out the dress. Thinking about that, she'd sunk down on the edge of the bed and stared at the ruby ring on her right hand. Like rose petals the rich red gems curved upward around the white diamond heart at the center. Although she'd wanted to wear it every day, she'd always been afraid that she might knock a stone loose, not be able to afford to repair it. Now that she needn't worry about that, she thought, she would wear it, this reminder of a love that spanned generations, handed down from mother to daughter. Since the ring and the mountain, those gifts from the past, were so linked in her mind, she again recalled the problem that kept surfacing even in her distraction—the conversation with the man at Murdoch and Associates. Rivers Alexander, yes, that'd been his name. He'd said, "You'd have to get legal advice." A few hours ago that had seemed impossible. Now she could certainly pay for it.

Ari jumped up and headed for the phone. She called Stewart Wellings, a lawyer who'd recently retired from the board of the Mountain and Plains Bank where she'd worked. Although she had not known the elderly attorney well, he had been an enormous help when Mrs. Mac died, refusing any money for his services, and he'd always inquired with interest about Ari's classwork when she met him in the hallways at work. She liked and trusted him, seeing in him the wisdom and integrity that reminded her of Gerald MacAllister.

A widower, Wellings lived a few blocks away in a stately red brick Georgian house. After his wife's death he'd moved to the quiet of Louisville, joining the bank's board, turning away from his highly successful career in Denver. Since he was a member of society's old guard there, and a cautious man, he'd become the trusted repository of their secrets. But as he grew older, he found he wanted to be around people whose secrets he didn't know. He was tall, with an aristocratic bearing only a little hunched by arthritis, and he invariably wore gray pinstriped three-piece suits, cut to disguise his stoop. Ari had often seen him turning toward his front door after an evening stroll through the peaceful streets. She hurried over at his invitation.

Showing him the ticket and the newspaper clipping, she said with a happy tremble in her voice, "I've several things to ask you. To begin with, what do I do first? After cashing the ticket, I mean."

As he looked at the numbers and the matching ones in the articles, Wellings's pepper-and-salt tufted eyebrows almost ascended to his stiffly curled gray hair. For a moment he said nothing, quietly eyeing her glowing face. There was no one, he thought, whom he'd rather see win a fortune. He'd always felt that Lillian Wyndham Lowell had been unfairly awarded Devin's estate. Nothing had been left for Ari, Devin and Bridey's granddaughter. He knew how tenderly Ari had cared for Lucy MacAllister in her last illness, knew how willingly the girl had taken on the funeral costs when she was already struggling to survive and attend school on a salary a little above minimum wage. But it occurred to him that she was in great need of protection. In addition to these riches she was beautiful.

Probably, he speculated, when she looked in the mirror, she could not see past the stain that spread around the eye, splotched across the cheek. But many men must also have noticed the warm golden-brown of eyes and hair, the generous mouth, a body that was both slim and voluptuous. He doubted that she'd had much experience. Would she be able to find a man who thought that she, and not her fortune, was the prize?

He could tell that she'd been gently bred, in the best sense. Although he'd only been slightly acquainted with the MacAllisters, it was a small town and he knew that Lucy and Gerald had raised her with loving care. They had given her their own firm beliefs in the essential goodness of people. Her upbringing had made Ari spontaneously kind, as he'd noted in the way she'd treated her fellow employees at the bank, but he wondered what kind of defenses she would have.

The innocence that Wellings saw in Ari was real. Growing up on an isolated farm, she'd had little contact with different kinds of people, and those in Lucy and Gerald's small circle were as benevolent as the old couple themselves. She'd been unprepared for the envious fear that had spurred her supervisor at the bank, Betty D'Amato, to get rid of her after Ari graduated and became a threat. While she'd suffered from the unwanted stares that her birthmark drew and from the unconscious cruelty of her childhood classmates, the MacAllisters had been sturdy bulwarks for her in dealing with it. Yet the port-wine stain had made her shy and standoffish with men. In any case, her rigid schedule of work and school had left her little time for social events. At twenty-three Ari was still a virgin.

A twinkle now in the sharp eyes above his gold-rimmed half-glasses, Wellings said, "Many years ago, when I began my practice, my best legal advice to a young woman who'd suddenly come into wealth would have been to find an intelligent, personable young lawyer and marry him." He smilingly raised an arthritic forefinger. "Now, I know what modern women would say to *that*. And no doubt they're right. So, failing that, you can hire me. I'll overcharge you, of course, but less so than other attorneys who have expensive offices to maintain. You'll need investment advice, too, and help with tax planning."

Here he paused, hesitating over the next question. When he had helped Ari settle the MacAllister estate, he'd asked if there were any members of her own family who might assist her. But she'd shaken her head, saying that both her parents had died young, that she didn't know of any relatives. Although the lawyer had moved to Louisville only a short time before that, gossip about the beautiful Gregory women was still whispered, and he'd learned that Ari was illegitimate. Now he wondered if the "dead" father was a fiction and had to consider whether the man might want to reacquaint himself with a newly rich daughter. Choosing his words carefully, he said, "I think you told me that your father was dead. Was he from Colorado?"

"No." Ari looked down, tracing a pattern in the Oriental rug with her sandal. "He was an artist. He died . . . before I was born. An accident. On a trip to Canada. His name was Christopher Roth."

At that name Stewart Wellings sat back in his chair with an almost visible jerk. He had every reason to know that Christopher Roth was dead, for he'd sat in Montreal some twenty years ago at the boy's bedside, watching him in the coma from which he'd never awakened. As Ceci Caley's executor Wellings had spent weeks after her death searching for her grandson. Ceci had tied the principal up tightly in a trust, not due until Caley was thirty-five, but there was the matter of how the money could be invested and where the interest payments should be sent. At last the lawyer had been notified that Caley Sutherland had been admitted to a hospital in Canada.

On arriving, however, Wellings had to tell the administrators that this young man who had Sutherland's wallet and did bear a superficial resemblance to him was not Caley.

The lawyer had stayed, hoping that Christopher would regain consciousness and be able to tell him where Caley might be. But although the boy had choked out Sutherland's name once in what sounded like accusation, his jumbled words were incoherent.

Later, when Caley wrote from Europe asking for money, he had an explanation. He said the two of them were friends and had exchanged wallets to allow Caley to get a passport to go abroad because of the drug-dealing charges. The Canadian police assumed that young Roth had been mugged and scuffled with the thief, who had been frightened off before he could get the billfold. There was no evidence to the contrary. Sutherland's roommate at the hostel swore he was with Caley that evening. Ten years passed before he came back, and then a high-priced lawyer took care of the old charges in Boulder. No mention was made of Montreal.

Still, when at Denver social functions Wellings saw Caley, sleek, blond, well tailored, he moved to another corner of the room. That story was a secret he preferred not to know. The lawyer decided it was not one that Ari needed to be told either.

He handed her back the ticket with a serious expression. "One kind of assistance you should get, even before cashing that, I think, is from a firm that handles publicity. In your case you need 'antipublicity,' a media screen. Reporters will besiege you for interviews, cameramen will push their equipment in your face. Under Colorado law it's no longer possible for Lotto winners to hide their identities behind a trust. Their names are matters of public record and must be disclosed. So you had best prepare yourself, go in and cash the ticket, and get it over with."

He leaned farther back in his velvet wingbacked chair. "A publicist can handle the incessant phone calls and letters from people you know only slightly, or have never met. Everybody will ask you for money, my dear."

He saw dismay at his words in her honey-colored eyes, but he wanted her to understand the problem so she would accept his solution. "Besides the appeals from the deserving, con artists and grifters will be trying to separate you from your cash. To spare yourself you should have your mail and phone calls screened. You need an accommodation address. Although I'm not sure, perhaps public relations firms deal with such—"

"Janie!" Ari exclaimed, then added apologetically, "I didn't mean to interrupt, Mr. Wellings. But my best friend just went to work for a national firm in Chicago, and I know they have a Denver branch because she was hoping that eventually she could be transferred back here."

"Check with her, right away," he replied. "And please call me Stewart." Although Wellings had given no sign of it, he'd caught Ari's nervous reaction to his reference to cameramen. She'd automatically raised her hand to her birthmark, but had then dropped it back onto the armrest of the upholstered chair. He now added gently, "You can easily wait a few days before cashing that ticket. Let your friend accompany you when she arrives if that would make you feel more comfortable. And sail into that office with all flags flying, ready for those cameras. First thing tomorrow, buy yourself a new dress. Or three. You do have a credit card?"

"Well, yes, but—" Ari stopped, then she laughed ruefully. "Do you know, I was going to say I didn't like to use it unless I could pay off whatever I charged at the end of the month."

"You'll be able to do that now. But you'll find the habits of a lifetime, the thought patterns, won't change overnight." A small crease furrowed his brow. Very few people, he considered, went through the experience of having the rules of the game changed in the middle of their lives. That was fortunate, he thought dryly, because very few people could handle it. But at least she was a bright young woman.

"You must be nice to yourself," he went on. "After all, such an enormous change is likely to put you under some strain, give you 'the jimmies and jingles,' as my wife used to say." He stood up and crossed the living room to a polished library table that held a cut-glass decanter and wineglasses. "Now a small celebration is in order. Champagne would be appropriate, but I haven't any chilled, so we'll toast the occasion with a glass of sherry."

After pouring the wine he handed her one of the small Waterford glasses and touched the rim with his. "To all the dreams that may now come true. And I want to hear about them."

"Thank you, Stewart." Ari was surprised at how easily his first name came to her lips, as if the very idea of wealth lent her assurance.

She sipped the sherry, which she'd never tasted before, pleased at its sweet warmth in her throat.

Settling himself back in the armchair, Wellings scanned the clipping again. "Your first check will be very nice indeed. Ten million dollars. An interesting gamble on the part of the Colorado Lottery itself, wasn't it? By giving a huge sum up front instead of spreading it out over a number of years, they attracted national attention and hordes of out-of-state ticket buyers. In two years you will receive another fifteen million. With that much you should be able to realize a few dreams."

"I am going to need your help with the most important one, though." Ari took another sip of sherry and began the story of Bridey's Mountain, giving a brief account of her family's history so that the lawyer could understand how deeply she felt about blocking any development there. She concluded by telling him about the phone conversation she'd had that morning.

When he heard the name of the developer who wanted to build on her land, Wellings's eyebrows climbed back up to his hairline. "Jonas Murdoch," he said, almost whistling. He tugged uneasily at the front of his vest. "Well, you have picked yourself a formidable opponent, Ari. A billionaire. And not the man to take kindly to having any of his plans obstructed. I think his employee was being quite accurate in telling you that Murdoch would never give away land with that kind of money-making potential." His mouth had a wry twist as he asked, "Did your caller laugh when you suggested it?"

"No," Ari replied, remembering the brisk practicality in that voice. She sipped from her glass. "I suppose he was being polite."

"Give me his name." As he jotted down *Rivers Alexander* on a small pad on the side table, it occurred to the lawyer that this must be Thomas Alexander's son. He hadn't known he was working for Murdoch. "It might be worth talking to him. And," Wellings went on, "I know a fine real estate lawyer in Denver. I'll call him this week so we can learn more about what might be done. But I have to be honest with you. Although I never thought I'd have occasion to say this, twenty-five million dollars may not be enough." Seeing Ari's distressed look, he added hastily, "Still, you must let me worry about this for the moment. Let me refill your glass. Tell me what else you're planning now that you've struck it rich."

Walking home in the twilight beneath a sunset that turned the edges of the clouds saffron and tinted the atmosphere itself gold, Ari still felt as if her feet were at least two inches off the ground. This illusion was heightened by the effect of sherry on an empty stomach.

She'd quite forgotten to eat anything since the croissant at breakfast before she'd looked at the newspaper. But after letting herself in, she went directly to the phone. This time, when she dialed Chicago, Janie answered.

For a full five minutes all her friend could do on hearing the news was whoop and gasp. Caught up again in excitement, Ari basked in the shared joy. Janie's spontaneous warmth always burst out, although she tried sheltering her feelings with a skeptical wit. She had the coloring of a Dresden milkmaid figurine, the creamy skin and robin's-egg blue eyes, and a too-rounded figure that was her despair. Her appearance and her open manner caused people at first to expect a certain guilelessness. But Janie was rose-thorn sharp and had a shrewd business sense. She'd chosen public relations because, she told Ari, it was one of the rare fields that had some women at the very top. Janie hoped to follow in their footsteps as rapidly as possible.

At last, Janie managed to finish an entire sentence. "God, Ari, how does it feel to be so damn rich?"

"I don't know." Ari paused in confusion, running a hand through her hair. "If this isn't seventh heaven, it's got to be sixth. But still, I sort of feel like I moved and forgot to leave myself the forwarding address."

As she heard that, Janie thought how true of Ari that must be. This sudden freedom would make her head reel simply because she was so unused to it. Through her college years she'd had no family, no money, and no one to depend on but herself. Janie remembered when they'd met at the start of their sophomore year. Ari had been at the university for two years, but had only been a part-time student. Janie's parents had finally given in and allowed her to transfer from the small religious college in Indiana that she'd hated. Hearing her moan over the enrollment forms, Ari had offered to help. Janie had looked at this likable girl with her wild mane of hair, the face of a Ralph Lauren model with its purple-red birthmark. But what she noticed most were the serious eyes, the earnest mouth. Since she herself had always been a little worried about her own impulsive nature, she thought Ari would be a good influence on her.

Since then, more than once, she'd considered that *she* was a good influence on Ari, who had to be reminded to have fun. And now she could. At that idea Janie's euphoria bubbled up. "Hey, you sound a little tiddly too. Great! But the least you could do is pour some of that champagne down the telephone line."

"All I've had is some sherry," Ari protested with a laugh, thinking how much she wished Janie were here with her. "At the lawyer's. And this is Sunday. Remember Colorado? Liquor stores are closed today."

"Okay, MacAllister, but promise me. Tomorrow, buy yourself a bottle of Dom Perignon, raise your glass in the general direction of Chicago and me, and drink the whole damned thing."

"A bottle of what?"

"Dom Perignon. Now that you're rich, Ari, men will be drinking it out of your slipper. It's the best champagne. I had as many glasses as I could snatch at a fancy wedding and I thought I'd died and gone to heaven. I just *wish* I were there—"

"You will be. At least I'm going to do my level best to get you here," Ari interrupted. She told Janie what Stewart Wellings had suggested about hiring a publicist and the reasons for doing that. "I really *need* you. You can help pinch me so I'll be sure this isn't all a dream. And you know how I hate getting up in front of people and . . . being stared at. Couldn't I call the Denver office of your firm and get them to send you out?"

Janie considered the idea, hope rising in her voice. "Well, Blackburn and Barton might let me come, figuring that even I—new to the game—could handle that. The usual thing, though, would be to have somebody there do it. So they'd really soak you for it." She paused and laughed outright. "Not that you have to care, do you? Yes, yes. I'll ask. I can't wait!"

"While you're here, you'll have to help me think about something," Ari said, her seriousness returning as she recalled Wellings's last words. "My lawyer says I may have a problem that even twenty-five million won't solve. Remember my telling you about my mountain? Here's what else happened yesterday." Ari explained about the offer from Murdoch.

Janie listened and then responded with real excitement in her voice, her words tumbling out. "I can help on that. Because you really *do* need a PR type. Look, if you got everybody who lives in that town on your side, they might kick in to help save that canyon. It'll be tough to come up with enough cash to buy this Murdoch out, but it could be done."

The enthusiasm in Janie's voice made Ari realize how worried she'd been by the lawyer's remarks. She'd been wondering how to even start thinking about the problem. Now her spirits revived. "Yes!" she replied. "Public pressure."

"We can do this," Janie returned. "The best thing, the absolute best thing, is that when you turn in that ticket you'll be surrounded by all those media people and you can start telling them—"

Ari felt the familiar stomach twinge that the very mention of the words *oral report* had given her from the fourth grade on. "Can I just say that I'm going to give to environmental groups and—"

"Sure." Janie said, soothingly. "No speeches." Although Janie was already busily planning a later press conference, she decided it was best not to tell her friend that at the moment. She knew from their classes together that Ari was able to forget her self-consciousness and argue with zeal when she was swept up in an idea.

Had Stewart Wellings overheard this optimistic conversation, he'd have been afraid that such expectations would end in painful disappointment. But he was a man who had not forgotten what it was like to be young and sure of success. He might have reflected that sometimes it was better not to know how heavily the odds were stacked. After all, in life, as at the racetrack, long shots sailed across the finish line. The horse didn't know it'd come out of the gate at 30–1.

Full of ideas, talking at the same time, Ari and Janie had eventually gone on to other topics. At first Ari had found herself guiltily checking her watch because it was a long-distance call. Before, when Janie and she had been separated in the summers, they'd always set the oven timer so they wouldn't run up a big bill. This time, it was early in the morning before they'd quit talking and Ari tumbled into bed.

Now, the sky was silvering with Monday's approach, but Ari at last slipped into the first light layer of sleep. Yesterday's dream recurred. Her hair was elegantly up, and she was wearing the white dress, the lace that was as delicate as a moth wing framing her face, falling over her wrists. The lavender and white columbines lifted their trumpets beside the canyon's stream, and as she knelt down beside it she could again see that lovely face, that was not her own, smiling at her. The mountain bent low to her touch.

Ari nestled warmly into the mattress's hollow just as she was settling into the dream itself. It would turn out right this time because she would be able to preserve her heritage, she was sure. There was no danger that an earthquake would threaten her mountain.

But the fear started again, creeping like spider legs up her body. Since she was only half asleep, she argued with its coming, "No, no, I have the money. I can do it."

Still, the dream events unfolded relentlessly. She reached for the submerged pocket watch, noticing this time that its case was incised with curlicued initials. Just then the stream ran an ominous red, as if the mountain were bleeding. Her ring slipped from her finger. She dug frantically in the sand for it. The watch chain snaked tightly up her arm. The man called out, "Ari, Ari."

Fear crawled up her back, along her shoulders. Again, the white hand thrust up from the water with the jeweled ring in the palm. But again Ari could not grasp it because of the coiling watch chain.

And she felt she must stop the rest from happening. She had to.

Yet it all unreeled just as before. The earth shuddered. Fog stained the mountain's face. The wolf howled like a soul in torment. Now the terror that gripped her whole body was colder than the peak's wind-blown snow.

She was sitting upright in her bed, shivering without the quilt's protection on her shoulders. Her breath was still ragged when she understood that she was awake. Her room, made unfamiliar by the piled-up sacks, slowly took on its recognizable shape. The images that had so frightened her began to ripple away.

For a moment Ari forced herself to hang on to the dream, to understand it. Perhaps the sudden changes the lawyer mentioned had brought it back, although the explanation didn't satisfy her. If these images reflected her fear about saving the mountain, why were they identical now that she'd won the money?

Stretching to relieve the tension, she saw the early light through the window. The day's awaiting pleasures began to surface, beguiling her. Ari decided that, for the first time in her life, she would do only what pleased her. She heard the magpies' cheerful croak, and it sounded like an invitation to join them.

Quickly she dressed in the shirt she'd saved and a pair of jeans and headed for the kitchen. She smiled to herself, thinking that the birds deserved a feast too. She'd give them the rest of the chicken. Then she'd go for a bike ride and take herself out for breakfast. Carrying the pock-marked metal tin with the magpies' food, she walked out into a dawn flaming with promise.

CHAPTER 2

The morning sky was taking on its usual uninterrupted blue as Rivers Alexander stared out of his office window in Denver. He'd come early, awakened from a restless sleep, and had enjoyed his walk through the city, washed by last night's rain, looking at glass skyscrapers turned momentarily into golden towers by the rising sun. But the sense of contentment that had brought him was gone. After arriving he'd opened his rolltop desk but hadn't been able to sit. Now, he rapped the solid oak of the window frame with the heel of his hand as he thought.

He turned and resumed a leopard pacing across the shining hardwood floor. He moved with the muscular grace of those animals, who are both wary and sure of themselves. His dark-lashed, light eyes even had the tinge of green of that large cat's, but his were unlike the leopard's enigmatic ones. Rivers's eyes reflected shifting moods, were more readable than he intended.

As he strode, he pushed up the turned-back cuffs of his pale yellow shirt. His brown-flecked silk tie was still crammed in the pocket of his tan sport coat, tossed carelessly over a cane-backed chair. His own high-backed black leather chair with its swivel base had been his father's; the desk had belonged to Patrick Alexander, his grandfather. When Jonas Murdoch had bought the Alexander mansion for his downtown offices, he'd wanted the fine old furniture as well, and except for a few cherished pieces, Rivers had sold it all. His own loft in Lower Downtown Denver would hardly have accommodated what amounted to several floors of solid Victoriana. He had, however, stored his family portraits.

With uncharacteristic tact Jonas had allowed Rivers to choose whichever of the upstairs rooms he'd like as an office. This front room on the second floor had once been his mother's sitting room. Then it had been decorated in a pale Wedgwood blue. The soft swag drapes had been replaced by efficient Levolor blinds, the delicate secretary with its pull-down top was now in Jonas's own home. But Rivers had kept the clean-lined reproduction Adam bookcase with its glass front and carved scrollwork at the top. His mother had died when he was only seven, but he remembered well her opening it, choosing a book to read him a story, and smoothing his hair as they sat together, her arm close around him.

At the moment he was thinking of a woman he'd never met. Although his phone conversation with Ari MacAllister yesterday morning had been brief, he was trying to imagine what he could have said to make her see sense. After all, the sale would benefit her as well as Murdoch. She *needed* money.

His father had been idealistic, and Rivers remembered the cost. He'd loved the man, but he resented Thomas Alexander's wholehearted dedication to public service. Rivers was very skeptical about the good that could be done that way, and it was mixed in his thoughts with all those lonely hours he waited in the window seat, a small boy who desperately wanted his father to come home. Then, too, Thomas's concentration on his work had meant the decay of the family fortune. There was just enough to pay for Rivers's education. He'd attended Denver's best private schools and later an Ivy League college, but he had always been surrounded by friends with money and choices. He felt like an outsider.

So he'd decided to get money. Murdoch paid him well, and Rivers knew he could learn from the man, could become a financial power in his own right. His past had given him a hungry edge. He saw money as necessary. Usually he liked his job, found it varied and interesting. Jonas gave him a wide range to find ways to invest money productively.

Rivers resumed his pacing, smiling as he thought of a recent proposal of his that had turned out quite well. Studying various companies whose stock seemed lower than it should have been, he'd liked Consolidated Chemicals's, a relatively new company formed by a merger of several old-line eastern firms. The stock price was low because Con-Chem was responsible for restoring ground saturated with what was now known to be hazardous waste. The Wood Canal disaster had been laid at their door.

Still, Consolidated Chemicals had a solid line of products and a huge cash reserve set aside for the cleanup. That pile of money alone made the company attractive for a takeover, which would send the stock soaring. Rivers saw it as a good bet. Jonas agreed and bought all the outstanding shares. The stock obligingly rose in price.

It had also crossed Rivers's mind that, with Jonas holding a thin majority of the scattered stock, Murdoch and Associates would be in a position to oversee the cleanup. He had no illusions that Jonas would be interested in doing good unless he was also going to do well. But at least his employer was always careful about not breaking laws, however he might stretch them. White-collar crime was now often prosecuted, and subordinates were caught in the net as well.

That idea caused Rivers to stop in his circlings around the room. This scrupulousness about the law did not extend to one Murdoch employee. Jack Dexter. It certainly didn't apply to the man Jonas was talking with downstairs right now. Caley Sutherland.

Everything Rivers knew about Caley caused him to distrust him. Although Caley had escaped prosecution in the spectacular collapse of Denver's biggest savings and loan, it had been a close call. That he was in a meeting with Jonas at all was unusual. In a sense he was a competitor; Caley had his own firm, Sutherland Investments.

Rivers frowned, rolling his yellow shirtsleeve another turn over his muscular forearm, trying to imagine what Caley would be doing here. Then he glanced down at his piled-up desk and decided he'd probably learn soon enough. But the image of Caley remained in his mind. Eyes so light blue they were almost transparent—yet they were somehow impenetrable. No hint of gray in his blond hair, although he had to be in his mid-forties. He looked even taller than he was because he, like many Denver businessmen, invariably wore cowboy boots. The impression he gave was of absolute smoothness, which hid the sharp edge of his thought. No, Rivers didn't like the idea at all of doing business with Sutherland.

Flicking at the Telluride file on top of his desk, he remembered that he hadn't wanted to work on that project either. But Jonas had pointed out that Rivers knew the mountain resort well. And he did, having gone there many times from grade school on. The Wyndhams, an old Denver family with sons his age, had a place there and had taken him along on ski trips. This very familiarity, his love of the town as it was, had made him unhappy about the development of Ute Rise Canyon. Still, preserving it now that the price of land had soared was, despite Ari MacAllister's wistful hope, out of the question.

Rivers had pushed the idea aside while he climbed Torrey's Peak near Denver later in the morning, his whole attention focused on inching his way up the difficult couloir. In that narrow gorge the summit was not even visible. He'd had to concentrate on jabbing the pick of the ice ax firmly in, then using it to pull himself up as he dug the sharp points of the crampons on his boots into the slick surface. Still, as he'd stood on the top, looking over the sea of lesser whitecapped peaks rising up below him, the problem had come back. Always, after completing a climb, he had a glorious the-world-is-mine feeling. On Sunday, along with that triumphant sensation, he'd been reminded of her sense of responsibility.

He'd heard again that soft voice with the iron of conviction saying, "I'd always have to feel that I sold my birthright for a mess of pottage. Or, in this case, sewage pipe. I would be the one who lost it." But now, as he drummed his fingers on the file, he knew there was no way to stop the oncoming bulldozers. Only a dollar-hard wall before them could even slow them down. Rivers remembered the shabby frame house on the main street of Louisville whose basement Ari MacAllister rented. There was no way *she* could manage it.

He was just grateful he'd have no further part in the Telluride project. It would be turned over to the lawyers at this point. One of them could negotiate with the woman. Just as he was about to shove the file away, a discreet buzz sounded, indicating that Murdoch wanted to talk to him. Rivers picked up the manila folder and started for the stairs.

Jonas Murdoch lifted his finger off the built-in button on the side of his desk and almost, but not quite, leaned back against the support of his leather chair. His straight-backed posture and imperially slim figure delighted his London tailors, for he showed off their meticulously fitted suits to advantage. In fact, Jonas could well have posed as lord of the manor in estate ads of the glossier English magazines. Not, of course, as a full-cheeked, comfortably tweedy squire. The Murdoch men, father, son, and now grandson, all had spare features, fleshless eyelids, aquiline noses, almost disappearing lips. In Jonas's case it resulted in a pared, patrician handsomeness. He did not look fifty.

The elegant, high-ceilinged room he'd chosen as his office was equally sparsely furnished. Once the parlor of the Alexander mansion, it had been filled with solid pieces of mahogany and rosewood and pleasant overstuffed settees. Luckily, Patrick Alexander had bought most of this attractive furniture before the eclectic excesses of the 1890s. It fit well in the Victorian mansion Jonas had recreated in southeast Denver for his home.

Looking at Jonas, one would have imagined he'd have preferred the more disciplined Georgian style of architecture. But to him the Victorian spoke of his family's past, reminded him of the gloomy but substantial pile belonging to his grandfather William, which had not been torn down until the 1960s. Jonas had a real interest in his family's history, as well as that of Denver and Colorado. While he considered himself fortunate in being the heir to an immense amount of capital—accrued before there were income taxes—he did not think luck had that much to do with it. He considered it a matter of superior genes. He'd always felt that his study of history bore that out.

The subject made him glance, almost unconsciously, at the door through which Caley Sutherland had just left. The financial past of his family had been intertwined with that of the Murdochs for most of the century. But Caley did not have anything like the Murdoch fortune. Here, Jonas quite consciously smiled, making a habitual gesture. He enclosed all the fingertips of his right hand over the black and gold ring, set with a diamond, on his left hand.

It was not, he mused, that they hadn't started roughly equal. Stanton Caley's father had done extremely well in meat packing. While Stanton hadn't applied himself to business, he was good at conserving. No, his real mistake, in Jonas's view, was in his choice of a wife, the mother of his child. Not only was she penniless and not of his class, but her background showed what could be considered an inborn taint. Ceci Caley, of course, had become Denver's grande dame before her death twenty years ago. And she'd been very, very careful with money. Managed it amazingly well for a woman, Jonas thought. But there was her past.

Jonas's thin lips stretched even wider. He was sure that he was the only man in Denver who knew that Caley Sutherland's formidable grandmother had started as a whore in Telluride. Even Caley himself had no idea. But the Murdochs liked secrets, almost as much as they liked money, and they hoarded them. When Enos had passed this one on to his son, he'd pointed out to Jonas that keeping Ceci's secret would, in the long run, be profitable. If she even suspected anyone knew, she would certainly have moved away. And she had her millions deposited in the Murdoch bank.

Murdoch usually recalled Ceci's past when he saw Caley Sutherland. It soothed him. For, despite the other man's lesser fortune, Jonas was more than a little jealous of his competitor. Caley, through his own business acumen, had certainly increased his holdings. In the ten years since he'd returned from abroad, he'd doubled and tripled his inheritance, which had been stagnating in the Murdoch Bank Trust Department. He'd done, comparatively speaking, much better than Jonas had in his investments. And Jonas insisted on winning across the board.

Moreover, Caley's reputation as a financial wizard made him much sought-after for advice. In the Denver Country Club locker rooms, at the Cherry Hills Men's Grill, the other members gravitated toward him. Pretending casualness, they asked his opinion on a real estate deal or the stock market. In the past they'd always deferred to Jonas's experienced voice.

Although Murdoch, in private conversations with these men, mentioned that Sutherland was reckless, that he sailed too close to the wind, they still gathered around him. It was true that if Caley should be so much as indicted for an infraction, they'd drop him. Denver society honored convention and the letter of the law. Misdeeds that might have been shrugged away by the upper classes on both coasts were frowned on in this western capital. But as it was, there were only insider stories and rumors, and Caley's bold style was much admired.

He had equal success with beautiful women, many of them rich in their own right. It seemed that he escorted a different one to every society event. Some were the divorced wives of men in his own set. These women could now go to the Denver Country Club only as guests. After the separation, no matter whose money had originally bought the high-priced membership, it remained with the husband. Caley had never married, but everyone agreed he could take his choice when he was ready.

And, there was that irritating manner of his, cocksure no matter how he disguised it with charm.

That morning Caley had arrived, crossing the expanse of office with an outstretched hand and a smile of fellowship. He'd immediately inclined his head back toward the conference room, where there were padded chairs, and actually ushered his host into it. Suppressing his temper with an effort, Jonas led the way, too curious about the reason for the call to object. But in his annoyance he found himself thinking that, since Caley was making himself so much at home, it was a wonder he hadn't also brought his dog, said to be a fixture in his own office.

The dog was a cross-breed, a mix of German shepherd and wolf, and Sutherland was almost never seen without it. Even on the street it was not kept on a leash. Meeting Caley by chance one day, Murdoch had commented on that, and the man had raised an unconcerned shoulder, saying it was "in control." But Jonas thought the animal had an unnatural way of avoiding one's glance. When it did look up, it had the colorless, unreadable eyes of the wolf.

Seating himself, Caley had said, with what seemed enormously good-humored candor in his pale eyes, "Jonas, I have a proposition you'll like. One that would make us partners, for a change."

Murdoch, folding his fingertips around his ring, had listened impassively. He hid every sign of his growing interest as Sutherland continued. Caley had met a young man named Frederic Steiner, whom he described as a brilliant "gene engineer." Steiner had bred a very useful bacterial form, one that lived on the waste products that Consolidated Chemical was having such difficulty getting rid of.

"Jonas, think of a voracious little Pac-Man, gobbling up all that noxious chemical soup now spoiling what could be valuable ground. It can chomp on *inorganic* compounds. Think what a patent like that would be worth to Consolidated Chemical. Your stock would quadruple in price."

Immediately, Jonas also thought of an enormous advantage that just the possibility of this "Pac-Man" would give him, even if it proved unable to gobble. But he didn't mention that to Caley. Instead he said, his thin lips approximating a smile, "Why so generous? Why let me in if you have this prodigy in your pocket?"

Caley lifted his palm in a rueful gesture, with a certain grace in his acknowledgment of Jonas's superior resources. "I can't capitalize this kind of operation. Especially now. I'm heavily into long-term investments, and I'd lose too much if I cashed them in."

Giving his ring a quarter turn, Jonas wondered if that were true. It could be. The man had a lot of irons in the fire. And Murdoch felt a certain smugness because Caley was so foolish as not to keep more liquidity.

"Steiner," Caley went on, "wants to call his company GeneSys, short for Genetic Systems, pronounced like *genesis*. By the way, you can check with his former professors at CU. They speak very highly of him, thought he was a genius when he was an undergrad. Of course, he has no business background, and setting up something like this calls for expertise I don't have. You do. In this field *you're* the genius."

Jonas knew he was being flattered and for a reason. But there was the way Caley did it. He made his compliments sound like simple statements of fact. Jonas began to feel expansive. He might have agreed even without the additional advantage to the deal that he'd seen but hadn't mentioned.

Caley flashed his disarming smile. "Of course, what I also want is a stock trade. Half your shares of Consolidated Chemical for GeneSys stock."

Normally, Jonas would have balked at this. Because the ConChem stock had gotten spread out before the merger, he now had a majority, even though he owned only fifteen percent of the shares. Selling half to Sutherland would cause him to lose that majority. But he had a piece of information that Caley didn't. Murdoch's stockbroker had murmured quietly on Saturday night at the country club that he'd located a widow willing to sell a substantial block. If he bought that he'd still have a controlling interest.

So although Jonas frowned at the mahogany conference table and seemed to be reluctantly deliberating, he was already half persuaded. What he said was "I'll have to think *that* over. In the meantime I'll have Alexander check out Steiner and his idea. Rivers did some research on hazardous waste before I bought ConChem. I'll need to hear what he has to say."

But after Sutherland had left, Murdoch sat unmoving at his desk before pushing the button to call him. What was uppermost in his mind was not simply the proposal that he'd just been offered. He was brooding over the idea of changing his entire investment philosophy, choosing stocks that were riskier but potentially more profitable. As a matter of fact, he'd be adopting Caley's high-roller approach to the market, although he didn't put it that way to himself. He *was* aware that if he succeeded, he would again resume his rightful place as the business leader in Denver. But Jonas had another reason, one that he found very hard to swallow, for considering this change.

He'd been taught, and he believed, that the Murdoch money was a sacred trust to be managed carefully so it could be handed down from one generation to another. There had only been one snag in this dynastic plan. Jonas had no sons. His wife, Faith, née Manningham, had had a complicated second pregnancy and the doctor had said it would be unwise for her to attempt another. The doctors consulted at the Mayo Clinic had concurred, as well as a famous specialist in San Francisco. Jonas rejected the idea of divorce, having inherited along with the Murdoch money a quite rigid system of beliefs that had little to do with established religion. The values he'd acquired in the past were not, to him, open to question. Even having a mistress could lead to expensive problems. And divorce interfered with the orderly flow of money.

Besides, he thought Faith was well suited to him. She came from what Jonas regarded as almost an old-line Denver family. Her grandfather, Theo Manningham, was English, with a reasonable claim on a peerage, and he'd come to Colorado shortly before the turn of the century. He'd married a woman of good family, Elizabeth Bender. Theo had worked hard and had acquired a solid fortune in Colorado real estate. Faith had inherited, along with other property, that now very valuable mountain canyon named Ute Rise.

Outside of her failure to produce a son, Faith was a perfect wife, as Jonas formally complimented her in toasts at the annual country club dinner. She ran the household and managed servants with a fixed eye on Jonas's comfort. At his request she invariably cooked his breakfast herself and very often dinner as well. She'd kept her neat figure and was always properly dressed. When their older daughter, Judith, had displayed a distressing tendency to plumpness, Faith had conveyed her own and his displeasure without overt nagging. Jonas had had to step in when their second daughter, Heather, had taken up with the wrong crowd from a public high school, but he could see that the decorous Faith had been staggered by this teenaged wrongheadedness. Heather had even dated steadily an Italian boy from the North End, but her father dealt with the situation firmly. In all other respects Jonas was pleased with the way Faith had brought up the girls. At the time of their marriages he'd thought they were both a credit to him.

But now, thinking about his sons-in-law, Jonas leaned all the way back in his chair, drawing a slow, dissatisfied circle with his forefinger on the glove leather armrest. Judith's choice had initially delighted him because he saw it as a merger of two distinguished families. Quentin Wyndham IV was an heir to the family sugar-beet fortune, and the Wyndham men were always tall, blond, and very handsome. On her wedding day Judith's pale prettiness had for once been transformed into beauty, and she and Quentin had made a regal couple. Jonas looked forward to the birth of his grandsons, knowing he was young enough to be able to teach them about the business world.

But, after five years, there were none. No children at all. Judith had spent time working with the Junior League, and now was talking of pursuing a graduate degree in art history at the University of Denver. Although Jonas had given Quentin an office on the ground floor, his son-in-law rarely appeared there. Being a Wyndham, he had a trust fund of his own, and he much preferred golf. He was very good at it. Before playing with him Jonas had put in an occasional eighteen holes and enjoyed it as much as he could enjoy a nonbusiness activity. But Quentin had defeated him so resoundingly that Jonas gave up the game. He didn't like to lose at anything.

Worse, when Jonas brought up the subject of grandchildren, Quentin merely gave him a bland smile and shrugged, as if it were not a matter of concern. Murdoch's forefinger increased the speed of its unhappy circle. He considered now that the Wyndham history had its dark corners that might indicate weaknesses to which he should have paid more attention before the marriage. Quentin's father had died piloting his private plane into the side of a mountain, and there were rumors he'd been drinking. Then, too, there was his great-aunt Lillian. Jonas recalled that his father, Enos, had been scandalized because there'd been much talk of divorce between her and her husband, Devin Lowell. He'd overheard his parents discussing it in hushed tones as he had entered the dining room. Seeing him, his father had dropped the subject abruptly as an unsuitable one for the young. But Enos had not been able to resist adding with a tight mouth, "Mind you, Devin Lowell had a promising future. I always thought her a silly woman, unable to be a proper wife. Now she's gone off to Washington alone, imagining herself able to influence political events as a society hostess. Bah!" His father had, of course, been right about Lillian.

His second daughter, Heather, was married to Scott Askew, who mystified Jonas and angered him. The young man had a fine background, old eastern money, although there was no longer a lot of it. Still, he had a good lineage and had graduated from Princeton. He was pleasant looking, solidly built, athletic. But he was content to coach at Graland Academy! It was Denver's finest private elementary school, but still a grade school. Teachers' salaries at such schools were very low, and without Heather's trust the couple could never have afforded to live anywhere near the school, much less indulged in their ski trips and vacations abroad. Scott seemed untroubled by the fact that he couldn't maintain his life-style on his own money.

Heather had lately devoted herself to women's causes, and when Jonas mentioned grandchildren to Scott, he'd smiled cheerfully and said that when the first one arrived, he planned to cut back to part-time coaching so he could care for the child. That way, he'd added, Heather could continue her volunteer work. Murdoch had looked at him, his thin lips vanishing completely, immediately suspecting a lurking femininity. He shuddered at the example his grandson would be given by a stay-at-home father.

Jonas was still musing on his disappointing sons-in-law when Rivers came into the office. He crossed the large room and sat in the window seat, stretching out his long legs. There were no chairs before Jonas's uncluttered desk, which focused the room on the man behind it. When Murdoch's fellow investors came, they met in the adjoining conference room with its padded armchairs. Jonas's employees stood before it when talking to him.

It had never occurred to Rivers to do that. He was accustomed to sitting before that bay window as he had as a child. Although Murdoch was not used to thinking about other people at length, because of the way his mind was running now he looked more closely at the young man across from him. The Alexander men, he considered, had a flaw. Patrick had acumen and failed to use it. Rivers's own father, Thomas, had not paid proper attention to business. Jonas found that he could still vividly recall the beautiful face of Helen Rivers, who'd had no background. Seeing their son, he contrasted him with Quentin Wyndham and Scott Askew, his daughters' choices. Somehow, he felt obscurely betrayed by history.

For this young man had ambition and a force of energy that reached across the long room, even as he sat looking through his notes in a file. Even when he'd hired him five years ago, Jonas had been impressed with his ability to state succinctly the advantages of a particular investment. He'd listen to any objection, his light, clever eyes assessing the point, and more often than not argue his case again. He'd been wrong several times, but not often.

Shortly after Rivers had begun working for him, Murdoch had also taken on Jack Dexter, a local boy whose parents had only moved to Denver after the Second World War. Dexter, too, was ambitious and he had a quality that Jonas, and Enos before him, placed a high premium on. Loyalty. Jonas had never precisely defined the term to himself, but it took in more than just a single-minded devotion to the family's interests. It encompassed as well an understanding of their business principles, that making money was paramount, that nothing interfered with that.

Jonas recognized that attribute in Jack Dexter. He was not sure that Rivers was capable of it, since he had his own ideas. Dexter never pursued any investment that Jonas expressed doubts about. And he always stood deferentially before the desk while they talked. Yet it was usually Dexter that he sent on the road and Alexander that he kept near him. Rivers had polish, knew how to get people to see things his way.

Murdoch immediately launched into an outline of Sutherland's proposal. He finished by saying that replacing the stock in Consolidated Chemicals that Caley wanted was likely so that the slender majority wouldn't be lost.

Rivers only asked, "What do you think he's *not* telling us?"

Murdoch hesitated briefly, recalling the advantage he'd seen that he himself had not told Caley. It was this: the hope of a scientific breakthrough in dealing with chemical waste would be a good reason to delay the hazardous-waste cleanup. It would take a congressional bill to do that, since the courts had already ruled that Consolidated Chemical was at fault. In the meantime Jonas could imagine good uses for the huge cash reserve set aside for the cleanup. But he decided against telling even Rivers about that plan. After all, Rivers would be the ideal man to lobby U.S. senators for the extra time, and it would be much better if he didn't know everything.

Jonas gave his ring a quarter turn. "You're right to be suspicious of Sutherland. We'll have to find out how good this "invented" bacteria is. Go see Steiner. And talk to the experts."

Rivers grimaced. "One thing I found when checking out Consolidated Chemical, Jonas. Experts don't agree. Nobody is sure how to clean up that goddamned mess."

Jonas pursed his lips, then replied, "Find a consultant that you can at least understand, even if we have to pay through the nose. Make sure he's discreet." He glanced down at his notes for the day before asking, "Telluride in place?"

Rivers shook his head slightly. "A problem. The young woman who owns the mountain square in the center doesn't want to sell. I've talked to her. It's not a matter of money; she wants the area left undeveloped."

Jonas's eyes flickered. He said, "Surely this is just an attempt to hold us up for more money."

"No." Rivers's tone was decisive. "But she's not able to pay her share of the costs of roads and other improvements."

Murdoch waved a commanding hand. "Then she has nothing to say about it. She can't even become a nuisance."

Rivers's mouth twisted a little at the way that last word was pronounced. Jonas abhorred what he called "nuisances," and for him, that was any obstruction—big or small—in his plans. He rarely ran into an obstruction. He was cocooned by his wealth, and Rivers had seen how all his employees, as well as his wife and his daughters, scurried to protect that webbing. When it was disturbed, Jonas had a nasty temper.

Rivers replied, "Let one of the lawyers explain to her how expensive roads are."

Jonas raised his eyebrows fractionally. "Lawyers are also expensive." Like most rich men he was very conscious of costs that could be avoided. "Dexter's in town. He'll talk sense to her."

Rivers ran a thumb over his full lower lip. This was one of Jonas's favorite ploys. He liked to set Dexter and Rivers against each other, perhaps as a way of ensuring loyalty to himself. If one of the two men didn't arrange things to Murdoch's satisfaction, Murdoch would imply that the other one could have. It worked, partly because Rivers didn't like Jack Dexter. He thought the man was obsequious to Murdoch and his investors, but overbearing with everyone else. He certainly would be with a penniless idealist.

Then Ari MacAllister would get her back up even further. Rivers had a mental image of her, although he'd never seen her. Despite the lovely voice she was probably plain, a little dowdy. A sense of humor, yes, but she was earnest, no doubt one of those champions of causes, a good many losing ones. She'd have to sign in the end, but with Dexter handling it, it would all take a great deal of everyone's time. And Jonas would blame Rivers for not having dealt with it in the first place.

Standing up, he said reluctantly, "I could try again. I'll drive over and talk to her now. It's still early. I should catch her in."

Murdoch slid open the slender, almost undetectable drawer in the front of his desk and glanced at a leather-bound engagement book. He kept his own appointments and disliked hovering secretaries. He nodded. "The architect and lift engineers are bringing the final plans in at the end of the week. Take care of her."

CHAPTER 3

Ari was having one of the most delightful mornings of her life. As she drove, she kept glancing blissfully down at her new outfit. Her silk shirt was a pale amber, and she'd liked the style so much that she'd bought another in a periwinkle-blue to wear with a crisp white suit on Wednesday. Her linen pants were an oatmeal shade and her shell flats were the same color. Her hair was tied back with an amber and apple-green scarf.

She was surrounded by the smell of the car's pristine leather, the delicate but pervasive odor of the huge spray of roses on the seat beside her, the hint of perfume from the tissue enfolding her purchases in their elegant boutique bags. Against her skin she felt the luxurious swish of the just-bought satin and lace lingerie, the cling of the silk shirt. Although it was not yet noon, she was marveling at all she'd accomplished.

After a long bicycle ride past fresh June fields, she'd taken herself out for coffee and homemade pastry at the just-opening bakery in Louisville. The most expensive car the small rental firm in town had was this shiny four-wheel-drive Blazer and she'd driven home in that. Pull-

ing her bicycle out of the back, she'd hurried in to the phone and, after
a pause in which a kaleidoscope of emotions held her still, she slowly
dialed the number of the plastic surgeon. Within a moment she had an
appointment with him. As she replaced the receiver, she knew she'd
firmly launched herself into the river of change. Then, since she and
Janie had agreed that Wednesday would be the day to appear at the
Lottery, Ari called and spoke to the Denver office of Blackburn and
Barton about getting her friend here.

She'd sunk down at the kitchen card table and taken three deep
satisfied breaths while she considered the rest of the day. After shopping, she'd decided on a picnic lunch. Although yesterday's could
hardly have been bettered in one sense, she recalled she hadn't gotten
around to the actual eating after she'd read the newspapers. Today
would be different. She planned on buying the champagne Janie had
suggested and picking up something suitably expensive at Alfalfa's
wonderful deli. She would toast the mountains.

She'd quickly folded up the quilt from her bed and pulled out the
old square of canvas to spread beneath it, going back to the kitchen for
the one remaining crystal goblet she had squirreled away on a high
shelf. Then she remembered the half-eaten apple pie that she'd baked on
Saturday and frugally packed it too. Clutching her credit card, Ari had
sailed out the door and headed for the stores on the Pearl Street mall in
Boulder.

Now she turned onto the asphalt of the two-lane back road, thinking that she had only one more thing to take care of, and that was the
most important. Soon she reached the wrought-iron gates of the old
Louisville cemetery, and even from there she could see in the distance
the tall scarlet maple that had been planted as a sapling when her
mother and grandmother were buried. Beneath that tree Isobel Ewen
and the MacAllisters had plots next to those of Devin Lowell, Bridey,
and Trish. With the future so brand new, Ari felt the need to be reminded of all that was good in her past, to grasp on to it almost fiercely.

Carrying the roses, she went past weathered headstones, some
leaning askew, until she reached the maple. Through the years Mrs.
Mac had brought her to the cemetery and they would fill the metal
vases at the foot of the graves with the season's garden flowers. Since it
was June, Ari thought, they'd have had huge, nodding peonies and
velvet-mouthed snapdragons.

She pulled a regal red rose from the spray and laid it on Isobel's
grave. On the shining gray marble of her headstone was etched a wide-
petaled apple blossom. Ari read again the familiar words: SHE NURTURED
THE EARTH, DREW BEAUTY FROM IT, GAVE IT TO OUR LIVES.

As Ari glanced at the engraved hearts above the plot of Devin and Bridey, she spread two roses on the grassy earth. She felt a warmth of gratitude welling up for all she'd been given, and she suddenly realized that it was *she* who needed the mountain to save and not the other way around. It was a true North in the quivering compass of her new world. She murmured, almost aloud, "I'll do my best to protect it. I promise. I'm the fourth generation. It's true our family didn't stay in that valley, but *I* am going back."

Putting another flower on Trish's grave, Ari looked at the engraved date, aware that, at twenty-three, she was almost as old as her young mother had ever been. All Ari had of her were the snapshots and a remembrance of enveloping arms, a scent of herbal soap, a sense of safety. She thought that if she herself could do something worthwhile, it would make up for this unlived life.

Just as she'd straightened from laying the spray between the two MacAllisters, blessing them again for their unstinting love, she heard a timid "Excuse . . . me?" behind her. Startled because she'd not heard anyone approach, she whirled around.

The older woman before her was wearing a speckled black-and-white dress with a tatted lace collar. She had on short black gloves and an upside-down-saucer straw hat with a perky bow in front and a bit of veil that covered graying brown curls. Ari had often seen that kind of hat at the Thrift Shop. It seemed somehow to suit this small, birdlike person and her diffident, old-fashioned manner.

"I am sorry . . . to disturb you," she said, her words coming so hesitantly that she seemed to be considering every one before she let go of it, "but I seem to have misplaced my glasses. And . . . the other pair is in the car so I can't find them. The lost pair, I mean. And without those I can't locate the car. I've been wandering all around, looking at the old tombstones, and so I've forgotten where I parked. Would you mind very much just glancing around . . ." she let the sentence trail off, an apologetic smile lighting soft brown eyes that had the blurry look of someone who badly needed glasses.

"Sure." Ari smiled back. "Where were you?"

"Well . . ." One neatly darned gloved finger pointed backwards, and she started to accompany Ari, but almost tripped over an exposed root of the maple.

Ari caught her arm and said hastily, "You wait here. I'll go look." She'd already seen something glinting in the sun on top of a salmon-pink marble headstone and went off to check.

When Ari returned with the glasses, the woman slipped them on and peered at her gratefully. "Now I can see you. At first . . . I thought maybe you were part of the sunlight because of your hair and your blouse. Such lovely colors on you, my dear. Thank you."

As she was moving off, she paused and glanced down at one of the inscriptions. "Bridget," she murmured. "That's a wonderful name. So powerful, you know."

"Powerful?" Ari asked with interest.

"The name itself is Celtic and means 'strong.' It was originally spelled B-r-i-g-i-t, and she was a ruling goddess, far older than Celtic Ireland, her worship having come with Gaelic Celts from their original home in Galatia." Now that the woman was on a subject that absorbed her, her eyes lit and her words came rapidly. "When the church found it impossible to eradicate her cult, they tried making her a saint, declaring she was nun who had founded a convent at Kildare. But the convent was noted for its heathenish miracles and evidences of fertility magic. It was said that cows never went dry there, that flowers and shamrocks sprang up in Brigit's footsteps." She beamed, adding, "It's hard to reduce a goddess to mere sainthood."

"I didn't know any of this," Ari replied in surprise. "And that's my middle name. Ariana Bridget."

"That's another Celtic name. Ariana. It means 'pledge.' "

"It's appropriate," Ari said musingly. "I've made a promise. One I hope I can keep."

Tilting her head to one side and fixing her bird-bright eyes behind the thick lenses on Ari's face, she answered firmly, "You will. You have a glow, as if you've been touched by good fortune. I'm glad to have met you. My name is Sybil. Sybil Morris."

Ari reached out to shake her hand and grinned. "I know the origin of your name because of the Greek myths. Yours means 'prophetic,' doesn't it?"

"Yes." Sybil gave a chirpy laugh. "But it's a little amusing that anyone with such bad eyes should have a name that's synonymous with 'seer.' Still, I pride myself on my inner vision."

"What does Morna mean, do you know?" Ari asked, stretching out her hand toward her mother's grave where the full name—Morna Patricia Gregory—was engraved.

"Yes, indeed," Sybil replied. 'Beloved.' I gather your family came originally from Ireland. Mine too. I've always believed that one day I'd go back, look up the records, trace the whole family tree. I can't be wrong about that. I can positively see myself getting off the plane at Shannon Airport."

Ari sighed. "It wouldn't do me any good to try, I'm afraid. My great-grandmother was called Morna Gregory, but that wasn't her own last name, we're sure. She'd left her husband and didn't want to be traced. And she never mentioned his name either. I'd love to know who she was, what happened to her before she came to America."

"Without a name," Sybil said thoughtfully, "it would be hard. Do you have any clues at all? Where she came from, for example?"

"Bridey—my grandmother Bridget I mean—said her mother told her stories about Castle Connemara, and in the family we always believed that's where she grew up."

"But if that's true, you're well on your way, my dear," Sybil returned confidently, "although it wouldn't be easy. Still, as a member of the Irish aristocracy, she'd be listed in *Burke's Peerage*. You can at least narrow it down to families from Connemara. And if that was the actual name of the residence, and you can approximate her birth date, you'd know. I'm a genealogist, you see, and I'm very familiar with that book. It will also give her husband's name and both of their death dates."

"Would it give *where* they died?" Ari asked, almost breathlessly. "None of us knew what happened to my great-grandmother after she left Colorado."

"No." Sybil shook her head. "But, because they were landed people, you might be able to find that out. People have long memories back there, especially in villages and small towns. I know it's hard for you to imagine, since you're young, but your great-grandmother, well . . . we're only looking at ninety years. A lot of people in their eighties would remember stories they heard about the local gentry when they were ten. In fact, they recall those better than anything they might have heard yesterday. It's only a matter of listening to them, asking the right questions."

"Is that what you do, Sybil?" Ari asked in growing excitement. "For a living, I mean."

"Yes." The older woman's head nodded with such enthusiasm that her hat's small veil fluttered. "I pore over official records, go through libraries, examine old tombstones. That's what I was doing today. Then, the best part, I go talk to the elderly with time on their hands. They so enjoy an interested audience. Unfortunately, it takes a great deal of my time, and most people can't afford to pay much. Sometimes there's travel involved. But"—she waved her gloved hands cheerfully— "not always. The Church of Latter-day Saints has wonderful computerized data from all around the world. And they're very willing to help, even if you're not a Mormon. In any case, it's work that I love."

"Sybil," Ari said, jubilation in her words and shining in her face, "please give me your phone number. You're right in thinking I've had a stroke of luck. And it means I can afford to pay. Go back to Ireland and while you're there, you can trace your family tree. But I want you to find my great-grandmother for me. I want to know who she was and what happened to Morna Gregory."

Reveling in this new hope that she might find more of her past, glorying in the perfection of the summer day, Ari sped away from the cemetery. She took the Eldorado Springs turnoff west toward the mountains, since that way lay open fields and wide vistas. It was after one o'clock and her picnic lunch was uppermost on her mind. She'd bought the Dom Perignon in Boulder, although she'd been absolutely shocked at the price. While paying for the champagne, she'd thought in alarm that it probably worked out to be about three dollars a sip. Then she'd caught herself and grinned, wondering how long it would take her to stop worrying about money.

But Ari slowed momentarily, wearing a half grimace. She'd forgotten to stop at Alfalfa's for food. All she had to eat was half a pie. On both sides of this road were only scattered farms and greening pasturelands between the foothills, their rounded purple bulk shading the long expanses. But she didn't want to turn back to the city. She wanted to live in this moment, with the sun warming her bare arm on the car's open window and the nostalgic scent of fresh-cut hay surrounding her. On the radio a sweet jazz saxophone lulled her, making her decide to play the rest of the day by ear, do whatever took her fancy. Shrugging happily, she kept driving, thinking that a champagne that cost that much ought to go with any food.

Soon she found that she was far more sleepy than hungry. The buoyancy that had kept her awake all of last night was now giving way to a pleasant drowsiness, and it occurred to her that she'd not slept in the open air since she was a child. Swinging the Blazer onto the edge of a sloping field, she saw not too far off a grove of cottonwoods in a small hollow, and she gathered her canvas and quilt and set off in that direction. There she spread them on the fresh shoots of springy grass showing through the wispy clumps of drifted cotton from the trees. With a sigh of satisfaction Ari lay staring up through the lightly swaying leaves at a hyacinth sky. She dozed off almost immediately.

What woke her sometime later was a chattering match between two red squirrels in the tree above her, and she sat up, refreshed. Pulling her silk scarf from her hair, she let the cooling breeze further tangle the flyaway curls. The sun through the leaves dappled the new grass, and the wind lifted the feathery cotton from the trees and sent it flying about her like warm snow. Feeling the peace of nature made her aware of the exhausting swing of her own emotions, made her grateful for this calm slope.

It was not until she stood up for a luxurious stretch that she saw the man in the middle of the uneven field, his back to her. He was pacing, his long strides even and deliberate. As she watched, he stopped and pulled an orange-tipped stake from his pocket. He bent and shoved it into ground soft from a recent rain, then used one foot for a hammer.

The late afternoon sun streaked his brown hair the tint of the stalks of goldenrod near him as he stooped. He was lean in brown slacks, the long sleeves of his yellow shirt turned back at the cuff. He moved energetically, his motions efficient and sure. Startled, Ari stepped back, although she guessed that he'd not seen her because the surrounding trees were in a low, bowl-shaped depression. She felt a rush of anger, imagining a tract city here with asphalt roads and concrete driveways. She looked at him with the narrowed eyes of a more experienced Eve seeing another serpent.

Just then, as he was measuring his steps along the top of a drop-off in the hilly field, he disappeared abruptly from her view. She stared blankly for a second and then, realizing the spongy earth had collapsed beneath him, hurried in his direction. But even before she reached him, she heard his low voice. Approaching the ledge gingerly lest she go slipping down as well, she peered over. Flat on his back in the eroded hollow, he lay laughing.

CHAPTER 4

Rivers Alexander did not see Ari on the ledge above him at first. He was casting his eyes to the heavens, thinking it was time to put in a complaint to the powers above. Since his reason for being in this field was unselfish, he didn't feel the ground should have given way beneath him. He was doing a favor for a friend while he was waiting for Ari MacAllister.

He had repeatedly called her, then driven to Louisville. But her phone seemed off the hook, and she was nowhere to be found.

Then, planning on trying her again later, he'd decided to stay nearby. As he was in the area, he thought he'd inspect this field. The land was owned by a high-school friend who desperately wanted to sell it, and he'd pleaded with Rivers to take a look at it in the hope he could offer advice. Preoccupied with his task, he hadn't paid sufficient attention to the porous ground, although he was now reminding himself that as an experienced climber, he was used to testing the surface. Laughter seemed the only answer.

Ari looked down at him, her concern giving way to her previous irritation. He seemed quite unhurt. The strands of blond-on-brown hair fell neatly over his forehead, the handsome, angular face was creased in a smile. Even his tie, although loosed at the throat, was straight. The yellow of his shirt was bright against the sandy soil with its rock out-croppings, clustered like mushrooms, that spotted the dry streambed in the hollow.

Under other circumstances she would have caught the self-mockery beneath his unexpected laugh. But her hackles had been raised by what he was doing. Moreover, she recalled with annoyance the confidence in his manner, measuring the earth as if he thought that was his unques-tionable right. A few pieces of mountain wilderness, she fumed, could certainly be left for the future.

Before she realized it, she bit out the question, "Are you a devel-oper?" Then she noticed the way his right knee was twisted sideways and added, "Are you okay?"

Rivers raised himself on his elbows and stared up in surprise. The sun behind the woman illumined her mass of curling hair, transforming it into a cloud of brown and bronze, added shades of red and gold. He took in the birthmark on her cheek, but his attention was caught by the expressive, wide-set eyes, the generous mouth. Her silk shirt was stretched across what looked to be perfect breasts and was tucked into the top of slacks that skimmed shapely hips. *Very nice,* he thought. He continued to stare at her, observing ruefully that his current position was hardly the way to impress her. Worse, she seemed to dislike him even before she'd met him.

With a slow grin at the way the day was going, he said, "Why is it that I get the feeling that if I say yes to the first question, but no to the second, you're not going to rush to my rescue?"

Ari flushed, feeling that she was really in the wrong by not having asked first whether he was hurt. She began to stammer, "I'm sorry. I should have . . . it's just that I . . ."

Rivers sat up, liking the genuineness of her response. He cast about for something to say, thinking there should be some book on the mar-ket that listed conventional phrases one could come out with in unusual and awkward situations. The author would say helpfully, "You've just fallen into a dry creek bed and a stunning woman appears. Say the following." But all Rivers found he could do was stare at her. When in doubt, he thought, try humor. But he couldn't summon up one scrap of wit. At last it occurred to him that her gloriously curling hair reminded him vaguely of an old movie. He brushed off his hands, saying lightly, "Thanks, Ms. Frank. I'll live."

"That's not my name," she replied, taken aback.

"Your hair," he said, trying to look as if sitting here was the way he'd planned to spend his afternoon. "It's quite lovely, but it reminds me of the actress in *The Bride of Frankenstein*. You know, what's-her-name."

"Elsa Lanchester," Ari responded automatically, looking in vain for the scarf she'd left back on the quilt. She tried tucking some of her hair behind her ears. He was one of those extremely good-looking men, she thought touchily, who never seem at a disadvantage. Such men had always made her more than a little nervous. She'd treated them with stiff coolness, and it had never crossed her mind that their response to her was due to her manner and not her birthmark. "Aren't you going to get up?" she asked, with an edge of exasperation.

"Yes, ma'am, Ms. Frank." He began to rise effortlessly without using his hands, but halfway up, he sat down, twisting his lips in pain. "No, I'm not. Damn! I've reactivated my bum knee. Probably strained it yesterday." He pulled up his pants leg, exposing a muscular calf and a knee crisscrossed by surgical scars. Wincing, he explored it with his fingertips.

She looked around for the safest way down the embankment, then hesitated, wondering if he could be faking an injury. They were quite alone and there wasn't a house for miles, she remembered.

Noticing her indecision, his easy grin returned. "I haven't mugged anyone this week. Honest. I'm a mountain climber. And look"—he pointed to the embroidered kneecap—"I've got the scars to prove it."

"That doesn't necessarily mean—" she began severely.

"The next thing you'll say," he interrupted, holding up one hand, "is that Ted Bundy looked trustworthy."

"Just what I was thinking," she retorted, telling herself that there was absolutely no need for her to have to justify such an idea to him. She was, after all, only being sensible. Nonetheless, a twinge of guilt made her scramble down hurriedly. Too quickly, she realized, as the slippery soles of her new leather shoes sent her skidding to his side and in danger of toppling over him.

He reached for her reflexively, catching her upper arm in a rock-hard grasp. Then his face twisted at the injured knee's contact with the ground. "And Jill came tumbling after," he murmured. "Sorry."

"I'm okay," she replied shortly, and bent down to offer her other hand. His skin was cool, and she felt again that amazing strength in his hands as he concentrated on pulling himself up and standing, flamingo fashion, before her. As he stood, still clutching her tightly for balance, Ari was at first only aware of his physical presence and a vitality that seemed to surround her, to come from the ends of his fingers. She was not sure whether the quiver in her arm was from his grasp or a tremble of her own.

Since he was just under six feet, Ari's upward glance met his quickly, and his eyes, neither blue nor green, were vivid, darkly lashed. She looked down immediately, her gaze sliding over the curves at the edges of his expressive mouth. He let out a ragged breath, and she thought she could feel it as well as hear it. Only on the rare occasions when she'd been reluctantly persuaded to attend a dance, had Ari been so near a man's embrace. In this case she wanted to stand exactly here and yet step back from the force of him.

Finally releasing her hands, he scooped one long arm around her shoulders. "Well, now," he said pleasantly, ignoring her surprised start, "what next?"

The crisp scent of his ironed shirt, the faint odor of sweat, was in her nostrils and Ari moved her head, angling to look up and down the streambed. The shelflike bank extended in both directions, the soil steeply cut. They'd have to get closer. "How does the idea of crawling grab you?"

"By the throat, Frankie, especially because I'd have to do it on one knee." He leaned harder on her, working his good foot in the sand to turn toward the bank.

"Don't call me that," she answered, trying to focus on the problem. His closeness was more than unsettling.

"Why not? You could call me Johnny," he returned.

The line from the song—"Frankie and Johnny were lovers, and, Lordy, how they could love"—flashed through her mind instantly, and she guessed from the quirk at the corner of his mouth that he was recalling it too.

"Can you hop until we get to the steep part?" she said tartly, sure that a warm flush was rising to her face. "I could try to push you up from there."

He nodded, and she encircled his back with her arm, a little taken aback because it seemed so natural to do so. She could feel the perfectly defined muscles above his waist. His fingers dug deeper into her shoulder as they staggered forward over the soft soil.

At the incline he tilted forward, caught himself on his palms, and, clutching the few rocks available, began hauling himself painfully upward. With only a second's hesitation Ari pushed him from behind, two hands squarely on his buttocks. Then she scrambled ahead of him and pulled with all her strength on his forearms. He groaned when his injured knee grazed a rock, but he lunged forward, at last lying prone on the grass. He let out a breath and closed his eyes.

Ari quickly knelt beside him. There was a faint sheen of sweat on his forehead, and what the effort had cost him showed plainly on his face. His mouth looked vulnerable. She noticed that he had two sets of creases near it, as if he smiled when he thought of something, and then smiled at himself for thinking it. A real sympathy overtook her. "Okay?" she asked anxiously.

He opened his eyes slowly. "You sure know how to show a guy a good time, Frankie."

Ari smiled down at him in relief. That glint of humor she saw reflected in his eyes also covered more than a little embarrassment. "Tell you what," she suggested, "I've got a four-wheel drive. It won't get stuck. I'll bring it here."

By the time she'd returned with the Blazer, he'd inched toward a nearby thick-trunked pine, evidently planning to pull himself upright.

"Wait," she said, getting out quickly. "I'll help you."

Rivers sat up, flicking pine needles and dirt from his shirt. "Sorry, but I think you're going to have to." He touched his knee carefully. "Do you mind waiting a minute till the nerves stop jumping?"

"Sure. I'll get my stuff over there."

When Ari returned with her canvas and quilt, he had his pants leg rolled up and the swelling was now obvious. "That does look bad," she said, eyeing it. "Maybe we could tie something around it?"

"No." He shook his head. "I know the drill. Ice, unfortunately, is what we need first. Later, I can wrap it."

"Do you know," Ari said slowly, "I just might have some." She remembered the liquor store owner lovingly packing ice around the Dom Perignon in the foam cooler she'd bought there and went to get it. Lifting the cooler from the middle seat of the Blazer, she also picked up the T-shirt she'd worn to the boutique. Next to him she laid out the canvas and then the quilt and, kneeling on the cover, spread out the T-shirt and began scooping ice into the middle.

He watched her, looking at the bright hair blown loosely by the wind, the long eyelashes that now hid the eyes flecked with gold, the curve of her full lips. Nature, as if wanting to compensate for the stain on one cheek, had given her flawless skin, he thought, his eyes moving down her throat to the blouse's opening. As she bent over, the lace of her bra did not quite hide the swell of her breast, and the lace's whiteness was a contrast against her glowing skin. He was struck by a shining about the girl herself, separate from the sheen of her shirt, the sparkle of the glittering stones of her ring. He grinned to himself, deciding he'd complain to the universe more often if it made amends in this fashion.

"If you can lift yourself onto this," Ari said, patting the quilt, "you can stretch your leg out." He did so, and she handed him the ice pack. At his smile her self-consciousness returned in full force. To avoid his glance she looked down quickly and, seeing the bottle of champagne, held it up. "I have something to celebrate, so I bought this. Maybe if you drank some, it'd go right to your knee."

He whistled, a low laugh in his throat. "You *must* have something to celebrate. Now, that's an idea—Dom Perignon as a painkiller! And the ice. You must be the legendary Woman That Has Everything."

"Not quite. Only one glass. We'll have to share. I'll get it."

As she moved to the Blazer, he noticed it was brand new. He remembered her asking, with a prickle in her voice, if he were a developer. The environmental movement, he mused, seemed to be attracting interesting women. But this one, he *knew,* given the car, the ring, the clothes, didn't live in any basement apartment in Louisville. Just as he decided that she probably was at the University of Colorado, which had a lot of rich students, it occurred to him that with her, he didn't want to start the usual conversation that ran on rails of "how-do-you-do; what-do-you-do?" What surprised him most was that she did not try to hide her thoughts, her quick feelings. Perhaps she could not. Each was mirrored faithfully in the eloquent eyes, the responsive mouth.

As she brought back the sack she'd packed at home, Ari was only aware of the fact that, in walking back to him, she had to concentrate on the motion of her legs, as if her body could not be relied on to move in its usual manner. It was partly the way he looked at her, making her feel as if she'd just been created, risen from white sea foam. But, too, it was his very presence, which made her intensely aware of herself, and yet absorbed by him.

Because of that she knelt next to him, although she realized the only practical way to share a glass was to sit beside him. This was a safe compromise. She held out the goblet. Unhooking the top wire, he twisted the bottle in his strong hands, rather than the cork, and it slipped out with a sigh instead of a loud pop. "You can't waste a drop of this stuff," he said as he poured the sparkling wine. "You take the first sip, but I'll make the toast. I owe the gods one today. Here's to 'answered prayers.' "

His direct gaze was so forceful, it was almost a touch on her cheek, and she looked instead at the golden liquid. "Perfect choice for a toast," she murmured, and hurriedly took a sip. Then she gasped. "Why, it doesn't feel as if you're swallowing anything! Except bubbles."

"Right." He grinned. "Try again. Wait till that effervescence hits your veins."

"Mmm," she said with delight after a second sip, "that champagne tastes like a Fourth of July sparkler looks. Here, your turn."

"Mmmm," he echoed, after drinking. "It tastes like the feeling after you finally get to the mountaintop."

"What's that feeling like? Is that what you climb for?"

"Yes and no." As he explained, she settled next to him, but she was still so conscious of him that she didn't let her arm so much as graze his sleeve. Yet his words recalled her own spinning high on the ridge yesterday, and they seemed to be sharing a memory.

"Yes, I see what you mean. The challenge, the concentration needed. But when you get there, I know how *that* feels," she said slowly. They sat together in silence. He refilled the glass a little at a time, and they handed it back and forth, occasionally holding up the crystal and seeing through amber bubbles a green sky. Ari thought that if ever she was asked to define happiness, she would describe this sun-drenched afternoon, this sensation he gave her of nerve-tingling difference and absolute oneness.

It was only when she had trouble taking the goblet back from him that she realized she was a little dizzy and should eat something. "I'm starving," she said, reaching for the sack. "Would you like a bite of apple pie?"

"Pie," he replied in amazement, a dark eyebrow rising. "You have *pie* too?"

"Well, I made it on Saturday," she replied, bringing out the tin and fork, "but it should be good. Better warm, of course. Open your mouth."

It seemed perfectly natural to hold out the fork for him, one hand cupped beneath it to catch flaky crumbs. When he cupped his around hers, though, and she felt his fingertips, her mouth went dry. She quickly took a bite herself and put the plate on his lap.

"My God," he breathed, cutting a huge chunk. "I don't think I ever had homemade apple pie before. No wonder it's a national symbol. Look, next picnic, I'll bring the wine and the silverware. *You* bring the pie."

She could see it was an effort, but he saved a piece for her. Somehow she wanted to giggle as she ate, watching him take a thirsty gulp of the champagne. When she followed suit, the most mundane remark made them both laugh uproariously. Soon he slid down, stretched out on his back, readjusted the ice pack, and sighed peacefully. Still hiccuping a little with laughter, Ari did too.

It was only when the late afternoon mountain chill slid along her arm that she opened her eyes. He was resting on one elbow, looking at her. The blood rose to her face, and she was sure both cheeks were the same bright red color. The idea of anyone staring at her birthmark made her acutely uncomfortable, and she felt her whole body flush and prickle with heat. She sat up hastily. Starting to gather her things together, she asked, "Where's your car?"

He gestured to the far end of the field. She stood up, afraid that her embarrassment made her clumsy, and saw the rakish lines of a low sports car in that direction. "Down there," he said, adding as he stared at the swollen knee, "but I can't drive it. Stick shift. Could you give me a lift back in to Louisville so I can catch a cab to Denver?"

"Oh, I can take you home." Her tongue felt thick. "It's no trouble."

"Thanks," he replied, his smile delighted. But the genuine pleasure in his voice and in his eyes did not reach through the wall of her insecurity. As she helped him to the car, even though he circled her shoulder tightly and her arm wrapped his waist, she could only feel her separateness. The closeness she had sensed disappeared. She'd never known anything like it before, and now it was gone. He said nothing, seemingly absorbed in an effort not to put too much of his weight on her and yet none on the injured knee.

When she climbed into the driver's seat and switched on the ignition, she brushed her hair, almost unconsciously, over her cheek. He reached over and smoothed it back. "What are you hiding," he asked gently, "the birthmark or you?"

Her fingers tightened on the rim of the steering wheel as she realized how aware he was of her feelings. She turned the car in a wide semicircle toward the road. For a second she couldn't imagine what words could get through her constricted throat. But then she relaxed into his awareness and the terrible grip of shyness miraculously unclenched its hold. Her voice sounded almost normal, she thought, and she was not even surprised at the straightforwardness of her reply. "For much of my life I've felt that most people only saw *it,* and not me at all."

His answer was quiet. "I can't believe that's really true. You're so beautiful—they'd have had to notice. But I can imagine that *you* believed that." As if to save her a response he went on. "In those teenage years, anyway. Why did we have to feel we had to be exactly the same as everyone else? Above all, why'd they tell us those were the best years of our lives? They have to be the worst."

He half laughed, half groaned. "Do you know, I still cringe over certain memories, even though, looking back, I can see how funny they were. Or would have been, if they'd happened to someone else. I have to tell you about my dancing class."

Later, Ari couldn't remember the details of his story. It involved his stuffing his pockets with macaroons, and a disastrously spilled cup of strawberry punch. He told it well, and soon she joined him in his rueful laughter. They covered the miles to Denver in what seemed minutes.

CHAPTER 5

When Ari stopped before the address he'd directed her to in Denver, she thought that, engrossed in their conversation, she'd not heard him correctly. It was unmistakably a warehouse in Lower Downtown, an area whose name was shortened, sometimes disparagingly, sometimes affectionately, to LoDo. True, this narrow rectangular building had had its warm red brick scrubbed, in contrast to the grimy exteriors of some of the surrounding old factories and boarded-up storehouses. The carved molding beneath the roof, too, had been freshly painted a deep gray to match the outer doors.

It was located a block from Market Street, a main thoroughfare once called Holladay Street. For much of its early history bordellos had lined the sidewalks. The bawdy houses were near Union Depot and convenient for all the new arrivals, although a mile and more from the once-proud mansions of Capitol Hill. A few blocks of bustling Market Street had been refurbished, but the process apparently hadn't spread here.

Just as she was turning to him questioningly, Rivers said, "Pull up to those loading doors on the side, will you?" He took out an electronic key, and the metal doors slid back to show an enclosed courtyard for parking. She drove into one of the lined spaces, saying slowly, "Weren't you telling me about a Victorian house on Grant Street?"

"Yes, that's where my office is, in the house where I grew up," he replied matter-of-factly. She imagined a family business, thinking that must be how he'd acquired that ingrained air of self-confidence, that sense of place in the scheme of things, both the past and the future.

But then he added with a grin, "Living here fits into our tradition too. I've been told that my grandfather Patrick was a generous supporter of the Holladay Street madams. More than a bit of a rogue, although he was said to be charming. He eventually settled down and married my grandmother, but that was after she'd borne him several sons."

Ari could see the double smile lines on each side of his mouth deepen. He went on as she cut the motor, "I didn't know my grandfather—my dad didn't marry until he was fifty—but when I look at his portrait, it's a little like looking in a mirror. What impresses me, though, is the detachment in his eyes, as if he were diverted by what he saw, but not touched by it. My father was the opposite. He felt everybody's pain, and had to do something about it."

He turned to face her, and Ari had a startlingly vivid image of a small boy spending lonely hours in a window seat, waiting for his father. Before she could take it in or sort it out, he asked, "Don't you think Patrick had the best of it?"

"Not really," she replied, with fervor in her voice. "He had it easier, maybe. That is, if you're judging him right." As she said that, she could now imagine the man beside her in a stiff wing collar, the hair a little longer and brushed back, a more ironic but equally vulnerable mouth. Ari almost blinked, as if the past had materialized from the old bricks surrounding them. She continued with a rush. "I'm not sure you are, you know—it would be hard to guess what his life was like. But if the question is, should you commit yourself to something outside yourself, greater than you, I think yes. Otherwise, you don't live at all. Of course, if you care that much, then you're open to the pain and . . ." She paused, feeling the color rising to her face again, then bit her lip. "Why *is* it that when you try to say what's important to you, immediately you think of how much better it's been said before, and that you sound like you picked it up at a bargain basement at the After After-Christmas sale."

"It's all in the *way* it's said. You clearly mean it," he answered. As she met his vivid blue-green gaze, Ari was again seized by the sense of intimacy with a man she did not know.

And the tone of his next words had the sureness of a friend's. "I hope you don't mind helping me hop in, but I want you to see the inside. I think you'll like it."

On the second floor the elevator doors slid directly open onto a huge two-story expanse that at first seemed all window. Because the west and south walls were glass, the room was decorated by the front range of the Rocky Mountains and the intense blue of the sky above them. Shaking her head, Ari said, "You're not sure if you're outside or in."

"A great view," he agreed, letting go of her shoulder and supporting himself on the kitchen counter. "I never get tired of it, even though the railroad tracks clutter up the foreground a bit." Ari turned full-circle in the room. A kitchen area with oyster-gray appliances was built against the east wall, separated from the entrance to the elevator by a curving counter. Swooping down against the stripped brick of the north wall was a spiral staircase that started at the high ceiling with its exposed pipes and disappeared downward into a circle in the floor. All the colors in the soft organic furniture were quiet neutrals, as if to emphasize the mountain's granite grays and muted blues as well as direct one's attention to the sky's brilliance and change. The Indian rugs scattered on the floor had only winks of red, flashes of old gold.

Rivers had edged his way to the comfort of a couch and had his right leg stretched out straight. As Ari approached him, she could see fine sweat again glistening on his forehead. Below his pulled-up trouser leg the knee had swelled to twice its size. "Ouch," she said, grimacing. "Don't move anymore. Let me get you a fresh ice pack."

She scooped up her dripping T-shirt, crossed to the sink, and wrung out the cloth. Intending to swing open the freezer door of the double-sided refrigerator, she grasped the wrong handle and found herself staring at shelves and shelves filled with cartons of fresh pasta and nothing else. Smiling at him over her shoulder, she remarked, "Based on the contents of your refrigerator, you must be three-quarters Italian."

"Well," he said, raising himself up on his elbows, "we mountain climbers *need* complex carbohydrates. And I like pasta. And I know how to cook it." He lowered his head back onto the pillow, adding cheerfully, "And that's *all* I know how to cook."

When she handed him back the ice, now covered as well in a thick hand towel, he grinned up at her and explained, "See, what I do is boil it up, then I throw whatever else I've got in a frying pan with this really good olive oil, and then mix it all together with grated Parmesan. If I had two working legs, I'd make it for you." He stopped. "Wait. I'm starving. There's a really good Italian restaurant a few blocks away. They don't deliver, but—"

"We *definitely* don't need take-out Italian," Ari interrupted, holding up her hand, a laugh bubbling up. "I, too, can boil water. What else have you got?"

"You'll have to look in the bottom drawers. Some vegetables, probably." He crossed his hands over his chest contentedly. "I'm beginning to see the advantages of this knee."

Ari's head disappeared into the refrigerator and then she began lining up the contents of the crisper on the counter separating them. "One green pepper, one really nice red one, a glorious yellow one, celery, two usable cloves of garlic. But I don't see any Parmesan."

"No nice little triangles in the cheese drawer?" he said, with a small frown.

"Nope," she replied, sliding that open. "There's only a square of feta cheese, plus a container of Greek olives and a package of walnuts."

He clicked his fingers in dismay. "That's right. I went to the Greek Market on Tenth yesterday instead of the supermarket."

"But this will be good," Ari returned enthusiastically. "We'll use the peppers, the feta—and the walnuts." At the surprise in his face she nodded firmly. "You'll like it."

"It's a deal," he said, sliding to a sitting position without moving his leg. "You boil, I'll chop."

Afraid that he was about to move to one of the stools at the counter, Ari started to protest, but he gestured to the polished gray of the marble dining table near the west wall. "That comes apart in sections. If you'll slide one over and bring the peppers, I'll slice and dice."

Glancing at the table, Ari saw that each slab had an individual wrought-iron base rather like the scrolls of old sewing machine treadles, and she moved the nearest to him. As she piled on a cutting board, a knife, and the vegetables, he said with a charming smile, "I do my best work with wine. The good reds are downstairs. Cellar temperature, you know. The Italians are on top of the wine rack in the corner."

Ari wound down the spiral staircase, stopping at the bottom step because her heart felt as if it would leap from her rib cage. He had the same effect, she thought with a grin, as aerobics or bicycle riding, but this was a great deal more fun. She glanced around without seeing a wine rack.

The lower floor was all bedroom, the corners stacked with various kinds of sporting equipment. The king-sized bed had giant pillows against the headboard, and a down quilt in a patterned cover that imitated blue-veined marble had been thrown in that general direction. It almost made it over the bed.

One long wall was a compartmentalized closet, with hanging baskets for sweaters, separate divided sections for shirts and trousers, a tie rack, and built-in drawers. These were neatly filled, but there were several shirts tossed over a nearby chair, ties draped over those, and a pair of trousers spread on the floor. A blue cable-knit sweater lay crumpled behind a lacrosse stick, an ice ax, and Nordic ski boots.

Pushing open a door at the end of the room, she saw a white-tiled bathroom the size of a locker room with a sit-in shower. As she turned back, the reflection in the wide mirror startled her. For a second she didn't recognize the entranced stranger in the golden shirt smiling back at her. Even her eyes and hair had picked up that sheen. She thought, *Because he sees me as pretty, I am. No . . . I am because I see myself that way. Or is it just that I'm happy?* She smiled again at the direction of her thoughts, deciding that at least she looked nice.

Going back to the bedroom, she was sure of the joy of meeting him, and enormously glad that it'd happened today, when she was still certain of who she was. If the future and her fortune changed her, and changed the way men would see her, she would know that *he* liked who she'd been, this Ari. "Frank," Ari heard him call, "I forgot to tell you, it's in back of the skis." She had to move three pairs of assorted sized skis to get to the wine rack.

When she handed him the bottle and the corkscrew from the pegboard on the kitchen wall, he said musingly, "I don't suppose that I neatly shut the doors of my closet before I left this morning."

"No," she replied, trying not to grin, "but I didn't trip over any wet towels. I think you get points for that."

"The trouble is," he complained, pulling out the cork, "those closets are made for clean clothes. What do you do with the half-clean ones? Three fourths of those compartments should have hooks for what you know you'll wear again, so you don't want to confuse yourself by mixing them in together. They don't design closets for real people. Next time, I'll—"

"Stuff everything in every which way and shut the door," she finished. "Just like everybody else."

"Right," he agreed, holding up his glass for a toast. "To next time. My treat, and you get to choose the restaurant."

Before she sipped, Ari raised a finger. "And dancing after. I intend to buy a wonderful dress."

"Couldn't you just eat in it? The dancing part would let out tomorrow night"—he gestured toward his injured knee—"which I was hoping for." He pursed his lips. "But dancing when feasible. Promise?"

"Promise." She touched her glass to his.

They later agreed that the pasta was perfect, and the wine just right with it, since it was smooth but strong enough to stand up to the olive oil and the creamy cheese. They found they agreed on almost everything: that an English major (hers) was a better choice than economics (his) because one got to read novels and poetry rather than study bars and graphs. He complained that since graduation he'd never had the need to look at either, let alone a pie chart. And, as they stared out at the evening sky, they were united in saying that Goethe was wrong in observing that one tired of the loveliest sunset after a quarter of an hour.

The sunset flamed into the room, first with sunflower and coral, then crimson and vermilion, then lapis and mulberry. The tinted clouds obligingly changed their forms from dragons to alligators to salamanders. The two of the them lay back on the soft cushions and named the colors and the cloudy shapes until the sky above the mountains was a deep and even marine blue.

They disagreed on the necessity of doing the dishes, but Ari insisted, and Rivers lay in the semidarkness, at last able to stare at her without making her shy. He watched her neat, swift movements, noticing how the track lighting of the kitchen shone on her hair and caught the sparkle in her golden eyes when she looked up to smile. His eyes lingered on the swell of her breasts.

When she returned with a fresh ice pack, Ari realized she was relieved that his sprawling on one couch meant there was no question of sitting near him. She remembered her shiver at only the graze of his hand when he gave her his glass and thought it odd that, as she'd helped him in from the car, his body seemed familiar, circling his waist an easy thing. Yet each unexpected touch reminded her he was an exciting stranger.

She clicked on the lamp and inspected his knee. "It's really gone down, I think," she said.

"Yes." He nodded, lifting himself up to look at it. "That's a good sign. If ice and elevation work, I probably don't need an X-ray. And I can wrap it, which really helps the pain, not to mention the walking."

"Got an Ace bandage handy? I'll get it," she offered.

"In the bathroom. Under the sink."

But as she headed for the spiral staircase, she stopped. "Well, I probably should help you downstairs now," she said. There was regret in her tone, and his answering look held it too. The moment before she spoke, they'd both felt there was still a little more time. But then, at her words, they knew the evening was over.

"Probably best," he answered resignedly, raising himself up on his elbows. "These couches are just a little too short for sleeping."

He slid down each step carefully, his right leg stiff before him, his weight on his arms. By the time she'd returned from the bathroom with the bandage, he'd taken off his trousers and was stretched out on the bed, gingerly lifting the leg. She saw the heavy muscles of his thighs below his shirttail and quickly averted her eyes. Raised on a farm, she was hardly ignorant of male anatomy, and she reminded herself as she stretched the elasticized cloth around his knee that she'd often wrapped the horses' legs. But when she'd finally secured the binding with the metal clips, her palms were sweaty.

"Is that better?" she asked as she finished. He was leaning back on the overstuffed pillows that formed the headboard, his eyes closed, the bedside lamp showing the contrast between the dark eyelashes and the sun-streaked hair on his forehead. She noticed for the first time that the leanness of his jaw was punctured by a slight cleft, that his lower lip was much fuller and softer than the straight upper one.

"Much." He opened his eyes and grinned at her. "Thanks."

Ari slid forward toward him on the edge of the bed, intending to hold out her hand and introduce herself. That seemed impossibly silly, and she impulsively leaned forward to brush his cheek with her lips, to wish him a good night first. But just then he sat up, and instead their mouths met. The kiss was soft and long and infinitely sweet.

She had imagined a hundred times what it would be like to kiss a man just like this. But she hadn't known what it would be like to have his lips move beneath hers, to feel the caress of his arms enfolding her, the hardness of his chest against the fullness of hers. She would stop in just a moment, she thought, but first she wanted to touch his cheek, and she slid her fingers down its length, aware of the faint stubble beneath the smoothness. His embrace tightened.

And she didn't want to stop just yet. It was delicious, the way she was relaxing, although every part of her body seemed suddenly more keenly alive. He sank back against the pillows, pulling her with him, and she lay spread across his chest, in the crook of his arm, their mouths refusing to part. His fingers stroked and tangled her hair, his hand turning so the knuckles again and again lightly grazed her chin, the side of her neck. His lips seemed to murmur endearments although they never left hers, even as his long arm scooped her legs onto the bed, even as he clicked off the lamp, leaving only a slit of light from the door to the bathroom.

He kissed her into sleepiness and back to tingling wakefulness. In neither state could she will herself to stop. *Not* just *yet,* she told herself. *Just a little longer,* she thought, part of her sinking deeper into the mattress, all of her straining against his length.

One moment she was sleepily, blissfully warm, and the next instant much too hot. Her shirt clung oppressively, stickily, and she slowly unbuttoned it, shrugged it off one shoulder, then the other. Then her bra seemed too tight, digging in above her rib cage, and she raised herself to unhook it, but her mouth couldn't part from his even for that instant. When he slid out of his shirt, and their bodies met, his flesh was cool and hot, and she rubbed her breasts against him, in catlike ecstasy, murmuring back at him beneath his kiss.

There was a sound deep in his throat, and his mouth lost its tenderness, became demanding. She knew then she could not make herself leave. She felt her bones would not hold her weight were she to rise up, as if the sizzle and heat of her blood had melted them. She wasn't going to leave. She wanted him desperately but with an odd clarity, as if he was a gift she'd give herself, for no man could ever again make love to the woman she was at this last moment of her old life. But beyond all of that, she wanted him.

When his lips finally left hers, to move, as soft as summer, along her chin, she tried to urge them to the swollen tightness of her breasts. But instead he nuzzled her ear, lightly licked the edge, pulled her lobe between his teeth. He whispered to her, and his words quivered through her veins. He ran his tongue along her shoulder, down her arm, pressed his mouth on the inside of her elbow. There was no part of her left untouched, unkissed. As he moved, she ran the tip of her tongue on his skin, amazed at the saltiness of the taste, but noticing that he smelled just like her. His body seemed again new, strange, and yet familiar.

When his fingers and then his seeking mouth finally reached her breast, her back arched in exquisite relief, her fingers dug in his hair, into his back. She lay absolutely still in this pleasure, not quite breathing. She was saying something, something, she did not know what. But she could not now stand the pressure of the waistband of her slacks, the rub and stricture of the fabric against her legs. Unbuttoning and unzipping with a sense of deliverance, she pushed the pants and underpants down and away from her body.

When he moved away, just for an instant, Ari could not stand his absence even that long, and curled anxiously next to him, pressing against his back. She heard the slide of a drawer, the snap of plastic, and then felt the consolation of the return of his mouth, his hands, and then his naked embrace. She held his head, exulting in that meeting, willing his lips not to leave hers again.

His fingers stroked her stomach, circled her navel, and at last they probed her, and she gasped at their delicate and insistent touch. Her body shuddered, trembled, loosened. Soon, even her arms fell limp onto the pillows. She felt an almost embarrassing wetness between her legs.

But she couldn't resist then sliding her hands along his length, down the hipbones, across his stomach. Perhaps it was that he sensed the surprise in her fingers as she grasped his thickness, perhaps it was the tentativeness with which she touched him. Suddenly, he rolled onto his back, staring at the ceiling, and his voice was hoarse, his question a statement. "You haven't done this before. Ever. Have you?"

"No," Ari breathed, shocked at the sudden coldness without him. "But—"

"Look," he said, and his voice was harsh and gentle, and she could feel the effort it cost him to say it. The muscles jumped in the arm that lay next to her, his breath rasped. "Then you shouldn't. No. Not now. You'll—"

"Yes," she said, putting her fingers over his mouth. "Oh, yes. Now." She slid unabashedly over his body, her erect nipples tantalizing against his chest, her moist legs wrapping his left thigh as if to ease that way the ache he'd aroused. She breathed in his ear the words he'd whispered in hers.

The low growl in his throat was immediate, unthinking. He grasped her shoulders, rolled her onto her back, his full weight on her. His kiss was urgent, rough, but she returned it, opening her mouth beneath his as if to take his breath itself. And her legs opened wide to him.

Ari didn't know how long she'd slept or what wakened her in the darkness of his room. The streets outside were quiet, and there was only a sliver of light from the bathroom. She glanced around, remembering, and immediately sat up. As she did so, she jerked from the scrape of pain between her legs. But to her surprise that chafing had the effect of arousing desire again. Shaken by that hunger for his mouth, his arms, his weight, she twisted toward him.

He slept on his side, with one arm outstretched to where she'd lain, his tousled hair almost dark, his eyes closed, only the outline of his lean face, the strong line of a shoulder, visible. Staring, she thought that the force of him, the energy, should have been blunted by his sleeping, should have been lost in the darkness. His gaze was hidden, his body relaxed. But she felt as if he were reaching up to her, pulling her down to rest on his arm, to adopt once again the rhythm of his breathing. For that moment she did not think she was able to resist, was not going to. It was only the sudden, but unmistakable, shock of fear that sent her almost tumbling from the bed.

Even later she didn't clearly understand it, but then she was telling herself as she hurriedly gathered her crumpled clothing that morning would come, that it would be better if he called her. She would write a note upstairs with her name and number. Now she was only filled with the urge to go as quickly as she could, afraid that he would waken, and then she wouldn't go.

It was only at the top of the spiral staircase that Ari paused to catch her breath. A three-quarters moon swung over the mountains, illuminating their peaks, the silver light pouring into the dark room, and she almost walked to stand in it, as if it could cool her skin. But that unreasoning need to hurry overtook her and instead she turned to the kitchen, whose lights still burned.

Picking up a pen by the phone, she fanned out a stack of mail, looking for a stray piece of paper or envelope on which to write. Then she caught sight of the name and address on those letters, and she let them fall through her fingers to the floor.

He was Rivers Alexander.

She'd talked to him only yesterday. He wanted to buy her mountain.

She felt the brief, hopeful thrust of denial. Ari almost groped for the counter, leaned against it, trying not to believe what was very clear. Then the questions started. Could he have known who she was? But no, even she hadn't known where she'd be or that she'd stop just there. And the car was a rental. Had she said anything that might make him suspect? All he probably had was a Louisville address; she was sure that she hadn't mentioned the town, had implied that she lived in Denver by her offer to take him there.

One thought cut against another as she tried to find a way out. He *personally* didn't want to buy the mountain; he'd even said he understood. It was the man he worked for who did. . . . But that was bound to affect the two of them. Of course, it was unthinkable that Rivers himself would try to persuade her, based on . . . Was it unthinkable? What did she know that made her sure of that? And what on earth would she say now when he phoned, knowing he had another reason to call?

Anger arose, and Ari shut her eyes tight, wanting to pound on the counter tiles in frustration. She had no idea at whom that anger was directed. It wasn't at herself, and it was absurd to level it at him. But there it was, clawing at her stomach.

She tried to concentrate. What *would* she say . . . ? But then in quick relief she realized he couldn't call her. He didn't know who *she* was. Although, what if at work, he tried to call Ari MacAllister . . . ? She wouldn't answer the phone. And she couldn't leave a note. She'd have to sort this out in her own head first. She had to leave immediately. Grabbing her purse, she hurried to the charcoal-gray doors of the elevator. She was still anxiously punching the button when it silently arrived.

As the doors slid shut, she clenched the wide metal support bar. Her eyes were dry, but the salt of tears stung her throat. She tried painfully to will away her confusion. Then she made up her mind that the best thing to do, while she considered all this, was to go to Telluride. Yes, she would leave immediately after going to the Lottery Office. That thought made her remember the photographers who would be there.

She'd have to leave because he'd see her picture and know who she was. Just the thought of hearing his voice caused her to shiver. She'd go to Telluride right away.

CHAPTER 6

Halfway through the article on the front page of the *Denver Post,* Caley Sutherland put down the paper and shouted with laughter. The woman who'd won the Sweepstakes owned a mountain right in the middle of Telluride's Ute Rise Canyon. He knew to the penny how much Murdoch had already spent on start-up costs there. He checked for her name while he thought, *She's got twenty-five million bucks and she doesn't need to sell. Up yours, Jonas, you son of a bitch.* There was no humor in his fierce smile.

"Loki," he said aloud, reaching down and tugging on the dog's ear, "we've got to get ahold of this girl. She's going to need help investing that money. A commission for me. And a little tighter screw job on Jonas."

He let go of Loki's ear, and the dog sank down on the redwood deck. For a moment the shepherd-wolf cross fixed its startling light eyes on Caley's ankle, then they closed.

Caley put down his coffee cup and lit a thin cigar. The deck of his house in the foothills overlooked Denver. Glass skyscrapers shimmered in the bright morning sun, giving the center of the city an insubstantial look, as if it were all a mirage. The house behind him was a modern A-frame, jutting out from the hillside, not set back in the pines. It was more glass than redwood, and birds often flew into the two-story windows, falling stunned to the deck. Loki disposed of them.

The sunlight restored the natural gold to Caley's hair, which had faded, his only sign of aging. There'd been no softening of the squareness of his jaw or telltale wrinkling in his smooth skin. He'd always avoided the sun, since it bothered his eyes, which were almost colorless except for a touch of blue. That Nordic fairness was inherited from his father's side, the thick blond hair, light brows and eyelashes, and he'd managed to escape the male pattern baldness of Stanton's line. Although a little thicker-set than in his youth, he was fit. In his mid-forties, physically he was stunning.

Caley blew out a stream of smoke, thinking that Jonas was overdue for some hard times. He himself had had plenty. It'd taken a high-priced lawyer to get rid of the drug charges in Boulder. Then all the years Caley was forced to stay abroad during the Vietnam War draft, his trust money had sat earning three percent interest in the Murdoch Bank, while they'd charged him eight percent in management fees. Jonas was not directly involved in the bank by then, but Caley held him responsible.

It had been Ceci who put that in motion by tying up his inheritance until he was thirty-five. He'd found the good life in Europe wasn't possible on the stingy amounts forwarded by the bank. So he'd gone back to selling drugs. But he'd had the bad luck to be caught. To this day his nightmares still replayed those months in the Turkish prison. No one here knew anything about that, but he was sure that someone should have to pay for it. His grandmother was beyond his reach.

To find his fortune eroded when he returned was more betrayal. Then, he'd been made to feel he'd have to reestablish himself, even though his family was as old in Denver as Murdoch's. And of probably better stock, he thought. Ceci had often referred to her own family as related to the French aristocracy. Yet, to gain admission to the Cherry Hills Country Club, he'd had to sit through interviews by the Membership Committee, while their eyes wandered over the furniture in his living room, glanced over the tailoring of his suit. At the Denver Country Club he'd even had to wait two years for an opening. It had taken longer to become a member of the Zebulon Pike Society. But Caley had succeeded with a vengeance.

Still, Murdoch had more money. *His* worth was whispered of in awed tones.

Caley viciously stubbed out his cigar. He knew he couldn't top

Jonas in that regard. What he *could* do was make trouble for Jonas while he made money for himself. He'd already bought Jack Dexter, one of Murdoch's investment scouts. So he got insider information. But sometimes Jonas got ahead on points, and Caley had to scramble.

The current scheme involving Consolidated Chemical had started with Caley's decision to buy the stock. But he found that Murdoch and Associates had beaten him to all the outstanding shares. Caley had detected the quick eye of Rivers Alexander behind that transaction, and he reflected that it was the second time young Alexander had unknowingly gotten in his way. He'd also scooped Caley on a software company's initial offering the year before.

It had become important to Caley to acquire some of ConChem. Meeting Frederic Steiner with his "Pac-Man bacteria" provided a way to do it. Caley had little interest in genetic tinkering, and Steiner's enthusiastic lectures bored him. This awkward young scientist, he could see, would have a hard time raising capital on a very experimental idea. But with someone of Caley's resources and reputation behind him, Steiner's dream of a company called GeneSys could be realized.

Not that Caley intended to put any of his own money into it. He was merely going to talk it up, palm the stock off on some of his investors—and get Jonas to trade half of his Consolidated Chemical stock for it. Caley didn't see how he could lose. He could acquire the solid shares he wanted: ConChem's price was not likely to go down. GeneSys, on the other hand, was very speculative. Its price would surge at the initial public offering, then no doubt rapidly decline. Caley could shrug, pointing out that he'd said it was very risky, and that he'd decided not to invest himself. He would make sure, however, that everyone knew Murdoch held lots of worthless GeneSys stock.

And now it seemed that Murdoch was going to suffer another setback on his Telluride project. Caley smiled broadly. Ms. MacAllister would surely be able to delay it, which would cost money. Wondering how she'd gotten that piece of land right in the center, Caley returned to the news story he'd only half finished. The article ended, "She is a native Coloradan. Ari MacAllister's great-grandfather, Berkeley Glendower, gave the Telluride property to her great-grandmother as a gift on the birth of their daughter. Both her grandmother, Bridget Gregory, and her mother, Trish Gregory, lived in the Boulder area. Following her mother's early death Ari was adopted by Mr. and Mrs. Gerald MacAllister of rural Louisville, who were longtime friends of the family."

Caley sat up with a jerk. She was Trish Gregory's daughter. And

Christopher Roth's. Had to be. He remembered the last time he'd seen Trish, and the glimpse of rounded stomach beneath her open coat.

Quickly he folded the paper back to look again at the picture. Before he'd only glanced at the face shown in half profile, thinking she was quite pretty. Now he studied it. There seemed to be a smudge on the photo, blotting the area above and below the eye on the partially concealed side of her face. He looked again. No, it was some sort of birthmark that marred her good looks. She deserved to be marked, he thought venomously.

Caley had always believed that Trish was the one who had turned him in to the authorities. The resentment still coiled within him. *That's when everything went bad.*

But this all made the game even more interesting. His smile returned as he considered the possibilities. Trish's daughter would definitely need help on her investments. He could say he was an old friend of her father's. There was no way she could know that wasn't true. She would trust him to provide the financial advice she needed. Perhaps, with her environmental interests, she'd be eager to buy shares in GeneSys.

Reaching for a pad on the table next to him, Caley started a letter. She'd be a little difficult to reach, but he had contacts everywhere. He wrote, *I knew your father.* Caley paused, thinking that he might as well lay it on thick. *I was with him when he died. He was my best friend. But I didn't know he had a daughter. Seeing your picture in the paper was like finding him again.*

CHAPTER 7

As it happened, Ari didn't get to Telluride right away. There was too much to do in Denver. Her friend Janie reported on arrival to the Denver branch office of Blackburn and Barton, her public relations firm. She'd been assigned half a desk; she would be sharing with another person, since the management was sure she was only in town temporarily. They had no idea of the campaign for Bridey's Mountain their new employee and their new client were jointly plotting. The two were enjoying their plans, which they discussed at all hours of the day and night.

They decided to take an apartment together in Denver. Stewart Wellings had arranged appointments for Ari with another lawyer, as well as conferences with two accountants, and several bankers. The ten million dollars, minus the government's substantial slice, had to be put to work earning interest right away. Ari told Stewart, only half laughing, that she couldn't believe how much time it took to be rich.

Janie had gotten her through the harrowing, camera-clicking day at the Lottery Office wonderfully. Moreover, Janie's background in business courses was a help to Ari in poring over the papers before signing them. She was determined to understand what she was doing, but it occurred to her that Rivers had perhaps underestimated the advantages of his degree. While it was true that bars and graphs were boring, Ari wished she knew the difference between a stock and a bond, why an investment was good, and *who* it was good for—her or the stockbroker. Still, she reminded herself that she'd learned a little in her years at the Louisville bank, and that she'd trained to read carefully at the university. She went through the files, trying to make sense of them.

Ari was sure, at least part of the time, that her decision to spend these first weeks in Denver had nothing to do with the nearness of Rivers Alexander. One moment she ached to see him. The next she was not sure she wanted to. She couldn't forget the power of his attraction —or her own fear of it. And she reminded herself repeatedly that he worked for Jonas Murdoch.

In discussing an apartment Janie had said, "We *have* to have a Jacuzzi." Ari added, "And a mountain view." She located a condominium with both. The penthouse of the tallest building in Cheesman Park, very near downtown, it had a three-hundred-and-sixty-degree view, and two Jacuzzis. Originally, it'd been two units, and during Colorado's high-flying days of oil the owners had bought both and combined them. When the price of oil plummeted, they couldn't sell the penthouse and had moved to California. The units could still be separated easily into two, but one now had a huge living room; the other a gleaming expanse of kitchen.

Rushing happily from one side to another the day they moved in, Janie at last collapsed onto a creamy leather couch. A forelock of her short haircut flopped onto her forehead. Janie's thick blond hair always looked as if it'd been trimmed just the day before by an inventive hairdresser. Her short-sleeved black linen suit not only was slimming but emphasized her porcelain complexion. Her cheeks were now pink with excitement, her blue eyes alight.

"Ari, I'm crazy about this place," she chortled, kicking her low-heeled pumps off her feet and up into the air. "The sheer decadence of the bathrooms! Forget about singing in those glass showers—they're big enough to dance in. And the marble Jacuzzis. I'm going to soak every night until nine. We could even have swimming parties in them— invite every good-looking bachelor in town. As soon as I lose fifteen pounds, of course."

Ari was standing in the kitchen before the restaurant-sized gas range with its black Lucite hood, lost in admiration. "Janie," she called, "come and look at this. It's even got a barbecue grill in the middle. We can make the most wonderful meals!"

Janie swooped in and glanced around at the pristine white and shining black of the kitchen, which looked as if it'd never been used. The glass-fronted cupboards jutting from one end were perfectly empty, as were all the cabinets above and below the counters, which Ari had opened. Everywhere the tiles sparkled at them.

"Ari, let me explain," Janie said kindly. "A kitchen is a shrine and should be left in its original immaculate state, untouched by feminine hands. We can visit here briefly, of course." She swung open the freezer door and gestured. "On this side one keeps the ice and the Häagen-Daz's. The other side is for the champagne and a few nice little Chardonnays, for a change." She tapped the glass of a cupboard with a rosy-enameled nail, careful not to leave a fingerprint. "This shelf will hold the wineglasses, ice cream bowls, and two cups for instant coffee when we're getting dressed to go to brunch. We put the garbage bags for the take-out food containers under the sink."

"And what would you do," Ari said, laughing, "with this glorious stove?"

"Perfect for plants," Janie responded promptly. "They'd flourish under the hood light. And we need a little greenery here."

"I can see," Ari returned, folding her arms, "that I'm going to get the half with the kitchen. Let me think what we'll need for—"

Janie interrupted. "I know what we need. And Saturdays are made for shopping. Let's go."

"We have to get kitchen stuff, even if you're only thinking of glasses," Ari agreed. "There's a Williams-Sonoma in the Cherry Creek mall—"

"Please." Janie was already going to the front door. "The only double-barreled names I want to hear are Neiman-Marcus, Saks Fifth Avenue, Lord and Taylor. Since you are so generously paying the rent, that frees up a good part of my salary for better things. We can stop at the gourmet caterers on our way back. They give you plastic silverware. Come on."

By the following Monday, Stewart Wellings had gathered information on the problem of the development surrounding Bridey's Mountain. The elderly lawyer, wearing his tailored three-piece suit even in the heat of June, adjusted his vest and looked rather gloomily at Ari and Janie. "I've had a long conference with Paul Whitney, one of the best real estate lawyers in town. You'll have to meet with him soon. But what he's had to say isn't encouraging."

Wellings's tufted gray eyebrows dipped together forebodingly. "The only way you could stop development is to buy Murdoch out. He has the land free and clear. It was bought by his wife's grandfather. Just as in your case, the land has been owned by the family for several generations. The mining claims were always renewed. Therefore, the federal government has granted both of you patents on the original Indian land. But you personally can't afford his asking price, Ari, which is considerable because it's based on the profits he would realize from a ski area with homes on site. Even if you put your entire fortune into this effort—which I could never recommend—you would still have to come up with additional millions."

Wellings focused through his half-glasses on the papers before him, afraid that he would see disappointment written on their eager faces. "There's one other possibility. If you would be willing, Ari, to keep only your mountain from development, you could give it to the town of Telluride or The Nature Conservancy. It's true that there's no access to it without crossing Murdoch's land. But he would be forced to grant right-of-way if your land is owned by a public entity, instead of by you." Wellings grimaced as he continued. "Even on this point we already know he will fight all the way. He wants the area kept exclusive because he's building very expensive houses—he doesn't want hikers and climbers wandering through. Worse, he really wants your mountain. Building the ski areas contiguously would save him a great deal of money."

Ari could not keep still any longer. "But, Stewart, I want to save the whole canyon. It should be left wilderness, as it is, all of it!"

Janie chimed in after Ari's passionate outburst. "And it's possible to raise that money. We can—"

Wellings at last came close to smiling. He made a tent of his arthritic fingers. "Why is it that I was sure that's the response I'd get?" He was certain that any adviser who took a straightforward financial view would shudder at the idea. Ari could increase her net worth substantially by taking Murdoch's offer.

But it was clear that the two were determined to make the effort, and of all the things those millions could buy, this was what Ari most wanted.

Feeling young himself somehow, Stewart Wellings put aside any further lawyerly words of caution. This time he did smile. "I've already made an appointment with Whitney. He's suggested we could buy some time by asking for an Environmental Protection Agency audit on the development. That will take four to six months. We could ask the Army Corps of Engineers to investigate the wetlands on the property. If they determine these wetlands deserve protection, Murdoch could be stopped. The town of Telluride will have to rule on the additional number of wood-burning units, which could affect air quality. But he isn't building that many houses. It's only a small hope that these actions will work—to be honest. But since Murdoch was poised to begin, they will at least delay the start. We should see Paul Whitney right away and file the papers with the EPA."

As he was gathering his papers to go, he looked keenly at Ari. "By the way, I called Murdoch's office and spoke to Rivers Alexander. A very knowledgeable young man, and I find upon checking that he has a position of some responsibility at Murdoch's. He was pleasant, but persistent on one point—he wanted to get in touch with you. He said he needed to talk to you and that he had something of yours to return."

At the mention of Rivers's name, just the sound of it, Ari could feel the blood rising to her face. Both Stewart and Janie clearly noticed her reaction. Wholly uncomfortable in the ensuing silence, Ari said, with an awkward wave of her hand, hoping to dismiss the subject, "That's right. I did leave my T-shirt."

Further unnerved at the thought of how that might be interpreted, she added quickly, "I made an ice pack with it. For his knee." There was still that silence. Ari finished, "I met him . . . accidentally. I didn't know who he was."

Wellings put his papers away neatly, saying, "I gave him the post-office-box number for the mail that Blackburn and Barton will collect for you." He directed a glance at Janie. "And the phone number at the agency." The lawyer clicked his briefcase shut and continued carefully, his attention seemingly on replacing his half-glasses in his pocket. "Pursuing a friendship with Alexander would have its problems. You must avoid mention of any of our . . . plans to block the development. As I told you at the beginning, Jonas Murdoch will be a formidable opponent. The fact that this audit was done on your initiative will soon be apparent. Since he was prepared to break ground, the delay alone will irritate him. You must keep all of this in mind, Ari."

After Wellings had left, Ari sat at the polished table, adjusting the files in front of her in perfect alignment. Janie wandered around the room, twiddling a pencil between her index and middle finger. At last she slid into a chair across from her friend and asked, "You want to tell me about this guy, Ari? It sounds as if I might be talking to him."

Ari became busy gathering the files. She very much wanted the benefit of her friend's experience, and Janie had always been open and easy in their many late-night discussions about men. Ari couldn't get Rivers Alexander off her mind. But even to Janie she could not bring herself to admit that she'd slept with a man whose name she hadn't known. Heading toward the door, she replied, "He . . . seemed really nice. I didn't get around to asking him what he did."

That afternoon Ari had her first visit with Dr. George Herron, the plastic surgeon. Shortly after she returned, Janie came flying in, an overflowing tote bag in each hand. A dozen stalks of fresh-opened white and purple iris bloomed out of the top of one of them. Catching sight of the flowers, Ari thought she'd never seen anything so exquisite. Then it occurred to her that perhaps every color seemed brighter because she was so happy.

Janie slid onto the nearest couch and, without catching her breath, began, "Quick, tell me. What happened? What did the doc say?"

"We can't *know* yet." Ari's words tumbled out excitedly. "But he's pretty sure the laser will take it all off. I mean, the odds are good. Really good. It works like ninety-seven percent of the time. He has to try a little patch first. See?" She brushed back her hair to show a dime-sized, brown, roughened edge on the birthmark.

Janie hurried over and peered at it. "Did it hurt?"

"No." Ari shook her head. "Only a little when they put the anesthetic needle in to deaden the skin. Like Novocaine. You can't feel the laser."

Ari had thought as she'd sat in the dentistlike chair that afternoon that it was like a wizard's wand, granting her lifelong wish that the stain would go away. The doctor bending over her in his goggles had looked more like an earnest grasshopper than a sorcerer, but the effect was the same. She added, "When the scab falls off, if it looks like new skin underneath, that means it'll work. Then the whole process will take a few months because one section has to heal before he does the next."

"This calls for a celebration. Oh, there's more good news. Your friend Sybil called. She seemed very happy about your great-grandmother for some reason. But she was so excited that I'm not sure *what* she was saying. Anyway, she said she was going to write it all because she had some book pages she'd photocopied to send her notes with." Janie started unloading the contents of the tote bag onto the coffee table. "I brought all of our favorite foods from Goodies-To-Go and there's champagne in the fridge. And these flowers, with a note attached, came to the office. Then, right before I left, this package came." She put a square box in Ari's lap. The return address read: *Rivers Alexander.*

For a second Ari's hands hovered over it, not touching it. She said, as offhandedly as she could, "It's probably my T-shirt."

"A T-shirt would fit in a padded envelope. This is a box. Open it," Janie urged.

The contents were hidden in layers of tissue paper. The card on top was thick, and as Ari pulled it from the envelope, a section of a map fluttered out. She read the card once and then again.

"What's it say? Come on." Janie was just stopping herself from reading over her friend's shoulder.

"He's holding my T-shirt for ransom." Ari felt a laugh slide by a catch in her throat. "To get it back I have to follow these directions exactly. Bring what's in the box, along with an unmarked apple pie in a plain brown sack, and come alone to the place circled on the map." She looked up, but not at Janie. "I know where that is—it's where I . . . ran into him. He says I'll recognize him because he'll be the man in the middle of the field holding a bottle of Dom Perignon. I get to specify the date and time."

Janie leaned back on the couch, twitched some blond hair out of her eyes, and smiled measuringly. "Nice," she said, drawing out the word. "I like it. If you want, I can send your answer from the office by messenger. What're you doing tomorrow?"

"Oh, I couldn't," Ari answered in quick alarm. "Well, not that soon. And you know what Stewart said. About a . . . friendship and—"

"Ari," Janie interrupted firmly. "That EPA audit will take months. This guy might even have quit his job with Murdoch by then, and in the meantime, you can see whether—"

"Besides," Ari cut in a little desperately, "I'm supposed to stay out of the sun, and I'm not allowed to put on makeup." She tugged her hair over the hardening scab.

Janie threw her hands up in the air in protest. "Your face looks fine. You can buy a big hat, or tell him you'll meet him in a dark restaurant." Janie had her romantic side. "What else is in there?"

Ari began to carefully unwrap the tissue paper. First one thin champagne flute emerged, then another. They were so fragile, they seemed made of air, not glass.

"Wonderful," Janie exclaimed, snatching one up, and holding it up admiringly. "A perfect housewarming gift—just what we need. I love this man. I was getting so tired of the plastic stuff I was even thinking of accompanying you to Housewares. I'll fill them right now." As she disappeared into the kitchen, she added, "Those flowers were brought to my desk personally by an exec at B & B. Who sent 'em?"

When she returned, Ari was staring at the card that had come with the flowers. "I can't believe it. These are from someone who knew my father." She shook her head dazedly. "I know so little about him, Janie." She looked up, shiny eyed. "I can't wait to meet this man. I'm so happy!"

The next morning before leaving for a session with the accountant, Ari sat down to write two notes. The first took a long time and she tore up two versions. At last she simply thanked Rivers for the glasses, saying how much she liked them. She said that she was rather busy at the moment. When she read that over, she decided it sounded a little stiff. She added that she hoped his knee was healing, but that he should keep the T-shirt for now in case it swelled up again. She signed the note *Frank*. Then she tapped its edge on the desk for a while before she sealed it, wishing she were sending another message—one that went *Yes, tomorrow*.

The second was quickly done. Ari addressed the envelope to Caley Sutherland and in her note mentioned how perfect the irises were. She accepted his invitation to lunch.

CHAPTER 8

From Caley Sutherland's note Ari
had expected a younger Stewart Wellings: paternal, approachable, reassuring. Janie, always cautious, inquired at Blackburn and Barton, and
reported that he was rich and respectable.

Yet at the last minute, before leaving for their lunch at the Denver
Country Club, Ari went back and put on a hat. It was a large lacy straw
one that matched her short-sleeved linen dress. The hat, she felt, softened the severe lines of the dress. But also, the brim dipped slightly on
the right, shading the birthmark and completely hiding the pink of the
healing skin. She was nervous about meeting Caley Sutherland, although she didn't know why.

Perhaps it was, she thought, that she was going to meet an unknown past. Her father existed for her only in a few faded Polaroids
showing a fair-haired, laughing young man. But he'd been this man's
closest friend. Caley had made it plain how he cherished Christopher
Roth's memory and anticipated meeting her for that reason. For the
first time she would encounter someone who'd known her father. What
would he think of her?

She was not what he'd expected. Caley was waiting on a couch near the maître d's stand and immediately decided when he saw her approach that this striking woman couldn't be Ari MacAllister. The newspaper account indicated she'd grown up on a Louisville farm. That and the accompanying photo had made him think of Trish in a long flowered skirt, her hair loose. And all that dreamy-eyed visionary crap.

He'd decided to meet Ari for lunch here to impress her. The Denver Country Club, as *Time* magazine had pointed out, was one of the most exclusive in the nation. Moreover, Caley was sure that their lunch would be interrupted by other members seeking stock-market advice. That should encourage her to ask for his help. But he had requested a back corner table, since he wasn't at all sure she'd be something he'd want to display to his peer group.

When she gave her name to the headwaiter, Caley hid his surprise. Ari couldn't hide hers. The man clasping her hand looked more her age than her father's, and he was astonishingly handsome. "Ari," he said, his pale blue eyes drawing her to him. "Caley Sutherland."

After they were seated, he leaned back, smiling at her through thick blond lashes. "I have to say this. I could see even from the newspaper that you'd inherited your mother's looks, but I didn't imagine how lovely you'd be." He almost meant what he said. If it hadn't been for the birthmark, she'd be stunning.

Although compliments usually added to Ari's shyness, his words sounded so spontaneous that she had to believe them sincere. He further relaxed her by sharing stories of his college days with her father. "I wish you could have known him." Caley's smile was filled with nostalgia. "How can I tell you what he was like? He was an artist. Impractical, too caring. He felt so strongly about things."

He seemed to look beyond her, then continued, "You're bound to think we were naive, imagining we could change everything. You have to remember it was the sixties, and we really believed we could create a brave new world overnight." To her, his shrug indicated regret for lost idealism.

As he told her about Trish's cabin and described the commune down the road, his eye kept returning to Ari's ruby ring. At first he was sure it couldn't be the same one. But he thought he'd have remembered it—the design was distinctive. He'd never forgotten the look on Ceci's face when *she* saw it. He didn't mention the ring. His voice was affectionate as he finished, "All I can say about your mother is that I'd never met a woman who was so . . . alive. Not since, either."

If there was a hint of "until now," in his tone, Ari didn't really catch it. But she felt warmly included in that past, as if she, too, were a contemporary. Her sharp sense of loss for the mother she'd only known through Mrs. Mac's stories, for the father she hadn't even been able to imagine, was, for the first time, softened. She was grateful to Caley Sutherland.

As they were waiting for the raspberry mousse and coffee, a thick-fingered hand was laid on Caley's shoulder. When he looked up, he saw to his satisfaction that it was E. L. Bascomb, a member of the board of Murdoch and Associates. An affable former Texan, Bass was a man who carried a great deal of weight in Denver, figuratively, and at 275 pounds, literally. "Caley," he said smiling plummily, "sorry to interrupt but . . ."

Ari looked up at the waiter as he set the creamy mousse before her. Caley could see Bass eyeing her as if *she* were the dessert course. As he introduced them, Caley mentioned lightly that congratulations were in order, since this was the new Sweepstakes winner.

"Well"—Bass's smile grew wider as he clapped Caley's shoulder—"you've sure found the right man here to advise you on that money, little lady." He was thinking with some envy that Sutherland's pick had once again hit pay dirt, but he put it to himself a little more coarsely. Caley knew exactly what he was thinking. "I won't keep you," Bass went on, "but I just dropped by the office and heard about that new GeneSys company."

Caley replied consideringly, "Well, of course, it's highly speculative. We could lose." He paused, as if he were going to say a great deal more, but grinned instead. As Bass strolled off, Caley was certain the man was calculating how much he would risk, sure that it was a very good bet. Turning to Ari, he said conversationally, "Bass is one of the associates of Murdoch and Associates."

As he'd expected, she took the bait, bringing up Murdoch's offer on her Telluride land. He drew her out, and she told him the history of the mountain, how important it was to her. Caley could see that, since her whole face spoke. And he could see the fervor in her honey-colored eyes. So like her mother, he thought with sharp anger. Maybe a tendency to miss the point could be inherited too. Colorado had a lot of mountains, and Ari wanted to spend millions to save one.

He already felt a proprietary interest in her money. After talking to her he realized that a big chunk of that first ten million could be wasted on this effort. Murdoch was going to win this one, no question. The game wouldn't be worth the candle if it cost a lot. In his way Caley was as careful about money as his grandfather Stanton. Capital should never be spent.

He took her hand in his and said slowly, "I understand. But I know your parents would want me to keep an eye out for your interests. Jonas Murdoch will pay you a great deal for that land." Much more than he'd like, Caley considered, now that he himself was in the picture. He continued, "If you sold, think what you'd be worth."

"In the ways that count I'd be worth less if I sold Bridey's Mountain for development," Ari replied firmly. "We're running out of wilderness, and it can't be replaced. Sometimes I think the reason I won the money is so that I can do something about it."

Caley's lips tightened, but he only asked, "Have you talked directly to Jonas?"

He noticed that her eyes slid sideways as she answered. "No, to someone in his office. Rivers Alexander."

The eyes, the expression on her soft mouth, did not escape Caley. So, he thought, she's met him. Dangerous. Alexander was very attractive and was probably looking forward to spending that twenty-five million himself.

Caley let his worry show. "He's Jonas's right-hand man and they think alike," he said slowly. "Of course, Alexander will tell you what you want to hear." Looking at her, Caley could see he was on the right track. "He's"—he stopped as if searching for words—"smart, on-the-make. Has to be. Old family, but no money anymore."

No, Caley realized as he watched her, he was not on target there. Her face gave everything away, and it wasn't Rivers's lack of money that was bothering her. "And," he added, "a man who'll get it one way or the other. He's very successful with women. Dates a lot of rich ones —different one every time I see him." Yes, he congratulated himself inwardly, a direct hit.

"Ari," he gently squeezed the hand he still held, "you probably think I'm being overprotective. I know you don't have to be told that some men are fortune hunters. It's just that your father isn't here. And I am. As to your Telluride land, I'll see what Jonas might consider. I know him well, and he isn't going to donate that land. Still, maybe I can come up with an approach you can use."

Ari was knocked off balance by what Caley had told her about Rivers. Every fear she'd had was suddenly confirmed. But this offer cheered her. "I'd appreciate it. I know this will be difficult. Stewart Wellings said—"

"Wellings?" Caley interrupted her in surprise. "How do you know him?"

Ari explained and ended by telling him how helpful the lawyer had been in choosing investments.

Caley slid his hand back and stroked his jaw, hiding his sharp displeasure at this news. That stodgy old bastard might have already tied up her money, he thought. For some reason Wellings disliked him. This was going to take time, goddammit. But control of twenty-five million made it worth it.

A muffled chime sounded, and he drew out a pocket watch. It was heavy gold and the case had curlicued initials engraved on it. Showing it to Ari, he remarked, "This belonged to my grandfather, Stanton Caley. Same initials as mine, but reverse order. I like to hold on to the past too."

Ari stared at the case. She'd seen a watch like that, although just then she couldn't remember where. Her mind was filled too completely with what he'd been saying.

Caley pressed the case open and glanced at the time. "I'm glad I set it. I had no idea it was so late, and I have an appointment." He took her hand again. "There's so much more we have to talk about. Are you free tomorrow night for dinner? Best food in town is at the Brown Palace. Historic building. Perfect for us."

His pale blue eyes held hers, and she said, "Yes."

When Ari went back to the condo, she saw a stack of mail that Janie had brought when she came home for lunch. Scooping it up, she sailed her hat onto the opposite couch and sank down without even glancing at the envelopes. Ari stared at the ceiling and tried to sort everything out. For a start, having lunch with Caley had been reassuring and fun.

Through her childhood she'd had Gerald MacAllister's steady love, and she knew its worth. But sometimes she'd wistfully eyed girls with young fathers who swung them up on their shoulders, steadied wobbling bicycles as they learned. And Gerald had died before she'd confronted the confusions of adolescence. Now, just when she stood uncertainly before a new world, there was Caley, powerful and very much at home there. He'd offered to escort her inside. She felt as if she were being given all that she'd missed before.

Yet he hardly seemed a generation older. He acted as if they were equals. She liked his gentle enclosing of her hand, the slight fragrance of his expensive men's cologne. But he was safe, almost a family member.

Ari blinked, stopped by her own thoughts. Less than two weeks ago, before she'd spent that night with Rivers, she'd hardly been aware of men's touch, their smell. Now, she was intensely aware of both. The thought of Rivers brought up what had so disheartened her during lunch with Caley.

She knew she needed to hear what he'd said about Rivers. Caley would know. She'd seldom dated, never had a close relationship, so she'd been easily misled. Although that experience had sent her reeling and had haunted her nights ever since, maybe now she could be objective and sensible. Caley had called him smart; she herself could have added a few more adjectives to explain just *why* Rivers was so successful with women.

No doubt he was only really interested in the ones with money. Of course, he hadn't known she had any—there was no way he could have known that. But he could simply have been after sex. Look where he kept the condoms, handy in the bedside drawer. That thought had knifed her every time it occurred. Recalling Caley's words, she could just imagine how many other women had shared that bed.

Still, she considered, if that's all he'd wanted, if he hadn't cared about her, why had he stopped their lovemaking? Even then she'd felt what that was costing him.

Ari snapped upright on the couch, telling herself this would not do. Her logical head was supposed to guide the wayward heart, not to mention other parts lower down, and instead her mind was making a case for Rivers, not against him.

Determined to leave the subject alone, she fanned out the pile of mail. There was a letter with his return address. Of course, she thought angrily, there would be a letter from him. She hadn't returned the phone messages he'd left at Blackburn and Barton, so he'd written. Her name must be at the top of his list now. Not only did she have millions, she was an easy lay. Not again. After what she'd learned this afternoon she was not even going to read the letter.

But it was a business-sized envelope. Maybe Stewart Wellings had wanted the exact asking price on Murdoch's land, and she'd just been sent a copy of the information. She tore it open.

As she read the letter, she had the uneasy feeling she could hear his voice. He said: *When I woke up that morning and you weren't there, I thought for a second I'd dreamed you. When I rolled over, hoping to go right back to sleep and find you there, my knee hurt. I hobbled upstairs, but there was only the mail on the floor. No note.*

But I thought you'd call. The next two days and nights were the longest of my life. I was sure you had regrets, as I'd been afraid you might. I tried to wish things had turned out differently, but I couldn't make myself wish that.

Ari winced. It would really be better not to read this. Even now, when she was trying hard to regret it, she couldn't. She ran her finger over her own lips and felt his mouth.

He wrote: *But then Thursday's paper came. I knew why the mail was on the floor. You knew who I was—the guy you'd hung up on just the day before. Then there was that twenty-five million. A man who desperately wants a date with a woman with that much money is kind of suspect. Still, I can at least say I knew you when. Before you were rich and beautiful. When you were just beautiful.*

He *had* made her feel that way, and for the only time in her life. But now Caley's words echoed in her ears: "Alexander will tell you what you want to hear." She knew she wasn't beautiful; one look at her birthmark in the mirror was all it took. When Caley paid her a compliment, it was different—he was seeing her as her father might have. But from Rivers, well, he was "on the make." She didn't have to be told he thought like Murdoch. He must. He was his "right-hand man." All that sympathy she'd sensed when she told him why she didn't want to sell her land was just part of his pitch.

Rivers's letter ended: *So, I work for Jonas Murdoch. There's no reason we should discuss business. There are sunsets, for example. I know several restaurants with western views, and they do the dishes. You made me a promise—dinner and dancing after. My knee's fine. Call any time.*

Ari's hold on the letter loosened as she decided. She wouldn't call. She'd believed he cared about her. She was smarter now, she thought. But Ari didn't think about why she was so sure of Caley, or so doubtful of Rivers. If she had, she might have seen that it was not Rivers, but something in herself she didn't trust. Her sexual feelings had overwhelmed her, frightened her. Those feelings were dangerous. And it was Rivers who'd called them up. By contrast Caley made her feel safe.

Hastily, Ari put Rivers's letter away and snatched up the next envelope, which was from Sybil in Boulder. That letter drove every other thought away. There were three photocopied pages from an old edition of *Burke's Peerage,* and the lists of how each British title was passed from father to son through the centuries marched down one eye-straining column after another. At the top of the first page was emblazoned an exact reproduction of a coat of arms. It showed a warrior's shield and, rising from that, an arm triumphantly holding up a laurel wreath. But on the shield was an open book and just above that the outline of a mountain range. The name over the coat of arms was O'Connell.

Ari's fingers trembled as she turned to the handwritten letter enclosed. Janie's description of Sybil's bubbling excitement was clearly an understatement. Although the script was tidy, the genealogist's eagerness made the train of thought a little hard to follow.

She wrote, *Oh, my dear Ari, I've found her! The only daughter of this particular family must be Morna Gregory. I can't be wrong. You said that she'd told her daughter Bridey stories of Castle Connemara.*

But, although the 1890 edition of the Peerage *lists a baron of Connemara, he didn't have any children and in any case, his residence was given as Government House, Madras, India. Still, there were several noble families from that area of western Ireland, and Morna might simply have been describing a castle in Connemara. And, as you can see, she was. Really, it says so much about your great-grandmother that she came from there. Connemara is a section of Connacht, in County Galway. Do you know what* The Touring Guide of Ireland *says about that area?*

Sybil had copied out a paragraph. *"Connacht has been described as the most Irish part of Ireland . . . a place of mild rain and mountain mists that magnify the brooding qualities of an introspective landscape. The strange, otherworld aspects of its mountains and lakes, boglands and stone scattered flats . . ."* Although Ari was reading as quickly as she could, anxious to get on to Morna, those words reverberated. That cool, green, remote land rose before her. She could even imagine the rocky seashore and a towered castle made from those old stones.

Sybil's words tumbled on. *I started with the 1890 edition of* Burke's, *because the next edition didn't appear until 1903, which was wise of me. Drat! That doesn't make sense. I mean, in 1890 your grandmother was only fifteen and still living at home. She didn't get married until the following year. My, sixteen is young to be a wife, isn't it? Of course that was common, then. But by 1903 her family itself is no longer included in* Burke's. *Immediately, I turned to a separate volume,* Extinct Peerages, *which says that Liam O'Connell, the only son of this branch, was without issue when he drowned in 1897 and the line was extinct for want of a male heir. Now, although women couldn't inherit the title, the editors do tell us the year of marriage of any daughter, as well as the name of her husband. So I knew who your great-grandmother married! Since he, too, was a gentleman, I hurried to look him up. His date of death—and hers—would be given in all likelihood. Sometimes the editors even put down the cause of death, as in Liam's case.*

Here Sybil interrupted her own narrative. *Sorry. I'm getting ahead of myself. You must be anxious to know how I came up with her maiden name to begin with, and why I sound so positive when I have no real evidence. The volumes of* Burke's *are only alphabetized by name or, very occasionally, by title, and they are very fat because each child born is listed. I began with the names starting with* C *because the Irish, like the English, often used places for surnames. John (who lived by the mill) became John Mill. So I spent some time wandering around the names starting with Conn with no luck. Then it hit me that the O's so common in Irish names could mean* from, *so I looked there. She was, after all, from Connacht. And O'Connell leapt to my eye.*

Now, Ari, run your finger down the pages of this old, old family to the nineteenth century. You'll see that in 1890 there is a Sir Greagoir O'Connell, Bart., of County Galway. His first name *is the Gaelic spelling of Gregory. His residence is Errislannin Manor, Connemara. His wife, who died in 1875, was named Morna. When your great-grandmother needed to hide her identity, she could have chosen her parents' first names as an alias! What's more, this couple had a daughter the right age. Actually, they had two children: a son, Liam, born in 1873, and a daughter, Arienh, born in 1875, the same year as her mother died, probably in childbirth or shortly thereafter. And, my dear, think of this.* Arienh *(pronounced A reen) is a Gaelic spelling of Ariana.*

Ari stopped. It could be coincidence, but it sounded so right. She realized how much she wanted it to be true. It was as if finding Morna's identity would help her find part of herself. They even had the same first name. Maybe her *middle* name had been Morna, after the mother who died at her birth, the mother whose white lace dress was stored in the trunk. It could be true, Ari thought, at least the birth date was right. Morna had given her age as twenty-five when Bridey was born in 1900. It could be true, she said, almost aloud.

Sybil's handwriting showed the speed at which her pen moved. *I can't prove any of this, of course. But we can* disprove *it. It shouldn't be too hard. Arienh O'Connell of Connemara married Sir Cullan Dunham of Daire. That's an island off Donegal, between Ireland and Scotland. He was called a laird; as his name indicates, he probably was Scots-Irish. That peerage is now in abeyance because no male family member has been found, but his date of death—and his wife's—is given as 1906. Your great-grandmother left Telluride, didn't you say, in late 1905? Surely we could find someone on the island who might know if the lady of the castle left Daire some years before she died. Or even where and how the laird and his lady died.*

Ari, you will have noticed that I keep saying "we." You and I should go together. Shannon Airport is not far from Connemara. We could rent a car and try to find the O'Connell seat. There is no sizable house listed in guidebooks by the name of Errislannin Manor, so the name has been changed, if it's still standing. Somebody ought to know. We can talk to the old people. And we must go to Daire, find out what stories they know about the last laird. Do say you'll come with me. As soon as you can.

CHAPTER 9

The rain was a barely visible mist. The windshield wipers on the Land-Rover seemed to slide to the sound of "A reen, A reen," drawing out the *ee*'s. Arienh O'Connell, who might have been Morna Gregory. On the long flight to Ireland, Sybil and Ari had speculated endlessly, going over all they knew about her. By the time the 747 was circling Shannon Airport, they'd convinced themselves that not only would they find Morna's true identity, they'd also come up with some idea of what had happened to her after she'd left Colorado.

As they looked down from the skies on the island, the ocean's foam had seemed impossibly white against the high dark cliffs, and each field an unimaginable, welcoming green. The streams and lakes gleamed silver, and the brown of the bogs made the purple moorlands brighter. They were both almost shivering with anticipation.

Now it was the start of their second day, and Sybil was at the wheel, since she preferred driving in the morning. A new hat with a fringe of veil perched on her tight curls. Despite the thickness of her glasses she was quick to spot a wandering sheep, and she smoothly cornered the good-sized British car on the miles of narrow coastal road as they sped toward Connemara. Ari was delighted that they were here and were together.

Without Sybil she was sure that she'd have mistrusted her emotions. Ireland's primeval pull had instantly grasped them both, giving them that sensation of returning to a place they'd never been and still remembered. "Funny," Sybil had said yesterday, a crinkle of surprise on her forehead, "but I've never before believed in racial memory, the idea that what my ancestors knew could be imprinted in my mind." But there seemed no other way to explain their feeling of intimacy with the land, their sense of acquaintance with these mountains, so different from Colorado's. Here, the mossy slopes wound to cloudy tops that were rarely more than suggested, a dream of mountains. In the Rockies each upthrusting granite peak had a knife-point sharpness in the dry, vivid air.

"Yes," Ari murmured, sniffing the green-scented moisture through the Rover's open window, settling a little wearily back in the leather seat. As much as she'd looked forward to coming, leaving Denver hadn't been easy. In the rush of the two weeks needed to pack and get her passport, Caley had become part of her life. He called every day with invitations to brunch, lunch, or dinner, often including Janie. They attended the theater and concerts. He had decidedly not wanted her to go, finding a new reason each day for her to stay.

"Wait," he'd insisted. "I want to show you Europe myself. I lived there a long time and I know it well."

"I'm not going to set foot even in London," she'd replied. "Just Ireland and back. For only a little over a month."

"Now's hardly the time for you to go," he'd then argued. "You have business affairs to look after." Starting with their dinner at the Brown Palace he'd urged her to consider more speculative stock. He'd pointed out that everything Stewart was doing was overly conservative, that a few greater risks would bring higher profits. Caley had, however, suggested she not mention that it was he who was advising her. "Wellings is sure to think *I'm* too much of a risk taker, despite the fact that it's always worked for me," he'd said with a small smile.

"But all my affairs are in order," Ari answered. "Stewart has put my short-term money in commercial paper, and that won't be free for six weeks. Besides, it'll take me some time to study the stocks you like, to read their annual reports and so forth."

Caley had been quiet for some time, then he'd run a finger down her cheek, saying, "And why wouldn't you trust my judgment?"

"Oh, I would," she'd reassured him. "But I want to learn from you, have you explain how you make your choices. Then I can see if I agree."

For a moment Ari had been afraid she'd angered him, although she couldn't imagine how. But his blue eyes were dispassionate when he replied, "My dear, you never cease to . . . amaze me."

Although she'd been busy, Ari had also taken the time to write Rivers. There was no point, she thought, in his constantly calling Janie, or expecting an answer to his dinner invitation. And if, at some later time, they met, this way they could do so comfortably. She'd intended only to say that she'd be abroad for over a month, but she ended up explaining why she was going and telling him about Morna. In spite of herself she wanted him to know how she felt.

After what Caley had said, she was aware this would make no difference, that it was unlikely that Rivers cared about her motives, or her as a person. That still stung, because she had really believed that he did. But a man as attractive as he was must have learned a long time ago how to convince women. He'd probably noticed her ring, the car, and thought it worthwhile to check her out. Fortune hunters had to be sharp eyed, she told herself.

He had stopped their lovemaking. She considered that. Maybe that was supposed to be a proof of his sensitivity. He probably thought he could do that any time, knowing a woman with her sort of birthmark didn't get much attention from men. She'd be a pushover. Ari bit her lip. She had been.

What surprised her was that this new way of regarding Rivers did not change certain feelings. Each night, when she tried to fall asleep, he was there, and she remembered again how it felt to lie in his arms, the weight of his body on hers.

During daylight hours she reminded herself that this was understandable. When she'd met him, she was already spinning with the news of the Sweepstakes, and then there was a strong sexual attraction. Songs and stories said it could hit like a lightning bolt. But she was sure its effect would wear off. All she had to do was avoid him until it did. For a real relationship she would need to respect and trust the man.

These were feelings she had for Caley, although she only saw *him* as a friend. He could not talk to her of her father's death without showing how much it still pained him. Several times he'd started to tell her how he'd sat night and day by Christopher's hospital bed, hearing the labored breathing, hoping against hope. But he'd been unable to finish the story and turned away.

Caley's kindness and concern for her made Ari grateful too. With every gesture he let her know that having her with him was what counted. His reluctance to have her leave for Ireland, Ari found endearing.

Sybil's cheerful comment, "Just another fifty miles to Roundstone," broke in on Ari's thoughts. *Fodor's Ireland* recommended several bed-and-breakfast places there. The two women had decided that, since these lodgings were usually owned by local people, they should stop at one for the night. The owners would be the best sources of information in their search for Errislannan Manor, which had once been the residence of Sir Greagoir O'Connell. There was, after all, a bit of land that jutted into the Atlantic nearby called Errislannin Point.

But on reaching that postcard-pretty village on a curve of Bertraghboy Bay, the proprietors smiled regretfully at each place they stopped. They had no rooms. "It's the Connemara Pony Show, ye see, and sure the entire western end of the county is booked." Worse, they said that they knew of no residence of any size called Errislannan Manor. There were no large houses near the Point.

The next town, Ballyconneely, lacked the charm of Roundstone village, but besides its lyrical name it had another advantage—one room available for the night. The owner of the pub where they stopped to ask directed them to the prim, lattice-windowed cottage of a widow named Mrs. Laffan. She had geraniums in the window, anemones by the door, and she was wearing three assorted sweaters when she came to let them in. Her smile, as broad as her brogue, could have adorned a tourist poster.

Over tea she was more than glad to speculate about the location of Errislannan House. There were several possibilities. "But it couldn't be Kylemore Abbey," she said flatly, brushing back some of the fluff of gray hair that had strayed onto her forehead, "built by an Englishman, that place was, in the Twelve Bens. The mountains, ye know. And the Abbey's new—couldn't be much more than a hundred years old." Ari and Sybil had already decided that the Twelve Bens were probably the mountains pictured on the O'Connell shield, since the range was drawn in two rows of six peaks. So the Abbey had seemed logical when they'd seen it pictured. On the other hand, the name Errislannan did smack of the seacoast.

"And ye're sure ye've the name right?" Mrs. Laffan's brow puckered.

"Oh, yes," Sybil responded positively. "It was the residence given in *Burke's Peerage,* and besides, I wrote to the Custom House in Dublin where they keep the birth, marriage, and death records. Errislannin House is where Sir Greagoir died in 1892."

Mrs. Laffan set down her rose-painted teacup with a distinct tinkle. "I'm a foolish old woman. Sure, and I am. We could be talkin' about the place my mither and all called the Castle. It wasn't one, grand as it is, but when it was put up some two hundred years ago, they built it around a tower from a ruined castle. From the thirteenth century, that was, they said. When my mother was a girl, it was bought by a brewer from Liverpool, who'd bring his family now and again for the summer. *He* called it Anaserd Place. Right near Lough Anaserd, ye know. And so they call it still. That's how they put it in the adverts when they want to let it. Empty now."

"You mean," Ari sat bolt upright, "that it could be rented? Perhaps we could take it for a short term. We need to stay near here, and there's no place open and—"

Mrs. Laffan's genial face crumpled in distress. "But, it'll cost the heavens and earth. I'm that sorry my room's booked for the weekend. The Pony Show people, ye see. And that's a huge place for only the two of you." She thought for a moment. "I do know the estate agent down the road who looks after it. Mr. Boyle, that is. He'll be knowing the name of the gentlefolks who sold it to the brewer. I'll give him a call and see what he can do." She disappeared into the next room.

Ari and Sybil squeezed hands, incredulous of their luck.

"It *could* be Morna's house," Ari said, hardly able to breathe, "and we'd be staying there!"

Sybil's eyes sparkled as she wiped her glasses. "We can check the parish records, hear old stories from the people around here. But it sounds dreadfully expensive." She was as careful of Ari's money as of her own.

When Mrs. Laffan returned, she was frowning in dismay. But she said, "Mr. Boyle will be round in the morning to show it to you. It's the O'Connell family house, but the present owner wants a dear price." When she told them the amount, even Sybil was relieved. For three weeks they could rent all of Anaserd Place, for the price of three nights in a New York hotel. Although Mrs. Laffan's small beds were comfortable, Ari barely closed her eyes that night.

The next day Mr. Boyle, a man in his sixties in well-worn Irish tweeds, relaxed when he saw their expensive rental car and Sybil's hatted-and-gloved respectability. Still, he was a man of definite opinions, and he could not stop himself from quick sidelong looks at Ari. He was suspicious of any woman quite that attractive. Her hair curled wildly in the moist air, tumbling over the scab on her forehead. Her eyes shone with an excitement that touched them with gold, and both smooth cheeks bloomed with pink.

Seated next to her in the front of the Rover, the estate agent began without preamble. "Now, the previous tenant was much given to *parties*. A writer, he was, with that sort of friends coming to visit. Within the first week the char—a steady woman—had given her notice. She said, if you'll pardon me, that one of the men walked out into the upstairs hallway without wearing a stitch. In midmorning. She's willing to come in today to air the linens, and will do up for you the entire time if—" He didn't finish the sentence, glancing again at Ari, as if to impress on her the importance of not allowing any guests to shock the daily cleaning woman. She nodded, concentrating on the rutted road, quite oblivious of his suspicions of her, eagerly hoping that around every bend the house would appear.

Sybil broke in from the backseat to ask if the woman's wages were included in the rent, and was told they were. She also inquired carefully about any gardener's salary, and the terms of the deposit. Satisfied at last, she explained why the two of them had come. Reassured by this information, Mr. Boyle beamed and dutifully tried to recall anything he knew. He was sure that the original family's name was O'Connell, because that was still inscribed in the thick file at his office. But although he talked at great length, interrupting himself every few minutes to say to Ari, "Well, it wouldn't be much farther now," he had nothing else to add. He himself was originally from the outskirts of Dublin and plainly missed that city's companionable crowds. He eyed Connemara's wild, windswept beauty and saw only barrenness in an unpeopled landscape.

"The priest here wouldn't be able to help," Mr. Boyle said emphatically. "A young man, and he only comes for the Sunday mass, and the funerals and such. More than one parish he has, with the sad shortage there is of priests, although he'd be willing I'm sure to let you see the old records. But the National Library in Dublin has those on microfilm, you know. And the property records of all the house sales, why, they're in Dublin too." He had a habit of telling Sybil a great many things she already knew, as well as of parading the glories of Ireland's capital city.

When he stopped to catch his breath, Sybil pointed out that records were useless, since Arienh O'Connell might not be the woman they were looking for. Instead, they felt they would have to talk to the older inhabitants and see what they remembered having heard from their parents about the O'Connell family. But Mr. Boyle returned, "Well, the old ones you'd be wanting have moved in with their children, now, haven't they? And *they'd* not be living nearby because of the lack of work."

Both Sybil and Ari waited for him to tell them that every old resident of Connemara lived in Dublin now, but instead he said thoughtfully, "They could even be in America, although how you'd be finding them I'm not sure."

They'd climbed upward from a pond-dotted boggy stretch and there before them stood a massive Georgian structure, beautiful in its simplicity, outlined against the cloud-striped blue sky. On its downward slope on one side was a shining lake, in the distance what looked like another but was, in fact, the Atlantic.

"A little plain outside," Mr. Boyle remarked, as if that were a defect, "but inside there's a deal of carved wood you'll be liking. Large for the two of you, but most of the rooms can be kept closed and you'll be enjoying the size of them all." He was still in the car fishing out the keys from his pocket while Ari was already at the solid door of the house, gazing up at the semicircle of small windows above it and then at the surrounding white stucco as if to memorize the walls themselves.

Once in, she could barely restrain herself from flying across the black-and-white marble floor and up the balustraded stone staircase, running from room to room and throwing open shutters to see the views in all directions. But the estate agent was determined to demonstrate the domestic comforts that he was convinced both women would be most interested in. He hurried them past a dining room that was fifty feet long, thirty wide, and twenty high to show them the brick-floored kitchen. Like the rest of the house it had clearly been updated at the end of the nineteenth century, probably by the brewer from Liverpool. A coal-burning Aga, a kitchen stove of formidable size, was dwarfed by the nearby fireplace. Here, as in all the enormous rooms, the large, brooding Victorian furniture seemed almost fragile.

At last he'd stepped outside to inspect the grounds, with a warning that Mrs. Kearney, the char, would soon be arriving on her bicycle. Ari and Sybil were in the tower room, looking into the distance where paths led over stony little hills to magically golden beaches. From this vantage they could see six mountains as well as the ocean. They hugged each other in delight and then embarked on an excursion from one giant bedroom to the next, trying each canopied bed for comfort.

The next week was a source of constant pleasures, as they roamed through the castle, rambled down to the beaches, drove to the Twelve Bens, and took in the Connemara Pony Show in lovely nearby Clifden. Mrs. Kearney arrived early each morning and insisted they breakfast on the rashers of thick bacon, tomatoes, and mushrooms she fried up, along with the fresh brown eggs she got from her neighbor. A sturdy woman with graying hair and red cheeks, she had a habit of almost running from room to room in her war with what she referred to as "the damp," opening shutters everywhere at the merest hint of sun.

When she stopped to pour herself a cup of tea, she was willing to chat, but she told them that she was from County Limerick and hadn't grown up in the area.

Sybil and Ari found that Mr. Boyle had unfortunately been right about the scarcity of people in their eighties and nineties still living nearby. In the evenings he helped by canvassing the pubs, Mrs. Kearney prodded her husband's memory for names, and Mrs. Laffan from the bed-and-breakfast spent a great deal of time on the phone talking to her friends. But no one they turned up remembered *their* parents saying much other than that old Sir Greagoir spent all his time with his books, that his son died young, and that the daughter had never come back, not even when the estate was sold up by a nephew who went to Australia. No one could tell them what Arienh looked like. Over and over Ari asked, "Do you know, did she have black hair, gray eyes? Did she sing?"

While Ari had no picture of Morna, she had heard many times from Mrs. Mac what Issy had told her, and what Bridey had said. Issy's repeated stories had made Morna's looks almost legendary, but Ari was sure that her great-grandmother must have been a beauty because she had so often studied the photographs of Bridey and Trish. Every day now she imagined a lovely girl, wearing that white dress with its impossibly tiny waist, coming down the staircase, walking through the rooms she herself was walking through now. Although she firmly believed it, and the very walls seemed to whisper it, she had no proof that Arienh was Morna.

When she and Sybil stood in the graveyard by the small stone church, staring at the mossy headstones of Sir Greagoir, his wife, Morna, and his son, Liam, Ari longed to know if they were her family. The obliging young priest showed them the records, which noted that Arienh O'Connell, a spinster of the parish aged sixteen, had married Sir Cullan Dunham, Bart., aged thirty-two, of the Isle of Daire. He'd added that, of course, Arienh would have been buried on that island with her husband. Both Sybil and Ari knew they might find more information on Daire, but they wanted to know *now,* while they were in this house. The brewer from Liverpool, or the O'Connell nephew, had apparently taken away all the possessions of the original family, every book, every picture. Late-Victorian furniture now filled the rooms. But Ari wanted to know that at least she was looking out the same windows that her great-grandmother had, wanted to walk down the staircase knowing it had been hers.

In the end, and Ari was forever convinced that this was so, Morna found her. At the start of the second week, in the middle of the night, an Atlantic storm had rushed in, battering the solid house, which must have been used to that. But there was a noise that awakened Ari, and because of the thick walls it sounded more like a persistent tapping, and she sleepily thought it might be someone at the front door. When she put on her robe and stepped out into the chilly hall, she realized it was a loud banging, and wondered if she ought to wake Sybil. They were, after all, a long way from the nearest house. But while Ari stood, hesitating to disturb her, she suddenly became aware that its source was upstairs and hurried down to the last bedroom of the wing. Opening that door a little uneasily, since that room was unused and had little furniture, she clicked on the light. Then, although she could not see through the dark window, she relaxed, sure it was one of the heavy shutters that had become unfastened from its inside catch.

When she threw up the sash, the wind and rain tore in, soaking the front of her robe as she struggled to close and hook it. The small table in front of the window was wet by the time she finished, and the lace runner that covered it had blown off. Ari picked that up and, tucking it over her shoulder, she carefully sponged off the wooden table with the bottom of her thin fleece robe. Then she hurried back to her bedroom to get out of the wet garment. The lace strip she spread on a chair and gratefully climbed back into the warm feather bed. It wasn't until she was dressing the next morning that she glanced at the lace and recognized the pattern as that on the collar and sleeves of the white dress in the trunk in Colorado.

But, used as she was to identical machine-made fabrics, Ari wouldn't have thought of that twice. The delicate lace was still a little damp, and she brought it down to dry by the huge stove that Mrs. Kearney faithfully fired up each morning for cooking breakfast. As she turned from the Aga and saw what Ari held, she said in surprise, "Wherever were you finding that?" When Ari explained, she nodded, "That end room. I decided not to open it up, since there were only bits and pieces in it. But that lace, now, that's handmade Limerick stuff, and sure I've not seen that design for years. My grandmother used it, made lace when she was a girl and Limerick's was all the style, she said. But then all the business went to Carrickmacross, way over by Dublin. They had different patterns."

Just as she was turning back to the bacon, she remarked reminiscently, "There was a woman lived down the road from me when I came to marry Kearney, and she used it too. Maybe she made this."

"Where is she now, do you think?" Ari asked, staring at the star-shaped flowers and wide leaves of the design. Someone's needle seemed to have enclosed air itself with silk thread in the gossamer fabric.

Mrs. Kearney wiped her hands on her apron and reached for the teapot to pour both of them a cup. "Let me see. Biddy. That was her first name. Curragour was her last. Queer how you remember things. We only talked a time or two about the lace, but I'd been born near Curragour Falls in Limerick. I've never heard that as a person's name before or since. Biddy went, thirty years and better ago, to live with her daughter, Tessie, who worked for the post office, I seem to think."

Stirring milk and three teaspoons of sugar into her tea, Mrs. Kearney wrinkled her brow, and then she added slowly, "They're not right round Ballyconneely, I'd say, for I haven't seen either of them since. But Tessie wasn't married. She might be on the phone, but it'd be not likely her mother is still with us."

After breakfast Ari disappeared for a long time. When she came back, it was clear that she was somewhere between laughter and tears. Rounding up Sybil and Mrs. Kearney, she led them without explanation into the huge dining room and seated them both at the long polished oak table. "Sybil," she asked, "tell Mrs. Kearney about my mountain and how it got its name. I'll be right back."

Somewhat mystified, Sybil did so, saying that Ari's great-grandmother had named it after Bridget, the woman who raised her since her own mother had died at her birth. Ari came in carrying a bottle of champagne from the cool wine cellar and three glasses from the kitchen cupboard. Mrs. Kearney's red cheeks paled a little, since it was mid-morning, but, looking at Ari, she had to smile.

Ari let the cork shoot joyously down the length of the room and then filled the glasses. Then she said, "When we came here, we thought that maybe the young woman who was the last of this family was my great-grandmother. But we had only a coincidence of age, place, and names to base it on. Now we have something more—something that can't be just another coincidence. I talked to Tessie Curragour, who lives on the other side of Clifden with her ninety-year-old mother, Biddy. We've been invited to tea with them. Tessie told me that her mother's given name was Bridget, and she'd been named after her aunt Bridget, who brought up the motherless girl who lived in what she called the Castle."

Now the tears slid down Ari's cheeks as she held up her glass and said, "Here, in her dining room, I want to propose a toast to my great-grandmother, Arienh Morna O'Connell."

CHAPTER 10

The next afternoon, promptly at
four, Ari and Sybil pulled up before a line of well-preserved row houses
of red brick. The small gardens before each doorway were full of flowers, but the Curragours' had been planted to within an inch of its life.
Since September was near, it was blooming with bright zinnias, feathery
asters, and showy dahlias. The woman who was engaged in cutting
deadheads must once have had hair as coppery orange as some of her
zinnias, but it was now subdued with gray.

Tessie Curragour introduced herself with a shy smile and it was
clear that she'd been waiting for them. Her eyes were a gentle gooseberry green, and she had a telephone operator's voice, quiet but clear,
with only a trace of a brogue. "I wanted to tell you," she said, "before
introducing you to Mother, how excited she is that you're coming to
tea. Now, that's good because it perks her up so, but even at the best of
times she does get a little . . . confused. But her memory is generally
good about the early days. It's what happened last week she can't recall."

"We're looking forward to meeting her," Ari said warmly. "I can't tell you how happy we are that you invited us." Sybil nodded so enthusiastically in agreement that her hat's veil fluttered.

Putting her secateurs neatly in her wicker basket with the flower heads, Tessie went on diffidently, not quite looking at Ari, "All morning Mother kept saying, 'Miss Arienh's granddaughter is coming to tea. Think of it!' I did keep reminding her that you'd be her great-granddaughter, but that slips her mind. I should explain that her own mother, whose name was Nora, worked at the Castle, too, after Aunt Bridget died. Bridget and Nora were sisters, but at opposite ends of a very large family. Bridget died just before Miss Arienh married, and Nora did the housekeeping until the old squire passed away. When my mother was growing up, my grandmother Nora would tell her stories about the O'Connell family while she was teaching her the lacemaking. In the end my mother thought of Miss Arienh as . . . well, a princess, you see."

She looked up now, her smile still a little self-conscious. "Forgive me for keeping you standing here, but I thought I'd better tell you so you won't be . . . surprised at her carryings-on. She'll be ninety-one soon."

The front room into which Tessie ushered them was tiny. Although there was little furniture, it seemed crowded with people because on the walls and on every surface were group family pictures. Into the corners of the frames of these were stuck colored snapshots of small children, apparently born after the formal ones were taken. There was a great deal of lace in the room too: squares of it on the back and arms of the matching love seat and chair, runners on the side tables beneath the pictures, and a starched piece on a coffee table with piecrust edges.

By the window, almost lost in this profusion, a frail old woman sat in a canebacked rocker herself wearing a lace collar fastened in front with a tortoiseshell brooch. Her white hair was thin in front, pink scalp showing through, but it was wound neatly in a netted bun in back. Deep lines crinkled her face everywhere except on her rounded apple cheeks. She beamed with delight at the visitors when they came in, and even made to get up, but Tessie hurried over and urged her to stay seated.

When Ari put out her hand, Biddy would not let go of it, but tugged her to the seat beside her and ran her other hand over the back of Ari's, stopping only to pat it. The old skin felt baby soft, though the hand itself seemed all bone. "Think of it," she said as if to herself, "Miss Arienh's girl. Another Arienh." Her pale cloudy eyes brightened with tears. At the sight Ari found her own springing up, and she stroked the old woman's hand.

"Now, Mother," Tessie said patiently, "this is Miss Arienh's great-granddaughter. *Her* name is Ariana."

Biddy waved her hand, as if her daughter were still a small child bringing up a small point. "And isn't she just her picture? Though the hair's not the same. Dark as midnight, hers was. But beautiful as the day, she was too."

"So Aunt Bridget *said,* and Grandmother would have told you the same," Tessie interjected, gently determined to help her mother sort out her memories. "You weren't born until ten years and better after Miss Arienh left."

The old woman's eyes darted sideways as if to recall something just out of reach. "But—" she began. Tessie patted her shoulder, smiled apologetically at her guests, and said, "I'll just get the tea. The water's boiling."

By the time Tessie returned with the teapot, a platter of thin cheese-and-tomato sandwiches on light-as-air soda bread, and another of tiny homemade tarts, Biddy was well launched into her memories. She told them as they came to her mind, and her daughter, who had obviously heard these stories many times, added whispered asides so Ari and Sybil could put the events together. It wasn't until the two of them were driving back to Ballyconneely that they managed to make a coherent tale out of it all, but at the time Ari simply drank in the words, trying to remember each one.

As they stood to leave, Biddy fixed her eyes firmly on Ari and said, "You must come again. I'll get out the box." Walking them to the car, Tessie repeated her mother's invitation, saying, "Oh, I do hope you will. She can't go out herself anymore, so company cheers her. I haven't seen her this alert for months. And, my, I enjoyed meeting you."

Ari thanked her again and assured her they would come, adding that they'd bring the pictures of the Castle and the town that they'd taken. They set a date for the following week. Before Tessie could turn away, Sybil asked thoughtfully, "What does she mean by her box?"

Lifting her eyes to the sky, Tessie half winced. "She has more than one. A great saver, she was. When I was transferred here by the post office, she'd spend hours sifting through her things while I was at work. But she'd no room to turn round and at last I got her to decide on what she wanted for the living room—well, you saw *some* of the pictures— and her bedroom, and I stored everything else in the shed out back. Now and again I bring in one of the topmost ones because it makes her happy. I've no idea what she's thinking she wants to show you, but I'm afraid she doesn't either."

As they drove out of Clifden, Sybil remarked, "Wasn't that amazing? It's just what attracted me to genealogy in the first place. Hearing the actual stories. And the way Biddy would phrase things sometimes, you knew she was repeating exactly what *she'd* heard. When she said, 'Why, people would walk twenty miles through the snow to hear Miss Arienh sing,' you were sure she was quoting her mother, Nora. In fact, the only thing she was the least confused about was her idea that she'd herself seen Arienh O'Connell. And that's easy to account for. She'd become real in Biddy's imagination after listening to her history all those long days, sitting there sewing lace."

Ari's response was a little slow in coming. She'd traveled to Ireland to look for her great-grandmother, whose life she'd heard from Mrs. Mac while the two of them gardened and cooked or just sat on the porch. Then, it had had something of the sound of a fairy tale, like the other ones they'd read together. Only, now the woman Ari would always think of as Morna was flesh and blood. And this part of the story held her pain.

Finally, Ari replied, "Her marriage must have been really unhappy. I can't get over what she said in that one letter she sent to Nora. Biddy never forgot it either."

"The bad part was that Morna was afraid of it before it happened, telling Nora of the bad dreams she was having," Sybil said sadly. "And then Nora herself describing the laird as having 'a trim black beard and eyes as cold as the devil's heart.' But you can see why Sir Greagoir was for the marriage, urging it on Morna, his only daughter. He was probably ailing already, since he died so soon after the wedding. He wanted to see her settled. After all, her brother was away most of the year in Dublin at Trinity College. And the Castle, before cars were common, must have been so isolated. Bridget was dead, and Nora wasn't that much older than her mistress."

"Yes," Ari said, staring at the Twelve Bens, their rounded summits made indistinct by shifting white clouds, "and Morna's father had scolded Nora more than once, and probably Bridget before her, for paying attention to what he thought were his daughter's foolish fancies. They thought Morna had 'second sight,' but *he* thought she just had too much imagination."

"Well"—Sybil nodded—"and Sir Greagoir was a scholar of Gaelic, studied the 'old language' as Biddy put it. A man who probably wanted to categorize, to separate Ireland's myths and her history, to begin with. Then along comes the laird of Daire, a substantial man, fifteen years older—which Sir Greagoir would have seen as a real advantage—and he speaks Gaelic. He probably charmed the old man."

"Maybe Morna too," Ari added slowly, "until she started having bad dreams. Nora's description doesn't mean he wasn't handsome. So many of the Irish are." She stopped here, plainly thinking about this. "A handsome and charming man," she repeated. "She wouldn't have known him well. And the only thing against the laird that Sir Greagoir would be able to see he'd dismiss as women's silly ideas."

"Or," Sybil put in, "he might have thought the dreams were caused by a very young girl's fears about marriage. Heaven knows, no one would have told her a thing about"—she paused delicately, but then went on—"sex. These people were not only Victorian, but *Irish* at that. Besides, Bridget was a spinster, Nora unmarried then. What happened on the wedding night was barely hinted at, I suppose. Still, Sir Greagoir might have considered she could have overheard something, and would have thought such fears 'natural,' the kind of feelings a properly raised gentlewoman 'should' have, no matter who she was marrying. While Nora said he idolized his daughter, he was probably sure *he* knew best."

"So she finally agreed, ignoring her own intuition, and she got married in that bare church," Ari said, swallowing hard as she imagined it, "and was taken to the Isle of Daire. She was only sixteen."

"And after that," Sybil continued, her own voice somber, "she never came back. Not even for her father's funeral. There was only the note from her husband saying she was too ill to travel just then. Her brother, Liam, got worried because he hadn't heard from her either. So he went to Daire. But only his drowned body came back, and the men who brought it said his sister was prostrate with grief. That was probably true enough, because Bridget had always said they were great friends growing up together. Nora took care of the burying of Liam."

Ari rolled up the car window. The late afternoon fog was coming in off the sea, and she thought that was what was making her so cold on that summer day. "Biddy told that so well," she said slowly, ". . . about how frantic her mother had been all this time, with no word at all, starting to be sure that Miss Arienh wasn't allowed to write. And when the one letter came, it sounded as if only Nora would have known what she meant."

Both of them were silent as they now drove up the road to the house, and they remembered Biddy's voice with its quaver. "A short letter, just saying she'd not been well, but she finished it, *My dear Nora, dreams and true visions may be hard to tell apart, but when you have the true one, you must believe it. You were right.*"

Just as they came to the top of the ridge, Ari said, shaking her head slightly, "You know, Issy always said that Morna left Telluride because she had a true vision. How could she have been so sure that she'd seen the real future? In fact, how did she even have the courage to live with another man, after what she'd been through?"

The older woman didn't reply for a moment. They'd come out of the lowland fog, and the last slanting rays of the sun illumined the white-walled manor before them, investing its solid grace with a castle-like air. Mist drifted around the base, but the roof and windows were touched with gold. The light reflected off Sybil's thick glasses as well, as she turned to Ari and answered only her last question. "But she loved Berkeley Glendower. She had to think about what she knew about him *and* how she felt about him. You can't forget that second part. As the old saying goes, The heart has reasons the mind knows not of. In the end she had to trust herself in choosing him. And from what you were told she never regretted it."

Looking at the manor, she added comfortingly, "Remember what we heard today about how happy she was here, tucked up with her books on rainy days, or out on the moors on horseback with her brother. As Biddy said, 'Come in laughing, she would, with the bottom of her skirts soaked through every time, no matter how Bridget fussed about her death of pneumonia.' "

"Yes"—and now Ari smiled as she followed Sybil's gaze—"I'm so glad we came."

But their three-week stay in Connemara was almost at an end. Both of them were very interested in seeing Daire now, and a good many of Sybil's relatives were in nearby Donegal. She'd done a great deal of research, had some names and addresses, and she'd started corresponding with a cousin named Rose McGerrity. There was a lot to do. Because their suitcases were already hard to close, they had to mail their purchases home. Ari had bought Waterford crystal, tweeds, lace tablecloths, hand-knit sweaters. She'd found a wonderful crocheted one for Janie. And there were postcards to be sent. She'd written a number to Caley. And, in the end, she wrote one to Rivers.

Since they were due at tea with the Curragours the day before they left, Ari wanted to choose the right parting gifts for the two women who now meant so much to her. She found a soft pink mohair shawl for Biddy, and a rose-covered bone-china teapot for Tessie, since she'd noted the spout on the one she had was chipped.

When they arrived, Tessie opened the door with an air of barely suppressed excitement. She could not seem to stop smiling. And Biddy, upright in her rocker, had the same expression. They exclaimed over their presents, and Biddy insisted her shawl be put that minute over her shoulders. Tessie, touching the fragile pot as if she were afraid she'd rub off the roses, said, "We'll have the tea in this today. But first, we've something to show *you*."

She picked up a large white envelope from a side table. "This is all mother's doing. She wouldn't rest until I'd brought in box after box from the shed. I think she had the original hair ribbons my sister and I'd worn to grade school. She hadn't seen much of it for years, and wouldn't tell me what she was looking for. Probably she wasn't sure she remembered right. But"—and she turned to the smiling Biddy and patted her knee—"you did. Among all those old pictures there was this one. We want you to have it." Tessie gave the envelope to Ari.

Inside was a gray-backed black-and-white photograph of a girl in a lacy white dress, dark hair piled on her head. The dress was exactly the one Ari owned. She could only stare at the picture in silence, alive only to the odd impression that she'd seen it before. "Turn it over," Tessie urged. On the back, in delicate copperplate handwriting, was the inscription, *To my dear Nora, from her loving Arienh*. And Ari turned it back, looked again at the lovely young face, and burst into tears.

The next day Sybil was at the wheel as they drove northward, and Mrs. Kearney waved at them until they were out of sight. Ari still had the picture of Morna on her lap, as if afraid to let it out of her sight. It lay on top of a thick mailing envelope from Janie that Mrs. Kearney had brought up from the post office on her way to the house, saying in relief as she handed it over, "Just in time, or sure you'd be back in America before it found you."

Janie's fat letter was on onionskin, and her fast half-print script seemed to race over page after page of the thin paper. Her letter was dated a week earlier: *Sorry that all your mail*—most *of which looks like boring business stuff—was held up. I was in Telluride for longer than I planned. But, Ari, I wish you were here so you could see me smile. I'm so happy about what we're doing, so grateful that I'm in it with you.*

As she scanned the next paragraph, Ari's own spirits soared at Janie's enthusiasm. Saying to Sybil, "You have to hear this," she read it aloud: *"The flight to Telluride is heart stopping. I mean because of the scenery, although you can see into the cabin and at first I kept one eye on the pilots to make sure they were looking at all those dials and weren't as entranced at what was below us as I was. You fly low enough to see range after range of mountains. Then, the plane drifts down toward Telluride and the view close-up is so beautiful that . . . Well, you'll see because you've got to go up as soon as you get back."*

Ari stopped for a moment, realizing that the emotion she was feeling could best be described as homesickness, even if pictures and other people's words were as close as she'd yet come to that mountain town. She returned to Janie's letter. *"First thing, I rented a car and drove through town to Ute Rise Canyon. Right away I picked out Bridey's Mountain, and maybe you wouldn't at first see a woman's face on its peak if you weren't ready for it, but then that's all you can see. All of a sudden I felt the way you must about the need to leave this place just as it is. Before I was doing it for you. Now I'm doing it for me, too."*

Sybil reached over and patted Ari, whose voice trembled a little here, although she read on quickly: *"The second thing I did, which was extremely sensible, was go to a bar. The one at the Sheridan Hotel, to be specific. It's exactly the way it's always been. All that old mahogany and dark wallpaper and beveled glass for partitions in the back. I started talking to the bartender because I figured he'd know some of the stuff I needed to know about the town, and it was four o'clock and he wasn't busy. Well, let me be honest here. I took one look at him and would have waited to talk to him even if he was busy until three A.M."*

Grinning, Ari looked up at Sybil and said, "Now, I haven't looked at the next page yet, but I would make a substantial bet that this bartender has shoulders like a Russian weight-lifter."

Sybil replied sedately, "My mother always approved of large men. She said it was a sign of good health." Her eyes remained on the road, but they were twinkling behind the thick glasses.

Ari continued aloud, *"He's a big grizzly-bear man, reddish-brown hair and beard. He's a sculptor—didn't you say your father was a sculptor? Anyway, this one says he tends bar to eat. Got the biggest hands I've ever seen and, when he describes something, he moves them around and you can even see what he's talking about. It's a good thing because, while he listens beautifully, he doesn't say much. Except about saving Ute Rise Canyon. Now, there's a topic he's interested in. So I took him out to dinner. And lunch. I put it on your tab, of course. Well, it was business, even if he has shoulders wide as Wyoming."*

Ari chortled with satisfaction and went on with the letter. *"Everyone calls him 'Sticks' because of the Roman numerals after his name. He's Sam Goler III, and his grandfather ran the stable down on Pacific Avenue. It's gutted now, but the walls are still there. Unfortunately, old Sam the First didn't own the land, or any in Telluride, and Samuel (which is what I call him) grew up in Norwood. But he's lived here for ten years now and he's got a lot of information (and ideas) for our campaign. You'll have to talk to him first thing."*

The letter finished with a postscript that Ari did not read aloud because her eye was caught by a name halfway through it. *P.S. Your man at Murdoch phones the office regularly. This Rivers is clever. He got your address somehow. The enclosed letter from him came to the condo. Caley says to give you his love with this note.*

Ari opened Caley's first, and as she did, she recalled their evening together right before she'd left. As they made their way to the patio of the Cherry Hills Country Club, Caley's protective arm was outstretched behind her. The nubby sleeve of his raw silk jacket just brushed her skin in the backless dress. A three-quarters moon turned the trees on the golf course silver and the manicured greens a deep emerald. Because he was there, the whole world seemed like a safe, enclosed park. The candles on the table lent warmth to his eyes, touched his hair with gold.

He'd made it very clear how unhappy he was that she was leaving him.

His letter, although short, still conveyed that message. In fact, if Ari had not been reading it with the memory of that evening uppermost in her mind, she might have recognized a real irritation because she was gone. In her absence Caley said he'd called Stewart Wellings and strongly suggested that some of Ari's money be put into a new company called GeneSys. Stewart's almost abrupt refusal had plainly gotten his back up, and he added that, as he'd told her before, such a conservative investment policy would end up costing her money.

He ended, "You belong here. With me." Even as she glanced through it again, a little sorry because the note was almost all business, Ari smiled. Caley was concerned about everything that touched her life.

Still wrapped in that thought, Ari almost absentmindedly opened the next envelope. Rivers's letter began abruptly. *I couldn't wait any longer to see you. When I got your address I went right to your condo. All I could think was that when the door opened, you'd be in my arms.*

The words themselves seemed to reach for her as he would have done. It even took her a moment before she resented his assumption that she'd respond that way. Then she had to wonder whether she might have done it at that. She could picture him standing there so clearly. And she could feel his disappointment as he went on, *But the door didn't open, and when I got home, there was your note saying you were gone. I should have guessed—the whole damned town seemed empty on my way back.*

She didn't want to think about all this. That opening had caught her off-guard, but she knew she couldn't trust a man who was after money and happened to be very good with words. She'd keep *that* in mind as she read.

He went on: *What you had to say about your great-grandmother and Berkeley Glendower got me curious, so I asked an expert on Colo-*

rado history. Jonas. You don't usually want to bring up this subject with him—it can shoot a good part of your day.

But he finally finished, "Glendower could have gotten his hands on Laughton Powell's fortune. What's amazing was that he turned it down. And he ended up with nothing. Wasted his life."

You made me start thinking about my family and I got out my dad's letters to my mother, written when he was working in Washington and she was here in Denver. She died when I was only seven, and he wrote me from there too. I wish to God I'd saved those letters. But I have what he wrote to her. She kept every one.

Sometimes he mentioned his own dad. He really loved Patrick, even if Granddad wasn't your pillar of society. Here's the funny thing. He wrote to my mom that one day when he was small, right before the First World War, he went into the parlor and there was Patrick sitting in the dark, and he was crying. That scared Dad because he was little and he'd never seen his father cry before. So he crawled into his lap. Patrick patted him and said, "I had bad news today. My best friend was drowned in a flood up in Telluride." Then Patrick took out a handkerchief and wiped his eyes, and said, "But I shouldn't be sitting here bawling. Alive, he was the just the luckiest man." My dad said he always remembered it because he never saw Patrick cry again.

Ari, do you know that the only man killed in that 1914 flood was Berkeley Glendower?

Silently, Ari read through it again, no less moved the second time. For a minute she found herself imagining that Rivers was thinking over those two different views of her great-grandfather's life. His only comment was *I guess I wouldn't expect Jonas and Patrick to see eye to eye on things.* Then she remembered that Caley had said Rivers and Jonas thought alike.

His last words were *Hurry back. I'm going to have to spend a few months in D.C. on a project. I can't face the idea that I won't see you before I go.*

Jamming the letter back in the envelope, she let out a ragged breath. How could he always sound as if he really cared about seeing *her* when what he really wanted—

Sybil was saying, "Research on the Glendowers will be easy to do when we get back. The Church of Latter-day Saints has all the records of Massachusetts on file. I'm looking forward to checking that, but nothing will ever be better than what we've found here."

Nodding, Ari looked again at the photograph of Morna. The dark cloud of hair was arranged loosely up on her head, and it framed the delicate oval of her face. The heavily lashed light eyes did not quite meet the camera, almost as if she thought its unblinking stare could also see into her thoughts, and she didn't want them known. The nose was fine drawn above closed lips, which might have opened readily to a smile, but not on this occasion. The full mouth, except for its perfect form, could have been regarded as a little too large for those even features. As it was, it seemed only to add to her beauty. But again, Ari was struck by the thought that she'd seen this face before. At last she mentioned this to Sybil.

"Well, you have. In the mirror," her companion returned placidly.

"But I don't look anything like her," Ari protested.

"Yes, you do," Sybil insisted, equally surprised that Ari had not noticed the real resemblance. "Biddy saw it right away. It's the first thing she said. Don't you remember?"

"But I thought that was . . . just a nice thing to say. And then I didn't know she had the picture or had ever seen Morna. Besides, *she's* beautiful."

"True," Sybil nodded in a matter-of-fact manner. "The only real difference is the hair. Yours is lighter, and a lot curlier, especially in this humidity. My, I always wanted hair like that. Mine tends to frizz."

Dumbfounded, Ari leaned back in the leather upholstery of the Rover's front seat, and this time she didn't notice that her silence lasted all the way through the broad expanse of County Mayo. Growing up, she had pored over the family albums, looking at the snapshots of Bridey and Trish, wishing she'd resembled them. Both the MacAllisters had often remarked how much she looked like the Gregory women, but she had been sure they were seeing her with the blind eyes of love. As she gazed out the window, she tried to take in the idea that all through the years she had looked in the mirror and never seen her own face. Only the birthmark.

Even now when it had almost disappeared from her cheek, she still somehow imagined it there. When it had been, maybe people had seen past it when she herself couldn't. Closing her eyes, she fervently thanked Lucy and Gerald MacAllister for the love that had sustained her when she was rejecting herself.

Ari was only brought out of her jumble of preoccupations when Sybil stopped before a charming tea shop with sparkling squares of mullioned windows. Over their steaming cups they checked the *AA Guidebook* for a bed-and-breakfast place for that night. They wanted to get as close to the Isle of Daire as possible so they could go there in the morning. That meant driving straight across County Donegal to Malin Head, the northernmost tip of Ireland.

By now they were longing to see the island that Morna had fled from, and to find out anything they could about its cold-eyed laird. The *Guidebook,* usually so helpful in describing any point of interest, from secluded crumbling monasteries where one might see a splendidly incised cross of St. Patrick to pleasant inlets with sandy beaches, had almost nothing to say about Daire. The editors only noted its remote location in the Atlantic near the North Channel between Ireland and Scotland.

But Sybil had great faith in finding out more about the island from the owner of lodgings in Malin, since it was the closest place. Remembering their experience with the crowds drawn by the Connemara Pony Show, Ari called for a reservation. The woman who answered at the bed-and-breakfast there seemed likely to meet Sybil's expectations. In a voice tinged with a Scots burr she reeled off efficient directions, ending by saying it would be late when they reached Malin. She promised to keep, as she said, "a bit of dinner" for them.

When they arrived, they were weary and hungry, but stuffed with feasting on scenery. Sybil had been proud of her home county's beauty with its high headlands, vast sweeping strands, and sunken valleys resembling fjords. Malin itself was a small village with high-roofed houses of dapple gray, oyster, or white. Mrs. Balfour, a very tall, sandy-haired woman with a forthright manner, had their bags upstairs and a glass of sherry in their hands in what seemed seconds later.

Dinner was as quickly served, and delicious. The fish, she said, was salmon trout, and it had the pink flesh of the one kind and the delicacy of the other. The parsley potatoes were meltingly good. The vegetable that their landlady referred to as "mange-tout" was a bowl of crisp snow peas. That was followed by fresh-picked berries and clouds of whipped cream. Since they were the only guests on this weekday, Mrs. Balfour seemed happy to join them for coffee and a chat in the parlor.

She'd grown up nearby, so both Sybil and Ari settled back comfortably to hear about Daire. But as soon as they brought up the island's name, Mrs. Balfour shook her head firmly. "Ye canna' go there." There was a ferry that went twice a week, but not the next day, and it only called there briefly in the morning with mail and supplies for the few inhabitants. Once there, one had to stay, she said, and she made it perfectly plain that one didn't want to do that. "Nothing to see but an auld ruined castle, no roads fit for a car—they still use pony-traps—and no lodgings to be had. Those still there fish a bit and live off the dole, mostly. I was on a boat last year going to the Hebrides. We stopped and I got off, looked round, and got right back on. Ye don't want to go."

Ari explained in some detail why they needed to go, and ended by saying they wanted to talk to some of the older people who might know where and how the last laird had died. But Mrs. Balfour still stubbornly shook her head. "I canna' think ye'll find out a thing. Oh, aye, at the time you're talking of, there were more folk there. Smuggled for a living, more than likely. But they went their ways when that didn't pay. It's odd. Those still left keep to themselves, a close-mouthed lot—or so our fishermen who stop there now and again say—as if they still had something to hide. And it's a nasty cold place for old bones. I wouldna' think there'd be but one or two of them out there."

Ari waited patiently until she had finished, but one of Mrs. Balfour's remarks interested her. "If there are fishing boats who go near, would it be possible for us to hire one to take us out and pick us up tomorrow?"

Seeing the determination on Ari's bright young face and in Sybil's level gaze, Mrs. Balfour sighed, nodded, put down her coffee cup. Having been convinced that they were resolved to go to Daire, she briskly organized the expedition. By six o'clock the next morning Ari and Sybil were boarding a trim wooden-hulled fishing craft by Hell's Hole on Malin Head, carrying an enormous Thermos of tea, crumb-coated Scotch boiled eggs, and blueberry scones.

The handsome young fisherman who helped Ari climb on seemed little inclined to let go of her hand. He had on a thick white turtleneck sweater and Ireland's smile in his black-lashed Celtic eyes. The first half hour he spent trying to persuade the two women not to go to Daire at all, using the same arguments Mrs. Balfour had. Not only did he seem to think the people there had the brains of sheep, he was convinced the women would find their day a waste of time, as well as boring and uncomfortable. He appealed, with his eyes on Ari's, "Sure, you'd have more pleasure spending the day fishing with us." His father nodded glumly in agreement, as if that were the very worst thing one could say about Daire.

They reached the island without knowing it. Although on the open sea the fog was lifting, leaving only patches on the slate-gray water, they seemed to go through a solid bank of it and then they were at a pier. The son pointed out a path leading up a rocky slope, saying that if they kept to that, they'd reach a small country store and post office run by a man named MacDougal. Then, a worried frown on his brow, he said the boat would be back at three. "Four o'clock," his father corrected. "Three," the young man insisted. They watched as Sybil and Ari picked their way carefully upward.

Five minutes into the conversation with the storekeeper named MacDougal, Ari was thinking that the young fisherman had been right, except that this particular island resident was not so much sheep brained as pigheaded. A man in his middle forties, he had coarse black hair with a widow's peak and boiled fish eyes. When they'd come into the minuscule shop, part of which was divided by a dingy open curtain into lodgings at the back, he'd been leaning on the dusty counter with his arms folded. So he was still, his undershirted elbows showing through ragged holes in the sleeves of his heavy plaid shirt. But he was saying, again, that he was too busy a man to be spending his time gossiping with women about the old days. All their questions had been answered with an uncivil shrug.

Ari was about to give up when Sybil took her billfold from her purse and pulled out a five-pound note. She laid it on the counter and said, replacing her former politeness with asperity, "Mr. MacDougal, I'm sure your time is valuable. But we'd like a cup of tea"—and she glanced back through the curtain where a stove was visible. "Perhaps while we're drinking it, you could give us a minute."

Seeing the five pounds, MacDougal uncrossed his arms quickly. The money disappeared in a twinkling. "Aye," he said, adding a grudging, "Mebbe," and he leaned his head toward the back to indicate they should follow him.

The tea was surprisingly good, and MacDougal even rinsed the chipped cups before filling them. But for the rest of their five pounds they at first got very little information, and that doled out sparingly. His shop had been built with stones from the old castle, but when asked what had happened to its former inhabitants, he shrugged. The laird and his lady were not buried in the old graveyard by the now-unused church, he said. At last MacDougal added, "Weel, of course, there's Mad Fergus," and proceeded to tell them about him.

His grandfather, also named Fergus, and his grandmother had been servants at the castle, and their son Geordie had lived on there for some time before building his own house nearby from its crumbling stones. Mad Fergus, a very old man himself now, was in that house still, although he could usually be found up at the castle's ruins. MacDougal concluded, with another of his shrugs, "But he's daft. Ye'll get no sense from him. Mention the auld laird to Fergus, and he'll be saying that he hears, on a dark night, the dead man laughin' madlike. Ye know"—and here MacDougal hesitated, looking at Ari, apparently trying to remember just how she was related to the castle's owner—"the laird was *glaikit*." And here he tapped his temple.

Because Ari said nothing, could only stare at the storekeeper with parted lips and a stunned expression, Sybil interposed, "You mean the laird was not in his right mind?"

"Aye, the talk was that now and again he was . . . queer in the head. Downright queer. But as for Mad Fergus, he's only daft. Nowt to be scared of, though he looks—" MacDougal stopped, as if the picture in his head was not at all pleasant. "But nac, he'll not harm a flea. As for him sayin' he's hearin' the laird, that's just the north wind screechin'. I'm only tellin' ye there's no sense to be made of what the auld man says. He'll just be goin' on about his own father and the money. If ye see him about the castle, go your ways."

As they got up to leave, the storekeeper suddenly became almost hospitable. He told them that he kept the small pub as well. "Come back after ye've had your look-round at the castle and all and I'll have a bit of bread and cheese ready. Mebbe a pickle. I've a good stout on tap. Happen the wives here will be in the store to pick up a tin or two and I'll ask them for ye, though most are no older than me. The men are all off fishing, but they'd not know. They all closed their ears long ago to Mad Fergus's talk about the laird."

As they went up the road, Sybil wiped her hands off carefully with a handkerchief and replaced her gloves. "I've a definite feeling," she said grimly, "that the cheese and pickle will cost quite a bit." Trying to distract Ari from her brooding on Morna's situation, she went on, "I wonder why this Fergus should talk about his father when the laird's name comes up. Surely it should be his grandfather that he'd connect with him. And *what* money?"

Ari only shook her head. Her heart hurt as she imagined Morna here, and with a husband who sounded not only unbalanced, but dangerous. Morna had come from her green Connemara to this gray, rock-strewn island. At home she could look from her windows at the sun-washed sea or the purple bright moorlands, race down a shining beach on horseback, laughing with her brother. Here the fog would wall one in, and the ocean seemed to be scrabbling at the stony shore. Even now, when it was just past high summer, the chill dampness made the air itself heavy and sodden. As the two women walked up the narrow road, the mist curled around their ankles like a cold wet cat, and they could only make out the blank-windowed cottages when they were directly in front of them.

They were both startled when they suddenly looked up and saw the castle looming before them. It was huge, and the grim medieval battlements of its front lowered over them. Drawing nearer, they could see that it was only a façade; the rest of the walls reached at most to a second story. The small windows were empty eyes; there was no door in the high-arched entrance.

Stepping through this, they could see piles of rock everywhere, as if the walls hadn't simply crumbled over time but had been flattened by a giant fist. To the left, what would have been an enormous hall was filled with rubble. A stone staircase before them led eerily upward to nothing.

"Oh, dear," Sybil said, drawing out the word in shocked sympathy. "Poor Morna. At its best this place could never have looked inviting. And to think . . ." She didn't finish the sentence.

Ari shivered, sharing Sybil's unspoken thought. Then she went on with little hope in her voice, "Even if Fergus is here, how would we find him without breaking an ankle?"

Then they heard, even over the sea's quarrel with the shore, the creak of a wheel. It was a rusty persistent sound, followed at last by a shower of loose stones. It came from some distance at the rear of the ruins.

"I'll go around the outside to the back and see if that's him," Ari said. "Maybe you'd rather wait here."

"No," Sybil said, "I'll come too. But we'll have to go single file and I'm going to take it slow. You go ahead and see if that's him."

Ari could make out a faint path, winding around lichen-covered rocks and then into a roofless room that, given the size of the still-standing fireplace, might have been a kitchen. The old man before the hearth, with his back to her, was painfully digging into the side of the fireplace with a small pick. When he set that down and turned to put a stone in his wheelbarrow, he saw her and came shambling up eagerly.

His shaggy hair would have been white if it were clean, but he was dirt from head to toe. A fine dust coated his thick eyebrows and had worked its way into each age-etched line of his face. He was wearing layers of filthy shirts and sweaters, one pulled on top of the other. As he approached, Ari could see that his eyes had almost no color, as if age had robbed them of blue or cataracts covered them. Her mouth dry, she opened it to speak, but he startled her by reaching out a grimy hand with black-rimmed nails and grasping her wrist.

"Mr. Fergus?" she asked uncertainly.

He dropped his hand immediately, as if astonished that her arm was flesh and blood. "I thought mebbe you was her," he mumbled, and his disappointment was plain. "I'm always hearin' him, so I was thinkin' she'd come back now to tell me where the pouch was. Me father"—and here he turned and spat—"may the devil poke him a guid one at this moment—said she was a kind lady." At the mention of his father his milky eyes narrowed with anger.

Sybil now came up beside her, and Ari said as calmly as she could, "My friend and I would like to talk to you. Maybe we could buy you lunch at the pub and you could tell us about the castle."

"Nae," he shook his head decisively. "I canna'. There's work to be done." He started to turn back to the fireplace.

Now Ari laid her hand on his arm. "Please. We'd be glad to pay you for your time."

"Nae, lassie," he returned, and a proud smile touched his lips. "I've guineas of me own. In the pouch, if I could but find it. The auld laird, when he went off to America, gave it to my grandda', and *he* was a careful man. Take one out at a time, he would, and we always had a bit of mutton with our bread, even when others dinna'. But me father"—and again he jerked his head to the side and spat—"went straight to the devil without telling me where it was. It'd been kept in the auld chest, but when I went to look, there was nowt there. Nowt. Hid it somewhere else, he did."

With trembling fingers, tracing the shape in the air, Fergus described a leather pouch with drawstrings, and he kept repeating that it was full of the solid gold coins called guineas and that rightfully they belonged to him. Then he wheeled around, trudged back, and began clawing out the stones at the back of the hearth.

They followed him and talked to him as he worked. But all Sybil and Ari's questions about the laird and where he went in America and how he died only prompted the old man to take up his litany again about the pouch. Grunting as he worked, Fergus told the story each time in much the same words, sometimes stopping to demonstrate the size of the pouch.

At last Ari decided it was no use. Perhaps, she thought, the storekeeper might have found out something from his customers. Even the cheese and pickle with MacDougal seemed better than this sad conversation. She thanked him and, before leaving, said one last time, "I do so wish I knew what happened to the laird when he went to America. Can anyone here tell us?"

Throwing a stone into the wheelbarrow, Fergus muttered and waved his hand, "Earth just opened up and swallowed 'im." He looked at them in confusion. "Hard tellin' how he could get out. But he does. I hear him. It's no' the wind."

CHAPTER 11

Caley's Ferrari growled quietly down a tree-lined street near Denver's Cheesman Park. The streetlamps were haloed by a soft October rain, and flickers of their light came though the glass of the sunroof, touching Ari's shining upswept hair. He glanced sideways again at her with satisfaction. She would do him credit at the gathering tonight at Jonas Murdoch's.

She'd arrived from Ireland only the day before. At the airport he'd told her how important this event was. Still, she hadn't seemed eager to go, asking if this was the best time and place to meet Murdoch. Hiding his impatience, he'd assured her that it was ideal, since business could be conducted better with someone you'd met socially. He pointed out that *everyone* in Denver wanted to go to this dinner commemorating the hundredth anniversary of the founding of the Zebulon Pike Society. And very few could. Caley had mentioned that it was black tie and her dress should be elegant, but conservative.

When he picked her up, he was pleased at how she looked. The remaining traces of her birthmark were almost invisible. The jewelry she'd chosen was, he thought, a nice touch. Pike's Peak or bust had become the slogan for the gold seekers who had swarmed to Colorado, despite the fact that the actual ore had been found in what was today downtown Denver, eighty miles north of that mountain. Her earrings were long strands of gold, as was the delicate chain that wound around her slender neck. It was set here and there with seed pearls. The dress's shawl collar, which dipped rather low in front, set off her shoulders. He'd checked the neckline discreetly, considering the occasion, and decided it wasn't *too* low, since you could imagine more than you could see.

Even at less ceremonial affairs Denver society women dressed with some restraint, except for one or two of the younger ones. This was not New York or Los Angeles. And the Zebulon Pike Society was quintessentially Old Guard. It was Colorado's version of the Daughters of the American Revolution. Perhaps because it was Colorado, however, it was a men-only society. One had to be a native of the state and have either contributed in some significant way to its betterment or had an ancestor who did. Prominent businessmen, with a sprinkling of former politicians, made up the select membership. The wives were invited each year to the anniversary dinner. Plans for this centennial year had been going on for months, and everyone thought it was fitting that Jonas Murdoch had decided to host it at his Victorian-style mansion, itself a storehouse of Colorado history.

Ari was staring at the droplets on the windshield, feeling a little disoriented, as if she were still somewhere between here and Ireland. The unusual gentleness of the rain, where thunderstorms were the rule, contributed to the effect. Probably just jet lag, she told herself.

Sybil had decided to stay in Donegal with her cousin Rose. The two of them had burst into laughter at their first meeting when they saw their identical thick spectacles also had similar frames. Rose, a retired schoolteacher, was overjoyed at the prospect of introducing Sybil to, as she said, "more Morrises than you can shake a stick at, and with some of them, that's what you'll want to do." They'd immediately set to work on an elaborate family tree.

Nor had Sybil been downhearted at the sparse information gathered on Daire. She'd assured Ari, "I'll find out what happened to Morna, or at least the laird. As close as we are to Malin Head, Rose and I can take a day trip back and have another talk with old Fergus. His grandfather must have known how the laird died, because he certainly knew *when* he died. He knew when it was safe to spend the guineas. And somebody gave that 1906 date of death to the editors of the *Peerage*. It's unlikely that Mad Fergus has forgotten what must be a part of his family's folklore. Besides, as Shakespeare put it, 'he's only mad north by northwest.' "

Their experience on that misty island had stayed in Ari's thoughts on the long flight back alone, and as she walked into the terminal it was Denver's brilliant sunshine that seemed unreal. But Caley's welcoming smile and reassuring hug gave her a sense of solidity.

That night, staying up late talking to Janie, Ari found another reason to be grateful for his presence in her life. The warm, steady affection she felt for Caley always brought her comfort and never a moment of unease. That had begun to sound unusual in any relationship with a man. She'd found that knowing Rivers had caused her as much despair as pleasure. The thought of him woke her from deep sleep, left her staring at the darkness. And now *Janie* was in love, and painfully so.

She'd begun telling Ari about the groundwork for the campaign she'd done in Telluride during the summer. Sipping champagne with her legs tucked up on the bed under her, Janie said, almost offhandedly, "You remember I mentioned the bartender at the Sheridan. The sculptor. Samuel Goler Three? I've spent a lot of time with him. He'll be a big help to us. Knows everybody."

Then without warning she spoke as if the next words hurt her throat, "Oh, Ari, I'm crazy about him and that's not the way he feels."

Immediately Ari had hugged her, saying, "What makes you say that? If you've been together a lot, he must—"

"*He* thinks we're good buddies." Janie grimaced at the bedspread. "We have lunch and think of ways to raise money for Ute Rise. And we caught parts of most of the Telluride Festivals—Art, Chamber Music, *and* Film. When he's working, I spend my nights at the Sheridan Bar, even though he usually doesn't have much time to talk. Does he think I do that because I'm addicted to pretzels and beer nuts?"

"Doesn't he ever say anything . . . personal?" Ari refilled their glasses, trying to remember if Janie had ever sounded this serious before. Although she'd dated a lot in college, a new man was usually what interested her. Now she was trying to bring her sense of humor to her rescue, but there was no hiding the depth of feeling.

"We talk and talk, Ari. Well, I talk more than he does, but still. And not just about saving Ute Rise. I told him my life story. Highly edited, of course. I left out the whole year my folks sent me to the Bible college in Indiana in the doomed hope that I'd straighten up. He told me his. He describes his sculpture. And I can't take my eyes off his hands. Except when I'm looking at his shoulders. God!" She sipped gloomily from the flute.

"Don't you invite him in when he brings you home?"

"Sure." Janie raised her eyes to the ceiling. "I stay at the Sheridan to make it handy. I sit on the edge of the bed and he sits in the chair across from me. The rooms are not too big. I even keep his favorite schnapps in my dresser drawer with two little glasses. So we chat some more. When he gets ready to go, I walk him to the door. If I stuck my hand out, he'd probably shake it, but that's it. He's never invited me to his cabin down the road in Sawpit." She stopped and added, "But that could be because he once said he didn't like anyone to see his work until it's finished. Says he's started something he really likes but he isn't sure yet whether it'll be any good."

She'd nibbled on one of the Swiss chocolates Ari had bought at Shannon Airport. "I just don't have *any* idea how he feels about me." She put down the half-eaten candy. "Maybe he thinks I'm too fat."

"Oh, Janie!" Now Ari was really upset at her friend's expression. "He would hardly spend all his time with you if he didn't think—"

"You don't know him," Janie interrupted. "He takes our campaign seriously. Samuel would spend that much time addressing envelopes if you asked him. He takes everything he cares about seriously. And Ari, he's so big and quiet and . . . well, he's a complex person. Without knowing how he feels, I don't know what to do. Except sit at the bar and smile."

"I can't wait to meet him," Ari said, trying hard to come up with a helpful idea. "I'll really look at him when I bring up your name. I'll see if *I* can read his expression."

"He'll probably think you're trying to catch his eye because you want your drink freshened. And he'll pass the pretzel bowl. He's a great bartender." Janie got up and slid her feet into her slippers. "Let's go see what's in the kitchen. I've tried this drowning-the-sorrows stuff and it doesn't work. Food helps, though." She aimed for a grin and added, "And having you to eat it with."

Janie had remained on her mind as Ari hurriedly shopped in the afternoon for a dress for this evening. Now, catching the streetlight's gleam on the skirt, she smoothed the soft material that the saleswoman had called *"peau d'ange."* It was sherry colored with that wine's golden tint, and she'd liked the draping lines of the design.

Glancing at Caley, she thought how wonderful he looked in a tux. It seemed to intensify everything about him, his blondness, his masculinity, his sophistication. Even his light eyes seemed more transparent, although she always found them unreadable. It was the gentleness he turned toward her that made her sure she knew him.

As if he were following her thoughts, Caley took his hand from the gearshift, lifted hers, and pressed a kiss in her palm. He said, "I hope you're not nervous about meeting Jonas. Just remember that your Telluride land may be a cause to you, but it's only another business deal to him, one of many. I really wanted you to come with me."

In fact, he had a scheme that would give Jonas an upset stomach, and it required Ari's presence. Caley didn't see how it could fail. He intended to suggest to Jonas, quite privately, that he sell Ari *his* Telluride land. For fifty million. It was a sweet idea, Caley thought, because whether Murdoch agreed or refused, he would be embarrassed before the assembled members of the Zebulon Pike Society, a group devoted to Colorado causes. Caley would make sure that everyone there knew about the proposal.

Now, suppose Murdoch agreed. Jonas stood to lose a lot at fifty million. Over the years the interest on the mortgage payments on the sumptuous homes he planned would bring him in double that amount. But that "bargain price" wouldn't sound like a really generous offer from a billionaire, especially to save a piece of Colorado wilderness. Worse, everyone in that group would know that the lovely young Sweepstakes winner didn't have that much and couldn't begin to raise it from a campaign. Yet Caley would announce "the gift" and solemnly lift a glass of after-dinner port to the host, praising his altruism and civic-mindedness. Jonas wouldn't be expecting a public disclosure and would turn green around the gills.

Suppose, on the other hand, that Murdoch refused. Caley had every intention of introducing the beguiling Ari to each individual member, letting the man see the fervor she brought to this cause. After she'd moved on, he would ruefully drop the news that he'd suggested to Murdoch that he help her preserve the land, the heritage of all Coloradans, but Murdoch wouldn't even consider offering a low bid.

Either way Murdoch would look grasping and selfish to the other members of the Zebulon Pike Society. Caley himself would look like a hero to Ari for his effort to persuade Jonas. Maybe *that* would get her to lean on Wellings to cut loose some investment money, he thought, speeding the powerful car around a corner.

It had taken all of Caley's willpower when he had picked her up at the airport not to comment acidly on how much her notion to take off for Ireland just then had cost her. And, in an indirect way, *him*.

For, despite Caley's certainty that GeneSys was doomed to failure, the stock in that new company had taken off at the first offering—and gone straight up from there. There was worse news for him. According to Jack Dexter, Caley's inside informant, Rivers Alexander had liked what he'd heard from the young scientific inventor and suggested that

Murdoch invest heavily in Frederic Steiner's company. Jonas had lots of shares. Caley didn't have any.

So, along with his dinner tonight, Caley was going to have to eat crow. Jonas knew that Caley hadn't bought into GeneSys, nor could Caley counter by saying he'd invested on Ari's behalf, at least earning a nice commission.

His voice, however, gave no hint of his irritation. "Murdoch's house," he remarked, "is something to see."

"Like one of these?" she asked, glancing at the enormous new homes of Cherry Hills Farm on their left. Here, a ten-bedroom French château stood within arm's reach of an equally massive mock-Tudor dwelling, which was itself bordered by a sprawling red-tiled Spanish hacienda. Only a few trees surrounded them.

"No." Caley shook his head. "His is new, too, but he's spent a fortune making it look old. To see it you'd think he picked up one of the old Grant Street mansions on Capitol Hill and plunked it down out here. He's got acres. And he needs it. The place is half museum. And then Faith has what she calls her conservatory, although that's an understatement. She has two full-time people taking care of all those rooms full of different plants and flowers. It's more like Botanic Gardens South."

"Really?" Ari replied with interest. "I'd love to see that."

"Probably won't get a chance. Not at night. Faith doesn't like to turn on the lights—says it disturbs the growth patterns or something. And I wouldn't be the one to ask her." He smiled, looking straight ahead. "I don't think she likes me very much."

"Why not?" At his casual shrug she added, "Did you ever ask her?"

Now Caley looked at her, his smile widening. "Do you know, I think I should." Like Jonas his wife didn't appreciate the unexpected curve from left field, even in conversation. Caley could imagine her startled face at such a question.

"Do you like *her*?"

"Never thought about it," Caley replied. "She fits in with the Victorian house. Like she's wearing a corset from the neck to the toe, even though she's small and wouldn't need it. Jonas is pretty straitlaced too."

At her silence he said encouragingly, "But you'll enjoy some of the people tonight. Let me see who all will be there," he continued. "Their daughters, of course, with husbands in tow. The older one, Judith, married well. Quentin Wyndham IV. Sugar-beet fortune. Really good looking. Every debutante was baiting the hook for him."

"Wyndham," Ari said slowly. For some reason the name made her think of Mrs. Mac's stories. "That sounds familiar. What does he do?"

"Make a point of asking Wyndham that, would you? I'd love to know what he answers." Even Caley's pale eyes held amusement. As far as he could tell, when Quentin wasn't on the golf course, he was screwing all the ladies he hadn't married.

"Judith's okay," Caley commented, turning off Belleview onto a country lane. "But she's one of those girls you always feel is looking back to see if Daddy thinks she's doing the right thing. Too bad for her. Jonas is Daddy. He *expects* all A's. Now, Heather, the other one, makes sure Daddy *doesn't* like what she's doing. Works for all those feminist causes, instead of the Junior League."

"But, Caley," Ari protested, "maybe that's what really interests her."

"Maybe," he answered absentmindedly, mentally going over the guest list. There would be two former governors, but one, he thought, would just make speeches at Ari, and the other would try to fall down the front of her dress. No point in mentioning them. He wanted her to charm everyone, not be intimidated into silence.

He smiled to himself, since that last part wasn't likely. Not if he knew Ari. If asked, she'd tell them exactly what she thought. But the way she looked tonight, the men weren't even going to notice what she *said*. And the women would dislike her at first sight. Bound to be an interesting evening. The Murdochs had no idea she was coming, although he'd implied to her that they did.

"Who else will be there?" Ari asked.

"Primarily the old families." He hurried to add, "Quite a few of them are young people, of course. I'll introduce you around." Rivers Alexander wouldn't be there, he considered. By this time Jonas should have packed him off to D.C. on the ConChem project.

"The Farnsworths will definitely come. Since their marriage they're referred to as 'Beauty and the Beast.' Everyone likes Willie, but he does remind you vaguely of a warthog. *Quite* a bit older than Steffi." The Testarossa flashed through intricate metal gates, now standing open. "She was Stephanie Trimble," Caley went on. "And she really likes being called 'Beauty'—maybe that's why she married him. That, and the Farnsworth money. The Trimbles don't have a bean anymore."

That wasn't quite all there was to the story, Caley thought with a inward grin. Steffi put a very high price on her good looks and had thought they entitled her to Quentin Wyndham—or Caley Sutherland. But then Quentin had married Judith Murdoch. Steffi had turned to Caley, imagining that all she need do on a date was smile and look pretty. Not in Caley's view. With him she had gotten more than she'd bargained for, and the price had been higher. A lot higher. She didn't have any money and he didn't have to be nice. She still flirted outrageously with other men, even though she was married. But not with him.

Ari started to respond, but then the Murdoch drive curved and the mansion, discreetly floodlit, came into view. Although recognizably Victorian, it had none of the exuberant gables and furbelows of that period. It was almost austere, and surrounded by tall trees, it looked forbidding by night. Even with the bay windows lit Ari thought it looked like the turreted manor from a nineteenth-century novel with a depressing ending.

CHAPTER 12

Ari was about to take the two steps down into the long, crowded room when Caley gripped and held her elbow. She had to pause, and in that instant she felt as if she'd been turned into a statue. People seemed to be staring at her as at an object that had just been put on display.

Not that anyone there looked openly toward the front of the room. There were no direct, appraising glances. The murmur of low, modulated voices continued, and in any case the solid Victorian furniture absorbed sound, as did the heavy velvet drapes across the far wall. The gathering of tuxedoed men and women in formal dress lifted crystal glasses, nibbled on the toast triangles spread with caviar, and went on with the rituals of cocktail hour. Nevertheless, Ari had never felt so thoroughly inspected. And there seemed a tension in the room.

Part of it was that Caley had now arrived. It was, oddly enough, like the coming of the predator on the African plain in the evening. The zebra, giraffes, and antelopes who were the prey—even the massive elephants who had nothing to fear—were suddenly aware of his presence. They did not stop grazing or drinking. And even the sharpest-eyed couldn't spot him in the long golden grass. But they all knew he was there.

Whoever Caley brought would be of interest. He was always accompanied by an attractive woman, but one of their group. Someone they all knew, usually a recent divorcée with a large settlement, someone who couldn't otherwise attend. Tonight, at the anniversary dinner of the Zebulon Pike Society, that was what they certainly expected. Instead, he'd come with an outsider.

Jonas Murdoch, taking a sip of dry wine, did fix her with assessing eyes. He registered that she was beautiful, saw the shining that didn't just come from the sheen of the dress and jewelry. But he was more caught by Caley's manner toward her. It was quite different, something about the possessive way he held her arm. His first gnawing thought was that if Sutherland married a young woman, *he'd* have plenty of time to have sons. Then Jonas noticed her profile and knew immediately who she was. After reading the article on the woman who owned a part of Ute Rise, he'd studied that face. He'd been particularly interested because of her history.

His sharp temper flared. His anger wasn't caused simply by her presence. Instead, he guessed that she was involved in some little scheme of Sutherland's. Jonas wanted everything to go perfectly tonight.

Normally he didn't concern himself with organizing social events. But the Murdochs were founding members of the Pike Historical Society. He had gone over, and approved, all of Faith's efforts and was pleased with the elaborate arrangements for what she referred to as a "lovely surprise" for the guests. He was well aware that Sutherland didn't confine his connivings to turning a profit. He also used his talents just to sow chaos. Jonas could not tolerate people who didn't follow the rules.

Actually, most of these were *his* rules. But Murdoch didn't think of it that way. He'd learned at his father's knee that there was a right way and a wrong way to do everything. He expected his family, his employees, and his friends to observe the set procedures. Even the associates in his business—rich men in their own right—went along, at least in his presence. Jonas had more money than they did. And he had that rattlesnake temper.

But as he wound his way though the assemblage, stopping here and there to make sure the guests were comfortable, his venom was hidden. His spare features were pleasant, his fleshless eyes good humored. With his graying temples and perfectly tailored evening clothes, he was the model of a gracious host. He was not, however, making his way to the front of the room to welcome the new arrivals. He was thinking that though Caley's hide was impervious, the girl was vulnerable. He was going to find out just how much.

Faith Murdoch was near the square arch, positioned to greet people as they came in. She was petite, but her bearing made every inch count. Her silver sequined jacket above the pearl-gray chiffon skirt picked up those tints in her hair. Her eyes turned to steel-gray when she looked at Ari.

Faith Murdoch didn't know who she was, didn't recognize the name when Caley introduced them. She had an entirely different reason for the frost in her voice as she remarked, "I didn't know you were coming. Your name card at the table merely reads 'Guest of Caley Sutherland.' I'm sorry."

She didn't sound it, and Caley was a little puzzled. Faith was always standoffish but she made an effort on social occasions. He apologized, explaining that Ari had just gotten back from Europe, and he hadn't known if she could make it tonight. Raising a blond eyebrow, he thought to himself that Faith had honed her finicky ways. But then Caley's back was patted heartily by another man, and he turned without seeing the reason for his hostess's wintry look.

Judith Murdoch Wyndham stepped forward. She was wearing the same dress as Ari. Her own was a deep pink rather than a golden brown. But it was identical.

Faith's annoyance at this turn of events was directed at Ari. Judith, however, took a different view. Being Jonas's daughter had made her quick to feel that if something went even slightly wrong, it was her fault. Her father had already remarked on her dress, saying that he didn't consider pink a formal color. It was that flash of worry in her eyes that made Ari hasten to say, "I sure like your dress." She added, "And that rose shade is perfect with your coloring."

Judith responded with a relieved laugh, "Next time we'll have to go shopping together."

"In that case," said her husband, who was standing next to her, "*I'll* come too." He took Ari's hand, saying, "I'm Quentin Wyndham."

It was obvious that he was a man used to being the center of attention with women. Quentin Wyndham could have sat for the Renaissance artists. Their archangels were beautiful, but definitely male. Next to him his wife's pale prettiness faded into the muted wallpaper.

His blue eyes looked invitingly into Ari's as he said, "I noticed in the article about you that your grandmother was Bridget Gregory. So we're related."

"How?" Ari answered in surprise.

"By nonmarriage," he said with a smile. "My auntie Lil's husband ran off with your grandma. To be exact, she was my great-aunt. Lillian Wyndham Lowell. Everyone was still talking about it at her funeral. I remember because I was about ten and wanted them to quit eating and drinking so I could go home and get out of that itchy black suit."

"Really, Quentin," Judith said with flushed cheeks, "I don't think you should bring up—"

But Ari broke in laughingly, "Why do funerals always require itchy suits?"

"I never liked Aunt Lil, anyway," Quentin responded, his smile deepening, his eyes not leaving hers. He was quite ignoring Judith. "And if your grandma looked anything like you, one could hardly blame Mr. Lowell. Let me get you a drink."

He stopped a circulating waiter. Just as he was handing Ari a glass of champagne, a peremptory voice at his elbow commanded, "Quentin, introduce me. I haven't met this . . . guest."

Wyndham glanced at his father-in-law, murmured names, and then took his wife's arm, saying to her, "We haven't said hello to the Farnsworths yet."

Ari was left alone with Jonas Murdoch. He said nothing for a moment, only looking at her with hard eyes.

She'd heard a lot about him. As she and Janie talked about the campaign, his name naturally came up often. Still, he'd been a faceless figure to her, almost an abstraction, though she wasn't sure she'd like him from what she'd heard. Seeing the coldness of his expression and the tightness of his thin autocratic lips didn't erase that feeling. Nor did he come out with any of the usual polite phrases to ease the situation.

But she was interested in his study of Colorado history, and she was about to bring up that topic, when he said abruptly, "Did the newspapers have it right? Was your Telluride land originally a gift from Berkeley Glendower?"

Ari thought his tone was almost rude. She felt he should have said, 'your great-grandfather.' The phrase was rapped out as if she had no connection with the giver. But it did occur to her that Murdoch might be one of those reticent men who genuinely lacked social grace. So she smiled and replied, "Yes, and it's been in my family ever since."

Murdoch began, "Your *family*—" and his stress on that word suggested he hadn't even recognized the word when she used it. But he was interrupted by someone behind her.

"Sorry, Jonas. I have to break in. This woman passes herself off as someone named Ari. But her real name is Frank. I'll ply her with champagne until she confesses." An index finger indicated the archway in back of Murdoch. "The governor is here."

Jonas wheeled without apology. And Ari felt a warm hand clasp hers, turning her around.

It was Rivers Alexander.

Looking up at him, if she'd been capable of thinking, Ari might have thought that lightning really did strike twice. Even the faint bulbs behind the antique wall sconces seem to dazzle her vision, and she was aware of her skin's tingling. She hadn't seen him for several months. But she hadn't forgotten how vivid his blue-green eyes were, how dark the lashes, how direct the gaze. She remembered exactly the double-bracketed smile and the expressive mouth. She couldn't think of a single thing to say.

It was the way Rivers was looking at Ari that caught Caley's attention across the room. The thickset man in front of him continued talking and gesturing, but he no longer heard him. It was possible that Caley didn't even recognize the emotion that clutched him. But it was jealousy. He felt instead as if someone had boldly snatched one of his prized possessions before his very eyes. He'd watched Jonas talk to her with some amusement, but he wasn't amused now. He began to move toward her, but the jowly man held on to his sleeve, making a persistent point.

Rivers asked her, "When did you get back?"

It was a simple question, but Ari again had the impression of such intimacy with him that his unspoken words were louder than what he said. Those words were "I missed you. I missed you every day."

She shifted her gaze to his black bow tie so he wouldn't guess she'd heard them. If, in fact, that's what he'd thought and it wasn't her imagination. "Last night," she answered.

"Then I'll forgive you for not calling. This time. How was Ireland?"

Because Daire was so fresh in her mind and because she needed to talk so she couldn't hear the silent conversation between them, she launched into that story.

When she finished, he said, "Mad Fergus? You couldn't make up anything that good. What—" But he interrupted himself, with surprise in his voice. "Ari, your birthmark is gone!" He leaned a little closer.

"Well, not all of it." She almost stammered. He was too near and the warm smell of him brought everything back. Once again she was in his bed, in his arms. His skin was cool and hot to her touch. His mouth was soft and hard on hers and then his lips moved down her throat, down—

Her mouth was dry but she had to talk, to say something, anything. "There's still the outline left. I put makeup on it tonight even though I'm not really supposed to yet. See?"—and she brushed her finger above and below her eye.

He ran his thumb lightly over her cheek. "Ari, I can't see anything." *She* saw that slight cleft in his chin, the full lower lip that she'd caught between her own teeth, and heard the words he'd whispered in her ear. She was sure that her arms of their own accord would reach—

"Alexander, stop that. This woman is *my* dinner partner." The short, squat man beside Ari had black triangular eyebrows, a squashed nose, a gray mustache, and a gap-toothed grin. His ugliness was pleasant and so was his voice.

"How do you know where she's sitting, Willie?" Rivers challenged him with a grin. "The dining room is shut up tight as a drum."

"Ignore him, my dear. I'm Willie Farnsworth. You'll be much happier sitting next to me, even if I'm not half as handsome as he is. *I* know all the insider dirt." He tucked Ari's hand firmly under his arm as he said this.

Across the room Caley paused just in the act of jerking his arm from the stocky man's tight grip. He relaxed but his mouth was grim.

With a guilty twinkle in his eye Willie went on, "I know I'm sitting next to this gorgeous creature because I fixed it. The wife and I snuck into the dining room, and I changed my name card. No one saw us, so don't tell Faith. Riv, have pity. I was planted next to the gov's wife."

He turned to Ari, explaining, "The woman's nice enough. But she is deeply interested in day-care. Besides, she doesn't drink and when she moves her hand over her wineglass, the waiter sometimes takes that to include mine as well. And poor Steffi was stuck by Jonas. One look from him and her cream soup would have curdled. So she changed hers. It was Beauty's idea to begin with."

Farnsworth made a move to go, taking Ari with him, but Rivers's mock-stern voice stopped him. "Willie, who did you put in your place? Me?"

"No," Willie replied stoutly. "They'd have known if I'd done that. You're next to the boss's daughter, as usual. I put Caley where I was supposed to be. He'll have a grand time. He has Faith on the other side. *She* can talk potting soil and fertilizer to him. Or drop more hints about the lovely surprise she's planned for us tonight."

To Ari he said, "Now, come along. We've just time to get acquainted over another drink before the dinner bell tolls."

As they sat down, Ari was glad to have Willie's comforting presence beside her. The wide table, laden with crystal, stiff white napkins, gold plates, and matching flatware stretched down two long rooms. Conversation was limited to those people sitting close by. But she had little chance to talk to Willie or talk at all. Heather Murdoch Askew, Jonas's second daughter, was on his other side, and she only paused in her remarks for an occasional bite of food.

She had pale, pearly skin and wore little makeup. Her ash-blond hair was worn in separate ringlets chopped off at her jaw. It looked as if she had just run her fingers through it after a shower, although it might have been the result of an expensive hairdresser's art. The black strapless dress was unadorned and tight across a flat bust, but around her neck were strands of magnificent pearls. Her manner was assured and forthright, almost blunt.

Heather's first words to Ari were "Judith says you're really an addition to the group. And she didn't mean it as the left-handed compliment it could have been." She waved a dismissive hand all down the table. "Honestly," she went on, "the same old gossipy crowd and the same old parties—here and at the country clubs. Boring! I think I spend more time with these people than I do with my own husband. Scott couldn't come tonight because he had to coach his basketball team. Dad would have raised Cain—and Abel—about him not being here, but luckily Riv was free and he brought me."

That sentence cheered Ari considerably. Whenever she'd had the chance, she'd tried to guess who his date was. Her heart had sunk to her kneecaps when she thought it was a spectacular woman with a mane of dark tousled curls. She had on a black dress that seemed more like a slip and it outlined her bosom and hips as if the designer had that wonderful figure in mind when making it. She'd been surrounded by men all evening and her low laugh had wafted through the drawing room like rich perfume. Ari had been relieved when Willie introduced her as his wife, Steffi. "Usually known as 'Beauty,'" Farnsworth had added proudly.

Leaning across Willie, Heather went on to Ari, "I hope you can stick to your guns on that Telluride land. I'd speak to Dad myself but"—here her smile was as thin lipped as her father's—"*that* would only hurt, not help. He disapproves of everything I do." There was more than a little pride in that statement. "And I have to devote my time and funds to the women's causes. We really need your help there."

As she described her work, sipping Perrier rather than wine, she kept eyeing Willie as if she included him in the list of battering husbands or employers who paid women minimum wage with no chance of promotion. Heather rounded on him when she got to the subject of how chauvinistic Denver society itself was. "You know, Willie, what

I'm talking about. Women who graduate from the Ivy Leagues still can't join the University Club. They can't be members in their own right at the country clubs. And just remember the Black Diamond Ball."

"Well," he protested feebly, a hunted look in his eyes as he reached for his wineglass, "that's put on by a few of the younger men, the unmarried ones, and they see it as a bit of fun, my dear. That's all."

Nettled, Heather stressed her next word. "*Sure.* Ari, do you know what I'm talking about? Every year these well-off bachelors get together and invite about nine women for every man to this ball. And do you know how they refer to the women being invited? The Bimbo List!"

Ari felt some pity for Willie who, after all, wasn't single and didn't look like an abusive husband. She changed the subject by mentioning the table display, which had entranced her. It was exquisite, each blossom a Colorado wildflower. The small pots in which they were planted were hidden by native ferns and sprigs of meadowsweet. From the head where Jonas and the governor were down to the end near Faith and Caley, they were arranged according to their time of blooming from spring to fall. Amid the larkspur, primroses, sego lilies, wild iris, cinquefoil, and tansy were scattered everywhere fragile stalks of the Colorado state flower—the columbine. Their starry white inner petals were juxtaposed with the blue-purple outer ones above their spurs of nectar.

"Nice, isn't it?" Heather replied, nodding indifferently. "From Mother's conservatory. I wonder if this is the surprise she's been going on about. This must have been a lot of work—for her gardeners, anyway—but the way she's been talking for a year, I expected something more elaborate. Maybe it's yet to come." She took the smallest bite of fish and set down her fork as if she were now finished with that course, adding, "The conservatory, although really it should be plural since there are several rooms, is built right onto the house. From the drawing room you can walk into your own private rain forest. Costs a fortune to keep it up."

Willie put down his fork, having finished the salmon, and commented on how very good it was. Heather raised a bare shoulder, saying, "The menu was copied from a dinner given at my grandfather's. His old-maid sister saved the recipes and course lists from his parties for the 'Sacred Thirty-six'—all the people who counted then. These plates were his. Twelve courses were common and the sheer amount of food they ate boggles the mind. I don't know how they did it. A salad fills me up for the day. And they served a different wine with every course!"

Ari heard Willie's low voice in her ear. "Times've changed. No one here will eat any of this. Except me, of course." He patted his round tummy with satisfaction. "I told Steffi I didn't see why we bothered all the time. Might as well give the guests soda water, a dry rice cake, and a lettuce leaf and have done with it. They're all watching their figures. One thing's the same, though." He wiggled his bottom disconsolately on the antique, harp-backed chair. "Same uncomfortable seats."

His glance was stealing with increasing frequency down the table toward his wife. Steffi Farnsworth was seated next to Quentin Wyndham, and neither of them was interested in the food. Their heads were together constantly, and whatever Quentin was whispering in her ear seemed to be very funny. Willie almost gulped down a glass of Pouilly-Fuissé.

Heather talked on through the courses, taking an occasional bite, but sending the food back largely untouched. Ari couldn't decide what her attitude toward her family was. Her voice displayed no affection, and she was openly critical of her parents and the way they lived their lives. Yet she seemed to share in it and certainly could be said to brag about their history and their money. When Willie excused himself right before the dessert course to, as he said, "Step out for a cigar," Heather slid into his chair and leaned forward conspiratorially to Ari.

Caley Sutherland had been watching them throughout the dinner. He had little else to do other than eat. When he found he was seated next to his hostess, he was quite surprised, and he noted that she was too. Faith directed only a few remarks to him. The first wasn't designed to make him happy. "You know, Caley, while I was planning this party and going through our old papers—my family's and Jonas's—I realized that we owed some gratitude to your grandfather Stanton. Before Theo Manningham arrived and took over the business, my great-grandfather was in some trouble over his real-estate dealings. He owned all of Montclair." This was now part of central Denver and the site of some of the most expensive houses.

As she lifted her crystal glass for an infinitesimal sip of wine, Caley noticed that her lips were as meager as her husband's. She continued, "His name was George Bender. He offered the land to Stanton for almost nothing. But your grandfather thought it was much too risky. Imagine. You'd have more money than Jonas if he'd bought it."

Caley hadn't heard of his grandfather's involvement in this deal before, although he knew the general circumstances. But he had a smooth retort. "Well, it's just hard to see into the future on these deals, isn't it? Take Bosley over there, for example. Now he's begging Jonas to help him out over in Durango. Bosley bet that it would be the next big ski resort, but that turned out to be Telluride instead. So Bosley's choking. He offered Jonas land at a very good price. Jonas turned him down.

Someday, your grandkids might really regret that." He paused, then added, "But then you don't have any grandchildren to worry about, do you, Faith?"

She stared at him for a long, cold moment, and for the rest of the evening she encouraged the governor's wife to tell them more about the cost of day-care.

It had been a mixed evening for Caley. The men's eyes had sidled enviously over Ari, and some had made joking remarks about how quickly Caley had appropriated the Sweepstakes winner. Then, those he'd encouraged to buy GeneSys stock praised him to the skies, but that only reminded him that he had no shares of his own. After dinner he would still have to waylay Jonas on the Telluride land, and Jonas was sure to bring that up. At least that would put Murdoch in a better frame of mind to listen to Caley's new little plan. He couldn't believe the bastard would see the pitfall yawning before him there. He reminded himself that when they talked, he'd have to get Jonas to pack Alexander off to D.C. as soon as possible.

Suddenly his thoughts took a new and strategic turn as he watched Heather whispering to Ari. He could see that these women, even the Murdoch daughters, would accept her. At that moment Caley decided to marry Ari. The more he thought about the idea, the better he liked it. That way he could get rid of old Wellings and get control of the money with some speed. It was time he settled down, anyway. Since he was the last of the Caley line, he should start his own family.

The next thought he had on the subject gave him even greater pleasure. Stanton and Ceci would turn in their graves when he married this particular woman. Ari had told him that her great-grandmother was an Irish aristocrat, but she lived in a whorehouse in Telluride when she arrived. A "singer," Ari said. Caley had some trouble hiding his smile over that idea. He could just imagine Ceci's horror at the thought of the blood from her distinguished family mingling with that of a lady from a whorehouse. Not to mention that none of the other Gregory women had ever got around to getting married either. His expression darkened. Trish, wherever she was, wouldn't like the idea any better than Ceci. Everyone else would think it a brilliant marriage for Ari. As did Caley.

Yes, he thought, that's what he'd do. It would be a while before he told Ari. Some things would have to be worked out. But that's definitely what was going to happen.

What Heather was whispering to Ari while Willie was gone concerned the behavior of his wife and Quentin Wyndham. "I can't imagine," she said indignantly, "what Mother was thinking of, putting those two together. But that's so like Mother. If she doesn't want to see something, she refuses to look. Really, over the years, I've come to the conclusion that her naïveté is terminal! Steffi's all but climbing into Quentin's lap. And both his hands are under the tablecloth."

"I'm sure Willie noticed," Ari replied. "He hasn't seemed very happy."

Heather shrugged. "Well, he's used to Steffi acting outrageous. Everybody encourages her, say what they will. The men want to tell her off-color jokes, and the women want someone to talk about, to disapprove of. I think they imagine it's all show on her part, that she just does it to get attention. But maybe not this time. Steffi's always wanted Quentin. Poor Judith."

Ari looked down at the far end of the table where Judith was talking intently to Rivers. He was looking down and nodding, the sun-streaked hair on his forehead, the dark brows drawn together as he listened. With her eyes still on him, Ari bent her head in that direction, and said, "Where she's sitting—and on the same side of the table—maybe she can't tell."

"Even if they were right next to her, she'd make every effort to look the other way. She takes Mother's see-no-evil approach. You know, I once remarked to Mother that most of the men she knew had a mistress tucked up in one of the high-rises near downtown, and she was shocked. What's more, she said she didn't believe me. Not that my father has one." Heather almost giggled as she added, "He'd think his time was too valuable to waste."

Now she looked at her sister, who was smiling, and sighed. "That's who Judith should have married. Rivers. They went together for a while in high school. They were too young then, though. But my father really likes him, thinks he's whip smart. Whereas Quentin . . ." Heather brightened as a thought struck her. "Who knows? Maybe this will all turn out for the best and it'll work out now. Rivers would be perfect for her. And he's one sexy man."

Ari was glad that the waiter's arm was now between her and Heather as the dessert was served. But she pushed it aside and picked up her coffee cup, realizing her stomach hurt.

Jonas stood up, and although he made no gesture, the table gradually quieted. "I promised you no speeches tonight." There was laughter and a thin smattering of applause. He almost smiled as he went on, "But the governor and I did want to propose a few toasts on this very special occasion. And I have just the wine for it. We are going to have one-hundred-year-old port. It came from the cellar of Laughton Powell, who was one of Denver's important men at the turn of the century. He was a wine connoisseur as well, and my grandfather William had the foresight to buy the contents of his house and his cellar when his widow, Amelia, moved away. I had the port decanted today, and I assure you it's drinkable. This will be served shortly in the drawing room." He paused and added, to more laughter, "Since times are different now, we invite the ladies to join us."

As he was leaving the room, Caley put a firm hand on Murdoch's arm. "A quick word, Jonas. Could we go to your study?"

As Murdoch's eyebrows darted together in irritation, Caley pressed, "It's business, and it won't wait."

He finally nodded curtly and led the way down a long hallway hung with old-fashioned portraits. By the time he'd shut the door in a book-lined room, his temper seemed to have improved slightly. His evening had gone well, and Caley had behaved himself. Moreover, as he walked down the hall, he'd remembered something. He sat at his desk, saying, "Your tip on GeneSys was so good that I suppose I should listen to you now. But it's a shame you didn't benefit from your own advice on that stock." He had the manner of a man handing over a platter of crow—uncooked.

Caley was prepared. He gave a rueful shake of his head and said, "Liquidity problems. I should have listened to *you* on that front. But it was your brilliance in setting up the company that made it take off." He acted as if that was hard to say. And it was. He slouched down in the leather chair and put his hands in his pockets. He rubbed his gold pocket watch as he continued, "I have another suggestion. You should offer your Telluride land to Ari MacAllister for, say, fifty million."

"What?" Murdoch almost stood up again. "Sutherland, you know that Ute Rise built out and finished is worth twice that. You can't be thinking that the EPA will rule against me. They won't. The announcement won't come until January, but I know. Why would you suggest I sell at a low price?"

Caley countered with a question of his own. "Isn't ConChem a far more lucrative project, considering everything?"

"Of course." Murdoch's eyes narrowed. "What has that got to do with it?" He immediately worried that Sutherland suspected that he had designs on ConChem's huge reserves.

And Caley did. He leaned forward, speaking earnestly. "We both have a lot invested in ConChem. We need a delay on the toxic waste cleanup, but that requires congressional approval. Don't you want to look like a concerned environmentalist to the good senators?"

"I see." Jonas picked up a pencil and tapped the eraser on his blotting pad. "Image." He often envied his grandfather's situation when elected officials listened to businessmen, as they should, without all this worrying about what the public would think. In those days the militia had been sent in immediately to subdue the recalcitrant miners. Usually he didn't have to bother with public relations, but in the Con-Chem case . . . He tapped the eraser again while he brooded. "But what if she comes up with the fifty million?"

"Be serious, Jonas." Caley smiled and stretched out his legs farther. "She hasn't got it. Where's she going to get it? Even the richest of the environmental organizations can't earmark that much for one project. And the owners of vacation homes up there aren't going to give big bucks. They like to spread their charitable contributions around. Now, all you have to say is that you'll sell only if it becomes a designated wilderness area. It's just a verbal offer—no signed contract." He stopped and added thoughtfully, "I can guarantee she won't come up with the money. Does that make you feel better?"

Jonas was, of course, highly suspicious of a proposal from Caley, but he reminded himself that, in this case, they both stood to profit from the ConChem deal. Nor could he see how there could be aces up Sutherland's sleeve. But he stipulated, "If she hasn't got the money by spring, then she sells to *me*. I want construction started by then. It's a short season for building up there and I want a *written* contract."

"Done." Caley stood up. By then he and Ari would be married and he'd make sure they got a fancy price for her land from Murdoch. "I wanted you to agree to this before you send Alexander off to bargain with Congress. It'll help if he mentions your real interest in environmental issues. He is going soon, isn't he?"

"Yes. Maybe tomorrow. I wanted him to spend time with Steiner at GeneSys so he could explain why we need the delay." Jonas was still turning over the idea in his mind. This last point clenched it. "All right. Fifty million. And you make sure she doesn't get it. It won't do my image any good if I have to *force* her to sell."

"Guaranteed." Caley put out his hand to shake on the deal. Ari would be happy at this news. And he was looking forward to proposing a toast to Jonas before the assembled members of the Pike Society. Jonas was bound to look like a piker.

As the waiters were circulating with the port, Ari was standing before the massive moss-rock fireplace talking to Judith. Jonas's older daughter had come up to her immediately after dinner and seemed eager to talk to her. She was suggesting they have lunch the next day. When Caley came in and saw them together, he blew Ari a kiss but joined the group around the governor. He wore a pleased smile.

"Mother's so excited," Judith said. "She's spent night and day thinking about tonight. Just before dinner she finally told me about her surprise for the guests." Although Judith's fingers were twitching at the skirt of her rose-colored dress, making small pleats in the fabric, she didn't seem upset. Ari thought with relief that she must be unaware of Quentin's attentions to Steffi Farnsworth. Glancing around the room, she couldn't see Quentin, Steffi, or Willie, for that matter. Probably he'd decided to have a second cigar, she guessed, or had at last found a comfortable chair somewhere.

"I guess there's no harm in my telling you about her surprise now." Judith grinned. "You'll see it in a few minutes. She's had a huge diorama of Pike's Peak built in her conservatory." She made a small gesture to the heavy red drapes on the near wall. Jonas was standing before them. Ari's eyes had been straying in that direction because he was deep in conversation with Rivers, who seemed to be trying to persuade him of something. But his employer didn't seem to be agreeing.

"Mother says she's *really* pleased with it. The gardeners have put in the same flowers we saw on the table, and she's got stuffed figures of the wildlife there too. Bighorn sheep, mountain goats, cougars, and down on the plain before Pike's Peak, there are antelopes and wolves. It must have taken her forever—people from the Museum of Natural History, the Botanic Gardens, and the Zoo have been out here. Not to mention all the workmen. And, being Mother, she swore everyone to secrecy. No one here will be expecting this, you know. She has strict rules about not turning on the lights in the conservatory at night because she says that disturbs the plants."

"Sounds wonderful." Ari tried to put enthusiasm into her voice. Rivers was arguing rather forcefully with Jonas. Perhaps, she thought bitterly, Rivers hadn't heard that the man might soon become his father-in-law. No doubt that would make him agree with anything Jonas said. Under the circumstances she found it hard to even look at Judith, but she made the effort.

"So the plan is," Judith was continuing, "for Dad to speak, then the drapes will open, and the governor can stand in front of the scene to make his toast. Dad's been busy too. He commissioned a book on Denver's leaders for the last hundred years, and he says the research has turned up all kinds of interesting stories."

At that moment Faith Murdoch, who was standing well behind her husband near the drapes, gestured to a waiter carrying a tray of port. He handed glasses to Jonas and Rivers, and Jonas stepped forward. "Ladies and Gentleman"—he raised his glass toward the gathering—"to the one hundredth anniversary of the Zebulon Montgomery Pike Historical Society. And to another one hundred years of progress."

After the room again quieted, Murdoch went on. "Although I don't have a long speech, I have a story to tell. Lately I've been doing a lot of reading in Colorado's history, and this is a factual account. It said something to me about how important it is for those in positions of power to think ahead for the future's sake." Here he outlined that future as he saw it.

Ari listened unhappily because his vision inevitably meant more mountains leveled, more plains paved over, and the aquifers under Colorado's dry mesas drained of their water. Probably his wife was right to display a papier-mâché mountain tonight, Ari thought grimly. Given his way, soon that's all they'd have to remind them of natural beauty. She didn't look at Rivers. As Caley said, he thought like Jonas.

By now Murdoch had launched into his story, which started with Laughton Powell. "Unfortunately, he was cut off in his prime, and his great fortune was left to his wife, Amelia. That is her portrait displayed this evening above the fireplace."

His audience followed his gesture. Ari had to crane slightly to glance up at the ornately framed picture. The woman wore feathery plumes in her piled-up hair, but that seemed all that was soft about her. Her eyes were chilly and seemed to command the onlooker's attention. The graceful neck was set on imperious shoulders above the prominent, corseted bosom.

"Amelia Powell," Murdoch intoned, "now had one of the nation's great fortunes at her disposal. But she was a woman and she made a mistake."

Ari wondered if his other listeners had the same impression she did: Jonas would have *expected* a woman in charge of a fortune to do that very thing.

"Her wealth would have stayed in this state," he emphasized, "building industry *here,* where all our citizens could have benefited. But she chose the wrong man. She'd set her heart on Berkeley Glendower."

Ari stared at Jonas in amazement. Why was he bringing this up? There was no mistaking the fact that Jonas was looking directly at her.

He continued. "Although a brilliant engineer, this man could not see what power for good a concentration of money gave. Not only for himself or any family he might have, but for his home state's future. He refused her. She ruined him, and he lost forever the chance he might have had."

Ari could hear the satisfaction in Jonas's voice, as if he believed Berkeley had received his just desserts for such a foolish decision. Her eyes sparkled with anger. Amelia Powell had clearly been vengeful and vindictive. On that ground alone Berkeley's refusal to marry her had been wise. Ari saw that the gap between the way she and Jonas thought extended to personal choices as well. Berkeley had chosen love over money. Jonas never would.

Jonas went on, "Amelia left Colorado. Her fortune went with her. And I see in this a telling point. We all have to look at the broad picture, to think beyond ourselves. History provides a frame of reference, gives us this overview. At present we are all concerned with narrow, immediate goals. Yes, we need to protect the environment, to provide for the homeless, to improve education. But we cannot lose sight of how best to accomplish this. We must draw more industry to this state. It's as simple as that. And here in this room are the powerful men with the right vision. We are the heirs of the past, of those men who came here and built fortunes in mining, banking, and agriculture. And we are the ones who must think ahead for all of Colorado's citizens."

He lowered his voice. "Now, to remind us of what we are working for, the heritage we wish to preserve, my wife and I want to present Pike's Peak and Colorado in all its beauty."

Faith pushed a button behind the velvet drapes and they opened to display the impressive summit of the mountain with a dawning sky behind it. On its slopes were real wildflowers and realistic figures of Colorado mammals.

But in the foreground were two astonished people. Quentin Wyndham at first had his back to his new audience. His tuxedo trousers were around his knees. It might have looked as if what he was interested in was a bighorn sheep. But there were two bare white legs entwined around his waist. And when Quentin half turned to face the group, they could all see Steffi Farnsworth spread on the sheep's back, staring at them in horrified surprise.

CHAPTER 13

Ⓣhe sleek white Beechcraft gathered its force and threw itself into the sky. Although Ari was staring out of the porthole-sized window, she didn't notice they'd taken off. She hadn't bothered to open the book in her lap either. The events of last night's party at the Murdochs' were still unreeling in her mind.

The drapes had opened to their full width, drawn silently by the electric motor. And no one moved. As if in unison, the onlookers took in their breaths in a single gasp. An impulsive guffaw, which was quickly stifled, came from somewhere in back. A glass slipped from startled fingers and shattered on the wooden floor. But even that didn't seem to break the stillness.

Rivers was the first to react. He'd been standing by Faith, and he jabbed the button to close the drapes again. As they slowly pulled together, he moved forward so his body partly blocked the view of Quentin and Steffi's retreat. His action spurred Jonas and in seconds, while his guests still stood open mouthed, he'd taken his wife's arm and disappeared through a side archway. Then Judith, who had at first clutched at Ari's hand and almost crushed it, was gone as well.

But again, hardly anyone else moved. Some still held their crystal glasses half-raised. Ari turned to set hers on the mantel and Caley's voice was in her ear. "I don't think there'll be a second act. Let's beat the traffic to the cars."

He took her arm and only stopped long enough on their way out to murmur to a silver-haired man, "The Murdochs do put on quite a show, don't they?"

As they drove, much too fast, down the dark lane, Caley's lips were firmly pressed together, and his eyes, when he glanced at Ari, only glinted. Finally, he remarked, "Judith and Quentin's wedding was spectacular. Must have cost a mint. The divorce won't come cheap either. Jonas will hire the best lawyers."

"You don't think they could—" she began.

"No," he interrupted, shaking his head firmly. "Not if Quentin gave her half of Tiffany's. Even if Judith could forgive him, her parents wouldn't let her. We'll have to go to the country club for lunch *and* dinner tomorrow. Can't miss the postmortem on this one."

"What'll Judith do?" Ari asked slowly, remembering the painful pressure of her hand.

"Faith said at dinner that she and Jonas were leaving soon for a cruise to the Galápagos. Bet they move up the departure date. To tomorrow morning. *And* they'll take Judith. She can look at those giant lizards and think about Quentin."

"I'm sorry about Willie," Ari said. "I like him."

"Best thing that ever happened to him." Caley sounded quite cheerful. "He won't divorce Steffi. But she'll have to be really nice to him, and for quite a while. He'll whisk her off too. But you watch. She'll reappear with a nice tan and a new hairdo. They'll be back in time to dance at our"—he stopped suddenly and cleared his throat—"celebration party for Ute Rise." He snapped his fingers. "With all this I forgot to tell you the good news. Tonight I talked Jonas into selling to you. And at a low price."

"Caley." Ari leaned back in the seat in amazed pleasure. "You're wonderful. How did you do that?"

"It took some fancy persuading on my part. But I did point out that a portion of his loss would be a tax write-off." He shook his head, adding, "I was worried when I saw Alexander arguing with him, though. Afraid he'd talk old Jonas into reconsidering. Those two *are* alike—they look at every dollar. But that's why Jonas is rich. Still, we shook on it and Murdoch will stick to it. Fifty million. Of course, *that's* a lot of money to raise."

He looked at her ruefully, and she slipped an arm around his shoulders and squeezed. "But you've given me hope, and a starting place. Thank you, Caley. No one could be a better friend than you are."

"I wouldn't be a good friend, Ari, if I didn't insist that *your* money be used only to seed the campaign. This should be done with public contributions. The environmental organizations will be a lot of help. But tomorrow you and I have to talk seriously about seeing that your funds are invested the way they should be."

When he kissed her good-night, Caley cradled her face and said, "Sleep well. Let me take care of your worries. Your dreams too."

He sped off and reached the road to the foothills fast, all the while thinking that nothing *he* could have dreamt up would have topped this perfect evening at the Murdochs. Because he'd opened the windows, the wind caught his uproarious laughter and sent it echoing through the canyon.

Ari slept hardly at all. Janie was still awake, and though she made Ari repeat the events of the evening three times, the two eventually went on to discuss the beginning of the Ute Rise campaign. "Now's the time for you to get up to Telluride," Janie concluded. "We've got to hit the ground running in January if the EPA doesn't find any problems. I can come up on weekends. And Samuel will be a lot of help, introducing you to people you'll need to know. Tomorrow's not too soon to start."

But when she got up and saw Ari packing, Janie raised her eyebrows and said, "I didn't mean that *literally*. You just got here."

"I want to go," Ari responded. Now that she had a set goal, she was anxious to start. She wanted to see Bridey's Mountain.

That would give her something productive to think about. She found herself brooding over Heather's words about second chances and the sight of Judith talking intently to Rivers. But as she readjusted her seat belt slightly and leaned back in the narrow seat, closing her eyes to clear her mind, she suddenly remembered that she'd had the dream again last night. It made her feel as if an urgent message were being shouted at her in a language she didn't understand.

It had begun as beguilingly as always with the sunlight and columbines as she walked up the canyon. But this time she recognized the familiar face smiling at her in the pool as Morna's. The mountain bent low to her touch, but almost immediately the water ran crimson as if with its blood. When she tried to retrieve her lost ring from the upraised palm, the chain of the watch handcuffed her more tightly.

That nightmare panic was vivid even now. She could almost feel the shaking earth, see the smoke-stained mountain, hear the man's call and the wolf's howl. For a moment she thought that it was Rivers's voice, but she was pretty sure she'd first had the dream before she'd ever talked to him. Of course, she'd also seen the face in the stream before she saw Morna's picture. That could be explained by Sybil's comment that she herself resembled Morna.

But the dream still made no sense. To distract herself, she looked out the window. The magnificence of the view lifted her heart. Except for the glisten of snow on the peaks of the Sawatch Range, the mountains were green with pine. Even now in October, they had a springtime promise in their colors, she thought. The bare summits were lilac gray. The autumn aspens, intermixed with the pine, were almost jonquil yellow. The glittering ribbons of rivers were quicksilver fresh.

As the plane slid lower, following the river to Telluride, she had a sharp feeling of homecoming, of a return as well as an arrival.

That stayed with her, although she told herself it had probably arisen because she'd been in Morna's Ireland only two days before, and she had the notion she was following in her footsteps. Anyway, Ari considered, the canyon's encircling shoulders of stone and the town were bound to look familiar to her. She'd seen so many pictures. Photographs of Telluride adorned hundreds of Colorado posters. Its Old West buildings hadn't been changed, and they remained in the dry preserving air as if in a time capsule. She'd read two histories of the town as well. Then, too, there were Issy's stories, faithfully repeated by Mrs. Mac. Still, as Ari drove the rental car beside the clear-running San Miguel and over the Cornet Creek bridge, her sense that she'd seen it all before made her skin prickle.

The mountains seemed to be right in downtown Telluride. The white top of the steepled courthouse with gold stars scattered on its red brick echoed a neighboring green peak. She stopped across the street from that building and stared at the clock-faced tower and then at the granite steps to the doors. Bridey, as a little girl reaching up for her father's hand, had gone in there to renew the mining claims on the mountain. Almost adjoining the courthouse was the three-story Sheridan Hotel. Patrick Alexander would have stayed there when he came to town, would have gone next door to the Opera House with his friend Berkeley to hear Morna sing. There was the red-brick Opera House by the hotel.

Abruptly, dizzyingly, time seemed to bend back on itself.

Even Ari's vision swam. She looked down the main street, empty because October was a "shoulder" season after the summer festivals and before the winter snows brought the skiers. But she felt for a second that if a woman stepped out of the nearby shop she'd be wearing a saucer hat and a high-necked dress with long skirts. She rubbed her eyes, thinking that in the last forty-eight hours she'd had very little sleep, that she wasn't over her jet lag, that too much had happened.

Taking a deep breath of the thin air, she glanced up Oak Street, which ran steeply past the Opera House. She stopped. How did she know that was Oak Street? She couldn't see the sign. Because, she reminded herself firmly, she'd read that some of the houses near the top had been washed away in the Cornet Creek flood in 1914. Berkeley had died in it—that's why she remembered. And she must have seen pictures of these restored houses with their frames and turrets painted in bright pastel colors and the filigrees white-trimmed. More were dotted along the north slope. A few were new, although they were also Victorian. She'd read all this, she repeated inwardly.

The history of Telluride was well documented. Part of the Ute curse seemed to have come true—families hadn't stayed for four generations. But, if the curse was the reason for the long period of the valley's misfortunes, perhaps it had also preserved the town for the future. As the mines, one by one, closed up, the original settlers moved on. A few people came and went, but most of the stores were boarded up and tumbleweeds blew unimpeded down the wide main street. Nobody had any money to change anything and there wasn't any reason to. In the 1960s hippies found their way here, but all they had was enthusiasm for the amazing beauty they found.

Then, right around a hundred and some years after the Indians were forced to leave, an enterprising man from California came to take a look at Telluride and saw the mountains that came right into town. He built the lifts, and the skiers brought their own gold.

Of course, the valley was still difficult to reach by an overland route. Driving from Denver took the better part of a day, *if* the roads were snowplowed and the mountain passes open. But the plane trip was less than an hour, and it offered that spectacle below. Brochures proclaimed, "Easy to get to, hard to leave."

That proved true for a number of people. But the town itself changed little because of its geography. It nestled almost at the eastern end of a box canyon where a craggy barrier of cliffs with hanging waterfalls rose up. Below these, at the east end of the canyon, was Pandora, the site of the old Smugglers Union Mine. A mining company still occupied the site.

So the developers built the palatial homes and lodges high above Telluride and well away from it. Mountain Village, as the subdivision was called, wasn't visible from the town. Its twenty-five hundred acres provided ample sites for those who liked skiing from their front doors. There were gentle slopes for beginning skiers, and Sunshine Peak for those with more confidence. The breathtaking plunge down the Telluride Face almost to the main street required real experience.

Even without the map in the guidebook beside her, Ari knew she'd have no trouble finding Ute Rise. She could see that that canyon led from the town park, which had always been a gathering place for Fourth of July picnics and other events. The park had been greatly expanded since the early days to include a band shell, an ice rink, a Nordic ski area, stone tables, and small bridges over the wandering river.

As she drove down Colorado Avenue looking at all the old brick and wooden storefronts, it was hard to resist the temptation to pull off onto the next block and explore Pacific Avenue. Then she could see what had once been Miss Freda's place and Popcorn Alley. There, too, would be the house where Berkeley and Morna had lived, Issy had cooked and gardened, and Bridey had grown up. Ari hadn't asked Janie to look it up. She wanted to find it herself and buy it immediately if that was possible. But she wasn't even sure it was still standing.

She felt she had to hurry to Bridey's Mountain. Leaving the rented Blazer near the empty park, she walked quickly beside the translucent water of the San Miguel. In her excitement she couldn't imagine it could ever be more beautiful, not in winter white or spring green. The bright red twigs of willow, like candles, lit the riverbed, and leafy branches bent over the water like molten gold. Along the canyon trail, where the creek joined the river, the aspen's brilliance seemed to shout from amid the dark pines.

Then she rounded the curve, saw the rising mountains, and stopped. Her view of Ute Rise had been formed by her grandmother's picture, and although Ari could see that the sketch was accurate, the feel of this place was quite different to her. Mrs. Mac had said that Bridey had drawn it from memory when she was living on the ranch in Norwood, and it was plain that the artist had recalled a place where she had been surrounded by love. She'd imparted that atmosphere, quite without sentimentality, to the protecting mountains.

What struck Ari instead was the power of these stony fortresses, and it was an awe-inspiring power because it was untamed. Bridey's Mountain was one of four, and it was the tallest and the most remote, a commanding presence. Two jagged-topped peaks were on one side, one on the other. With an outstretched finger she traced the rocks that formed the sky-lifted face. It was a human profile, but human in the sense that the ancient people had when they transformed their deities into their own likenesses to make them understandable and accessible. This was a depiction of Brigit, the Earth Goddess.

Perhaps, Ari thought, Morna had had that idea in mind, as well as the name of the loved woman who raised her. When she looked at nature here, she, too, saw a formidable strength. That didn't mean that Bridey was wrong in her remembered portrayal of the safeguarding mountain. If *she* saw it as a protecting force, it had to be strong.

She'd come home. Bridey's Mountain claimed her. Staring upward, Ari realized how much she needed the mountain. And this wilderness, so close to the town, was what others needed, as a reminder of what once had been.

She said, half aloud, "I'm the fourth generation. I've come back. I'll keep this, as it is, for the fifth."

CHAPTER 14

Leaving the mountain didn't lessen Ari's feeling that she had to hurry. Now she was thinking of all that needed doing. Checking her watch, she realized this would be an ideal time to talk to Samuel Goler III. The bar at the Sheridan Hotel would be almost empty in the late afternoon.

As she walked in, the room was quiet. The only light came from the windows that faced Colorado Avenue and a few old-fashioned sconces at the back next to beveled glass partitions. The thick raised pattern of the dark red wallpaper above the wainscot looked as if it were the original design. The man arranging glasses behind the polished mahogany bar could only have been Samuel.

Ari thought that it wasn't just the thick mat of chestnut hair and trimmed beard or his size that had reminded Janie of an approachable bear. Although he was now relaxed, one could imagine the heavy muscles beneath his long-sleeved lumberjack shirt. When she introduced herself, her hand was enveloped warmly. His mouth in the rather solemn face didn't curve in a smile, but his eyes were suddenly lit from within.

"Welcome," he said. "Although from what Janie tells me, maybe I ought to say, 'Welcome back.' "

"Thanks." Ari slipped onto the barstool feeling as if she'd just met an old friend. "My grandmother was born here. And your grandfather, wasn't he?"

"Sam the First," he agreed. "And the stable where he worked—and slept—was right near Miss Freda's."

"Our folks were neighbors," Ari said with a grin, "and in the *right* part of town—the south side—even if some people then would have disagreed."

"We come from the right sort," he replied, the crinkles around his eyes deepening. "No matter where they lived. Let's drink to that. What'll you have?"

"Just club soda," Ari answered, adding, "I've got a lot of exploring to do yet."

He filled two glasses, added twists of lime, and touched hers with his. "Glad you're here." After a quick sip he said, "Janie called. Said to tell you if you came by that she reserved you a place at the Doral up in Mountain Village. One of the penthouses. Think you'll like it."

"We talked about that, but now that I see the town, I'd rather get a place down here." Since Janie's name had come up, Ari was trying to guess what Samuel's feelings about her might be, but he didn't have an expressive face.

He stroked his beard and answered, "Well, in a few weeks, with the lull before the ski season, a lot of places in town close up. Up there you got everything you need. And a great view. You think you can see clear back to Denver."

The Doral was brand new, an enormous European-style luxury hotel with apartments and a complete spa. Ari had seen the brochure, listing the steam and massage rooms, the tennis courts, two restaurants, and four pools. "Sounds perfect," she remarked. Still carefully watching his expression, she asked. "Did she say whether she was coming up this weekend?"

He grinned now. "Yeah. Said you should get her an appointment for a massage and facial, but you could skip signing her up for the Nautilus machines." Samuel held up the glass he was drying, checking to make sure it was sparkling as he went on, "We've got a lot of hard work ahead of us, Ari, to raise enough money to buy Ute Rise. Now, Janie's smart, real smart. She saw our problems right off."

As he explained, his face was grave, although his eyes were warm with affection for his town. He pointed out that if Telluride sprawled westward along the banks of the San Miguel River, not only would that natural beauty be lost along with its wildlife, but the small-town benefits would go as well. "Here"—and his big hand seemed to encompass protectively the stores, the library, the period houses—"we got a real place, and you can walk to anything. People live here and their kids go to school here. If they just keep expanding, put a bunch of lodges and chalets on stilts by the river, this will be just another old-timey shopping district in another ski resort, spread out all over the valley."

He had passion in his voice when he talked about how Telluride looked now, about being able to drive all along the tree-filled river meadows that were free of fences and houses, and come down a street that had hardly changed in a hundred years. "If they turn Ute Rise into another subdivision, there'll be no wilderness left. Now, not just the people who live here, but the tourists, too, they can all go out their doors and be *outdoors,* not in some little park."

As he waved his hand, Ari could see satellite dishes on Bridey's Mountain, an asphalt road paved over the wildflowers, the aspen confined to neat little groves. "But," he went on, "we've been lucky here so far. They put all the new stuff up in Mountain Village. And that's fine. I even like to go look at those places. People build those great houses, and it's okay with me if they just want to live in them a few weeks a year. But if they put them down here, well, they're what we call 'dark houses.' I mean, you don't have neighbors anymore, just an empty place next door. And there aren't any kids in them, and no parents to support the schools."

He ended bleakly, "There are a lot of rich people here, Ari. But I don't know if they'll give a lot of money to save Ute Rise. If Telluride gets all built up and changed, they might figure they'll just go someplace else."

Ari traced with her forefinger the vanishing circle of her wet glass, and her face was grim. "Eventually we'll all run out of places to go. And there's no handy universe next door. So we've got to save this one. I'm so glad you're here. Janie said you were such a help." It occurred to her that she'd found out a great deal about what he thought about Telluride, but nothing of what he felt about Janie.

Before she could pose another question along those lines, he asked, "Are you going to buy a house in town?"

"I want to buy *our* house. The one my family had, I mean," she explained. "It's on Pacific. A big old house. Used to be yellow. But I don't know if it's still there."

"Oh, yes." And this time his whole face smiled. "Down in what used to be Finn Town. It's boarded up. An old lady who just died lived there for years, and her name was . . . Hm, well, it'll come back to me. She had a couple of good offers to turn it into a bed-and-breakfast, but she didn't want to move. I don't know who she left it to."

"I can't *wait* to see it," Ari said eagerly.

"Now, don't be put off," Samuel answered worriedly. "She probably just had enough to pay the taxes, so she couldn't really keep it up." His hands moved, suggesting a house huddled in on itself, sagging a little on one side, with peeling paint. "But it'd fix up fine and be a great place." His fingers recreated proud gables, sparkling bay windows, a wide porch with newly restored filigree trim.

As she watched those hands, Ari thought that if Samuel could mold stone half as well as he could shape the air, he must be a magnificent sculptor. She remembered that her father had been a sculptor and she wondered if he, too, could sketch castles in the air.

So absorbed had she been in their conversation that she hadn't noticed that it was twilight. He glanced through the windows and said, "If you hurry, you can still get a good look at the outside."

She thanked Samuel and quickly walked down the block to Pacific Avenue. She wanted to stop and look at everything, go down to Miss Freda's, which was now a restaurant, see Popcorn Alley. But first she wanted to find the house.

As she rounded the corner on Pacific, she could see it even from two blocks away. Its six-sided tower rose above its smaller neighbors, most of which were the one-story houses that the Finnish miners had once owned. Some of these had been renovated and painted in cheerful colors, like charming doll's houses; others were in real need of paint. The roof of the tower was even visible above the elaborately turreted and gabled new bed-and-breakfast inn across the street.

But as she stood outside the rambling Victorian she'd heard so many stories about, it was hard to find any traces of its former glory. The yellow paint had come off in strips, leaving exposed raw wood. There were gaps like missing teeth in the delicate wooden frieze around the roofline. The windows had plywood nailed over them, and the front porch sagged dispiritedly. Even the lawn had given up, showing only a few clumps of green amid brown thatch.

The disheartened look of the place made Ari suddenly want to whisper to it, as if it were a living thing, to say, *"I'll* make you beautiful again, grand again. It won't take long. It won't."

Going around the side, hoping for a window she could peer through, she went past beds with the flattened dead leaves of daylilies and saw a door above two concrete steps. Its old-fashioned knob with an engraved lion's head was hanging from its post, ready to fall off. She thought it would be a pity to lose it and stepped up to try to tighten it. As she jiggled it back on, the door slowly swung open.

She put her head in, calling, "Hello? Anyone here?" Her words echoed through empty rooms, but she thought she heard a rustling sound from high upstairs. She walked into the kitchen, in darkness from its boarded-up windows, raising her voice. "Anyone home?" Only the word *home* seemed to reverberate off the walls and dusty floors.

She clicked the light switch by the door several times in vain. Then the noise above was repeated, making her a little uneasy, but she decided it was probably squirrels scampering across the roof or birds nesting in the eaves. She could make out another door at the far end of the kitchen, which probably opened onto the back and, if it weren't nailed shut, would provide light. As long as she was here, she did want to see what she could, at least of the downstairs.

That door was the entrance to a sun porch and, although most of its small windowpanes were full of jagged cracks, they'd been left uncovered. Ari stepped out onto the dingy surface, only covered by tarpaper. Drooping clotheslines ran down its length, and she ducked under them and gazed out onto the devastated garden. The gazebo had collapsed in on itself. A back lane now ran behind it, and beyond that was an open lot that probably had once been part of the garden stretching to the river. But she smiled, seeing there was still plenty of room for flowers. Already she was mentally planting daisies by the gazebo, laying out a strawberry bed, and a corner for herbs.

Then she glanced around the sun porch and remembered hearing that a room had been added on for Issy's winter garden. So this was it. In her mind's eye she, too, filled it with sweet-scented white gardenias and jasmine, bright orange hibiscus and blooming rose-throated amaryllis. She could envision their colors against snow-trimmed panes.

Turning back to the kitchen, she now saw the monstrous coal-fired range back against a wall next to a capacious pantry. On the other side of the stove a metal hip-bath with a curved lowered front still stood. She imagined a little girl splashing in its bottom, in a room filled with light and warmth, while Issy kept one eye on her and the other on the cooking.

Carved molding, now thickly painted over, outlined the entrance to another room, and peering in, Ari realized it was the back parlor. The vaguest memory of lilacs was in the air. Silk wallpaper hung down in shreds, but there were still glints of gold in its fragments. Looming on her right was the jutting mantel of a huge fireplace, and straight ahead she could just discern through another door rows of built-in bookshelves on high walls.

That was the library, then, where Berkeley worked at his rolltop desk. Morna and Bridey would have curled on a thick sheepskin before the fire, reading a bedtime story. Mrs. Mac, about to read one to a small Ari tucked on her lap in a rocker, had sometimes begun by telling her that, adding that Bridey had surely read this one to Trish by another fireplace, and it was time to hear it again. Ari stood with tear-filled eyes, remembering.

Again she heard the faint sound from upstairs, but knowing those rooms must be in total darkness from all the plywood she'd seen, she was sure no one could be there. Still, she went back through the kitchen and groped her way down the passage to the front hall. Her trailing fingers felt another closed door, which she assumed was the dining room. Finally, there was a molding and then only empty air. An archway, she assumed, into the front parlor. She moved sideways across the hall until she touched the balusters of the staircase and stopped to listen, looking up, although she could see nothing at all.

Ari breathed quietly, and the musty, shut-up smell filled her nostrils. Then the air was laden with the scent of lilacs. Even as she wondered, a left-behind sachet . . . she heard the unmistakable swish of silk. She could almost feel someone, something, waiting.

There was a sighing, creaking noise. She stiffened, shivering. But that was the house settling wearily on its foundations, as if it didn't want its hopes raised. Without thinking she spoke aloud, "I'm here now. It will be the way it was."

When she went out, she again tightened the knob, and tried again. This time, the door stayed solidly locked.

CHAPTER 15

Caley's explosive anger was hidden. His voice sounded calm, controlled. His hands were fists, thrust deep in his jacket pockets. His temples pulsed, but the chill November wind blew his thick blond hair over them. His eyes, which normally gave away nothing, were behind mirrored sunglasses.

"Understand, Ari. You'll have to put a great deal of money into the renovation of that house. And it won't appreciate the way the ones on the north slope might. There, on the south side, you're not surrounded by other expensive houses, but by bed-and-breakfast places and rental condos."

They were unsheltered from the wind on a rocky ledge overlooking Ute Rise, but the morning was bright. Ari's hair was tangled by the sharp breeze, and her honey-colored eyes were alight with sun and happiness. "I'm sure you're right. But this isn't an investment for me, Caley. Well, of course, a house is. But I love this one. It's my family's house. I'm going to live there."

"The problem"—Caley returned to the attack, jamming his hands even farther into his new parka's pockets—"is that it's on Pacific Avenue. The lot is valuable because of the commercial zoning. So you had to pay top dollar, regardless of the condition of the house. Anyone else who bought it would bulldoze the place, put up a good-sized lodge, and make it pay that way. The cost of real estate up here is as high as downtown Manhattan." He tightened his lips, trying to see if the situation could be salvaged. "It's too bad you've already signed the papers. Still, if you let it sit until summer, you could add enough to get the realtor's commission back, turn around, and sell—"

She ran her hand affectionately down the padded sleeve of his parka. The material disguised from her the coiled tightness of his thick forearm. "I know how concerned you are about me, Caley, and about making financial mistakes. I appreciate that. But this is what I want."

He couldn't trust himself to reply to such foolishness. All he could think about was the incredible waste of time and dollars. In his mind her money had become his, especially since he'd decided on their marriage. When he'd seen the location of the dilapidated house, he knew she must have had to put up close to a million. And he'd yet to get his hands on any funds for investments of his own choosing. Turning his head away from her, he looked down on the steep drop below them.

The narrow ledge gave a magnificent overview of the canyon, but they had to climb down to it above a deep crevasse that looked as if it went to the earth's center. They were seated on two rounded boulders, surrounded by a few wind-twisted Ponderosa pines. Loki had refused to step out onto the shelf with them. The dog remained on the overhang above, stretched out on the stone, its head on its paws, its blank, silvery eyes slit against the wind.

Ari knew that Caley was unhappy about her buying the house. But she believed that, to him, it meant she would spend all of her time in Telluride instead of in Denver with him. She hadn't been able to get back there for a month because she'd been busy arranging the purchase, as well as getting ready for the Ute Rise campaign. He'd called almost daily, trying to persuade her to come back. For that reason she hadn't discussed the matter with him at all, guessing what his reaction might be. She wanted to explain to him in person. Stewart Wellings had overseen the contract. He was satisfied that she'd gotten a good price from the owner, an heir who lived out of state and wanted to sell.

When she'd met Caley at the airport last night, he'd caught her to him so tightly that she could hardly breathe. At dinner at the Doral they'd had so much catching up to do. He'd hardly let go of her hand. Ari told herself that when he'd had a chance to really see Telluride and then the house, heard her plans to renovate, he'd share her pleasure. She was still sure that would happen when he thought it over.

But things hadn't gotten off to a good start. This wasn't the ideal time to visit the resort. The aspen leaves were gone, and the snow not yet arrived. Although the pine-filled valley had a brooding beauty, most of the restaurants and stores in town were closed for the season. It had been an exceptionally dry fall, and the local residents each day worriedly eyed the cloudless sky. Their fortunes depended on heavy snow. Machines could only do so much. Caley had commented when he arrived that he wouldn't risk money where everything depended on the weather.

After a late brunch Ari had driven him by the house, but he'd merely looked at the neighborhood. They hadn't stopped, because she wanted him to see Ute Rise right away. He'd barely glanced at the mountain. On the winding trail he'd remained quiet, the only sound the crunch of his cowboy boots on the dry leaves. But she reminded herself that the elevation—nearly twice that of Denver's—took some getting used to. This was the first chance they'd had to talk.

It was clear that now wasn't the time to go into all she'd done already to start work on the house. But it was hard to keep from telling Caley her excited plans.

She'd had an enormous amount of help from a young couple named Kevin and Kate Hennings, who'd just finished redoing their own Victorian home. They were friends of Rivers. When he'd sent Ari his Washington address, she'd responded with her Telluride address, mentioning in her reply that she'd bought the house and describing its condition. Several days later Kate Hennings came by, saying that Rivers had called her. Her arms were full of catalogs. Laughing, she'd held out the top one to Ari, saying, "This one's full of period door hinges and knobs you can order. Invaluable. Honest."

The Hennings had shown her over their own house, stopping in one room or another to say, "See what we did here. Don't do that. Here's what we should have done." They'd helped her find a contractor who was knowledgeable about putting in modern plumbing, heating, and wiring. Ari was overwhelmed with the decisions only she could make on light fixtures, faucets, sinks, tubs, flooring, paint, and wallpaper. But Kate was as eager as she to pore over the catalogs, and they spent hours doing that.

Weekends were even busier. Janie came up each Saturday, and she and Ari and Samuel went through the tax lists of Telluride property owners, discussing how to approach various people to get contributions for Ute Rise. Ari had to smile, watching Janie look at Samuel, patiently bent over the computer printouts, scribbling comments, hearing her sigh as her eyes moved over his shoulders. Last Sunday she'd grimaced at Ari and sent her pencil skittering across the table in protest. "What happened to the idea of the *idle* rich? We should be downstairs in the spa, up to our necks in a mud bath or a hot tub." Samuel only grinned and handed her back the pencil.

One of their projects was a huge party to be given during the Christmas season in the Doral ballroom. Ari thought it would be a good way to get acquainted with people who cared about Telluride and whose support she could ask for later. "If the EPA says Murdoch can't build," she said, "then it'll be a good way to meet my neighbors." They were planning on mailing the invitations this week.

When Janie arrived this morning, she said cheerfully that she'd already handed one over. "Rivers came by the office—said he was in town only overnight and wanted to hear how you were. Nice to finally meet him in person. I invited him immediately. Why didn't you tell me about him, Ari?"

"I did." Just the sound of his name always caught Ari a little off balance.

"You said he was *nice*. Listen, if I'd known what he looked like when he and I were having those chats about you on the phone, I'd have told him that unfortunately you were dead but I was free for lunch. Lifetime option available. Now, I've met Samuel, of course, but Rivers will be a real addition to the party. I don't care who he works for."

It was moot anyway, Ari thought glumly. Caley had been right. Judith had filed for a divorce from Quentin Wyndham weeks ago. She'd moved to the East Coast, taking an apartment in New York. New York was too close to Washington, D.C., for comfort.

Caley's back was to Ari, and he said nothing. Only a magpie's piercing call broke the quiet of the wilderness.

Ari tucked her wind-tangled hair behind her ears. She still hadn't told Caley she'd be working on the campaign that afternoon and wouldn't be able to see him until dinner. She tried again to think of a way to cheer him, remembering all he'd done for her. She wanted to reassure him that having the house wouldn't change things between them. They would still be able to see each other. She'd go to Denver. He could come here. She was determined to maintain their connection. He was far more than a friend. He was family.

It was true that Caley didn't enjoy skiing, skating, hiking, climbing —all the outdoor activities that Telluride offered. But he might if he tried, and he should get away from business pressures.

As she considered, she glanced around and saw Loki. They could at least take the dog on long rambles, although she had to admit Loki hadn't bounded in delight through the woods today. He'd stayed at Caley's heels, following almost sullenly. Caley had told her not to pet him. He was beautiful, with those light eyes and silvery coat. But she thought that perhaps the shepherd/wolf hybrid wasn't a good mix, neither tame nor wild. Its instincts would be at war. The animal wouldn't know if it should protect or prey. Even his name wasn't one she'd choose. Loki was a malicious Norse god, always trying to undermine the other gods. When she'd asked Caley about the name, he'd merely replied, "He's always been called that."

The silence between them continued.

Caley had planned this visit carefully. When it had first occurred to him to marry Ari, he'd opted for a spring engagement. By then, he considered, she'd have given up on Ute Rise, knowing that raising fifty million was impossible. He'd be spared the worst of the campaign. If he were her fiancé, she'd expect his support. Large amounts of money, as well as a certain amount of time. He couldn't imagine anything more absurd.

He'd assumed that cautious old Wellings would watch her spending so that *he* needn't worry.

But talking to her on the phone made it increasingly clearer that Wellings was doing no such thing. Caley could see that she was spending recklessly on saving the canyon. Getting to Telluride became a priority for him. Then, he had only worried about the campaign expenditures. She hadn't even mentioned the house.

Last week he decided that he would have to tell her now about their future. Moving up the date would have several benefits. Wellings could stiff-arm him on the investments as long as he was only a friend of Ari's, but he couldn't pull that once they were engaged. Having her mind on wedding plans, Caley thought, should distract her nicely from fund raising.

And he could bed her now. It wasn't easy putting that off. Coming back with her from the Murdochs, he'd almost pulled over onto a dark side road. But he felt that control of twenty-five million was worth a little patience. With a wedding ring offered it'd be interesting to see what she'd get used to in bed, and how fast.

He hadn't brought a ring with him because there was one of Ceci's he was going to have reset. With the sudden change in his thinking he hadn't had time. But the proposal, he was sure, would make her happy. He could say the ring was at the jewelers, but he couldn't wait for that. He'd planned on champagne in her penthouse after dinner.

But he'd seen Jack Dexter in the almost empty restaurant and instead arranged to meet him later in the bar. Caley was curious about what Murdoch's man was doing up here in the off-season. As long as he kept slipping checks to Dexter, he'd tell him. Saturday would do as well for the engagement. Maybe, he thought, he could even find a florist open in this godforsaken place.

In Denver, Caley and Dexter had usually arranged their infrequent meetings where they'd be unlikely to run into anyone they knew. Even so, Dexter had a habit of glancing uneasily over his shoulder. He did so last night, despite the fact that the hotel lobby was deserted and the only person in the room was a yawning bartender. At last Caley had said irritably, "For Christ's sake, Jack, even Jonas wouldn't be suspicious if he saw us having a drink together here. We know each other, and the damned town's empty."

Dexter ran a hand over the thinning widow's peak that emphasized the narrowness of his face. "Yeah, but I'm supposed to meet the guy hired for construction supervisor on Ute Rise. This Payton Cross . . . well, you don't know what he'd think or say. He's real loyal to Jonas for taking him on at all."

Jack shifted his eyes to the doorway. "The day we talked about giving him the job, Riv Alexander was against it. He thought Cross was a loose cannon—kept pointing to things in his record. You should have seen Cross when he heard that. You don't want to get on *his* bad side."

Caley swirled the Scotch in his glass. He was interested in hearing that Murdoch was going to be all ready for ground breaking in the spring. He said, "So what if this guy sees us? Didn't Jonas tell you that he and I had a . . . little agreement on this deal?"

As if assessing that to see if it were true, Dexter waited before he finally responded, "No. But he's still on his South America cruise. All he said was to get things set up without making any noise. Besides, wasn't your girlfriend at dinner the one who's causing the holdup? Waiter said she's staying here and she's the one that won the lottery." His smile had a smirk in it as he lifted his glass. "Always the way—the ones who win don't need it. *She's* already sittin' on a gold mine."

Ignoring his remark, Caley drew out a thin cigar case. He lit one, slowly blew out the smoke. "Going to be a little hard, isn't it, to get a big project off the ground and keep it quiet? You have to line up the crews. A mountain project like this, you're going to get a mixed bag of workers as it is. Not your family men from town wanting a steady paycheck. You'll have to bring them in."

"Yeah," Dexter agreed. "That's why Jonas wanted Cross. Some of the hard hats we'll get spend most of their nights in the bar. Payton'll be right there on their ass. And they won't give him any shit. He's an ex-con. He's got that mean Doberman look. You know what he does?"

As he spoke, Dexter adjusted his Armani jacket. Even its looseness didn't hide the barrel torso that went oddly with his gangling arms and too-thin face. "On the site Cross keeps this piece of heavy chain hangin' out of his back pocket. If he's talkin' to a hothead, he wraps it around his hand while he's lookin' at the guy. He's even got a tattoo of a chain on his wrist. Sometimes all he's got to do is finger the tattoo, and the guy backs off."

Over Dexter's shoulder Caley could see the man approaching them must be the one Jack had been describing. He was tall, with a dark crew cut and a weathered face. He did have the look of a Doberman—a fitted skin without an ounce of waste. Like the dog he had no need to *appear* intimidating. One glance at him would convince.

Caley shook Cross's hand almost cordially. He had the feeling that if you bought him, he'd be thorough and you could count on his mouth staying shut. It was hard to be sure about Dexter. He needed money *and* reassurance. Worse, he had unrealistic expectations. Dexter thought that Murdoch would accept him into the social circle, like Alexander. Dexter probably even hoped Caley would help him there. It was out of the question. Not only did he lack the background, he lacked the polish. But Dexter wouldn't ever be able to figure that out.

Now Caley continued to look broodingly at the canyon's wilderness. He could see that once Ari had lost her campaign and they were married, he could put the screws to Jonas on the price for this acreage. Custom houses, close to town—Murdoch would still clean up. But the thought of upping her share didn't cheer him. There was no point in making money if she was busily stuffing it down a rathole. The house, the cost of the campaign. Then whatever she contributed to the goal itself. It'd be gone fast.

He couldn't stop her. He had no control. Caley couldn't bear that. It hadn't happened often. When it did, it brought back old rage. Ceci. Trish. The Turkish prison and his face pushed against the cell's stone floor. His anger now made his whole body a clenched fist. It even made his groin hard.

Ari stood up. "Let's walk to the top of the trail. You can really see Bridey's Mountain from there." Caley didn't answer, didn't move. She brushed a foot through the dry tangled grass and scattered pine cones. Then she said, "I'll meet you here on my way back." Turning, she reached for a handhold near the overhang to pull herself up. Above her, Loki quietly got to his feet.

"No!" Caley got up fast. She was going to learn it right now. There was only one way for the two of them to do things. His way. His fury cut off all other thoughts. It choked his breathing, made his legs heavy.

Behind his sunglasses his pale eyes were blind ice. But the blood in his loins was scalding, stretching the skin to pain.

He was going to slam her against that rock wall and put it to her. Shove it clear up her belly. When she felt it *there,* she'd pay attention, all right.

Maybe it was his abrupt movements that made Loki growl, a low vibration in his throat. Caley didn't hear.

He yanked at the heavy snaps of his parka, dragged his belt open. Ari only looked at him with a slight puzzled crease in her forehead. She had no fear in her eyes.

That maddened him further. Just like her mother. Some people didn't get the message easy. Then she'd get it hard. He'd pump the hot sperm right into her veins. His arm lashed upward for her hair.

The next instant he was sprawled on the ground. It was as if his feet had been jerked out from beneath him. He hadn't had time to catch himself on his hands. He was stunned by the force of his fall.

"Caley." Ari knelt by him immediately. "Are you all right?"

He had no breath to talk. He rolled over, then sat halfway up, trying to take in air. She looked at his pointed boots, saying worriedly, "The toe must have caught in the grass. Before you get up, we'd better check your ankle. You could have twisted it."

Loki's head was back, the sound in his throat more a howl than a bark.

Caley rasped a command to the dog. At the dark threat in his voice it quieted instantly.

Letting his breath out, Caley reached down, felt his ankle through the thick leather. "I'm okay." He brushed aside Ari's outstretched hand and got up. He flicked the weeds from the front of his turtleneck jersey.

Then he looked down at her. "You were moving too fast toward Loki. These dogs can attack when that happens. They're unpredictable. He could have hurt you." Caley glanced at his undone belt. "I thought I might have to . . . discipline him." He hooked the belt, snapped up the parka.

In the mirror of his glasses, all Ari could see was her own image.

CHAPTER 16

On the evening of the Christmas ball Ari hummed as she hurried down the stairs from the penthouse loft. On the last step she realized she'd completely forgotten what she'd been intending to do. She was too nervous to concentrate. The butterflies in her stomach seemed to have moved right up to her throat. But she was too happy to care.

She let cool water run over her wrists, partly for the calming effect, partly because she realized she'd spritzed perfume on twice in the last half hour. The delicate lily-of-the-valley scent of Joy filled her condo as she paced, still in her terry-cloth robe.

Part of her tension stemmed from the fact that Janie had drawn up a list of Very Important People who would be attending the party. People who might be future contributors to the campaign. Ari was to make a point of meeting and talking to them.

Which—she grimaced as she checked the typed sheet again—was easy for Janie to say. *She* was at ease with strangers. Ari was not.

What she was really anticipating, however, was Rivers. He'd told

Janie he'd be at the party. He'd ended his last letter to Ari, *Can't wait to see you.*

One moment she was sure that he would come. But the next she doubted it. His last notes from Washington had been brief. Even his first letters, full of amusing stories about the Capital, had been impersonal. She'd begun to wonder if, absorbed in his new life, he considered her just another friend. A friend he'd like to see if he had time. He'd said that his vacation would be short. Probably he'd have a lot to do in Denver while he was there. Friends and relatives to visit. The Murdochs would be there for the holidays. Judith and her parents. Judith, who was getting a divorce. Ari tried to ignore that last idea. Besides, he might not even be able to get here. All the skiers were clamoring for air tickets to Telluride now that the snow had fallen in glorious abundance.

Still, he had said he'd come.

Ari had decided that there was no reason she couldn't talk to him, dance with him, enjoy his company. But, knowing what she did about him, it could go no farther. She would be coolheaded.

Caley, of course, would be there. She welcomed the idea of his reliable presence. It troubled her, though, that their relationship was not on the old comfortable terms. She'd been to Denver twice in the last six weeks, but he'd not come to Telluride since his one visit. And he'd left that afternoon, saying he'd had an urgent message. Although her trips to the city had been filled with errands and shopping for the house, the two of them always met for lunch or dinner. But now it was never just the two of them. He always brought people he wanted her to meet.

He was hurt, she was sure, over her decision to live much of the year in Telluride. He refused to talk about it. When they were together, he treated her . . . carefully. It was the only word she could think of to describe the change. He seemed to look at her differently, and he never even gave her a peck on the cheek. She missed the easy affection that had provided the warmth and acceptance of the family she didn't have.

The real problem, she decided, was that the campaign work took up so many hours. When she had more time to spend with him, they could work things out. From what he said, he seemed to assume that would happen too. A few weeks ago he'd mentioned that he preferred warm beaches to icy mountains in the winter and suggested a trip to Mexico. She'd hated to say no, but she pointed out that everyone who owned property in Telluride was there over Christmas and she needed to be getting acquainted.

He'd replied with a half-smile, "Then you owe me. We'll go in the spring. It'll still be snowing here, and you'll want some warm sun. I'll find a perfect place for us when I'm down there. A deserted sunny beach."

She'd laughed. "I'm so short of sleep now that by then what I'll probably need is a week in bed."

"I'll insist on that," he answered expressionlessly.

Ari trailed into the downstairs bathroom to have another look at her hair. When she'd described what she'd be wearing to the party, the hairdresser had brushed it all to one side, making a cascade of glistening curls. She scattered tiny golden pins to hold it that way. When she finished, she'd said, "Right. Sophisticated but sexy." Although Ari had been unsure fifteen minutes ago, she decided now she liked the style.

And the dress was perfect. Janie had been up a half hour ago, and she'd agreed. She'd come rushing in to give an account of the ballroom decorations, since she'd come early to check everything over. But before she could launch into that, Ari had to stop her, turn her around, tell her how wonderful she looked. Janie's dress was white, with an almost Grecian simplicity that both suggested the roundness of her figure and subtracted from it. Her blond hair was, for once, not severely cut. Instead the smooth top loosely and gently framed her face.

"Thanks, Ari, thanks." Janie's cheeks were flushed, her eyes like Christmas. "I can't wait to see your dress on you. This is going to be an event. The room looks terrific. Only this afternoon I was saying, 'It's wrong. It's all so tastefully sterile!' But now, with the little lights on, it works. Samuel agrees. And he's an artist."

She uncovered the small plate she'd brought in, saying, "Wait till you see the food. This is Samuel's personal favorite. Try it. Glacier cheese tart. Egg whites, whipping cream, and three kinds of cheese. It melts in your mouth. *I* even asked for the recipe."

As she was leaving, she added, "And don't forget to get downstairs by eight-thirty. Some people might come early." Janie had paused. "Ari, you should see Samuel in a tux. The tailor must have taken out all the padding to fit his shoulders in. I'm way past propositioning him. I'm thinking proposal." A little of the light went out of her eyes. "If I can get his attention." Then her grin returned. "Anyway, *he* thinks he looks like a bear in a monkey suit and he keeps trying to loosen the shirt collar. Tell him he looks like Fred Astaire, will you?"

Going upstairs, Ari thought that all she could wish for was that Sybil were here. On her Christmas card she'd written that on her second trip to Daire, Mad Fergus had even stopped digging long enough to drink a bottle of stout with her and Rose.

Smiling, she slid open the closet door and took out the dress. It was Christmas red, but it was gold, shimmering first one color, then the other. She slipped it on and its perfect sequined fit outlined her body. The matching shoes reminded her of the ruby slippers from Oz.

She'd always dreamed of a gown and a ball. Here it was. Soon, soon she was going to dance. She could not wait to dance. Ari twirled around her half-lit bedroom. She spun to the full-length mirror and stopped.

She'd caught a glimpse of her profile with the hair brushed back. Looking again, she saw the resemblance to Morna that Sybil had mentioned. That was unsettling, as if it were not her own reflection.

Dr. Herron had said, "I can take scars and birthmarks from people's faces. I can't remove them from their mirrors." She touched the glass at eye level. If she looked like Morna, she told herself, she must be beautiful.

Again she whirled in a dance, stopping dizzily by the glass doors to the balcony. If she kept this up, she thought, she wouldn't remember all she was supposed to do. But there was plenty of time to take another look at the list of names. Most of the people would come late. Caley said he certainly would because Ari would be busy greeting guests and he knew few people in Telluride.

Ari pressed her hands, which suddenly felt clammy, against the cool glass. It didn't help. Nor did the sight of Mount Wilson's majesty under a low moon. She shoved open the sliding doors and tried deep breaths of cold air.

The door chime sounded. Sure that it was Janie with another report, she ran down the stairs and threw the door open.

It was Rivers.

He wore a dark cashmere coat over his tuxedo, a white silk scarf around his neck. In his hand he held a very small cellophane box. She stared at him with widened eyes and said nothing at all.

Nor did he for a moment. Then his smile flashed. "Now, that is a wonderful dress. You did promise me one when we first met. And that included dancing. Here I am."

Ari stepped back, still trying for the right words, or any words at all. He walked in, closed the door, and leaned against it, folding his arms. After another moment when all he did was look at her, he said, "You don't need flowers to wear. You don't need anything. Still, here's one if you want to wear it." He held out the box.

It was a tiny golden-throated orchid, and the small red bow just matched her dress. She swallowed as she looked at it, but her mouth was still dry as she said, "It's lovely. Perfect. Yes, I do want to. Thank you. How did you know—?"

"I asked Janie about the color." He slit the tape on the box, lifted out the corsage, tried positioning it in several places before finally pinning it on her right shoulder near her throat. As he did so, she stood a little stiffly, her eyes down so all she could see was his plaid cummerbund, trying not to even breathe, but she smelled the cold outdoor freshness of his coat, felt the warmth of his breath.

Finally, he stepped back. "There. Not many women who can outdo an orchid, but you can."

The hallway seemed much too narrow, and she was much too close to him. But she was thinking of just lightly brushing her lips against his cheek to say thanks when he added, "And orchids are scentless, whereas your perfume is wonderful."

"Not too much?" she asked quickly, running an unsteady thumb over her wrist.

"Not at all." He paused, taking in that motion. "A little nervous about the party, are you?"

"Oh, Rivers." Ari turned and walked into the living room, rescuing herself from his nearness. She clasped her hands together tightly. He followed her, and she went on, "I went past 'nervous' at six o'clock. High-level stress set in at seven. Now it's panic."

"What's the problem? Sounds like it's going to be a great evening."

She explained about the list and remembering people's names when her own shyness tied her tongue, ending, "For Janie this would be simple. She'd even enjoy it. But there'll be just me standing there and—"

"Let me see the list." He shrugged out of his coat, putting it and the scarf on a chair. "I spent a lot of time here while I was growing up, and I know the locals. Probably not that many of the newcomers."

Heads together, they went through the typed sheet. He tapped one of the first names. "Red Deaver and his wife, Pam. One of the few times you'll see them off the slopes. Pam taught me to ski when I was six. They bought Mountain Village when it was mountains and no village. Now they have more hotels than a Monopoly board. He's graying, but he's still got hair like a forest fire. You'll pick him out."

He ran a thumb over his lip. "Don't know these next two couples."

"The trouble," Ari answered, "is that one owns General Mills and the other General Foods. I keep mixing them up."

"So." Rivers grinned. "We'll give them both military titles." As they went through the names, they came up with catchphrases to help them remember. They were still whispering some in the elevator, and trying not to laugh at the funnier ones even as they walked through the ballroom arch.

The huge room glittered, the candles and small lights gleaming on the glass walls and bouncing back. The snow everywhere outside and the white everywhere inside made the glass seem to disappear. Ice sculptures of mountains floated in bowls on tables laden with food and flowers. Transparent Christmas ornaments swung from the ceiling and hung like icicles from the enormous tree in the corner. Each round table on the sides held an upright aspen branch, like a cupped hand with fingers, decorated with smaller versions of the ceiling's shiny translucent flakes and moonstone balls. Here and there were green boughs with a hint of red, a touch of silver.

The first guests were people Rivers knew, and before Ari had time to worry about choosing her words, she was chatting with them, a champagne glass somehow in her hand. It was easy because he was there, his hand on her elbow.

People then began arriving in groups, and they were soon separated. But she found that people's names sprang to her mind, and she was enjoying herself immensely.

"Ari"—Janie's whisper was urgent in her ear—"look who's here. Maximilian King! Movie studios, oil wells. He has fifty million in his petty cash drawer."

"Where?" Ari stood on her tiptoes, scanning the crowded ballroom.

"Near the front. The guy the size of Mount Massive. I heard a rumor he was thinking of buying here. And he's with the Deavers. Quick, go talk to him before half the room gets there."

By the time Ari reached them, Rivers was shaking hands with a jockey-sized man whose carroty hair identified him as Red Deaver. Before she could catch her breath, she was being introduced to him and his wife. Pam Deaver, a brisk, compact woman, said, "My dear, I'm so happy you bought that beautiful old house. Red was always eyeing the lot to build on. I said he just couldn't tear that place down. You'll have to tell me about it. But let me introduce you to the Kings. Told them about your winning the Sweepstakes."

Barbara King, a sharp-featured, ageless blonde, smiled briefly and held out three cool fingers. Her diamond necklace seemed to stretch from her neck to her shoulders. The movie mogul's enormous hand enveloped Ari's. "Lady Luck," he said, with a broad smile. "Call me King. We have to talk. You'll have to tell me your system for winning money."

Ari grinned. "I will, if you'll tell me yours for making it."

Rivers was beckoning them all to a nearby table, while talking earnestly to Red Deavers. It was clearly business. All Ari heard was Rivers repeating the word *GeneSys*. As soon as the Kings were seated, everyone there who had a nodding acquaintance with the Deavers was lining up to meet their guests. Ari saw Caley come in.

He stood in the ballroom arch. The lights in back of him gleamed on his hair, but shaded his face. When he leaned forward to brush his lips against her cheek, the reflected candles gave his eyes an uneven glitter. He said, "You look lovely. Like a Christmas present." His voice was almost harsh as he added, "Just what I want. I should have put my foot down and taken you off to Mazatlán with me."

"I'm sorry too," she began. "Break a piñata for me and—"

He interrupted, "If I get out of here. There's more snow coming. Telluride flights are already scheduled to take off from Montrose. I'll have to leave early in the morning."

"We still have tonight." Ari could see the discontented twist of his lips, and she felt an almost guilty twinge. "Dinner's a midnight buffet. Dancing until almost dawn."

Before he could respond, Red Deaver laid a light hand on Ari's arm. "Now, you'll have to introduce me. Heard this is the man who set up GeneSys. I want to hear what he's doing next."

Caley's obvious interest increased as Red added, "You'll have to meet my houseguest. Maximilian King. He wants to hear too."

Ari watched as Barbara King made room for Caley next to her. Then she surveyed the room and immediately caught sight of Rivers on the dance floor. She thought how different he was from the other men here. All of them were wearing black tie, and the tuxedo was a uniform of sorts, a very civilized one. That should have made him blend in. Instead, he seemed as conspicuous as a leopard in a drawing room. Those big cats were elegant, and could stretch out before a hearth, but it was difficult to look away from them.

While Ari was listening to the stories of an attractive, uniformed Air Force major-general, Rivers came up, holding two laden plates. He grinned, gracefully apologetic, at the clearly disappointed officer, saying, "She always has to eat at midnight, or she turns into a pumpkin."

As Rivers led her away, Ari realized that it was twelve o'clock. "I can't believe it's so late," she said, amazed, "and I *am* starving. But I told Caley that—"

"Oh, he's eating. I'm sure that Barbara insisted he stay with them. King doesn't dance, and she needs a partner. Caley will like that. Barbara's a good dancer. Now, grab my arm and walk purposefully so no one will stop you. Here you led me to believe you'd be hanging around all shy and wallflowery by yourself, whereas I haven't been able to get within waving distance. I knew it'd be that way. Janie and Samuel have saved us a place in a quiet corner where they promise to do all the talking while we eat."

As they sat down, Janie scooped up the last raspberry in creamy vanilla sauce and smiled with enormous satisfaction. "Party of the season. Guaranteed. Everyone looks like they're having a great time. I know I am."

"Me too," Samuel agreed. While his answer was wholly sincere, everyone else had to try not to grin at the note of real surprise in his voice. He'd finished eating and was sitting back with his chair pushed out, his big hands lying loosely in his lap. His top shirt-button was open beneath his tie and he seemed quite at ease. Rivers asked him if the marble eagle in one of the Telluride galleries was his.

"Yes." Samuel leaned forward, his face lighting up. "I thought they were asking way too much for it, but it sold right away. Floored me. Pretty soon I can quit tending bar."

"I'd have bought that even if I'd had to take out a second mortgage," Rivers responded. "It's truly good, the essence of eagle. The cock of the head, those hunched wings. What are you working on now, or don't you like to talk about work in progress?"

"No, I don't, but this one's almost done." Samuel's hands came up eagerly. "I wasn't sure it was going to work, and it took me months. But it's bound to be the best thing I ever did. It's the figure of a woman in marble. A couple of years ago I picked up this great chunk of stone in Marble, Colorado. As good as that from the Italian quarries. It was alabaster, but it had just a thin blue vein." His big hand delicately traced a thread like embroidery silk in the air.

"And it sat there in the corner of my place in Sawpit. I knew it had a form inside it, but I didn't know what it was, how to free it. It's that way sometimes with sculpture. You have to take away all the stone that *isn't* the statue inside. Every day I'd look at it and think. I wanted to start on it, but I couldn't because I might make a mistake. All I could do was wait. Then about six months ago, it came to me."

He went on talking, but his hands were far more eloquent. They made rounded motions, conjuring up all things warm, desirable, yielding. His palms seemed to shape hard marble into soft flesh before their eyes. The form he drew in the transparent air was white, rose-petal white. It was a woman who seemed to be bending to embrace something. Samuel's fingers hovered near Janie's features as they created the face. She was mesmerized as she watched him with parted lips.

Ari was spellbound, too, but she was watching Janie, wondering if she could see that Samuel's heart was in his hands, and that those talented fingers had just portrayed the woman he loved.

When he stopped, Rivers said, almost conversationally, "You know, it seems you almost could have used Janie as a model for that. Or don't you use models?"

"No, no, I don't." When Samuel's hands rested on the table, he seemed handicapped in his speech, and he added slowly, "But I've got her . . . memorized. I could see her as I worked just like she was sitting there."

The brightness in Janie's eyes might have been amazement, might have been tears.

Caley's hands rested on Ari's shoulders, and as she lifted her face, he leaned down, saying, "The Kings and Deavers want me to go with them to the next party, and I—"

Rivers broke in, "Best to do it, Caley. Strike while the iron's hot. They couldn't hear enough about your coup with GeneSys. Business first, I always say."

When he saw Rivers, Caley's eyes took on a metallic glitter. "Speaking of that, I'm surprised to see you here, Alexander. Very surprised. Jonas told me only this morning that he was expecting a full report from you on ConChem." He paused, then asked pointedly, "Not going to disappoint him by staying for skiing, are you?"

"As much as I'd like to," Rivers responded cheerfully, "I won't have the time."

"I'll come with you to the door," Ari said, rising quickly, "and say good-night to everyone." It suddenly occurred to her that it must have been Rivers who told the Deavers about Caley's success with GeneSys.

As she turned away from the departing guests, Rivers was there, taking her hand. "It's time you came to your own party. Dancing now."

The orchestra was playing "The Way You Look Tonight," and he smiled as he reached for her, as if it were the song he'd have requested. As his arm encircled her, Ari was afraid he must have noticed the quick tension in her back. She knew she was moving a little stiffly, because she was trying to maintain a respectable inch between their bodies and that wasn't easy. She had to concentrate on that. And there was the question of where to look. For safety she kept her eyes level where she could only see one of his faille lapels, a corner of his mouth, and the wing of his bow tie. But then she had to shut them because she found herself wondering if the whole tie would come undone if you just tugged on that end.

Closing her eyes helped, although her other senses got a little confused. She thought she could smell the warmth of his skin, and she certainly could feel the music as well as hear it. The music relaxed her, then it took over, or perhaps he did, and they moved together in time.

His hand was only lightly on her waist, her arm barely resting on his shoulder. They were not pressing against each other, but they began to seem to her like one dancer. She knew exactly when he would turn her, when he would pull her to him, and there was no thought required.

She had only one idea in mind and it was that this would never end. Now and again it had to because someone else cut in. Ari would smile at her new partner, even recalling the right name, nod at his remarks, find a phrase on her lips. But then Rivers would return, and as soon as she slipped exactly back into his arms, there was no need to talk. Music was the language, and their bodies spoke it, whether there was a loud and pulsing beat, or a quiet, melodious tune. Music was the only time, too, and so there was no tomorrow, no questions about ever-afters. There was only this moment, and they were dancing together.

She had no hesitation now, during a slow piece, in laying her cheek against his, in fitting her palm inside his. Her body's curves shaped along the hardness of his length. She could sense the pulse of his heartbeat in the artery of her throat, feel the softness of her face on his. Yet in that perfect blending she'd never seemed more herself. And even the music suggested it would never end.

But the orchestra began playing what had the unmistakable sound of a final song. Over Rivers's shoulder Ari could see the last guests departing. She hurried to the door, shook hands, thanked people for coming, returned smiles. But somehow she was still in the bright cloud of music.

When she turned back to the ballroom, the musicians were packing up. There was no sign of Rivers. The caterers were wheeling away the tables that had held the food and liquor. A waiter went around the room blowing out the candles, one by one. Janie and Samuel had slipped away some time ago.

She could hardly breathe for disappointment. Crossing the hotel lobby, she tried telling herself that this was just as it should be. If he'd waited and gone up with her, she might have weakened, asked him in. As she pushed the elevator button, he rose from an armchair, hidden by the towering Christmas tree.

Smiling, he said, "I left my coat upstairs."

CHAPTER 17

As Ari was taking the key from her small evening bag, Rivers asked, "Can I come in for a minute? I want to talk to you." His tone was unexpectedly serious, and that caught her off balance. The key slipped from her fingers and onto the passageway carpet.

He scooped it up and, possibly misinterpreting her expression, said as he turned it in the lock, "I mean *talk*, Ari, and I hope you'll listen. I'm going to say something I've never said before." He threw open the door, ushered her in, and shut it behind him before adding, "I'm going to propose."

It was very cold inside, but Ari was too shocked by his words to remember that she'd left the upstairs balcony door open when she'd gone downstairs to the party. Of all the things he might have said, those were the last words she expected. She stood numbly, rubbing the sides of her upper arms in her thin sequined sleeves, staring at him.

"You *really* keep your heat low," he said. "Is it all right if I light the fire?" He flicked on the low living-room light, saw his coat and wrapped it around her shoulders before crossing to the fieldstone hearth. Shivering, she followed him and, because her knees no longer wanted to hold her weight, sank wordlessly onto the edge of the couch before the fireplace.

He knelt, lit the paper surrounding the kindling, and waited to see that it caught. Still on one knee, his arm resting on the other bent leg, he turned, saying, "Let me say at the beginning that I can imagine, if we were engaged and the EPA gave Jonas the go-ahead, you would object to my job. Still, it's a little hard to propose to a millionairess if you're out of work. Throws some doubt on your motives."

The rising flames behind him touched the sun streaks in his brown hair. The lamp at the far end of the couch illumined his face, raised toward her. Both creases near his mouth were distinct, as if he saw the irony in talking about love and money in the same breath.

Ari was still too stunned to get her thoughts in any order. His job, money, or the lack of it, was hardly the first issue on *her* mind, but it was the one he'd brought up. She had to say something. Tugging her curls free from the heavy coat around her, but pulling its warmth more closely, she replied, "Well, to ask people for large contributions to buy land from Jonas Murdoch while you—" She stopped herself abruptly and then burst out, "That isn't the question. Rivers, this is only the third time I've ever seen you in my whole life. I—"

"What about the line from Shakespeare?" he interrupted, not getting up, but holding her eyes with his. " 'Whoever loved, who loved not at first sight?' And I did. I knew it the day I met you, and I would have been camped on your doorstep the next morning, if I'd known where you were. It wasn't just that you were beautiful, it was you. Everything you think, and believe, and are, just shines out all over you. Since then, what you write to me, what you tell me about what you want from life, makes me *like* you more, but I couldn't love you more. And I couldn't stop if I wanted to. I want to marry you."

Joy began to fill her veins. She'd never guessed how much she wanted to hear him say that.

At some level in her mind she held on to Caley's words that all Rivers wanted was money, that he would marry to get it. She knew, too, how much she wanted him to make love to her. So she would be persuading herself to believe him. But despite that tangle of thought and feeling, at that moment she did believe him.

His compelling gaze wouldn't let go of hers, and she was caught in the force of him, drawing her across the room to him, willing her to say what she herself wanted to say. Trying to think, she crossed her arms in front of her, then found herself rubbing his coat sleeves, the smell of him in her nostrils. Now she was too warm, and hearing the fire's roar, she slipped off the coat. She ran her tongue over her dry lips, saying at last, "I don't think we know each other well enough."

He stood up, came nearer, made her look up at him. Both lines of his smile held amusement. "That's the beauty of my plan. If we were engaged, we could do what couples do. Have dinner, talk, go to galleries and movies, discuss."

His lips twisted and the humor was gone. "As it is, you won't return my calls. You answer my letters but you never mention how you feel about me. Still, when you look at me, I get my hopes up because it seems to me that you feel the way I do. I know you've been busy, but you're avoiding me. Why?"

Hastily she glanced down, plucking at the crimson sequins of her skirt. After what he'd said, and her own reaction to it, she couldn't accuse him of being interested only in her money. And she couldn't tell the truth. How could she say that she couldn't talk to him because she'd make plans to see him, and if she saw him, she would end up in his arms? He'd regard that as a quite convincing argument for his case. To answer she would have to lie, so she said nothing.

When she didn't answer, he paced down the living room, his voice intense as he tried to explain, to persuade her. "It's true that I'll have to be in D.C. for a few more months. I can't quit just now. I've begun the talks with the congressmen. I want to persuade them to give ConChem time to see if these new genetically engineered bacteria can be developed. I feel I have to stay until the negotiations are over. It's an important environmental project and I believe in it. I know you have to stay here because you believe in what you're doing. But we could write, talk every night on the phone. It's only a few hours by plane. You could come to Washington; I'd come here whenever I could. You'd end up knowing me all too well. Then you might want to change your mind. But I'd take that chance, any chance, if you'd say yes."

She thought about what he was suggesting. They could go to the Smithsonian, see the Capitol, walk beneath the cherry blossoms in the spring. They could catch the shuttle to New York to the theater, dance in the shine of that city's lights. And then, and then, she could spend the nights in his arms, turn to him in the mornings. During this time she would certainly learn—

Her inward voice, interrupting this train of thought, had an edge to it. It reminded her of how little time she had before summer, when development on the mountain would start, the long hours the campaign would demand. It asked again if she thought that in this dream of lovemaking she would see him or herself more clearly, or if the opposite wouldn't be more likely, that she would keep her eyes closed.

He came back and stood before her, but this time she was not going to meet that blue-green gaze. "Oh, Ari, when I met you, I knew you." He smiled a little ruefully. "And you have to admit that even that first day, *you* learned a lot about me. You saw my messy closet, my rather bare cupboards"—his smile was replaced by longing—"knew my bed."

She sprang up, the flush that burned her face part embarrassment, part overwhelming memory. "Rivers, don't. It's not fair to mention that now." She tried anxiously to explain. "I mean . . . I always wanted to tell you that . . . well, you said in a letter that you thought I regretted that. I didn't. I don't. But you have to remember that that day I'd just found out about the Sweepstakes and I wasn't myself. You have to realize that I wouldn't normally—"

His hand closed on her wrist. "Ari," he said firmly and very low, "who knows *that* better than I do?"

"Well, yes, of course, you knew—" The blood came more furiously to her face. "But I mean that it's confused me ever since about how I feel." She wanted to tell him about not being sure she knew herself well enough. But her thoughts wouldn't fit into the right words, and he was standing right there. Her fiery flush made even the thin fabric of the dress too warm, and the crackling flames sent out too much heat.

The silky tone of his next question made her sure he'd misunderstood. "Are you saying that you think your response that day, your making love to me, was possibly just a result of your other . . . emotions? That it didn't have that much to do with me, with us?"

She shook her head so quickly that some of the gold pins in her hair scattered. But she couldn't even get out a simple no. She looked at him helplessly and forgot all the words she ever knew.

His fingers on her wrist tightened. His other hand reached up and, with one sharp pull, undid his tie. He abruptly raised her face to his. "Then let's try it again. You didn't win the Sweepstakes today."

But this time it was very different. His mouth was hard, not soft. His embrace was almost crushing, pinioning her uplifted arms against his chest. And her desire for him did not come in sweet and easy stages as before. It shook her immediately, as if it had been gathering force all those months, lying in wait. Having been let out, it wasn't going to wait anymore. It moaned in her throat, and she gasped like a swimmer at last shooting to the surface as she opened her mouth to his.

With her arms pressed upward she could only reach the buttons on his shirt, and she almost ripped at them in her hurry to feel his body against hers. Her dress was easier, and he had it, with one quick zip, pooled around her feet. Everything else was fast, despite their unwillingness to let their mouths part. When her naked breasts were against his bare chest, she wrapped herself around him, trying, even as they stood, to take him into her so they'd be closer.

The sound he made was somewhere between a laugh and a groan of pleasure. He raised her only high enough to take her feet off the floor, and to swing her to the couch. As they pressed down together into its hollow, she could feel him, rigid and straining against her belly, and she thrust her hips eagerly up against him. She breathed, "Now," in the heat of their kiss.

He might have tried to say, "Wait," but he couldn't get out the word. He raised his head, seeing her eyes opaque with desire, like crystallized honey. This time he did groan, thrusting into her.

When at last he slipped from her, he knelt by the couch, took her face in his hands, kissed her hair, said painfully, "I'm sorry, I'm sorry. Did I hurt you?"

"No." Ari could hardly get out the word through lips that felt thick. "Oh, no." She raised her head and saw the red marks of her nails cross-hatched on his back, and she reached out gingerly, to tenderly touch them.

She noticed something else, that his shoulders were goosefleshed, and that without his warmth she was chilled to the marrow. Just as he said, "God, it's cold," she jumped up, saying, "I'm freezing!" The fire was only embers and the air was glacial.

"Quick," she said, reaching for his hand. "I don't know what's the matter, but it's got to be warmer in the loft." She pulled him toward the stairs, and they raced up together. Then Ari saw the balcony door open on the crystal night and flew to slam it shut, as she urged him, "Hurry, get under the quilt."

The smooth sheets were like ice on their bare skins, and the goosedown quilt, light as snow, was every bit as cold. Laughing and gasping, they rubbed each other's upper arms, shoulders, back, intertwined their legs. Soon there was a cocoon of warmth around them as they lay locked together, but they didn't let a stray foot venture yet outside this small enclosure.

"Hold still," Rivers said, "I want to make sure your circulation is fully restored." He kissed her forehead, her eyes, the tip of her nose, the sides of her mouth. Running his index finger over the curve of her upper lip, and again and again over the lower one, he murmured, "They seem all right for now. I'll check them later to make sure."

His mouth skimmed down her throat, and his tongue lingered in the small hollow at its base, licked along her collarbone. "Shoulders need work," he mused, nibbling at them. A little later he added, "The breasts will take some time."

Ari's breath grew shallow, almost stopping in her pleasure. She had that sensation of her bones liquefying, dissolving, while her skin prickled with life beneath his fingers. When his tongue was feather light inside her, her hips writhed. He leaned one hand on each, and she heard a low laugh in his voice as he said, "Not following directions. I said 'hold still.' "

But soon she couldn't. "Rivers, *please*. You have to, now. Really. Please."

He uncoiled himself, stretched full length beside her, pulled her to him. "On one condition. No moving." He entered her, velvet smooth and hard.

"Now, Ari," he whispered, "we're going to talk." But they didn't. They lay on their sides, warmly pressed together. They took turns, rolling one way or the other, never parting, to stare through the glass wall at the indigo sky filled with huge stars so white, they burned in the cold night.

At last their kisses grew longer, deeper. Then he stopped, pressing himself on top of her. "You're cheating," he said sternly. "Swiveling of hips is out." He clamped his body full length on hers, each of his long arms grasping one of her wrists, even putting one instep on each of her feet. His lips went to her ear and what he said now was not quiet or soothing. The words made her shiver with heat, and she tried to thrust up against him.

But she was fixed by his rigid force. Finally, she constricted her inner muscles. His words came faster, but he would not let go of an inch of her. So she put her mouth to his ear, and what she said made him forget everything, except how to move. Even after they had pulled apart and tumbled into sleep, their bodies stirred and touched.

So deeply was she wrapped in this euphoric sleep, that when the dream started, Ari did not even remember its usual ending. There was only the rising sun, the exquisite columbines, the glistening stream. The hem of the white dress whispered through the grass as she approached the water. But when she looked into the pool, it was her own face, and she was not smiling. And the mountain was not limned in the background but was rising upward, sharply outlined.

Even the attack of the fear was different. It gripped her suddenly, shook her awake, and the sound of Rivers's voice calling to her was still urgent in her ears as she sat up. For a second she thought his shout was real, that he'd gone downstairs, but a quick glance showed the top of his head deep in the pillow beside hers. Even her abrupt movement had not caused him to stir.

The meaning of the dream was no clearer to her. But what she guessed caused her to hurry into her heavy bathrobe and slip down the stairs in the pale morning light. Still she couldn't sort it out. Her fear for the mountain didn't explain why she had heard his voice calling her there. If anything, he stood in the way of her saving it.

All she knew was that she couldn't consider an engagement. If she said yes, she knew she would be waiting for each week to end so that she could catch a flight to Washington. And there would always be the temptation to stretch the weekend an extra day. Yet, if the campaign were to succeed, each day would matter. She would not get a second chance. The bulldozers would come in late spring and gouge into the canyon's sides.

But she stood there at the foot of the stairs with him warmly asleep in her bed. She'd worried last night that such an arrangement might not be the best way to learn whether she really loved him. Inwardly, she found herself arguing that it was the only way to discover that. Then there was the thought that made her shiver, despite her thick terry-cloth robe. What if he grew angry at a refusal and she never saw him again?

She put her foot on the staircase to go back up. The only sensible thing to do was slip back into bed and they could discuss it later in the morning. Ari had actually gone up two steps before she was struck by the realization that she was not going to be thinking clearly on the subject while lying in his arms. There wasn't much hope, in fact, of doing that while they were seated, fully dressed, across a breakfast table. Even if he were looking away from her, glancing at a menu, reading the newspaper, and she found her eyes resting on his mouth, her own lips would never frame the word *no*.

An unwanted vision rose in her mind. Suppose that the two of them were seated in a restaurant in Washington, knowing she had to leave the next morning, both dreading the parting. What if he echoed Jonas's thinking? What if Rivers urged, "Be reasonable, Ari. Building in Ute Rise is just a business deal. There are a lot of mountain valleys. Buy another one. Save it. Then you could stay here with me."

She turned from the staircase abruptly. No, *he* wouldn't. In her agitation she tied her bathrobe belt so tightly, she could hardly breathe. She said, almost aloud, "He knows how I feel about Bridey's Mountain, that I have to try. He loves me, he said so. So he'd want me to do it." All her emotions sprang to his defense as she paced. Shaken by them, she almost frayed the terry-cloth tie she was twisting in her hands.

But the mention of love brought to her mind again how hard its demands could sometimes be. *You have to be so sure,* she whispered to herself. She thought of all the Gregory women. And her own life reflected its pains. People died, and you were alone standing with all the leftover love.

Ari was trying hard to think clearly, to use her head. She was convinced of the power of reason as a guide. To her, emotions were untrustworthy. It didn't occur to her to wonder why she believed that. If she'd questioned it, she might have seen she was afraid of her feelings. Among them lurked sexual desire, with its threat to overwhelm her. But she thought the problem was whether she could trust *Rivers.* And the right answer depended on asking the right question.

Taking a ragged breath, she decided there was only one thing to do. She would leave a note, but she would go. Ari went quickly into the downstairs bedroom where her big closet was and gathered a few things in a tote to take with her downstairs to the spa. She shoved a sweatsuit into the canvas bag. She could shower, sit in the Jacuzzi, perhaps sleep on a couch in the massage room. But she could not come back until he'd left.

She wrote hurriedly, *Rivers, I'm sorry but an engagement isn't possible now. Not yet. I'll write and tell you why I feel this way, what I think, and I hope you'll write back. But please don't try to see me or call me. Right now I don't know what I think.*

As Ari laid the note at the foot of the stairs where he'd be sure to see it, she noticed her spangled dress tossed on a chair, the corsage dangling from it. Slowly she walked across the room. Taking the orchid off and pinning it to her bathrobe, she pricked her finger because the tears made it almost impossible to see.

CHAPTER 18

Pacing outside Ari's penthouse door, Caley was chafing with impatience. She wasn't there but he didn't know where else to try. It had only been late that afternoon that he'd decided they should get engaged now. He'd picked up the reset ring from the jeweler's. Before he caught the plane to Telluride, he'd called her from the Denver airport. The only person still at the campaign office was a volunteer who thought Ari had gone back to the Doral. She told him that Janie had left a few minutes ago.

When he'd arrived, he'd gone by the house just in case, but even the workmen had quit for the day. At the hotel, when she still hadn't answered her phone, he'd had her paged. No reply. He checked both restaurants, looked into the crowded bars, walked by the boutiques, glanced in the art gallery.

Ari hadn't known he was coming. Caley hadn't either. But he couldn't wait any longer. In the last three weeks everything had gone wrong because he'd been distracted by images of her. Everything, starting with the trip to Mazatlán. In the warm sun he was feverish, thinking of her. None of Mexico's voluptuous, dark-eyed diversions had taken his mind off her. Quite the opposite.

Maximilian and Barbara King had pressed him to visit them on his way back, so he'd gone to Los Angeles. But there he could concentrate on neither business nor pleasure. He'd ended up telling King he'd get back to him on investment opportunities. He couldn't make himself listen to Barbara's endless stream of Hollywood gossip. Worse, part of the trip was mortifying. His lack of interest in the nubile starlets King provided was all too evident. He couldn't get an erection. That hadn't happened to him in years.

Caley laid all this at Ari's door. If she hadn't so angered him with her waste of money, he knew they'd have been engaged in the fall. And he could have required her to go with him. Having Ari in Mexico would have settled him down, calmed him. He could see that now.

But after what had happened in October, he'd felt just the opposite. His loss of control on the mountain had really shaken him. He'd almost made a bad mistake there. It wasn't like him to get carried away when there was real money at stake. It wasn't like him to get carried away at all. If prison had taught him anything, it was discipline. And if he were going to get his hands on the money, he knew he'd have to handle her, for a while, with kid gloves. So he'd thought it through and made what he was sure at the time was the right decision.

Since Ari wasn't going to give up on the campaign, he was going to distance himself from it all. That way he wouldn't get worked up. She'd make inroads on the first ten million from her winnings, but she couldn't get her hands on the second fifteen because it wasn't due from the lottery board until next year. By then they'd be safely married and it would be in his control. Caley was himself going to demand a prenuptial agreement, and Wellings would handle hers. But there were a lot of ways around that after the wedding.

In the meantime Caley had known he'd have to play it safe. When he was with her, he brought along other people, and that had worked well. He planned on continuing that strategy through the spring.

But two things had changed his mind. Seeing Rivers at the party had given him a shock. Alexander needed money, he was good looking, he was very quick. Even though he was out of the way, there were too many attractive young men in Telluride, drawn there by the skiing and the women they might meet. If Ari didn't know that Caley meant marriage, she'd have a line outside her penthouse door.

What was even more disturbing was that, in Mexico, all he could think of was having her, about getting her used to the way he liked things done. He could see the sweat on her face, see it sliding between her breasts. He could feel his fingers tangling in her damp hair, pulling her head back. He could see the shadows grow in her eyes. Eventually she'd do what he wanted. He couldn't quit thinking about it. It hadn't gotten any better since he'd returned.

There was only one thing to be done. So he was here. It meant he'd have to watch himself. Take it easy. He'd have to let her spend her time and money on the stupid campaign. Maybe he could prevent the worst of it. But he wouldn't let it get to him. Too, he had real hopes of stopping her on the house. Talking to Red Deaver about that location had been enlightening. If she could be persuaded to hold off on further renovations until spring, a profit on the lot might be possible. He could tell her that the two of them should go antique shopping in Europe first. Point out that when she had the furniture, she'd be in a better position to know what to do to the house. That should work. Eventually she'd see they should bulldoze the damned place.

Caley walked down the corridor to the elevator. He could hear it constantly stopping at the lower floors. The hotel was jammed. Mid-January was peak ski season. Walking through the lobby he'd seen a half-dozen people he knew. Heather Murdoch was waiting, skis piled around her, for her husband to check out.

"Caley." She'd waved him over. "You look wonderful. Isn't this the best? The snow's perfect. Scott and I hate to leave." Then she'd taken in his tailored jacket and Gucci loafers, and she'd grinned. "But then you're not here for the skiing, are you?"

With a half-smile Caley replied, "I don't ski."

"You know," she said, adjusting the sunglasses in her hair, "there were a lot of disappointed women in Denver because you weren't there for any of the Christmas parties. Then we heard Ari was having a big do up here. Lots of talk. I think all of us will be a little put out when you finally get married. It's such fun wondering who you're going to show up with next. But I said I thought this time was it."

Caley's smile grew wider as his fingers slid over the small box in his jacket pocket.

"I knew it!" Heather exclaimed. "You're engaged!"

"It's still under wraps," he answered.

"I see—you want to make the announcement with a flourish. I won't tell a soul. Well, just Scott. This is too good to keep. And Judith."

"How is Judith?" Caley inquired with interest.

"Well, they"—Heather always assumed everyone knew she was referring to her parents when she used a certain inflection—"were worried because she was just hanging around her apartment in New York. Thought she'd get over things if she were busier. But they decided she shouldn't come back here until the divorce was final. And there was Rivers down in D.C. doing the lobbying bit for Dad. That requires a lot of entertaining. So she's gone down to help him." Heather arched an eyebrow and emphasized the word *help*.

"Maybe there'll be more than one wedding this summer." Caley's hand stayed in his pocket.

"I wouldn't be surprised, would you?" Heather raised both eyebrows. "Let me be the first to offer you my congratulations. Ari's a sweetie. I'll give her a shower."

Caley heard the busy elevator as he paced back to the penthouse door. There were no rooms available anywhere in Telluride. But he didn't need one. He'd stay here. With Ari. Even if *she* didn't know it yet.

That thought brought a glitter to his eyes, and he rubbed a hand along his tanned jaw. But he'd have to keep a tight rein on himself. This waiting for her didn't help. It was making him irritable. He was finding his leather jacket too warm. For the third time in five minutes he checked his pocket watch. Snapping it closed, he ran his thumb over the incised initials on the case and slipped it into his pocket next to the blue velvet jeweler's box.

He heard the elevator door slide open, and Ari stepped out in a terry-cloth robe with a towel wrapped around her head. "Caley!" she called, running down the hall so fast, the towel flew off. He swung her up in his arms and her wet hair fell around his face.

"Why didn't you tell me—" she began.

"I had you paged everywhere. Why—" he said at the same time.

"Swimming. With my earplugs in. I'm so happy to see you. You look so good. That tan with your hair—"

"I brought you something," he interrupted again. "Something you'll really like."

"I'm getting you all wet." She laughed, brushing the drops from her hair off his jacket shoulders.

"Yes," he said, his arms clenched around her hips, feeling her nakedness beneath the robe. "You are."

"Then put me down. I'll get you a drink while I dry off and get dressed."

"Don't bother," he said, letting her slide down his body. "No need to do that. We can have dinner sent up. Later."

As she opened the door, Ari was already launching into stories about all they'd already done at campaign headquarters. She continued talking while she got glasses and filled the ice bucket in the kitchen. "It's wonderful having Janie here all the time. I have to tell you about her and Samuel. They're getting married this summer! Wait till you hear what she has—"

As Ari started to twist the corkscrew into a bottle of white wine, Caley interrupted from the living room with a laugh, "By then Judith Murdoch will be getting married too. Probably be a little quieter affair than the first one."

"So soon? Who to?" She set the bottle down on the counter, although she hadn't pulled out the cork.

"Alexander. She's moved down to D.C. The word is that she's helping him with the lobbying. But everyone knows. And it's a good match. They even went to grade school together. Jonas and he agree . . ."

Caley went on, but Ari wasn't listening. There seemed to be a roaring in her ears, and suddenly not enough oxygen in the room. She closed her eyes against the inner image of Rivers bending down to kiss Judith.

The only idea in her head was that he hadn't meant all those things he'd said. Not really. He'd meant he wanted to marry a woman with money, but if one didn't show the proper interest, there was always another. She hadn't heard from him since the night of the Christmas party.

Of course, she'd told him not to call or write. It'd taken her all of three weeks to come up with a letter to him. He probably hadn't even gotten it yet.

Not that it would matter now.

But she hadn't been able to figure out how to put down on paper all the things she wanted to say. One thought twisted into the next, and she didn't know which thread to pull in the tangle of her emotions. She felt joy, fear, desire, hope, an incessant longing. And Ari was ashamed. Once again, she'd fallen right into bed with him. She didn't even know that she wasn't pregnant. Pressing the cold bottle of wine to her forehead, she was thinking that she still couldn't believe that she'd—

"What's taking so long?" Caley leaned against the kitchen door frame, one blond eyebrow raised.

Ari looked at the wine bottle. "The cork . . . I guess I didn't do it right."

"What we need is champagne. I'll call down for some later." The corkscrew came out with one smooth pull of his fingers. "But this is fine. Come on."

Ari hurriedly piled things from the counter onto the tray—napkins, the ice bucket, three glasses, a bowl of nuts—and followed him into the living room. As she set it on the coffee table by the fireplace, she tried to clear her thoughts, saying, "Tell me about Mexico. What did you do?"

"Oh, the usual. But I found a great house overlooking a deserted little cove. Big, but no live-in servants. Ideal for our honeymoon."

It took both of them a few seconds to realize what he'd said. Ari stared at him with parted lips. Then Caley gave a little laugh, set down the bottle, raised a rueful shoulder. "Guess I really got things in the wrong order, didn't I? You'll have to forgive me. I've never proposed before. But I mean it. I want you to marry me."

Ari didn't so much sit as collapse onto the edge of the couch. Her lips were still parted. If anyone had asked her how she felt about Caley, she'd have answered, "Oh, I love him." She would have meant he was more than a friend, but rather like a family member. She'd never thought about *marrying* him.

It wasn't the difference in their ages, or the fact that she'd only known him a few months. It seemed to her that, in some ways, she'd known him much longer. But she'd been so involved in her feelings for Rivers. The idea of Caley as a husband simply hadn't occurred to her.

Her absolute surprise didn't displease him. He'd almost expected that. But he also expected that once that passed, she'd do just what she'd done in the hallway a few moments ago. He spread his arms for her.

Ari didn't move, couldn't move. Now she was looking at Caley as other women must always have done. The sun had turned his skin golden, lightened his hair, made his eyes sea colored. But she wasn't thinking that he was handsome, rich, powerful. She was remembering what she owed him for all his kindness, for the generosity and gentleness he'd displayed, the comfort and safety of his presence. Her gratitude included what he'd done for her father.

All she could think was that to accept Caley would be to cheat him. She couldn't honestly say she loved him as she should if marriage were the question. She might even be pregnant with someone else's child.

Looking down at her hands tightly curled in her lap, she finally managed to bring out, "I can't."

Now *he* stared. "What do you mean, you *can't*?" The specter of some teenaged marriage to a Louisville farm boy rose in his mind.

"I mean—" Ari stopped. She wanted to be truthful. She wasn't going to mention a possible pregnancy. But she did want Caley to know how much she cared about him and what it meant to her that he'd offered marriage. She began again slowly, choosing her words, "I do love you. . . ."

"Well, then?" He smiled, raised his shoulders in a question.

"But the kind of love . . . I'm not ready for marriage. I—" She was up quickly, walking to the far end of the room.

When she turned, he was taking a small box from the jacket he'd thrown on the couch arm. "That's what engagements are for. We both need to know each other much, much better."

There was no mistaking the look in his eyes, as he added, "I'll convince you. Come here. Let me put this on."

"No. I can't." She meant that. Ari could not go right from one man's arms to another's. She pulled so hard on the robe's belt that it dug into her waist.

He could hear that she meant it. But at the moment anger only bordered the edges of his impatience. "Ari! For God's sake. Is that all you can say?"

"Caley, please." There was pain in her eyes, in her voice. "Let me think. Not now. I—"

"When?" His angry voice cut across her words. He put down the box, ran one open palm across the knuckles of his other hand.

The front door swung in. "Ari," Janie called out, "that massage was—" Seeing them both, she stopped herself, twisting the towel tighter over her hair. "Caley, hi. Great tan! When did you get back?" Then she felt the tension in the room. "Well, catch you in a bit. I'll just get dressed." She disappeared into the downstairs bedroom. A few seconds later she heard the front door slam shut.

CHAPTER 19

It all hinged on timing. The way Ari thought about Caley's proposal might have been different if she'd written to Rivers sooner than she did, and he hadn't responded when he did.

But after she received his reply, she began to see accepting Caley as possible. Then, over the next days and weeks, it seemed probable. She had a list of reasons. The fact that he'd asked her to marry him meant that he loved her. Caley showed every sign of caring about her, and she was grateful that his negotiations with Jonas Murdoch had given her a chance to save her mountain. She admired Caley's acumen. She was impressed by his knowledge of the world, and she could see all he offered in terms of stability. Their children, and grandchildren even, would be given a secure place and loving support.

But she did see that thinking that one *ought* to love someone was different from feeling it. She couldn't understand why, when Caley was clearly attractive, she herself was not attracted to him.

Ari had talked the matter over with Janie that January night, telling her what Caley had said and explaining why he'd left so abruptly.

They'd stayed up late discussing it. When Janie asked Ari how she felt about Caley's proposal, Ari kept repeating, "I don't know." When Ari asked Janie what she thought about it, Janie replied, "What *I* think about it is neither here nor there. *You're* the one being offered the ring."

The third time Ari asked, Janie said patiently, "Caley's got to look like the answer to every maiden's prayer. He's very handsome and very rich. With his social background there are women in Denver who'd marry him even if he were a toad. And he isn't. He's bright, witty. He presses desserts on me at dinner. I love that in a man. What more can I say?"

Ari looked at her for a long moment and said, her forehead creased, "It's what you're not saying."

There were a few things about Caley that troubled Janie. But no matter how tactfully phrased, these would sound like criticisms. If Ari married him, she'd remember what Janie had said and it might cause a wedge in their friendship later. The truth was that Janie didn't like Caley. She didn't feel it was wise or helpful to say that.

In terms of any major objection to him as a husband, Janie knew that she herself could summon up a reasonable defense. What bothered her most was that she didn't think Caley and Ari shared certain basic assumptions or even many interests. It was obvious that he didn't want to hear about the Ute Rise campaign. But that could stem from a fear that Ari would be in pain if it failed. He'd been the one who got Murdoch to agree to a sale in the first place, so Caley must agree with what she was doing. As for their interests, Ari would want to hear about his business life, would be willing to learn. She'd worked hard to understand her own affairs. After marriage they could probably find other areas of mutual interest.

Then, while Janie thought that Caley was all charm if things were to his liking, she wondered if he'd be so if he were crossed. He was not used to that happening. He was an older man, and powerful. But surely Ari herself could see that would be the case. Besides, who knew what he would do for a young wife whom he loved? She was convinced that he loved Ari. And Ari's affection for him was real, even if it wasn't the stuff of songs and poetry.

Janie had heard several things about Caley from a vice-president at Blackburn and Barton. When the executive at her firm learned she knew Sutherland, he made several admiring remarks. He thought Caley very clever to have avoided prosecution in Denver's savings-and-loan scandal, and he commented enviously on his fast cars and rich girlfriends. Janie had to admit that there was no reason Caley shouldn't have dated a lot—he hadn't found the woman he wanted to marry. The women in his circle all had money. She knew that he'd never been actually accused of business wrongdoing, so she wouldn't repeat the gossip. She saw no point in bringing it up. In any case, that was not what Ari was asking.

Janie dodged the question again. "Before you ever had lunch with Caley, I did what I could to check him out. I even looked up his Dun and Bradstreet rating. Ari, there's rich and then there's rich. Caley is loaded. While he may not be able to just toss Ute Rise Canyon in your lap for a wedding present, he wouldn't miss a good part of the purchase price. He must love you. I can't see why he'd be marrying you for—"

"That's not what I mean, Janie, and you know it."

Janie ran her fingers through her hair and at last answered, "I don't think this conversation is about what I think of Caley. Or even your feelings about him. It's about Rivers, the way you feel about *him*. When you look at him—"

Ari burst out, "Can you tell just from my face? Does he know—?"

Leaning back on the couch, Janie spread her hands with a smile. "Let me put it this way. You told me your great-grandfather was crackerjack at poker. Well, *you* shouldn't play. You didn't get the gene that's a requirement there. As to what Rivers knows, what does he say?"

Following the Christmas party Ari had simply told Janie that she and Rivers danced until late and talked, but she hadn't been specific. It would have involved bringing up what had happened afterward. Ari wasn't prepared to admit that she'd done what she'd done. Or that she might even be pregnant. But also Janie and Samuel had gotten engaged that night, and when they told her, Ari just wanted to share in their happiness. Besides, she wanted to write Rivers before she talked about it.

But trying to figure out what to say to him had taken those three weeks. Ari knew that she was sidestepping in her letter, unable to be honest about feelings she didn't trust. She did tell him how much what he'd said meant to her, but repeated that they didn't know each other well enough. In the end she said, *Rivers, this isn't fair to you. But I can't make this decision now. Please don't try to convince me otherwise. Just write.*

Ari was a truth teller, and she was a little suspicious of some of her last words. Probably she hoped he would convince her—and sooner rather than later. Still, she regarded her approach as the most sensible thing to do.

His answer came immediately. The words seemed to be etched in bitterness on the page. He said: *You're right. It isn't fair. But it's your decision. I can't believe it's what you should do. But then, I can hardly be objective. So there's no point in writing what I think. So there's no point in writing. Best wishes.*

Rivers was not replying to what Ari had written to him. Instead, his angry words sprang from what Judith Murdoch had told him. Her sister, Heather, had passed along the gossip about Caley's engagement to Ari. Judith saw no harm in telling Rivers, her only Denver friend in Washington.

He could see that Ari had written the letter before Caley proposed. But he'd heard she'd accepted. Worse, he assumed she'd merely been putting him off until she knew whether Caley would propose. That was scalding water on a fresh burn.

Ari read his reply three times. She didn't know that he'd heard she was engaged to Caley. So at first, she was a little confused. After all, she hadn't said no. Then she was angry. Finally she was furious. She was sure she knew the reason he wasn't going to take a "maybe." Since she hadn't eagerly said yes, he intended to regard her answer as no. That's what he meant. He was taking back his proposal. Now he could pursue Judith Murdoch, who might show definite signs of interest. He couldn't afford to let her get away while he waited for Ari to make up her mind.

Shortly after his letter came, Janie asked what she'd heard from Rivers. After seeing Ari's face she didn't bring the subject up again.

At night Ari lay in bed staring sleeplessly through the glass at the stars burning in the frigid night. She shivered with heat as she remembered Rivers lying beside her, the hardness of his body, the softness of his mouth. Then she remembered, too, that she'd been told about Rivers, that his first interest was money. She told herself that she'd been naive to have believed anything else. She'd been foolish, but at least she wasn't pregnant. If things hadn't ended this way between them, she might have gone down the path toward him, even knowing she'd come to grief. She was lucky, she'd repeat, that things had ended this way.

But she couldn't escape from the cycle of hot desire followed by cold thought. She'd see his face, the blue-green eyes lit by amusement or darkened by his desire. Ari could even visualize his hands, and she ached when she recalled what those hands could do. Then she'd remind herself that her family's history showed that love was more than that sweet and desperate making of love. For Morna, Berkeley had had to give up his career, his position. In the end Morna had even had to give him up. Devin had repeated the sacrifice for Bridey, and she'd had only him, since no society would accept them. Trish's world with an illegitimate child would have been very narrow, too, and her choices limited. Then, Ari would remember Lucy pushing Gerald's wheelchair, and the MacAllisters' long and tender care of herself.

If love cost so much, Ari tried to think coolly, the man must be one who was worth it. He had to be one who shared her values. It was clear that what Rivers wanted most was money and for her that was not what was primary. There were things that were priceless.

But some nights, although Ari wrapped the pillow around her ears so she wouldn't think it, an idea recurred. If what Rivers wanted was money, she could offer it. That and herself. All she had to do was pick up the phone, say she'd changed her mind. It would be dawn in Washington, but he might be very happy to be awakened by that call. He'd said he loved her and whatever he meant by that, he certainly seemed to like her and to enjoy the sex. She could imagine his smile, hear him say, "I'm on my way to the airport."

Then what? Her money would have bought him. But she'd have had to sell herself. Could she live with that? Or with him, knowing what she'd paid?

With this came a related thought. Suppose he was in bed with Judith when the phone rang. At that image Ari found that every inch of her hurt. Even the light goosedown quilt chafed her skin. Supposing he hesitated when she called, weighing in Judith's possible inheritance. What was worse, Ari began wondering how much money Judith had right now. More than she did? At this point she realized that *she* was thinking just like the Murdochs. They had all that money, but it was never enough for them.

It was true, she had to admit in despair, that she could see how people could keep wanting more and more dollars. When she'd won the Sweepstakes, she'd thought twenty-five million was an unimaginable fortune, that it would buy anything and everything she could ever want. But she'd learned immediately that she needed more than that to buy her mountain wilderness, which was what she wanted most.

Since then she'd begun to see exactly what it would buy. One small Van Gogh painting. Or five Learjets. Or twenty-five of the best houses in Telluride. Or jewelry, clothes, cars, and trips. It was amazing how fast you could spend it on things like that. But then you wouldn't have invested for your future. If you spent it, there was no security for you or your children. So you invested it and still lived on a budget, even if it was a generous one. Ari had read that one of the Rockefellers used to pace his house in frustration thinking of all the works of art he couldn't afford that Onassis could. But Onassis wouldn't wear an overcoat to New York restaurants because then he'd have to pay to check it.

When she'd first met Caley and remarked that winning the Sweepstakes meant money was no problem anymore, he'd laughed out loud, ruffled her hair, and said, "There's no such thing as too much money."

And Ari's thoughts would circle back to Caley. He had no reason to care about her money. He valued her. All the Gregory women had wanted a man they could love and had given up everything for that. *She* was being offered security and love from a man she could admire.

Caley waited for a few days, sure that Ari would come to her senses and call him. But she didn't. His temper grew worse, and when he entered a room, Loki slunk out the other door. Finally, Caley decided to swallow his pride. She had millions. Then, too, the image of her with the sweat streaking her face filled his mind. He could feel his fingers in her damp hair. He recalled the fullness of her breasts and the tight roundness of her hips naked under her robe as he held her. At last he called her.

"Have you thought over what I asked, Ari?"

"Oh, yes. Of course. It's just that I don't feel . . . ready for marriage. Not yet. I wouldn't hold you to—"

He tried to push his anger down. "It isn't a question of that." He couldn't quite keep the hoarseness out of his voice as he added, "You're what I want." He didn't finish the thought out loud, "and I will have you." Caley was good at getting what he wanted, one way or another. He did say, "When?"

Ari didn't know, couldn't answer. The conversation ended soon after. She felt pain at having caused him pain, and perhaps a little guilt, too, although she couldn't have said exactly why. His "when?" began to haunt her.

But then Maximilian King called Caley, inviting him to come to Los Angeles and look again at his investments. He didn't want to go, but it wouldn't have occurred to him to turn down an offer like that. He knew that now was when he ought to go. Barbara King, who was partially responsible for the invitation, wouldn't have welcomed him so warmly if there were a lovely young fiancée in the wings. He told Ari he'd be gone for several weeks. That way she'd have time to think.

The thought was always in Ari's mind, but she had very little time. The campaign had gone into high gear.

Samuel had proved invaluable, and not only because of his willingness to do whatever was required. His "before-and-after" sketch of Bridget's Mountain was displayed on the wall of every shop in town. One side showed the majestic mountain above the canyon's panoramic wilderness, the other gave only a brief glimpse of it hidden behind satellite dishes and chalet roofs. Also, Samuel designed the pin with the outlined face of the mountain that all the visiting skiers bought and took home for a Telluride souvenir. The proceeds went to the Ute Rise fund.

There were so many volunteers that the rented office on Colorado Avenue bulged at the seams. The overflow went into the partially completed downstairs rooms at Ari's house a few blocks away. It would be some months before she could move from the Doral, but having the spacious kitchen restored delighted her, and it was a useful room. The campaign staff often gathered there for morning meetings. Although Ari had the hip bath moved into an upstairs bathroom, the wood-burning range warmed the kitchen almost instantly on the winter days. An old-fashioned blue kettle always stood on top, keeping water ready to be brought quickly to the boil for tea or coffee.

The original oak flooring in the back parlor needed only a final finish, but Ari hadn't yet bought furniture. In the meantime there were cardboard boxes of brochures and computer printouts of donors stacked on card tables in these rooms. But even so the parlor glowed again. New gold silk wallpaper shone on the walls, and the polished Woodbury mantel of hand-carved basket-weave above the hearth gleamed even when no fire was lit. There often was one. Ari had found a huge old sheepskin rug left in the attic, and with its thick fleece newly cleaned, it was comforting to sink down on it in the evening with a cup of cocoa and watch the crackling logs.

She and Janie usually sat there to worry out loud. For it looked as if a total of fifty million would be very hard to raise in a few months. Stewart Wellings said, "Time is your enemy here, Ari." She could hear the concern in the old lawyer's voice. "The terms of your contract with Murdoch are plain. If you can't raise the money for his land by the end of May, *you* have to sell your land to him. He wants to start construction in June."

Neither Janie nor Ari said the word *impossible,* but by February it was in their minds. Late at night, alone, Ari told herself that it would not be a waste of spirit and effort even if Ute Rise Canyon couldn't be saved. The money would then be used to preserve the San Miguel River.

But she would lift her eyes to Bridey's sketch of the mountain, and she would see superimposed on it Samuel's vision of the clutter of satellite dishes and rooftops hiding its upthrusting beauty. "I have to save it, I *have* to," she'd whisper. She'd put aside the book she couldn't concentrate on anyway and get up and pace for hours, trying to think of ways to come up with the money.

She herself had donated six million, and she was paying all the fund-raising costs. But Stewart had firmly tied up the rest of her winnings. Even if she gave it all, it didn't seem likely that the total could be gotten.

Most of the residents, even the newcomers just building palatial homes, were willing to donate, but they were asked to contribute to so many causes. They had their favorite charities that they gave to regularly. Some of them gave as much as five thousand to the preservation of Ute Rise. Caley had sent that amount, and so had several Denver people.

But it took a lot of those checks to make up even a hundred thousand dollars, let alone *one* million. Several corporations, especially those with executives in the valley whom Ari asked personally, gave reasonable sums, but there were guidelines on large gifts. Those usually required lengthy proposals and months of notice. There certainly wasn't time to do that before summer when construction would begin.

However, although time was important, small incidents can affect outcomes. The campaign was changed because Samuel worried about what Janie had for breakfast.

CHAPTER 20

Samuel came into the kitchen of the yellow house on Pacific Avenue, melting snowflakes glistening on his thick chestnut hair and beard. Smiling, he pointed an accusatory finger at Janie, saying, "All you had this morning was coffee. You should never miss breakfast."

Grateful at the sight of food, Ari hurriedly cleared a space on the table where she and Janie had been working. Samuel had brought ripe-red California strawberries, a carton of milk, and a box of all-natural cereal. As they sat eating, Janie tapped the box, and mentioned the president of the firm, who had hosted a party in his home for the campaign. She asked musingly, "Do you think, Ari, if you and I both promised to have very large families and feed the kids only this brand of granola—I'm talking breakfast *and* dinner—that he might consider getting the company to write a really big check?"

"Well"—Ari stared at the strawberry on her spoon—"he personally has been generous, and I'm willing to ask. I don't know." She put down her spoon and winced. "If he sees me at his door again, he might hide behind the couch and then move to Aspen in the middle of the night."

Although all three of them came up with a part of the final plan for saving Ute Rise Canyon, it was certainly Samuel's next remark, which he insisted he'd meant as a joke, that sparked it. He said, "What you ought to ask for is space on the cereal box. Every morning millions of Americans stare at it and if even half of them sent a dollar to save the mountain—" He stopped in surprise because Janie and Ari had both jumped up, looked at each other, and started to dance around the kitchen.

That weekend Ari, carrying a portfolio of sketches and ideas, appeared at the executive's door. He liked the concept so much that he was on the phone to his marketing director by Saturday noon. Everything had to move fast because their plan was centered around Mother's Day, which meant the boxes would have to be on the shelves by April.

The cereal company's design came quite close to what Ari, Janie, and Samuel had in mind, although the company's marketing people and artists refined the approach. On the front of the box was the astronauts' photo of the luminous blue planet that was their home. On the back was a drawing of Bridey's Mountain with its sky-lifted face. The brief history printed below started with the departing Utes turning back in sorrow to look at the valley and their hope that its beauty would remain forever undiminished. It recounted a little of Morna's romantic story, telling how the beautiful Irish noblewoman named the mountain after the woman who had raised her. It ended with her desire that this be forever preserved as it was. *She saw it as a gift of love not only to her daughter Bridget, but to the future,* the copy read.

Even on a cardboard box, the message had the dignity and simplicity of truth.

Above the picture were the words *Send Mom a card from Mother Earth*. By contributing $2.50, one could have the card mailed in time for Mother's Day, and most of the proceeds would go toward conserving this part of America as wilderness. The envelope would be postmarked in Loveland, Colorado.

The card itself, although not expensive to produce, was attractive. On the cover, at the top, the silvery script read *The Face of Love*. A color sketch of Bridey's Mountain in blue tones was framed in a silver oval, a common Victorian design. On the inside flap a short version of the mountain's history appeared. It was followed by this: *Love can move mountains, and* save *them. Because someone loves you, this one will endure as part of our natural heritage.*

The verse on the facing page was short:

Mountains born of Mother Earth
Trace the face of love
Across a span of blue.
That love is strong, will last as long
As, Mother, what I give to you.
In their hearts they hold
Earth's shining riches, too
But all the gold and silver pales
Beside the love I feel for you.

The success of the entire appeal was probably related to the growing concern in America over conservation. Here was something people could do. They could preserve one mountain valley. The history of the Utes also recalled an earlier television image of the Indian, a slow tear on his face, as he eyed a despoiled landscape.

It certainly was a success. Stores could not keep the box in stock. In order to send out all the cards, Blackburn and Barton had to hire a huge temporary staff. The post office in Loveland had to rehire their Valentine's Day workers. On Earth Day in mid-April a poster of Bridey's Mountain was displayed at all the celebrations.

A song entitled "The Face of Love" had a meteoric rise up the charts. It featured a number of well-known folk singers of the sixties, and the lyrics spoke of the love displayed in the beauty of mountain and prairie, in the blossoming of each spring, and how that love should be returned to the earth by its people. It had the warmth of "We Are the World." And its profits went to save the mountain.

Ari was invited on one of the network morning shows before Mother's Day. It drew a large audience. She was a Sweepstakes winner with an absorbing story about her family and a mountain. Not only was her face lovely, it shone with earnestness. Her hands also trembled with nervousness, but no one noticed.

Janie told Samuel when they returned from New York that she'd been afraid Ari was going to shake her fingers loose before she got off-camera. "And," she went on, "even on the way back I couldn't tell if the plane was vibrating or whether that was just Ari. I haven't had the heart to tell her that the producer would like to have her on again when the campaign is over."

These months had telescoped into one for Ari. Time lost its divisions of weeks, days, and hours. She and Janie and Samuel sat up late in the kitchen drinking coffee and making lists of the things that needed doing. Then they would catch a little sleep, get up, and start drinking coffee and making lists. They knew it was morning because phones began their incessant ringing. Winter's shine and whiteness became spring's sleety rain and tentative touches of green. One minute it seemed the main street was crowded with skiers in bright parkas and so many cars, it was impossible to cross. When she looked again, she saw one local resident going into the post office and a stray dog trotting down the middle of the road.

Even the exterior of the house seemed transformed overnight. The six-sided tower that had tilted slightly and huddled in on itself now rose grandly above its neighbors. The paint glistened sunny yellow. The white filigree trim was mint new. The doors with their stained glass windows swung open from the solid, sweeping veranda. But Ari only stopped a minute to admire before hurrying into the spacious rooms still filled only with card tables and business forms.

Caley had repeatedly urged her to buy furniture before renovating the house. But she couldn't, although she'd have felt foolish explaining that neither she nor the house wanted to wait.

Her personal life was confined to the phone and the mail. Sybil sent cheerful updates from Ireland. She wrote, *I've pulled a real switch. The Irish always went to America to make their fortune, but I came here to make mine. There are so many Americans over here who want help finding their ancestors that I'm in real demand. Cousin Rose is the biggest help. We're going back to Daire in May to try again with old Fergus. Maybe this time we'll have the best of Irish luck.*

Caley called regularly from Los Angeles, but their talks were usually strained. To reach her he often had to try the hotel, the downtown campaign office, and the house, only to be told Ari was in between them. There was always irritation at this in his voice when he got her, and she felt his discontent almost weighing down the phone line.

He said he was satisfied with the investments he was choosing for Maximilian King, and more than satisfied with the commissions he was earning. Sometimes he could be coaxed into telling her amusing stories about Hollywood parties and all the celebrities he met. But there was usually an underlying edge in his words to remind her that he hated being away from her, that it was she who'd decided they'd be apart. It was becoming impossible for her not to feel guilty at causing his unhappiness.

Ari longed for the way things had been between them, remembering the lighthearted laughter and the easy closeness. She was more than ever convinced that once she had time, it'd be that way again. Each day she was more and more sure that she would marry Caley. The idea had become part of her framework of thought. But she never said, "Yes, I will, when this is over."

"You could at least agree, Ari, that we can be *engaged* at the end of this . . . campaign of yours," he'd argued more than once. "Surely you could take one weekend off. Just forty-eight hours. We could meet in Denver, stay at the Brown Palace. We had our first dinner there." His voice became rough with insistence. "You need a rest. I'll have them serve all our meals in bed."

The last time he called, he'd said, "I knew you before you were born. You know we belong together." The words sent an odd shiver along her arms. She had the feeling that in marrying Caley she'd complete a circle. But she couldn't even give him a date for an engagement. Ari couldn't persuade herself that it was fair to him until she was able to be wholehearted in her acceptance.

She hadn't heard from Rivers, but she'd heard *of* him. On the last weekend of the ski season she'd been opening the outside door of the downtown office when she heard a woman's voice calling to her from across the street. Heather Murdoch pulled off her headband and shook out her curls as she came toward her, saying, "I just left a message for you at the hotel. Scott and I flew up on the spur of the moment to ski and we were hoping you'd have dinner with us tonight. Lots of gossip and things to talk about. Are you free?"

"Oh, I'm sorry. I'm not." Ari did have a dinner scheduled with a donor and his wife, but she wasn't sorry. She didn't want to hear about Judith and Rivers.

Heather rushed right on. "Well, I know that *you'll* be back in Denver soon. We can get together then. We're all looking forward to great parties this summer. Is Caley here?"

There was a certain archness to her tone, but Ari didn't notice because she was trying to think of a quick and graceful way to end the conversation. She replied, "No, he's in Los Angeles. Business trip." She opened the door partway, adding, "I should get going. So nice to see you and my best to Judith."

"But, speaking of Judith, I have to tell you." Heather put her hand on Ari's arm. "You wouldn't recognize her! I didn't and she's my own sister. She's blooming. I've never seen her look so good. She's working so hard in Washington on the lobbying. It's what we women have always known, right? We need work, a cause, something to devote ourselves to just as men do."

She rushed on, hardly drawing a breath. "I'm always saying to

Scott that this divorce will be the best thing that ever happened to her. Before, what did she do? Her little committees. Then, she waited around for Quentin to come home. Well, she had her sports. She really misses the skiing here. But she and Rivers get away to Vermont, even though it's nothing like—"

"That's our phone inside, Heather. I better get it. Staff's not in today. Good to see you." But Ari let the phone ring for a bit before she reached for it with a shaking hand. She was trying to dispel the image of a romantic lodge in snowy Vermont.

Yet she had too much to do to dwell obsessively on it. The campaign was succeeding. By the second week in May they'd gone past the halfway point and were closing in on thirty million. Still, they had a long way to go to fifty.

Blackburn and Barton called with weekly reports, and the contributions from the cereal boxes were pouring in. Many people sent far more than the two dollars and fifty cents asked. But after Mother's Day there were naturally far fewer donations.

By the third week in May the only question was how far short of their goal they would fall. Ari could no longer look at Bridey's sketch that hung so proudly in the back parlor. All she could do was worry about money. Walking through the house, stopping to touch the old range for luck, she winced as she remembered a year ago when she'd won the Sweepstakes. On that sunny hilltop she'd thought she'd never have that worry again.

There was only one more week. Under the terms of the agreement, if she didn't have the money, she'd have to sell Bridey's Mountain to Jonas Murdoch.

CHAPTER 21

Bur Ari had one last plan. She'd
always known what she would do to save her mountain. She was quite
clear in her own mind that she wanted to do it, and she felt lucky that
she had the chance. But she was sure that other people were not going
to accept her decision readily.

The campaign was some fifteen million dollars short. And, in a
year's time, the lottery board would give her the fifteen million of her
winnings. She was going to offer it all to Jonas Murdoch. She couldn't
imagine that he wouldn't be willing to wait for the final payment.

When she'd told Janie and Samuel, Janie had groaned, put her
head in her hands, and without looking up, said, "We knew you would.
It's kept me awake nights. Ari, a year ago you had a fortune. You won't
have much left. You already gave so much. I can't bear it." Whooshing
out her breath, she added, "Knowing you, I'm not going to waste time
trying to talk you out of it. Maybe I even agree. I just don't know if *I*
could do it."

Samuel simply embraced Ari and said nothing.

They had, of course, looked at the problem from various angles, suggested alternative solutions. But all three had known this was the only way. It was the last week of May. They had no time.

It took Ari a few hours of pacing before she finally called Stewart Wellings to tell him. She felt she had to marshal her arguments against all of his possible objections. During the campaign they'd become fast friends. He'd always been ready with sound suggestions and legal advice. He'd listened to her worries, encouraged her efforts, and sent a very generous contribution of his own. But what had meant most to her was his interest and his unmistakable pride in what she'd accomplished. When she'd returned from New York and her appearance on the network, she'd found flowers and a card from him reading, *What I would have wanted in a daughter, I see in you.*

Still, she didn't believe he would agree with her decision. He'd too often counseled investments for the second lottery payment that would assure her future and that of her children.

But when he picked up the phone, he sounded unhappy even before she'd told him. "Ari," he said, "I had lunch at the University Club in Denver, and I heard the news. It bothers me that we didn't discuss this before now. The legal work alone takes time. There's the change of will, pre—"

"What are you talking about, Stewart?" Ari interrupted in astonishment.

"Your engagement," he answered. She heard the reproach in his voice as he went on, "I knew you were friendly with Caley Sutherland. He's called me several times. But you should have told me of this."

"But I'm not engaged to Caley," Ari answered quickly.

"Oh." Stewart's relief was clear. Hearing that she was had spoiled his lunch, and he'd been upset ever since. "My friend must have been misinformed. He was so positive that I didn't question him. Mere gossip, then."

"Not exactly. I am thinking of it." When Stewart said nothing, she continued, "Caley's a wonderful man. And he's done so much for me."

Stewart's surprising silence made her feel that she had to explain the fact that she'd hesitated at all in the matter. So she went on, "It was just that I wasn't sure I was quite ready for marriage. All the changes I've already gone through in the last year made me want to consider it carefully. But I think the world of Caley. Maybe I didn't tell you but he was a good friend of both my parents. In fact, he was with my father when he died."

Stewart's dislike of Caley had begun at that bedside in Canada. And his opinion of the man had never gotten better. He'd heard of some business dealings that had really disturbed him. When he'd

learned of Ari's friendship with him, he'd debated dropping a discreet
hint to her. But a lifetime of caution had held him back. He had nothing
but rumor to base his misgivings on. Even his belief that Caley was
partly responsible for Christopher Roth's death was just a belief. But he
certainly knew that Sutherland wasn't with him when he died. That was
something he was going to say.

"I'm afraid you've been misinformed there." Stewart explained
that he'd been Ceci Caley's executor, had been searching for her grandson, and had himself sat with Christopher. "I didn't want to tell you,"
Stewart finished, "because it added nothing to what you knew. And I
felt it might cause you pain."

Whenever Ari thought of her father—that laughing boy in faded
Polaroids—she'd felt real pity. The idea that he'd had only a stranger to
mourn him did cause a wrench of the heart. She recalled that Caley had
never been able to talk about his death. Now she guessed he'd been
overwhelmed by guilt because he *hadn't* been there. Somewhere in the
back of her mind was a regret that Caley hadn't been able to tell her
that himself. But just then she was imagining the scene Stewart had
described. It did hurt. She was quiet.

Stewart immediately felt remorse that he'd brought it up. "I'm
sorry. Maybe you didn't need to hear that."

"No, I am glad you told me," Ari answered slowly. "As a matter of
fact, you aren't going to like what I'm going to tell you either."

But when she said she was going to use the rest of her winnings to
buy the canyon, Stewart's reply was prompt. "Yes." He drew out the
word. "I've been watching this campaign like a bettor with his last
dollar on a horse, knowing what you'd do if it didn't completely succeed. You know I can't approve. You'll be left with your house and a
sufficient income. But very few people ever get the amount of money
you have, and the choices and freedoms it would have given you will be
gone. But from what you said in the beginning, I was sure you had your
mind made up about what was important to you. Even the most skilled
advocate can't change that kind of thinking. I wouldn't try. But I have
two things to say that you must listen to, even though you won't like
them."

"I will. Fair's fair," Ari agreed.

"First, my dear"—he paused hesitant before going on—"because
I know you, I'm certain that your decision here wouldn't influence your
choice of a husband, but—"

To the lawyer's surprise Ari interrupted him with an affectionate
laugh. "You're tiptoeing, Stewart, aren't you?" She imagined him raising his tufted eyebrows and adjusting his half-glasses as he carefully

picked his words. She explained, "You're worried that, since I'm giving away my money, I might be more inclined to marry Caley because he's rich. No. He's been genuinely good to me. He's a fine man."

Stewart listened to her with foreboding. His view of Sutherland was very different from hers, but he couldn't say that. It bothered him, too, that in the entire conversation Ari had never said she *loved* Caley. Still, he bit back his words. He tried telling himself that many an older man had proved a doting husband to a young and beautiful wife. That might happen here. Sutherland must be rather different than he'd imagined him to be if he accepted this decision of hers. Then a thought struck Stewart, and he asked, "What does he think of your signing over the rest of your winnings?"

"I haven't told him yet," Ari replied. "He's working in Los Angeles. I'm going to call him this evening."

This cheered Wellings enormously. While he personally thought that any man would be lucky to get Ari, he had the distinct impression from his phone calls that Sutherland was equally interested in her money. That had probably never occurred to Ari simply because he already had so much. The young cannot help their lack of experience, he thought, but maybe Sutherland would give himself away. Stewart smiled for the first time since lunch. It'd be the best thing that could happen. It didn't seem to the old lawyer that Ari's heart was in real jeopardy now, and he could not imagine her happy later with Caley Sutherland.

"You must tell me what he says. He's . . . an astute businessman." Then Stewart's smile faded. He was dreading what he had to say next. "Ari, you have to consider that Murdoch might not be willing to wait. The second installment is not due for a year, and you cannot borrow against lottery winnings from a bank."

She was taken aback. "Jonas knows that I'll get it, though. It's only a matter of months. Are you thinking he'll want interest on the unpaid balance?"

"That's something we'd have to work out with him. But I mean that according to the terms of the contract, he has the right to refuse. I talked to him several times while we were negotiating that contract, and Murdoch has never wanted to sell. At fifty million he still loses a lot of money."

"But he agreed to do it! Why would he change his mind just because he doesn't get it all now? It's just a . . . technicality."

"He can argue that you now have to sell to him. That's probably what he wants. *You* agreed that if you didn't have the money by June first, you would do so."

"Stewart." Ari's voice was tense with worry. "He can't back out. Think of the national attention, the . . . media coverage. People would be furious. They bought cards, gave their money, thinking they were saving the mountain. His company would get the kind of the publicity that would ruin—"

Stewart cut in. "He doesn't have to worry about that. Not really. His firm's stock is not sold over the counter or on Wall Street. He doesn't run a business that could be affected by public opinion. He invests money—his own and that of his associates. He can reasonably assert that this is not a good investment for any of them."

"I don't understand. I don't." Ari could hardly swallow around the lump of fear in her throat. "Well, I can see that he can use this to get out of the deal. But why did he agree in the first place?"

"Because he didn't think you could raise anything close to fifty million. Then, you'd have to sell to him without any further delay. It'd never occur to him that you'd put in *all* that you had. Maybe, too, he wanted to appear concerned about the environment, thinking it wouldn't cost him anything. As a matter of fact"—Stewart stopped, and then sounded even more concerned as he continued—"that's the second thing I heard at lunch. Congress granted a delay on the cleanup for Consolidated Chemical. Alexander was successful in his lobbying. Murdoch has no further need to care about how he looks to the senators."

"Wait." Ari struggled for any hope. "What about these associates of his? Surely they might urge him to preserve the canyon, given all that people have done."

Stewart wanted very much to console her, but he didn't want to offer thin straws. "I know two I can call. They're the kind that might see it your way. But I'm afraid that most of them will rubber-stamp whatever Jonas wants. Certainly E. L. Bascomb, one of the richest, will support him. None of them likes losing money. That this is a good cause won't sway them." Stewart's voice grew harsh with his own disappointment. "These men know the public memory is short. In three or four years when the project is completed, newcomers will buy houses in Ute Rise, only remembering it was famous for something or other."

Ari didn't respond to this, and Wellings could imagine her pain, the slump of her shoulders. He found it very hard to bear. At last he added, "Let me see what I can do. I'll speak to him right now. But I'm sure we won't know for a few days, in any case. He won't say no outright."

After she hung up the phone, Ari simply sat, stunned, twisting her ring around her finger. She'd always seen the rest of the money as a fallback. No matter how she'd worried, she'd never believed she could fail because of that. Part of the force of this realization that she could fail came from her feeling that once again she hadn't understood how things were, how they worked. She hadn't ever examined what lay behind Murdoch's offer. She thought she'd learned so much in the last year. Now she could see she could be wrong about that.

But she was determined not to give up. Hope came back. She'd ask Caley to help. He'd know how to talk to Jonas. Yes, Ari told herself, this would work. Caley might well offer to loan her the fifteen million. From what Janie had said, he could afford to do that. Of course she'd insist on interest. It wouldn't have to have anything to do with their relationship. Straightforward business. She glanced at her watch. He might be available now.

"Ari," he said, with pleasure in his voice. "I wasn't expecting you to call." He waited with anticipation for what she'd say next.

She told him that she was offering the second fifteen million dollars to Jonas Murdoch.

The words burst from Caley before he could think. "I can't believe it. Have you gone—"

"Please, Caley. I know how this will make you worry about me. Don't. I've thought it through. I'll have enough money. But first, just listen."

It was all he could do. He was clenching his teeth. His throat was closed with anger. The blood pounded in his temples.

Ari went on to explain that Stewart felt Jonas would use her request for a year's wait to enforce the contract. She begged him to talk to Jonas, to persuade him to wait.

As she spoke, Caley began to calm down. He realized it wasn't bad news, it was good news. He rubbed the back of his neck, telling himself he'd gotten hair-trigger over the last months and wasn't thinking clearly. Jonas wouldn't wait—not one day. He must have been praying for an excuse not to sell. If Ari hadn't been spending so much on the campaign, the whole thing would have amused Caley enormously, since he knew Murdoch had to be sweating it. The cereal boxes, her appearance on the network show. People responded to that sort of thing by sending money.

He had kept close track and had known that she wouldn't make it. It'd just never crossed his mind that she'd want to pledge the rest. He still couldn't believe it. But Caley realized this was all going to play to his advantage. He'd just have to think it through.

"Jonas will listen to you, Caley," Ari was saying. "You're my only hope. I'm sorry to ask you to do this, but I've never wanted anything so much."

He saw he should get off the phone immediately. "I can't imagine what I wouldn't do to make you happy, Ari. I'll certainly talk to him, and in person. I'll catch the first plane that I can. It might be late when I get into Denver tonight, but I'll call you. Now, don't worry. Let me handle this. I can't promise that it'll work out, but I'll do all I can."

It was going to work out and just the way he wanted it, Caley thought, grinning and leaning back in his chair. Now Murdoch was going to have to buy the mountain from Ari. That would help her net worth some. She wouldn't want to live in Telluride with her mountain gone, and the house would make an ideal bed-and-breakfast. Should be able to clear some more on that.

Jonas, of course, would be hard to deal with for a while. He didn't even like the word *media,* and reporters from all over would be clamoring at his door. His associates, who were putting up part of the construction costs, wouldn't like it either. All of them preferred a low profile and most of them even kept their names out of society columns. They'd be bitching. Good ol' boy Bascomb would be getting his knife into Jonas. And Jonas would blame Caley. As he recalled, he'd guaranteed she wouldn't come up with the money. Well, she hadn't.

He tried to think of other problems. The ConChem delay was settled, so there was no worry about public relations in the Capitol anymore. Two of the associates might urge Jonas to honor the spirit of the agreement and sell, especially when they heard Ari was giving all she had. That'd get his back up even more, and he wouldn't listen to them. No, Jonas would be hard to live with, but he'd be prepared to ride out the storm.

Caley knew Jonas didn't give a damn about the man in the street. He did enjoy having the good opinion of his peers. In Denver's little pond he was a giant frog. He wanted the bowing and scraping at the Petroleum Club, at the country clubs. He'd think that in the case of Ute Rise, other businessmen would understand if he said he'd have to take too large a loss on the land.

As Caley stood up and began to stuff papers into his attaché case, he was thinking of ways to soothe Jonas so he could wrangle a better price out of him. But then another idea struck him and he sat down again abruptly.

Suppose that Ari suggested he himself loan her the money. He drew out his cigar case and lit one, blowing out the smoke slowly. He'd have to forestall her by bringing it up himself and explaining that there was no way he could get his hands on that much right now. He could tell her he was tied up in real estate and long-term investments. He could even say fifteen million was beyond his reach in any case. Yes. There was no way she'd know how much he was worth.

Caley checked his watch and snapped the case shut with a satisfied click. He'd tell King and Barbara he'd been called back to Denver on urgent business. It was urgent. His grin grew wider. Ari was bound to appreciate his efforts, even though she'd be very unhappy at the way things turned out. He'd insist that she needed to get away. Mexico would be hot now, but the house was on the ocean. On a deserted beach. Clothes would be unnecessary. He closed the attaché case with an even more decisive snap.

CHAPTER 22

The house itself seemed to be waiting with Ari that night. She'd had that feeling ever since she'd walked up the path, that it was sharing her apprehension. The lilac bushes along the veranda still had tightly curled buds, not yet ready to relax into bloom. Glancing around inside, she thought the sensation might be due to the emptiness now that the card tables, stored boxes, and computer forms from the campaign had been removed. From the front parlor, through the dining room, to the back parlor, there was only an expanse of shining floor. The sheepskin rug before the fireplace had been rolled up. The air in the deserted rooms was filled with anxious expectancy.

The absolute quiet heightened her impression of held breath. Pacific Avenue was dimly lit and silent. The festivals that attracted the crowds of summer hadn't started. She looked through the stained glass of the front doors and could see no lights on in the neighboring houses. Within her own, not a floorboard creaked or faucet dripped. Even the birds nesting in the eaves had settled in for sleep.

It was late, but she hadn't wanted to go back to the hotel. Caley would call here if she didn't answer there. Ari knew that he wouldn't have anything to tell her tonight, but she looked forward to hearing his reassuring voice. A hundred times that afternoon and evening she'd told herself, as well as Janie and Samuel, that he would persuade Murdoch or know a way to solve the problem. There was nothing anyone else could do. She was enormously grateful that he was part of her life.

When the phone rang at last, Ari was in the kitchen and she leapt for it. "I'm back," Caley said, and there was more emotion in his voice than she'd ever heard before when he added, "and everything here reminds me of you."

"I'm so happy—and relieved—that you're here." Ari meant exactly that.

He hesitated, as if the next words were hard to say. "There's only one thing that bothers me, Ari, and I have to tell you this up front. I did some intense figuring on the plane, hoping that I could come up with the cash for Jonas. But I'm not Jonas, and I haven't got anything close to fifteen million myself. It would take several months for me to realize any substantial sum from my Denver real estate, and at that it'd be a fire sale and I'd lose heavily."

She swallowed hard. She'd seen a loan from Caley as a real hope, since Murdoch couldn't back out if she had the cash in hand. But she appreciated that he wanted to offer it, and she said so.

"Ari, I'd give it to you if I could. You know that. But there's still real hope. To persuade Jonas I've got a carrot and a stick. I'll consider his tax situation tonight. If I can make him see that there'd be substantial tax savings if his loss is regarded as a charitable donation, he'll have to rethink."

Caley sounded quite cheerful as he went on, "The stick I've got is the size of a two-by-four. His refusal to sell when you're only asking a year's grace will hit the front pages. Reporters will characterize him as a Scrooge of a billionaire and splash his actual holdings in full view. His associates will also get scrutinized, and some of them have dealings in their past that they certainly won't want raked up. E. L. Bascomb walked away from the Texas savings-and-loan crash with millions, and the American taxpayers had to pick up the check."

Ari let out her breath. "Caley, you are wonderful. I knew that if anyone could, *you* could do this. I'll always be grateful."

"I only wish I could *guarantee* that it'll work. Still, there's a very good chance. Now, remember, I don't want you to worry. I'll work on the figures tonight—all night if I have to—and get to Jonas first thing in the morning with my ideas. And win, lose, or draw, I'll be in Telluride with you tomorrow night. Chill some champagne for us."

After Ari hung up, she sat at the kitchen table, still wrapped in the warmth of his words. She decided then that she would marry him. In fact, she'd call him back now and tell him so. If she waited until tomorrow night, he might feel she was simply moved by gratitude. She wanted him to understand that her yes was based on her feelings about him. She wanted to tell him how much he meant to her.

Standing up to go to the phone, she remembered that there was an open bottle of sherry in one of the cupboards. She could tell Caley that she was proposing a toast, even though he wasn't there. But there were only coffee mugs on the shelves and two champagne flutes. Ari hastily took out a mug. Those were the glasses that Rivers had given her.

As she poured the wine, her hand shook a little at the thought of Rivers, of the day they'd met. But she'd gone over that so many times and had sorted out to her satisfaction why she must have been so attracted to him. She was very lonely. For four years after Mrs. Mac's death all she'd done was attend classes, work at the bank, and then return to that small basement apartment. She wanted someone to love, someone to love her. Even at the time she'd probably not guessed how much she wanted that. Then there he was with that smile. There was the way he looked at her that made her feel he was wrapping her warmly in his arms even when he wasn't. When he did, she mistook that for the love she wanted.

But Ari was sure the feelings she had for Rivers couldn't be trusted. On his part they must have been superficial, easily transferable to another woman. He seemed so sincere that anyone could have been fooled. She had been.

Rubbing the sides of her arms, Ari thought about how much Caley loved her and all he'd done that showed that. She respected him, admired— Suddenly, she felt goose bumps through the thin linen sleeves of her shirt. It was cold in here. Very cold. There must be open windows in the back parlor, and the mist off the river was coming in. Spring nights in the mountains could feel like February. She hurried in to shut them.

Even before she ran her hands over their tightly sealed frames, the fear started. It was exactly that irrational fear that gripped the sleeper waking from a nightmare. Everything the eye lit upon had a threatening shape, even a harmless chair. She was immobilized by it, and it was a phantom her mind couldn't grasp. There was no reason for this nameless panic.

Groping, she clutched the fireplace mantel and tried to take in air through her open mouth. When her eyes focused, she was staring at Bridey's drawing. There was no comfort there. It was shadowy in the light from the kitchen, and the mountain looked ominous. The face couldn't be recognized on the stern dark summit.

Then she smelled the lilacs. The scent was unmistakable and as insistent as the first time she'd entered the house. But the flowers by the porch hadn't opened, and she could hardly have smelled them back here. She knew that. But she was going to go look at them again, to check. It would at least make her move from this spot she'd seemed rooted to since she'd stiffened with fear. There was an explanation, there had to be.

When she reached the front hall, Ari heard a sound that stopped her abruptly. It was the rustle of fabric, of silk on silk. She strained her ears. She was certain. It was the sound she had heard the day she arrived. It came from upstairs. But there were no drapes on the windows, not even shower curtains in the bathrooms. The upper two floors were absolutely empty.

Trembling, she leaned against the newel post of the banister and closed her eyes. She did her best to push down her dread, to think. She took a few deep breaths. That helped. She inhaled again, telling herself that the tension she'd been under was responsible for this. It was making her imagine things. Probably a classic panic attack. That was it, of course.

She opened her eyes, arched her back, revolved her shoulders. She would be calm. As she turned to head back to the cheerful kitchen, she saw a gleam of gold, a chain pooled on the hall floor. Thinking it must be one of Janie's or that a volunteer had lost it, Ari bent down to pick it up. The fear leapt out in nightmare force. Her hand froze halfway to the floor. That was what happened in the dream each time she had it. She would be leaning over, searching the water of the stream for her ruby ring, and the white hand would come up holding it, but the chain would manacle her wrist. This one, too, would coil upward, clutch her.

She couldn't move her arm. The smell of lilacs grew more insistent. The silken fabric whispered to her, saying, "No, no, no." Now she couldn't breathe at all.

The sound of the ringing phone seemed the bell sound of that incomprehensible dream. When she realized it was the phone, she ran, stumbling against the table, knocking over the mug of sherry. "Hello." She swallowed, tried to repeat the word.

"Ari. Is that you? I can hardly hear . . . have we got a good connection?" Sybil's voice reached across the Atlantic, sounding as if she were in the next room.

"Yes. Yes. Oh, Sybil, I'm so glad you called." Ari sank down into the wooden chair, her legs unable to hold her weight.

Excitement made Sybil's words run together. "You'll have to tell me all your news, my dear. But now, I've known for two days, and I'm going to burst if I don't tell you mine. I know what happened to Morna! I know all about it."

All Ari could manage was "How? Did Mad Fergus finally tell you?"

"He told us, you and I, the first time we met him!" Sybil gave Ari no chance to interrupt, rushing on. "But first of all I have to tell you what happened on this last trip. This time he recognized me, and I think Rose, too, but he had to start all over again on the guineas. We tried to rush him through the story, but he was as determined as ever to convince us that they existed. So he went on about how the pouch was always kept in an old chest and how he went to look in it after his father's death. You remember."

Ari could again see the old man, eyes milky with cataracts, standing in a roofless room gesturing with grimy hands. "Maybe not his exact words, but—"

"He said that when he looked for the pouch of guineas, 'there was nowt.' But this time, he insisted Rose and I follow him into the great hall, with the idea, I suppose, that if we saw the chest, we'd have to believe there were once guineas in it. He scooped rubble out of that enormous fireplace, pulled out a battered leather case—more a box than a chest—and opened it. "Nowt," he repeated. But that case wasn't empty. There was no pouch, but there were papers."

"Papers?" Ari repeated.

"I mean documents, old deeds on parchment, and some letters. One of them the last the laird ever received. He must have just shoved it into that case with his important papers for safekeeping until his return. That letter was sent from London, and it made him leave immediately. It told him where Morna was."

"Sybil," Ari breathed. "Who wrote it?"

"It's only signed 'Colette.' No last name. It's on that old-fashioned rag paper, and the ink is only a little faded. I'll read it.

"Mon cher Monsieur. *I have information that I understand you want very much. It is regarding your wife. You will do me the favor of not revealing my name, but I wish to sign this letter so you will take what I say as my word.*

"*She is using the name Morna Gregory and she is in Telluride, Colorado, in the United States of America. If you go there, you will have no trouble finding her as it is a small mining camp.*

"*I do not lie to you. I lived under the same roof as this woman.*

"*There is no need for you to feel further anger toward Monsieur*

Stanton Caley. He will no longer pursue the idea that you will divorce her. He no longer has any personal interest in your wife. I promise this. He is leaving England on the next boat, and he is not returning to the United States.

"*I repeat. As you are a gentleman, you will not reveal how you have discovered her.*

"That's it," Sybil finished. "Then she signs her first name. Not much guarantee that it's the truth, but she sounded like she somehow thought it was more believable than no signature."

"Who was Colette?" Ari burst out. "And—"

"And why did she do that to Morna?" Sybil interrupted. "That's what you're wondering. Right? Me too. She must have known Morna was trying desperately to keep the laird from finding her."

"Well," Ari went on slowly, "if she lived with Morna, it must have been at Miss Freda's."

"Yes." Sybil sighed. "And you're not going to find employment records from that place at the Town Hall. I had two days to think this over, and I've thought of nothing else. Obviously, though, she wants to keep the laird away from Stanton Caley, whoever he is."

"I know who he is, Sybil. I told you about my friend Caley Sutherland here in Denver. He's his grandfather."

"Really?" Sybil was all interest. "Do you suppose he'd know anything?"

"I'll certainly ask," Ari replied, "but he would have told me if he did. I told him about Morna, and he's talked a lot about Stanton. He's mentioned his grandmother too. She was French, but her name wasn't Colette. And from what he said about her, I *know* she didn't work at Miss Freda's."

"At first," Sybil went on, "I guessed that maybe Stanton Caley was a friend of Berkeley's, maybe trying to talk the laird into a divorce on his behalf. But that's not the impression Colette gives. She says that Stanton no longer has a 'personal interest' in Morna. And if he was only a go-between, she'd point that out, as worried as she sounds that the laird will come after *him*. But we can talk that over later. I want to tell you the rest, even though I don't think it'll make you happy. I know how she—and the laird—died."

"Tell me. Hurry," Ari replied. "It's amazing that you could find out."

"It's as I said. Mad Fergus told us the day we first went to Daire. He said the earth opened up and swallowed the laird. Remember?"

"Well, yes," Ari said slowly. "But, Sybil, that's just a common expression that people use when they don't know what's happened to someone. It just means the person disappeared, vanished off the face of the earth, or something like that. Doesn't it?"

"Of course. And that's what we both thought. But a few weeks ago I started to think about that, mainly because of what Fergus said next. He wondered how the laird got out to come back and haunt the castle."

Puzzled, Ari pushed her hair back off her forehead. She couldn't imagine what Sybil meant. "But he's called Mad Fergus and that does sound a little—"

"Yes, yes," Sybil broke in. "Loon crazy. But suppose Fergus was speaking *literally*. That makes a kind of daft-sense if he believed that the earth really *did* swallow the laird. And, Ari, we know from the *Peerage* that Morna and the laird died in 1906. What happened that year?"

The repeated sound of the word *earth* was what caused it to spring into Ari's mind. "The San Francisco earthquake . . . But what would they have been doing in San Francisco?"

"Exactly what bothered me!" Sybil returned. "We always assumed that once Morna was aware her husband knew of her whereabouts, that she wrote to tell him to meet her. And she'd obviously want it somewhere at a great distance from Telluride. But New York would surely be logical. That's where the laird would be arriving from Ireland. So I put it out of my mind for a couple of days. But it kept niggling at me. If I'd been at home, I'd have gone right to the library to check old newspapers for the lists of those killed. Finally, I couldn't stand it and Rose and I went off to Dublin to the university libraries."

Now, mixed in Sybil's voice with the joy of her discovery, was a catch of sorrow. "Their names were both on the list. There was even a short side article headlined 'Irish Nobleman and Wife Killed/Visitors to City.' "

As Sybil read it aloud, went on recounting the sparse details, tears began to slide down Ari's face.

". . . Valencia Hotel," Sybil was saying. "It was on the waterfront, where the worst damage was. That hotel was wooden, and it collapsed completely, killing almost everyone instantly. Now, if they'd been staying on Nob Hill at the Fairmount Hotel, which had just been built, they would have been in no danger. And, Ari . . ." Sybil paused, as if unsure whether she ought to go on.

"I know what you're going to say," Ari said, with tears even in her throat, "you're going to say she knew. That that's why she told him to meet her in San Francisco. She didn't feel Berkeley would ever be safe as long as the laird was alive. Somehow she knew, she saw something, and she went knowing she'd die too."

"Yes," Sybil answered slowly. "We're both Celtic, so we can believe that. And don't forget, Morna had to worry about Bridey too. She was still married to the laird when the child was born. Legally, he might have had some claim. Certainly, if he could spirit her away to Daire, where he was the law, he could have kept her always."

Imagining a child on that grim island, Ari shivered with cold. Rubbing her hands, she saw the rubies' blood-red shine on her finger. "She left the ring here, Sybil. She wouldn't have left Berkeley's gift if she hadn't known she wasn't coming back. She wanted Bridey to have it."

"I hope, Ari, that I haven't made you sad. I sat down to write all this so I could send you copies of what I have, but I couldn't wait." Sybil was quiet and then, trying for her usual friendly tone, asked, "Now, what news of the campaign?"

"I'll know tomorrow, Sybil, so let me call you. And thanks, thanks again. I think I needed to hear this tonight."

After she'd hung up, Ari sat still at the table for a long time. The force of all the day's emotions left her exhausted and drained of any. At last she reached around to the counter in back of her, picked up a dish towel, and wiped her eyes.

It was then she was aware that she wasn't alone. Morna was there. Ari knew it. She didn't smell lilacs or hear a skirt's silken whispers. But there was her presence, here in the house where she'd known those happy years. It was comforting.

Ari felt none of the fear that had gripped her before. That had nothing to do with Morna. It seemed quite natural to talk to her. She said, "I don't have your courage. Or your love." Ari even absentmindedly mopped up the spilled sherry with the dish towel as she went on, "But I'm trying my best to save your mountain. Our mountain."

Getting up, she rinsed out the mug and put the damp towel in the sink. "I just wish I had your way of knowing things. If only I could have inherited your second sight, along with the ring and the dress. I can't even understand my own dreams, especially the one that keeps trying to tell me something." She turned to face only empty air. Then she smiled at herself. It was time to lock up the house, go back to the Doral at Mountain Village, and see if she could get some sleep.

Then she recalled the gold chain and that it needed to be put someplace for safekeeping. It wasn't on the table, so she opened all the drawers near the phone, thinking she'd stuck it in one of them while she was talking to Sybil. They were empty. She checked under the table, on the counter tops.

Probably, she thought, she'd just never picked it up and it was still on the hallway floor. But, although she turned on all the overhead lights and looked everywhere, it wasn't to be found.

CHAPTER 23

"Jonas." Caley's tone was sardonic, but there was a hint of chill amusement in his voice at the idea. "Do you really think I'd bring fifteen million to the meeting this afternoon so you'd have to sell Ute Rise to her? I'm going to marry the girl, so her money will soon be mine. Why would I give it to you? Especially for rocks and trees."

Murdoch had tried to keep his own emotion tamped down. "You have an inclination toward fun and ga—"

"That'd be pretty expensive fun," Caley had cut in. "No. It's all going to go the way I just laid out. I'll come this afternoon and persuade your troops not to panic. I've got a couple of good arguments for them. Everyone has to be reminded that the shouting will be over in a very few weeks. You can go ahead and build now. I'll put some of *your* money in my pocket when you give Ari a nice piece of change for her mountain. We're together on this. It'll work. Relax."

After he hung up, every pore of Murdoch's skin felt irritated. Despite the fact that his perfectly tailored shirt was made of the finest cotton broadcloth, he felt as if he were wearing a hair shirt. His left eyelid twitched, and it seemed to be sandpapering his eyeball. He couldn't swallow around the incipient rage that had solidified at the base of his throat. Massaging his temples, he tried to get his thoughts in order, knowing that this afternoon it'd be far better to get the unanimous support of his associates on the Ute Rise deal. And he had to put his trust in Sutherland, of all people.

Thinking about developing that land had for several years brought Jonas nothing but pleasure. Telluride had gone from a dead end to the most expensive box canyon in all of Colorado. His wife's family had owned the property for two generations, it was free and clear, and it was ideally situated. All of his associates were eager to be included.

The fact that the MacAllister girl had part of it hadn't even been a cloud wisp on his horizon then. But the spring floods and winter avalanches that had once torn through that valley were no more destructive to it than she'd been to his interior landscape. Now, the best possible outcome Jonas could envision was painful to contemplate. For if he held her to the contract and she was forced to sell to him, he and his associates would be at the mercy of fire ants, locusts, and grasshoppers in the form of reporters. Unfavorable publicity would not normally disturb him, but some of his associates were vulnerable.

Bascomb had been calling three times a day, and there wasn't any need for a telephone to hear him bellowing from the other side of Denver. Most of the others had rung almost as frequently, some with fear in their voices. Business could not be conducted at this level without some locked closets full of bones being discovered. The national press had a way of finding keys. Murdoch's spare features tightened almost into fleshlessness as he wondered how well several of his own unpleasant secrets were secured. Even what was standard sharp business practice looked unsavory when dragged onto the front page.

Abruptly he pulled his memorandum book toward him. This kind of scrutiny would even affect his present operations. He'd better speak to the two ConChem executives he'd been involved with regarding plans for the use of the cleanup reserve fund. They mustn't speak to *anyone* about it.

He rapidly jotted down several other notes. Rivers was due back anyway, but now he would have to come tomorrow to handle the reporters, and that job would take a couple of weeks. Dexter certainly couldn't do that—he couldn't think on his feet. But that meant Alexander couldn't be at Ute Rise when construction started. Payton Cross was competent and loyal but no good at the financial end. So Dexter would have to look after—

Jonas sent his expensive pen sliding across his onyx desk in outrage at the next thought. There would be pickets at the construction site. Environmentalists from all over would show up, and some of the Telluride residents would be bitter. They couldn't legally interfere with the work, but Dexter would argue with them instead of smooth them down. Cross was explosive, as Rivers had said. And then there were the hard hats always spoiling for a fight.

Trying to relax his rigid back, Jonas leaned into the Moroccan leather chair. All through the last weeks of Ari MacAllister's campaign, his shoulders had steadily tightened. At the outset the deal Sutherland proposed seemed the best way to acquire her land without further delay or aggravation. Even when the campaign was high flying, he'd been able to reassure himself that she wouldn't have time to get all the money she needed. So that would have been that. The money she raised would go to another environmental project and no one could blame him. At the price he'd offered, he still stood to lose a great deal. Any businessman could see that.

He was stunned at how close she'd come. Still, it wasn't enough. But who on the round planet could have imagined the woman would offer all she had and was going to get? The tic in Jonas's eyelid jerked convulsively. The press loved it. They'd all be here.

The only thing worse would be selling to her at that low price. Jonas couldn't conceive of that. He wouldn't even see very much of the fifty million he'd get. He had no cost basis in the land because it had been acquired so many years ago. So the capital gains tax would take most of the profit away. And he would lose the magnificent profits of having Ute Rise Canyon fully developed with palatial homes. Profits that could be spread out over time and not be subject to heavy tax. There was no help for it. He and his associates would just have to endure the upcoming plague of reporters.

And *that* was the best he could hope for. Again the recurring anxiety made Jonas straighten up in his chair. Sutherland could walk into the meeting this afternoon and slide a check for the shortfall across the conference table. He could come up with that fifteen million. Murdoch knew it. And the land would be all hers.

Sutherland had ridiculed the idea, and as he'd said, it was too much money for one of his twisted little games. But what if he were obsessed with the girl? Jonas's forefinger circled on his desktop as he brooded over that idea. He thought about Farnsworth and his precious Steffi. The two of them had shown up at the country club, all smiles and cooings, not three months after the Pike Society dinner, an evening Jonas blocked out of his mind. But he couldn't see it. Caley was not

Willie. If Steffi had been married to Sutherland and pulled that, she'd better not go home with him.

Yet the news of Caley's engagement had been all over Denver for the last few months and still hadn't been formally announced. If the girl had enough sense to hold Caley off so that he would help her keep her mountain if the campaign failed . . . Jonas's finger stopped. No. If she could figure that out, she'd know Sutherland was not the man to try it with.

He reached for the black stiletto-shaped pen. If only Sutherland had stayed in California. He even looked like one of those financial golden boys who flew in from L.A., then turned up bankrupt when a deal was arranged. Out there, the sunshine glinted on the knife in every man's hand. It was not that different in Denver. Except for one thing. The cuts could be deep, but everyone was careful not to give fatal wounds. There were some rules here, at least. There had to be. The families stayed on. They intermarried, and usually they closed ranks against outsiders. They all gathered around the same tables, played on the same golf courses, attended the same parties. And Caley was smart enough to know there was safety in smaller numbers.

Yet the image of Ari and the way she had looked at the Pike dinner rose in Murdoch's mind. He ran a mental eye over her form, remembering the hair, the eyes, the breasts, the hips. Jonas was aware that he'd never understood what some men would do for women, especially one like that. Her own family history showed it. From all accounts Berkeley Glendower had been a brilliant engineer. The Bridal Veil Falls project still operated—a testament to his genius and foresight. There was no doubt he could handle money. Then, Enos Murdoch always said Devin Lowell could have run the state and maybe the nation. Those two men, Jonas thought, were *ruined* by Gregory women.

Jonas nodded. History gave an overview, and he believed that it provided some insight into people. He wouldn't have gone so far as to say there were genes for behavior, but there was something there, something in the bloodlines. Look at Sutherland. And Jonas knew he himself should have looked more closely at the Wyndhams before he allowed Judith to marry one. They'd had the brains not to spend their money, but they were unpredictable people in other ways that mattered. What a man did behind closed doors was one thing, but Quentin couldn't even keep his pants zipped in public!

The Alexanders were even harder to read. Patrick couldn't take anything seriously, and his son Thomas was all too serious about *public service*. Rivers wanted money and he had Patrick's shrewdness, Thomas's dedication to work. He did have the habit of saying "on the other hand." That was an ideal way to look at investments, but Jonas had sometimes wondered if Rivers might not someday take a look at the whole setup and say that.

Still, he had admirable qualities. Murdoch had the feeling he'd always regret that Rivers and Judith hadn't gotten together in Washington as he'd hoped. His grandsons would have been just what he wanted. And Judith was more than willing. She'd mooned over Rivers for two years in high school. Jonas had made his own wishes as plain as he could to Alexander. He'd anticipated having dinners with a son-in-law who could talk about important topics instead of golf scores and grade-school soccer. He couldn't understand what could have gone wrong. If anyone knew what the Murdochs were worth, it was Rivers Alexander.

Jonas ran his fingers over the slim pen in exasperation. If money didn't motivate people, he couldn't imagine what would. That idea brought him back to Caley. His skin prickled at the decision he'd made. But at last Jonas felt he had to bet that when there was real money on the table, and some of it was going to be Sutherland's, the man would sit down and deal. He'd asked him to the meeting this afternoon.

Caley had said he'd present a good case for Murdoch. The associates would listen to him, and it was important that they agree if they were going to be facing those prying reporters. A unanimous decision not to sell to Ari MacAllister would look much better. If they all stood together, then the important people, their peers at the clubs, would accept what they were doing.

But Stewart Wellings had already talked to John Wallace and Leland Ames. They were substantial men and had called already to voice their reservations, even though Jonas had no reason to think those two were running scared of the press. That was another thing he couldn't understand. Wellings had a fine mind and unless he'd become a doddering old fool, why would he go along with this girl's foolishness? She couldn't be paying him that much. Maybe he was besotted with her too.

Jonas sent the pen skittering again. He fingered his eyelid, adjusted his shirt collar, shot his cuffs. It was essential he keep his temper this afternoon. This waiting—which was all he could do—wasn't helping.

At noon Ari was also convinced that there was nothing she could do but wait. Caley had called early and sounded so positive that she'd sung in the shower afterward. "In my view," he'd said, "you can't really lose on this deal. I'm convinced of that. I'm invited to the meeting, and I'll present a good case. See you tonight. I'll have to bring Loki

—I've left him too long as it is. But he doesn't drink champagne. Just us. I can't wait."

Stewart, however, had been completely pessimistic. He'd called two of Murdoch's associates who had listened to him carefully, but both had said Murdoch wouldn't wait. When she'd told him of Caley's optimism, the lawyer hadn't responded for a long moment. His answer was dry. "Perhaps he knows something I don't."

Turning this over, Ari walked up through the canyon and amid the burgeoning green, she found the dried husk of a milkweed with a few gossamer seeds still clinging. She blew them toward the mountain and wished with all her heart. Then, almost without intending it, she found herself back at the house. But no sooner had she opened the door and stepped into the hall than she had the immediate idea of going to Denver.

She didn't even debate it with herself. She just left. On the way to the airport she did wonder what she could say to those men that Caley couldn't say better. Murdoch could certainly say—and probably would—that she hadn't been invited. But she knew she had to go.

It wasn't until she'd stepped into the deserted outer offices of the Grant Street mansion that Ari had even a moment of indecision. She remembered that just a year ago when she'd thought of confronting Jonas Murdoch, she'd been unable to imagine making herself do this. And she heard men's loud, angry voices coming from behind closed doors down a hallway. Still, she walked steadily toward those doors and put out her hand to turn the knob.

But before she touched it, Bascomb's amused Texas drawl came through clearly. What he said stopped her, made her shrink inside her light suit jacket. "Sutherland," he was saying, "I am surprised at you. If I had a chance to get my cock in that little lady, she'd be screwed to the bed. And way too busy to be makin' all this trouble."

The remark took away Ari's resolve. She looked down at herself, buttoning her jacket all the way up.

Caley replied coolly and without animosity, "Just try using your other end for a change, Bass. Listen. There's no reason to sell to her. I agree, those reporters are going to cause you grief. But try telling them this. You're not going to develop *her* mountain. You're going to let it remain untouched. I guarantee you that in three or four years those lots that overlook—what do they call it, the 'Face of Love'?—will go for double the price. People forget fast. This campaign will end up making you money. And in just a few weeks the reporters will be hot on some other story."

Outside the door Ari was thunderstruck. She wondered if this was some sort of strategy of Caley's that she wasn't grasping. How could he have said that?

A quiet cultured voice that she didn't recognize cut in, "The press isn't noted for gullibility, Sutherland. And a good few of their readers, too, are well aware that the point was to save the entire area as a wilderness. If we try to get away with saying we're preserving her mountain, they'll come back with that picture they have. The one that shows the mountain hidden by satellite dishes and lodge roofs. And in the meantime they'll be turning over every leaf in our front yards, trying to find the dirt. And who hasn't got some?"

Maybe that's Caley's plan, Ari thought with shaky relief. *He wants them to refute his argument, make their own case to sell to her.*

Murdoch's tone was icy. "That sort of muckraking hardly influences anyone who matters. In the long run we'd be foolish to throw away the kind of opportunity the development of Ute Rise represents just because this girl has the media on her side. She's getting their attention by bankrupting herself. I consider such behavior irresponsible. She's improvident, not thinking of her children and grandchildren."

A deep voice rumbled, "Wait a minute. What I don't understand, Caley, is why you're siding with Murdoch and telling us not to wait for her money. From what I hear, you've got good reason to want her happy. And I saw her on TV. She's serious about her beliefs. She'd have to be to offer what she's offering. Is this maybe a little scheme on your part to make us look—?"

Bass interrupted, "Wallace here's got a point. But when I was thinkin' about that, I had to say to myself that if ol' Caley here wanted her happy, all he had to do was make up the difference. Now, fifteen million *would* hurt, wouldn't it, old son, but it wouldn't cause you real pain. So, boys, I'm just sayin' that if he'd brought a check, we wouldn't be havin' this talk. She'd have Ute Rise. That's some ground to trust him. But maybe the best reason's this. When Caley marries that little gal, her money's as good as in his pocket. He wouldn't want her to hand it over for a pile of boulders and some Christmas trees."

Caley's tone was dry as he answered, "I guess I'll take that as a vote of confidence, Bass. I'd argue that what I'm doing here is really in *Ari's* best interests, no matter what she thinks now. You'd all be doing her a favor by not selling. Giving away her fortune is something she'd be bound to regret later. She's a young woman"—he stressed each word heavily—"and later she'll see it was a mistake."

Ari was halfway in the room and almost next to Murdoch at the head of the long table before they all saw her. Her voice was calm

enough, but her eyes were burning. "I did make a mistake, Caley. A big
one. *I* trusted you. That wasn't the speech I thought you'd make."

Jonas stood up quickly. "You've no business here. Leave. Right
now."

A thin, silver-haired man stood up. He was the owner of the cultured voice. "I disagree with you, Jonas. This is her business. It's her
land. She's said she's willing to give all she has, and it's a considerable
sum. Quite enough to let her stay."

Murdoch's fleshless eyes became slits and he started to speak, but a
heavy-set man's deep voice carried the floor. "Leland's right. Let her
talk. We got time."

Ari didn't have time to think, and she began quickly before anyone
else could speak, "You agreed to sell if I had the money. I'll have it all in
a year, and I can pay interest on the shortfall until then. You're businessmen, so you can understand that.

"I want to make you understand why I want to save the canyon.
It's only a small corner in a big state. Why not pave it over, put up some
nice houses? But in a lot of America there's no end to the pavement
anymore. Nature's dead there because we never stop. We know how to
pave and we know how to level mountains. There's fifty-four of them in
Colorado over fourteen thousand feet. How many should we settle for?
Forty-nine? Twenty-three? Two?

"What do we need mountains for? Or wilderness? The American
Indians believe we're all part of the earth. Our own best scientists agree
that we need the mountains, and the rain forests, and the wetlands.
They say we have to stop and take care of them or we'll all die.

"So I don't think I'm some crazy voice crying for the wilderness.
Or that I'm being irresponsible and not thinking of my grandchildren.
Their first requirement is a livable planet. If I leave them dollars, what
are they going to do—sew the paper together to make an umbrella to
keep out the ultraviolet rays?

"If I don't spend my money to save what they need, and you won't,
who will? The poor people can't. This is how I want to use my money.
Nothing else I could get with it would be worth as much. I'm only
asking you for a year, but it would take several lifetimes to bring back a
wilderness full of birds and trees and flowers once you pave it over."

There was a brief silence and Murdoch asked, "Have you quite
finished preaching, Miss MacAllister? We'd like to get on with our
meeting."

Leland Ames stood back up. "I don't need to stay for the meeting.
Even if she wasn't right—and she is—a deal's a deal. The year is a
technicality. I recommend you sell, Jonas."

John Wallace rumbled, "Preaching can be hot air. Words. But she's putting her money behind those. I'm agreeing with Leland."

As some of the other men gathered their papers together, Jonas glared at them and almost hissed at Ari, "Some men can be swayed by a pretty face and a pretty speech, Miss MacAllister. I'm not one. And it's *my* land. Under the terms of the contract I don't have to wait. You'll notice that none of your supporters here have their checkbooks out to make up that large difference which is due tomorrow. Even your fiancé is firmly sitting on his."

Ari looked at Caley and her eyes still blazed. "He's not my fiancé."

"Ari." Caley got up and reached for her arm. "I'm only thinking of you. Of us. You'll see I'm right. Let's go and talk this over."

When he saw Ari jerk back her arm, Murdoch began, "She's doing you a real favor by dumping you, Sutherland. Women in her family—"

"Shut up, Jonas." Caley wheeled toward him and there was a certain desperation in his pale eyes. "You're only causing more trouble—"

"You're the one who started the trouble," Jonas shot back, unable any longer to keep down the rattlesnake of temper. "You persuaded me to try this, and you promised you'd see she wouldn't come up with the money. Lies, deceit, I swear it's in your veins. The whore's blood in your veins."

"What are you saying?" Caley's tone was more surprised than threatening.

Jonas's gesture included Ari. "You two deserve each other. A perfect match. Your grandmothers started out in the same brothel in Telluride! Oh, yes, Caley. We all called her 'Ceci,' but it probably stood for C. C.—Colette Caley. Stanton told Enos. We wanted her money, but we always knew it was a French whore's money."

For a moment Caley didn't move, couldn't move, and when he looked, Ari was gone.

CHAPTER 24

That same afternoon, as he pulled onto the valley road into Telluride, Rivers felt like pounding the steering wheel of his Saab. Anger clawed his spine.

Damn Jonas Murdoch. At this point he did whack the dashboard with the side of his fist. His rage, however, had nothing to do with the associates' meeting regarding the sale of Ute Rise. He hadn't known it was scheduled, let alone what had happened. Rivers had been driving for the last seven hours.

But last night in Washington he'd found out that Jonas had deceived him thoroughly on the plans for ConChem. An executive from Consolidated Chemical had pulled Rivers aside for a few quiet words during the noisy dinner celebrating the granting of the congressional delay. The man had been sure that Rivers was privy to all of Murdoch's plans, including the diversion of the reserve fund.

Jonas, true to his family tradition, had kept that secret from all those who didn't absolutely have to know. It was a nasty little secret. The money set aside for ConChem to clean up polluted ground and water could be put to other uses now that a postponement had been granted. Rivers had thought that this delay was necessary because GeneSys was not yet ready to set their new bacteria to work on pollution. But as he listened to the whispered words at the party, he learned the real reason. Jonas wanted to get his hands on that fat cash reserve.

Two other things became instantly plain. The money might not be there when the time came to unpollute. And Murdoch had preferred that Rivers not know that so he'd be a more effective lobbyist. That way he wouldn't have to lie.

But as he stood there, watching the executive's eyes dart like a wary rodent's, Rivers *felt* as if he had lied, as if he himself had been splattered with toxic garbage. He'd left immediately and caught the late plane to Denver. Although it was the middle of the night, he intended to go right to the office and leave his resignation on Murdoch's desk. But throwing his suitcases down in his bedroom, he saw his climbing gear. And he realized that what he wanted most was to clean himself. On top of a high mountain he thought he might rid body and mind of the sense he had of being covered with muck.

Some of his anger stemmed from the fact that he had *not* been told —he'd merely been used. Underlying that was the troubling question of what he'd have done if he had known. Would he have gone to Washington to lobby under those circumstances? Rivers wasn't sure. He'd have to face that, think about it.

In his bedroom he'd also seen the bulk of a package he'd long wanted to deliver to Ari MacAllister. So he decided to climb in the San Juans, telling himself that the long drive there would give him time to think. And it might help calm him. He knew that the very idea of seeing *her* would have the opposite effect, but he intended to do it anyway. He had something to say to her.

During the months in Washington, Rivers had gotten secondhand reports on the effect of the Ute Rise campaign. Jack Dexter had complained on the phone about how bad tempered Jonas had become because of it, even though no one at the office believed that the fifty million could be raised. The question of Ari pledging the rest of her winnings didn't seem to occur to anyone. It was information that should have been taken into account. Rivers knew she would. He was as sure of it as if he talked to her every day instead of not at all. However, he wasn't on the spot and no one asked him.

What Rivers didn't imagine was that Jonas would use the strict terms of the contract as a way out. He assumed Jonas would *have* to sell, given the circumstances. Certainly it would burn the man's soul because he'd bet a valuable property and lost. But that Jonas, blinded by anger, would enforce the exact terms of the contract didn't cross his mind. After all, in this situation it wouldn't be just the man in the street who'd take a dim view. Because of Ari's good fight in a good cause, the men in the country clubs would look at Jonas differently too. It was no longer just a business deal. Their opinion meant a great deal to Murdoch. Had he been on the scene, Rivers would have tactfully reminded him of what he would lose in the eyes of his peers.

As it was, Rivers had no way of knowing that during his long drive Jonas had refused to extend the time limit. Or that, at this moment, Ari was staring at the drawing of her lost mountain in despair.

Rivers was thinking about her. Sometimes he felt that Ari was all he had thought about in the last year. She'd become the prism through which he now saw the world. Before he'd met her, his future had seemed clear. He'd known what he wanted and how to get it. Now, light had broken into its bewildering array of color, and everything looked different.

As he drove along the San Miguel, Rivers was musing that, if he hadn't met Ari, he might have married Judith in the end. He could remember when she wore pigtails in grade school. They knew all the same people. They liked the same sports, and he liked *her*. She had a genuine sweetness. Jonas had dropped enough hints to the effect that this match would please everyone concerned. But, because of Ari, Rivers had learned how love felt. He couldn't forget it.

And because of Ari he was pretty sure he wouldn't have gone to Washington under false colors. A refusal would effectively have ended his career with Murdoch and Associates. On the way to Telluride he'd had to recognize that he would never know what he would have done if Ari hadn't come into his life. He might *not* have said no. But he'd met her before that decision arose. So Rivers was convinced that he wouldn't have been able to lobby if he'd known Murdoch was only after the cash reserve. She'd become his conscience.

Yet she, who had changed his thinking, was going to *marry* Caley Sutherland. Rivers had been trying to understand it for six months, and he couldn't. Before he heard that news, his feelings about Sutherland were confined to distrust and dislike. Now he'd slipped into hatred. Caley had everything—the brass ring, the gold watch, the rainbow fortune. And the girl.

Rivers surveyed his own prospects. He was now out of a job. What he'd heard last night had considerably diminished his self-respect. But he didn't doubt his ability to make money. He could do that. The letter of resignation to Jonas that he'd been mentally drafting during the drive would help restore his self-esteem. He could take care of that. But he still wouldn't have Ari.

Traffic was inching along the two-lane road into Telluride. Rivers whacked the steering wheel sharply with the heel of his hand. *Why would she marry Caley?* The simmering stew of his frustration boiled back into anger. *Why?*

One night over dinner he'd posed the question to Judith as if it were a subject of mild interest. He'd never told her he was in love with Ari. Judith paused in raising her salad fork to her mouth, considering before she answered, "Maybe she doesn't know him very well. She can't have known him long. Besides, look at all the men at the clubs who've been acquainted with him for years. They admire Caley and follow his business advice. Myself, I think he's . . . well, unpredictable at the very least. He scares me. Caley makes *me* think of that road sign —Proceed at Your Own Risk."

Her eyes were troubled as she went on, "But, Riv, if Ari were sitting here right now, I wouldn't say that to her. It wouldn't be . . . fair. After all, it's only my *feeling*. It's based on little things one person or another has said over time. Just gossip, really. I couldn't point to anything he's *done*."

Judith had put down her salad fork. "You can just bet he's always on his best behavior around her. Smooth as cream. She's bound to think he must love her. She probably says to herself that any man that rich wouldn't be marrying her for her money. Still, our feelings about him are right." She ended firmly, "I wish somebody would tell Ari that Caley isn't the man she thinks he is."

It was at that moment that Rivers knew he was going to tell Ari that. Even if she didn't listen, he was going to warn her. Not that she'd believe *him*.

Glancing up ahead, Rivers could see that the incoming cars were being held up by the lumbering pace of giant trucks pulling flatbeds with bulldozers and road graders chained to them. He eyed them impatiently, wondering why the equipment was needed, since the lots near the Doral in Mountain Village were ready for construction. But he went back to trying to sort out the puzzle that maddened him.

Once or twice he'd wondered if Ari had agreed to marry Caley because she needed to save her mountain. She didn't have the money. He did. Those pieces fit. The trouble was that the picture on the jigsaw box didn't resemble the Ari that Rivers knew. It was hard to imagine Caley handing over millions for a wilderness, but it was impossible to envision Ari trading herself for it. True, she'd now given Jonas all her money. Maybe she couldn't stand to be poor again.

Rivers crossed the Cornet Creek Bridge into Telluride. The image he couldn't bear was Ari in Caley's bed. He'd been trying to keep that idea out of his head for months. Nothing worked. That was what was in his mind as he pulled onto Pacific Avenue.

Ari had gone to her house directly from the airport, caught up in the firestorm of her emotions. She had no memory of leaving Murdoch's or of the flight back to Telluride. When she came in, she immediately stripped off the linen suit and silk blouse, tossing them onto a kitchen chair as if they were reminders of her defeat. She slipped into the blue jeans and thin sweater she kept in a downstairs closet. Pacing, she made the circuit from the kitchen, through the bare downstairs rooms, and back again. As she counted her losses, she twisted the ruby ring, chafing the skin on her finger.

She'd lost the mountain. Despair parched her tears. She'd tried her hardest, but she'd failed. *Her* daughter wouldn't have the bulwark of Bridey's Mountain. Those who came to Telluride would never see the wild beauty it had once possessed. If the spirits of the Utes returned, they would wander directionless in a landscape forever changed.

It wasn't fair. She repeated that going through the back parlor. Jonas had weaseled out of the deal on a technicality. He'd been playing the game by different rules. She should have imagined he would.

But Ari knew that wouldn't have changed the outcome. She couldn't fault herself there.

What made her writhe was her face-value acceptance of Caley Sutherland from the first. She'd been a fish in a barrel. He hadn't even needed a net. She could not believe her own stupidity. It didn't matter that he already had a lot of money—he was angling for hers as well. Why did she never suspect, she asked herself. Hadn't he laughed, telling her, "There's no such thing as too much money"?

He told her other things as well. He was willing to be what she wanted him to be. She longed for a father. He offered her that. Not content, he'd gone further. She'd almost gone with him. Ari firmly shut the door on that thought.

Marrying Caley, she'd imagined she'd be completing a circle, one begun with her parents. But the circle was older still, one made up of lies, deceit, and greed. Colette had used Morna for her own purposes. Caley tried to repeat that cycle.

Now Ari felt she could not trust herself. That *was* a loss, and it was the last, worst fear. She twisted her ring as she walked, scraping her skin. Her instincts had played her false. Hadn't she always fallen into Rivers's arms? So she'd clung to reason, seeing in Caley the promise of safety. Staring at the sheep's clothing, she hadn't spied the wolf.

She could not calm her rage or quiet her self-reproach. And she couldn't stop pacing.

As she went through the hall, Ari glanced through the stained glass of the double doors and saw a man carrying an enormous brown-paper-covered package up the walk. Only his blue-jeaned legs were visible. Although she wasn't sure she could even speak civilly to a deliveryman, she opened one door, then reached up to unlatch the top of the second. Just as she did so, he set the parcel next to the door. She found herself facing Rivers.

He had a light stubble on his cheeks, and there were signs of sleeplessness around his eyes. Tension creased the double lines near his mouth. He wasn't smiling. Pulling at the bottom of his windbreaker to straighten it, he said a little stiffly, "I didn't know that you'd be here. This is for you. I traded Jonas some of mine for it because it really—"

He was a perfect foil for her anger. Now it could be directed outward. Ari didn't hesitate. "Something *from* Jonas? What a switch. But he knows *I've* got nothing left to offer. I gave at the office. His office. *Your* office."

That thrust hit a fresh wound. Rivers banged a fist on the closed door. Unlatched, it flew open. He followed it in, saying with bitter precision, "Not *my* office. I quit." He spun toward her. His eyes had darkened to slate. Emotion had erased all color. "I want to tell you something. I admire your giving up all your winnings. But you're paying too much for that mountain if marriage to Sutherland is part of the deal."

Those words had the force of a backhand to the face. She even took a step backward. For a moment Ari couldn't get her mind around the accusation, let alone find words to refute it. She stuttered, "You think . . . I'm not going to . . . I wouldn't . . . for money?" Then her fury found a voice. She lashed back, "Of course *you'd* think that way. When are you and Ms. Big Bucks Murdoch tying the knot?"

His face went almost blank. "Judith?" His voice became low and cold as he came closer. "Where the hell did you get that idea? Caley?"

"Never mind. I know." She needed more than a shield from his nearness. She grabbed for words that would have a sword's cutting edge. "You're up for the highest bidder. She's got more money than I do."

But that seemed to glance off Rivers. He was staring at her. He'd heard the unmistakable sound of jealousy behind the words. It was sweet. It was rain on dry earth. Taking off his windbreaker, he tossed it over the newel post. Ignoring what she said, he looked at her face. He saw the flicker of vulnerability in her eyes, in the quiver of her mouth.

He pushed up the sleeves of his cotton sweater. Taking one more step forward, he said, "God help me. *You're* the only woman I ever wanted to marry. And the only one I ever asked. And that proposal stands."

Ari refused to hear *what* he was saying. Still burning with a rage fueled by self-blame, she fell back on the one thing she was sure of. Rivers must know she still had fifteen million dollars. That's *why* he was saying it. She returned to the attack. "What's the matter? Did Judith take Quentin back?"

Rivers lunged forward, almost shoving her against the banister railing. His hands clenched around the stair balusters on either side of her. The tendons in his muscular forearms stood out. He bit out each word. "Enough. Listen to me, Ari MacAllister. I don't have much money. Now neither do you. But I can make it. I'll never have as much as that lying son-of-a-bitch Sutherland. Believe me, that's what he is. But I can make enough, if money's what you want."

He was too close. Even now, when she was trying to imagine what possible reason he could have for saying she had no money, she felt her instincts ready to betray her. It must be some kind of trickery on his part. Yet half of her burned to overlook any deception, to join him. Divided, she could only summon up sarcasm. "Well, we can probably scrape by on fifteen million, Rivers, can't we?"

Almost touching, they'd never been farther apart. "What fifteen million?" he demanded.

Her words were now as distinct as his had been. "The fifteen million dollars Jonas wouldn't take for the mountain because I don't get it until *next* June. As if you didn't know."

For the first time he saw the defeat in her face, the hopelessness in her eyes. The tension in his arms lessened. "Jonas won't wait?"

Ari pushed past him. She didn't stop until she reached the far side of the front parlor. She faced the fireplace, grasped the mantel, and then let her hands drop. "Why are you doing this? What's the point?" All she could think of was Caley's frantic effort to salvage the situation between them at the end of Murdoch's board meeting. Was Rivers trying the same thing? She hardly felt the pain as she viciously twisted her ring.

He didn't respond. When she half turned her head to look at him, he was in the middle of the room. His eyes were on her, but he was clearly assessing what he'd heard. "Something must have set him off, made him lose his temper. He'll regret this." He ran an open palm down his jeans as he thought.

This time she winced as she spun the ring. Tugging it off, she almost sent it sliding down the polished mantel.

He walked down the length of the room before coming to stand next to her. "I've been driving for seven hours. I didn't know. I'm sorry." His voice was quiet.

Ari wouldn't meet his eyes, but kept hers on the swept tiles of the empty hearth. He slid his fingertips along the mantel, still considering. Then he picked up the ring, saying, "Don't leave it here. You might forget it." Lifting her unresisting right hand, he saw her chafed skin. He put the ring on her left hand. "It belongs on this finger." He gently cupped her hand in his.

Rivers could see how even her vivid coloring had dimmed. He asked, "How was everything left? What did Jonas say?"

Ari felt drained of all emotion, even the anger that had sustained her. Her body seemed heavy now, as if lead, once molten, were hardening inside her. She replied dully, "Tomorrow is June first. If I don't have the money by then, he gets the mountain."

He couldn't bear the pain he heard. "Why didn't you get the money from Caley?"

She needed to get the words out before her lips were sealed shut. "For the last time, I am not going to marry Caley Sutherland. I have never been engaged to him. If he offered me the money, and it meant I had to talk to him, I wouldn't take it."

Rivers reached one hand toward her. Ari didn't jerk her arm. She merely moved it away, across her body. She said, sounding as if her throat were closing, "And I won't marry you. I'd have to trust. I can't." She had to make him leave. "Find yourself some other rich woman."

His footsteps had a hollow sound on the bare floor. She heard the finality of the door's lock clicking behind him.

Maybe it was better this way, she thought. She stood, dry eyed, recalling how much the Gregory women had given up for men over the years. Morna had left even her child for Berkeley. In the end Bridey had lost everything. Trish, as well.

Still, she couldn't stop herself from crossing the room, opening the door, to see if he was gone. All she saw was the extra huge paper-wrapped package on the veranda. With difficulty she pulled it into the parlor. As she ripped the paper down, her eye was caught first by the glint of a metal plaque at the bottom. BERKELEY GLENDOWER read the inscription at the base of the intricate gold frame.

The man in the portrait looked almost ready to step from the frame, to speak to her. Although he was wearing late-nineteenth-century clothing, a rich brown frock coat, wing collar, scarf tie, he seemed ready to go on with a conversation that had only briefly been interrupted—not by years, but by minutes. His dark hair was brushed back, except for a piece that had come loose across his forehead, and there was animation and warmth in the brown eyes flecked with gold. There was a shining intelligence in that handsome face.

Ari looked at him, and now she began to cry. With the relief of tears came a softening of defeat. She didn't know how long she stood there. Gradually the chill in the house made her shiver.

Rivers's jacket was on the newel post and she went to get it, throwing it over her shoulders. As she came back into the parlor, Ari continued a conversation she didn't realize she'd begun. "Everything's gone wrong," she said to Berkeley. "Everything. I would have given all I have, and that hasn't made any difference." Spoken aloud, the words didn't convince. She tried again, remembering a proverb—*Take what you want, God says, and pay for it.* "I did," she protested. "I offered all my money." The words hung in the empty room.

She needed to be warm. It occurred to her that a fire had been laid in the back parlor. Unrolling the sheepskin rug, she knelt on it and held a match to the kindling. As the flames grew, she folded the windbreaker into a pillow, stretching out before the fire.

Illuminated by the twilight, Berkeley's portrait watched her. This time she thought about the other half of the story—what the men who'd loved the Gregory women had given to them. All the things . . . Ari drifted off to sleep.

CHAPTER 25

Caley hated Telluride. He shoved his back against the hard wooden bar chair at the Sheridan. To make matters worse, he'd had to charter a plane to even get here. By the time he'd gotten out of Murdoch's and calmed down enough to plan a little, the last flight had left. *It was all Jonas's fault.* He wanted to kill that son of a bitch. Kill him. Making that crack about Ceci in front of Big Mouth Bascomb and the rest. Probably planned it that way. Be all over town tomorrow.

Glancing around, clenching and unclenching his hand, he realized he hated this place too. He needed light and company. It was easier to get hold of himself with other people around. All this had was deserted tables, that dark red bordello wallpaper, a long empty mahogany bar. When he'd walked in a half hour before, the thin blond bartender had waved Loki in as well, saying, "You and the dog will probably be the only two customers I'll get tonight. Summer rush doesn't start till next week." The only distraction here was that they stocked Glenfiddich, his favorite Scotch.

After the fiasco at the board meeting Caley knew he had to try to smooth the edges. But he couldn't drink too much. He had to be careful. His hand trembled slightly as he lit his third cigar.

Hearing the truth about Ceci had tilted his universe, more than he recognized. His grandmother had been the sun around which Caley had reluctantly orbited. Even after her death his thoughts still gravitated to her precepts. He always tried to please—or displease—her. All *that,* he was thinking to himself in disgust, for the estimation of a whore.

She had told him to be an entrepreneur. *Go out there and make money. Sure.* If she hadn't tied up the money, he wouldn't have had to sell drugs, get in all that trouble. She'd been one for business herself, he fumed, in the world's oldest profession. *What could you expect from a woman? They were all whores.* He gulped down the rest of the Scotch. *And the Gregory women—talk about being done in by a bunch of sluts.*

Trish had turned him in to the narcs. He was sure of that. *The beginning of real bad times. Canada. Turkey.* He wasn't going to think about that. Then Ari. *A bitch from the first. And this afternoon*— His hand tightened into a fist that he could almost feel clutching around a handful of her hair. *Her fault.* She was going to pay. He lingered over the idea of the sweat running down her face, between her breasts.

But first he had to get her back. That called for some strategy. He inhaled the smoke of the cigar deeply. He'd have to take it easy. Plan. Caley beckoned toward the bartender. A third drink wouldn't hurt.

How could he get around Ari? Apologize? *Seriously kiss ass.* He could say, *I was wrong. But I was only thinking of you and our children. I was so afraid you'd regret it later. Even blame me for letting you do it.* No. She'd say some goddamned thing about it being her decision. He'd have to do better.

As he picked up his fresh drink, his knuckles whitened against another tremble. *Damn the Gregory women to hell. Even with their heads up their asses, they still caused*— Caley stopped. He felt an unexpected twinge of fellow feeling for his grandmother, and wondered if she'd bested the first of that lot, the one Ari was always going on about. What was her name? Morna. If Ceci—

Then an idea struck him. Strategy was the word. He could say his speech at Murdoch's was a ploy—one to get them to argue back. He could say, *I was playing devil's advocate, Ari. You heard what I said. I told them not to give in, that the reporters were no problem. Then Bascomb and the boys would have to start thinking about what a real pain those reporters were going to be. If I'd walked in there and told them to sell to you, they wouldn't listen. They know how I feel about you.* Caley took another sip of Scotch. Would she buy that?

He nodded to himself. Yes. That would fly. It had to. He rubbed one fist inside a cupped palm. It had to. He'd waylay her tomorrow morning.

"Caley," a voice behind him broke in on his thoughts. Jack Dexter had come in the side entrance from the hotel. "What are you doing here? Jonas said you were going to be at the associates' meeting this afternoon."

Caley shrugged. "I was there. You up here to start on Ute Rise?"

Dexter pulled out a chair. "We're as ready as we can be. Payton Cross should be along soon to go over some last-minute stuff. What happened at the meeting?"

"Ames and Wallace aren't going to back Jonas. And some of the others won't either."

Dexter's narrow face creased with worry, his shoulders moving uncomfortably under his ill-fitting shirt. "Too bad. Be a lot better if everybody hung in there. Now those friggin' reporters are going to be on *us* like a pack of dogs."

Caley waved it off. "Let 'em yelp for a couple of weeks." He lifted his drink to his lips, but then he set it down. Catching the bartender's eye, he pointed at his glass, nodded at Dexter. "You know," he said slowly, "two can play at this game. It's all smoke and mirrors, anyway." An idea was forming. And he could use Dexter.

Pretending real regret, Caley said, "Jonas *is* going to look bad on the front page. Can't you see the headlines, Jack?" He moved his hand in a broad gesture. "SWEEPSTAKES WINNER PLEDGES ALL; BILLIONAIRE SPITS IN THE FACE OF LOVE!'"

"Oh, shit." Jack's face paled.

Caley waited until the bartender put down the two Scotches before continuing. "The trouble is, everybody knows she'll give him the money. He only has to wait a year. That makes for real bad press. Most people see fifty million as a lot of cash. They don't realize that Jonas would lose at that price." He shook his head. "It isn't fair. Why should they get all the good coverage? The environmentalists, I mean. Look at some of the things they've done—spikes in the trees, sabotaging construction machinery . . ." Caley looked at him assessingly. Would he take the bait?

Dexter circled for a bit and then rose like a trout. With a sideways shift of his eyes he began, "Our bulldozers came in this afternoon. If they were sabotaged and everybody thought the environmentalists . . . sand in the gas tanks, maybe . . . like the Monkey-Wrenchers, the Earth-Firsters."

Caley's smile was genuine. "Brilliant, Jack! I'd never have thought of it. Yes. Do it yourself and blame the environmentalists. Then *they* won't look so good in the headlines." He had to nail it down. "I'm going to have to start writing you bigger checks, fella. That's a major-league idea. You can't tell Jonas until after the shouting's over, but then I'll make sure he knows whose idea it was." Caley laid it on thick, holding up his glass. "Welcome to the Club."

Jack's glow of pleasure deepened as the front door opened. "Here comes Payton. He's the guy I can get to do the job. And he can keep his mouth shut."

Cross was wearing a plaid shirt with silver studs and jeans that fit his lean, tough frame exactly. As he got to the table, he nodded curtly, "Sutherland." He signaled the bartender. "A beer." Hooking a chair with his boot, he sat down, keeping his eyes on Caley. The tension in his movements hinted at a leashed antagonism.

Dexter couldn't wait to let him in on the plan. But the flat silence of the other man made him hurry his words. When he finished, Cross shifted his hard stare to Dexter. "What does Jonas think?"

Caley put in, "It's not something he *should* know. Not now." He tapped the table meaningfully. "But he'll be real grateful. Later." He leaned forward, adding, "You've got to do it tonight. Around dawn might be best—you can see what you're doing. The lynch mob forms tomorrow. Jonas will make the announcement in the morning about refusing to sell. The pickets will be out in the afternoon. And your chance will be gone."

While he thought, Cross fingered the chain tattooed on his wrist. "I owe Jonas," he said finally. His eyes warned them. "But if it goes sour, I'm not takin' the heat."

Jack assured him. "No problem."

Caley pushed back his chair, and Loki got to his feet immediately. Throwing down a fifty-dollar bill, Caley stood up. "Have another round on me."

As he left the Sheridan, Caley swallowed down laughter. If all went well, the bulldozers would be wrecked by dawn. But no one would know until someone tried to start an engine. When Jonas announced his refusal to sell the land, reporters would gather. Then, within hours, Dexter would tell him he could counter the bad press with outrage over environmental terrorism. He'd be happy—for a few minutes. Then Caley would call him.

Outside the bar the air was chilly, but Caley breathed it in with pure pleasure. Now everything had been set in motion. All he needed was a grandstand seat—and a camera with a zoom. He'd get photos of a Murdoch employee sabotaging that equipment, trying to make it look as though protesters had done it. Any of the major TV networks would feature the pictures. They would be delighted to expose Jonas after the popularity of the campaign to save Bridey's Mountain.

But the networks were never going to know the photos existed. When Jonas heard about them, he would pay anything to suppress them. Even he wouldn't be willing to ride out that storm on national television.

It was blackmail, Caley thought with satisfaction. But it was in a good cause. What Jonas was going to have to give for those negatives was his land. He was going to have to sell it to Ari—at a fire-sale price.

Caley considered the figure Jonas would now have to take for Ute Rise. Thirty-five million. Just what she had raised in the campaign. Then she'd get to keep her fifteen million.

After that there'd be only one thing left. He'd have to make sure Ari knew it was he—Caley Sutherland—who had saved her mountain. And he would accept her apologies. For now. She would accept his ring gratefully. Everything would be back in balance.

He was a patient man, he told himself. Later, there'd be time for her reparations.

In the bar, Cross had drained his beer. He set the mug down hard. Jerking his thumb toward the door Caley had just gone through, he said, "I'd feel a lot better about this if Slick there wasn't in on it."

"It was my idea, Payton, not his." Dexter was still riding the wave of Caley's approval. "He's a good friend of mine. We've been in on several deals together. He's okay."

"I don't like him. He's got one of those tricky minds." Cross struggled to explain. "You know the kind of guys—they sit there talkin' to you, but they got somethin' else goin' on in their heads. They're seein' stuff you don't." He flicked the fifty-dollar bill in distrust. "Just like that Alexander. You clued me in on that. He badmouthed me to Murdoch. Why'd he do that?" His voice rose. "I was lucky I got hired. But I've been straight with Jonas. And he was straight with me. I owe him, I guess."

Dexter tried to calm him. "Have another beer." He scooped up the money. "Have a couple. We got enough."

Cross kicked back his chair and dug in his pocket. He tossed some crumpled bills on the table. "I'm buying my own. I'm goin' to get some tools. Sand won't do it all—you gotta' cut the hydraulic lines. Stay here."

Rivers had walked down Pacific Avenue, past Popcorn Alley, ending back on Telluride's main street. In spite of it all he felt better than he had in months. Ari was not going to marry Caley. Everything was still possible.

She thought she'd lost her mountain. He himself wasn't so sure, even if he couldn't see at the moment what to do. Perhaps Jonas could still be made to listen to sense. It was obvious he'd forgotten what was important to him. The idea of losing money in the Ute Rise deal had blinded him to what else was at stake. The regard of his peers. Even the judgment of posterity. Rivers smiled ruefully. Could he try that line on Jonas?

His smile died. It wasn't just a question of a telephone call. Once Jonas got his back up, *Jonas* had to be the one to back down. And how could he make that happen?

He had to try. Ari deserved her mountain. He couldn't stand the idea that she'd lose it. His job status at Murdoch's—that could wait.

Rivers saw the lights of the Sheridan bar. Maybe Samuel would be at work; he might have some ideas. And he thought, *I could sure use a drink.*

Jack hailed him as soon as he'd stepped through the door. "Rivers!" Motioning him toward his table, Dexter was thinking that this *was* his lucky day. Not only had Caley welcomed him to the inner circle, now he could get one up on Alexander. He couldn't wait to tell him his idea.

He was smiling as he picked up his Glenfiddich. It was his third. He waved the bartender over with an expansive gesture, saying, "Drinks are on me. What'll you have?"

His manner puzzled Rivers. Jack must know that Jonas's action would mean some bad days ahead. Sitting down, he said, "Just a beer. I don't see what we've got to celebrate."

"If you mean the reporters coming, I can take care of them. Two can play that media game. It's all smoke and mirrors, Riv." But then Dexter set his glass down hurriedly as a thought occurred to him. Suppose Alexander found some way to take credit for this. He'd better not say too much. His eyes narrowed. "How come you're up here? Jonas send you?"

"Visiting a friend." Rivers could see a look of triumph about Dexter. He knew that, if goaded, Jack would lay it out. "But when I tell him I'm here, he'll probably want me to stay. Talk to the press. He'll have *me* do that."

"I can do it. I've got a handle on it." Jack took a swig of his Scotch and leaned back, determined to say no more.

Rivers put a certain skepticism into his voice. "I don't know. Calls for quick wits. We're the bad guys. Plenty of people bought those

Mother's Day cards. The song got a big play. The reporters are going to take us apart. Do you really think you—"

Dexter broke in. "Those environmentalists have sometimes pulled some radical stuff that doesn't look so hot in the papers. Monkey-Wrenchers. Responsible businessmen don't like to hear about sand in the gas—and how about them putting spikes in the trees?"

"So what? That's old news. The reporters aren't going to remind people of that." Rivers caught the shine of excitement in Dexter's eyes, and he began to suspect he was on the right path.

"Well, maybe they won't have to *remind* them," Dexter retorted.

"You're saying the best defense is a good offense? Got a tame Earth-Firster in your pocket? How are you—?"

But Dexter had stood up abruptly. Over Rivers's shoulder he saw Payton Cross coming out of the hardware store on the other side of Colorado Avenue. Not only would Cross get the wind up if he saw Alexander, he'd tell Rivers he knew what had gone on during the discussion about hiring him as construction supervisor. He stood up hurriedly, shoving the change to the middle of the table. "Have to go. See you later."

After he'd left, Rivers tried to sort out what he had heard. Jonas was going to start building as soon as possible. Summer was short up here. Those bulldozers he'd followed into Telluride were Murdoch's. It'd be easy to disable them. As Jack had almost said, sand in the gas tanks. It would seem an outraged response on the part of the environmentalists.

But it was a stupid idea. It wouldn't take that much pressure off Jonas. And it was dangerous. To make it plausible, claims would have to be put in to the insurance companies. That made it fraud. Jonas would have to be crazy to risk— That was it. Murdoch didn't know. It was Dexter's plan. He wanted to look clever, do something on his own initiative. He was always trying to prove himself.

Rivers finished his beer. Dexter was going to do it. He could believe that. The odd thing was imagining Jack coming up with the idea. But somehow he had. Mulling it over, Rivers saw this could be turned to Ari's advantage.

The only question was *when* Dexter planned to do it. If he was smart, he'd do it tonight. Tomorrow night the local residents of Telluride might even be holding a vigil. Tonight would be safe.

Rivers rubbed the back of his neck wearily. He'd been up all the previous night and driving the whole day. This would mean camping out by the bulldozers. He couldn't take the chance that they'd wait till the early hours of morning. But if he could get a photo of Jack wrecking the equipment, he'd have real leverage with Jonas. It was worth losing a little sleep.

He stood up. He had everything to gain. Ari.

CHAPTER 26

It was almost dawn when Caley lowered himself to the ledge overlooking Ute Rise Canyon. Lucky he'd been here that day with Ari, he thought, and knew where it was. But this time he held all the cards. As before, though, when he snapped his fingers at Loki, the dog refused to come down, stretching out on the overhang above. Caley shrugged. His boots crunched through dead pine needles as he approached the edge. Lifting the camera, he cradled the zoom lens and pointed it toward the bulldozers below. *Perfect.* Even in the gray light he could focus on the ridges of the first machine's track. Getting a clear enough shot to show a face would be easy.

Caley congratulated himself. Everything was back in his control. He sat down, settling his back against a boulder beneath two Ponderosa pines. Their stunted branches were wind twisted, barren of new growth. As soon as Cross showed up, he thought, he'd have a great view.

Shifting uncomfortably on the layer of dry needles and grass, Caley shivered in his leather jacket. *At least it was dry.* Maybe the chill would keep him awake. He wished he'd brought a Thermos of coffee. Yawning, he stared down, unseeing, at the green canyon.

It wasn't until a magpie swooped down from the trail above, startling him, that he realized he'd been dozing. The bird, its black-and-white wings extended, dived over the brink of the ledge into the deep fissure beneath him. Pulling his watch from his pocket, Caley snapped open the case. Cross should be here soon.

The night had been long and cold. Uncomfortable as he was, Rivers kept nodding off. It was only when his head fell forward that he jerked himself awake. Going without sleep the night before made his need for it now almost painful. He hadn't brought enough coffee. Only taking time to grab his parka from his car, he'd bought the first camera he could find—a disposable one. He couldn't be sure when Dexter would sabotage the machinery and he had to be already in place. As dawn neared, he could no longer risk standing up and taking stretches to ward off the drowsiness.

He was jammed behind the huge tire, taller than he was, of a road grader. It was the only possible cover, but it was hardly an ideal situation. The two bulldozers were directly opposite him. Another road grader was angled ahead of this one. The camera lens was fixed, so he had to be close to get an identifying shot.

During the slow hours of the night Rivers had thought it over. Dexter would be foolish to let anyone else in on this scheme, so he'd do it himself, but he had to be caught in the act. Rivers planned to wait until one of the machines was wrecked. Then he'd have evidence to use against Murdoch to force him to sell.

Ari would see finally that he was one with her. She would trust him. With that warm thought he plunged into a deep sleep.

When Payton Cross came, he came alone. He'd left Jack Dexter as a lookout in the car at the mouth of the canyon. *You only need one man for this job, anyway,* Cross thought. Dexter had had so much Scotch the night before that he'd trip over his own shoes.

Reaching the clearing, Cross almost sniffed the air, alert for danger. Not that he expected any. If there'd been any real chance of getting caught, he wouldn't have agreed in the first place.

But last night this plan had sounded better. *Still, you were only talking ten minutes.* He patted the wire snips in his parka vest pocket. The bag of sand was in his left hand. After he finished with the gas tanks and hydraulic lines, it would take only a few seconds to spray-paint the Earth First symbol on the machines. As he drew near the bulldozers, the chain in the back pocket of his jeans shifted, the heavy links clicking against each other.

* * *

It was the coldest Ari had ever been. The lace of the white dress had frozen as solid as frost patterns on winter windows, and it was scraping like icicles on her unprotected throat and on her bare arms. The cold turned her lungs and heart to dry ice and penetrated to the pit of her stomach.

Although Ari was running, it was that dream-running where there was no forward motion. But she had to keep trying because there was a desperate need for hurry. This time the nightmare fear was already there. It was inside her, like the cold. Her own movements didn't warm her at all, and the temperature in the canyon dropped lower as she went higher.

There was no snow on the ground, but the columbines by the streambed were bent and frost-killed. The water was not frozen because she could hear it, and one glance showed her it flowed a dull and pitiless red. The white hand thrust upward, in its grasp the gold watch swinging from its chain. This time she could see on the case cover the intertwined *C* and *S*.

Looking up at the mountain, she saw the face was stained by smoke. She could not even breathe in this fearful cold. If she didn't do something, she would never be warm again. When she heard Rivers's voice, she knew what it was she had to do. She had to wake up.

Ari jerked up. It was not yet dawn, but very nearly, and there was a gray glimmer of light in the back parlor. The fire had gone out long ago. She'd fallen asleep on the sheepskin rug, using Rivers's windbreaker as a pillow. The early morning chill was in her bones. She reached around for his jacket, and as she slipped it over her thin cashmere sweater, she heard his voice again. It was quite close.

Sure that she was awake, no longer dreaming, Ari pushed herself to her feet, peering through the long dining room to the front parlor, thinking he must be there. But the room was empty, and she could only just make out the gold edges of Berkeley's portrait. Still, Rivers was calling her. That was clear. Her movements seemed dreamlike, but she was fully awake and she knew what she had to do. She had to go to the mountain. He needed her.

Without thought she walked to the door, down the porch steps, and hurried along Pacific Avenue toward the canyon. The town was absolutely quiet, and the only sound was the waking chirps of small birds. In that first gray, colors seemed to stand out. The pastels of the houses she went by were bright, and their tulip beds were masses of reds and yellows and purples.

Ari didn't notice. With each step she took, the meaning of the dream became clearer. It was about love.

But it had always become a nightmare. There was the fear. She'd always assumed the fear was for the mountain, a reminder to save it. This morning, even half running as she was, she knew. It was fear *of* the mountain, of its power. She was afraid of love.

It was always a risk, with the highest stake of all. Yourself, Ari thought. You had to put yourself on the line—not just money—and Fortune spun the wheel. Losing meant joyless days and nights of misery.

She'd been afraid to gamble. She hadn't trusted her feelings about Rivers. And she hadn't trusted Rivers. She didn't believe that a man would love her. Her birthmark disfigured her. Despite all the MacAllisters' best efforts Ari had taken in an idea that was all around her, in books and magazines and movies. Men only loved beautiful women. And she was not beautiful. Not like the other Gregory women. All she saw in her mirror was the port-wine stain splashed on her forehead, down her cheek. Without questioning the idea she believed that no man would really love her. If she allowed herself to care for him, he would leave. And she would be left with all that pain.

But that was wrong. Not only was the birthmark gone, the idea had always been wrong. She knew it now, speeding through the town park. Rivers did love her. He'd looked right past her birthmark. Love didn't ask for a perfect face. That was not it, that was not it at all.

For Ari saw clearly the lesson of the final dream. All the Gregory women knew it. Love was always a risk. But not to choose it was really to lose. It meant a life forever in the cold.

Crossing the arched wooden bridge across the San Miguel, she knew she loved Rivers. And she was going to tell him just as quickly as she could get to the mountain. But even covering the ground at a fast pace, it didn't seem fast enough to reach him. Why he should be there in this chilly dawn still did not occur to her.

As Ari started up the canyon, she saw a parked car with a man dozing behind the wheel. His eyes were closed, his head thrown back, displaying a narrow face, a widow's peak of hair. But she barely glanced at him because she was in too much of a hurry. She rushed past, her sneakers making no sound. When she saw the stream, she didn't even glance at it, and only took a quick look at the mountain. Now she was running full tilt.

CHAPTER 27

Caley wanted to go home. When he'd made the decision to handle things this way, he'd liked the strategy. Now he was cold, he was cramped, he was tired. All that was on his mind was how much he'd like to be in bed.

He could, he thought, be in bed with Ari, instead of sitting here on prickly pine needles. He dug at a knot above his shoulderblades. *Sure. It only would have cost me fifteen million dollars.* Letting go of that much would be stupid. It'd put him under ninety million. Last time he'd checked, his total worth was something over $100 million, and he liked the sound of that figure. *And what would he get for his fifteen million? A tumble in the sheets?*

He wasn't used to being uncomfortable. Perhaps that was why Caley found himself, for a moment, feeling that right now it didn't seem such a bad bargain. Ari turning to him sleepily, his fingers stroking through her soft hair, her eyes warm with welcome.

He clenched a cigar between his teeth. *Hell, yes, you get a lot of welcome for fifteen million bucks.* He remembered how he'd had to kiss

Ceci's grasping hands to get a lousy fifty. Lighting his cheroot, he blew smoke out impatiently. *Where was Cross?*

From the overhang above him Loki growled low in his throat. He half turned toward the dog, but his eye was caught by a motion near the bulldozers. Payton Cross was loping toward the first one.

Throwing down the cigar, Caley quickly focused the zoom lens. The shutter clicked, once, twice. *Got it.* He waited for Cross to make his next move, steadying the long lens on his bent knee. As his quarry turned, his face clear in the viewfinder, Caley pressed the shutter release. *You're on Candid Camera.* Behind him a thin tendril of smoke spiraled from the dead pine needles. Loki eyed it silently.

Intent on Cross's actions, Caley suddenly caught another movement from the road grader farthest from the trail. He swung the lens toward it. Rivers Alexander leapt into view. *What the hell?* He snapped another picture. *Doesn't matter.* He had two Murdoch employees on the scene.

Caley saw Rivers raise a camera. In one deadly motion Payton Cross reached behind him, whipping forward a length of thick chain.

But behind Caley fire flared in a burst up one of the pines on the ledge. Caley jerked around, the heat hitting him in the face. Scrambling to his feet, he lunged for the handholds in the rock to the overhang.

As his fingers clutched frantically at the top, Loki slashed at them with his teeth. Stunned, Caley fell to the ledge. Flames crackled near him, sparks hitting his boots. "Back," he hissed. The dog, tensed just above his head, stared him in the eye. Loki didn't move.

Had the fire made him crazy? A threat in his voice, Caley snapped orders as he struggled up the handholds. This time the dog ripped the back of his hand open. Caley jumped down, slapping a palm over the wound. The fire flashed up the other tree. *If I try again . . . get my head up . . . he'll go for my throat.* Cornered, Caley spun to his right. The trail was twelve feet over his head atop a wall of uneven rock. Below was the deep crevasse. *I could hang by my fingers, edge along . . . maybe work my way up.*

Caley looked down. The gray rock plunged into blackness. He fumbled to twist the zoom lens off the camera. He hurled it at Loki. It missed and Loki snarled, motionless. The fire's hot breath brushed his legs. In panic Caley pulled out his watch. Taking careful aim with trembling hands, he threw it at the dog's head. It grazed his muzzle, but Loki didn't give ground.

There was no other choice. Caley reached over, scrabbling for the rock wall. His fingers clung desperately to one cranny, then another. He swung his legs, trying vainly for a purchase with the narrow toes of his boots. Without a foothold he couldn't raise himself up. He could only hang by his hands, safe from the fire, but just a few feet away.

It roared, consuming every dry blade of grass on the ledge. The heat made the wound on his hand sting; blood trickled down his arm. His weight dragged at his fingers, stretching the tendons of his forearms. His cheek ground against the stone wall. *Nothing is worth this,* he thought in despair.

He couldn't hang on long enough. His fingers finally went numb. When Caley lost his grip, he may have cried out as he fell, but the sound was swallowed in Loki's howl. The wolf-dog turned and, running now, headed for the wilderness. The fire continued, reaching up hungrily. But the trees on the trail above were out of its range. There was no wind, and there was nothing on the surrounding rock to feed it. It began to die back, sinking into glowing ash.

The first rays of the sun slanted into the canyon. One glinted on the gold surface of Caley's watch as it swung from an exposed root near the overhang.

CHAPTER 28

The clink of tools was what aroused Rivers. By that time Payton Cross was at the bulldozer directly across from him. At the first sight of him aiming the camera, Cross reacted with the speed of a striking snake. He didn't say a word. He was already edgy, primed, and his first instinctive move was for that length of heavy chain in his back pocket. Rivers wasn't used to men whose immediate response to any threat was violence, and only his quickness saved him from its brutal blow along his head.

Even as he jerked back, he knew how badly he'd miscalculated. This was no Jack Dexter. Cross was not going to be caught, by anyone. If Rivers, a Murdoch employee, was found dead on the scene it would be a better case against any Monkey-Wrenchers. Rivers had no place to go but backwards, against the first angled machine. The tip of the whizzing chain clanged into the side of the road grader behind him, reverberating through the canyon.

"Doin' me in again?" Cross snarled, whipping the chain back to his hand. Just as he raised his arm to lash it out again, both men heard Ari.

"Rivers, where are you?" Her voice was frantic and close by.

Only an unthinking fear for her made Rivers lunge toward the foreman at that instant. And only that leap and Cross's second of distraction made the lethal end of the chain miss its mark. But the side of it was vicious enough. More than enough. The chain slammed into Rivers's temple and he crumpled to the ground. He lay motionless, absolutely still. Cross, sure that Ari hadn't gotten by Dexter, but had come from higher up the canyon, maybe with others, stopped. Then he scrambled off down the slope.

Rounding the bulldozer, Ari saw Rivers lying unmoving on his side and the blood, the amazing amount of blood, pouring down his face. Even as she ran forward, she'd begun an agonized prayer under her breath. She knelt, patting pockets frenziedly, finding his handkerchief in the windbreaker she was wearing and pressing it tightly against the gash along his forehead and temple. "Please, Rivers, please. Don't die," she begged, "I love you. I love you."

Somewhere she heard a car start, the peel of tires, but Ari noticed only that the handkerchief she held was soaked almost immediately. Then she did know fear. Waking fear that was much worse than nightmare. She was too late. She'd had reason to be afraid of love. So she'd held back. She was too late. The warm blood stained her fingers, ran down her arm, and all she had was cold reason.

Only a moment ago she'd been prepared to accept that Fortune always had a hand on the wheel, but she couldn't bear to lose him now, now when she knew he was all that mattered. It would smash all dreams to dust. It would break her heart.

Lifting her eyes, she looked wildly around. The canyon was deserted and still. A smoky haze drifted through it. Above her rose the benign face on the mountain, and she pleaded with it. "Don't let him die. Help me, help me."

But as Ari looked back down, the bright blood was pooling on the new grass. The image of the red-running stream flashed before her appalled eyes. She shivered as she heard a wolf howl. Stripping off the windbreaker, she held its sleeve as tightly as she could to his temple, trying to keep the blood in. The only clear thought she had was that it could be an artery, and she knew how quickly fatal that was. One only had a few minutes. Even as she stared, his face seemed to be losing color, the lashes too dark against the pale skin.

Her body shook with an inward scream that could not get out. Like a heavy bell clapper the words *Too late, too late* thudded in her brain. Desperate to shut them out, she fought to think.

Tears were running down her face and scalding her throat. But words rushed up brokenly. "Wake up, Rivers, wake up. I love you. Please. I love you."

As she patted her trembling hand almost roughly on his cheek, his eyes opened. They were blurred, out of focus, but instantly he tried raising his head, saying, "Where is he?"

"Don't move," she said. "Don't. He's gone. They . . . I heard a car. Don't move just yet." His eyes did not clear, but he let his head sink back on the soft grass.

"We have to get to the doctor." She was talking as much to herself as to him. "Right away. You're bleeding a lot. Just don't faint, Rivers, don't faint."

"Okay," he murmured, sounding lucid. "I won't." She leaned over to hold the jacket more tightly against his head. When he looked up at her, he was even managing a slight lopsided grin. "But only if you say it again."

"Don't faint," she repeated, again unsure that he was coherent, worrying about getting him down the canyon.

"Not that," Rivers said. "The earlier bit. I heard an 'I love you.' You won't take it back when the doctor says I'm going to live, will you?"

"No. Never." Ari leaned down, kissed his cheek, his mouth. "I do love you. That's what I came to tell you." She added, blinking back tears to smile, "And it's too late for you to take your proposal back. I accept."

She wiped smears off his face with the rest of the jacket. The blood was flowing, but not spurting, from his temple. It wasn't an artery.

"Do you think you can get up?" she asked. "You're going to need stitches, at least."

The first flares of sunrise were flaming the sky and the light touched Ari's hair. Relief warmed her tear-starred eyes. He smiled at her. Although pain roared through his head and pounded in his ears, Rivers knew he'd never been this happy.

He raised himself on his elbows. "Right now I feel like I could even climb that mountain to announce our engagement to the town. But"— he did turn white as he struggled to a sitting position—"maybe you'd better help me get up first."

As he stood, swaying a little, his arm around her shoulders, he reached out and patted the yellow bulldozer almost affectionately. "That's a wonderful machine."

Startled, Ari glanced up at him, thinking that he was, after all, confused. She tried to urge him forward, but he stood his ground.

"I mean it," he insisted, his blue-green eyes alight. "First time in recorded history that a bulldozer *saved* a mountain. When Jonas hears what we can now say to the press, he'll give in fast." He leaned down carefully and scooped up the camera. "One of his men was wrecking these, and they were going to blame it on environmentalists."

Ari stared at him. Grinning, he nodded at her. "We'll give him just the amount you raised in the campaign—not a penny more. He can make the announcement this morning, saying he's pleased to donate his land to such a worthy cause."

He tightened his arm around her shoulder. "When I call him, how about I tell him you'll put up a nice little plaque thanking him for his unselfish contribution? That way history will remember him."

All Ari could do was smile. She looked at the mountain, its skylifted face illumined by the sunrise. It was strong, secure, the gift from the past that would be given to the future. She could tell her children the stories and say it had been bequeathed by Morna and Berkeley to them, but it belonged to everybody. Each person who looked at the mountain would own its unspoiled beauty.

The Utes had looked back at it with longing. Bridey had shown it to Devin, Trish had carried its memory in her heart. Ari thought then that love had its way of lasting. Her father had died before she was born, but his blood flowed through her veins.

She tucked her arm more firmly around Rivers's waist and looked up at him. For the moment her sheer happiness even overrode her worry about him. "Why not?" she answered at last, her voice still unsteady. "Jonas deserves a plaque, because if it hadn't been for him, I wouldn't have met you."

"Yes, you would have," he replied with conviction as they started toward the trail. "I'll always think we had an appointment to meet in the field that day. You even had the foresight to bring champagne. And I had the good sense to fall at your feet. Although"—Rivers winced as he dabbed at the blood—"I don't think we should make a habit of that."

Now she felt she'd won the prize. They were together. As they walked down, with his arm around her shoulder, hers wrapped around his waist, the light gleamed on the canyon walls and lent a rose color to the rushing stream. It was dawn.